LOVE, YUMI

The Romantic Life Of A
Japanese Idol

Hildred Billings
BARACHOU PRESS

LOVE, YUMI

Copyright: Hildred Billings
Published: 1ˢᵗ January 2016
Publisher: Barachou Press

Part 1

TWO GIRLS FROM SEKI

関市からの少女たち

If you don't know me, that's okay. There were many days I didn't know who I was either.

My name is Chiharu Morita. Of course, that is the name on this blog, so that is who I am. But I feel detached from that name – not because it's a stage name. No. It's my real name. I get bills in that name and it's what I sign my contracts with. I never even changed the *kana* when I entered the entertainment industry at eighteen. I've always been Chiharu. To hear Chi-*chan* makes me happy.

However you came upon my blog, whether as a regular reader (thank you) or through some link in a comment section, I feel the need to properly introduce myself. The Chiharu you know is only a shadow of who I am. Yes, I was in a group called Butterfly Tops. Then I was in a group called Celestial, in which they tried to make me like a hip-hop star. It didn't work. Now I am a composer, the person responsible for some of the pop songs you hear on the radio. I've worked with many celebrities and up and coming singers.

Those aren't the reasons you know me, though. You know me because of YUMI.

Yes, that YUMI. The eponymous one. I call her Yumi, but the big letters are the ones I see on variety shows and the news. I don't need to tell you who she is. You know who she is. She's the woman who comes into your living room every night on dramas, music shows, and radio request lines. Maybe you read her blog too. She hasn't posted on it in a long time.

Yumi, as you may know, is my childhood friend. We grew up together in a little town called Seki in the middle of Japan. We graduated high school and went to audition for a new girl group they were creating. The rest is history.

For you, anyway. For me, I still breathe this every day. Because I love Yumi. I have since I was a young girl too stupid to know the words for what I felt.

This is my confession. This is the story of not only me, but Yumi too. Of how we left our town and became household names. Of how I fell in love with her and did everything in my power to protect her from the evil in this world. I did not always succeed.

She knows I am writing this. Yumi doesn't deal much with the media these days, but I told her that this story needed to be released to the world. I am tired of holding it in. She gave me her blessing and only asked that I not make her look weak to you.

Please support me – support us – as I take my time telling you our tale. Maybe I'll write it all in one day or maybe it will take me a month. I will not rest until you know the truth. All the lies the agencies and labels tried to make us spew will be known.

I know there will be hate. I know many people won't understand. Maybe this will mean the end of what career I have left. But I don't care. If I don't tell this story, I won't know who I am anymore. I want to be more than "the girl who loved Yumi," and yet it's the only identity I can ever remember having.

For better or worse, let us begin.

Chapter 1

"*Mou,* Chi-*chan,* try to keep up!"

Yumi's voice distracted me enough to make me cross my ankles and fall over onto her bed. The music continued to play in the background, but Yumi, my best friend in the whole world, stared at me as if I had lost my balance on purpose.

"If you do that during the audition, you definitely won't pass." This was the most exasperated I had seen her since her mother was in the hospital a year ago. "How can I become an idol without you?"

I got to my feet and brushed off my plaid skirt. We had come straight to Yumi's house to practice after school, so she and I were both still dressed in our uniforms. "We already promised. If one of us passes but the other doesn't, then we have to support that person."

"I know! And I will support Chi-*chan.*" Yumi clasped her hands on my shoulders, shaking me in her fervor. "If you can't get in, I don't stand a chance!"

That was a lie, even if Yumi didn't believe it. She was beyond more talented than me. True, I could play the piano around her about five times in a second, but in all other areas Yumi Nishikawa was one of the most gifted girls in the world. She was a lead vocal in the school choir until she switched to theater and was cast in every lead role she tried out for. Since she was a child, she attended ballet lessons every week, something that I also used to do before dropping out because I was too heavy and have two left feet.

Yumi was also far more beautiful. She was lithe, airy, with a grace in her movements that made other girls at school sigh. Whether she grew out her hair past her shoulders or chopped it off for the summer heat, she found a way to make her cheekbones stand out and her large, double-eyelid eyes take in the world around her. Her skin was milk-white pale with barely a blemish. I was envious of her. Later I would understand that I was simply attracted to her.

Well, perhaps not *later*. I already knew I wanted her in ways that were not natural.

"I think you can do it." That was all I said. "Come on, let's try one more time."

Yumi started the song over and we attempted our hasty routine once more. Part of the audition was moving in a group. Our invitations said that we should prepare to split off into groups, given a rough choreography, and then not only perform individually but as a unit as well. We didn't know who we would be with or what the routine would be, but practicing was nonetheless a good idea. An idol who didn't put in the time for her skills was one who wasn't an idol for long.

I should say right now that it was Yumi's idea to apply for idol groups. Ever since our first recital she was bitten by the performance bug and dreamed of becoming a famous singer, dancer, and actress. She wanted to be the whole package – an idol. Me? I was content envisioning a future of college. I was going to the junior college in Minokamo and then applying to the Performance Arts school in Nagoya. They have an excellent piano program. If I couldn't become a professional pianist, my next best bet was to learn how to teach in turn. It wasn't much of a plan, but it was more practical than dreaming of stardom. I was always more practical.

Then word got out that an independent agency in Nagoya was putting together a new idol group and having open auditions. Yumi was the one who printed off the applications and rushed to my house on the edge of town, claiming this was our last chance before becoming adults. I don't know why I filled out the application, other than as a lark to appease Yumi. When we were invited to the in-person audition, I was shocked – but not as shocked as Yumi, who reportedly wept in her kitchen until her mother called me to find out what was wrong. That was the difference between us.

Here we were, practicing for an audition when I could have been reading a book.

We took a break after a successful round, Yumi going downstairs to fetch some lemonade from the kitchen. I sat on her bed, fanning myself even though it was a good ten degrees outside. Yumi's home never lacked for warmth. Her mother was a successful author of non-fiction, and her father worked for the city hall. Between the two of them, Yumi was a spoiled child for most of her life. Her room was bigger than mine, with carpet instead of tatami and a wrought iron bed frame that looked like it came from a fairytale book. She wasn't allowed a TV, but she had a small laptop and a large stereo on her shelf. Rows of CDs and records lined the walls where you could see a poster of some famous idol from years gone by. Her latest obsession was Kumi Koda, who wasn't an idol, but who had made a name for herself by using sex to sell her songs. Yumi often said she was jealous of Kuu-*chan's* confidence in her body. I wasn't much into the singer's music, but I am not ashamed to admit that I watched her music videos and often stared at those sexy posters on Yumi's wall. It was rare for me to see a Japanese woman who showed off her body so much.

"Are you going to break up with your boyfriend?" Yumi asked as we drank our lemonade and flipped through magazines. "I remember you talking about it."

I pursed my lips, and it wasn't from the lemons. "Ah, I forgot about that. I guess I'll have to do it soon. Make it clean before graduation."

Before anyone thinks I'm coldhearted, let me tell you that this boyfriend and I were not serious. His name was Junpei. Junpei Tachibana. Maybe you have heard of him, since he plays minor league baseball in Chubu, or so I heard.

Junpei and I never did anything. We never kissed, we never hugged, and we never held hands. I had no interest, and he never brought it up. I'm not sure how we came to be in a relationship for most of high school. One day he asked me if I wanted to check out a movie with him, and like the spineless wimp I was I agreed. After that, people assumed we were a couple, and neither of us denied it. What's funny is that we only saw each other at school and sometimes around the neighborhood we both lived in.

I can look back on it now and laugh. I was so gay! This boy was a shield to keep me safe from other boys who might ask me out. People wouldn't question my sexuality if I could say I was dating Junpei and he didn't deny it. Sometimes I wonder what he got out of that relationship. If you think I am quiet and sullen, then you've never met him. He made a monk seem like a great conversationalist.

Either way, I had to break up with him. It would be easy, even though Yumi mistakenly thought that he and I were serious. I never even met his parents outside of the supermarket.

Maybe it was because Yumi was boy crazy and couldn't understand how other girls weren't. Of course I don't want to speak ill of her, but most of those things you see in the papers about her relationships with men are true. Well, I can't attest that the certain men involved are truly the ones. There were lots of things even I as her best friend wasn't privy to. But Yumi liked to date boys, and during high school she dated a lot. Never for long. She once told me that dating boys was like ripping weeds out of a garden. There were so many to choose from, but it felt satisfactory to clean them out from around the pretty flowers. Silly me always took that as her admitting she liked girls too.

"It'll be good to be single again." Yumi's bed squeaked whenever I shifted my weight. It never did that when she was on it. That sort of thing made me self-conscious. "I mean…"

Love, Yumi

"Eh, Chi-*chan*, you wanna be a player?" The gap between Yumi's teeth was endearing when she smiled. "Excellent for when we're famous. All the boys we want. Famous boys!"

Nothing sounded worse.

"Hey, look at this." She tossed her open magazine to me. It was left on one of the pages in the back, where the comics and adult talk were. "Maybe we should learn some tricks before going to Nagoya."

I could barely look at the comic detailing how to give a proper blowjob. Not only did I think I was too young to care about such things still, but it grossed me out. I didn't know it was considered normal in many relationships. Why would someone want to do that with a guy? I thought about doing it with Junpei and nearly gagged. I never wanted to see his penis, let alone put my mouth on it. "I don't want to know this..." I closed the magazine.

Yumi pouted, as if I spoiled the fun.

Back in those days, I couldn't tell you if I knew I was gay yet or not. I knew the concept of "gay." I knew what the word lesbian meant. Except I grew up in Seki. Lesbians did not live in Seki. They were a Western idea. Hollywood. White women on TV could be lesbians, but the idea of a Japanese girl taking up such a label was nonsense to me. And if a Japanese woman *did*, then she was a strange creature indeed. I wouldn't think she was Japanese. Maybe not even a woman. Please don't think I hated myself. I just didn't understand back then.

All I knew was that I wanted to go with Yumi wherever she went. She was the only best friend I ever had. We had known each other since kindergarten – she knew my secrets. All but one. That I loved her in that way.

I didn't understand it yet. I wouldn't come to understand it for a few more years, as I gradually woke up to who I was, what my desires were, and how much I needed it in my life. I couldn't tell you the exact moment I realized what I felt for Yumi was both romantic and sexual. I don't think there was a single moment.

When I went home that evening – after staying at Yumi's for dinner, as I often did when my mother was working late – I thought about my future. If we were accepted into this idol group, what would happen? Would we become famous? Would we travel the world singing songs and bringing happiness to people? That's all Yumi could ever talk about. She lived to make people happy. If you felt sad, or lonely, or rejected, she would come up to you and tell you a joke or share a funny story with you. It was impossible to be around her and not become infected with her zest for life. If anyone should have become an idol, it was her.

I wanted to become an idol too. So I could be with her.

***

A big deadline passed a few days ago. Beppu, my manager, came by my home to pick up the music sheets I had written to personally deliver them to the label. Well, that's kinda a lie. Beppu isn't my manager anymore. Not since I was in Celestial. He still helps me and looks after me in the industry, just like I do for Yumi. Only he doesn't have to worry about some of the more heinous things with me. Just making sure my deadlines are reasonable and that I get the money that's owed to me.

He picked up the sheets, which I had neatly organized in an orange folder, and started telling me the latest gossip at the label. I didn't pay attention since I didn't care about the drama going on in such a place. So instead of listening, I sat at my piano jotting down notes on another music sheet. The song I was writing was for my own enjoyment. A bit more complicated than the usual pop or folk fare I submitted to the label for consideration.

Beppu stopped talking and watched me compose for a few minutes. I was surprised when he said, "It never fails to amaze me that you didn't do something greater with your skills."

"What do you mean by that?" I was an award-winning composer. What else was there to do with my skill other than what I was already doing?

"I mean you have a fantastic skill that should have never been left to rot in this industry. You should have gone to a conservatory and learned to be a great performer... on the piano."

I laughed at him. "That's what I wanted to do originally. Go to a music school and play piano all day."

"Then why in the world did you apply to be a damn idol of all things?"

My fingers remained poised over the keys. "Because of Yumi." I began playing one of her favorite songs, a ballad from the '90s. "I'm Proud" by Tomomi Kahala. Perhaps you know it.

"Of course." Beppu sighed in that way that said he knew he wouldn't get past my barriers. Years knowing each other took us to that place. "Yumi. It's always Yumi. You make all your decisions based on her."

It wasn't a scathing judgment. Once upon a time I would have believed it, but now I was able to smile at him as I played my way through the chorus of the song. It was loud enough that notes echoed in the living room, and anything else Beppu would want to say was instantly drowned out. So he leaned against my piano, staring at me as if I were the most fascinating woman in the world. I had a hard time believing that.

I abruptly finished the song after the first chorus. "There are worse ways to live a life."

"It's not healthy."

I ignored that. "I'm thinking about doing it. About confessing everything that's happened to us over the years. I just want to get it off my chest and let the whole world know what we went through." I waited for my old mentor to berate me for such a foolish idea.

"You're not interested in a career, are you?"

"There are more important things. I have enough money to last a while if it comes to that."

"Move back to Seki where the living is cheap. Move back in with your mother."

"If I have to."

Another sigh. Beppu is still a large man, so every deep breath made his buttons strain against his torso. "The media will be all over it. You know that, right?"

"I don't care either way. I'm tired of people having the wrong perception about us."

"And they will continue to have wrong perceptions even if you vomit up your history. Say the wrong thing about someone at the label, and you *will* be out of a job. Not to mention blacklisted. Not even porn-game companies will hire you to write their pre-pubescent fuck tunes."

I glared at him. Not because I was offended on my behalf, but because my living room was littered with Lica-*chan* dolls and a four-year-old snoozing in their midst. Girl could sleep through me playing piano all afternoon, but picked up bad words like a sponge. We had to stop watching adult movies when she was around at all, because the next day she would go to day care and start spouting the foulest words until the teacher's ears bled.

"Right. I forgot you're the greatest babysitter in the world now." He didn't finish the rest of his thought. *"Something else we can thank Yumi for."*

"Either way, this is something I have to do. You may not understand, but I'm willing to take the risk."

He leveled his eyes at me, and for the first time since I was in Celestial I felt the heaviness of his gaze. It stopped me where I sat. Almost made me look away like I was a twenty-year-old with something to hide. "Is she willing?"

I glanced at the girl clutching one of many dolls. "She knows. This is something we decided together."

"Ah, sure. Destroy your livelihood then. What's it to me? I don't make money off you anymore." He laughed, and I knew he was only joking, but sometimes words like that still stung. I never had reason to believe that Beppu saw either Yumi or me as disposable. In order to do such an emotionally and physically demanding job as his, however, he had to have a certain sense of humor. "Just be nice about me. I have a wife to feed."

"So you two made up?" The ballad of Beppu and his wife was a tale as old as my life with Yumi.

"Begrudgingly. When you reach this age, you don't have many options. I can't be single. I don't have enough time to take care of myself when I finally get home."

"Yet you have enough time to come over and run errands for me."

"You're different. You make stupid life decisions actually look mature. I wish half the girls I manage could make dumb life decisions look so altruistic. Did I tell you about the stupid sixteen-year-old I've got in this group? She keeps smoking, and to top it off she's got some twenty-year-old boyfriend buying her cigs for her. Kinda hard to do it on her own when you keep her in a school uniform all day. Still, I need to find this guy and scare the shit out of him. When do I stop raising other people's daughters for them?"

I gave him a look.

"Fine, fine, Babysitter-*san*, like I said, making dumb life decisions look like a Mother Mary sacrifice."

"I'm not a martyr."

"No. You somehow didn't die after all of that."

I gave him another look. No. I hadn't died, minus some attempts against my life. It was never me who I worried about. I don't have to tell you who I was always worried about.

Chapter 2

The audition came the weekend before graduation. It was the most inconvenient time, but perhaps the label thought it a way to weed out the girls who weren't as serious. Yumi was very serious, so we had to go.

Nagoya took nearly two hours to get to by train. Since the auditions began at ten in the morning, we had to take a train from Seki before the sun came up. I was yawning on the platform, but Yumi was acting like she had taken 100 ccs of caffeine. She kept practicing a dance routine until it came time to board the train. I struggled to keep my eyes open.

We didn't go to Nagoya often, not just because of how long it took to get there, but because of how much it cost. Nearly 2,000 *yen*, and that was only one way. I had to ask my mother for some of the money to make the trip. She groaned, told me I was a foolish girl for trying, but gave me money for the train and lunch anyway.

Love, Yumi

Some people think it's strange that two teenage girls would run off to Nagoya by themselves to do an audition. I don't know about younger girls, but we were eighteen, and the only thing we feared was making an ass out of ourselves in front of the panel. We knew there would be hundreds of girls there that day. Many of them would be prettier and more talented. Some had been trained in other parts of the world to become world-class entertainers. I knew we didn't stand a chance, and thought it was a waste of time. Yumi, though, wouldn't hear my pessimism.

As I had anticipated, the audition hall at the record label's headquarters was full of girls our age and younger. Each of them had been personally invited after submitting audition tapes. Yumi and mine's was of a song and dance routine that we came up on our own. I even wrote the song – she choreographed. Our talents always complemented each other like that. I could write songs and she could sing them. I could think critically and she could drum up the passion for an act. People often said that we were Yin and Yang, the perfect balance of two people. I didn't have to ask to know which one I was. All my life people made quips about my "manly" looks and deep voice. Perhaps I was doomed to be a lesbian from the start.

We were lined up with a row of girls dressed in their school uniforms. They must have come from some function, but it made us both self-conscious. We were auditioning for a teenaged idol group. We should have come in our uniforms as well. Project the right image to the panel. Instead Yumi was in flexible trousers and a loose cotton shirt. Perfect for dancing on command in, but not super fashionable. I wore jeans and a T-shirt. I was even worse off in the looks department. We looked like poor college students instead of excited high school girls.

"Oh my God, Chi-*chan!*" Yumi said, exasperated as we moved up in the line. "What if we don't make it? What if we screw up?"

I didn't like that look on her face. It was the same look she made before she went on stage for a school play, yours truly only having to care about the accompaniment piano music. Yumi was always a star. I was her attendant in the wings. Embarrassing how happy it made me.

"You'll be fine." I didn't say anything about myself. What was it to me if I made it or not? I had already decided that if I made it but Yumi didn't, I would turn it down. "You look great." I don't know why I said that, but Yumi didn't bat an eyelash.

The line slowly moved. I had no idea what to expect.

They were calling girls in two, three at a time. I went in with Yumi, who was shaking so badly that I had to take her hand and hold it between my fingers. I concentrated on breathing steadily, for both her and me, and by the time we reached the panel of judges she had covered my hand in sweat.

"Names," the man in the middle said. He was middle-aged, wrinkled, worn, and looked like he was about to pass out. "You." He pointed to me.

It zapped my nerves. "Chi... Chiharu Morita." I gave the customary greetings to the panel and took a step forward.

"So that makes you Yumi Nishikawa."

"Yes, sir."

The man asked Yumi to sit down in a chair along the side of the wall. Great. I had the honor of going first. I looked over the three people sitting at the table. Aside from the man, a woman with a mole on her nose and a younger man with sheen in his hair went over paperwork and glanced up at me occasionally. My throat was dry, and this wasn't even my deepest desire.

"What would you say is your main talent?" Only the man in the center spoke to me.

I glanced around the room. Instruments lined the walls, some of them disturbed from their placement. A grand piano faced me. "Piano," I said confidently. "I've been taking lessons since I was four."

The man remained unimpressed. I was probably the fiftieth girl that day who claimed to be able to play the piano.

"I can also sing pretty well. Alto." Singing was not my strong suit, and I was definitely not a soloist. I did fine in a choral arrangement or singing backup to someone else. "I took ballet as a child." Yumi was the one who continued with that.

"Says here you've applied to a few music schools. Get into any of them?"

"Not yet…"

"Very well. Sit down. You there."

I switched places with Yumi. So much for that.

She was doing a damn good job of not showing how nervous she was. Only I knew her tics, like her fidgeting fingers. She also bit her lip until it bled if she got nervous enough. Later I would see a little trickle down her mouth. "What is your main talent?"

"Singing. And dancing. Oh, and I can act too." Yumi smiled. It was pure nerves.

"You star in many school musicals?"

"Yes! All three this past year I had a lead role. I was also a soloist in the school choir."

"So I see. Impressive list of schools you've applied to as well. Get into any of them?"

"So far only Chubu Ongaku Gakuen."

"That's not a very big one." The man sighed. "Seeing things like The National Female Choir and Takarazuka Music School on here made me hopeful. Yet if you got into either of those, I doubt you would be here today."

The frown fell off her face. Oh boy. The National Choir was a few months ago. She didn't even make it past the first round. As for Takarazuka, that was a one-time application two years ago. They allow you to try again every year for about three or so, but the deal with her parents was she only got one shot. She didn't make it. They recommended she try again the next year, but her mother didn't let her.

"I didn't get into those schools, but I've studied ballet for twelve years and have lots of acting and singing experience."

"Play any instruments?"

Yumi shook her head. "I studied piano too, but gave it up for ballet." Yumi could dance as gracefully as a prima ballerina, but was never as good as me with the keys. That's why we were such good partners for recitals at school. I played; she danced or sang. Less pressure on me, and more attention for her.

Things weren't looking good. There was nothing about us that stood out, and the judges were about as bothered as a cat woken up from a nap. They had seen dozens of girls already that day. There was no way we could be memorable, especially with our boring résumés. Every girl there that day took ballet, piano, sang in a choir, and acted in school plays. Now if Yumi had actually managed to get into some of those schools and groups, maybe she would have stood a chance. Like the man said, though, if she had, she wouldn't be there that day... and I would've lost my friend a long time ago.

"All right. Show me what you two can do." He pointed to the both of us. "You get three minutes to perform and impress us."

Yumi and I looked at each other. That stupid routine we practiced for weeks was about to haunt me again.

Then the man pointed to the piano. "Over there, Mozart. And you better be as good as you make yourself sound. Girls who can play piano are a dime a dozen in this business."

Oh no. This threw more than a wrench into our plans. This was the whole damn toolbox and the kitchen sink for good measure. Panic overcame Yumi's already pale face as she looked to me for answers. We hadn't prepared for something like this. Me? I was just glad I didn't have to dance yet. My wider hips weighed me down whereas Yumi's lithe body could glide through the air, tutu or no.

"I'm Proud," I mouthed to Yumi before taking my place at the piano. Sometimes it was easier for me to make the decisions.

She looked at me as if she couldn't understand. I knew she knew my words, but perhaps they hadn't sunk in yet. Not surprising, considering she was probably the most scared she had been. This was one of her last chances to get into the industry young. If she didn't make it, she was looking at uploading songs to the internet and hoping someone clicked. This was in the days before that was a reliable way to start a career. So the idea must have been going through her head, and she wasn't having it.

Love, Yumi

We had little time, so I eased my way into the notes. I wasn't nervous. Piano was second nature to me, especially songs I played all the time. It wasn't like singing or dancing. When you play piano, the focus is not on you or what you look like, but the sounds you create from something beyond yourself. It wasn't like standing on a stage doing the usual performances. That's when people stare at your appearance and criticize what makes you, well, you. I became very familiar with this distinction when I was a young adult.

On the piano, I am merely a conduit for passion and musical enjoyment. Sure, people will critique my technique and how much emotion I am able to put into something, but that comes from my heart. It doesn't matter if I'm ugly or pretty. It doesn't matter if I'm not limber enough to raise my foot to my head. I can have a hoarse voice and play piano. The piano doesn't care.

The first few notes of the song entered the air without a flaw. Of course, this was not impressive. It was a simple intro that required little skill, but I was mostly here to support my friend. It was up to her to sing the lyrics to the best of her ability.

This is where I become embarrassed telling my story, because this next part is a moment I will always cringe at when I think back on it. Today I am a professional piano player who rarely makes a mistake as long as she is hale and healthy. Back then, when I was a naïve eighteen-year-old, I was prone to stupid mistakes. Usually I would just play over them. Yet the moment I heard my fingers slip on the keys and create a tremulous, heart-jarring sound that jerked half the room out of their seats, I instantly felt the power of dread filling my heart. My fingers stopped moving, and I gaped at Yumi with the most apologetic face I could muster.

The young man on the panel laughed. Yumi looked like she was going to come over, strangle me, and then barf her nerves on top of my head. Let me tell you, that was the guiltiest I had ever felt since I was caught stealing coins for a soda out of my mother's purse when I was a child.

"*Iya...*" Yumi's crestfallen countenance made me want to rip my own fingers off my hand. What could I do? I had ruined her dream. All I could think in that heart-pounding moment was how much I regretted attempting a song that I thought I could do on auto-pilot. Not in a situation like this. Some friend I was.

Before the panel could dismiss us as a lost cause, I hit the first note I could think of. It was a muscle reflex, to be sure. I told my brain to start playing the first song to come to its forefront, a song I could impress with while still being stimulated enough to pay attention. I couldn't sit idly at the piano and let Yumi do all the hard work. If I were going to help her dream come true, I had to play as if *I* were trying to get into the school of my dreams.

It was an original composition. Good in the sense that I could impress them with my skills as a creative artist. Bad in the sense that I wasn't intimately familiar with it yet. This meant that as I played I had to make some things up. I remembered the bones of the song, but I had to let my fingers make up the difference as they flew over keys, my body moving with my whole arms as I traveled from one side of the piano to the other. The air was full of the clamoring melody I produced. After I played this impassioned introduction, I looked fiercely at Yumi, counting out when I expected her to join in with her voice.

The song did not need lyrics. No one cared about lyrics. In this sort of audition, unless you are trying to impress with pure songwriting skill, the lyrics are a mere conduit like the piano. Lyrics only help you express your voice – the true instrument that Yumi wielded.

I believe I have mentioned that she was a trained soprano singer. And I was an alto. Between the two of us, we could harmonize a killer tune. It helped that we often sang together so much growing up. I let her lead, however. It was her time to shine, and the moment I counted "Four!" she burst into a high, steady note that matched the key I was playing in. As my fingers flew across the keys at a blinding speed, Yumi sang with the melody, her voice sliding through scales and holding notes that would leave most novice singers breathless. I didn't look at the panel. I was too focused on making sure I didn't flub again.

Just as I created a pattern with my melody, Yumi created a pattern with her voice. As she looped it along with my composition, I joined in with my deeper voice, holding back its strength in order to let her keep the stage.

I knew about when three minutes were up. I chimed in with a new part of the melody, anxiously working my way up a scale with finger work that would make the devil dizzy. Yumi heard this with her expert ear and held a long, high *fortissimo* note that used every part of her body as she bent down, building up her strength in her diaphragm while her throat only betrayed the slightest bit of breathlessness.

We stopped at the same time. The room went silent.

The panel didn't say a word. They simply studied us, looking at me, looking at Yumi. She was shaking, red in the face. I shook out my hands and cleared my throat.

The man in the middle stood up, his metal chair scraping against the floor. He rounded the table, stepping right up to Yumi and looking her in the eye. She cowered before him, like any teenage girl would. "Why do you want to become an idol?" he asked her with a serious tone.

She stuttered, trying to remember how to use her voice for talking. "I want to make people's dreams come true," she said. "I want to give them an escape from reality. I want to be someone they can look to so they can feel better."

He considered this, and then looked at me. "And you?" he asked. "I don't know any idol in the current industry who can play like that."

I said the first thing to come to my mind. "I just want to play. Don't care how I do it."

The other two people at the table looked at one another, and then at the man in charge. "We'll let you know," he said. We were dismissed to finish the audition elsewhere.

***

Beppu, with a flair for bringing up dreadful memories, always likes to remind me of that one time I completely butchered the opening notes to

"I'm Proud." He'll cheekily start talking about it, pausing long enough to see me groan, and then laugh like an elementary school bully. "How could you fuck up one of the simplest songs on the charts? Admit it, you were nervous."

"Who cares?" I always say so defensively. It's hard to rile me up like that, but this man has been pushing those buttons for *years*. "I blew your stupid mustache off with my follow up."

I have long since fine tuned and cleaned up that song into what you now know as "Lucky Dreamer." I released it as an original composition on one of my albums. Yumi actually covered it at one of her fanclub concerts. I dare say her voice suits it a lot more than mine. I had originally wanted her to feature on the track, but the label claimed there was a scheduling conflict. One day.

"Remember what you said when I asked why you wanted to become an idol?" Beppu always kept laughing. "Your answer was such fucking bullshit. 'I just want to play!' I saw right through you, but I wasn't going to let those shithead executives let talent like yours and Yumi's get away. Although I almost wrote you both off. Yumi looked like a scared chicken, and you were too cynical to be a happy idol. But then I thought that would make you more likely to survive this industry. And we weren't going to get you unless we took on Yumi as well."

In truth, I never knew whether or not to thank him for choosing us. Who knows what life would have been like had our dreams ended there? I probably wouldn't have the career I have today. So for that I am grateful Beppu saw my potential. Yet maybe Yumi could have had a better life if she went to a small music school and eventually became a performer some other, safer way.

We both know how everything ended. I wouldn't be here confessing my sins if it weren't for that fateful performance. Sometimes I really hate the song "Lucky Dreamer."

Chapter 3

Yumi was the first to find out our results, and because of it I didn't get any sleep that day.

It was a week after high school graduation. I had just returned from a trip to Kyoto to see my mother's extended family, and while there I contracted some mild bug that gave me a fever for a day. When Yumi came crashing onto my property, I was still in bed, achy but on the mend. My mother was at work, and she told me that if I felt better I needed to fill out my paperwork for the junior college in Minokamo. The deal was that if I didn't get into the idol group, I would start taking classes and work my way up to music school.

I was still too worn out from being sick to do any work. When pebbles started hitting my bedroom window, I groaned and tried to ignore it.

These were the days before cell phones were in every teenage girl's hands. Most girls I knew owned them, but I never saw the point. So even though Yumi had a phone she texted on all day, she couldn't text me, her best friend.

And her new group partner.

"Chi-*chan!*" she called from outside my window. "Wake the hell up!"

When I rolled over and didn't respond, I heard her kick up the dirt outside my window as she ran to the front door. I had lived in that house my whole life, and since Yumi was a regular visitor from the time we were children, she knew where we kept our spare key. The front door slid open downstairs, and I prayed for peace.

"Chi-*chan!*" My bedroom door flew open, and soon Yumi's hands were on me, shaking me awake. Moaning, I told her to back off as I shoved soiled handkerchiefs off my bed and grumbled about feeling like shit. Yumi didn't care. For her to not show me any concern meant something big had happened. "I just heard from the label! Did you get your mail yet?"

I looked at her through red eyes laden with sleep.

Yumi dumped the letter and flew back downstairs. She rooted through our mailbox, the metal lid slapping against the box. Her footsteps clobbered on the staircase and down the hallway. That whole time I stared at my bedroom door, wishing this could have waited another day.

"Wake *up!*" Yumi rocked the bed until I nearly fell out of it. "We've gotta find out if we made it or not!"

I mumbled something I don't remember now. Yumi almost kicked me in the butt and spat on me to get me moving. When it came to her dream, she didn't like waiting.

"Fine!" That was all the strength I had. I snatched the letter from her hand and tore it open, feeling fatigue already wash over me. Yumi hurried to catch up before I could read my fate.

"*Thank you for your interest. After consideration, we would like to invite you…*"

The shriek coming from my right nearly split my ear in two. After I jumped out of my skin, Yumi slapped her hand over her mouth and crumpled to the floor, tears springing from her eyes. I had no idea if that was a good sign or not.

"*Kita!*" she cried, sounding like an *otaku*. Her hand snatched for mine, even though it was grimy, sweaty, and covered in sickness. "It finally came! Our ticket to stardom!"

To this day I find it interesting that she assumed I got in too. In her mind, there was never any doubt we would go into this together. I once asked her about this moment. We were sitting in my living room, enjoying a beautiful afternoon as it came through my wide windows, and I remembered the day we were accepted into the entertainment industry. "Why did you assume I had gotten in too?" I asked, sprawled out on my couch as I stared at the sunshine outside. "You have always been bigger star material than me." For every album I sold of my original compositions, Yumi sold 500 of her pop fare. There was no reason to believe that just because she had gotten in, I had as well.

She looked at me, her face long and weary. Gone were the chubby cheeks and the gap in her teeth that I loved growing up. Sometimes I would still catch glimpses of the Yumi I used to know. For the most part, she was different. Beautiful. Gorgeous. *My Yumi*. Different, and not just grown and matured.

"I had to believe it. I didn't understand it at the time, but I needed you more than I needed that dream. I couldn't have one without the other."

***

I couldn't sleep the other night. I was up in bed, staring at my phone like so many people do now. Funny, considering I used to be the type of girl who thought she was above such things.

The glare hurt my eyes but I couldn't look away. I was reading comments from fans regarding Yumi's concert two years ago. The one where nobody could tell how sad, anxious, and troubled she was. Nobody but me. When I watched clips of that concert, I could see the pain in her eyes and the sorrow in her heart. She had everything, but she couldn't be happy anymore.

I don't like those videos. Being there in person had been enough for me at the time.

People being as they are, they like to go back after someone has a breakdown and try to see the lead up to it. Most people hang on this concert. They criticize the way she moves, sings, and even talks to the audience. All things that were endearing at the time. Now these people see everything as a sign. Even a sneeze between songs meant she was drugged out of her mind. Please, I have no reason to believe she was on those kinds of drugs that night.

It was reading those comments that made me want to write this blog. I almost did it right there, switching over to my blogging app to make some sort of announcement. Then I thought better of it. Until I started telling this tale, my blog was only to announce developments of new songs and to occasionally talk about my day. Post a picture of a beautiful scene or an especially delicious drink at my local café. People like to see that sort of thing.

Nothing meant less to me after I thought of how people talked about Yumi.

I mention this because I think this is where I will leave off for now. My time is limited today, even though I was impassioned enough to start this journey. If you read this, then I have posted it and gone to bed. I have turned off my phone so I don't wake up at 2am to phone calls from Beppu and others at the label. People telling me I'm fired, that I will never work in music again. I am prepared. I don't want to work in this industry if it means I have to hide the truth.

I will return tomorrow, for better or for worse. If I don't return quickly, then I will lose my nerve, and you will never know what really happened. I can't have that. Not if I'm dedicated to it now. Who knows what I will wake up to tomorrow? Maybe the world will be over. It wouldn't be so bad.

Part 2

GOODNIGHT KISS

お休みのキス

I was afraid to turn on my devices this morning. I had a restless sleep, partly because of the unseasonable heat (I still have the flannel sheets in my bed…) and because of what I did yesterday. When you confess something like that, it's normal to think you'll wake up to find out that everything has changed. That people who once were on your side will no longer look at you anymore.

The hateful comments I got were something to be expected. Yet the overwhelming outpouring of support from a majority of you almost made me cry as I drank my morning coffee and tried to eat some toast.

Thank you.

I cannot express how much it means for my regular readers to say things like, "Of course we will support you," and, "Now I know why you create such beautiful music." The fear I felt was not only the fear of rejection, which I am always familiar with. It was also a fear of having my life turned upside down.

No one from the label has contacted me yet, although there is a voicemail from Beppu on my phone. I haven't listened to it. No doubt he will admonish me and then give me about ten minutes' worth of advice. He still thinks I'm a teenager in need of his guidance. In truth, I do feel that way. I will probably need to hear his thoughts about how to deal with the label over this.

Yumi has not said anything. That's not unusual these days. Sometimes she doesn't talk to me for a long time. I have learned to not take it personally. After the things she has been through, well, I would probably be the same way.

As for all of you, thank you. I cannot say it enough. You have given me the courage to continue my story. To be able to say "I'm gay!" is already powerful enough. Please ignore the commenters who may say something cruel. They cannot hurt me.

I will continue my story. I am taking some time off from work just to talk, although I will need to leave in a few hours to run my errands. Until then, please listen.

Chapter 4

It was a month before we were summoned to Nagoya with our parents and to go over the offered contracts. The contracts were standard – our parents were not.

I haven't talked much about them before. My mother is a straightforward woman. She raised me by herself since she divorced my father when I was barely a toddler. I don't know much about him besides his name and that he lives somewhere else in Gifu. I haven't seen him. Even after I started appearing on TV, I have barely spoken to him.

My mother is strong in her own way. Not just in her body, which is stocky and where I get most of my form. People take her seriously because she has a serious look about her. Yumi used to joke that it's because of my mother that I too am so serious about things. That I'm too mature. She doesn't say that anymore.

Her parents, on the other hand, are quite the opposite. They are successful, fairly wealthy people. They tend to have their heads in the clouds. They are not bad people – please don't think I am saying that – but they don't tend to think ahead or about possible repercussions. So when my mother and Yumi's parents showed up in Nagoya with us one weekend to discuss the terms of our contracts, their reactions were completely different. My mother argued with them over everything while Yumi's parents accepted everything unconditionally. They signed so quickly that I thought stamps would fly from their hands. Beppu got to know my mother well that afternoon as she told him the contract was shit and I needed more than one day off a week.

Even though they accompanied us for the discussions, we moved into the dorms by ourselves. It was a sunny day in April, when the cherry blossoms have long since bloomed and fallen down the sewer drains. Yumi and I packed two bags apiece, hugged our parents goodbye, and got on the train in Seki to start our new lives – together.

She was a bundle of energy while I tried to conserve mine. For the hour it took to get to Gifu City, our main transfer to continue on toward Nagoya, Yumi talked and talked about what a great opportunity this was and how we would have to persevere even through the hardest times. She didn't know what she was talking about back then. Not unusual for her.

We were halfway to Gifu City when she tapped my shoulder. "Chi-chan, I have something for you."

I had to double-take as she pulled out a small box from her backpack. "What is it?" I asked. There was nothing I could think of as being something worth giving me. It wasn't my birthday, and I hadn't asked for anything.

Yumi giggled at my bemused expression as I took the box and opened it. A necklace. Simple silver chain and a *kanji* pendant. It was *tomo,* the Chinese symbol for friend.

"Please take it," Yumi said, one hand clasped on my wrist. The train staggered along the tracks as she looked at me expectantly. "See?" She pulled a pendant out of her shirt. Together, our necklaces said *yuujin,* or best friends. "I'll let you have the better one, Chi-*chan.*" She said this because her symbol simply meant "person" on its own. It was somewhat silly seeing a simple upside-down V hanging from her neck.

She helped me put on the necklace, talking about how this was a common thing to do in the West. "I saw it on TV," she said to me. "And when I saw these necklaces at the shop, I knew we had to have them. This way the whole world will know that you and I are friends forever."

Why did the world have to know? Knowing for myself was good enough. Yumi was that way. She liked to share with the world. I suppose it's ironic that I am the one writing this story, and not her.

When we transferred trains in Gifu City, Yumi's lost energy caught up with her and she slumped against my shoulder in our seats. Back then, I didn't understand the rush I felt when her breath hit my skin or her hair tickled me. Nor did I understand the significance of her playing with the necklace around my neck, her fingers pressing against my chest and teasing the buttons of my shirt. All I knew was that I didn't want her to stop.

"*Kore,*" she said, pulling a red string from her pocket. Ever since she was a child Yumi enjoyed making bracelets out of strings like that. It wasn't unusual for strings of every color to fall out of her pockets, because she would take them to school, on road trips, and of course on the train so she would have something to do. I thought she would make a bracelet on the spot, but instead she tied the string around my left pinky finger.

She tied the other end around hers.

I laughed. "What are you doing?"

The string remained taut between us. "It's the red string of fate. Now we're destined to always be together, no matter what happens."

I couldn't stop laughing. A few people looked over their seats at us. "That's for love, Yumi!" Romantic love. The kind I couldn't yet admit I felt for my best friend.

She frowned, untied the string from our fingers, and let it fall to the floor of the train.

Now that I think back on it, I wonder if she was trying to tell me something. Maybe she felt that pull between us as well. Something that transcended mere friendship. Yumi and I had known each other as long as we could remember. To live a life without the other felt like treason. Perhaps there was some sort of string keeping us together. Of course the red string of fate is for the person you romantically love. I didn't know if there was one for good friendship... for the person you would spill your heart to, cry on, and need for the rest of your life. Maybe that sort of thing didn't matter. All that mattered was that we didn't want to be apart.

I loved her so much back then. I still love her, of course, but now I can't believe how stupid I was to not act on it. Things could have been different.

A company car from the label was waiting for us at Nagoya Station. The driver confirmed our identities and phoned the company to say he had located us and would be bringing us in. Now, we could have gone to the office ourselves. It was in Sakae, just two subway stops away, and we had been there before. But the moment we entered Nagoya, we became the label's responsibility – their liability. So we were herded into this black van and told we would be there in fifteen minutes, traffic permitting.

When we auditioned, we were in the practice rooms in the basement of the multi-level building. When we signed the contracts, we were in a second floor conference room. Now we were taken to a room at the top of the building, where we could see the TV tower surrounded by the greens of Odori Park. The Sakae Ferris wheel was a wonder to behold, lit up in a variety of neon colors and moving through the air with steady grace. It was those kinds of shots that made the imagination of a teenage girl light up and take off for the stars. Everything was starting to sink in. I think Yumi felt it too as she composed herself just in time for three men to enter the room and take the driver's place.

The man in charge was the label president, Mr. Yamamoto. To his left was the head of the artist management and production division, Mr. Kawaguchi. While these men were important, I rarely saw them. It was the third man who would become a staple in my life.

Beppu, the man who asked me why I wanted to become an idol and later laughed at me when I was an adult picking up toys and folding tiny jumpers fresh from the laundry. Of course his name isn't really Beppu. I think it's Masanori. Everyone calls him Beppu because that's where he's from: that resort town in Eastern Kyushu that aunties sigh over and city kids like to pretend doesn't exist.

They told us what we could expect in the coming days, from settling in to our rooms, meeting our other group mates, and beginning our training. This would include classes in dance (mostly modern), vocal techniques, acting, instruments and musical theory, etiquette, and what they called "personal responsibility." That was a fancy word for nutrition and learning how to never gain a kilo on pain of expulsion.

Everything was heavily structured. While we took these classes, the label would be hard at work constructing our group from a marketing perspective. They would study our personalities and slowly introduce us to the masses to gauge interest. Meanwhile, songs would be written, skills assessed, and hopefully within six to nine months we would debut as a real idol group. The label wanted us to debut sometime in autumn, but Beppu stressed that it may not be until the new year.

After that, we were taken to our dorm, a room on the back streets just behind the label building. Most of the other girls were already there, and this was when we first met them.

If you were a fan of Butterfly Tops, then you probably recognize most of these people. There was Nezu, the incredibly short girl who was brought in solely to "rap," a novelty in idol groups back then. Her personality is just as boisterous as she comes off as in her interviews and performances. I liked her. She spoke her mind and didn't let much get to her. She was someone who could make her way through the industry. I just looked up what she's doing lately, and it seems she's part of an indie hip-hop label, performing and producing. I'm happy for her.

Her roommate in the dorms was Dahi, who went by the stage name Dolly because her real name reminded the public too much that she was Zainichi Korean. She was the only one in the group who could possibly out-sing Yumi, and was made the lead vocalist because of it. Dolly's selling point was her natural beauty. I could see right away why the label wanted her. Minus the Korean ancestry, she was a total package for a blossoming idol group: pretty, thin, well-composed, and talented. When I first met her she kept her hair its natural black, but when we had our image change she started dying her hair ridiculous pastel colors that made her look like, well, a doll. I believe she's a fairly popular fashion model and occasional actress now.

Reika is the last one you probably recognize. She was a vocalist, pretty girl, but very quiet outside of singing. Honestly, in the days of Butterfly Tops I found her rather expendable. (I am sorry if you are reading this Reika…) I guess she was a fan favorite.

She shared a larger dorm with the last two girls, Koto and Mayu. They were good-looking dancers for the most part.

Naturally, Yumi and I shared the third dorm. It was a cramped, Spartan place with hard twin beds and minimum storage space. We wouldn't be spending much time in there anyway. Only to sleep and spend the odd hour or two before the sleeping. The label made sure our days were packed, and on the rare day off we actually got, we either went out for fun or slept on the much more comfortable couch in the common area.

The dorm came with a large gymnasium style shower, which held a cubby for each of us to keep our hygiene supplies. There was a kitchen, never stocked beyond low-calorie foods, and a small recreational area with a TV and some books. It never got much use.

It's hard to believe I lived in that cramped space for so long. When I was there for an hour a day (aside from sleeping, of course) I was usually consumed with work. Or talking to Yumi. It was like a perpetual sleepover for us, especially in the early days. While it wasn't unusual for us to spend the night at each other's houses in Seki, this was somehow more intimate. Probably because we could easily reach across the gap between our beds to touch each other, which we sometimes did just to prove we could.

The next day, we began our training by meeting our female mentor, Anna Matsuda.

I'm not surprised if you don't recognize the name, although she would be appalled to hear it. Anna was an idol in the '90s, although these days she makes most of her money by doing commercials, variety shows, and the occasional low-budget drama. Oh, and offering her "mentoring" services to labels. I put that in quotes because Anna has never been very famous. Sure, she managed to make a living for herself in the industry, but she will never be a household name. Her main appeal was being half-American. She was from Hawaii, although not native Hawaiian. She spoke fluent English and often muttered in it under her breath when she was around us. Luckily, we only had to see her a couple of times a week.

That first morning she came into our dorms where we had lined up as instructed by Beppu. I don't know about anyone else, but I felt like a military recruit up for inspection. Probably because I was.

Anna went down the line, inspecting each of us. Physically, I should probably say. The label already knew what our talents were. Anna's job was to advise them on what to change about our bodies.

I knew this sort of thing went on in other industries, but I never thought about it in Japan. Here, our idols are presented as "natural," complete with flaws like moles and crooked teeth. Now I understand that the tactic behind this isn't to be kind to the idols. It's to market them to fans that are looking for a girl-next-door, someone they could easily see in their neighborhood – and fantasize about. I never thought about what kind of fans we would have. We knew that men were a huge demographic, but until I became an actual idol I had no idea they would be the vast majority. Grown men. Men who wanted to fuck me because of my plaid uniform skirt and energetic way of dancing around a field. Natural. *Pure*. It makes me gag now.

"She's quite plain, isn't she?" Anna stood in front of Reika, the girl at the far end from me. "Nice bone structure, though. Filled out. Give her a basic makeover, beginning with the hair. Give it some volume but keep the natural color. Make her shine and stand out. A bow would be cute in her hair. What's her name?"

"Reika."

Anna's nose scrunched up like she smelled a pile of shit. "Change it! No idols with a name that sounds like Reina on my watch…"

Muttering, Anna moved on to the next girl, Dolly. She had nothing but nice things to say about her. Something about seeing a bit of herself in the girl's beauty and the fact she wasn't fully Japanese. It made me exhale a sigh of relief. Maybe she would go easy on Yumi and me.

Koto and Mayu got a few comments about their overall style and the way they kept their hair. Since they were primarily dancers, they needed to be pretty but not so much since they would always be in motion. Plus, it sounded like Anna already decided that Dolly would be the main visual of the group. Possibly the leader.

When she got to Nezu, she started laughing.

"Are you kidding me? How old is this girl?"

"Seventeen."

"*Seventeen?* She looks eight!"

They bickered over the look to take with Nezu. Age her up? Make her look even younger? There was only so much to do with a girl who looked like she should be playing the recorder at a school recital. In the end they met in the middle and decided to give her clothes and makeup suitable for her age, but give her pigtails to highlight her youthful appearance. Hilariously, it's a style Nezu has kept since, and she's quite a bit older now.

I held my breath when Anna reached Yumi. She could be particular about what people thought regarding her appearance. A boy once called her "hawk face" and she cried all night.

"Hmm." Anna rolled her papers and tipped up Yumi's chin. "Plain, but there's a lot to work with here. Excellent bone structure. Give her a proper haircut... I'm thinking pixie... and we could take her to the next level. Don't skimp on the bangs, but keep them to the side. Add some colors. Start with a light red or soft brown and we'll go from there. Smile, girl." Anna chuckled. "Charm point: these teeth. We'll doll her up a bit and then make sure she smiles for the camera a lot. Mature but still holding a girlish edge. These aren't bad." Anna tapped Yumi's breasts as they poked through her T-shirt, making my friend stumble back. "Humble, but they suit her frame. Give her a padded bra from now on. She'll still look natural and like they fit her frame, just more attractive. Give her a cool style. Yes, she can be the cool one."

Yumi swallowed. Her entire look was just changed in an instant. The hair would be cut, dyed, and styled to highlight the structure of her face. The clothes she was to wear from now on were mostly jeans and stylish tops. So much for the cotton skirts she brought with her.

Anna's satisfied smile disappeared the moment she saw me.

"Oh my God." She looked as if she saw a hideous monster before her. "You lot expect me to work *miracles?* Who is this girl? An intern thinking she's funny?"

Beppu cleared his throat. "Vocalist."

"I hope she can sing like Liberace, because woof."

I feel like I must defend myself. Granted, I was a fairly homely girl, but I wasn't ugly. Just average. Eventually they would learn how to style me to give me my "optimum beauty," but in those early days Anna was looking at a sad, round face and a stocky body to go with it. I was the most muscular of the bunch. Not fat. Sure, I was a bit overweight at certain times, but for the most part I was merely built like a pack horse. I've since grown into it more, and people even tell me I'm "striking" when done up in makeup and fancy clothes, though I don't know if I believe them. I mean, I have never cared much about what people thought of my looks. They could think me beautiful, ugly, or think nothing at all. What was it to me?

But I wasn't a bad looking girl. Just average.

"Either put this girl so far in the back nobody can see her, or just start from the ground up. Clothes, makeup, hair, get her some fucking plastic surgery for the love of God. And definitely put her on a diet. It's her only hope."

I wasn't happy to hear that. I liked not being hungry, thank you very much.

The mood in the room changed after Anna left. Those of us who had been rebuilt like a custom doll were quiet and on the verge of tears. Those who had been relatively praised were quiet for our sake. Nezu complained that there was nothing she could do about her height. I said that I wasn't ugly. Some girls assured me that I was fine for a normal girl.

Yes, a normal girl. Not pretty enough to be a national idol, but I could do well on a regional level. Even I knew that back then.

It was Dolly who was a natural beauty. Even Yumi would soon be done up in a way that I had to admit was stunning. The first time I saw my best friend – the girl I loved – walk away from the dressing room, new hair, new clothes, and a new style of makeup, I was floored. For the first time I saw her not as the girl who got her school uniform dirty kicking up dust with her bike, but as a star who would be in magazines, on stages, and on TVs. The panic I felt wasn't jealousy that I wasn't as good looking or that now half of Japan would find her beautiful. It was the knowledge that my Yumi would soon be beyond my grasp. How could I protect her then?

***

Ever since I became an important person in a child's life, I've come to understand my protective tendencies. From the moment I first saw her, I knew I had to fiercely protect her from the horrors of the world. It's funny. I don't consider myself a maternal person, yet holding that baby for the first time awoke so many things within me. I felt a conflation of sadness, confusion, and anger. If she had been born a boy, I wouldn't need to protect her outside of how a mother protects her child. Since she was born a girl, there will always be people trying to take advantage of her. Like they did with Yumi.

It's common for mothers and guardians to gather around the gates of the school where the little one goes when it's time to pick them up. Ironically, I've become one of them. When my stomach starts growling for lunch, I know it's time to stick my wallet in my back pocket and start the ten-minute walk to the school. Since she's still so young, she only goes for a half day. I don't usually take her to school early in the morning, but I'm almost always the one waiting at noon to see her chubby face come tumbling through the gates, sometimes with the help of a teacher because she's always had some problems with her balance. The doctors say it may be something she grows into as her body matures, but there is a possibility that there were drugs in the system when she was in the womb. Even though I know I shouldn't, I blame myself.

She calls me Chi-Chi. The first time I heard her call me that, I almost cried, and I didn't know why. People think it's funny because my name is Chiharu and she's calling me "daddy" instead of "mommy." Well, if you look at me, you will see that I am quite unfeminine most days. People see me as a woman, but even the little one's teachers were surprised the first time they saw me. The only mothers waiting around the gate with a haircut like mine also compensate with skirts and flashy makeup. I haven't worn makeup since I had a photo shoot a few weeks ago.

It's best for her to not be too confused anyway. So she calls me daddy. There are worse things for a child you love to call you.

Playing with her, bathing her, and putting her to bed remind me of my training days as a teenager. At the time I didn't realize how much Beppu was looking out for us. He has two daughters, although they are almost grown now. I don't think he saw much of them growing up because he was "too busy raising you girls," or so he always said. Most of us were out of high school. To think of a strange man "raising us" was something else.

When I am tipsy or in a particularly funny mood, I will call Beppu my father. I didn't have one growing up, and he is the closest thing to a father I will ever have. He is more than a mentor. He was my guardian during those formative years in the entertainment business.

Girls fall in love. They make mistakes. They are like any other human being, except they are more vulnerable because of how they were born. I wonder if I look at my little one the same way Beppu looked at the seven of us when we were first assembled. He must have seen seven stupid, hormonal teenagers who were about to deal with things no normal young woman does. On top of that, we were going to make bad decisions and have people try to hurt us. Just thinking about it makes me panic and want to go grab the baby.

You see? I am a maternal mess.

I think Beppu knows what I am going through. We have the kind of relationship where he can make fun of me relentlessly and I either take it or throw it back at him. It's unusual for our age difference and him being my old manager. Whenever he comes over and sees me "babysitting," he'll laugh and say, "Remember that time your period was late?" and then he'll get a Lica-*chan* doll in the face.

Soon she will be at an age where I can start teaching her to ride a bike. I don't know why this excites me. It's not the first milestone a child has, and it'll be far from her last. I mean, I'll soon give her piano lessons, and that is something much more personal to me than riding a bike. I think it's because some of my first heart-stopping memories of Yumi were when we rode bikes in tandem. I can still remember pedaling through the empty roads of Seki, Yumi sitting right behind me with her arms wrapped around my abdomen. When she wasn't talking over the wind she would lean her head on my shoulder and whisper for me to go faster. She loved the thrill. I loved having her touch me like that.

The little one isn't quite ready for the bike yet. I know the moment she has that kind of freedom it will be hard to keep up with her. She will grow even quicker. Soon I won't know what she's doing out there with her friends, if there's a boy – or a girl, of course – who has stolen her heart. She will keep things from me, like I kept things from my mother for far too long. Someone will break her heart. She'll waver on what she wants to do when she grows up – striking a balance between her passion and my expectations. I'll be hard on her, even if I don't mean to be. I'll only want what's best for her. You mothers out there know what I mean.

She has the power to kill me with just one look. When she laughs, I see that gap between her two front baby teeth, and all of my love, my misery, and who I am today comes crashing through my heart. Only one other girl has made me feel this level of emotion.

Chapter 5

The next six months were devoted entirely to our training.

They were not glamorous. In fact, every day of rest we were given was one I, at least, took with no remorse. On average I slept about six hours a night. Doesn't sound too bad at first, but keep in mind I was still a teenager and could barely function without nine. Consider this went on for days at a time, and by my day off I would be a zombie wandering the halls of the dorm.

It was like being in school again, only instead of memorizing *kanji*, math formulas, and dates in history, we were tasked with "the arts." We were all divided into two categories: talents and "needs work." The stuff in between was largely forgotten on the individual level. The talent classes were meant to take our natural abilities beyond what we knew. For example, Beppu arranged for me to take at least one hour of piano lessons from an instructor every day. Likewise, my vocals were deemed "promising," and I took vocal lessons with Yumi and Dolly, sometimes by myself, sometimes as a trio. I was the only specified alto of the group, and it was my understanding that I would be responsible for lead backing vocals and the occasional solo line in our songs.

What I needed to improve on the most was my dancing. All afternoon, every afternoon, I met up with one instructor or another to go over my athleticism. They agreed that I didn't become easily winded, but I practically had two left feet. One even refused to believe I took ballet for many years. I didn't say I was good at it.

Yumi was almost the opposite of me. She excelled in vocals and dancing. They also had her take acting classes. While I never had dreams of starring in movies or even commercials, there seemed something easy-go-lucky about pretending to be someone else. Yumi was a natural. I would listen to her in our room or in the common area reciting lines of a play, her movements practically liquid as she incorporated the occasional pirouette or modern dance move. She was taking both in the afternoons, but not with me. She danced with Koto and Mayu while I was stuck with Reika and occasionally just by myself, I was that bad.

What she failed at the most was musical theory and instruments. I love Yumi, but she has never been great at playing instruments. For a while she played violin in school, but never got a solo and was pushed farther and farther back into the group until you couldn't hear her at all. In the beginning, Beppu had her take introductory piano to help her learn music better. I knew this was a lost cause. Didn't he think I had been trying to teach her to play even children's tunes for *years?* Growing up, Yumi would occasionally watch me play piano with a frown. For every second she admired me at recitals or in my home, the next second was full of jealousy.

We all took etiquette and "personal health" classes together, usually at the end of our days when we were exhausted from the rigorous physical training we went through. The instructor was a middle-aged woman who always wore a long skirt and turtleneck sweater, even during the sweltering summer months. Her job was to make sure we knew how to behave in public, especially when we were representing our group and by extension the label. She judged our posture, the way we spoke, and even the way we sat down. Yumi was a natural at looking ladylike and was the instructor's favorite student. She, Dolly, Reika, and Mayu were stars and set an example for the rest of us. Nezu often got into spats with the instructor while Koto constantly fell asleep on her desk. Me? I discovered that crossing my ankles while I sit with my hands in my lap was near impossible. It wasn't something I could do without thinking… although it's funny, now that I have been out of that business for years, I find myself doing it constantly. I'll be sitting in front of my TV and look down to realize I'm crossing my ankles to the side and holding my hands in my lap like *Uchi de Banzai!!* is going to storm through my door and interview me in my home. Where was this when I was in training? I would've been yelled at less.

While the etiquette classes were annoying, the personal health ones made me rage.

There were some aspects of it I agreed with, or at least didn't mind. The instructors who came to teach us on a rotating basis talked about the importance of exercise – which we got an abundant amount of – and eating a healthy diet. This isn't so bad. It's the same thing we learned in school. We even learned about our female bodies, although nobody would admit that they didn't remember fallopian tubes or how to treat a yeast infection from middle school health class.

We also learned basic sexual health, even though our contracts stipulated that we were not to date, let alone have sex. Of course, idols do those things all the time. They're just sneaky about it. Things weren't different back then. Even during training, both Reika and Mayu had boyfriends they saw, and Dolly would talk to any boy she came across when we occasionally went out on weekends. Nezu was the only one who openly said she wasn't interested in dating, only learning her trade. Koto, I gathered, was too shy. Yumi was like Nezu and focused on her dream. As for me? I was just as interested in boys during that time as I was as a teenager – or even now! I've only feared for my womb once in my life, and it was not during those times.

These things didn't bother me. They were factual, useful. No, it was the other shit that made my fingers curl and my face get so bothered that the instructors would stop teaching and ask me if I had a problem. The other girls would laugh at me for my "bitchy face" anyway. When we were alone in our room, Yumi would suggest that I take my etiquette lessons to heart and control my reactions. Grow a poker face. Well, I've never had a poker face. I'm either looking slightly happy or downright incorrigible. Even to this day I have people asking me if I'm constipated or about to punch someone.

No, what really pissed me off was the diet talk. As I said before, the instructors talked a lot about good diets and healthy exercise. That only applied to a small amount of people. For idols? We were supposed to take the recommended amount of calories and cut them in *half*. Absolutely no sugars or fat. There were so many salads on hand that I felt like a sheep. Rice became a luxury. And I got off easy, because I wasn't supposed to be "pretty."

Of course I was on a diet. Anna Matsuda had declared me fat, and lose weight I did. Between the lack of food and all the exercise, I went down a size in my first two months there. Yumi went down two. She couldn't get away with sneaking food like I could.

Outside of our dorm room, people from the label watched her and a couple of others like hawks. If she took too much food, they chastised her and took the excess away. If she ate the wrong thing at all, she was informed that she didn't care about herself. Yumi would come into our room at night, exhausted, her stomach growling and her voice whining about how hungry she was. "Chi-*chan*," she would say pitifully. "Snack?"

I had a stash of crackers, chips, and other goods that I kept beneath my bed to munch on when I was hungry. So, every night. I got these on my days off, since nobody inspected me as long as I continued to lose some weight, and my mother would send me whole boxes of them after I told her what they were doing to Yumi. Her parents didn't seem to care.

Yumi ate a lot of my snacks. She was like an endless pit. A vacuum. If I had a box of crackers, she would inhale them in one night before going to bed. Then she would retain water and get yelled at by either Anna Matsuda or a dance instructor. In the beginning she ranted about it, claimed that it didn't bother her, and then after a while she stopped mentioning it at all. I thought maybe they had let up on her. Then later on I realized she had given up. It was the first way they got to her.

Yet she was one of their darlings. Up for one of the top spots in the group once our training was looked over at the end of six months. Everyone guessed that either she or Dolly would be made leader and the center of the group. Those kinds of rumors made her happy. She would sing merrily in the common rooms and hum herself to sleep at night. Even if she didn't make center, she was still happy to know she was such a contender.

I was happy for her too. It was her dream.

Sometimes I sat and thought about my own dreams. This was especially true at the end of a long day, when I was sore, hungry, and tired of being yelled at because I couldn't dance as well as everyone else yet. I would stay behind in the instrument room and tap out some melodies on the piano while I sorted my thoughts. Why was I there? Just for Yumi? No, I wouldn't have come if I didn't want some of this as well.

True, I loved to perform. My preferences only lay in the piano and some light singing. Being an idol was more Yumi's idea that I went along with. As a child, it looked like fun. Who didn't want to practically sing karaoke in front of the world if it made them happy? As I got older, however, I grew more self-conscious, and kind of lazy. It was fun feeling my arms tone and become more muscular as I worked out in the company gym and learned how to dance better. The few times we went to the park on our days off to kick around a soccer ball were fun because the other girls would *ooh* and *aah* over how hard I could kick the ball. I wouldn't get that level of exercise without someone ordering me to. I didn't lose many inches on my body... nor did I lose many kilos. But I became a muscular young woman, and it made me proud to see how my clothes fell on my body. Especially T-shirts. For some reason I really liked looking at myself wearing a T-shirt. (If I admit... I still do.)

My dreams, though, never became clear in my head. So I continued with the training, assuming that things would improve once we actually debuted. We still didn't have a group name or any other information yet.

The label heads said they were still conducting marketing research and deciding on a style for us. Those days were quite the conflation of the times. Not only were schoolgirl type idols big again, but sexy, charming women were making the rounds as well. Since we were older teens, I had hoped for something more mature. I didn't want to wear a school uniform again.

That's it, I suppose. Life was much of the same every day for those months. Except for one day. There was one special day in August, when the heat was baking outside but my body was burning for other reasons. It was the day I first kissed Yumi.

***

One time, Yumi and I were climbing a tree in the encroaching forests just behind my house in Seki. I was stockier, stronger, but she was lithe and able to climb faster than me. She scurried up that tree faster than I could count, and I was counting – counting how many laughs she let out as she screeched every time a splinter entered her palm or a piece of bark scratched her bare leg. Yumi was a mess by the time she reached the sturdiest branch. I was farther behind, my feet losing purchase in the same places she had once touched.

"Chi-*chan!*" she called, straddling the branch as she waved down at me. Her dark hair obscured her face as the upper breezes blew by, but her smile was big and friendly behind every wisp. I was entranced, like the lovesick thirteen-year-old I didn't know I was yet. I wanted to spend the rest of my day attached to that tree trunk, my fingers digging into bark and sap as my head tilted up and gazed at her laughing figure.

"Do you need help?" She pushed her hair out of her face, that smile disappearing as concern took over her countenance. "*Mou*, Chi-*chan*, stop eating so many cakes!"

Easy for her to say. I was the one who hit puberty first, and my body had grown heavier with each passing month. My mother said I was filling out into a woman's form, but all I knew was that my breasts were lopsided and my stomach and thighs were covered in red streaks that made me think I was being tied down in the middle of the night. Yumi didn't have these markings. Nor did she have her full breasts yet. I don't even think she had reached menarche, something I knew she was jealous of me for having months ago. Anyway, eating a rice cake was as good as gaining a kilo in those days. She didn't know this yet. I miss the days when she didn't worry about what she ate.

"*Daijyoubu...*" I muttered, using the last of my strength to shuffle up the trunk and swing myself onto the branch. I landed behind Yumi, exhausted, my back slumping against the trunk as I hid my disdain for having a broken limb trying to shove itself into my ass.

Yumi didn't look at me. She was focused on the fields in front of us, each a beautiful hue of green as the farmers made their final rounds for the evening. The sun was before us, descending, its brightness muted by thick clouds as the final rays of daylight turned the patches of sky red and purple. Back then, I didn't think to savor such sunsets. When you grow up in a place like Seki, you assume that everywhere in the world has the same sunset.

I was too busy savoring my friend anyway.

Was that the day I fell in love with her? Those days of being fascinated with her aging form are a blur to me now. But I think that was the day. I barely knew what love was, of course. Only what the movies said about men and women kissing and getting married. I never saw my mother love my father before their divorce. The only frame of reference I had in real life at the time was my own beating heart and the blood that pounded in my ear as I thought about touching the small of her back through her white blouse.

I didn't, though. I was too embarrassed. Even though I had touched her a million times since we were children, this time it felt different. It's funny to look back on now that I'm an adult. Almost nostalgic.

"Chi-*chan*," Yumi sighed, glancing over her shoulder. "One day when we get out of here, I want you to write a song about this place. I'll sing it."

"What kind of song would I write?" Just the thought of it made me want to yawn. Who wrote songs about Seki? You laugh because of that song, "Nostalgic Town," that I wrote for Suzuka Ashida. What did it hit? Top twenty? It played on all the rural stations, and I got a lot of fan mail from aunties saying that I was an old soul. That wasn't about Seki. It is about the feeling I have whenever I am around Yumi.

"A ballad. Guitar ballad. Like Mariya Takeuchi!" She said it with such gusto that I thought she would fall off the branch and crack open her skull.

"Why would you sing it? I thought you wanted to sing like an idol. Idols don't sing songs like that anymore." Even when I was thirteen, I was cynical about the state of current music.

The way she looked at me was odd. Like she was considering something about me for the first time. "Because I want to sing all the songs Chi-*chan* writes."

She looked away again. It was an offhand comment, and yet it startled me. Before that day, I never thought about anyone singing my songs. I barely sang my own songs outside of the shower. When I thought of Yumi singing them, on a stage with bright lights like she would one day, I felt my heart stop in my chest as if someone put their hand there and squeezed it.

Let me put it this way. When you are a composer, you of course care about creating a beautiful melody and evoking emotions with nothing but a piano and a few words in your head. Whenever I create a new song, I sit at my piano and study the keys before pressing any one of them. If I hit the wrong note, I lose my inspiration. But if I hit the right one, I instantly hit the next, and then the next, and soon a song bursts from my fingers until I have a chorus and maybe a bridge down. When I play this song for the first time, I can imagine a singer taking me away on the journey I am actually creating. I don't think of myself as the person responsible for the song's creation. I think of the singer, standing on that stage and using the power of her voice to convey my feelings to you.

I could see Yumi, standing proudly in Budokan and enthralling her audience with my songs. I remember sitting in the VIP section of that concert, in fact. I am happy with the track Miss Ashida cut, but if I may say so, Yumi's live performance of my song in Budokan nearly killed me.

But that day I had no idea that soon Yumi would really sing my song like that. I didn't know a lot of things. Like that I was in love with her.

I was sitting at my piano years ago, hitting the same note over and over. I was worried about Yumi. Earlier that morning I saw the news report that said she was being warmly received in Taiwan. "The girl YUMI who has captivated the hearts of Asia," the headline said in Chinese. Even though the public loved her, I was afraid. I was always afraid for her. She has always been so fragile about how people perceive her. You should have seen her the day the homeroom teacher told her she had the hair of a dirty farm girl. She cried all day and told me she was going to cut it off. She wears her hair so short now, but she's still a scared girl sometimes who wants to prove her femininity. Which is why when I saw her on the news report, wearing a stylish pair of trousers and a beautiful blouse, I only saw her womanly form and the warmth she exuded. I wondered if anyone in the Taiwanese airport could see what I had always known.

It was a hard day. I was still in love with Yumi after so many years. And now without her around, I pouted at the piano until the news reporter said, "YUMI will be performing this Saturday, and she says that she hopes to reveal a new song from childhood friend Chiharu Morita, who has gained much popularity as a songwriter."

Was it true? Was she going to sing the song I wrote just for her? The label didn't like the songs I wrote for her. They could see my love in them. The perverted love that my mentor Anna said was like a curse on my name.

Yumi never realized. She thought all of my songs were brilliant and fought to sing them, but the label always won. Why did she think I retired from the idol life? I was tired of losing.

But that wasn't why I was pouting so much at my piano. Nor was it because I got the seventh noise complaint of the year from the neighbor with a barking dog. I am embarrassed to admit, but I was so depressed because they showed Yumi with that man. "We're just helping each other promote our projects," she always told me when we had the chance to get together. "It's not like we're really dating."

You know how that ended. I could sense it happening at the time. I was jealous. I would always be jealous of anyone – any man – Yumi spent time with. I always wanted to be alone with her, like we used to be growing up. I wanted to go back to that tree and watch the sunset with her sitting in front of me, talking about how one day our dreams would come true.

That was the day I wrote "Magnolia." She never had the chance to perform it.

Chapter 6

Yumi's birthday happened to fall on a weekend that year. It was also a weekend that we had off – both days! Even though half the girls went away, to go on dates or visit their families, I wanted to make the day as special as possible for my best friend, who had worked so hard those past four months.

We didn't have much money yet, but I bought her a cupcake from a bakery and nearly shoved it into her hand when a label person wasn't looking. We took it to our room, lit a candle in it, and I sang a birthday song for her. She made her wish and blew out the candle. Although I had bought the cupcake for her, she insisted on sharing half.

"Did you get something from your parents?" I asked, licking chocolate off my fingers.

Yumi had wolfed down her half of the cupcake faster than I could notice. "No. We're going home for *obon,* so I'm sure I'll get something then." I hoped so.

I had another gift for her, but waited until that night to present it to her. After dinner we had some fun in the common room with Koto and Nezu before heading to a karaoke place to have some *real* fun. Granted, we were all underage so we couldn't buy alcohol, so we ordered the most sugary drinks on the menu to really piss off the likes of Anna and company. As sugary drinks tend to do, we were so hyper within the first half hour that we were screaming lyrics to ridiculous songs, sure to make our voices hoarse for Monday.

When we ran out of time, we went back to the dorms and sat around the common area, acting like we were at some sleepover with pillows in our laps. Nezu started off suggesting we play truth or consequences. Since Yumi was the birthday girl, she had to go first.

"*Hora!*" she exclaimed, sitting back and smiling so her gap showed in my direction. "Truth!"

"When was your first kiss?"

She blushed; I blushed. Even though I thought I knew the answer, it was embarrassing to think about. Back then I didn't understand why. Now I do. It wasn't embarrassment. It was jealousy.

"*Fourteen. Ryuuta Matsumoto. Coolest boy in the second year.*" Her first official boyfriend. I saw them kiss before. I could only imagine what else they did, but she never talked about it for some reason.

"Seven."

The rest of us gaped at her. "Seven?" Nezu repeated.

"*Hai.*" Yumi was not perturbed. I was. My goal was to hide it from the others.

"Who were you kissing at seven?" Nezu's laugh was almost infectious, if it weren't for me keeping my mouth shut and my head pointed down. "Some boy in the schoolyard?"

Yumi tilted her head, neither humiliated nor struck with nostalgia. "Something like that."

"And what about you, Chi-*chan?*" Nezu asked me. "When was your first kiss?"

I was trapped in this strange world where I didn't know what way was up and what way was down. "*Seven*." I should have said. Instead, I lied. "Sixteen." It was when I started dating Junpei. Yumi wouldn't question it. Or would she?

You see, *I* was that person she kissed when she was seven. I don't count it as my first kiss or even a real one. We were seven! You know how children will emulate what they see adults doing? One day Yumi and I had the brilliant idea to practice kissing. At seven. I don't know if that's normal or not, but one day we were playing and suddenly pecking each other's lips like it was no deal. At the time, it wasn't. And never did we bring it up again, because why would we?

I unfortunately thought way too much about it the rest of that evening. The group split up, Yumi off to take a shower while I sat in our room and stared at the present I wanted to give her. It was a song, composed just for her voice. I had written it between piano lessons over the past four months.

When she saw the sheet music, she claimed it was beautiful and that she couldn't wait to practice it. I hoped she wasn't bullshitting me – she still wasn't great at reading music even after all this time. Better than she was growing up, but I doubted she could hear the notes in her head as she looked it over. Either way, she approached me on my bed and gave me a hug before changing into her pajamas and thanking me for a great birthday. Only one more year to twenty.

A summer storm rolled through later. Soon the window was lashed with rain while lightning lit up the world outside. Neither Yumi nor I were scared of storms, so I didn't think much of it.

"Chi-*chan*?" I could barely hear her voice over the storm. "Can I come over there?"

I didn't think twice. "Of course."

I've always wondered if other girls did what we did. Sometimes we would share a bed. Not just conveniently sleeping in the same space because it was easy or necessary, but purely because we wanted to. And I don't mean double beds or beds meant for two people. I mean twin beds and futons that we both had to squeeze into. When we were children it was easy since we were so small. When Yumi stayed over at my house, my mother would put us both in my bed and it wasn't a nuisance at all. Growing older and bigger, we didn't do it as often, but there were nights Yumi or I would crawl into the other's bed. There was nothing sexual about it.

These beds were even smaller than the ones we grew up with. They were barely made for function, let alone getting a good night's rest in them. So when I said Yumi could climb into bed with me on the night of her birthday, I was not thinking ahead. This was the first time she had asked such a thing since we came to the dorms.

"Oof, Chi-*chan,* this bed is narrow."

I was pushed up against the wall, on my side, face toward hers as she shoved even closer to me. My blanket barely covered us both. "It's the same damn bed as yours. Don't know why you are surprised."

"Feh, maybe I really am fat."

"Don't say that." I put my hand on her side, squeezing what fat she had those days. "You're perfect."

"You think so?"

I nodded, and hoped she could feel my forehead touching hers. "Happy birthday, Yumi,"

"Thanks."

I closed my eyes and focused on going to sleep. It would be a cramped night, and a part of me hoped she would slink back off to her bed within an hour or so. As I felt the waves of sleep begin to claim me, I heard, "Why did you lie about your first kiss?"

My eyes opened again. "Eh? Don't know what you're talking about."

"Please. You know it was you I was talking about. When we were seven. Or have you forgotten?"

"Oh, no…"

"That's not fair, Chi-*chan.* How can my first kiss be with you but yours isn't with me?"

Except it was. I hadn't said anything to the group because I didn't want them knowing what we had done. They would judge us. Think us weird. I hadn't come out to even myself yet back then, but I knew that much. The world didn't want to know about what Yumi and I did as children. My mother would have laughed, but Yumi's would have punished her. I would never see her again.

"I'm sorry." I didn't know what else to say.

"If you're really sorry, you'll kiss me properly."

My heart stopped, something she could have surely noticed being so close to me. Although the room was dark, I could still see her eyes looking back into mine, wide, mischievous. She was a beautiful girl with an even more beautiful smile.

She was my best friend. And she wanted me to kiss her.

Here is where I confess the sheer nerves plaguing my poor body. Yumi didn't know I had lied when I said my first kiss was at sixteen. I had never kissed anyone before. Least of all a boy. Until that moment I wasn't even sure I wanted to kiss a girl. I liked the thought. Girls were safe and easy to get along with. The touch of Yumi's hand on mine, as our fingers intertwined between us, was almost hypnotic. I wanted to feel her soft skin more. Feel *more* of her skin. My nails brushed against her wrist, making her shiver, and in that instance I knew what it meant to have such power over another person.

For all my confusion over the years, and for all I know now, back then there was only one undeniable truth in my mind: I wanted her. I wanted Yumi. I wanted my best friend. Always had.

My fingers caressed her cheek, tentatively. She may have been joking still. Yumi didn't mean for me to really kiss her. She liked boys. In school she was so popular with them that people joked she could have her pick. The jealousy I felt then was directed at her. That she could have her pick of her lovers. Why had she never picked me?

I wasn't jealous now. I was scared. Petrified. I had never kissed someone before. Now she, of all people, wanted my lips on hers.

There were two options. I could call her bluff and turn over, sighing at such a joke, or I could play it off with a kiss on her cheek and a laugh to chase it down.

In my endless stupidity, I chose neither. Instead I chose a third option that would change my life forever. I kissed her. For *real*.

Such a kiss started innocently enough. I gently placed my lips upon hers, savoring the taste of her skin as my fingers struggled to figure out where they should go. Her shoulder? Her face? The pillow? What did people do when they kissed in this position?

Then I leaned into it, which didn't take much work since the bed was so tiny. My hand clasped against her cheek as my breath stuck in my throat and I became brazen. My first kiss... and I was taking the lead!

There. That was the moment. When Yumi's hand gently held my arm while I gradually rolled on top of her, I knew it. Oh, God, I knew it. This was what I wanted. This was the sort of thing my body pined for, my soul called for. I wanted a woman. I wanted someone soft and pretty, someone who sighed like a goddess and caressed me as if I were her chosen acolyte. This potential was always inside of me. Had I kissed her earlier, or perhaps another girl, I would have known sooner. It wasn't until that night it all became clear to me. The scent of her soap and shampoo – of her – filled my nose as my fingertips played with her shorn hair.

What was I supposed to do next? I was inexperienced. A virgin to all things but love. In the movies the couple would make passionate love all night. Yes, I wanted to do that. With Yumi. No longer was she only my best friend. She was a woman, not a girl. A woman I begged to have as I wrapped my arms around her and allowed my body to roll on top of her. Amazing how well our legs twisted together. Yumi opened her mouth. My tongue slipped along hers.

It was all happening so fast.

I was going to do it. For better or for worse, I was going to take off our clothes and make love to her. Yumi didn't know it yet, but she was my first kiss. Now I wanted her to be my first in everything. My first love. My first partner. My first lover.

In my excitement, my hips thrust against her. Yumi turned her head away, and that was it.

"*Mou, ii yo.*" She laughed, turning over beneath me so she faced her own bed a few meters away. I had no choice but to slip between her and the wall. "That's enough of that silliness."

I wish I could tell you that more happened that night. The best thing was that I found out so much about myself. The worst was that Yumi never brought it up again. Not even when she asked me to hold her and I wrapped my arms around her and softly pressed my lips against her neck. None of that. None of this was mentioned again the next morning.

But in that tiny moment of my life, everything made sense.

***

The chance to ask her about that night never came up until a few months ago. We were sitting in a café, catching up on everything when I asked her what she thought of that moment. Yumi, dressed down in a casual T-shirt and designer jeans, looked at me with a forlorn face and said, "I wanted to know how Chi-*chan* kissed."

"And?" My hand shook around my teacup.

Yumi looked wistfully into the distance.

Before you ask, since I know it will come up in the comments and emails, Yumi knows that I am a lesbian. I told her a long while ago. I am blessed in that she has always supported me and never judged me for it.

Dealing with judgment is not easy, though. My fellow lesbians will know how hard it is to be someone like us in society. While I never broke down and cried over my sexuality, I did understand that it made me abnormal and a threat to some people. I would have to be careful who I told, both in the industry and out. Beppu knows. He was probably one of the first, since he's very observant and may have known even before I did. Most of the label knows, I guess. They don't care, as long as I don't make a scene. Like now.

Yet in my industry, whether or not you're a public celebrity like Yumi or a behind the scenes name like me, you have to be careful. Employers don't like it when your personal life is not the norm. Let alone in my industry. When I was an idol, I had to be very careful about my image. Not only was I not allowed to date boys, but girls would be even worse. I had to remain "pure." Our fans expected us to look available to them. They wanted to imagine us playing silly games in our rooms, eating sweets and whining about calories, and blowing off our studies even though we were of course immaculate students. A riot, since I had already graduated!

It took me many months, years really, to fully understand what kind of lifestyle I wanted to live. I had no access to information while I lived in the dorm. I only knew that I liked girls and wanted to do all sorts of adult things with them. Realizing that woke up that certain part of me inside. I went from repressing any sexual desire I had – because I thought it had to be directed at boys, and they didn't interest me – to imagining kissing every girl I came across. It was liberating. Freeing. Finally I understood what people were so obsessed about regarding sex.

This is very personal, but a big turning point for me was when I first started... oh no, it's so embarrassing. All I'll say is that I saw an increase in personal activity after I realized my sexuality, if you understand my meaning. I thought about girls. Not necessarily Yumi, although she was my frame of reference. Sometimes I just made girls up. Trying to determine who my ideal type was. A part of me became restless to experience sex with another girl.

Except the first thing you realize when you accept that you're gay is that finding others like you is nearly impossible.

Back then I didn't have access to the resources other lesbians had. I couldn't sign up for mailing lists or magazines. I couldn't search the internet. I was too young to sneak to the one gay bar I knew of in Nagoya. If I wanted to find a partner, she would have to be in my immediate circle. And none of the girls I trained with were like that.

Love, Yumi

The closest thing I had to any kind of partner was Yumi, and as I said, she never brought up that night again. I often wondered if she thought about it at all.

"Of course I thought about it," she said in that café. "My Chi-*chan* isn't so bad a kisser."

She was killing me, and she knew it. Yumi enjoyed making me squirm in embarrassment.

Since that fateful night, I have gradually come to know more about myself. There is no doubt in my mind that I am gay. My interest in men has never increased from zero, whereas there have been a few women who made my heart flutter. None as much as Yumi, though. She doesn't make my heart flutter. She gives me heart attacks.

I think this is a good place to leave off for now. I'm feeling a bit under the weather, and when we meet again I will be jumping into a new arc of my story. When the Butterfly Tops finally debuted and we first tasted stardom.

Thank you for sticking with me so far. Your support means a lot to me.

Part 3

INNOCENCE IS NOT A COMMODITY

Hildred Billings

Love, Yumi

純真は商品じゃない

Pardon my absence these past few days. I fully intended to jump back on the day after you last heard from me, but I woke up the following morning to a grumpy and very sick little one. Apparently she caught a bug going around her school. Next thing I knew, I was trapped in bed as well. Soon my whole household was coughing and sneezing.

This means plenty of time has gone by since my last confession. Plenty of time for the media to finally pick up on it. It was not pleasant to be lying on my couch yesterday morning, trying to recover from this bug, and turning on the TV to find out people were talking about Yumi again. This time I had no one to blame but myself.

It's kind of funny what people are saying. Apparently I am both a pariah and a brave woman. I'm either corrupting the youth or being a voice for a generation. Whatever. I only set out to tell my and Yumi's story so it would be known. I don't mean to do anything else. Whatever people take away from my posts… that's on them.

Perhaps it's my fatigue talking. Before I started writing these posts, I had been hired to write a short score for an independent video game. Well, so far they haven't fired me, so there's that. I should be working on it instead of doing this. My brain is so foggy from being sick that I'm not sure I can do a great job on it right now, so I'm here instead.

Beppu called me shortly after I posted that last entry. I got some great unsolicited advice. How I'm fucking myself over. How I'm probably fucking Yumi over, who is already working hard to rebuild her image and career. Now the world knows that we have kissed. Even if the story they know is from years ago, it's enough. She willingly put her lips on another girl's, and for that she must be punished.

We both knew going into this that people may say things. That in an extreme situation we may lose our careers. We were prepared for that. I have other things I can fall back on, and Yumi was always good with her money, even during her darkest times. Of course there is the little one to think about. That's why I wanted to do this now. It would be easier to make changes now that she's still so young as opposed to later when she has friends and a memory. I think she'll be fine, even with someone like me helping to raise her.

Enough about that. The time has come for me to sit down again and continue the story. Where did I leave off? Oh, right. The media will love this part for sure. The real story behind the birth of the Butterfly Tops.

Chapter 7

It was a drizzly, sleepy Tuesday morning when the seven of us were summoned to the downstairs conference room to hear our fates.

"Butterfly Tops?" someone said, after the logo and the name of our group was revealed. I had to concur with the question. Months' worth of marketing research, and that was the best they could come up with? It sounded like a sneaker brand.

"Yes," Mr. Kawaguchi said. "The seven of you are a rainbow of butterflies. You will each be assigned a color." He pulled out laminated papers and had us pass them around the table. Sure enough, there was my face on one of them, outlined in dark blue. Yumi, sitting beside me, got bright red. I didn't need to be told that I would be in the back of the group with such a subdued color – not that they ever did anything with these colors, mind you. "The Tops stands for 'being at the top of the world.' Every group must convey a sense of world domination."

I snorted. A few people glanced at me, including Beppu.

"Your first song has been decided." We next received the scores for the song, including a separate lyrics sheet. "Those of you who can read music, try to memorize it tonight. Tomorrow you will begin practicing for your debut. Next week is recording. After that, we are hoping to have you ready to go in four weeks."

Four weeks! We would be debuting so soon? Granted, we had been there five months already, but four weeks to be handed our destinies and then sent out into the world was no time at all. Were they marketing us already? We had very few photo shoots. Just our company profile pictures and then some nice ones to put up on the website.

We were informed that we were having a "soft debut." This meant we would put out a song, do some performances, and then work on our next single which would be more heavily promoted. I thought this was silly. Nobody remembers the soft debuts of other idols.

It didn't help that our debut song, "Forgotten Memories," was bland and too formulaic. The melody was simple. I learned to play it on piano in fewer than ten minutes, something I had to do to help Yumi learn how to sing it. The lyrics were just embarrassing. Clichés, overused words, and the generic idea that sometimes we forget things. Imagine that.

We spent the whole week learning this God-awful song. "Learning." Like I said, it took me ten minutes to master on the piano, so that meant it only took us a day to learn how to sing it in the practice room. Multiply this times five and that was the hell I lived in.

Sure, you think I'm whining over nothing. Think of the blandest song you know and how much it grates on you. It gets stuck in your head even though you don't want it there. What can you do? More than one night saw both Yumi and me humming it in our sleep.

Most girls would give anything to become an idol. It's true, most of the girls in our group were like that, including Yumi. Even they admitted that they could barely stand the song. It did not help that lines had not been distributed, so we each had to learn the entire thing leading up to the day of recording.

Love, Yumi

I admit, this day was rather fun… but not for the reasons you may think.

At the morning meeting we were given our line assignments. Yours truly received one line in the interlude. The rest was backing vocals or a duet with someone else. Everyone sang the chorus together.

"*Yatta*," Yumi said beneath her breath after counting up her solo lines. She and Dolly were alternating lines in the first verse – a sign that they would become the two biggest stars of the group. "Eleven lines. Can you believe it?"

I showed her my one. She expressed concern that my talents were not being used. While I agreed, I didn't care about singing.

The seven of us arrived in the recording studio at precisely ten. We had been there before to record demos of our singing abilities – or lack thereof, in Koto's case – but this was our first time recording an actual song. Most of the other girls tittered. Me? I was more interested in what was going on behind the glass.

When the producers and mixers weren't concerned with me, I would wait for my turn to record outside the control room. I wanted to see inside, particularly the large soundboards with so many buttons, knobs, and equalizers that I felt like I was looking at an old science fiction movie. Beppu was inside, discussing things with the producer and recording engineer. When he saw me loitering, he briskly asked if he could help me with something. I told him I was curious about what went on in there.

I thought he would shoo me away, but after staring at me for some time, he motioned for me to enter the room and watch Reika record her lines of the second verse. I behaved, standing off to the side and watching these men twist dials, move knobs, and give instructions to Reika in such a way that the sound quality was much better. It reminded me of tinkering with a piano. Something I hadn't had the chance to do all week for the first time in months. Withdrawal.

Eventually I had to leave the room and go record my lines. Yumi stood outside the booth, since her turn was after mine. I could hear her humming her eleven lines. If it were possible, I think she was the only one excited about this venture. As for me? I did my line in two takes and got the hell out of there.

There is nothing glamorous about recording a song as a group. Later on I would discover that we didn't even need to record on the same day. It wasn't unusual for us to never even hear each other's voices until the final product came out. When we could, Yumi and I recorded together. We knew how to harmonize with each other, which was to the label's benefit. Plus Beppu remembered our audition and how good we sounded. Too bad he had little say on line assignments.

We had the song recorded by the end of the day. Celebrations were had at dinner, and that night Yumi climbed into bed with me for the sole purpose of giggling into my ear and saying she couldn't believe our dreams were really coming true.

That was silly. It was her dream. If my dream were coming true, she would have been doing more in my bed than be giddy about the idol life.

Our debut single was released both in CD and digital format three weeks later. That was when the real work began.

***

While she was sick, the little one cried and cried for someone to help her feel better. She's still so young that she doesn't know how best to express herself. All I can do is hear her tears and try to decipher what she needs. Medicine? Food? A hug? When I came under the weather as well, giving her any of those three became too difficult, and I felt terrible the one time I slept through her outburst.

In some ways, it was the same with Yumi over the years. When we became distant after her fame, I had to learn to interpret her cries for help. She wouldn't always come to me when she needed someone to tell her she was fine. Sometimes I had to watch her television appearance and decipher the signs. Call it a sixth sense, but a flick of her wrist meant she needed someone to steady her. A wrinkling nose meant she wanted to rant in anyone's direction. Sucking in her breath was a cry for help. I could never get to my cell phone fast enough when I saw that sign.

It's in my nature. I have to protect and defend those I love. To this day I would fling myself over a cliff if it was the only way to give Yumi a happy life. Likewise, if someone asked me to rob a bank for the little one, I would probably do it. I can be brash like that.

Of course, I would rather show my love and tenderness in more... private ways. Before we got sick, I spent a whole afternoon on the floor with the little one, dressing dolls because they had a party to go to. When the baby tired of those, we pulled out a puzzle and laughed at old Chi-Chi putting in pieces upside down. For lunch I made *miso* soup and tiny sandwiches that she could eat in one bite. While I sliced the meat and bread, I sang her a song that I was in the middle of writing. Yumi is the only one who is a bigger fan of my work.

In the afternoon I was so tired I picked up the girl and took her into my room. We napped like mother and daughter for the better part of an hour. The way she clung to my shirt with a pout on her face was just like Yumi.

The love of a parent vs. a romantic partner is staggering, and yet they feel so equally strong. Don't ask me to rank them. The loves are profound, but so different that they're not even in the same league. The thought that one day this girl will be too old to want to nap with me breaks my heart. I can't even think about it.

So you see, when I love, I do it fiercely. This leads to me doing things that I would never otherwise do. Like join an idol group to make both Yumi and me happy. Her because it was her dream – and me because I wanted to be with her. At the end of the day, I am happy with anyone I love buried in my embrace.

Chapter 8

If I may say so, it was bullshit what they did to us for our debut.

Traditionally, an idol group is at least somewhat promoted before their debut. They will do public appearances, sing some songs, interact with fans to build a fan base, and do other types of promotions that are meant to make more CDs sell come debut time.

We didn't do any of that. I should have recognized right away that we were getting a raw deal, but at the time we didn't know. You know what they did to us? They probably thought it was cute. They handed us each a stack of our CDs, and after we got done being amazed at how far we had come, they told us to go out and sell them.

One-thousand CDs. We had to sell a whole thousand CDs. By ourselves.

If that makes you anxious, imagine how we felt. Seven girls – unknowns in the industry at the time – being told to go out and shill ourselves because the label was too cheap to do it for us. I'm not sure if such a thing would happen these days, what with how popular MP3s have become. Back in those days the physical sale was king. It wasn't uncommon for a new idol group to sell at least 20,000 the first week with a good media push from the label. Except we weren't getting that push. We had to push ourselves to sell one-thousand CDs. In a week.

There was another pressure as well that I only felt tangentially. This challenge would also determine who the leader of our group became. For weeks Yumi and Dolly had been vying for the spot. While being leader meant a lot of responsibilities, it also meant a lot more exposure and a bigger chance at stardom.

Naturally, Yumi chose me to be her partner. We were split into three teams and stationed around Nagoya with displays and microphones. This is when we also received our first uniforms. As I feared, they were schoolgirl uniforms – long-sleeved white blouses, green and black plaid skirts, and crimson bows to wrap around our necks. It was still too hot for a jacket, but we saw in the wardrobe department that the jackets were green as well.

I was not happy to be back in a school uniform. While I wouldn't call myself a tomboy growing up, I definitely did not find my uniforms practical or comfortable. At least in my girlhood days they were nothing more than uniforms. As an adult, I saw it and realized who we were really pandering to. The label officially marketed us to younger girls who would look up to us like big sisters, but those weren't the people who came to our shows. When I put on that uniform for the first time, I felt like I was forced back into a role I never wanted to perform.

At least now I understood how they were styling us. Yumi looked good in the uniform, as it hugged her body nicely but not in a risqué way. She had the kind of body that looked good in just about anything. Jealousy reared its head. I looked stocky, with my thick calves poking out and my face, which was still chubby with some baby fat at the time, bulging from the high neckline. My only saving grace was my professional haircut that framed my face in a flattering way. Yumi, who long had her hair cut into a cute pixie and occasionally dyed a dark brown, looked like a cool and chic schoolgirl. Very fashion forward at the time.

We were the only ones with short hair. It's funny to think about now.

Yumi and I were assigned a space in Sakae, not too far away from the label building. Every morning we set up our booth by ourselves, plugged in our mics, and begged for passersby to buy our CD for the low price of 500 yen. Now, that was a good price, and it still is. But we were unknowns with only one song and its instrumental on the disc. That first day, the only people who bought our CDs were a few businessmen and a group of guys who asked for a dance in return. When I glared at them, they ran off and Yumi told me to be more careful.

Our whole group's tallies that night were grim. Fewer than one-hundred sold, and most of that came from Dolly's partnership with Koto. Yumi was troubled, not just because of the low sales but also because of Dolly's success. That night my friend climbed into bed with me and made me promise we would try harder the next day.

I didn't know what to do in order to "try harder." I wasn't naturally charismatic. I didn't have a shrewd business sense. I still don't. When it comes to marketing, I leave it up to my label. They know what they're doing. Why would they hire me to sell myself? Look what I'm doing right now! I know nothing!

Yumi wanted us to perform our song. Sure, that sounded like the way to go, but there were only two of us for a seven-person song. While we could get by on the vocals, the dance was ridiculous with just the two of us. Add in the fact that I was still a somewhat stiff dancer, and without a bunch of other girls to cover up my mistakes it was an embarrassment.

Of course, me embarrassing myself endeared me to some new fans. While girls snorted and pointed at my awkward movements, men encouraged me and bought a CD to make me feel better. Yumi, who had a smile for everyone, thanked them with a fervent voice that fit right in with the idol image. Even with all of this, however, we still weren't able to sell more than a couple dozen CDs. When we came together that night to go over our tallies, it seemed hopeless.

I didn't want to dance again and get pity sales. When I complained to Beppu before retiring to the dorm, he said, "Then don't dance. Don't mock your real talents. You want to make it in this industry? Show them what you showed me."

Yumi thought I was crazy, but the next morning I went into the instrument room and checked out a portable keyboard to take with us a few blocks down to central Sakae. It took the both of us to carry it as well as our other goods, but the moment we were set up in our spot, I had a good feeling.

We rehearsed a couple of times before turning on the mics and selling our talents. Our real talents.

Yumi could sing, and I could play the piano. She could charm the audience while I supported her in the background. To this day I see people online who ask, "Where were you when YUMI entered the spotlight?" Every once in a while someone will reply, "I was there in Sakae, watching her perform in that schoolgirl outfit. I knew she would be a star!"

Nobody remembers me. That's okay. It's better that way.

Of course we mostly performed the song we were selling. A special piano version. Sometimes we played it fast, and other times I turned it into a down tempo ballad. Yumi could convey the emotion either way. She was on fire with energy one minute and then mournful about her forgotten memories the next. The first way got people's attention – the second way made them part with their money.

We also performed some of my original songs. The ones from back then weren't really good, and on that keyboard it was difficult to express the right sound like I did with the grand piano at our audition. Yet I tried, and Yumi more than made up for it using her voice. For the most part she made up lyrics to my melodies, and other times she just sang notes to show off her skill. It worked.

Thanks to Beppu's advice, we were able to sell many more CDs that day. However, it wasn't enough. By the end of the week we had only managed to sell 900 CDs as a group. We had failed.

Or so we thought.

As we received the final numbers at the Friday night meeting, something strange happened. The seven of us were melancholy and convinced that we were going to be disbanded before we had the chance to prove our real merit. In fact, Mr. Kobayashi and Mr. Yamamoto were both quite serious as they began to tell us this.

Then Beppu waltzed in with an open laptop and plopped it down in front of the men ruling our fates.

Someone had recorded Yumi and me in Sakae the day before and uploaded the video to the internet. That in itself was not special. What was included the amount of views – well into the thousands by now – and the many comments praising Yumi's singing ability and "pure face." One of the commenters asked where they could buy our music, and the uploader responded with a link to the official MP3. When Mr. Kobayashi checked its ranking, he was floored to see it had entered the top 100 on the J-pop list.

I was surprised as well. What didn't surprise me was the announcement that Yumi was our leader a week later.

***

My mother once told me that I am too easy to manipulate and take advantage of. She didn't mean it in a rude way. Just that she was concerned that someone would start using me and never let me go. Drain me of my life, money, and vitality. In a way that kind of did happen.

I'm not the type of person who can ignore when others are in trouble. It's not just Yumi either. If there was a kid on the way home from school who was crying because they got hurt or bullied, I made sure to stop and find out what was wrong. I don't like the thought of people being alone when they're upset. Doesn't everyone deserve a shoulder to cry on? At the time I didn't see how this made me easy to take advantage of. I have noticed that this has also not transferred to adulthood well.

We had a rough and strange day a couple of weeks ago, the little one and I. She had a check-up at the doctor's office and I was the only one who could take her. That always causes a mess, but thankfully this doctor knows me and my relation to the child. It's probably illegal what we're doing, but when you have the power of a big label and management companies behind you, anything is possible.

Anyway, they didn't do anything too upsetting. But the girl is very sensitive, so everything has the possibility of being more upsetting than it would be for a child her age. For example, when we were coming home from the doctor's, I had to stop at the supermarket to get something for dinner. Usually I don't like taking her there by myself because the music, the sounds of people working and shopping, and the bright lights can irritate her to the point of throwing a fit. She needs someone to take care of her when we go shopping. When I'm by myself, I can't do everything at once.

So of course she had a tantrum the moment we stepped out of the store and back into the sunlight. She stopped right in the middle of the sidewalk, plopped down on the concrete, and started wailing like the whole world was against her. After I realized how upset she was, I stopped and knelt beside her, asking her what the problem was this time.

"Are you hurt? Did you trip? *Kotae nasai yo.*"

Asking her to answer is always fruitless. Even though she is over three now, she still doesn't speak much. I don't know how normal this is. I feel like a child that age should be chattering? The doctors say that she may be a late bloomer. Like I said before, it is possible there were drugs when she was in the womb. I think about this fact constantly. Like it's my fault. In many ways I believe it is.

So here we are, a small child sitting on the sidewalk bawling her eyes out, and me, some big, masculine woman trying to get her to calm down so we can walk home. Of course people stopped and stared. They probably thought I was an unfit parent who couldn't control her looks or her child.

Just as I was seriously losing my patience and about to pick her up and haul her home, she lowered her fists from her eyes, stared at me through drying tears, and whimpered, "Mama…"

We were silent. A breeze kicked up and blew our hair into our faces, but I was too stunned to clear her strands away. They stuck to her sticky skin as she tried to breathe again, her chest huffing up and down as she puffed her cheeks and looked to me for answers.

Rarely do I feel so heartbroken. What could I tell her? What could I tell myself? In that moment I wasn't good enough. Me, the most consistent person in this child's life, wasn't going to be good enough. I had a parent's paranoia at that moment. What if this was to be our relationship for the rest of our lives? Would this girl grow up looking at me and thinking, "That's not my mother," or other such disparaging things? I love this child like I have no one else to love sometimes. From the moment she was born I knew I would have to protect her. What I didn't know was that I would have to protect myself from moments like these.

"You want your mama?"

She nodded, her frown glistening in tears and saliva.

I didn't know what to tell her. Lie, and make her no longer trust me? Tell the truth and hurt her some more? I couldn't win. She couldn't win. A three-year-old doesn't understand that she can't see her mother whenever she wants. And in our world, she doesn't necessarily understand that I can be there for her as well.

"What about Chi-Chi, eh?" I pointed to myself, to remind her of who I was. "We've both had a long day. Why don't we go home?" I didn't tell her I was going home to work while she napped.

It was apparent that while she didn't dislike me, I was not the person she wanted in that moment. Too bad. My patience was running thin, my frustration mounting, but being a parent in these situations brings out those sorts of feelings even in the greatest people. The hardest part was convincing a three-year-old that we needed to go home.

"Mama *inai*..."

"*Sou.* She isn't here. But you've got me."

Eventually she climbed into my arms and asked me to carry her home. She clung to my torso, arms looped around my neck as she rested her cheek against my shoulder. I'm not the strongest woman in the world, but I could balance her with one arm while the other carried the grocery bag.

Love, Yumi

We live in a thick residential area, full of single-family homes and well-off families that can afford to have a mother stay at home all day. Not all of them know me, especially a few blocks away from where I live. So on the way home that day I ran into some of the housewives in the area, and each one said, "Your daughter is so cute!" or, "Aw, is someone having a rough day?" I just said that she had come back from the doctor's. That was enough explanation for the women.

It made think about how the world sees me as this child's mother. Yet she doesn't see me as her mother at all. I never know how to take that. A child's love can be so pure and yet so scathing at the same time. She doesn't have a filter and is prone to saying hurtful things to me. I try to shrug it off, but sometimes it can be difficult when you put so much energy into raising another person.

I guess my mother was right. When she first heard that I was going to be a part of this child's life, she clicked her tongue and told me that I was being taken advantage of again. First by Yumi, then by the entertainment industry, and now by this child. Then again this was the same woman who quickly sent me a box full of things for raising children, as if I could not get them myself. In a way, though, I think she sees herself as a grandmother now. So while she gives me grief for taking on this role, she welcomes the little one with open arms when they visit each other. It makes me happy to see.

I'm sure that some of you have some opinions about this by now. Maybe you're like me and want to help those you love. What is the line between being taken advantage of and truly helping? I still don't know. Because when the little one looks at me and says, "I want Mama," all I can do is stroke her hair and try not to cry. "Me too," I say. Whenever Yumi is not near me, I miss her, and this makes me vulnerable.

Chapter 9

When I think back on those months before we debuted, I realize how easy we had it. Yes, we trained hard every day, and sometimes barely got time off, but for the most part we were left alone and we all got along pretty well. Once we debuted? Everything changed.

One thing that happened was Dolly and Yumi fighting all the time. From the moment Yumi was announced our group's leader, Dolly threw one tantrum after another. She claimed to be the best for the job since the beginning. She was older than Yumi by two months and had more training under her belt. Apparently she used to model for local chains back in her hometown. Dolly said that she didn't get the position because of her Korean ancestry. The label retaliated by telling her Yumi did more for the group's visibility.

This confrontation hurt Yumi to the point I could hear her sniffing at night sometimes. Not crying. Just tear-like sounds. The second time it happened, I got out of bed and went to hers. It was the first time since we moved into the dorms that I slept in her bed instead of her in mine. She did not kick me out. In fact, she pressed against me, one arm around my waist as she slowly drifted off to sleep.

The label decided that our official debut would happen at the end of the year. Once again we rushed into recording, only this time we also had to learn a more complicated dance routine since we were filming a music video. For the song I got two whole lines. Probably an upgrade because I was a part of that video that went viral.

Speaking of which, this was when we first started getting attention on the streets. The label had us doing "guerrilla lives" around Nagoya, sometimes in Sakae, and sometimes in other populated neighborhoods. At first we thought the small crowds gathering around us were passersby. Then we slowly began to realize that they were already our fans and had coordinated meetups to come see us live! There weren't many at first, but after a while more showed up, and by December we had a mini-fanclub forming everywhere we went. They cheered for Yumi, Dolly, and Nezu. Reika and Koto got some love as well when they got close enough to the audience. Of course they did. They were all pretty and cute. After this realization, the label moved Mayu and me to the very back line of our dance formation. She took it a lot harder than me. I didn't like those men leering at me like they did my friends.

We filmed the music video in a studio one week before my birthday. Besides dancing in a brightly lit area, we also had a loose story going on in a makeshift classroom. Of course, in this classroom everything went to hell as we caused mischief by clomping chalky erasers, drawing silly pictures on the blackboard, sneaking food out of our lunches, and making origami out of our homework. Every one of us took turns playing the serious but frazzled teacher. When it came my turn to put on the thick glasses and pencil skirt, everyone agreed that I was the scariest looking. If you look up that video on YouTube now, you will see that I had the most shots as the teacher.

I was glad to leave the tripe that was "Forgotten Memories" behind. The new song was called "Daydreaming" and a bit more complicated. There was a lot of word play in the lyrics that made it fun. There was a B-side too, but only Yumi, Dolly, and Reika were featured on it.

I had an interesting birthday.

It was in the middle of the week, and in the middle of our preparations for our big formal debut, so we didn't get to have any kind of party. We didn't even have cake, but that was mostly because we were afraid of getting in trouble. Even I was feeling the pressure to eat less, and I was considered homely enough to leave in the back row of the formation. To get caught eating cake? We were only allowed a few bites of sweets in our promotional shots, because of course teenage girls love to eat cake.

On the evening of my birthday we had a staff meeting to go over some scheduling for our debut. A few people wished me happy birthday, but for the most part we jumped right into things. What makes this meeting memorable wasn't the business end of things, but the personal.

Halfway through the meeting Dolly once again brought up her grievances about not being made leader. By now I had heard it all, so I tuned it out. For all I knew she was crying about Japanese superiority complexes.

At one point she got in Yumi's face across the table and accused her of sleeping with somebody. I was just as appalled as my friend, but the real shock came when Anna Matsuda stood up and slapped Dolly right on the cheek. The room went deathly silent.

"Control yourself," our mentor hissed. "It's disgusting how you prattle on about your dreams that don't mean anything in the realm of the world. Don't you think every girl in this business has the same dreams? I've been there. Twenty years ago. I was part of some nowhere idol group staffed with dykes and imbeciles. You're lucky you get to record music, make music videos, and promote yourselves outside of a theater. I wasn't so lucky back then. It wasn't until the group disbanded that I finally managed to carve a name for myself. Now sit down!"

Dolly promptly did. Anna turned to the rest of us.

"There is no room for your individualistic fantasies in this business. If one of you fails in a group, you all fail. Nobody cares if you're Korean or ugly as hell if it means you can still sell CDs and concert tickets. You want to go far? Then you get a leader who brings assess into the seats. Who's doing that for you right now? Whose name are they chanting at those corner lives you're doing? You can think you're the princesses of your own world all you want. It means shit if nobody is looking to be your prince."

Dolly slumped into her chair, hand still on her cheek. She didn't dare look Anna in the eye. Hell, I barely could.

"Leave your ideals and your issues at the door. This isn't summer camp. This is the real fucking world and outbursts like that will get you fired. You know what you do? What we tell you to do. If we tell you to kiss Yumi's ass, then by fucking God you are going to *kiss her ass*. Once you start doing interviews you will be nothing but gracious to one another. You inspire each other. You love each other. You're fucking sisters! And quite frankly, if this is how you conduct yourself within staff meetings, then you truly aren't fit to be the leader of any group."

Not the first time we got a speech about being selfless. Yet something about that incident really stuck out to me, and not just the slapping. It was what Anna said about doing what they told us to do.

Yet I was rubbed the wrong way. The way she said it... she implied that we had to do *anything* they said. In retrospect I now understand why I felt so weird. Such life lessons wouldn't come until later.

I couldn't sleep that night. There were other things on my mind.

Anna said that some of us were ugly as hell. In a way I accepted that she was talking about me. I had always accepted that I was not the prettiest in the group. Being pretty was never important to me. Yet after a while those kinds of comments begin to wear you down. I guess that was the night I began to feel the effects of being so "ugly."

"Yumi?" I said, unsure if she was still awake or not. I heard her rustle in her bed. "Do you think I'm ugly?"

"Eh?" She sat up. "No way. You're pretty. Don't listen to what those people are saying."

"You're just saying that because it's still my birthday."

"What's wrong?" Yumi sat on the edge of her bed, fingers curled around her mattress. "You don't usually care about that sort of thing."

"Ah, just something Anna-*san* said…"

"Don't listen to that wannabe who never got to be. She's obsessed with looks. She thinks everything is about how pretty you are. I like to think it doesn't count *as* much as people say."

"That's easy for you to think, because you're really pretty."

"*Hontou ni?*" Why was she laughing? Didn't she believe it? Even without the makeup and hair colors she would be known for later, Yumi was a conventionally attractive girl. She had a little but distinguished face, with wide-eyes other girls would kill for. Tiny lips that looked gorgeous with the right color lipstick. A nose that didn't need contouring. Her ears were proportional and her neck long enough to work any haircut. That didn't include the rest of her body. I mean, you've seen her. You know how beautiful she is, even if she's not your type. Now imagine her at nineteen.

"It's different for me," I said, turning over in my bed. "Even if I lost more weight…"

"Who said you should lose weight? You're not fat!"

"I don't have the right kind of body for this job."

"Don't say that. Just because you're more muscular than me doesn't mean I'm prettier. You're just a different kind of pretty, Chi-*chan*."

"I'm not pretty."

In the ensuing silence, I honestly didn't think Yumi would respond. She finally understood what I was trying to say. Then, "I think you're beautiful."

For some reason my eyes stung. A million people could say that they found me beautiful, but even if I believed them I wouldn't care. Coming from Yumi? A girl society found ten times more attractive than me? It was like being told I was the most loved person in the universe. It meant more to me than Beppu saying my piano playing could save our group.

Yumi came to me, sitting gingerly on the side of my tiny bed as she loomed over my head and stroked my cheek. In that moment, when her fingers touched my skin, I thought I knew what it was like to feel mutual love.

I held my breath when she leaned down and kissed the tip of my nose. "You're beautiful," she said again, softly. A single finger pushed against my chest before drawing a line down my T-shirt, between my breasts, and then to my navel as it lay exposed at the bottom of my clothes. "Don't let anyone make you think otherwise. If someone says you're ugly, tell them Yumi Nishikawa thinks you're a goddess."

"Why would I tell them that?" I asked.

All five of her fingers pressed against my stomach, warm and very welcomed. Everything became tight, taut, and taunting as Yumi slowly pushed up beneath my shirt, her hand dangerously close to my breast. I'm one of the only women I know who sleeps without anything on beneath her shirt. Maybe that's too much information, but I want you to imagine how close she was to touching something so forbidden to me. My breathing became frantic, my chest heaving against her hand as she bent down again and kissed my lips. The second time for a second birthday.

I wanted to cry. Not only did Yumi think I was beautiful, but she wanted to do this sacred thing with me. Back then, I still thought of it that way. I was a nervous virgin who didn't trust anyone else enough to touch or make love to me. Yumi was the only one. I wanted her to grab me, kiss me, and rub against me in ways I didn't even understand yet. I didn't know much about sex, besides what you learn in textbooks and from your dumb friends who think they're having good sex but in reality can barely move. But I knew I wanted to do those things with her. Anytime.

When she kissed my lips again, I thought I was going to die.

My fingers went into her hair. I had touched her hair many times before in my life. We were close enough that not only would I brush it for her when it was long, but we would also pick things out of each other's hair without even asking. Dust, dandruff, even twigs and grass if we were really roughing it outside after a long day at school. Yet this was different. I wasn't grooming her. I wasn't even staring in awe at the way another girl's hair parted and fell. I was being tender, sharing my feelings with her. I wanted to tell her, in that simple touch, how much she meant to me. What did she feel when I touched her like that? Did she feel the same rush I did when she brushed her knuckles against the side of my breast? Could I touch her there as well? Even though we were so close and this was happening, I was too afraid to ask to touch her in return. Because then she would know what I had been thinking about her these past few months, and that would make things weird.

I realize how silly it sounds now. Like I said, I was an ignorant virgin in both sex and love. I didn't know how to express either.

This sacred thing... I don't consider the sex I've had with other women as being sacred. When it's with someone you love, though, it's like going to another world and getting lost in paradise. I could barely comprehend it when I was that young.

Just when my arm was about to wrap around and pull her down onto me, Yumi pulled away, and I could have cried for different reasons.

"See? You're beautiful." Yumi patted my stomach and stood up. No. No she couldn't be leaving me already. Even last time she stayed in my arms all night. "*Omedetou tanjyoubi.*"

Happy birthday. Happy fucking birthday. God, I was such an idiot to believe she really wanted to do that with me.

If I had the spine back then that I do now, I would have asked her why she kept playing with me like that. She was my best friend. Didn't she know that she was messing with me in ways that couldn't be undone? I was bitter, irate. Both at her and myself. I didn't like the way she toyed with me, and I didn't like how I was falling for my best friend.

No, I had always loved her like that. She passed being my best friend such a long time ago. Two kisses later, I wanted to scream.

Instead I rolled over and tried to contain the sounds of my muffled sobs. I wish I could tell the me of back then what I know now. That for every time Yumi broke my heart she would love me even harder next time. Stupid girls like me need to believe in that sort of thing.

***

Two months ago I had the distinct "pleasure" of catching a late night show featuring Anna Matsuda as the guest. You can't imagine my great and undying joy as I saw her botoxed face on my television screen. High-definition. Large screen. Yes, I was so happy.

"Fucking asscrack," I muttered into my tea, my constipated face scowling at the screen. I could feel it. That's how intense it was.

The program was one of those adult-oriented things where has-been celebrities come on and gossip about "the good old days" and what really went on ten years ago. Okay, I don't begrudge them that much. They can be pretty entertaining, especially if they're people you've personally met like I have. There's a reason I had flipped to that channel that night. The rest of the household was in bed and I had my bath. All I wanted to do before turning in was drink some tea and eat some empty calories.

Then Anna Matsuda was on my TV, and I wanted to vomit.

The topic that night was the olden days of the idol industry. Back in the '90s, anyway. Like I said, Anna was an older mentor by the time I went through the system. The hostess asked her what it was like being an idol just before the digital age erupted. I had forgotten she was an idol in the early to mid '90s. Now I don't feel so old.

"Oh, it was so nice back then. You could keep your secrets secret. These days there are blogs, Twitter, and other such things that make it nearly impossible to have a private life. In turn people made a big deal when you didn't act the way you were supposed to. We were so coached back then. They still are now, but it's harder to adhere to those things when everyone can be stalked so easily. That's why you have to be careful! Girls these days don't know how to conduct themselves online. They also think the real world is the online world. They make fools of themselves on their Twitters and then fools of themselves on TV. It's foolish. Let me tell you, back when I was in the circuit, so many of the girls had skeletons in their closets that would only get out if they blabbed about it on TV. Or if someone told on them, of course. That's always been a danger."

The hostess nodded as if this were new information for her to parse. "*Sou,* people are so open about their secrets these days. Or even if they're not, it's easy to suss out if someone isn't careful. What kind of secrets are we talking about?"

"I shouldn't say. But multiple boyfriends, abortions, mixed racial ancestry, homosexuality…"

"Homosexuality? Really? I didn't know it was possible for an idol."

Anna turned up her nose. It's funny. She's half white, and back when I knew her she had her super foreigner nose. Now she's had so much plastic surgery to make it look more Japanese. "There are more dykes in the industry than you can imagine."

"How many did you know?"

"Just two, really. That was two too many."

While on one hand it made me feel better to know that there were other women like me in the industry, no one likes to hear such things. Casual homophobia, however, is still so common. I can't watch most variety shows without being reminded of this. Usually it's focused on men, but in this instance I felt it personally. Especially coming from Anna Matsuda.

"I don't understand why girls like that want to join the industry. Don't they know who they're pandering to? Do they think they're going to hunt for women? They're in for a sore surprise! Idol world has no place for a lesbian. And damn well it shouldn't. We don't need that kind of perversion in our wholesome entertainment."

That's when I had to turn off the TV. Or at least change the channel to the news. Watching wars break out seemed easier to bear than that sort of thing.

I wondered if Anna thought about me. She let slip more than once that she suspected I was gay. I don't know how she could have possibly known. Maybe those old group mates of hers who were gay taught her a thing or two about spotting them. Sometimes I wonder who those girls were. Are they happy now? What kind of lives are they living? Did they continue their careers? I wish I knew the answers.

I also wish we could live in a society where it didn't matter what your sexuality is in any line of work. Why shouldn't an idol be a lesbian? Why is it so bad? Is it because some fantasy has been obscured? That says a lot more about the dangers of that fantasy than it does the girls themselves. Besides, for as innocent and pure as idols are supposed to be, why are we even thinking about this? Wouldn't a lesbian idol be just as pure as a heterosexual one?

Or is it because we desire each other that we're dirty and impure? Because Yumi kissed me with that sort of meaning, does it mean I was made impure when I was eighteen? Impure in ways that a boy couldn't do?

A part of me is interested in knowing what you all think. Is there room for lesbians in our society, let alone in entertainment? Would knowing that an idol is a lesbian kill some sort of fantasy for you?

I'm thinking way too much about this. Not surprising, since it hits so close to home.

So I suppose I will leave you with this question as I head off for the night. I wanted to write more, to get further into the story, but I'm still feeling a bit sick and should probably rest instead of forcing myself up all night. I do not doubt that some of the things I said today will spark more commentary among the masses who read this. Oh well. I've opened the jar. All I can do now is finish.

Good night.

Hildred Billings

Part 4

WHEN THE FIRST SPARK GOES OUT

その炎を吹き消す

As you may have noticed, I took a day off from my tale again.

Not because I am feeling lazy, but because some emotional things happened once again. We weren't sick, physically. Instead it's a sickness of the mind and heart. My blog posts have made it to the national news. It's very surreal to open your laptop and see your name in the headlines. "Composer and ex-Idol Chiharu Morita Tells All," was just one example this morning.

Everyone has an opinion. The comments are not just from my loyal readers who always support me. Now I see commenters coming from all over the world to both deride me and say that I'm doing a good thing. Some of you are even gay and say you have found inspiration in my tale. That's sweet. Honestly. But I would like to remind everyone that this is not just my tale… and for that I am paying.

I went with Yumi to her therapist's yesterday. I don't always go with her. Maybe once a month or every six weeks or so. If she asks me to go with her, though, I do. When I go, it's mostly to talk about my relationship to her, and it's cathartic for me as well.

Yesterday we did not talk. Once we sat down, Yumi started crying. It's not unusual for her to cry there. Sometimes we go a whole session with her crying in silence. I think she feels that it's safe to cry there. After the things she's been through, I can't blame her. She just wants to be in a safe place surrounded by people who care for her and won't judge her.

It took a few minutes, but I soon realized that she was crying because of what was happening with my blog. Even though she signed off on me doing this, it's still hitting her hard. I guess she got a phone call from her manager saying that she needed to put a stop to this and issue a statement that none of it was true. I asked her if she had read the posts. She said she only skimmed them. So I told her what I had talked about, and she could only say, "Good, good." It didn't seem like it was good.

Eventually she opened up and told me that she was having a hard time dealing with the backlash. Backlash? Some people were rude about it, but they always were to her. If she went out wearing a surgical mask because of her allergies she got columns written about her insinuating that she was once in a gang. I don't think it's so much the backlash as it is her trying to process everything that has happened. I asked her if I should stop this, but she told me to keep going. "I'm not strong enough to tell it," she said through many sniffs. "It has to be you."

Yet how could I look at her so upset and not be upset as well? I started crying too. That poor therapist. Two crying women who didn't know what to do.

It's especially hard because I know what we're going to talk about today on my blog. Up until now, everything has been difficult, but this is when things start to get... well, rather upsetting. I'm going to talk about things that make me want to vomit just thinking back on. I can't imagine how hard they are for Yumi, who actually lived them. I will do my best... and tell her to not go online for a couple of days, as I'm sure many of you will explode in conversation from what I am about to unleash.

Chapter 10

Our official debut couldn't have been planned better if we all went to the shrine and prayed until our hands fell off.

We debuted at #52 on the Oricon Daily Charts. When we got the news, we were so happy that we told Beppu to screw off while we bought a bag of cookies and split them between us. Luckily he didn't say anything to either Anna or the executives. Instead he praised us, saying that we had worked hard and it was evident we had managed to capture the hearts of some fans.

These fans were the ones who came to our first post-debut performance held in the middle of Sakae. One day SKE48 would perform regularly in that spot, but that day it was only the seven of us from the Butterfly Tops twirling in our skirts and singing to the audience. Being in the back allowed me to be lazy, but I was excited too. While I didn't smile as wide as everyone else, I put in more energy into my performance and let pride overcome me when the applause erupted at the end of our song. I didn't even mind singing "Forgotten Memories" afterward or the backup chorus for the B-side. The day was sunny and beautiful for being winter, so I was really happy to share that kind of moment with our new fans.

The relaxing time soon came to an end. We had a lot of promotions to do, and the label was moving forward with a third single so we could quickly build up a discography and put out an album in less than a year. In this business, you can't wait too long, or else your sales dry up and your fans move on to someone else. As a new group, we were vulnerable.

That's why we worked nonstop for the next two months. When we weren't recording demos, we were having our photos taken and doing fan events that may have included a significant amount of radio interviews since they were easy to get on. We also did a couple of local channel promotions on TV, although that kind of thing made me nervous. I have always preferred doing radio interviews since I don't have the pressure of trying to look good. If I laugh and the radio host sees my teeth, it's not a big deal. But on TV I am trained to cover my mouth like a good woman should. Radio is so much more freeing, and I can be myself.

In truth, I don't remember much about those two months besides running around and performing the same song over and over again. They weren't bad times, but we were tired a lot. If I thought the training was tough, I had yet to pass out in my bed so quickly that sometimes I woke up to find Yumi huddled up against me. I was so tired I never noticed her climb in.

Of course, she reveled in the attention the most. I have always said that she is a natural performer, and I don't go back on that word now. When you put her on a stage of any kind in front of people who want to watch and listen to her, she will shine until you are blinded by her performance power. In those days, she was still green, but her natural talents made her popular with the crowds. They often took photos of her and asked for her autograph and to pose with her. Dolly was also popular, although she could be colder with the fans. Reika was considered cute in the traditional way, and Nezu had a few supporters who called her "Mini-Nezu" and often brought her Minnie Mouse gifts. The character became somewhat of a mascot for her over time.

Mayu, Koto and I were not as popular. Nobody chanted our names and few people asked for our autographs. I was fine with this, but sometimes I would see Koto looking sad and Mayu standing wistfully in front of the crowd, trying to attract someone's attention. In a group this size, it's impossible for all members to be popular. Those who don't have some huge role or ooze charisma are often forgotten in the background. I had no large role in that group. I couldn't dance well, and my voice wasn't powerful enough to be given more than a couple of lines.

Yet I shouldn't downplay the attention I did get. Every so often a fan would bashfullyask for a picture. I remember one man my age who stayed behind after a performance in Sakae to ask what kind of flowers I liked. The next time he came to one of our shows, he gave me a single pink rose. Yumi gave me so much crap for it. "Got a boyfriend now, eh?" she asked with a big smile on her face. I kept the rose on the shelf behind my bed. Why not? It was pretty. "You're gonna have a boyfriend before me out here."

To this day I don't understand why she would get gung-ho about boys paying attention to me. She was the same way growing up. When I started dating Junpei she would always nudge my side and click her tongue like a disapproving mother. I used to think she pitied me because I wasn't very pretty, and any attention I got should be reinforced. Except she still did it after the rose thing. Her, the girl who had made out with me twice. I don't understand.

The only time I felt really nervous was when the label executives came to watch us perform. Mr. Kobayashi made sense because we were already becoming a staple on their roster. But Mr. Yamamoto showed up quite often as well, and sometimes he clapped the loudest out of everyone in the polite crowd. One time he and some of the other executives took us out to dinner. Just us. No Beppu, and no Anna. They toasted to our upcoming success and encouraged us to keep working hard. At the time I thought my discomfort was from my own social ineptitude, but now I understand that I could smell some rats before they made a nest.

Things were coming along for our third single. There was a lot of anticipation since we had expanded our fan base and the label thought we could possibly debut in the top 20. The song was meticulously produced. We were called in multiple times to re-sing lines, and it was during this time Beppu first showed me how to use some of the buttons in the control room. He let me help the sound engineer process some of Yumi's vocals while she sang. This was after they made it clear I was not being paid for it.

We took pictures for the CD jacket long before we were due to shoot the music video. This time, instead of dressing up in our uniforms and standing against a backdrop, we were dressed in casual clothes. Not our own, of course. A stylist dressed us, some in jeans (like me) while others wore dresses or pretty skirts. Yumi wore a pair of denim shorts and a white T-shirt that hugged her body. Compared to the new light color of her hair, it was quite striking.

Of course, we needed drama for the video shoot.

Dolly couldn't let things go. Not even after Anna slapped her in front of everyone in the meeting. She was still bitter about the leader thing, and after two releases I guess she felt that she wasn't getting the attention she deserved. This culminated on the first day of the video shoot. It was to be spread over two days, the first on Friday and the second the following Monday. On Friday we were doing the studio shots. Well, Dolly wasn't happy that Yumi was in the center of our circle for the main choreography shot. She argued with Beppu and Mr. Kobayashi about it until she turned blue enough to freeze the room. Yumi came up to me in the middle of the studio and asked, "Is it something I did?"

"No way," I told her. "She's narcissistic. Lots of those types in the industry." Boy, don't I know it now. "They chose you to be leader for a reason."

She didn't seem to believe me.

It got to the point that filming was seriously delayed and Mr. Yamamoto had to be called in to settle everything. I think Dolly knew she wasn't going to get her way, but she did everything short of guaranteeing she was going to get fired. I was pretty impressed that she had the balls to do that. When I think about getting in the president's face and nearly calling his mother a donkey, I want to throw up. Yet that's how Dolly has made a name for herself in the industry. I guess when Anna Matsuda said that Dolly reminded her of someone else at that age, she wasn't kidding. I could easily see Dolly growing up to slap a girl in the middle of a meeting.

"Tell you what, we'll think about it." Mr. Yamamoto ended the discussion there. That sort of finality meant Dolly wasn't going to get her way at all.

After we finished filming for the day, we had an early dinner right there on set, since bentos had been brought in to feed to crew. It was cold, tasteless, and a bit greasy, but after exerting myself all day for the camera I thought it wasn't such a bad deal.

Yumi and I ate in a corner, alone, since she was avoiding Dolly. Halfway through our quiet meal, Mr. Yamamoto came up, forcing us to stand and bow politely in his direction. He told us to not sit down so quickly.

"Yumi-*chan*," he said with too much friendliness. Later on I would realize that he did not look at me much, but at the time I noticed his courteous glances in my direction. "I just wanted to let you know that you're doing a wonderful job leading the group. You're quite mature."

It didn't take much to get Yumi blushing. Her cheeks turned a rosy pink at the president's compliment, and she bowed again, thanking him in a hushed whisper. "I just want the group to succeed," she said. I believed it. Whether or not Mr. Yamamoto did no longer mattered. He was already going to get what he wanted.

"I would like to talk to you more about your future prospects. You know, you could be successful on your own one day. Perhaps some solo releases?"

You may think it's rude for him to say these things in front of me, but in that business, everything is matter-of-fact. Only the delusional don't know where they stand with the higher-ups. So to have Mr. Yamamoto imply that Yumi was worthy of such obvious things but I wasn't didn't bother me. In fact, I was excited for her. If anyone deserved her chance to shine in the spotlight like that, it was my best friend. My talented, pretty friend. I didn't need those things to be content. I still don't.

Yumi, understandably, grinned like the young fool she was. "*Arigatou gozaimasu!*" She bowed deeply, her eyes full of the possibilities. Endorsements. Solo singles. A small fashion line or fragrance. Magazine appearances. Yumi Nishikawa – we had no idea she would be YUMI one day – could be the girl all other girls wanted to be. You could see that in her happy face.

Even Mr. Yamamoto was smiling. "Of course that's a bit into the future, but it's worth discussing. Do you have time tonight?"

Yumi tilted her head. "I suppose so."

"Excellent. A few of the other board members and I are having a party down the street from here. You're twenty, right?"

"No, sir. Only nineteen."

"Oh. Well." Mr. Yamamoto cleared his throat. "No worries. Do come by, though."

She looked at me. "*Is Chiharu coming?*" We both knew the answer.

During that time, I knew but didn't have the words for what I realized. I knew that I was not desirable for those sorts of deals. I knew that I would never be more than a backup vocalist who could play piano on songs. There was no reason to invite me to those meetings. I also knew that I wasn't… appealing. Not just in talent, but in looks. Even now I know I am not what most men find pretty in a woman. I've thinned down since fully growing, but I still have that mean look and dress like I'm going to knock over a convenient store at any moment. This sort of knowledge makes me keenly aware of how little use I am to men. Especially powerful men. Even if I could sing opera or dance a full ballet by myself, I would never be invited to one of these "meetings" because I wasn't their idea of good looking.

Yumi was, though. Why didn't I have the words to explain this to her back then? I was supposed to be the observant one. What good is that if I can't help her stay out of trouble?

"I would be honored." Yumi did her best to keep her excitement contained. She didn't squeal, but I could see the corners of her mouth twitching into an outrageous smile. "Just tell me where to go and when to be there... oh, will Beppu-*san* be taking me?"

That smile on Mr. Yamamoto's face turned into anything but comforting. "No need to add on to his workload. Man needs to go home to his family sometime. Oh, by the way..." He tuned to us again as he walked away. "We will also discuss this matter going on with Dolly. Wow the other board members enough and you may never have to worry about being the center of the group ever again. Dolly will learn her place."

A flash of concern overtook Yumi's face. It was gone quickly, however, and I didn't think of it again that night. Instead I wished Yumi luck and told her to have as much fun as she could with a bunch of old guys in suits. Her smile was genuine, full of the hope for her promising future.

The next day she got the center position in the video. She had to force herself to smile.

***

Every day I regret not doing something. I don't get any peace from it. For a few seconds every day I go over in my head what I could have done, said, or tried the moment I realized something was wrong – when they didn't invite me too. That I wasn't vulnerable, but Yumi was.

It wasn't until years later I found out what happened that night. For so long I thought of only the worst. All those perverted men, dressing her up in some skimpy outfit and parading her around as their latest toy. I had heard those stories before. I had seen them for myself. Yet when Yumi opened her heart to me years later, she told me that my worries were overdone. They hadn't touched her. But they made her wear a maid uniform and serve drinks and snacks as they smoked cigars and leered at her. Many would "accidentally" graze her bare leg and ask her to pick things off the floor without bending her knees. I know those types of men. They could come just from seeing a pair of underwear.

Although they hadn't touched her, she knew she had been violated, even if it took her years to realize it. They had assaulted her with their eyes, their words, and their intentions. They debased her for being young and naïve, but legally old enough to take advantage of like that. I want to throw up thinking about it, but I promised I would say this. That I would out those executives right here for all of you to see. Mr. Yamamoto and his band of perverts. Arrest them. They've raped countless girls, and I hope those women can be brave and come forward.

So I often berate myself for not doing something. For that was the day the first of her innocence was truly sapped from her. Oh, she was still the same Yumi, but I could see wariness in her eyes every time a man in a suit spoke to her, paying her compliments and not me. "You're going to be a star," they kept saying. She cried. I thought at the time that it was because she was so happy. Now I know. She was scared.

You would think that because we were such close, lifelong friends that she would tell me. I don't think she had the words, or even the knowledge of what she was experiencing. She wanted to be happy and live the idol life. Everything was a beautiful world as long as she was near me. She didn't want to ruin it for me. What she didn't know was that it had been ruined the moment I saw her cry for the first time, late at night in our dorm room. She probably thought I was asleep and let her tears loose beneath her covers. Normally I would have gone to her, ask her what was wrong and hug her, but I had never heard that kind of crying before. It scared me to hear that fear in her voice... so I left her alone.

It's taken me a long time to work up to this part of my confession. It only gets more fucked up from here. Before, all of that talk about training and dreams and shit... those were the good days in this business. Those were the times to be naïve and only think of success. Not just before Yumi's popularity exploded and she became a household name. Of course even after the bad stuff started happening, we could still go to cafés and theaters and have fun together on our days off without anyone recognizing us. But they weren't the same as before. Yumi started holding things back, and little by little I stopped knowing what was going on in her life.

Love, Yumi

I know I haven't posted much yet today, but I think I need to step back for a few hours. It's still early in the day, so maybe I can continue later. It will depend on how I feel, what's going on here at home, and whether or not some backlash occurs. I am sure what I am about to hit publish on is going to ruffle quite a few feathers. I ask that you not worry about me. If you are going to worry about anyone, please send good thoughts and wishes to Yumi. I know that not all of my fans are her fans, but it's important to me that she makes it through this okay. Even though she's blocking out the media for a while, it's still possible for her to get anxious about this. I think I'll go try to check up on her after I pick up the little one from school.

Please take care, everyone. I will be back later.

Hildred Billings

Part 5

INTO THE FIRE

火炎に飛び込む

Whoa, I was not expecting such a response! I stepped away for five, six hours and came back to a flood of comments. I was scared to read them. After the sort of thing I just said, it would make sense if most of the comments were full of hate. Yet the support most of you are showing gives me strength. I will be sure to tell Yumi the good things.

Speaking of her, I managed to see her this afternoon. After picking up the little one I swung by Sakae (always fun with a toddler) and stopped by her management office where she was working today. Beppu was there too, although he does not work directly with her. It was nice being able to talk to both of them at the same time. Of course we talked about the reaction to my blog, although after a few minutes Yumi didn't want to talk about it anymore. Instead we talked about the album she is working on. I am proud to say that they are mostly my compositions. She's still in the recording stage but today they were talking about what to name the album and what kind of visual concept it should have. Naturally I'm not at liberty to say.

She got weepy halfway through our discussion. I hope Yumi will be strong enough to make it through a new album release and what might be coming her way. She got a new phone number before I did this so hopefully people can't harass her. Honestly, I don't think she'll do too much promoting with the album. She's talking about doing small venues for the tour. Probably fanclub only. I don't think YUMI will be performing in Budokan again anytime soon.

I told her I could cook dinner for her tonight, but I think she's going to just stay late at the management's office. They'll bring her a *bento*. It only sticks out to me because I was just talking about that moment when we ate *bento* and Mr. Yamamoto came up to us... I didn't mention it, but I sat there watching Yumi cradle a three-year-old, wondering if this moment would have existed if I had done something all those years ago.

Now I'm home again. Thinking about dinner. Also thinking about what I should say next. I suppose there's nowhere else to pick up than the release of the third single, huh?

Chapter 11

Our third single, "The Days of Sweet Mornings," managed to sneak in at #19. That was only on the first day. After we were done celebrating that small milestone, the single crept up and down the charts all week until it settled in at #18 overall. It was strange, loading up the website to see our jacket cover on the front page where the top 20 daily hits were recorded. For many people in Japan, this was their first time hearing about us, so sales were steady as those outside of the Chubu area became curious and decided to download our song.

It was the end of March, and the cherry blossoms were already blooming. I said to Yumi, "Can you believe that one year ago we started this journey? It feels longer than just a year."

She was over the moon and around Jupiter from how well our single was doing. Every day Yumi woke up with a smile on her face and was the first person in the meeting room, a practice room, or out in the common room practicing our songs. We were kept busy with street performances and appearances on the local broadcasts. The amount of people turning out to watch us perform in Sakae was quickly increasing in number. Soon I had three fresh roses on my shelf. I didn't know any of the men who gave them to me. Nor did any of my group mates get roses. I later found out that a small fanclub of mine (can you believe it?) had decided this was an appropriate way to show me support. Later I would get letters too, but for the most part this was a wordless communication between my fans and me. Some girls wanted to chat with their fans, to find out what they liked, how they were, what kind of lives they lived… me, I was content with not knowing such details. It was enough to know that there were people watching for me in the performances. Although, to be honest, it made me more nervous than usual.

The morning I asked Yumi whether or not she could believe it had been a year was a cold one. For some reason, the window in the conference room was open, and she got up to shut it, her sweater hanging loose on her body. I remembered that sweater. It was one she brought from Seki, a nice one she had for about two years. It used to barely fit her. Now it was so loose I couldn't see the outline of her breasts. No, until that moment I hadn't realized how much weight she had already lost. Then again, she had been laying off my snacks.

"One year is eternity in this business. Next year we could be out a job."

Such a cynical thing wasn't like her. I didn't mention it, because Beppu came in, followed by the stragglers that were the rest of our group.

Mr. Kawaguchi was all smiles when he walked in. "Ladies," he said, dropping some folders on the table while he opened his arms to us, "I have excellent news. We have been invited to perform on *Music Tonight* one week from now!"

I was drinking cold tea from a bottle when he said this. The moment the words hit my brain, I choked on the liquid, feeling it burn my nostrils as it came up the wrong way. Nezu reached over and slapped me on the back. Everyone at the table tittered, especially Dolly, whose face lit up for the first time since our debut. The only one not smiling like it was Girl's Day was Yumi, who looked relieved rather than happy. I figured she was tired. And hungry. She hadn't had breakfast yet. I later found out she was skipping her breakfasts altogether.

"We're driving to Tokyo Thursday for taping on Friday. Until then, you will be practicing extra hard with your instructors to put on the best performance of your new song as possible. This is your introduction to all of Japan! Celebrate!"

We did. There was an hour before we were due in the practice room, so we spent that hour huddled in a circle of tears and excitement. Mayu broke down crying as she called her parents and told them to tune in next Friday. Reika's makeup ran down her face even though you couldn't see any tears. Dolly talked about how to best style her hair for HD cameras. Nezu squeaked like the mouse she was named after, wondering if she should wear some Disney characters in her hair – apparently her fans had given her ribbons and barrettes. Koto was the type to contain her excitement while even I hiccupped at the thought of being on Japan's top music show. For the first time since entering this business, Yumi was the one to calm me down, putting her hand on my shoulder and saying, "Things can only go up from here, right?"

We were in training all day. That weekend we had appearances to honor, but the label canceled the small radio and street lives for the next week so we could focus on creating the perfect dance routine – something new to show the world next Friday. Even I, the girl with the balance of a two-legged tripod, put my all into it and was proud to have learned the routine in one afternoon.

It was dinner time when we were finally released for the evening. I stayed behind to go over something with the instructor before packing my things and heading back to the dorm. On my way by the instrument room, I heard a few pitiful notes and poked my head in – it was Beppu, playing a children's song on the piano.

"Ah, Chiharu," he said, looking up at me. "Come here."

You don't say no to Beppu. Even now, for as much shit as I give him, I am inclined to listen to him. I often disagree, and honestly, he doesn't understand me all that well, but he's the closest thing to a father figure I have. I suppose it's normal for a girl to disagree with her father. According to Beppu, that's all his daughters do.

"Do you know this song?" He played it again, his timing off and one of the notes completely wrong. I tried not to jerk my shoulders when it happened. My first piano teacher would have rapped my knuckles for making such a blunder.

"Of course. Everyone knows that song."

"So I'm not so bad at piano. Here." He stood up, gesturing to the bench. "I want to hear you play."

I stared at him for much too long, wondering why my manager suddenly had this kind of free time and why he was privately asking me to perform for him. Since I auditioned, I had no reason to believe he cared about my skills at all.

"What's wrong? Stage fright? In front of *me?*" He's the kind of large guy who laughs with his body, making him downright threatening if you're not used to it. "I heard you completely butcher poor Tomo-*chan's* song a year ago. You shouldn't be scared of playing in front of me."

I didn't like being reminded of my blunder, even if I had managed to make it this far in the business. Nevertheless I sat on the bench and glanced at the keys. "What should I play?"

He shrugged. "Whatever you want. You're the Bach around here."

I would never say that. I don't think I'm some genius with the keys. Sure, maybe I am naturally talented to an extent, but keep in mind I've been playing since I was old enough to sit up on a bench. Three lessons a week every week for most of my life. When my mom got us a piano, I played every single day. I loved it. I still do. So it's passion and skill. I was just fortunate to have those opportunities to be as good as I am. Except I wouldn't call myself Bach. It's kind of annoying to have other people joke about that.

Since it was stuck in my head, I decided to play our latest single. I added some embellishments to make it sound prettier on its own. Nothing special, or at least I didn't think so. Really, I was just covering my ass. More than once the piano teacher there told me that I shouldn't play straight tunes. "Make them something special," she chided. "Nobody wants to hear you recite a poem in front of the classroom. They want to hear when passion strikes you and freestyle whatever comes to your mind. Anyone can read music. Only those who can see beyond the notes will go anywhere in this business."

I still take those words to heart. And on that fateful day I played another song for Beppu. I'm sure he recognized it as "The Days of Sweet Mornings," but I made it my own. Before I got online to type up this post I sat at my piano and played it again. It was nostalgic. I don't like watching the video because even though on the surface it looks fun and carefree, I now know how Yumi felt in the outdoor shots. How even though the camera favored her the most it was because one of the men in suits who had leered at her made it so.

When I finished playing I didn't know what to expect. Not applause. Beppu only applauded ironically or by social compulsion. I thought he might harp on me for choosing that song. Instead he just looked at me, studying my angry face with an angry one of his own. He bit his cuticle and said, "How would you like to play piano on *Music Tonight*?"

It's hard to get a rise out of me. I'm the girl who heard her father was never coming home again and just went back to playing with dolls. That afternoon I laughed, uneasily, wondering why he would mess with me like this. "You're joking. Why would an idol play piano on a show like that?"

Later he would say that it was that reaction that told him he had made the right judgment about me. "I'm not asking you to play the next great musical masterpiece. Play one of the group's songs like that. We'll get Yumi to sing. Maybe a couple of others. Play 'Daydreamer' or the B-side. Strip it down to a piano ballad and show Japan how mature schoolgirl idols can be. There's a market for it. For fuck's sake, you're all out of high school now. Your fans know it. The label knows it. They won't be satisfied with just the bloomers and the squeaky voices. We have to give them something else. You're not young high school idols. You're older high school idols. Third year. Worried about the future and still hanging on to those carefree days you're never going to get again. See what I'm getting at?"

"Sure," I lied. "You think my playing is good enough for national TV?"

"I don't want to get your hopes up. The label could say no. But TV Gekka has asked us to perform two songs, with the first one being half the usual time. That means we could do a piano number without boring the audience. I'll try to make it happen. Just don't hate me if I can't."

As if I believed it would happen at all.

Beppu asked me to play an original composition next. After I played a couple of songs for him, he said, "Your talents are truly wasted in this group, Chiharu. Not in music, but in the idol life. Stick with this world and you will never grow as an artist."

I didn't know how to take that, so I didn't say anything.

"You're a good looking girl. Don't let anyone else in this business tell you otherwise. You're just not what people look for, generally. If you want to make it in music, you'll have to rely on your talents. Yeah, you have a pretty good voice, but your dancing is lacking. I suggest you concentrate on the music itself. Well, that's my advice."

I stood and thanked him for his consideration. As I was leaving, my stomach growling for my meager dinner, he stopped me again.

"Write down some of those songs and give them to me later. I'd like to see them."

So you see, Beppu was the first one to really believe in my capabilities. On a scale that could change my life, anyway.

***

My relationship with my music has always been strange. Since I was a child, I would think up songs and start tinkering with them on the piano. In the beginning, my mom would ask where I had heard such a tune. She didn't believe that I came up with them on my own until much later when I entered a local songwriting contest and won second place.

I knew how to read music before I knew how to read Japanese, but I didn't start writing my songs down until middle school. By then I had forgotten most of the songs I loved making up as a kid. You see, those songs were for me. Therapy. After a long day at school I would come home and play before doing my homework. It's my way to unwind, to unleash my emotions bubbling inside of me. Some people cry. Some get angry at video games. I sit at a piano and make shit up.

Obviously it's been good to me. I've been making a good living as a composer for a few years now. Not everyone accepts my compositions, but I am proud to say that it was a rejected song that Miss Yoshie Tanizawa picked up to perform as one of her early singles. You know, the one that made her really popular? At the office people joked that some bigger artist's leftovers were good enough to create a new star. It was a backhanded compliment, but it still made me proud to hear.

Usually I write lyrics too, but about half the time they're rejected and someone at the label or the artist who gets it rewrites them to be more personable. I don't care. The songs I sell to the label aren't really from my heart. Yes, I put a lot of work into them, but I don't spread any particular message with them. They're formulaic. Write what the public wants to hear on the radio on their commute home. After a while you know which chord progressions and words will appeal to people the most. I have this chart hanging up on my wall that Yumi and I made for fun. "Words For the Masses." Shit like sakura, happiness, tears, holding hands, the moon, laughter… that kind of thing. The goal is to put at least one of those words into every verse. I check off how many I've used and then try to keep them balanced. If you're bored, you should listen to the songs I write for others and count how many times such words appear.

The songs that mean the most to me don't go to the label for redistribution among their artists. Instead I keep them for myself or give them to people like Yumi. Usually I have them on hand and just give them to her. If she can't use them for some reason, she gives them back to me and I either sell them or hide them away in a drawer by my piano. I suppose I could sing them myself, but they're not meant for me to sing. The only ones I sing are ones I feel are so personal or have some sort of concept. For example, I wrote the entire "Transcendent Holiday" mini-album in one night when I was drunk on *sake*. I can't even remember why I was happily drinking that night, but I do remember the sweet summer breeze coming through my window as I sat at my piano and took shot after shot until I passed out for twelve hours and woke up in a stupor. I found the music sheets I had scribbled the day before and thought, "Wow, this is pretty good!" It amuses me that it's such a fan favorite.

Sometimes I read about other big name composers in the industry and wonder how they have so much endless creativity in their minds. I'll never be as prolific or famous as Tetsuya Komuro or Shun'ichi Tokura. Just thinking about how many hit songs they put out in their careers intimidates me. I'm lucky to create a sellable song a month. Sellable. Meaning the label will give it as a lead single to one of its artists. They scoop up everything else I create that they think they can use, but they turn up as B-sides and spare album tracks. Whatever. I get paid.

Then there are things like this video game project I am working on. It's not the first time I've done a soundtrack. I did that anime web series a year ago. I doubt I would be up to the pressure of a large production. Who am I, Yuki Kajiura? No, I'm just Chiharu Morita. I'm not much more special than other composers on the label's staff who also happen to do side work. Fifty years from now, nobody will really remember me. They'll remember YUMI, but they won't know who wrote some of her songs. To be fair, they won't remember most of the people who wrote her songs. They won't even know she wrote a few of those songs herself.

It doesn't matter whether or not people remember me. One of my greatest joys is playing the piano, and as long as I can do that, I will be happy to some extent. There are a few people I enjoy entertaining with it as well. I always laugh when the little one dances to my playing. Beppu is someone that is hard to read but always compliments me when I finish a piece. And of course, Yumi often comes to where I'm with a piano just to sit and listen to me play. I could entertain her for hours.

In a way typing these posts feels like playing the piano. I'm not creating music, but I'm creating something by moving my hands over these keys in such a way to convey my meaning. If I think about it too much I become lost in the existential implications. Language, intent... the human brain can be so fascinating. All around the world, since the beginning of time, people communicate using music. It transcends culture and time itself. There are people in this world performing songs that were written down thousands of years ago. Sometimes I dream of unearthing some ancient song in my backyard and teaching myself to play it the way it was meant to be played. I want to connect to someone who once lived, loved, hurt, and worried in this very spot. It doesn't matter how mundane their lives were. Those feelings were real back then, and perhaps that person's spirit echoes in the walls of my modern house even as I write this.

I wonder... will my spirit echo somewhere too one day? Will Yumi's?

I hope we will be happy spirits.

Chapter 12

We arrived in Tokyo Thursday evening, just in time to check in to a cheap business hotel that only had one double bed a piece. This meant we had to double up per room, so Yumi and I huddled together that night giggling about being on TV and getting to perform together, just us. Beppu had convinced the label that it was in the group's best interests to show off such mature talents. I assumed that Dolly and Reika would also sing with Yumi, but no… it was like Yumi and I were a sub-unit already. We joked about that in bed. What would they call us?

"Seki-Tachi," Yumi joked, thinking she was so clever to refer to us being the only two girls from Seki. "Or they would make some couple name for us. Yuharu. Chimi. Oh God, *Chimi!*"

After I finished laughing, I suggested that the *kanji* for Chimi be 'blood' and 'beautiful.' We would be strikingly gorgeous goth girls in sailor uniforms, our skin pale while blood dripped from our eyes. We would sing downtempo rock covers of classic idol songs. I hurt my abdomen laughing as I went to sleep thinking of Seiko Matsuda's "Red Sweet Pea" set to depressing guitar and bass. Fans wouldn't know what to make of us!

Nobody slept well that night, but between coffee and adrenaline we were energetic all day Friday. We went to the studio in Roppongi early, to meet the production staff and to do rehearsals. The head producer of *Music Tonight* told us that they were excited to have some fresh idols on the show. "We haven't seen an indie idol group do so well so quickly," he said. This was before AKB48 completely exploded, but only by a year or two. In those days, we really were exceeding expectations. I think the label only wanted the Butterfly Tops to be a regional sweetheart act that relied more on regular performances than album sales. So, kind of like AKB48, but on a smaller scale.

The producer was particularly interested in Yumi, who had her hair and makeup done naturally. The woman in the dressing room wet her short hair and gave it a sheen just right for the stage lights, while a man touched up her face to give her an innocent look with a hint of realism. It was mostly the eyes. Yumi's big eyes were narrowed to look more pensive than optimistic. A small tail of eyeliner hugged the edges of her eyes, bold and daring.

Me, they combed my hair and put some gel in it to keep shape. The only makeup they put on me was some concealer, a hint of blush, and eye shadow so I wouldn't look pale under the lights. That was me, Chiharu. Nondescript.

I am glad for the advent of rehearsals. Because of them I was able to step on the *Music Tonight* stage for the first time without the whole world seeing me nearly throw up. The only people watching were staff. The only camera rolling was a test camera to make sure we would be lined up correctly for the real broadcast. Our mics were on but not optimized yet. So when we sang, it was a bit chaotic, with my backing vocals overpowering both the lead and main vocals of Dolly and Yumi respectively. They told us not to worry about it – yet.

When Yumi and I rehearsed our piano rendition of the ballad B-side, I screwed up so many times that I could see the producer shaking his head and preparing to cut the performance from the program. It took Beppu delaying the inevitable for ten minutes before I finally got through the song flawlessly twice. I heaved a huge sigh of relief when the producer gave the go-ahead, and Beppu reminded me to try some of the stage fright exercises I learned in training.

We passed the time until show time in the dressing rooms, having our hair and makeup touched up while Beppu went over protocol until he was blue in the face. None of us were paying any attention to him. Half the girls were texting away on their cell phones, and me? Sitting in front of the mirror trying to control my breathing. I practiced my piano playing on top of the dresser, forcing the pattern into my mind so I could do it automatically when the cameras were rolling. *I can do it. I can do it.* Muttering that to myself, I almost didn't notice Yumi.

She was standing in the doorway of the dressing room, chatting with a young man on the label's staff. I had seen him before, around the office, at our lives, and now here. I think he was a grunt who helped move equipment. As far as I could tell he was nice enough. Never talked to him much. Just one of those guys in black you're not supposed to notice.

If Yumi had chatted with him before, I had no idea. She was a friendly girl and would happily talk to anyone. Yet the way they talked now was pretty chummy. Jokes. Light shoulder touches. I watched them for much longer than I should have. Normally I wouldn't notice her talking to anyone, but that day, while my heart pounded because of our upcoming performance for national television, I began to sweat because Yumi was talking to a boy.

She had many boyfriends before. Some lasted longer than others. I saw her kiss them goodbye when she came to meet me somewhere. Watched her get piggy-back rides down the street or across the schoolyard. It never bothered me before. I shook off my ill-feelings, blaming them on the bile in my throat. Because clearly that bile came from performance anxiety.

The boy had to leave, and Yumi spent her time until the cameras rolled fiddling on her phone and laughing with Koto.

Love, Yumi

Beppu summoned us half an hour before show time. We were on standby until the cameras rolled, standing in the back of the pack until the interview. Fine with me! I didn't want everyone looking at my constipated face and saying, "What is that girl's problem?" I tried, I really did, to relax my face and look pleasant if not happy. I was trying so hard that Yumi said, "You look ill."

So pissed and constipated it was.

The cameras rolled. The lights came on. The hosts stood at the front of the stage welcoming the viewers, while a man carrying a clipboard and wearing a headset stood in front of us, ready to give us directions out onto the stage.

The first guest called was a singer-songwriter from another label. She walked out with bushy auburn hair and a big smile that sparkled in the stages lights, twirling her floral skirt and bowing in greeting to the cameras. I knew this was her first appearance too, yet she looked like a natural, floating across the stage and waving to her adoring fans.

"Go!" the staff member said, patting Yumi on the shoulder.

The moment she took the first step from backstage, the announcer said, "Butterfly Tops!"

There we were, seven girls in matching sailor uniforms even though we were all too old to still be in high school. We were supposed to go out in single-file with Yumi and Dolly in the lead, but Nezu tripped over her own damned shoes and stumbled into Dolly. The girl had such grace that she barely flinched as she nodded to the camera and shoved Nezu behind her. It caused a ripple effect through the line, and soon I was stuck between Reika and Mayu, outpacing the former while the latter scrambled to keep up without calling attention to herself. A TV hanging above the audience showed that the camera only had eyes for our lead members anyway.

It was surreal, standing on that stage and walking toward some of the most famous hosts on TV while a seasoned male idol group was announced behind us. Another stage hand directed our group to a row of chairs, and soon I was safely sitting behind Yumi, enough people blocking my face so I could relax and pretend I wasn't nervous while Camera 1 focused on us.

You think a lot of strange things when you're sitting on stage, being filmed for national television. Naturally you think about your appearance, and concentrate on sitting up straight, looking pleasant, and speaking softly when prompted. I've been on TV quite a few times over the years. It never really changes. Sure, it becomes easier, and you realize what few things nobody is really paying attention to, but you still get those butterflies and you still feel self-conscious. The only thing I had going for me that first time was that I was so obscured and unknown that the only person in all of Japan focusing on me was my mother back in Seki.

The singer-songwriter was the first to be interviewed. I didn't know much about her before that night, but I remember thinking that she wasn't only pretty, but well-spoken. I would have never guessed that this was her first national appearance as well.

You may be wondering who it was. She's not popular anymore, but back then she had a string of mid-chart hits that got lots of radio play. I suppose you would call them mostly nostalgic as opposed to iconic. The kind of songs you never think about until you randomly come across them on late-night radio when stations don't care what's played.

It was Erina Tokawa. See, now you probably remember her. Real fancy on an acoustic guitar. She always wore long sundresses and wide-brimmed straw hats. Kind of hippie-ish, though I wouldn't call her a hippie.

Erina was warmly received by the audience, a sea of young women who were probably there for the male idols. I never noticed until that night how often the audiences tended to be overwhelmingly women. After a while I came to embrace it. What could be better than looking into a dozen faces at a time, each of them feminine and understanding? The few times I would make eye contact with a man I would flub whatever line I was trying to say to the interviewer. Something about men made me nervous.

The lights in the studio dimmed for Erina's performance. A happy acoustic tune filled the air, as well as her soft, melodic voice. I thought, it's not so bad, being on stage. If someone like Erina Tokawa could make it look like cutting cake, then I could do it too.

Good thing I thought that, because shortly after the applause we went to commercial and the stagehands prepped us for our interview.

I didn't have to say anything. That was up to Yumi, Dolly, and Nezu, our designated personalities. I just had to sit there and smile for the camera. It was easy to smile when Yumi cut a joke about being cold when we filmed outside for our recent video. Indeed, it had been very cold. When we weren't filming, we stood around the area wearing winter jackets and huddling together for warmth. The hosts expressed sympathy and asked, "What is it like to become popular so quickly? You only debuted a few months ago."

"It's very freeing, actually," Yumi said, which surprised the hosts. "When you're training, you worry about how the public will receive you. I feel that if it took too long for us to gain popularity, we would always be worried about it. Now we know that we did everything right. It gives us the ability to keep moving forward and better ourselves quickly."

Nobody could follow that. Dolly's mouth dropped open, and Nezu contained a laugh at how charming our darling Yumi was in the face of a camera. Off to side I could see Beppu smirking as if he couldn't have coached her better himself. Later I heard he actually had coached her to say something just like that. Combined with Yumi's genuine energy, and no doubt that half of Japan just thought, "Wow, that girl really sees the big picture."

Beppu's plan to make us look mature was taking form.

But not as well as it did when Yumi and I were called out of our seats to take our places on another stage, complete with piano and microphone. Dolly did her best to wrap up the interview, and I did my best to not throw up in front of Camera 3 as I sat down on the bench.

With only twenty seconds to spare, Yumi leaned over my shoulder and whispered, "You're the best piano player in the world."

Such a simple, meaningless phrase. Of course I was not the greatest piano player in the world. Nor did Yumi really think that. She was giving me a confidence boost, and a much needed one. Thanks to her, I was able to take a deep breath and put my fingers where they needed to be, careful to not actually hit a key yet.

The hosts announced our introductory song. They said it was the B-side to our single, designed to show off our "cool and mature" sounds. Hilarious, considering what I was wearing. What Yumi wore. I looked at her. She seemed so at ease in front of the camera, waving to the audience. This was it. This was her moment, not mine. I was here to back her up and make her truly shine in front of others.

The moment hinged on me. I could not mess up. I couldn't. Not if I wanted Yumi to succeed in the future.

My performance was flawless. I heaved the biggest sigh of relief when it was over.

***

Somebody in the comments asked about how I met Yumi. I think I mentioned it before, but we met in kindergarten. We've essentially known each other our whole lives, or at least as long as we can remember. Although I do recall the day and moment in which we met.

It's not a very special story, but since someone asked I may as well go over it.

Halfway through the school year, Yumi and her family moved to Seki from Ishikawa. She started school on a Tuesday. I know this because my mother used to coordinate my outfits based on the day of the week, and that day I was wearing a plaid jumper. My Tuesday outfit.

Fortune is the only word I can use to describe what happened that day. It's difficult for me to make friends, so if I didn't meet Yumi I may not have had friends growing up. Now that I think about it, I really haven't had any other friends. Sure, I've had good acquaintances I sometimes hung out with sans Yumi at school, but nobody I would spend the night with or do something as crazy as becoming an idol with. Even now I'm mostly a loner. Sometimes I think about trying to make friends with the mothers at the little one's school, but it feels awkward because I'm not really her guardian and they might ask questions. Plus I'm not interested in talking about toilet training and the best juice brand. The day I become a *juku* mother is the day I have a long think about my life. Beyond this confession.

Anyway, whenever we got a new student it was always a big deal because Seki is small and students are more likely to leave instead of arrive. Having a new girl was even more exciting because then it meant a possible new friend.

Yumi has never been shy. From the moment she introduced herself, she was yelling so loudly that the teacher asked her to quiet down. I vaguely recall her wearing a red outfit and hair in pigtails. Of course, every girl wanted to be her friend. Even back then I didn't think much about making friends. I was content to play by myself. Yet the moment we were given free time, Yumi came up to me and asked if I could show her where some blocks were.

You see, it's a boring story. We played with blocks that Tuesday. Then Wednesday. Then by the next weekend our parents were talking outside of the school and arranging a play date. We were inseparable from then on out. That's just how it goes for most children, isn't it?

Sometimes I think about what my life would be like without Yumi. Would I have really been alone growing up? Would I have been doomed to graduate by myself? It's not the end of the world to grow up friendless. But then I wouldn't have Yumi.

We were talking about our friendship a while ago. You know how it is when you've known someone for so long, and since you were so young. Nothing is sacred. You know when the other person had her first period and what she looks like when she's deathly ill. Sometimes we forget talking about such things isn't normal in public, and we'll get weird looks whether we're in some mainstream place or an exclusive joint. I miss the mainstream places like Mister Donut or Starbucks. Yumi is too easy to recognize, though.

"Do you remember when we went to the river and thought we were alone, so we stripped down to our underwear like it was nothing? Then when we got out and there were boys walking by with their bikes? They couldn't look at us Monday without dying!"

As much as I don't care for reliving those particular memories, I let Yumi talk about them since they make her happy, and it's rare to see her laugh out loud like that these days. Talking about things that happened before we entered the industry always makes her happy. The only time she laughs like that outside of nostalgia is if there's a really funny show on TV.

If the sullen, traumatized Yumi were the one I met twenty-five years ago, I wonder if we would still be friends growing up. Or would she have been like me and mostly keeping to herself? Would we be the two loners? Would that have made us friends as opposed to her deciding that first day to talk to me of all people? I should ask her why she talked to me. She probably doesn't remember.

While I'm answering questions – really, I'm just putting off the next post – there was something that kinda pissed me off. I shouldn't read comments, especially the negative ones, but you know what it's like. A damned car wreck on the highway that I can't look away from. I'm a glutton for punishment, as my mother would say.

More than one person insinuated that I am unfit to take care of the child because I am gay. That's so antiquated. Do you know how many gay people successfully raise children in this country, let alone the world? Well, I don't have a documented number, because the country doesn't care about that. I do know quite a few gay parents, and they are all just as competent as most of the straight ones I know.

Besides, some of those straight mothers and fathers you know probably aren't as straight as you assume. Just because someone got married doesn't mean they are heterosexual. I know quite a few of those too. Every time I go to a meeting place I am floored by the amount of married people in there. No, not married to another man or woman. Married to a person of the opposite sex. They do this to either establish a family or to save face while they have gay relationships on the side. Some are both gay while others are hiding it from their spouses. You can't judge someone just by what you see.

I couldn't do that though. Marry a man. Even if you put a gun to my head I don't think I could do it. The situation would have to be even more dire, like the little one's life on the line. Sometimes I think about these situations and freeze up in bed. I know I don't have to have sex with a man I am married to, but being married to one would make me think of it all the time. I don't want to do that again. Think I would actually throw up if I had to.

Or is this not so much about that but this preconceived notion that gay people are sex addicts? Do you think I would subject a child to my sex life? We are not perverts. Some gay people are promiscuous like straight people can be, but we are all totally different aside from that one thing. It's really nobody's business how many partners I've had, but I can assure the world that the little one won't ever have to know either. Why would she? Do you tell your children who you're fucking? Inside your marriage? Outside of it? Do you tell your spouse?

Forgive me. It's difficult dealing with this sort of thing on a large scale. I knew when I started writing these posts that I would be facing those kinds of comments. Yet it wasn't until I actually saw them that I realized what I had signed up for. Say whatever you want about me, but leave that child out of this.

I suppose I should get back to the story now. You may have noticed that I am dreading this part.

Chapter 13

Thanks to *Music Tonight*, we had our first Top 10 release. We made it all the way to #8 on the singles chart with "The Days of Sweet Mornings," and soon we had many media people knocking on our doors. Teen magazines wanted us to appear in last minute spreads. The first time my face was in a magazine was with "Teeny Popper," the kind of advice rag that talks about entrance exams and how to approach your crush. The bigger magazines weren't for me. Yumi, Dolly, and Reika had their faces plastered on those pages – the designated models of the group.

I had other things to keep me busy anyway. Outside of performances, we were preparing for our debut album, which had been moved up a month with a fourth single to release two weeks before it. The single had long been chosen – the original title track to the album. Production was cleaning it up while Beppu and the others argued what kind of concept it should have. Meanwhile, the songwriters pulled overtime coming up with songs for the album. Now that we were popular, they took extra care.

Love, Yumi

Since I was one of the least busy but most vocally skilled members of the group, I was called in many mornings to record demos of these songs. Later I learned that Beppu was the one who requested me. In between takes, he sat me down in the control room to show me how the knobs and dials really worked. At first I found it boring, but over the weeks I understood what he was doing: preparing me for my future after the Butterfly Tops.

I sang demos. I learned production. I took piano lessons and even recorded some piano for the album. I learned more complicated choreography that challenged me but toned my body in ways I did not recognize. I was exhausted most days.

We were all exhausted. Everyone had different roles to fill in the creation of this album. Yumi was making the press rounds as the leader, main vocalist, and one of the most recognizable faces of the group. Her first solo gig was for an older teen magazine. With summer approaching, she was put in a blue bikini and asked to play on an empty beach. We were envious that she got to spend a day *playing*.

To say I didn't see much of my best friend those weeks is an understatement. Sometimes whole days would go by before I had the chance to talk to her or even see her. She was kept so busy that we joked that we had never been apart so much. I was a bit envious that she got to do so much traveling. In time I would get to tour the country as well, but I was starting to feel the pressure of being cooped up in the label building so much. First free weekend I got I went back to Seki and enjoyed the peace and quiet of my house and my mother's attentions. Although it felt wrong without Yumi busting down my front door to suggest we go swimming in the river.

I was so busy that I never noticed what was happening to my best friend before it was too late, so to speak.

We were in Nagoya, but by some miracle the whole group had a Sunday off. It was hilarious watching girls like Dolly and Reika secretly make plans with boyfriends. I overheard Dolly in the bath saying, "I can't wait to get fucked finally. I'm so pent up I'll blow before he does this time!" Someone laughed. I think it was Mayu.

I was used to watching my group mates sneak out to see boyfriends or fool around on their days off. Obviously I did not have a companion. If we were not so famous in the area now, I would have gone out shopping or enjoy the sunny day in the park. Maybe play a sport and use my new muscles for other ventures. Too dangerous. I spent my day off in the dorms, snoozing here and reading a book there.

In truth I didn't know where Yumi was. She had disappeared early that morning and didn't come back until late. At the time I didn't think much of it. On her days off she would either spend the whole day in bed or say she was "going out to get some me time." I gave her the space she wanted. We still spent half our nights together in our dorm room – yes, sometimes in the same bed still, although nothing happened – so I didn't feel put out or ignored. I understood. On that day off I was glad to have the dorms to myself. The peace and quiet was a luxury after the constant braying of teen girls and the clatter of instruments.

I was in bed reading by the time Yumi came back. She grabbed a towel and went to bathe before I could say hello. When she returned, her hair wet and a towel clinging to her frame, she sighed happily and dressed while I wasn't looking. I was in love with her, but I wasn't a pervert.

The light went out after Yumi climbed into bed. I thought she would fall asleep without a word, but five minutes later she said, "Chi-*chan?*"

"Yeah?" I lowered my book.

The long pause was full of apprehension. It made me close my book. "I lost it tonight."

I turned my head toward her. "Lost what?"

Another stifling pause. "My virginity."

Let me tell you, I had never heard my heart pound in my head as hard in my life as I did in that moment. Within a second I had convinced myself that I didn't hear correctly. "What?" I couldn't say anything else. I was too shocked.

Yumi turned over in her bed, facing me. "With Tako-*kun*. You know. My boyfriend?"

"You have a boyfriend?" How did I miss this?

"*Maji de!* You don't remember?"

"I didn't know he was your boyfriend."

"Ah, maybe I forgot to mention it… we've been dating a couple of weeks now."

"The staff guy, right?"

"Yeah. He's cute, *ne?*"

No. No he wasn't. He was boring, bland, *male*. I couldn't remember what this guy looked like even though I had seen him a thousand times around the building. My blood was boiling. I saw him hanging around our dressing room at *Music Tonight*, chatting Yumi up like she was a prize to be won. Ask her out. Touch her breast. Fuck her. That's how quickly it played out in my head, the image burning behind my eyes.

I was washed in the flames of jealousy and all I could do was calmly say, "I didn't know you were a virgin."

It was the truth. I had assumed over the years that at some point Yumi tried sex with one of her high school boyfriends. She talked about sex enough. Always reading those comics and doing those quizzes in the back of those magazines. Why hadn't she told me about her having sex before? I had rationalized that it was such a non-thing she didn't care to share. Later I realized I had built this idea up about her in order to not feel jealous. Yumi had mediocre teen sex a couple of times. No big deal. It happened in high school. Not like I knew I was in love with her then. Why would I have cared?

But no, Yumi was still a virgin long after becoming an idol. Then she had sex with a guy on the staff. That was it. That was the reality. I hated that reality.

"I didn't do much with those other boyfriends. Kissing, some touching… tonight was my first time actually going all the way."

"I see." The next thing I was supposed to ask was something like, "How was it? Is it big? Did he fill you up?" God, even now I'm not sure what I'm *actually* supposed to say in that situation. I'm so detached from that world. Surely someone will tell me in the comments.

"It was good." Probably a lie. "Hurt, though not as much as I thought it would."

I bit my lip until it bled.

"Did it hurt your first time?"

Now that made me sit up in my bed. "Excuse me?"

"The first time you..." Yumi caught herself. "Are you still a virgin?"

"Why wouldn't I be?" I almost said it hatefully.

"You and Junpei..."

Oh, *gag!* "We never did it. I'm a virgin." I wanted it to be a badge worn right on my arm. No man, no boy had touched me. I didn't want them touching me. I wanted pretty girls with soft skin and giggles on their lips.

"Sounds like we both didn't know that about one another."

Strange, isn't it? Two best friends since kindergarten, never talking about our personal sex lives or lack thereof. Like I assumed about her, she had assumed about me. Even sex, a basic bodily need that I would understand soon enough, was too taboo to talk about. It was always an abstract. A hypothetical. Never a reality.

I went to sleep that night thinking about my own desires. I was jealous that Yumi was not only sleeping with some dull guy, but that I wasn't having fun as well. My own desires had long awakened since that first night she kissed me. I thought about girls a lot. Women, especially. I was nineteen and had libido tossing and turning every night in my gut. Yumi told me about her "okay" sex with her boyfriend, but I couldn't tell her that I had earlier fucked myself to the fantasy of some woman I saw on TV. It's embarrassing to admit, but even though I was still an inexperienced virgin, my fantasies were raunchy and even kinky. To think of them now makes me blush!

I wanted to know what it was like. To make love. To have sex. To fuck. I was jealous that Yumi could meet a boy and discover it for herself. It was so much more difficult for me. I had no idea how to find a girl to share my lust with. Who was to say one would even want me? When would I have the time to look for her? That's what I should have done. I should have snuck out and gone to the gay bar, looking to lose my virginity the same night Yumi lost hers.

You couldn't pay me to be an inexperienced teenager again. Those years of frustration were hell.

***

I just realized that I never talked about the moment I broke up with Junpei. I didn't say anything because it was such a non-thing that... well, who cares?

Now that I'm thinking about the night Yumi told me about her boyfriend, I start thinking about Junpei. I said before that I heard he is playing minor league baseball around Chubu. I looked him up. I wasn't too far off the mark. He played for a while after college and is now involved with small time management. Baseball was always his one true passion in life, so I am happy for him. I couldn't find out if he is married or has children. In truth, he never seemed like the kind of guy who would go looking for that. It would be something that just happened, kind of like asking me out.

It was a dusty evening when I told Junpei I couldn't be his girlfriend anymore. One week before graduation, after he got done practicing for the final game of his high school career. Since we lived in the same neighborhood, I ran into him while I was walking my bike home from music club. We stood on the dirt roads, my throat dry from both the dust and what I had to do.

"So I'm going to Nagoya to do this music thing," I said. I refused to say "idol" around him. Not that he would judge me. I doubt Junpei even knew the concept back then. If it had nothing to do with baseball, it was beyond him. "Don't know how it will go. Guess it means we're splitting up though. Easier that way."

He stood there, slouching because he was so tall, that baseball player haircut making him look like a sullen monk more than usual. A pitcher's mitt hung from his hand, and he was still dressed in his practice uniform. It was all I saw him wearing besides his school uniform. "Okay," he said, in that flat, monotone voice of his.

Okay. Just okay. We had been "dating" and all he could say was *okay* to breaking up. That only reaffirmed what I had known all along about our sham of a relationship. "So, uh… take care."

"You too."

That's it. The last time I saw him before graduation and since. No hard feelings. No love lost. The cleanest breakup in the history of Japan. Because we weren't really a couple.

Long ago on that night in the dorms, I thought about Junpei. How could I not? I rarely imagined what it would have been like to sleep with him, but Yumi inadvertently put it into my head and I couldn't let it go. I wondered what he looked like naked. I wondered if he could be a good kisser and lover. And then it got dark. I wondered what he would try to force me to do. What names he would call me. Even back then I was wary of men. I knew how they looked at women. Because sometimes I caught myself looking at them the same way.

I know that's irrational. I can't look at women the same way men do, even if we're both sexually attracted to them. I know what it's like to be a woman. To be leered at. To be harassed. I can fantasize about doing fucked up things in bed with a woman, but it's not the same as a man just assuming that's what happens. I am too aware of reality. Of my lack of agency in the world. Always on the defensive. Always vulnerable.

Sometimes I think of myself as a victim, and I feel powerless. I don't like that feeling, so I shove it down deep inside until I can put a smile on and go about my day. It's not easy to go to the grocery store, buy my food, and be amicable to the cashier while my brain is melting with, "One time, a man touched me." How badly I may want to say that, even though I know it's not acceptable. "You're looking at a survivor." A survivor of what? Did I really survive something? To what am I referring?

If you know anything about the Butterfly Tops, then you're probably thinking of the day a fan tried to kill us.

Chapter 14

The label decided to try something new with our fourth single. Since they were afraid it would not sell as much due to the album right behind it, the label bundled tickets to a "meet the idol" event into every CD. This was back when the charts still counted releases with those kinds of gimmicks. So when the fourth single came out and we hit the top ten, we were excited, and didn't care that it was only because of the tickets.

In all, it wasn't a stupid strategy. We had a strong first week sales and sold enough meeting tickets that the label rented a large convention space in the middle of Nagoya to facilitate it a week later. That morning I woke up to a raging headache because I hadn't slept well in days. No days off since we started promoting the single, which led right into album promotions. The recording was done, the videos shot, and now the company was putting everything together. Our job that day was to go meet fans and build solidarity with them.

"Meet," of course. It's impossible to sit down and talk to so many fans, even as the seven of us. The format went like this: we lined up for hours, shaking the hands of fans who came through. There wasn't enough hand sanitizer in the world for us, but every fan was required to wipe down before being admitted to the final line. Who knew what they were doing between sanitizing and touching us? I didn't want to think about it.

This was also when I knew for sure we were being marketed to men. These companies, they try to pass us off as idols for middle school girls, and sure, a good chunk of our fans belong to that demographic, but for the most part an idol is the object of a grown man's affection. We are the perfect girls next door they either knew growing up or wished they had known. We are a fantasy. Sometimes a sexual one.

Yumi was the first in line since she was our leader. Her job was to greet each fan individually, shake his hand, and smile the biggest of us all. I took the spot behind her, which made Beppu happy since fans knew we were best friends and was trying to get the label to play that up some more. "They love the idea of a pure and platonic relationship like that," I overheard him say to Mr. Kawaguchi more than once. "Plus they are a good foil to each other. She's outgoing and pretty, and the other is your stereotypical quiet girl. Look, for once we don't have to fabricate good feelings between members, so we should take advantage of it." I think he was trying to get the label to utilize more of my talents, such as playing piano to Yumi's singing.

It was a grueling morning. Standing in those schoolgirl shoes all day was hard enough as it is, but add to that the monotony of smiling at fans, shaking their hands, and intercepting gifts, and you have a trying day. Each man's hand was the same to some extent. Sweaty. Clammy. Shaking. Most of them wouldn't look us in the eye. Those who did came off as either too friendly or otherwise creepy. We couldn't win.

"This way, please." It was Yumi's boyfriend, whose name I still cannot remember. Everyone called him Tako, like the octopus, because he had long spindly arms and could twist his mouth into a big O. She was still dating him, although she didn't say much about those dates. Nor did she talk about their sex life, thankfully. I didn't know why Yumi was still sleeping with him. Looking at the back of his head as he directed fans to the line made me irate. Why did this mediocre fuckface get to date someone like Yumi? She was way out of his league. What did she see in him? Was he that funny? I had to keep containing my angry face every time I looked at him. It wasn't good for the fans to see me plotting to kill a guy out of lesbian jealousy.

After a while, you stop caring about the men – and occasional schoolgirl – coming through the line to meet you for five seconds. It sounds callous, but it's true. I'm sure most fans understand that it can be grueling doing that sort of thing. Me, at least? I had to completely zone out to save my sanity. I saw hand after hand coming my way. Glasses. Hats. Scruffy hair and clean cut guys. T-shirts. Suits. Uniforms. Men by themselves and with friends. My voice grew hoarse from reciting the same line over and over. "Thank you for taking the time to meet us today. I hope you enjoy our new song!" Yeah, sure.

Hence even today I do not really blame myself for not seeing it coming. I was so tuned out, in another world where my calves didn't ache and my hand didn't smell like five-hundred men that I didn't even notice the fluorescent lights shining off the tip of a box cutter.

Yumi's scream, however, will remain lodged in my memory for the rest of my life.

I had never heard her scream like that before. It wasn't loud, terrified, or even surprised. It was the kind of scream someone utters when they see something coming but can't put a stop to it. Disbelieving. Accepting. The only time I screamed like that was when I was a child and my mother fell asleep at the wheel. We veered off the road and almost rammed right into a thick tree. She woke up and managed to swerve out of the way before it happened, but I remember ten-year-old me letting out a long, breathy noise that could only be described as the scream of recognition.

In those slow, *slow* moments in which time all but came to a stop, I saw the box cutter stick out from this man's hand and slice the air in front of Yumi's face. She took a step back, but it was too late. Before security, or Beppu, or even I could tackle the attacker to the ground, the sharp tip of the cutter lodged itself right into the pristine white of Yumi's blouse.

Shrieks littered the air as the rest of my group mates ran away in a barrage of body parts scrambling to climb over one another, the other fans who happened to be there whipping out their cell phones while making their getaways as well. Tako, that useless piece of fucking shit, took one look at what happened to his girlfriend... and ran off like the spineless nobody he was.

I remained there, frozen, watching Yumi fall backward to the hard floor. My instinct was to cover her, and I did – I threw myself in front of her, blocking her with my body as she stared into my face on her way down to the ground.

I was just fast enough to save her. And I was just in time to feel a quick, searing jolt of pain hit my shoulder as the blade came for me next.

Later they would tell me it was a shallow cut. Two days in the hospital. The man was taken down by security and a raging Beppu before he could lodge it deeper into my back and possibly paralyze me. But let me tell you, it didn't *feel* shallow. I swore that the cutter was at least six inches deep and twisting around, mauling my flesh and making me see a sheet of red before my eyes. I had never been stabbed before. I have certainly never been stabbed since. Good God, it was awful.

Thankfully my brain shut down the pain for me by letting me pass out on the ground. The last thing I remembered was crumpling against Yumi's lifeless body, the chaos around us not enough to lure me away from unconsciousness.

I woke up in the hospital a few hours later. Because of where my injury was, they had me sitting up in the bed with enough space put between the wound site and the mattress. Uncomfortable, to say the least.

Nobody was there to see me wake up. Nobody could explain to me what happened. I was in a white, empty room...

No, not empty. There was a curtain drawn around the bed next to mine. Of course the label wouldn't put us up in separate rooms. They were too cheap for that. This way they could market us as the fallen best friends to the press – couldn't even be separated in the hospital.

We were both hooked up to many monitors and IVs, although in my case I'm sure they were unnecessary. I didn't know about Yumi yet. All I could hear was the beating of her heart as told by the machine. It was regular. Stable. I sighed in relief.

"Chi-*chan?* You awake?"

I was more surprised that she was conscious than I should have been. In my head I quickly built up a scenario in which Yumi was paralyzed, dying. You have probably guessed that I am quick to expect the worst in these situations. Can you blame me, when this is what happens?

"I'm awake." My throat was sore.

"You know what happened?"

"Yeah."

She reached out, wincing, and drew back the curtain the rest of the way so I could see more than her twitching brows. Her hair, usually crisp and styled to a fault, was splattered against her forehead and drenched in sweat. It looked so much darker than it usually did. Like the old Yumi I knew in high school. "It's bullshit, right?"

I wanted to laugh at how candid she could be in a situation like this, but my wound hurt, and laughing only irritated it. Luckily our voices had roused a nurse out in the hallway, and the next thing I knew a doctor, Beppu, and Mr. Kawaguchi from the label were in the room to explain things.

I would be staying two days to make sure my wound would heal fine. Yumi was staying half a week since her injury was more serious. They caught the man who did it and he was taken into custody, although nobody knew his motive yet. Beppu theorized that it was a crazed fan. That was the moment I realized just how popular we were.

Too tired to ask questions, I settled into my bed to take a nap as the men muttered to themselves and prepared to leave. Then the door to our room swung open, and there was my mother, a nurse practically jumping on her back for not listening.

"Chiharu!" One good thing about the size of the women in my family is that they can barrel over grown men like Mr. Kawaguchi. He didn't stand a chance against a mother bear clocking in at 90kg and swinging a purse that weighed half that. My mother was soon at my bedside, crying over the bandage on my shoulder and screaming at the men behind her. "How could you let this happen? Who is protecting these girls?" She shook me and pointed to Yumi, the girl she had fed countless times over the years. "How could a man like that... like that..."

Beppu did not advance on her, but he stood nearby, his hands up in apology, as if saying, *"What else could we do? I'm a father you know."* "I'm so sorry. Rest assured that we are looking into what happened and making sure that it doesn't happen again."

"Are you sure about that?" My mother put a protective arm around me as she faced the label. "I put my daughter's life into your hands. When she came here, you assured me that she would be protected and kept safe. Look where we are!"

"Accidents happen..."

"Fuck your accidents! This isn't an accident! This was some crazed lunatic *targeting* my daughter!" I didn't correct her. The man was after Yumi, and I only happened to get in the way.

The doctor insisted that the room be vacated. Beppu and Mr. Kawaguchi escorted my mother out of the room to "discuss" matters. She looked over her shoulder at me, her country face overwhelmed here in the big city where men in suits controlled the fates of girls.

"Don't let them hurt you," her visage seemed to say. *"Protect yourself. Protect your friend. Because I can't reach you here anymore."*

***

To this day I get chills when I think about the man who stabbed us. Not from the event itself, although that was certainly frightening, but what turned up. His manifesto.

He hadn't been a fan. Yumi – and not even Yumi, just the group – was a convenient target because he lived in Nagoya. Clearly, the man was unhinged. The police report said that he lived with his mother, which wasn't unusual itself, but he was a lowly office worker full of spite and a darkness that even his own mother said was "unnatural."

When we think of these types of men, we imagine the crazy fan with a million figurines in his room. The man who never leaves said room except to go to work and to stalk idols dressed as cartoon characters. According to the police this man's room was the exact opposite. Plain. Devoid of personality. Not a single figurine. Just a bed, a desk, a dresser and a laptop.

The laptop was the scary thing. On it he had thousands of videos. Grotesque, violent porn and creepy pictures of schoolgirls he must have taken on the sly. These videos and pictures were in the same folder labeled "Whores." Not just the porn stars. The middle school girls playing in arcades and standing around suburban sidewalks talking about homework and boys.

The evening news published the document the police found on the man's laptop. That manifesto that still haunts the back of my mind sometimes. So close to my subconscious that I've come close to writing songs about it.

"The girls of today are trash," he wrote. "You see them. They say they are women, but you cannot be a woman until you have served your God. A righteous God who punishes these women for being so deceptive to men. What woman do you know who has told you the truth? Their hair isn't really that color. Even their eyes change color. Do you think that girl is as pretty as she sets out to be? No, she is caked in lies, smeared across her face because she is a whore."

"And now we have these… idols. Corporations prance them out to entice you. You think those girls are really in high school? They're older than that. College aged, if you're lucky. They're as innocent as a fucking hooker. Penetrated by men who don't even love them. But they'll dance for you, flash you their underwear like you dream a good girl would do just for you. If you're lucky you'll get to see the outline of their breasts, the muscles in their legs, and some ice cream on their cheek. It's all sex. These corporations… they want you to see a virginal goddess who will spread her legs just once – because once is all she has before she's soiled – and she'll spread them for *you,* good sir. These idols are prostitutes. High-end ones waiting for you to pay their price. Buy our CDs! Buy our merchandise! Come to our shows! Give us money and we'll give you our bodies! They smile for you, good sir, but it's a trap. A honey-laden trap ready for you to lick up if you'll just come closer…"

I don't want to share anymore of it. You can find the whole thing on the internet. The point is that a man like this doesn't see us as human. Women aren't human to him. Girls aren't humans. We're monsters. Monsters that must be eradicated, like we're the Grendels to his Beowulf. Or maybe we're Grendel's Mother. It's been a long time since I read that.

The point is that it didn't have to be Yumi. It didn't have to be our group. This was a man who wanted to hurt all idols, maybe even all females in the industry. He saw us as a fake product. Back then, I didn't understand what it meant to be an idol. How true he was, in a way. Now I know. I look at these girls on TV. Sure, they're having fun, but do they realize what their labels are doing to them? They're sexualized to the point you don't even know if they're being sexualized. We're desensitized. It's hard to believe that even homely me was sexualized for so long. No wonder my mother gave me that look.

The fun and games were over. We were targets. We were victims. We were idols.

Chapter 15

Both Yumi and I were back to work within a week of the incident. There was no time to waste. The man had been caught and his guilt so clear that we wouldn't even be needed to testify. So the label, in all of its great kindness, gave us two days off to "recover" while they created a media shitstorm around the attack in order to boost sales for our upcoming album.

It sounds heartless. It was, really. There was no reason for Yumi or me to be anywhere but in the hospital or in a quiet place while we healed, emotionally and physically. Back then, though, I was glad to have the work. Some tracks were sent back to the studio for polishing, and Beppu called me in between dance practices to help the engineer.

"We want to make Yumi's voice more prominent," the producer of the album told me. "After what happened, she is the official star of the group."

I gave him a respectful "And me?" look.

"Yes, we will make your backing vocals more prominent as well. I had wanted to anyway, since you have a lovely tone that balances out all the soprano and squeakiness. The label told me the fans didn't want to hear such a deep voice from a young girl." I didn't correct him on the girl part. By that point, I felt quite womanly, even in those ridiculous schoolgirl outfits. I laugh now. What did I know!

Besides studio work, I spent a lot of time in practice. Yumi suffered the most here. The doctors told the label that she should not be doing those dance moves for at least a month while her wound healed. What happened? She was in the practice room three days later, spinning, jumping, and even doing a damn pirouette in front of the wall of mirrors. You would have never guessed she was *stabbed* a week ago. That's how Yumi was. *Is.* She wanted nothing more than to work hard at being a performer. In her mind she saw those disappointed fans. Fans who wanted her to get better, but fans who also wanted to see her cheerfully performing, saying, "I'm here! I'm okay! Let's have some fun!" Her injury was worse than mine, and yet she worked harder than ever. Even when she became winded and winced from the pain in her chest, she persevered, although at night I could hear her groaning every time she turned over in her bed.

I offered to let her sleep with me. She declined, saying she needed all the room she could get to keep her wound level.

It was hard watching her struggle to find a balance between getting better and dealing with what happened. She, like me, needed the escape work brought. Only in Yumi's case she was more pivotal to the marketing, so she was busier... doing interviews, getting shots taken for magazines, and interacting with the press. She had been the primary target of that man's attack. Me? I was the loyal friend who defended her. That was my angle. Sometimes a reporter asked me what was going through my mind. I would say, "I had to protect her with my life." It made for a great story. It also makes for a good truth.

Yumi dumped Tako. I wasn't surprised – relieved, really – after what happened. She told me that she was too busy for a boyfriend, but I knew it was because of how he acted at the incident. He didn't defend her. He didn't even visit her in the hospital!

So I thought she would be done with dating for a while and instead focus on her work. Yet one week later she started hooking up with another guy. Sex on the first date, she told me. "I just want to fuck." I had to excuse myself to dry heave.

From then on, I came to assume that Yumi always needed to be in a relationship. She always had a guy or two, even if it was just for sex. I shouldn't sound grumpy about it, because that would make me a hypocrite, as you will find out eventually... yet I couldn't help it. I hated the idea of her fooling around with boys, sometimes men much older than her. She would do so flippantly, picking up a guy here, sometimes over there, I couldn't understand it... I mean, I could understand wanting to have sex. Except this wasn't just about getting off for her. There was something else, something I couldn't put my finger on for such a long time.

This was going on while we prepared for our debut. In the beginning, Yumi would talk about it with me, but I would be so standoffish about it that she got the hint and stopped bringing up the guys. I probably just made her issue with them worse, but I honestly couldn't stand hearing about one guy's dick and another guy's propensity for oral sex. Ugh!

I drowned myself in more work. I took some of my compositions to Beppu like he asked, and he forwarded some of them to the label. Later I discovered he was taking my name off them and saying, "Ask if you want to know who they are." He did it so they would take the compositions seriously. And they did. One week before our album dropped, I was called into a meeting with the staff, who said they liked one of my compositions so much that they wanted to use it on a future release. Oh, and did I have anything else like it?

That's how I started my career as a composer: amidst the chaos of our first album release.

As you probably know already, our album debuted in the top five. However, we didn't have much of a chance to celebrate because we were always promoting, always performing, always interacting with the public (with triple the amount of security now) and always on the go. We were falling asleep in between performances, and more than once I tripped during a dance because my body was too tired to keep going. It's common for the idol life, but I was so naïve back then that I didn't think twice when the company doctor gave Yumi and me some weird pills. He said they were for our injuries, to make sure they didn't get infected while we were so active. Amazingly, these pills gave me more energy. So much energy that I couldn't sleep at night. I told the doctor and he gave me pills to take before I slept four to five hours a night. Pills for when I got up that made me get-going, and pills when I went to bed to help me sleep again.

See how stupid I was? It was so clear what they were doing. Now I look at what I just wrote and I want to go back in time and shake my younger self. "They're drugging you!" I would say. "They're turning you into their dancing machine!"

Label doctor my ass! I've heard they give girls abortion pills before they even tell them they're pregnant. They don't have the artist's best interests in heart. Only the company's bottom line. The company needed me to perform on minimal sleep. I worked hours that are actually illegal.

Because our first album was so successful, we were given a special live in the Nagoya arena. It was our first big concert, and we sold it out quickly. I wish I could tell you I remember the practices and the performance itself. I was so drugged, so busy that when I think back on it now all I can remember is some flashing lights and the deafening roars of the crowd.

We thought that's how it would always be. We were preparing our next single already, the one that would include my composition. I was growing as an artist, which was what Beppu wanted. I was making money, which was what the label wanted. I wasn't dead, which was what my mother wanted. What did I want? I couldn't tell you. Everything I've told you already is what I remember.

The next thing I clearly remember from those hectic weeks was when we were summoned from our beds at five in the morning – this was not scheduled, mind you – to attend an emergency meeting.

We were yawning, still drugged on the downers but trying to be professional. In a haze I watched the executives come in. Also some other men in suits I did not recognize.

Love, Yumi

Beppu stumbled in, dragged from his bed across town. What was going on? I tried to ask him this as he sat down next to me, but I didn't get an answer. I don't think even he knew yet.

Greetings were exchanged. A somber air drifted like smoke. I looked to my left, then to my right, waiting for the inevitable news – we were being disbanded and had to vacate the dorms immediately.

They didn't say that. Instead they looked us squarely in the eye and announced that the label had been bought out by another company.

Please picture a group of drugged up, sleepy teenagers who barely know what "bought out" means. If you picture a group of girls slumping over and saying, "That's nice," then you win the contest.

We were too out of it to understand what this meant. The only concern someone could drum up was, "Are we being disbanded?"

No, no, surely not, they assured us. The staff we worked with would largely be the same. Just some turnover during this brief upheaval and exchange of power. Mr. Yamamoto was gone. A new company president was taking over. He was one of the men in suits, although he looked just like the rest of them to my fuzzy eyes.

Nothing was going to change on our level, they said. I should have known that these types always lie.

The changes happened immediately. Once they started, there was no stopping them.

"Butterfly Tops is one of the strongest girl groups in central Japan," a man said in a business meeting. "It only made sense that we would swoop in and scoop up this independent idol factory." The imprint was the same, but we were now owned and distributed by a larger corporation. No more hometown Nagoya charm. Our group was too successful to contain to just Chubu. The new company wanted to make us Japan's #1 darlings.

They were going to do this by completely changing our image, starting with our fifth single which had already been recorded. It was scrapped, including my composition.

"These girls are too collectively old to be pulling the high school angle," the president said in that same meeting I overheard. "Do we want to rely on those types of fans? What happens when they age too much in five more years? We need to change direction entirely."

We were given a new song to record for our fifth single. It was called "Growing up," and the sound was a complete change from the poppy, bell-ringing schoolgirl chorus we had been putting out.

The production was positively polished. While the composition was still bubbly, we were instructed to sing closer to our actual registers, which were deeper and more mature thanks to our age. We sounded like an actual damned vocal group on the playback. Instead of seven girls straining their voices to sound cute and young over the same horns and electric pianos, we were seven girls belting out notes we didn't even know the others could hit. Laced between thick dance beats, the Butterfly Tops had gone from high school sweethearts to college vixens. Even I was astonished.

The video reflected our new change as well. We still wore our old uniforms, although they had been redesigned to be sexier. Shorter blouses, shorter skirts, and socks that went up past our knees because that's what men found sexy. For the first part of filming we did a more complicated dance (which put me far in the back because I could barely do it) in a studio setting. Then later on they turned on some sprinklers and doused us in water, making our white blouses stick to our skin while we danced and tried not to slip in the splashing water. It looked really cool in the final video, but the meaning was not lost on me. They were showing the world that we were not supposed to be girls anymore. We were fully sexualized.

Our local fans were aghast and disappointed at our sudden image change. Our new national fans – many of whom included women now – were delighted with the cool beat of the song and our "new" vocal talents. Between Dolly's sultry voice and the power behind Yumi's, this new single could very well blow the rest out of the water.

The new executives said that they had further plans for us. For now, we were to help our fans join our transition into a bigger, more mature act. It would not be easy.

Love, Yumi

***

I was interrupted while writing this last entry of the day. Not by the child, but by Yumi, who blew up my phone before stumbling through the back door, the one I always leave unlocked when I'm at home and awake.

"They put my album on hold," she said. She was neither exasperated nor distraught.

We had expected something like this to happen. The label is very reactionary about that sort of thing. Once they get whiff regarding some tension with an artist, things go on hold. This meant Yumi couldn't finish recording her songs or putting together her image for the new album. Photo shoots were postponed.

I haven't heard from the company I'm doing the soundtrack for in two days. We usually touch base about once a weekday so I can tell them how it's coming along and they can give me feedback. Simple five minute conversations. Except they haven't called me and they're not answering my calls. They're thinking about whether or not to fire me.

Before coming back to write this, I took Yumi into the kitchen and made us some tea. The little one was in bed already, so she was not a concern. Yumi went to see her, though, and when she returned she said that she wished she could sleep so peacefully tonight.

We drank tea in silence, looking at our cell phones in case we got "the call."

"They're gonna cut me. I can feel it," Yumi said over her mug. "I'm a liability now. Once you start posting the really incriminating shit, they'll blacklist me. Maybe it's for the best. I can leave the industry."

"You don't want that," I said. "This is your passion."

She laughed. "At what cost?"

Even if we were to lose our livelihoods, we still have enough money saved up to relocate with the child. Plus we will be getting royalties from our songs for the rest of our lives, even if sales plummet. We both have songwriting credits, which is where the money is, you see. If we move somewhere cheap, we can live okay for a long time. We've thought this through extensively.

It's different when you're actually facing the possibility.

"Tonight," Yumi said, wrapping her hand around my wrist, "I want to feel your heart with mine."

Sometimes Yumi and I are still girls – teenagers. She'll come to me in the night and climb right into my bed with or without my approval. Now that I have a large bed it's not as stifling as it was in the dorms or even back in Seki. It also means I don't get to feel her curled around me, nuzzled against my chest and breathing against my skin. Unless she asks for that. To feel our hearts together, which gives her peace. And me.

So I will leave off here for tonight. Yumi wants to go to bed, and she won't go without me. Look at me. Still a sucker for that woman. If she told me to jump, how high would I jump?

I don't care, because tonight I will feel her in my arms like that, and it's been a while since we last had the chance to remind ourselves that the other exists in this reality.

Part 6

THE CORRUPTION OF CHIHARU MORITA

森田千春の堕落

My apologies for my absence. Things have gotten crazy here.

I probably don't have to tell you that. Turn on the news or open a web page and there we are, our pictures splattered across every tabloid with sound bites coming from mouths we've never even heard of before.

Three days ago I woke up to the sounds of police cars on the street. Normally I wouldn't think anything of it, but considering what I recently posted I was afraid they had come for me. Paranoia, I suppose. I called out some powerful names. Who knows what they can dig up that would technically get me a warrant if the police's pockets were lined enough to consider it…

It wasn't for me. Well, not *specifically* me.

Reporters were clogging up my street. Like most neighborhoods around here, it's a one-lane street, so a slew of men and women carrying around cameras and booms are going to piss off the neighbors. I didn't even know the reporters were coming to my house like flies until I saw the police dispersing them. Now they're camped out on the street corner, buying coffee at the local café so they can stay there and wait for me to emerge. Must be good for business.

Of course, since Yumi was with me that first night, the press went nuts when she tried to leave the house to go to work. "Yumi!" they called, waving their mics in her direction. "Tell us what's really going on! Are you a lesbian?"

"Are you a lesbian?" was seriously the first thing they asked? Because I am a lesbian? So she must be one too. Guilty by association. Good to know that after all these years I have managed to turn my best friend into a dyke like me. It really is contagious. Case closed, the homophobes were right.

I'm astounded. Out of everything else I've talked about so far, they want to know, first and foremost, if she's a lesbian? Don't they know about the men in her life? Just two weeks ago some tabloid was speculating that she was dating another man on her label. But no. They saw my stories about her kissing me years ago… boom. Lesbian. Headlines across Japan.

No, "Yumi, are the accusations about the label true?" No, "Yumi, were you really given drugs to perform more often?" Not sexy enough. Although I guess I should be rather flattered.

Once Yumi ran back into the house, I woke up. That's when I heard the police sirens. Then Yumi barreling down the bedroom door in such a fashion that the little one woke up downstairs and started crying. In all of my confusion, I could only think of the sirens coming to get me, of Yumi on the run, and the little one coming down with the greatest infection of her life. It's not fun waking up like that.

Yumi couldn't go to work. Nor could I take the little one to school. Not with the vultures out. I had to call her in sick, and Yumi had to have the company car she takes meet her right outside the gate instead of at the end of the street. I never saw so many flashbulbs outside my house before. Yumi, dressed in black from head to toe, jumped into the back of the car and took off before anyone could get a clear picture. She has done things like this before.

Even though I was home all day, I couldn't bring myself to turn on my laptop. Nor did I turn on the TV aside from cartoons for the kid. I spent my whole day with her, baking cookies to calm my nerves and to give me something to do. I called my mother and told her what had happened. "Stupid girl," she said in that exasperated way mothers get. I know now. "What did you think was going to happen? *Ara.*" She said she would come visit me as soon as she could.

Yumi returned that night, but she wasn't alone. Two men were with her: her PR manager and a representative from the label. It wasn't enough to talk at headquarters. They wanted to involve me as well. Me. The whistleblower on our story.

"We humbly ask that you halt the blog posts," the PR manager said at my dinner table. To think I served him tea. "This is damaging to Yumi's career."

"And what has happened so far?" I dared him to say that the label was dropping her, let alone canceling her album. They would not do the former. Even if Yumi was never allowed to release original material again, she was still too much of a cash cow. To release Yumi was to offer her up to some other label. Probably some indie label that would salivate to have someone as big as her – even if tainted – on their roster.

The men looked at each other, sitting on either side of Yumi on the other side of my table. She did not look back at them. She did not even look at me. "Well, for one, the press is having a field day. Not the good kind."

"Over what? Bad men doing bad things to young girls?"

They shifted uncomfortably in their seats. I thought, "*Yes, come into my house and see how the big surly butch likes you saying shit about her.*" Well, I'm not big. I'm not surly either. Really I don't think I'm that much of a butch, but it's a fun image to paint. "The allegations over what happened that one night and you calling for vigilante…"

"Oh for fuck's sake."

"Plus, the uh…"

I stared that man down like he was plotting to marry the child.

"Say it," I said. *I dare you.*

He wouldn't say anything sexual about Yumi. Or me. The man was too cowardly for a PR manager.

"It's your job to make sure her career isn't ruined. She told me to do this." I looked to Yumi for backup, but she couldn't meet my gaze. "You can't stop me. You can't stop *us*."

Finally, she glanced up at me, hopeful.

That's when the rep from the label stepped in. He made sure I knew what kind of trouble we could be in. They were still playing nice because they thought that was how to shut me up. That and because they needed Yumi. Even "sales crashing" Yumi was more viable than half of their other artists. Sign in to their homepage and you will see her in the top five list of their artists. Out of *hundreds*.

"What you two do in your private life is up to you." Even he was assuming it! Funny how when you're gay suddenly every man on Earth gets to speculate on your sex life. "But when it becomes public, it reflects poorly on the rest of us. What do you *want*, Ms. Morita?"

Did he think I was going to ask for hush money? I didn't need money. "I want the truth to be known to the world."

"What truth?"

I could only look at Yumi. "Our truth."

The label gave me enough drama in three days for me to remain low. I am back now. The press has given up for the night and I can finally run out to grab my mail. Still no news from the game company. I work on the compositions, but I have to assume I've been fired. The first of many firings, probably.

As I've said before, we're in too deep. I can't stop now. All of this will have been for naught if I give up, if I tell you I'm crazy and I made it up like the label wants me to say. Though in all honesty I almost put this off another day. It was Yumi who came to sit beside me and say, "Don't leave those readers hanging. You're more eloquent than I am. It has to be you."

Then she fell asleep here on my shoulder. Even with her eyes closed, it's like she's watching me type. I'm nervous. Who wants to have someone watch them write?

Chapter 16

I remember the day the new executives started fucking with our fates.

Things had been good, sort of. Compared to the old guard. We didn't work as many hours. For the first time in weeks I slept more than six hours in one night. We got some days off. Our songs were better. The fan mail we received now came from all sorts of people, not just men. When I received a letter from a high school girl in Mie Prefecture, telling me how cool I was and how much she loved my voice, I felt validated by a fan for the first time ever.

Of course, things were not great still. And I can't continue until I talk about *that* day.

I was in my dorm room, door open, doing some cleaning on an evening off. I had already eaten my dinner of rice and vegetables and was looking forward to a long shower and turning in early. Although, to be frank, in my hormone-addled and still-yet-unsatisfied brain I was thinking of indulging in something I hadn't let myself touch in many weeks. I was long past due. I had earned it, especially since Yumi was at vocal practice that night.

Part of this cleaning included rearranging my pills. My "vitamins" as the doctor called them. It was while I lined them up on my shelf and counted out some pills into a container that Beppu stopped by for an impromptu inspection.

Beppu was allowed into our dorms whenever he felt inclined. As our manager, it was his duty to make sure we had no contraband and weren't up to any nefarious acts that could harm our bodies or our image. Except he wasn't the kind of manager who got into our business. He gave us privacy, and in fact rarely entered the hallway of our dorms unless he was waking up some sleepyhead or checking in on someone who was feeling ill. So to have him standing in my doorway, staring down what I was doing was not something I could have prepared for.

Of course, I was startled, not afraid. I wasn't doing anything wrong.

"Chiharu," he said in a flat voice. "What the hell are those?"

I finished counting my blue vitamins and snapped the plastic lid shut. "My vitamins."

"Vitamins. Who gave those to you?"

"The doctor, duh."

Beppu snatched the nearest pill bottle off my vanity and stared at it with wide, alarmed eyes, like a father who just caught his kid hiding marijuana in their underwear drawer. "God damnit," he muttered. "God *fucking* damnit." Before I knew it, he lunged at my pill bottles, knocking them all into the trash can before turning toward Yumi's messy vanity and cursing the amount of bottles on it as well.

"What's wrong?" I held myself against my bed. Never had Beppu acted like this when it came to my personal life. He saved this for when he found one of Dolly's boyfriends.

"Chiharu." That growl made it sound like I was in trouble. Suddenly I had the concerned, authoritative father version of Beppu in front of me, furrowing his brows and shaking one of Yumi's pill bottles in my face. "Do not take any more of these pills. Do you understand?"

I swallowed. "Yeah… why? They're just vitamins."

"These are not vitamins." He struggled to keep his voice even, his breath controlled. Imagine a burly man flaring his nostrils like a wild boar about to go in for a kill, and you've got Beppu cleaning out drugs. "These are amphetamines." He shook the pill bottle in his hand. "And those," he said, pointing to one bottle in the trash can, "are benzos."

He went through them all. Amphetamines to make us energetic. Benzos to help us calm down for six hours at night. Appetite suppressants. Diet pills.

I had been putting this junk into my body for months. Yumi had even more. Beppu marched up and down the dorm hallway, raiding our rooms and emptying pill bottles in sinks and toilets. Some girls were as naïve as me and thought he was dumping their super vitamins. Others, like Dolly, rolled their eyes and said, "Great, now I'll be a zombie for real." When Yumi returned from her lessons early, she found half her vanity cleared off and Beppu frothing at the mouth because *pills*.

"Those fucking jackasses!" Pills scattered all over the hallway floor as he dumped one of Nezu's bottles in a flurry of rage. "How long have they been doping you all up, huh? You girls like this shit?"

I didn't. I hated it. Until that point I thought my recent health problems, like my heart racing a couple of times a day and food being too gross to touch had to do with other things. I never thought to associate it with the pills. Later I found out that I could have suffered permanent heart damage if I kept it up much longer. A part of me was grateful to be rid of that junk.

And then Beppu came up to me and said, "Never take this fucking trash again. Understand, Chiharu?"

I nodded, my arms shaking in my T-shirt and my legs buckling beneath my yoga pants.

"You're going cold turkey. You're all going cold. It's the only way."

I had no idea what that meant. He didn't want me taking these pills? Fine. I trusted him more than the label doctor. I would stop taking them. Most of us would stop taking them once we knew what they were.

"Now listen to me, Chiharu." He grabbed my shoulders, shaking me against the wall as his eyes bore into my face and made me whimper in fear. "Tomorrow is going to be a nightmare. You stay strong. You stay fucking strong for yourself and these other girls. I'm getting you all the day off. You're going to be too sick to work anyway."

Withdrawal was the biggest bitch of my life.

Because you think you're taking vitamins, you never stop to think that you're dependent on these drugs the label gives you. You have no idea that you're addicted to god damned amphetamines and your body doesn't know how to function without them and the benzos. Something it used to do so naturally... and now you have to teach it all over again.

Beppu got us our day off after he chewed a new asshole into the label doctor and spat all over the executives, who claimed they had no idea this was still going on, a remnant of the old guard. Bullshit. They knew. They condoned it. They would have kept pumping us full of drugs until the police found out. Amphetamines are illegal, you know.

Not only did we have a day to wean off the shit, but our dorm was under lockdown. No one but Beppu and another doctor were allowed in, and we sure as hell weren't allowed out. Not that we would have gone anywhere but insane.

I woke up with a massive headache and stomachache. I was jittery, tossing and turning, sweating until I drove myself to the bathroom to drink half a gallon of water. Then I was hungry. Starving. My body craved food, and there weren't enough snacks in my room or food in the fridge to feed me – or the other girls, who had the same problem as they wearily shoved each other out of the way to get rice and cereal. We were like barbarians, our primal ancestors clubbing each other over the head to get a fucking grain of rice if it meant the difference between being famished from withdrawal or sleeping an hour.

Once we did sleep, we slept for hours. Koto was practically in a coma all day. (Shit, she got off easy!) Reika passed out in the common room and lay there for a good two hours. Dolly scratched at her face, slumping down in the hallway with a half-finished apple. If you saw us, you would have thought we were in an asylum, or that our dorm was pumped full of a poison that made us delirious. I certainly was delirious. Toward the end of the day the hallucinations settled in, and I am ashamed to admit I seriously screamed because I thought a giant spider was trying to break through the glass of my window.

I was lucky in the sense my body adjusted fairly quickly. Once the sweats broke and my stomach settled, I could think clearly. Just in time, too. Because Yumi had it worse than me.

I still don't know what other drugs they had her on, but she spent most of the day trapped in the bathroom, her head hovered over a toilet as she vomited half the contents of her stomach. Maybe all of it. I sat there when I could, holding her up so her head wasn't literally hanging in the bowl. I patted her back, rubbed her neck, and gave her a hug in between spasms of puke. She reeked of body odor and vomit. I've seen her deal with some rather heinous flus over the years, and none of them compared to that drug withdrawal.

Beppu came in and out, making sure we were still alive. He was glad to see me with my senses in the late afternoon, although my strength was sapped out of me. I was the only girl mostly recovered who wasn't passed out in bed. I had to stay with Yumi to make sure she didn't drown in vomit.

"I'm sorry you're going through this," he said softly, a kind, fatherly hand on my shoulder. "If I had known… damnit, I need to check on you girls more."

"It's not your fault," I said, weak.

Yumi's vomit extravaganza was over, and we were both cleaned up and taken to our rooms. Beppu helped me climb into my bed, the sun barely setting as I already closed my heavy eyelids and prepared to sleep for more than twelve hours. My manager, the only grown adult in that whole building who gave a shit about me, pulled a sheet up around my chin, smoothed down my hair, and muttered that he hated this part of his job.

"You're just kids." It was the last thing I heard before drifting off into my blackout. "Damn country kids with an exploitable dream..."

I have never taken those drugs again. Every time I have to pop a sleeping pill just to get my body to wind down, I curse the label, and my heart races. I'm convinced I'm going to die from heart failure. Well, that and my stupid best friend always giving me a heart attack.

Naturally our parents heard about our illness and wanted to know what happened. The official report from the label was "influenza." My mother called me, demanding to know if this was true. Ever since the stabbing, she called me every time I coughed.

"It's true, we were all sick." It was three days later, and I was mostly clean and sober. Yumi still looked like hell, but she was back in the practice room, passing out at seven and sleeping until six in the morning. She often forgot to eat dinner, so I would make her eat twice for breakfast even when she protested.

My mother didn't want to believe me at first. I told her we were all fine now, and eventually she relented. But I have noticed ever since she treats me with an air of suspicion if I say "we're all fine." Like when she called me last night to check in with the blog, which I am sure she is reading.

God, I don't want to think about that. If my mom is reading this, I don't want to know.

At least the label was upfront with us about what they were putting into our bodies. They had to be, since we were on to them. If we told our parents, they could sue, and that was the last thing the label wanted. So at the start of a long day of performances and media plays they would hand us caffeine pills and say, "Take no more than two today. Take the second one no later than three. You need your rest tonight!" As if they cared.

"Growing up" was ready for release, and that was our focus. We debuted the song at our one-man live in Sakae to an enthralled audience, a mix of our old fans and the new. Thankfully, most of them liked it. Our hope was that the old fans would come with us to our new image, whatever it was going to be. And of course we didn't want to lose the new fans because we were dressed in schoolgirl outfits. Very sexualized schoolgirl outfits. I blush to look up pictures from that single and see me in a wet blouse and a skirt that barely fell past my thighs.

I think the label was worried our lack of drugs would make us uncontrollable. Quite the opposite. Now that we were more clear-headed, we were also more energetic and personable with our fans. We were also able to better appreciate our chunk of fame, which made us excited girls and more willing to put up with the bullshit. A pleasant surprise for the label, to be sure.

Yumi and Dolly were the types to thrive on the attention. They were always at the front of the stage, waving to people, teasing them, and smiling so big that you would think they were sisters even though they looked nothing alike. During that time I would sneak online to see what people were saying about us, and of course those two got the most public attention. They were our chief singers and visuals. It was funny to see someone say, "Did you know that Yumi and Chiharu are lifelong friends from the same hometown," and someone else reply, "Ehhh? *Maji de!* They are nothing alike!"

Of course Dolly and Yumi were not the only ones with fans. They just had the most, and the most attention from the media. The rest of us had our energetic fans as well. Nezu's were from another planet, I swear. She had an actual fanclub that all wore mouse ears and chanted weird things during her solos. She loved them, but the rest of us were always confused. Especially when they stopped being grown men and became a mix of men and women who loved her style.

Reika's fans were quiet, as they mostly loved her for her look – after all, she was a pretty visual with only the occasional solo line and moderate dance skills. They preferred piling her with letters and gifts, tokens of their affection. They were mostly men. Reika was the one who had to be really careful about her boyfriend, because if her fans found out she was truly unattainable, they would have abandoned her.

Koto, Mayu and I had fans too, although they were unorganized and mostly gave us the occasional letter. We never had signs, chants, or club wear like the mouse ears or the *hangul* for Dolly's Korean name on hats and buttons. Koto loved her sparse fans the most, taking the time to learn their names and point them out in the audiences. Mayu was appreciative, but very shy, which attracted her fans. They didn't need her to respond to their advances.

As for my fans? They were the kind to show up to our concerts, wave, sometimes give me a letter, and then go back to their lives while I went back to mine. I rarely responded to fan mail. Didn't have the time or the energy. And to tell you the truth, I never knew what to say.

I guess you could say the symbol of my fans was a rose, thanks to that one fan. I got a lot of stationery with roses on it, lots of pens, hats, jewelry, etc. The other members made fun of me because I was so tomboyish but my side of the dorm room was covered in rose crap. Beppu bought me rose-scented perfume to wear when I met my fans to encourage this.

"Come on, Chiharu," he said when I originally rolled my eyes at him, "It's such a non-thing compared to some of the crap I've seen fans pull with other girls. Be grateful it's just this."

"Growing up" debuted in the top five. Well, at #5. That's still top five! We did the usual TV and radio tours for a month before having a five-live tour around Japan. It was my first time visiting Sapporo and Fukuoka. I wish we had days off so I could have been a tourist for a while.

I can't mention this time without talking about what happened to Koto. At the Osaka concert she collapsed, right on the stage, her body slumping in front of mine. I almost stepped on her. I remember my foot coming up for the next move and slowly moving toward her torso. By then I managed to stop myself, gasping, the rest of the group crowding around while a murmur went through the crowd. Staff people came out and helped her up, but she was so groggy they had to halt the live for a few minutes and cart Koto off somewhere. Exhaustion, they said. Apparently she was the one member truly functioning on those pills.

I wish I knew Koto better. She was a nice girl. Worked so hard she literally collapsed on stage. There were rumors flying that she had some disease, and the label went with that angle to divert attention from how crazy our schedules were. As far as I knew, Koto had no diseases like that. She was just tired. Thankfully, our tour came to an end shortly after that.

Usually we would have begun preparing for our next single, but we were so busy we figured that was the reason. Maybe the next single would be a double A-side. We hadn't had one yet so that could have been fun. Maybe they could have used my composition this time...

We were back in Nagoya when I was came back from dance practice and walked past one of the conference rooms. I could hear Beppu, his voice loud as he slapped his hands against tables. Mr. Kawaguchi was trying to reason with him about something.

"...You *need* her," Beppu insisted. I peered through the slit in the door and saw his big body sweating under whatever pressure he foisted upon himself. "She is the only member of the group who can fucking read music without someone holding her hand. Fuck! She's the only one who can play a god damned instrument!"

"Be that as it may," one of the suits said, "her fans are limited in number, and she doesn't bring much else to the table. She is a mediocre dancer, especially for what we have planned."

"She can sing," Beppu was quick to point out. "You need a solid alto in the group."

Oh no. They were talking about me.

"An alto is good, but we have to look at the big picture. We need to cut costs to give them a higher production value."

"Fine. Cut costs. You know one great way to cut your fucking costs?"

The suits were silent.

"She can compose. You know she can. She can write lyrics. Not only is that a fucking selling point with an idol group, but you could save a ton of money paying her to write songs for the group rather than bringing in your much more expensive staff. It's a win-win. Fans love it when idols write their own songs. You save some money, since that's all you care about."

I couldn't listen anymore. Deep down I knew they were discussing my fate with the group. Whatever the outcome, it wouldn't make a shred of difference whether or not I listened. I was better off getting some sleep.

One week later we were given the one-two punch. Koto and Mayu were cut from the group. Cue crying from everyone, especially the girls in question. Koto took it hard, her sobs echoing in the dorms as she packed her things. Mayu was quiet, even for her. Later we found out that she had been offered a different job at the label, becoming a dance instructor for the next new girl group they were working on. Eventually she would become a choreographer.

Koto... well, we'll talk about what happened to her later. It's inevitable.

As for me, my name was never brought up, but I knew I was almost cut as well. The label wanted a four member girl group, but Beppu convinced them that five was better and I was the one to survive the cut. Dolly and Yumi were of course keepers. Nezu was unique and had her ardent fans. Reika was one of the most beautiful, and even though she was not incredibly talented, she brought in money from the magazine modeling gigs and the fans buying her merchandise. Me... well, I guess they agreed with Beppu that I could be used to make money too. Mostly off my songwriting skills, as I was quickly approached to hand in five songs by the end of the month for consideration. They even gave me an hour every morning of private piano time to work on them.

I said it was a one-two punch. The first punch was cutting our two best dancers. The second punch was this:

"The Butterfly Tops are coming out of their cocoons. Say goodbye to the schoolgirl outfits, ladies. Head down to makeup and wardrobe. You're growing up."

***

I'm sitting here, writing this to you when someone wakes up, lifts her head, and says, "You're only that far in the story? Chi-*chan,* you're wordy."

I put an arm around her, my hand curling around her bicep. The both of us got used to being athletic, so it's not unusual for us to still be toned. For Yumi it's an image thing, and for me it's a...

"It's a sexy thing," Yumi fills in for me, squeezing my other arm and preventing me from typing until a second later. "Are you gonna write everything I say and do?"

"Yes." I can barely contain my stupid grin. Like we're twelve again, playing a prank in our homeroom back in Seki.

It's good to know that even though we're doing something like this, and even though the media is right on my doorstep, we can still be a little carefree. Yumi loves teasing me. She always has, although it disappeared for several years in between us coming to Nagoya and a year or so ago. I missed it.

"Did you, now?" Yumi shifts in her chair, stretching her arms above her head and puffing out her chest in the process. "Oops." She looks to the dining room window, which I have shuttered tight in case someone from the media manages to come in the middle of the night and try to sneak pictures. I've never had to do that before.

"Don't worry. Nobody can see us in here."

"That so? Well, then they can't see this." She leans over and kisses me on the cheek.

"Why, Yumi, are you a lesbian?"

"No comment." She takes off her sweater and leaves it on the back of her chair. "What do they say in Hollywood movies? I please the fifth?"

"Plead the fifth."

"Even better." She puts her hands on my cheeks and turns my head toward her. "I plead the first, second, third, fourth... I dunno, all of them."

"You do know one of those is about guns, right?"

Of course she doesn't. I'm the one who looks at stuff like American law because I want to know how I can work it into a song. The Occupational era of the 1950s is rife with inspi...

Her lips are on mine. I don't believe it at first, and then she nearly knocks me out of my chair from the strength of her kiss.

"You're too easy," she says, easing away. I'm still reeling from the impact, like she's shoved me and slapped me around. Her kisses have always felt like that. "No wonder I like playing with you. If you were a mouse and I were a cat, I would have outright devoured you years ago."

I have no idea what the hell she means. But I'm pretty sure I want to find out.

"Tell your readers that." She looks over my shoulder. "Oh, you have. Damnit, you're gonna make me sound like a slut. Thanks, Chi-*chan*."

"I do my best to tarnish your reputation. Just ask your manager."

She stands, leaving her sweater behind. Good. She's not leaving the house. "I'm gonna take a bath. That okay?"

"Do whatever you wish." The stupid part of me holds out hope that she'll invite me.

"No, no, we can't do that," Yumi chastises the moment she sees those words on the screen. "That would be too gay." Before I can get offended, she slaps me on the shoulder and says, "You need to sit here and finish for the night. Aren't some pretty good times for you coming up?"

I wrinkle my nose. "Define good times."

"Oh…" She's on the other side of the room, acting coy as she looks over her shoulder and bats her eyelashes at me, "You know what I mean. Player."

I throw a balled up napkin at her and she takes off down the hallway, laughing. Sometimes I hate her, because she makes me so embarrassed.

Chapter 17

We did grow up. We grew up too quickly.

The Butterfly Tops weren't just dropping two members, they were having an entire overhaul. If most of the members weren't staying behind, I'm sure the executives would have changed our name and be done with it. Although we did start going by B.T. to differentiate the new Butterfly Tops from the old.

It began with our looks. We spent most of the day in hair and makeup, listening to stylists and even Anna Fucking Matsuda discussing how to change us all over again. Make us adult. Make us *sexy*.

I'll start with Yumi. They bleached her hair. Not the first time they did it, but usually a week later they would dye it dark brown or something like that, so the blond was only temporary and behind the scenes. This time they gave her a yellowish-golden glow and trimmed her hair until her facial features were so stark I barely recognized her.

They trained her in new makeup techniques. Smoky eyes. Eyeliner until she cried. Blush, red lipsticks, and some kind of cream that made her forehead whiter. After they stuck her in a pair of shredded designer jeans and a skimpy tank top, I had no idea if I wanted to kill them or date her.

Reika had the most radiant transformation. They teased her hair, curled it, went through five hairstyles in one day until they settled on a few bouncy curls and flirty clothes made out of leather. Her overall look was a throwback to the bad girls of old Hollywood movies. She wore it well, and I could tell she would own it on stage and in the videos.

Nezu was allowed to grow up, although she still looked like a teenager and always would. The pigtails remained, but they added extensions beneath them to give her a long swath of hair that swished whenever she turned around. Her clothes became punkish instead of cute. Minnie Mouse was still there, but instead of hair ribbons and blouses it was belts and armbands.

Dolly had the most eye-catching transformation. They made her the most mature, the most adult out of all of us. After they bleached her long hair shocking white-blond, they doused it in a tie-dye of lavenders until her whole head sprouted lilac flowers. I couldn't believe it at first. I thought she was wearing a wig!

She was also given big hoop earrings, a sparkly makeup canvas, and skin-tight clothes that came out of the same closet as Yumi's. But while Yumi was still the cool one, Dolly was the big sexy sister, wearing crop-tops, studded white jeans, baggy jackets that offered lots of peeks of what she had beneath, and enough jewelry to knock out an attacker. When she first walked out of the room we thought a new member had joined our group. One who intimidated the hell out of the rest of us.

And me. Dear God. To this day I have no idea what to think of my look from back then. It was the kind of look that isn't so bad – kind of fit me, really – but when you look back on it you see how dated it was and want to cringe. The stylists said, "She's the tomboy. There is nothing to be done about this face and she has no hair to work with." So they snipped what I had and put in a ton of products to give it a cool style. Then they gave me a natural look for my makeup, minus the eyeliner slathered on. Next were the skinny designer jeans that made my ass look so prominent I caught myself staring more than once... and the boots. The damn cool but uncomfortable boots I was expected to dance in flawlessly. Sometimes they only covered my ankles, and sometimes they came up all the way to my knees. Whatever I wore down below, I always had some sleeveless shirt that either had a snazzy design or enough rips to make it look like I didn't care. My jewelry was sparse, black, and meant to accentuate, not draw attention.

These were the looks we were given and expected to maintain even in our off time. They were identities. The cool girl, the sexy big sister, the retro glam chick, the little feisty sister, and the tomboy. Once we were ready, they took head and body shots of us. I was to always look aloof and standoffish in my pics. My cranky face was used to my advantage, I guess. However, if I were to pose with Yumi, whom everyone in Japan now knew was my childhood friend, I was supposed to show juuuuust a little give in my personality. As if I liked her, or something radical.

The pictures were on the website by the end of the day. The next day, as we stood in front of our mirrors trying to remember how to apply our new makeup and hair gel, Dolly brought up the comments on her cell phone and showed us the responses.

Old fans were outraged and saying they were leaving. New fans were practically salivating to send us gifts and buy our new CDs. The label's mission was accomplished.

Everyone had a million comments for Dolly's purple hair. Even more people piped up about Yumi's sexy look. I was not expecting anyone to care about me, but some people said, "Who is that? Is that Chiharu? I had no idea she was so cool!" and "She looks like the kind of girl even this girl could crush on. Look at me, please!" and even "Some days you question your sexuality. Today is one of those days, because Chiharu looks like a really cool guy."

Yumi had comments about my look too.

"I never imagined you looking this way," she said, pointing to the sleeveless shirt that allowed my prominent muscles to show. "You look kinda..."

"Weird? Boyish?"

"Hot."

That took me aback. She wasn't joking. The way Yumi looked at me was unlike any way I caught her looking at me before. It made me self-conscious. And sometimes I wonder if I kept up that look for so long because it was something women were attracted to. When you're a nineteen-year-old desperate for affection, you are willing to try anything in the name of attention.

Musically we went in a new direction as well. The executives no longer wanted us to sound like classic J-pop. Even more money was pumped into the songwriting and production. Now I could see why Beppu took the angle he did when fighting for me to stay in the group. When a pair of Swedish producers showed up in the office one day, we knew things were going to be different.

Indeed, the day we were summoned into the recording studio, we almost passed out at the sounds of thumping club beats, sirens, and all sorts of noise that was not yet popular in Japan. Music was going in that direction in the West, but EDM had yet to hit us here. We were still playing classic love ballads and riding the RnB and Hip-Hop waves. For the label to decide to catch up with the West so quickly was a calculated risk. There was no guarantee that the public would be on board with it for another couple of years.

So we had this song, now known as "Toxicity," playing in our heads as we went over the relatively simple melody. Instead of singing it like we used to, however, we were encouraged to use our natural tones, to growl, to sound sexy and fierce. "You're young women declaring your independence in the world," the vocal director said. "You don't care what other people think of you. You're going to be the girls everyone looks up to because you don't take shit."

With fewer people to compete for lines with, I was given the second bridge. This may not sound like much to you, but it was a good four lines and included some power singing. For perspective, Dolly sang the first bridge, and she was our main power vocalist. In fact, our roles were soon settled this way. Dolly was still lead vocalist, singing the opening verse. Yumi was main vocalist and sang the choruses and some other lines here and there. Reika was given second verse or interlude, depending on the song. I was given a lot of bridges and the occasional verse. Nezu was taken off singing altogether. At first this concerned us, since her voice wasn't bad – better than Reika's – but Nezu was finally coming home, so to speak. She was now our official rapper, the skill she got into the group using. In all honesty, we were skeptical, but when she laid down the opening rap to "Toxicity" we were floored. So smooth, so melodic, and to find out that she wrote it herself? Impressive. Now I knew what she had been practicing for nearly two years.

The video was a lot like the previous one. Dark studio, lots of flashing lights, sexy dance moves… you name it, we did it. There was even a scene where we writhed on the floor, and I am still so embarrassed to watch it and see me pelvic thrust the ground right on a pivotal beat. Then a flash to Yumi's face and cleavage as she sang the chorus. Good God.

There was also a scene with rippling fabric. Silks, I think. A giant industrial fan blew against us, our hair spiking up, our clothes flying, and the fabric looking positively ethereal on camera. In real life, however, it was noisy and almost violent. Nezu got knocked over by one bolt of fabric that came off its screw. She was back in action fifteen minutes later, but for a moment we thought she had a concussion.

With a single as highly anticipated by the public as this one, it was only natural we would do heavy promotion. We had spots in all the major teen magazines, only the biggest national radio shows to debut our track, and of course TV. It would be our third appearance on *Music Tonight*, including the night I played piano and when we went on to promote our first album. It was also the night I finally got one of the things I wanted the most.

***

Some of you were kind enough to tell me that some of my old colleagues were talking about my confession. I admit I don't keep up with them very often. So when I went to Nezu's blog and saw a lengthy post about what I was saying, I was shocked. And scared. What if she was saying something terrible? I didn't want to imagine someone I used to work so closely with saying bad things about Yumi or me.

Hence my surprise when I saw her vehemently supporting the both of us. Forgive me for copying and pasting, but some things she said include, "I knew them both personally for a few years. Even back then, they were kind girls who would never hurt anybody. Why be so cruel to them because of circumstances?" and "Do you have any idea how hard this kind of life is on a person? A woman? I haven't been through half the shit they have, and there are some days I want to quit and drown myself in a bottle. You media types and haters are too much!"

Because of what Nezu was nice enough to say on her blog, I felt relieved for a day. Then early yesterday I received a call from her for the first time in almost two years. She invited me out for drinks in a place near her home. "Of course people will recognize us," she said. "But in that kind of neighborhood, nobody will say anything. I know some people who can fuck them up." I don't know if she was all bluster or not (sorry, Nezu) but when I arrived in that section of Shibuya I was surprised at how discreet everything was.

We had drinks in some underground place that was too dark to see people but bright enough to move around in. Nezu bought me my drink and started things off by saying, "You're fucking foolish for doing something like this, you know? You're all over the god damn news. Yumi's career is probably going to tank. And yet I can't help but admire your bravery."

"Thanks, I guess." I hadn't even started on my drink yet.

"Those fuckers in the industry need to know that they can't get away with their shit anymore. I just worry about your safety. They know people. I don't just mean you losing your contracts and gigs. I mean *getting hurt*."

"I'm not worried about that. This is more important than watching out for myself."

"Aren't you taking care of that kid now? What about her?"

I have thought about this. For the most part, I am the only constant in the little one's life. If something should happen to me, then I'm not sure where that would leave her. Of course I love her and want to protect her. Yet I also can't let this opportunity slip by. As I said before, it would be easy for us to start over somewhere else if I lose everything. Change our names, relocate... or maybe I will move to Guam or somewhere, even though my English is bad.

If something actually happens to me... then what? I worry about this a lot. I guess if I disappear, please come looking for me. I wish there was a way to entrust the child to my mother, but I don't have that kind of legal power. I don't trust her in the hands of her real grandparents. Even Beppu would be better, although he's probably groaning reading this. *"Two daughters were enough, Chiharu,"* he would say. *"Don't make me go through that hell again."*

Then Nezu shook her head and solemnly told me that she had no idea that "those sorts of things" were happening between Yumi and me. Nobody did, according to her. "I never heard a bad thing or rumor about you," she said, already on her second drink. "You were quiet and kept to yourself, but nobody had a problem with you. Didn't ask for more than you deserved in the groups. Tried hard even when you were falling behind. You were reliable. Dependable. Ah, I guess now I know why Yumi always stuck with you."

I could've told her that.

So I told her some things. Things I have yet to talk about here. Nezu nodded along, sometimes frowning, sometimes laughing or saying, "I can't believe it!" If it weren't for the circumstances of our meeting again, you would have thought it was just old times.

At the end of my spiel I took a long swig of my drink that I had barely touched, my throat dry and parched. Nezu stared at me, shaking her head and saying, "Boy, people are gonna blow up when you talk about that on the blog. You sure you wanna go through with it?"

"I don't have a choice," I said.

"Chiharu," she began, attempting to look serious. With Nezu, it's hard to be serious. "There is always a choice."

"No. This isn't something I can leak through songs or wait until I'm eighty to talk about. We made the decision together to do this."

She looked at me pointedly. "Except you're the one sticking her neck out. I looked. Yumi hasn't posted a damn thing on her blog or made any official statements. As far as the world is concerned, she could disown your ass and start doing damage control at any moment. She's at no risk." Nezu sat back, biting her lip. "Or is that part of the plan? Deflect all of the blame to you?"

"Maybe." That was the dangerous thing about Nezu. You let your guard around her childish charms and forget she is a grown, perceptive woman.

"Damnit, Chiharu. You're a good person. Way too good."

"I get that a lot."

"I bet you fucking do."

People tell me that all the time. That I'm a "good person." Too good for my *own* good. What that means, I'm not sure. I just do what I think is right. It makes sense for me to take the fall for this confession. After all, Yumi and I made the decision together, but this is my confession, not hers. I don't want anything out of it like a book deal or attention. All I want is to tell the world what really happened. What may still be happening in the industry today. Can't people understand that? This isn't just about the industry. About my life. About Yumi's life. It's about how it all comes together and creates this unbelievable story that I can't carry around in my heart anymore.

If my confession can touch anyone in any way, then I am touched as well. I don't care if I lose my career. There is more to life than writing songs for other people.

Chapter 18

I have never gotten used to performing on TV, but the night we performed "Toxicity" live on national television will remain the most nerve-wracking of my life.

It was the stupid dance. They weren't kidding when they said they were changing up the style. We went from doing cutesy hand movements and average footwork to bona-fide modern dance infused with hip-hop elements. Hell, we were doing the whole violent and jerky dance moves before they became really big a couple of years later.

Lest you think I'm bragging, I'm not. Quite the opposite. Because it was a difficult dance for me to do, and there was no way for me to cover up my lack of skill on national TV. Sure, the cameramen were probably told that I was not the best dancer and to not ever pan on my footwork, but the audience could still see my faults. It wasn't like the music video where they never showed a close-up of me dancing. I was doomed. Or so I convinced myself in the dressing room, too nervous to put on my makeup and having to hail Yumi to do it for me.

"You're going to be fine," she said, holding my chin still as she added eye shadow to my face. "You need to give yourself more credit. I know the label works you to the bone on your dancing, but you're good. You're more than good."

She admired her handiwork before letting me go. I turned to the mirror in front of me and sighed. One of the rare times I wished I had those pills again. At least they kept me numb to the stage fright.

I just had to do it. Didn't help that we were the second act once again. After... you guessed it. Erina Tokawa. She was back again, releasing a single at the same time we were. I saw her in the dressing rooms, and she smiled in our direction. Reika was a big fan of hers and asked for an autograph. Laughing, Erina gave her one and then asked for one in return. I doubt she cared about any of our autographs, but it was a nice gesture.

"Good luck," she said to us as we lined up to go on stage. Her eyes lingered on me, moving up and down my outfit. She did not do that to anyone else in line. "You'll do great."

I'm not sure about anyone else, but I certainly did not do "great." I passed, even though I nearly tripped and landed on Nezu in front of me more than once. Thank God the stage was dark and the few lights the stagehands concocted were reserved for anyone but me. I was now officially the least popular member in the group. My saving grace.

Never in my life had I been so glad for four minutes of a song to be over. When we left the stage, I heaved a huge sigh and wished I could go to bed in the room I shared with Yumi.

There is a lot of waiting at a music show. You wait for your rehearsal, you wait to go on stage, you wait for everyone else to finish their stages, and then, if you're like me and unpopular, you wait for the media frenzy to be over afterward. Even after the show was over I had to sit backstage and wait. Wait. *Wait.* Yumi, Dolly, Nezu, and even Reika were being interviewed by various media about our new single. Since we were leaving town the next day, this was the only chance for some interviewers to talk to them in the flesh. And there were a lot for everyone. Except yours truly, because nobody cared about the tomboy who couldn't dance.

I waited off to the side, dreaming of a shower and bed. You have no idea how much I wanted to wipe off my makeup and wash the gunk out of my hair, but we weren't allowed to do that until we got to our hotel rooms. We had to always be "on" whenever we left our rooms now. The label didn't want the paps catching us looking like, I dunno, commoners. It wouldn't have been awful except we had to buy our own products and they got expensive. I stopped saving so much money and started blowing it on hair gel and makeup. Joy. At least I got discounts on the clothes... when they let me pick them.

So picture me sitting in a dark corner, slumped over on a bench because I was bored and annoyed. Who knew how long those interviews were going to take. They could last an eternity if Dolly was incapable of shutting the fuck up. I suppose if I cared about interviews and had people who cared about interviewing me, I would have felt differently, but the fact remained that I didn't even have Beppu to talk to because he had to oversee interviews on behalf of the label.

Turned out to be a good thing for me.

"You look like you're having a good time." Erina Tokawa stood in the nearest doorway, fresh from her round of interviews. "I liked your performance."

I looked up from my cell phone, and the first thing I saw was the plunging neckline of her dress. Earlier she had been wearing a light, summertime sweater to cover it up. If a pap caught her like that, her wholesome singer-songwriter image could be in trouble. "Thanks," I muttered, trying to avert my eyes from *cleavage.*

Forgive me, I was a randy nineteen-year-old who couldn't help but think of boobs every twenty minutes. *Only every twenty minutes, Chiharu?* Well, I was busy. Not much time to think about boobsboobsboobs when you're wheezing in a dance studio or starving an hour before dinner. Besides, the only pair of grown boobs I had seen at that point in my life were my own and some on the internet. I had no real frame of reference other than some women had big breasts and other women had little breasts, and some women had brown nipples and others had pink. Regardless, they were all pretty great.

"I like your guys' new image. Been following it with some interest. We need more girl groups who are mature. Never was into the schoolgirl thing."

Her and me both.

"Me, I'm not allowed to change my image at this point. Not without a fuss." She was still talking, huh. Don't get me wrong. I liked Erina from what I knew about her. Had some of her songs on my MP3 player. She wrote whimsical, optimistic tunes about love, nostalgia, and cool spring days. People loved that crap. Including me.

"I like your image," I said, my tongue fumbling in my mouth. My problem was that I didn't understand why she was talking to me. Bored, and no one else to talk to? There were other performers milling about. An old famous rock band. A crooner male solo artist. A male folk duo that she had collaborated with before. Why wasn't she hanging out with them if she was bored?

"Thanks." She was closer. I could smell the vanilla scent hanging around her. God damnit, it was intoxicating, and sometimes when I'm in a candle or bath shop and smell that vanilla, I am taken back to that night.

Yumi likes to burn vanilla candles. I have never told her that they make me think of another woman.

"You wanna get out of here?"

I rarely use the word surreal to describe anything, but that moment was fucking surreal. Like you don't know if what you just heard was real, but why shouldn't it be? Why shouldn't Erina Tokawa be talking to me? Asking me to sneak out with her? At the same time, it was so random. Of all the people to ask that night, why me? I didn't understand yet. To tell you the truth, I still puzzle over it sometimes. I'm no one special. Not even when I was an idol. Women rarely come to me because I exude some confidence, some key sexuality that comes naturally to me. They come to me because I'm better than the other options. Because I'm in the right place at the right time. Like that night, I suppose.

Love, Yumi

"What?" It was all I could say.

Erina leaned down next to me, the darkness of her cleavage pulling me in like a Venus flytrap. "Ditch your group, ditch your manager, and meet me downstairs in ten minutes. It's fun being bad." She winked at me. Erina Tokawa winked at my sorry ass.

I'll be honest with you. I knew what she meant. I knew what she was implying. But it was so absurd, so *impossible* that I couldn't believe it was true. Was she flirting with me? Asking me out? Ofcourseshefuckingwas. Like I've stated a hundred times now, I was a dumb virgin who didn't know these cues yet. I can look back now and go, "Hey, idiot, that woman wants to fuck your brains out," because I've been around that block a time or two since. Back then I didn't understand. I didn't think it was possible for a woman like her to come on so strong, let alone in the dressing area of *Music Tonight*.

"I have an apartment near here. I'll make sure you get back to your hotel before dawn."

My heart stopped in my chest. My mouth went dry. My eyes grew so big I thought she would laugh at me.

"She's catching on. See you then." Erina buttoned up her sweater and sauntered toward her dressing room.

Yes, yes, I know what most of you are thinking right now. *Jesus, Chiharu, you've got to be kidding me!* I kind of wish I was. If you knew me, you would know I'm not the type of woman who makes these things up. I also am now aware exactly what Erina was doing. She was seducing me. Me. *Me.* Not only a woman, but some nobody from a girl group. Sometimes I forget that Erina was only a couple of years older than me. Her airs were so mature that I would think she was a good ten years older than me.

Plus the odds of her being like that… who saw that coming back then?

Now I was at a crossroads. How was I going to meet up with her without trouble?

I am, and was, such a goody-two-shoes. One of the reasons Beppu trusted me so much was because I never got into trouble. I was so naïve and obedient, it was no wonder he saw me as the responsible one of the group. Chiharu Morita did *not* sneak out like Dolly, Reika, and even Yumi. (Don't get me started on how many times I watched Yumi sneak out to go drinking with a boyfriend.) Chiharu Morita was a good girl who knew how to stay put and be dependable. God knew Beppu needed someone like that in the group.

Chiharu Morita wanted to get laid.

At the end of the day, I was still a gutsy teenager who was getting antsy for some life experiences. I could go drinking whenever I wanted even though I wasn't legally old enough yet. I could even get some drugs through the label doctor, though I can't say I ever did that. Getting sex as a lesbian, however, was a lot more difficult. When the opportunity presented itself to me, my brain started whirring in all the possibilities. Then I put a plan into action.

It wasn't much of a plan. I stood up, made sure nobody was watching – and who would be watching for good Chiharu? – and walked right on out of there.

On the way downstairs I texted Yumi, who wouldn't get my message until after her interviews. *Going out. Don't wait up for me. Tell Beppu something. Don't care.* Yumi was the better liar. Although I'm sure my message would throw her for a loop.

Erina joined me within five minutes. I tried to play it cool. Indifferent. Women were into that, right? Coming off like it was no big deal whether or not we went through with this. *"Oh, that's cool if you want to have sex. It's also cool if you don't. I can get pussy elsewhere."* I didn't want her assuming I was a virgin. Be cool. Go for it. Act like you had been to this dog and pony show a few times. Many times.

God, I was so embarrassing.

I thought we would take a car to her place, but she really did have an apartment nearby. Of course she did. She was successful and we were in Roppongi. It was a ten minute walk to her building. No wonder she was on *Music Tonight* once a month.

I had a jacket on, hood over my head. She threw on a trench coat, sunglasses even though it was night, and a cap. We looked like we were up to no good, and we knew it would be no good if the paps caught us together sneaking out. "Don't you have a manager?" I asked.

"Obviously. She doesn't give a fuck if I leave early after I've met my requirements. Don't worry about it."

So I didn't. I was already in trouble once Beppu found out I was missing. For that I turned off my cell phone.

Erina lived in a small but glamorous apartment overlooking downtown Minato Ward. Tokyo Tower shone in the distance, lit up like a Christmas tree in the middle of summer. But I didn't get to see much of the view. The moment I stepped into her apartment and slipped off my shoes like a good guest, she latched her door and threw herself on me.

Erina Tokawa *threw herself on me.*

Of course I knew that I was semi-famous. I was not a household name, but I had a certain level of fame that afforded me entrance to exclusive places for celebrities, especially if Dolly or Yumi were with me. Yet Erina was much more famous than me. She had successful singles and two Top 5 albums. It felt like she could have anyone she wanted. And she wanted me so badly she snuck me into her apartment and started…

Oh my God, I was making out with another woman.

That's how long it took to sink in. That I was against the wall of someone's *genkan,* their lips not only on mine but their tongue going wild as if she were famished for another person's touch. Until that point, the only girl I had kissed was Yumi, and she was slow, testing. Erina had nothing to test. There was no reason to be slow. Erina didn't want to explore and make love. She wanted to fuck.

I panicked. Vanilla was in my nose and hair was in my hands, and it overwhelmed me, the poor virgin I was. I pushed on her shoulders, not violently, but hard enough to make her stop. Erina stood back on her heels, snorting in disbelief. I think she expected me to slam her against the other wall. I was the masculine one, after all.

"Ah, so it's like that?" Her smile was coquettish, apparently understanding something that I did not. I still have no idea what she was talking about.

She took my hand. Flirty, but respectful. Like we were on a date. She led me across her small apartment in the darkness, turning on a dim lamp next to her wide bed. *"Oh God, oh fuck."* This was actually worse. Being slow. Even the way I landed on her bed after she pushed me onto it was gentle. And here she came, straddling my legs as I fought to get my stupid, stifling jacket off. She had long lost the hat and sweater, looming over me with that great, *fantastic* cleavage.

"So, Chiharu, what do we talk about?" She unbuttoned more of her dress, and Jesus Christ, she wasn't wearing a bra. *"Contain yourself, you horny bitch."* I was a stupid bitch in heat. Ever since Yumi kissed me the first time and I went, "I'm gay! I'm so fucking gay!" I had been waiting for this moment. For a woman to sit on top of me and show me her breasts.

I've gone this far. I might as well say that Erina Tokawa has a pretty great chest.

"Uh…" My tongue fumbled in my throat. If I drooled like a dog over clothed breasts, I was completely out of it regarding flesh and nipples. Goodbye, words. *"Uh."*

Erina enjoyed that reaction. She bent down, smiling, her lips gently touching mine as her chest rubbed against my shirt. *"Take it off. Shit fucking hell take off my shirt!"* "You're going to be a lot of fun."

This is going to sound morbid, but I liken losing one's virginity to dying. No, not like that. What I mean is that one moment it's there, a constant in your life. Sometimes it annoys you, sometimes you're relieved to have it around, but for the most part you don't think about it. Then it dies. And it can never come back, for better or for worse.

Erina assassinated my virginity within a half hour. Killed it, took it out back, dug a shallow grave, kicked it in and started casually flinging dirt over it before going back inside to make tea like it was no big thing. The only difference was that I could have said no at any time – no one can really say no to being murdered. Why in the world would I say no to this? Why would I say no to a pretty woman kissing me, touching me, initiating me into the world of sex I had long yearned to know? At the time I couldn't tell you how talented Erina was or not. For someone like me, though, I had no issue with her skills or her ability to make me see and feel things I never had the chance to before. It's one thing to know what you like, and learn over the months and years how to stimulate yourself. It becomes predictable, but reliable. With another person though, I quickly discovered that part of the thrill was never knowing how good it would feel and in what ways.

I don't want to give you a play by play of what happened. I will say that about fifteen minutes in, I was very sure that I was no longer a virgin. Twenty minutes in and I was seeing brand new colors. Twenty-five minutes in and I was already losing my mind to orgasm. (How many people can say they orgasmed their first time?)

And thirty minutes in I was taking everything she had just shown me and giving back to her, taking moments to study another woman's body, to revel in its differences from mine, every mark, every fold, every size difference and the way her skin and fat hung. Erina was not muscular like me. She was fit, but soft, someone I suppose the butches at gay bars would say was "the pinnacle of femininity." I loved it. Finding out how another woman tasted – and not just her flesh – how she kept her hair, and sounded when enjoying herself was not only a new experience for me, but an exhilarating one. Your imagination can only conjure so much on its own.

As much fun as I had, I would be remiss to not say I was nervous when it came to trying to please her. In my head I knew what to do, but actually putting it into practice was a different ordeal. Who knew if I was doing it right? Would she tell me? Would she let me know if my fingers fumbled, my tongue was careless, or my hips were too brash? The danger was falling into a spiral of nerves and messing up for sure. So I tried to put it out of my mind. Tried to show her the same pleasure she showed me. After all, I really didn't want her thinking that I was a virgin. Even if that had been true fifteen minutes before.

And just to make sure she took care of it, Erina was ready to go again within another few minutes. Hard. I learned that's what happened once the walls of propriety and, "Well, that's what our pussies look like, let's get to the real fun now that it's out of the way," fall.

Pardon me for digressing, but I've never considered myself really a top or a bottom. I know it's traditional for gay people to see themselves that way, but I never saw the point in it. I like both. It's one thing for me to take a natural role in appearances, but it's another behind closed doors. I like to dote and be doted on. I want someone to seduce me and then me seduce someone else. I want to feel a woman go at me like she can't control herself, and I want to do the same to them, to unleash my pent up energy and never ask for forgiveness, because it's not needed. But if I may say so, that first time I learned what the term pillow-biter meant. She did things to me that a man could have easily done, and yet I knew – I *knew* – that no man could make it feel as good as she did.

If I thought my first orgasm was enough to pass muster, then I had no idea what to expect from the second one. It almost hurt I was so far gone. Like my heart was going to stop and my poor mother was going to get a highly unexpected answer when she asked how I had died.

It was nearing eleven when we exhausted ourselves. I lay in her bed, naked, staring into the empty space before me and reflecting back on what I already knew – I fucking loved sex.

"Tea?" Erina asked, sitting up and pulling on a silk, barely there robe.

"No thanks." It was the first thing I said in over an hour that was not, "Yes!" "I'm coming!" or some variant of *Oh my God.*

She made herself tea in the kitchen several meters away, and I wondered what the standard procedure for a one-night stand was. Should I go? Excuse myself, put on my clothes and sneak back into my hotel room? I didn't want to. I wanted to lie there for another hour, indulging in the post-orgasmic feeling of relaxation that I hadn't been able to feel in months. Endorphins were taking over my brain and I was happy to have them. I had also not anticipated how nice Erina's vanilla scent would mingle with what we created together. Short of her coming over to pamper me in bed once again, things could not have been better in that moment.

"How did you know?" I asked when Erina returned, sitting on the edge of her bed and sipping her tea. "That I was... I mean..."

She smiled at me over her mug. "You mean you couldn't tell from me?"

"No."

"Aha, so I was right. You're inexperienced."

I sat up, the sheet falling away from me. "I'm..."

"Uh huh. I didn't necessarily mean like that. I mean, a girl who can..." she blushed. "Well, never mind." Good. I had fooled her, at least. "I mean when it comes to our world."

"Our world?"

"I mean homosexuals, Chiharu."

"Oh."

"After a while, you start recognizing women who are open to such things. I could tell tonight. That's all."

"And not last time?"

"Forgive me," Erina said, putting her mug down on an end table. "Last time you didn't interest me in the least. Like I said, never was into the schoolgirl thing."

I wouldn't hold that against her. Although a part of me felt like thanking the stylists back in Nagoya for making me a more conspicuous lesbian, even if that wasn't their intent.

Erina walked her two guitar-calloused fingers up my stomach and into my cleavage. The way she lightly scratched the skin of my breasts made me ready again, because damnit, I was a teenager and I was never satisfied. Not for more than five minutes anyway. "I knew you would be up for it because I just knew. Call it a gaydar. The faster you develop yours, the easier things will be to bear."

I wanted to ask her how one did this, but couldn't without embarrassing myself.

"Hang out with enough lesbians and you'll start noticing the signs. There's a place in Ni-chome here that caters to celebs on the down-low.

Granted, it can be a bit empty, but sometimes it's nice to have somewhere to go and know that the bartender won't blab about you to the paps."

"You go there?"

"Sure. It's not exactly common knowledge that I am this way, right?"

"No. Or at least I never heard any rumors."

She put her hand on my breast, and I tried to keep my breath still so I wouldn't give away how excited it made me. "Let's keep it that way then." She pinched me, and I got the point. Not that I was going to out her anyway.

I wish we could say we had more engaging conversation, but this wasn't a date. It was sex. I knew that going in, and I knew that when I left another hour later – after we did it one more time, for the road. I closed my hood around my face and stole toward the hotel on the other side of Roppongi, snuck in, and did my best to be quiet going up to the room I shared with Yumi.

I did my best.

"*Chiharu!*" That booming voice stopped me in my tracks in the middle of the dark hallway. Even with my hands in my pockets and my hood up over my head, that meddlesome man still found me, like he had been waiting in the wings, camped out by the elevator waiting for me to come back from my fuckfest. As he got closer, his voice got bigger, until the whole damned floor could probably hear. "Chiharu Morita, *where the hell have you been?*"

I don't like scaring Beppu. I don't even like angering him, although I give him a hard time here and there. So when he pounced on me, his brows twisted in scorn and his lips flapping with spittle, I knew I had pissed him off. Thanks, Yumi. Thanks.

He didn't really want an answer. He knew where I was – nowhere good. "Sorry." What else was I supposed to say?

"Oh my God, she thinks she can apologize." One of his big, thick fingers pounded my collarbone to the point it bruised. "The hell has gotten into you? I've been calling you all night!"

I didn't doubt that. I finally turned on my phone and saw five messages and missed calls, one of them screaming, WHERE THE SHITFUCK ARE YOU? "Didn't get them until now."

I thought he was going to strike me. Not that he raised one of his hands, but Beppu has one of those furious faces that practically backhand you anyway. I could feel myself swaying under that sturdy gaze. "Chiharu," he growled, his voice rumbling in the pit of my stomach. "I expect better of you."

So like a parent. *"I'm just disappointed in you."*

"I expect Dolly to be gone half the time I'm fucking looking for her. I expect Nezu to hide when she doesn't feel like dealing with me. God knows Yumi sneaks out with the best of them. But you? Don't do this to me, Chiharu. I need at least one girl around here I can trust."

"Next time I want to go out, I'll tell you then."

"Don't fucking sass me."

Then he sensed it. He had been so furious that he never settled down enough to let his senses kick in. He looked at me. *Looked* at me. He leaned in and sniffed me.

"Vanilla."

Oh, he was good.

"God fucking damnit. I hope the lay was worth it, because I'm gonna cuff you to me for the rest of your fucking life and you will never have sex again."

I don't know how he knew. I don't want to know how he knew. Being in this business for twenty-five years taught him everything, I suppose.

"Get out of here." He shoved me, disgusted. I felt guilty for a bit, if only because I had broken his trust in me. Deep inside I knew this was the real source of his anger. Beppu trusted me. I was the dependable one. The one he knew would behave and watch after the others. How could I be that way if I was sneaking off to smell like vanilla and sex? At least I didn't smell like alcohol. Yet.

Without a word, let alone an apology, I went to my room and slammed the door behind me. I listened to Beppu's heavy footsteps stop outside the door before going on to his room. We had to be up in a few hours to drive back to Nagoya.

"Chi-*chan?*" Yumi sat up in her bed, gazing at me in the darkness. "Where did you go? What happened? Beppu was so pissed… I'm sorry, I couldn't think of anything believeable…"

"It's fine." I sat down on my bed, slowly removing my shoes and socks before taking off the jacket. After being undressed by a beautiful woman earlier, this felt wrong, to undress myself. "He'll get over it."

"*Mou,* what happened?"

I shrugged. I wasn't going to tell Yumi. I had yet to tell her about the lesbian thing, although she had probably guessed. In truth, we didn't get to chat and share secrets much anymore. We were always too busy. "I went to meet someone."

"I don't like you being so secretive."

Me? Who was the hypocrite? Yumi had enough secrets to fill a whole closet. Most of them had to do with her boyfriend of the moment and what they did on the dates she snuck out to have. Things I made clear I didn't want to know about. Ah, now was my chance.

"I did it." My clothes were strangling me as I tore them off and changed into the single set of pajamas I brought. I should have taken a shower, but I washed up at Erina's, letting the makeup run down her drain and the gel stink up her bathroom. "I lost it."

"Lost…" Even in the darkness, Yumi still had eyes big enough to see. The whites of them glowed as she realized what I was talking about. "Chi-*chan!* When were you going to tell me something as important as that?"

"Right now."

I climbed into bed, tired and weary. Too long of a day. Too much sex. Too much yelling. I didn't want to share details. Not yet. I wanted to curl up in bed and go to sleep thinking back on my first experience.

"Chiharu." I was really getting tired of my name. "Tell me. Everything."

That's the thing. I couldn't. I couldn't tell her that I went and fucked and was fucked by Erina Tokawa of all people. For some reason I was still nervous about telling my best friend in the whole world that I only wanted to make love to women. That they were beautiful, amazing, interesting… and that was just their bodies.

I felt ill when I realized I couldn't tell her these things because of my feelings for her. I was afraid she would make the connection, and that would be the end of everything.

"Come on!" Yumi got out of bed, flung back my covers, and climbed in next to me. These beds were much larger than the ones back in our dorm, but she still held close to my body, and I was afraid she would smell the vanilla. "How was it? Tell me at least that."

I sighed, remembering. Even with Beppu yelling at me I still had some endorphins filling me with joy. "Good. It was really good."

"Really? Lucky."

"Great, even."

"Ah…"

"Fantastic."

"I got it."

"You asked."

"So I did."

I thought she would ask for more details, but all Yumi did was cling to me, forcing her way into my hold as if she were the one I made love to and not Erina. "Sorry if I made everyone worry," I said.

She was silent, her breath hot against my throat. "You have a hickey," she said.

"How can you tell?"

"I know about hickeys, Chi-*chan*."

I kept waiting for her to say something about the vanilla. Anything. Yet Yumi said nothing about it. In fact she said nothing but, "Who was it? Anyone I know?"

"No one in particular."

"Why are you being so secretive?"

Because you'll judge me. "You don't know them."

"I want to know the kind of boy who can seduce you."

And that was why I couldn't tell her.

It's clichéd, but you do see the world a bit differently after you lose your virginity. Nah, nothing has really happened other than you had a good time (unless you were unfortunate, I suppose) but you feel like you're a part of this big adult club. I got up the next morning feeling the usual things I felt until I remembered what happened the night before. I could still smell Erina on me, prompting me to go into the bathroom and properly wash up. Yumi was up by the time I got out of the shower. She looked at me weird. I looked at her weird back.

Because I was out so late and didn't sleep much, I decided to do most of my sleeping in the van. Yumi and I sat in the backseat as usual, my head resting on the back while she slept against my shoulder. The other girls were in the single seats in front of us, and Beppu drove with his eyes constantly on me in the rearview mirror. Fuck him.

Somewhere between Tokyo and Nagoya I snapped awake, that kind of awake you can't explain. I took in a sharp breath, woke up Yumi, and stretched my arms up until I touched the ceiling of the van.

"Tired, eh, Chiharu?" Beppu's voice was full of sarcasm. So he still wasn't over it?

I rubbed a kink out of my neck. "Something like that."

"Uh huh."

Dolly turned in her seat, her lilac hair falling toward the van floor. "Where were you last night? You freaked everyone out by bailing on us."

I glared at her, daring her to say something else to me. "None of your business," I said.

Now Nezu was looking at me, those stupid pigtails bouncing with every movement of her head. "Beppu was so mad," she hissed, like a kid tattling. "I thought he was going to kick your ass when you got back."

I yawned as if none of this mattered to me.

"Oh good grief," Dolly said, turning around again. "She got laid."

Laughter that could only belong to Nezu sounded. "*Hontou?*" She had a gap in her teeth, bigger than Yumi's. "Must've been good to ditch us."

Love, Yumi

Beppu was still glaring at me in the rearview mirror. Wasn't he supposed to be, I don't know, watching the road?

"Thank God," Dolly muttered. "Maybe that stick will finally be out of her ass."

The knowing chuckles that went around the van – minus Beppu – told me one thing. That before last night, I had been the last virgin in the whole group. Better late than never.

***

When I heard Erina retired from music, came out, and moved to Australia with her girlfriend, I was happy for her. It's not very often a Japanese celebrity comes out, let alone a woman. That's why I didn't feel too bad about saying Erina was my first. It can't affect her anymore. In fact she's probably somewhere reading this and saying, "I knew she was a virgin."

In the years since, my relationship with sex has taken some interesting turns. I'm not going to turn this blog into a list of every partner and encounter I've ever had, but I think it's important to be able to openly talk about these things. I'm sure there are many people judging me for what I've shared already, whether because of self-righteousness, insecurity, or even jealousy. Why do people feel this way? I want to live in a world where a person can talk about sex freely. Of course, some things should stay private, particularly if they're intimate to a certain extent. Talking about sex in general, though? I don't find it sacred.

When my mother had "the talk" with me in middle school, I already knew much of what she was telling me. Yet her conversation was hooked on boys – don't do this, don't do that, any guy who asks you to do anal is a jerk and watches too much porn, etc. – and only some of it ever applied to my life with women.

I often think about what I might tell the little one if I'm tasked with telling her these things one day. I want her to know that sex can be joyous and a great way to feel good for a while, but to also know that giving your heart away – especially while young – is dangerous. Yet every parent who says this as a warning knows that they're a hypocrite. We all gave our hearts away when we were much too young by our parents' standards. Deep inside we know that our children will do the same. We don't want them to, but one day we will find them crying because someone broke their heart and now they don't want to live anymore.

How do you help them get through that pain? How do you tell them that there is always someone else to fall in love with?

I don't know how. Because I have yet to fall in love with anyone but Yumi. Even if she were to die and officially be out of my life forever, I don't think I could love anyone else like I love her. Our bond runs so deep, so far back, that it would be impossible to replicate. The things we went through together are the things that either destroy relationships or make them stronger. We are still around each other to this day, so it must have strengthened ours.

So I guess I'll tell the little one that, at the very least, Chi-Chi thinks sex is fantastic (cue disgusted look on her face) and should be had as often as possible (cue dry heaving). She doesn't have to "save herself" for someone special, but she should be safe and make sure that it's what she really wants to do. I will also make sure that she knows it's okay to fall in love with a boy or a girl. Or a man or a woman, if she's a late bloomer. (Cue her insisting that I will never, ever know about her sex life. Even though I will, and I will be dry heaving as well.)

At some point she'll want to know more about my experiences. Not too many details, of course. Just enough to get a feel for what kind of person I am and what she might expect in the real world. I'll tell her that I met many wonderful women who had different ways of loving. Some were hard, some were soft, others quite filthy in their desires and others sticking to the ol' standbys until they died. Everyone is different. Every encounter is different, even with the same person. Especially if you love them.

Until she reaches a certain level of maturity and knowledge of how the world works, however, I'll have to field questions like, "Did you help make me?" She knows that babies come from the mother's body, but she only vaguely understands that a man helped put the baby there. When she asks me that question, I can only answer truthfully, "Sometimes I wonder." And then she asks, "Are you my papa?" I ask her, "Do you want me to be your papa?" The smile on her face says yes, but her words say, "No, because you're a girl like Mama." How astute. I'm not sure how it makes me feel though.

I once asked Beppu if he knew it was a woman I had been with that night. He looked at me, snorted, and said that he knew the moment he smelled the vanilla on me. "Rumors had been flying around her ever since her debut," he said. "I had already suspected that you might be that way, but the moment I smelled that vanilla I knew for damn sure."

"Did it bother you that I was gay?"

"Not on a personal level. But I did think, shit, one more thing I have to keep secret. The wannabe gangster, the alcoholic, the strung out slut, and the dyke. What a group. Who knew Reika, with her steady boyfriend of five years, would be the easiest to manage the image of?"

Who knew, indeed?

Chapter 19

Amazingly, the public liked our new image enough that "Toxicity" debuted at #2 on the weekly charts. Granted, it was a slow week for sales, so it was a low-volume #2, but it was still #2 and we celebrated by pouring sparkling cider with the staff and *sake* in Dolly's room.

Mr. Kawaguchi told us that for every fan lost with the image change, we gained five more. That sounded like an inflated number. However, I was glad that many of the fans were now women. In fact, most of my fans were women. I had more female fans than anyone else in the group. They thought I was cool. I reminded them of their boyfriends. They liked my lower voice and thought pianos were sexy. When the label caught wind of that later tidbit, they sat me down at a piano at one of the concerts and gave me a five minute solo to wow the audience. By then I had enough confidence to pound out something off the top of my head. There was a clamor for the MP3 to be available the next day, so I recorded it in the studio and I had my first solo release.

Love, Yumi

"You're so amazing," one girl wrote me. I liked to read my fan mail from girls and women before I went to bed, and Yumi would tease me that the fame was going to my head. Really, I just wanted to close my eyes and think of women. *"When I see you on stage, Chiharu-san, I imagine that you're singing to me."* Most of my fan mail was like this. Suffice to say, the content of most of my mail has changed over the years.

Yumi was right though. Many things were going to my head. My popularity was increasing, although still nowhere near the levels of the rest of the group. If I had a letter in my hand, Yumi had a dozen more from men all over the country. Even outside of the country. She was building quite the following in China and Taiwan, just like Dolly had fans in South Korea. There were talks that if our next album went to #1 we might do an Asian tour. Beppu said that rumor was leaked only so we would work harder.

Ah, Beppu. After that first night I snuck out – and it became a habit once we were back in the dorms and it was easier to do without getting caught – he didn't treat me with the same amount of confidence he used to. He still thought of me as the most mature one, but that didn't mean much anymore. I often talked back at him. Not always, but enough that now I think about it and cringe. I thought I was hot shit for many reasons and didn't need to listen to him. Not just the fans, but because the label was asking for more of my compositions (that they had yet to do anything with) and because well...

I kind of had a girlfriend.

It happened completely by accident. Also I should say that the word "girlfriend" is used generously. We weren't serious. In fact I think she may have had a boyfriend. I didn't ask. She didn't divulge. It was more about fooling around than forming lasting bonds.

She was a backup dancer who sometimes performed with us, but mostly she danced in videos. The relationship began in the practice room, actually, when she and another girl were called in by an instructor to help me with some moves I was having difficulty with. We got to talking, and like Erina suggested, I looked for signs. When one night she bashfully asked if I was seeing anyone and I said no, she became flustered, and I saw my chance.

Her name was Ichiko. She was a pretty girl. Nothing spectacular. Not drop dead gorgeous, but I liked her. She was soft-spoken everywhere but in the bedroom, where I could get her to squeal in ways I didn't know women could. She was a year younger than me. Barely out of school, but then again it was hard to believe the same could be applied to me.

I saw Ichiko for a couple of months. We were never anything more than casual friends with benefits, although I called her a girlfriend because it was a novel idea and because she was sweet enough that I was open to it being something more. I wanted a distraction anyway.

The other girls in the group always had something else going on. Yumi was becoming a hot commodity in magazine modeling. She went to Guam, Okinawa, and even Australia to do autumn photoshoots in beautiful places. Dolly, Reika, and Nezu were also traveling around and doing individual promotions. Nezu even hosted her own hip-hop radio show that broadcast both online and on radios across Chubu. Dolly and Reika were often chosen to appear in music videos for other label artists, and there were talks about both appearing in a drama. When Yumi was offered an endorsement deal to advertise a makeup brand, she and I celebrated by going shopping and having lunch in a fancy restaurant. The paps caught us holding hands. The media and fans dubbed us "adorable friends," because back then that's all two girls holding hands meant. Ichiko asked me if something was going on between us. She never knew about us occasionally sharing a bed. I figured that would give her the wrong idea.

Since the other girls were often busy with deals, I was always alone in the dorms. At first I enjoyed the peace and the ability to hog the TV all I wanted in the evenings. Then it got lonely, even with Ichiko sneaking in and out of my room. The label kept me busy at the headquarters by writing songs and apprenticing in the studio. More of Beppu's ideas. At least my insolence didn't make him think twice about training me for important endeavors.

I didn't begrudge my group mates for their travels and endorsements. I had the occasional photo shoot for a magazine, but nothing much, and I never had a cover. Happily I stayed in Nagoya and got sucked into the world of songwriting and producing while the label prepared our next single. My group mates were gone when I first heard the music of our seventh single, a sizzling Latin tune called "Passion" that was meant to add some spice to people's winters. I didn't know the melody or the lyrics yet, but I started training with Ichiko and the other girl in the dance room. I needed all the help I could get.

One particularly lazy Sunday was spent having an even lazier date in the building. After we did some voluntary dance practice I played some songs for Ichiko on the piano, which she found invigorating. And stimulating, since she quickly insinuated that we should go to my room and fool around.

So we did. That was not lazy. I was still at that stage where all sex was animalistic whether I was on the top or on the bottom. With Ichiko, I was always on top. She got off on me overpowering her, and I got off on it too. While the sun set outside my small dorm room window, I climbed on top of my girlfriend and fucked her brains out. I'm sorry that's not romantic. We were not a romantic couple, and I was too eager to realize I needed to slow the hell down sometimes.

When I got like that – okay, when I get like that still – I was so lost in the moment that a skyscraper could collapse outside my window and I would never notice. Especially when I was on the brink of bringing someone to orgasm, like I was the day someone opened the door and came stumbling in with a rolling suitcase.

Time slowed. Practically stood still. I jerked my head up, gaping like a suffocating fish, my fingers two knuckles deep into a woman I barely knew.

"Holy!" Yumi dropped her suitcase, hand slapped across her mouth as she stared at me and what I was doing. Even though a blanket was wrapped around us, it was still obvious what was going on.

"Oh my God!" Ichiko shoved me off her and curled the sheet around her bare breasts. Her face was so red I thought she had a fever.

And then there was me, still too dumbfounded to function.

"Yumi!" I finally said, leaping out of my bed and stumbling in the small open space. I still had my shirt and underwear on, thank God. "The *hell* are you doing here? You're supposed to be in Okinawa!"

My friend, the travel weary but still beautiful Yumi Nishikawa, stared at the girl in my bed as if she had never seen another naked human being before. "Finished a day early."

I shoved Yumi out of the room so Ichiko could throw on her clothes and bail. My girlfriend was so embarrassed that she pulled her sweatshirt on backward and scurried away, tail between her legs. Only then did I let Yumi back in. And only then did I realize what my best friend now knew.

"Chiharu." Her big eyes were already wide, her cheeks pale. "That was a…" She looked at my bed again. The scene of the crime.

"I'm gay." Seemed like a good time to go ahead and say it.

Yumi turned to me again, her designer dress hugging her hips and chest, making her legs look a kilometer long. Damnit, why did I go thinking that? Oh, right. Sex on the brain.

"You're what?"

Was she serious? All that kissing and touching we did and she was going to pretend that she had no idea I swung that way? "I'm gay. I like girls. Sexually."

She considered this for a while, as if her brain were ticking away the things she knew and didn't know about me. She looked up, down, and then back at me again, her face softening from shock to mild concern. I hated it when she looked at me like that. "When were you going to tell me?"

Seriously?

I held my hands out to my sides. "Not exactly something to bring up over dinner."

"This whole time I thought you were seeing a guy…" I had told her I was seeing someone, but no details. Just like she didn't give me details about her love life.

"Well I'm not. I never have. I've only been with girls."

Something contorted on Yumi's face, but I couldn't tell you what. I couldn't even tell you why she was reacting this way, as if what I said was impossible. Did she not pay any attention? "For how long?"

"What do you mean?"

"I mean for how long have you been this way?"

I furrowed my brows. "My whole *life*, Yumi."

"What? I mean... you never told me?"

"To tell you the truth, I didn't really know until a..." I stopped. I didn't want to say a year ago, because she was quick enough to think of that night she kissed me. Her birthday. "A while ago. It's not a big deal."

"The hell it's not!" Finally, Yumi closed our bedroom door, no longer shocked. No, she was pissed now, but not at me. Not at the situation either. I didn't know what she was reacting to as she bundled her hands into fists and scrunched her face. "It's... it's..."

I was afraid she was going to say "an abomination." Or "a disgusting thing." I prepared myself for those words to come from my best friend's mouth. The woman I loved's mouth.

"It's a big deal," she said, softly. It surprised me, and her gentle hand on my arm was even more surprising. "Chi-*chan*, these secrets have to end. I want you to be able to tell me everything. I want to tell you everything... but I haven't! Because I..." She wiped something from her cheek. "I'm afraid you'll judge me."

I bit my lip. "I'm afraid you'll judge me too." Judge me for being in love with her.

"How can we possibly judge each other? What has happened that we feel this way?" To my surprise, she hugged me, her body warmer and firmer in my arms than Ichiko's ever was. "I want to know those things about you."

Tears welled in my eyes. Tears I did not expect. I blamed hormones. After wiping them away, I sniffed, my soiled fingers digging into the back of her designer outfit. "I'm gay!"

This wasn't a defiant declaration. It was scared, pleading, yet hopeful. I cried into her shoulder, her fingers stroking my hair and patting me on the back. It was in that moment I knew what else I had been so afraid of. Not just Yumi rejecting me or thinking that she had made me gay and that she was somehow to blame, but a fear of society. The press. The label if they found out. The stigma I could face not only in my culture but in the professional world. When I thought about how much I had been hiding from people for so long, I sobbed it out, relieving my heart and my soul in the process.

Yumi nuzzled my cheek with her nose. "I don't care. Whether you date boys or girls, you'll still be my best friend. Just…" She pulled away, smoothing my bangs. "Be careful."

Funny for her to say that. She had no idea how careful I had to be around her the most.

***

Coming out has always been a major topic of discussion wherever I go in the lesbian world. Non-famous women have to be careful about their jobs and families finding out, but we women of any fame have to be more careful. We have paps on our tails every time we go out the front door wearing anything but a black jumpsuit. Whenever I went to Ni-chome in Tokyo, I had to dress like I was going to rob the nearest bank just to avoid pictures. I would dress up beneath my heavy coats and hats even in the sweltering summer months, and so did many of the other women I met in that celebrity-oriented bar. We would look nondescript as possible until we passed through those doors and ripped off our covers in relief.

I've always hated being in the closet. Why should I have to hide my relationships and my attraction to women? Why do I have to listen to other women go on about their boyfriends, their boyfriends' dicks, and their boyfriends' manner of showering them with affection… when I can't even say a girl is pretty?

Why should I sit in a bar, relaxing with a drink, having a conversation about lesbian sex with someone I never expected to see there because I see her on TV every night… and then have to pretend the next time I see her on a variety show that I don't even know her?

You already know that I am gay, but I feel like I want to say it one more time. I am a lesbian. I have been my whole life, even if I didn't know or understand before I left Seki. I tell the world this for many reasons. For one, I am tired of hiding it, and feeling like I have to hide it when no heterosexual woman has to hide her attraction to men. Second, I want to send a clear message to other women like me that there's nothing wrong with us. Most of us are still good people. Are there lesbians who also happen to be the scum of the earth? Of course, but it's not because they are gay. The only thing that changes because we love women is that we kiss them good night instead of men.

Third, I am stupid enough right now to think that any of this can make a difference. I want to believe it, but I know all I've really done is hurt myself. And Yumi.

Please do not ask me about Yumi's sexuality. That is a private matter that she can choose to share if she wishes. It is not my place to tell you with any definitive reasoning that she is this or that. I can't give her a label. I can't tell you what she thinks about gay marriage. I can only tell you what I think. As much as this confession is about her too, in the end all I can share are my opinions.

My opinions are about to get rather dark. This next phase isn't as hopeful as me losing my virginity and coming out to my best friend.

Chapter 20

By the time the rest of the group caught up with me in the choreography for "Passion" and we began recording, something else was stirring in the office.

A few months before, the label debuted an all-male group called Boytasm. They had a good debut, cracking the top ten with hardly any effort. Unlike us they were based out of Tokyo, so we rarely saw them, and they definitely didn't sleep near our dorms or use our practice rooms. For the most part, I ignored their existence. Boy bands never interested me, for obvious reasons, and there was nothing particular about them that appealed to me. Dolly and Reika appeared in their debut music video, but that was my only connection to them besides sharing a label.

Now we were in the meeting room, going over the treatment for the music video for "Passion," and discovering that all five members of Boytasm would be appearing in the video so they could piggyback off our success.

Love, Yumi

This sort of thing isn't unusual for labels to do. It's a smart business move, really, but nineteen-year-old me was annoyed at the prospect of having a music video set covered in guys my age. Boytasm was marketed as our brother group, the male foil to Butterfly Tops. They had five members similar in age to us, and from what I could tell they had a similar fashion and music style. I often wondered if they would sing any of the songs I gave to the label. That was the only way I would ever take an interest in any of their music.

So I thought, "Great, well, at least I'll only have to deal with a bunch of guys for a day. What will they do? Dance around in the background and maybe make pained looks at the camera?" And then we got a second treatment saying that we would be paired up with a member each and dancing tangos with them in the music video.

Fuck me.

The boys came to Nagoya to practice. They had just finished recording their debut mini-album and had some time to promote themselves in our video. Overall, they weren't bad looking guys. (I'm gay, not blind.) Tall, muscular, an assortment of hair colors and jackets. Ah, it sounded familiar. Like who I saw when I looked in the mirror.

I was paired with the member named Junya. Thankfully, he looked nothing like Junpei, whom you may recall was my high school "boyfriend."

Junya was quiet and respectful. That made having to touch him for hours every day somewhat bearable, because at least I didn't worry about him making lewd jokes about my body or grabbing something he shouldn't. That didn't mean I liked having to learn the "woman's" side of the dance, which was quite intimate. I often had to curl my leg around his and drape my torso as if I wanted to make passionate love to him. It was so stupid. The first day of practice I got into it with the choreographer because this was so not me. Chiharu did not ooze her sexuality all over a guy. I lost the argument, of course. I had to follow the choreographer's instructions or face the wrath of the label. Since they knew I already had a lot of trouble with dancing, let alone looking vulnerable and feminine with a *guy*, the director came in and assured me that we would not be getting much screen time with the pair dancing.

"People don't want to see you dance like that anyway," he told me in private. This was the director of half our videos, so he knew what a lost cause I was when it came to dance moves more complicated than the Macarena. "We'll be focusing on the visual leads."

That was code for Reika, Dolly, and Yumi. Nezu would get camera priority when they needed someone looking cool and cute at once. The only time I got priority was during my solos (sometimes) and when they needed to meet their member quota. Since those days I have noticed that I mostly got random shots when it came to humping the floor or shaking my hips. I guess they knew how I best sold myself.

The sad thing is that I actually liked "Passion." It had an updated Latin beat and the lyrics were quite raunchy if you chose to read them that way. The melody was fun to sing, and if it weren't for the pair dancing, the choreography would have felt fresh and maybe entertaining. The moment I found out about the video, however, I started to hate that song. When I showed up on set for the video and found out I was going to wear a *dress*, I wanted to die.

Wearing skirts and dresses never bothered me until the image change. Once I embraced my new masculine look and started using it to get girls, I saw it as my own style. Asking me to put on a dress at this point was ridiculous.

Right away everyone started teasing me because of my muscles and the look on my face.

"You look lovely," Yumi said, wearing a dress similar to mine. I thought she was teasing me as well, but then she said, "That cut suits you. It brings out the best parts of your body."

I never got to find out what she meant by that.

Although I had read the video treatment a dozen times, I missed the part where half of the video was filmed in a live music club. The extras and background dancers dressed in half-suits and flirty dresses, their conversations drowning out the music playing over the speakers at times. I thought that it was an interesting concept, and all I had to do was sit at a table and pretend to talk to Junya.

Ah, I was still so naïve.

The director had us girls rub ourselves against the tables, angst for dick against the walls, and crumple on the floor as if being separated from these guys was a worse punishment than death. I think we were supposed to portray women who wanted to have sex with our boyfriends so badly that we had to writhe against tablecloths and candlesticks to get our kicks. I laughed when Dolly got the great idea to run her tongue around the rim of a wine glass. Her hair had been dyed a rosy pink for this single, so she looked like a cartoon character trying to grow up.

Then the director asked me to ball my fists against the wall, which I did, conjuring up the most pained expression possible. (Well, I did hurt my hand.) Then I had to slide to my knees and fling my head back. *Then* a makeup artist applied fake tears to my face so everyone in Japan knew I was sobbing for cock. I nearly got kicked off set when I stopped halfway through this stupid motion to crack up. The director was not impressed, especially when Junya was brought in for me to rub my ass against. He stood there like a robot while I fought the urge to break out into a dance just to show the producers how ridiculous this was. They could put me in a dress and big hoop earrings, smooth down my hair, and pad my bra to make my breasts look bigger, but I was still the tomboy of the group.

After the video shoot I assumed I would rarely see those boys again. Yet once we changed into our street wear and returned to the dorms, Dolly said, "Hey, we're going to Athens tonight. All of us. Let's go."

Athens was one of the trendiest nightclubs in Sakae, catering to the privileged like us. Cameras were strictly forbidden and everyone was searched going in and out, so it was a friendly place for celebrities living in or visiting Nagoya. While I don't mind a nice nightclub once in a while, I do prefer the lesbian ones... for glaring reasons. Regular nightclubs with men are boring. They're always hitting on you, wanting to dance with you, and loading you up with alcohol.

Oh, alcohol. Something I have yet to mention. Back then I was still such a goody-two-shoes. I may be talking back to authority figures and having casual sex when I could, but I still rarely drank and never did illicit drugs. My group mates, however, had livers of steel. Even Yumi, who had turned twenty a couple of months before, could down alcohol like a champ. I knew she drank some beer and wine in high school – I rarely partook since my mother would have kicked my ass – but somewhere between Seki and stardom she built up a high tolerance for alcohol. I rarely saw her drink it since she was smart enough to not keep any in the dorms, so I suspected this ability formed from dates with boyfriends.

So the ten of us, plus Reika and Dolly's boyfriends who showed up for the party, sat at a large table in the middle of the club. Back then Athens was brightly lit enough to give off a white, friendly glow, but dark enough that you weren't in everyone's business. We had to bring chairs from unoccupied tables, which meant we were crammed close together, me between Yumi and Junya, of all people. Our stupid group mates were either inadvertently or directly trying to shove us together. Or maybe it was coincidence.

I just had a beer that night. Even though I could get in enough trouble being in a club when I was underage, I still thought, gee, I better not drink too much! I had yet to ever be drunk and I didn't want that night to be the night I chased a hangover.

Everyone else, naturally, collectively drank enough alcohol to down a herd of elephants.

Shit got rowdy pretty quickly. Smoke lit up everywhere as Dolly and half the guys fished for cigarettes and went to town puffing on them. Even Yumi took a cigarette from Yohei, the leader of Boytasm and her partner in the video. When she lit up and took a healthy drag without choking, I was awestruck.

"Since when do you smoke?" I asked, ignoring the stench.

She looked at me as if I were about to run and tattle to Beppu. "I don't smoke, Chiharu." She only said my full name when she was angry or trying to put distance between us in public. "I am socially having a good time."

Love, Yumi

Yumi can get belligerent when she's drunk. When it's just the two of us drinking in private, she's bubbly and giggly, her wobbling a sign of laughter. In groups and alone, however, her drinking gets angry. She is easily offended and liable to make brash, harmful decisions. I did not know this yet. God, I wish I did. I would have kept a closer eye on her.

The party was fine for the first hour. I was not necessarily having a good time, but nothing bothered me and my beer wasn't even that bad. For the most part, I was bored. So many men, so much smoking, and topics I knew nothing about or cared for. I couldn't even tell you what they were talking about because I was that bored, and because speech started slurring left and right the more they drank.

After that first hour I started becoming irate. I wanted to leave and get some sleep, since I'd been functioning on five to six hours of sleep a night all week.

I spent most of the evening texting on my phone. Do you know who I was texting? No, not Ichiko. She and I had broken up a couple of weeks before, shortly after Yumi walked in on us and it freaked her out. No, I was talking to Koto. Amusingly, we became better friends after she was kicked out of the group. I didn't talk about the group because I knew it depressed her, but we would talk about her new job at a dance club and how she was trying to get into the local performance arts school. "I want to study under Shiho Nakagawa," she often said. "She is so strong and elegant." I knew her well. She had taught a few lessons to us. She was also really gay. (She's openly married to another woman now, so I feel okay saying that.) I don't think Koto knew that though. Not sure. Not like we can ask her now.

Koto eventually had to go to work and I was left sitting among a group of loud, drunken teens and early 20-somethings puffing on cigarettes and making dick jokes. Every once in a while Yumi would slap my shoulder after some joke amused her, but I wasn't paying attention. I was waiting for a good moment to slip away and be the buzzkill of the evening. Who really cared that I was there anyway?

The mildest form of entertainment came from Dolly and her boyfriend, a sluggish guy with greasy hair and a bad boy persona that totally fit her tastes. He rode a motorcycle, okay? Not a scooter. A motorcycle. (She made sure we knew this.)

They had been arguing off and on all night. The more they argued, the more alcohol they both slammed back. Every once in a while they would shout so loudly that it drowned out the rest of the conversation, and everyone would stop and stare at them. They didn't care. They kept going, sometimes pouting in silence, sometimes bringing up old grievances like toxic couples tend to do. Finally half the table got up to go check out something at the bar, leaving me with Dolly and her boyfriend and a couple of the guys from Boytasm. Like Junya.

"So, uh…" he began, scratching his head and picking at something behind his ear. Like me he hadn't drank as much, although certainly more. "Yeah…" Boy, he was good at flirting.

"Yup," I said.

"Do you wanna…"

I didn't know what he was going to suggest, but I knew my answer was no. "I'm seeing someone," I lied.

"Oh."

Before things could get terribly awkward, I stood up and wandered toward the bathroom.

It was late enough that things were getting busy even on a weeknight. I saw some people I recognized but didn't personally know. Some people who were famous then but not famous now, and some people who weren't famous yet. Back then I didn't get excited over this – I guess I was becoming numb to being around other celebrities – but I did notice them and thought that meant people were more careful about their conduct so the rumor train didn't zoom out of the station.

I was so wrong.

In the dark hallway leading to the restrooms I found a pair going at it. At first I had no idea what they were doing other than making out like a couple of idiots, but then I realized that she had her pants halfway down with her legs wrapped around the guy's hips. It was dark so it was hard to tell at first… but as I got closer I could hear the grunts of sex and was instantly soured. Who wants to stumble across *that?*

Just as I turned around to go back to where I came from, I recognized Yumi's head of blond hair and Yohei's stubble.

I zipped out of there, my heart slamming in my chest and my breath caught in the back of my throat. No. Nope. Couldn't handle it. It was one thing to hear these stories from Yumi… it was quite another to walk upon her having sex with a guy in the middle of a public place.

You may think I sound like a hypocrite. After all, she walked in on me having sex and I wasn't bothered. That was different. Do I have to tell you why? I was a jealous, heartsick dumbass who could barely stand the thought of my Yumi fucking guys. Seeing it for myself? I wanted to throw up. I wanted to cry. I had to hold myself together until I got back to the table, trying to find something to distract myself with. There was nothing, except Junya, who was playing on his phone, and a couple of other guys. Men. I couldn't be around them.

So I grabbed my jacket and told them I was leaving. They ignored me, and I darted out of Athens, putting as much distance between me and there as I could.

The cool night air felt good on my face. I zipped up my jacket and inhaled, thankful to no longer be smelling cigarettes and booze. It grounded me, giving me the renewed energy I needed to meander back to the dorms and sneak in without Beppu or someone else noticing.

"Ughhh, Chiharu, it's you."

I looked to my right, where someone huddled on the ground by a small dumpster. Someone hiding from any paps who may be lurking around the corner, trying to catch minors drinking and couples holding hands. I didn't recognize the voice at first because it was riddled with cigarettes and drinking, but the moment I saw that pink hair I rolled my eyes.

"Yeah, it's me," I said to Dolly. "What's your deal?"

She looked up at me, her face blotched in red. "I can't move."

"Why?"

"I'm too drunk."

Sighing, I bent down to help her up, her dead weight hanging on me as she made no effort to grab the dumpster or push herself up with her lower muscles. Luckily I was strong, so lifting forty kilos onto her feet was easy, dead weight or not. Dolly stumbled back and forth, grunting, her hair limp and greasy like her boyfriend's as it fell in front of her puffy face.

"Where's your boyfriend?" I asked.

"Fuck him. He's not my boyfriend anymore." She swung one arm around my shoulders, and I made sure I had a good hold on her before we walked down the alley, my feet steady while hers stumbled around. "Men are shit. You have the right idea, Chiharu. Fuck women."

I stopped. "What are you talking about?" I'm so bad at blustering.

"Come off it, I know you're a queer."

I didn't say anything. Just readjusted my hold on her and started walking again, dragging her for a few steps before she caught up.

"Who else knows?"

"Eh? I dunno. The others aren't as observant as I am." She sniffed, still haughty even when she was fall-over drunk. "I wish I liked girls. Must be fun to lick pussy sometimes."

"*Maa*... what else have you observed?"

The laughter falling out of her mouth was both sadistic and just drunk. "With you? You're so boring. Even when you're telling Beppu to fuck the hell off you're still a goody-goody. Although..." she looked up at me, batting drunken eyelashes, "you need to get over Yumi. That girl ain't ever gonna spread her legs for you like she does for those bozos."

I almost let her go so I could watch her fall on her face.

"See? It's true. You have it so bad. She ain't queer though. Sorry."

The image of what Yumi had been doing with Yohei burned behind my eyes. That was what she looked like having sex. That was how her face looked. How her body stiffened. How her... I had to stop thinking about it. "She's my best friend."

"Yeah, yeah, the story the media loves to eat up. Your whole fame is wrapped up in her. If it weren't for her, you wouldn't even still be in this group."

"What are you talking about?"

"Don't think I don't know they were going to cut you too. You can't dance and you're about as charming as a lamp. But Beppu fought for you. And then Yumi fought for you too."

"She did?"

"You don't know? She and I had a meeting with the execs about the group going forward. We were the first ones to know about the downsizing. They said they were cutting three people, and she just knew you were one of them. You should have seen her face." Dolly tried to imitate it, but I somehow doubted Yumi looked like a cackling witch having digestion issues. "She begged them to let you stay. She said she would do anything."

"*Sou ka...*"

"Yup. And then one of the execs said they would discuss it with her at a private meeting. You know what that means, right? Or are you so low on the fame pole that you haven't had to even suck cock for something yet?"

This time I did let her go. It was so, so satisfying watching her crumple to the asphalt, cursing at me while she struggled to retain some dignity. She crawled over to the side of the street, threw up in a gutter, and then crawled back to me, her hand grabbing my pant leg. Yes, I felt vindicated enough to help her stand up with a giant jerk to her arm. I could have dislocated her shoulder, but I didn't care.

"Fuck you, Chiharu." Dolly's breath reeked of vomit. "No. No, fuck you." She was belligerent enough again that, had she been more sober, she would have pushed me. Except she needed me to stay standing up, so she merely spat words at me. "You're not above it. Don't act like you're better than us because you never had to fuck for what you have. Do you know how many girls have to get splashed in the face to get their breaks? How many boys, for God's sake? Yumi's probably taken more in the eye than I have, and that says a lot!"

I wanted to be angry at her. These allegations about Yumi were ridiculous. But I could hear a thin layer of pain in Dolly's voice, and sure enough, I looked down to see her wiping a tear from her cheek. "I'm sorry." It was all I could say.

"Fuck you. Must be nice being fully Japanese. Even me fucking half the executives wasn't enough to make me leader of the group. I don't know what kind of powerful pussy your friend has, but it's enough to put a spell on you for so many years, so... what chance did I have?"

"Stop it." My grip on her tightened, and it wasn't to keep her safe. "If you want me to get you back home, you'll shut the fuck up."

She did. Laughter bubbled behind her lips as we continued our slow trek back to the dorms, keeping to the protective shadows. I was able to contain my anger until we arrived, and I stayed with Dolly until she was in her room, falling into her bed, still laughing. "Who will I have to fuck tomorrow?" she asked the air as I closed her door. "Who?" The last thing I heard was a slew of drunken tears hitting her pillow.

I took a shower and went to bed. As I lay there, trying to sleep, all I could think of was Dolly's accusations. I felt sorry for her. Truly. I didn't doubt that what she rambled about was true for her. I had heard of girls having to do sexual favors to get a turn in the industry, but I didn't think – naively, so fucking naively – that it wasn't happening in our group. To Yumi, too? Surely she would have told me. But like I said, I didn't even find out about the maid costume until years later. We weren't supposed to be keeping secrets, but we still did.

"I'm afraid you'll judge me."

Since that day, Yumi and I had been better about sharing our secrets. We would lie in bed together, me patiently listening to her talk about a fight with a guy while she asked me about sex with girls. What was it like? How often did someone orgasm? I had been afraid that she would reject me for my sexuality, but she either never brought it up or talked about it curiously. Like I was a specimen to observe. I was afraid that she wouldn't want to curl up with me anymore. It would be too sexual, or something... but she still did. Not often, but when we slept together I always felt better.

I wondered if she came to sleep with me when something bad happened. Was I her escape? Her comfort?

That night I heard her come home as I was drifting off to sleep. She staggered in, grumbling, burping, and making all sorts of other unladylike sounds. Hilarious if you knew how stylish she looked that night, wearing nearly-sheer leggings and a designer jacket over her braless top. Her hair was coiffed just right and recently touched up at the roots, her makeup so flawless ever since she learned how to apply it like the pros. She looked more like the Yumi you know today than the Yumi I knew growing up.

I wasn't going to say anything. I could smell Athens on her, and it reminded me of what I saw her doing with that guy.

"Chi-*chan*," she groaned, sitting on the edge of my bed and putting her drunken, weary head down to my chest. "Can I sleep with you tonight?"

The stench was terrible. Cigarettes. Beer. Liquor. Musk of man and God knew what else. I squirmed beneath her weight, the sudden need for her to get the hell away from me atrocious. How often did she do it with Yohei already? Were they fucking from the first day they met? Was that their first time? How many men had she been with? Was she having sex with executives to get her endorsements and magazine shots? I had heard of models being sexually coerced by photographers. Was she doing that too?

"No." I shoved her off me, listening to her limp body thump to the floor.

I was disgusted. Disgusted with her. Disgusted with my disgust for her.

***

Yumi is out of the bath now. She has been for a while. I can hear her bare feet padding around the house, her throat humming a tune that I don't recognize. She comes into the dining room where I'm still typing, smiles at me, and asks, "Can I read?"

I tell her to wait a second. I need to publish an entry.

The baby starts crying. Yumi tells me to finish what I'm doing. I'm surprised to see her duck into the little one's room, and am even more surprised to hear her singing a soft song a few seconds later.

She comes back out once I publish an entry. Hanging around me, she's trying to read over my shoulder again. I get up and let her sit down. This is weird. She doesn't want anything to do with the blog posts, and yet tonight she can't tear herself away from them. Of all the nights!

I sit and watch her read for a while, until I can't take it anymore. I go into the kitchen to make some tea. The kettle whistles, me chewing my cuticles and listening to laughter behind me. She's reading the entry about Erina.

The tea is poured. Chamomile. We'll both need it.

I put a mug down next to her. Yumi waves it off, engrossed with my metaphor about virginity and death. There's a stupid smile on her face, the kind I haven't seen in a while. "Eh, you had such a good first time!"

I can't sit there and drink tea while she's reading my blog. So I take it over to the window, forgetting it was shuttered already. Then I wander to my piano, but I don't want to play while the little one is down for the night. Yumi reaches the part where she walked in on me and Ichiko, and she's mumbling about the memories.

No, I can't be around for this. I steal upstairs and look for something to clean. Laundry to pick up. There's nothing, since I'm such a fastidious housekeeper.

I wait twenty minutes. Downstairs I hear Yumi get up and walk around. Pacing. Something slams against the table. Her hands. I wait for the sound of my laptop smashing through the window, but it never comes. No more laughter. She has reached the end of my posts for the day, and I hear her sob.

It only takes a few moments, and it's over. I wait another five. After tiptoeing downstairs I find her sitting at the dining table, tea in hand, although she doesn't drink it. Not until I walk in.

"Wanna talk about it?" I ask.

"*Iya da.*"

I sit in the chair next to her, facing her, watching her leg jiggle and her face contort in thought. She still has blond hair. Sure she changes it sometimes. Black. Brown. Remember when it was shocking pink for her single about the color? She says she likes blond or black the best. The two extremes. Nothing in between. Like her emotions.

"I'm sorry," I say. "But I have to tell the truth."

"Uh huh." She sips.

"I don't feel like that now. Why, do you remember it?'

"Yeah. I was shocked."

"I don't blame you."

Yumi relaxes her shoulders. "Even though it was years ago, it feels like yesterday."

I put my hand on her arm, squeezing her through the white silk of my robe she's borrowed. "It might as well have been."

"Except it wasn't yesterday. That's what I have to remind myself. It was a long time ago, and that's not my life anymore."

She shakes me off her and resumes her pacing back and forth. "Yumi…"

"It's not!" She's so vehement that my robe, which is loose on her thin frame, shakes. The baby whimpers in her room. Yumi lowers her voice. "You gonna publish that?"

"I already have."

"Jesus." She laughs. "No wonder people are pissed."

She comes and hugs me, her nose against my scalp as I wrap my arm around her. I can smell my soap and shampoo on her, infused with her natural scent that I recognize so well. She smells like me, and yet it's her at the same time. I can't tell if it's comforting or disconcerting.

My head tilts up. She kisses me.

Not like before, when she was just joking. This is the kind of kiss that ruins a girl like Chiharu Morita.

It's over just as quickly as it began, like every kiss she has ever given me. Even though she now knows how much it fucks with me, neither of us can help it at times. Is it weird for us to be like this? For her to come to me, kiss me, and then walk away again? Is it friendship or something more? Is this normal for girls who have known each other since they were six?

"I'm going to bed," she says, walking away. She stops at the foot of the stairs and looks around the corner of the wall at me. "Well?"

I clear my throat. "Well what?"

"What about you?"

"In a bit."

That's not good enough for her. She frowns, drumming her fingers against the wall. "After you just got done tarnishing my name some more? You know I'm going to get another angry call from my manager in the morning, right?" She puts an angry foot on the next step. The look in her eyes is unmistakable.

Come make it up to me.

Part 7

SEX, LIES, AND SUICIDE

セックス、嘘、そして自決

It's been a crazy week.

Yumi didn't just get an angry call the next morning, while she slowly crawled into her day clothes and mumbled about how hungry she was. She got a summons to the office and a thousand cameras in her face when she left the house. This time a slew of body guards from the label stood at my gate to keep the horde back. Nobody cared about complaints now.

So to say that I had to relocate is a bit of an understatement.

Obviously I won't say where I am staying now. No, I'm not at my home. No, I'm not at my mother's. Even my mother isn't at home, so don't bother trying to harass her. She came to take the little one somewhere safe a few days ago. There was no way I could keep the both of us shielded from the press for however long this rides out. So my retired mother drove down from Seki, took her granddaughter, and got the hell out of Nagoya. We went in opposite directions. I talk to them on the phone every day, but I still worry.

I haven't seen Yumi in two days. She called me once, long enough to tell me she was glad that everyone was safe. My life is not in danger, but I am finally really nervous. The news, when I could bear to watch it, was nothing but conversations about our morality. I lost my job with the video game. A curt message left on my phone.

My career is over. I am sure of it.

Even though I was prepared, it still hurts. You want to believe that you live in a world where you can tell your life story and nothing bad happens. Maybe some people get angry, but that's it. Who cares? It blows over in a few weeks.

I knew this wouldn't blow over. I also didn't think it would be a national thing. It's a digital, global society now. There are people in America talking about this. They don't know who we are, but they're talking. Most of them don't understand why it's a big deal. So what if some grown woman is gay and has a crush on her best friend? I wonder what it's like to live in that kind of society.

I feel sorry for the girl house-sitting for me, making sure that the media doesn't barge into my home. She's one of my students. I'll talk more about her later, but I trust her enough to not go through my things or to deal with the media. She's the only non-celebrity who could do it.

So I am holed up in some non-disclosed location. I feel safe enough here. At least I don't have to worry about cameras outside my windows. But I am lonely. Without the little one, Yumi, or even Beppu nearby I feel like I'm all alone. So I guess I will be updating this more often.

Where was I in the story? I don't remember now.

Chapter 21

The craziest thing to happen over the next few days wasn't that Yumi was invited to star in her own nighttime drama, but that I was invited to take on a regular part in it as well.

It seemed that the marketing of our friendship had worked. When the network propositioned the agency to hire Yumi as the starring actress, they countered with adding me as well. There was nothing altruistic about it. They simply wanted to make more money by having me on the cast. When the network okayed me having a recurring supporting role, we were enticed the sign the dotted line.

Yumi and other members had various roles in dramas in prior months. Dolly had been the closest to a lead role, having scored herself a supporting role that appeared every episode in a popular drama. When it was announced that Yumi would have a starring role – opposite a seasoned young and popular actor, no less – there was much celebrating. Nobody cared that I was also in the drama. Nobody except Yumi, who said we would have lots of fun debuting as "serious" actresses, and my mother, who loved watching dramas and was tickled at the thought of her daughter being in one.

At the press conference announcing the drama, Yumi and I wore clean white and black outfits that matched our marketed personalities. She in a white skirt and black blouse, and me in black trousers, jacket, and white collared shirt. I didn't care much for the outfit, since it was stuffy and a bit formal for my tastes, but Yumi insisted that I looked sexy, and well, that kind of compliment from her could stroke my ego for days.

"What kind of role will you play?" the media asked Yumi.

"I will be a strong young woman in search for a career." That was the synopsis we were given. In the drama called *The Secretary of Shibuya*, Yumi would play a young woman who was a struggling college student looking for a job after graduation. Eventually she would land a job as a secretary at an ad agency, where the lead actor worked. I played another secretary at the ad firm, a man-hating (of course) stick-in-the-mud who befriends Yumi and tries to keep her away from the male lead because of some trauma I went through relating to a man. It was one of those dramas that was both dark and light-hearted, depending on the episode. Such things were fashionable in those times, as networks tried to appeal to the college demographic.

Shooting wouldn't begin until after the new year with a target release in early spring. In the meantime, we continued to prepare for the release of "Passion," and I had my twentieth birthday shortly before that. Nothing special happened, other than Beppu giving me a beer and saying, "Congrats on surviving this long."

We appeared on a few variety shows to promote both the single and the drama, which we hadn't even started filming yet. Sometimes we went as a full group and other times it was just Yumi and me. Even though I had no camera charisma, show hosts thought I was hilarious because I was so "surly" and "serious." I don't know what they meant. That was just how my face looked. Yumi was the one always laughing and clapping and smacking me on the arm every time she was embarrassed by the hosts. Like it was my fault she couldn't speak English or remember the name of her pet turtle when she was eight.

One time we went on "Role Reversal," that show that makes known pairs of people – friends, married couples, comedian duos, band mates, etc. – switch roles for an hour. For Yumi and me, that meant our roles in music. They had Yumi pretend to be me by dressing her up in my boyish clothes and trying to play piano in front of the entire nation. I got a bit smug when she laughed so hard she had to excuse herself off the stage because she couldn't remember how to even play Twinkle Twinkle on the keys. The hosts brought her back, chastised her as hosts do, and asked her to read some music. When she sat down she tried to compose herself, but laughter kept bursting forth and all she could play was a mess of notes that sounded like the piano was being dropped from the top of a building. The audience loved it.

They made me put on a chiffon dress. Everyone ooh'd and aah'd at my makeover, commenting that I "actually looked like a girl." Then they unearthed some photos from my school days when I wore skirts all the time. I said, "Do you think it's special that I wear a dress now? A dress means nothing." My annoyance went right over their heads, and I proceeded to sing Yumi's solo song from our group's first album. We lowered the register so it fit my voice, and the audience was surprised I knew how to sing. When it was over, the hosts said, "Wow, they should just kick Yumi out of the group and make Chiharu take over both roles."

That night Yumi asked me if I thought she was expendable in the group. I snorted and told her she was the most valuable member. I was the one who had almost been cut. When I brought that up, she only frowned harder.

We promoted "Passion" for two weeks on TV and then left the rest of it up to our group mates since Yumi and I were due on set for our drama. Before we left, we attended the Coming of Age ceremony in Nagoya to celebrate that we had turned twenty the year before. Our parents came in from Seki to be there with us, my mother helping me put on a rented green furisode while Yumi's mother insisted she wear a bright, vibrant orange with gold sashes and an ermine collar. Individually we looked good, but together the green and the orange clashed together so badly that we joked we should be apart all day. The label sent a professional photographer to take our pictures. I still have some of them at my house.

The drama was being filmed in Tokyo, since it was supposed to take place in Shibuya Ward. Because of this, the network put us up in a nice hotel room in downtown Shibuya, letting us steal a peek at the great crossing outside the station whenever we felt like it. At night all of Shibuya, including the 109 building, lit up in a riot of colors that made us giddy. With our big double beds to keep us comfortable at night, we both got some of the best sleep we had in months. It was also the first time I let Yumi crawl into bed with me since the ordeal at Athens. Once again, just because it was a bigger bed didn't mean she kept her distance. On the first day of filming, I woke up with Yumi wrapped around my torso, her legs kicking out from beneath my covers. Everything smelled of her.

I didn't think filming a drama would be so boring. Then again I had only a supporting role, which meant I spent hours sitting around on set while Yumi filmed her copious amount of scenes. I spent my time working on compositions to give to the label. After my appearance on *Role Reversal* the public was reminded that I was an actual musician, and they clamored for more of my work. The label decided to make our next single a double A-side, with the second A-side being one of my ballads. Even though I had already sent them many, they wanted more to choose from. Lyrics included.

Acting is not one of my strong suits. So in a way it was a blessing that my character was just an extension of my personality. I didn't have to smile, change my accent, or act bubbly. I did, however, have to wear stiletto heels for the first time in my life… because a confining pencil skirt wasn't enough.

I could not walk in those heels to save my life. From the first day I walked out of costuming, I was rolling my ankles and wobbling around, sometimes falling and catching myself on a desk or an unwitting cameraman. The director was often exasperated with me because of my terrible balance. Didn't he know I couldn't dance? What made him think I could walk in heels? Many scenes were re-blocked so I was sitting or standing in place. If you go back and watch *The Secretary of Shibuya*, you will see this for yourself. The few times I did have to walk for a scene they finally put me in more manageable heels.

The drama was a customary ten episodes, and I appeared in every one. Some episodes featured me more than others, but for the most part I sat on sets all day waiting for my scene or got the whole day off to screw around. Yumi rarely got a day off. She would come back to our hotel room so exhausted that one time she fell asleep in a bubble bath.

One day, about halfway through filming, I sat on the sidelines as I always did when I wasn't having a scene. I was too tired to compose so I read a magazine, ignoring the world around me.

"*Ano*, Morita-*san*?"

I looked up from a riveting article about motorsports. The person handing me a bottle of iced tea was Honoka, one of the production assistants whose job was to get whatever anyone wanted. Earlier I had asked for something cool to drink since it was warm on set.

Most of the time I would say thanks and get on with my day. Production assistants are meant to blend in with the scenery until you need them. But that day, when this young woman's fingers brushed against mine as she handed me my drink, I felt something touch my cheeks. I looked at her, a messy bun of dirty blond hair spilling from its casement, and her rimless glasses slipping off her nose as she leaned forward. There was a peace to her face that I didn't see often on set. Her smile before she bowed her head and wandered off to take care of someone else made me blush.

It was Valentine's Day when I was getting lunch at the *bento* bar, dressed in my characters' clothes, including the fake glasses. Even though there was a copious amount of chocolate that day, Honoka still came up to me and presented me with a small box of handmade chocolates.

She had given all of the actors something, but when she looked at me she nearly spat out her words. "Happy Valentine's Day, Morita-*san*," she said, looking as if I wouldn't take her gift.

I accepted with a smile. "Please. Call me Chiharu."

She said she was on break, so we talked for a while. I learned that she was half-American on her mother's side, with dreams of one day working on a Hollywood set. This was her first job out of college – which meant she was about three years older than me – and she admired me for being so successful at my age. In turn I wished her luck in her endeavors. We came to an impasse in the conversation, but neither of us turned and walked away.

When I was with Erina that one night, she gave me some other advice on how to approach women. *"If some girl wants you, you'll know. Trust your instincts. She'll get flustered around you, look for reasons to touch you. She'll go out of her way to be in your sight. She might make you do all the work, but play your cards right and you'll have her in your bed just like I got you in my bed."*

Honoka brushed against me as she reached across the table for a napkin she didn't need. Her cheeks were red as she glanced at me. I may have been seeing things, but I could have sworn...

She slipped me a note. I unwrinkled it, saw the words, *"I want to fuck you,"* and quickly tore it into a bunch of pieces, my skin flushed in embarrassment. Honoka giggled.

"I, uh... don't really have a place..."

"Love hotel?" The girl was pretty, but she said that so loudly I couldn't help but feel she was a bit stupid. "Sorry, I live in a share house. Too many people."

"Oh!" Beside us, Yumi appeared. "I will be out late tonight..."

Honoka looked distressed by my friend's presence. To Yumi I asked, "Hot date?"

"Not as hot as yours, I'm sure." She scurried away in her stiletto heels.

By the time Yumi returned to our room late that night, Honoka had already left, and I was dressed in my pajamas. I heard the door unlock and thought nothing of it, but Yumi crept the door open and peered inside. "Is it safe?" she asked.

"It's just me."

Love, Yumi

The door swung wide and Yumi entered. The moment she closed the door again she said, "I didn't want to interrupt again. How was...?"

I looked up from the script I was studying on my tussled bed. "How was what?"

Playing dumb was on purpose. I wanted to hear her say it. "*How was the sex?*" For the first time in my life I got laid on Valentine's Day, and I had no complaints. "How was your evening?"

"It was good. Yours?"

She put her hands on her hips and cocked her head to the side, as if she couldn't figure me out. "Fine."

I held my gaze with hers before she finally glanced away with a huff. Yumi turned to her bed and dumped her tote bag on the comforter. Within a few seconds the bag fell over and spilled some of the contents: tissues, makeup, loose coins, a copy of today's script, pads, and one of those discreet condom cases. It was open. And empty.

A hypocrite I most certainly was. Even though I had just hooked up with a woman from the drama set, I was still jealous at the thought of Yumi having sex with someone who required a condom. (Okay, with anyone that wasn't me.) I somehow doubted she was meeting up with a woman who preferred the use of a strap-on.

"*Oi,*" she said, facing me with a scrunched nose. "*Nani sore?*"

She pointed behind me on my bed. I glanced over my shoulder, choked, and snatched the pair of lacy pink underwear Honoka left behind. Probably on purpose.

"My Valentine's Day present," I said, swinging the lace from my fingertips. Yumi turned away again, picking up the contents that had spilled from her bag. "Wanna try 'em on?"

"No thanks." Yumi removed her jewelry and stacked it on the nightstand between our beds. Bracelets, necklaces, dangly earrings. "Don't think they'll fit you either." A long, manicured nail poked the air right in front of the pink lace before she slipped off her heels and walked toward the bathroom. "I'm gonna take a bath. Enjoy your present."

Before she could disappear behind the bathroom door, I pelted her with the underwear, just to hear her shriek and watch her leap forward on the balls of her feet.

I never said I was above childish pleasures.

***

I don't like it here. As I said before, I am lonely, and even if I were not in such a place as this, I still could not go out and do anything even if there was no chance the media would spot me. I thought about inviting some friends I trust to keep me company, but that would be too obvious. Gee, there are two of Chiharu's students coming in and out of that place. Maybe she is staying there? My assumed name will only get me so far.

It's funny. I'm such a private person that this is almost too much to bear. It's a miracle I can even publish my confessions. When I published the first one, I was very nervous. I kept second-guessing everything. How stupid would it be for me to say the things I wanted to say? Apparently very stupid.

Yet I do not regret any of this. When I am overwhelmed with loneliness, when a phone call to Yumi or my mother isn't enough, I remind myself that this status is only temporary. Sure, it will have life-altering effects. Effects I will feel until I die. This hiding out is only temporary. Soon enough I will be back in my home with my family.

Part of the reason I am going crazy is because I have no outlets but this blog. A woman can only take so many baths and read so many magazines. The internet and TV are dangerous for my mood right now. There is no piano for me to play to pass the time, to work, to release my pent up energy. There is no one here to talk to besides some aunties who are so nosy and gossipy they'll know who I am if I'm not careful, and one foreign woman who can't speak Japanese, and I can't speak English well.

So I will keep writing. Even when I can't bear to type another word of my confession, I will find something else to write. Perhaps a letter to someone I love.

Chapter 22

We had a break in filming as is customary in the industry, and were sent back to Nagoya until the drama debuted. The network would make changes to the second half of the script depending on viewer feedback. This rather annoyed me, since my character was scripted to only have a minor change as of yet. But I knew the public would want to see her heart healed by a man, and the thought of my old lovers and even people who barely knew me watching that made me want to retch.

I was still insecure about my sexuality. Once I was in bed with someone, I could handle myself, but getting to that point and feeling confident talking about it was a different issue entirely. Part of my problem was that I had sexual experience, but no romantic experience. Ichiko had been my girlfriend in a sense, but we didn't go on dates besides watching some movies before having sex. We never went out. We never kissed for the affection of it instead of as a lead up to intercourse. I didn't yet know what it was like to cuddle with someone, to have them stroke my head tenderly, to whisper sweet nothings whether we would make love later or not. I could only still fantasize about going on a date with someone, holding her hand, looking into her eyes and thinking *I'm in love.*

Luckily I was twenty and didn't *need* romance since I was young and busy. Unluckily I was twenty, so I thought sex and romance were often the same exact thing.

Honoka visited me in Nagoya. We weren't girlfriends, but we liked each other enough to have both conversation and more private times together. Since we worked on the same drama and she had family in the area, it was not strange for us to be seen together in a café or out shopping, although we did not hold hands like Yumi and I would when the mood struck us. We weren't known best friends for a lifetime, after all.

We only hooked up once while she was in town. I went to her hotel room where nobody could walk in on us. I realized that a part of the thrill from the past few occasions was the chance that Yumi would, in fact, walk in on me having sex with another woman.

Therefore the sex with Honoka a second time was not as good as the first. I didn't feel the need to perform as well, and didn't think much of it when everything was lackluster. However, Honoka thought differently.

"Is it me?" she asked, pressing her hands against her body. "Oh my God, it's me."

"No, no. I'm just not really into it today."

"Because of me?"

This was my first time dealing with someone else who was apparently insecure, but for different reasons. No matter what I told her, Honoka was convinced that I found her unattractive and didn't want to have sex for that reason. In a way, she was right. Not that she was unattractive, but she wasn't the one I wanted to be with. Hard to explain even now, but I would not be satisfied with anyone but one person at that time. It was a feeling that came and went over the years. Sometimes I never thought of Yumi when I was with someone else, and other times she was all I could think about.

I ended up having my first fight with a lover. We traded some insults — well, she mostly insulted me and I lazily made shit up about her — and I left, trying to tell myself that it didn't bother me as I went back to the dorms.

Yumi was there, napping on her day off. I had told her I was going out with Honoka that day, so we made no plans.

When I slammed our door closed, she woke up with a start. What, did she think it was the fire alarm? I would have laughed at her surprised face if it weren't for the bitter feelings inside of me.

"What is it?" she asked. "Why are you like this?"

I sat on my bed, head in my hands. "Had a fight."

"With that girl?"

"Yeah."

"*Mou,* what did you do?"

I glared at her, dressed in a long-sleeved T-shirt and sweatpants to fight off the winter chill. She often didn't look this sloppy, even when sleeping. Her stylist enforced how important it was to be ready to be photographed at any moment. The only time Yumi completely let herself go was in our room.

"Who said I did anything?"

"That kind of look means you did something and now denying it."

"What?"

Yumi tossed back her comforter and swung her legs over the side of her bed. With such baggy clothes, it was the first time in a long time I saw her looking so, well, fit. Recently, she had been losing quite a bit of weight, to the point she was constantly buying new clothes because the others were too baggy. The one time she borrowed a sweater from me because she was so cold she practically swam in it, and I was the skinniest I have ever been at that point.

"You're funny. You think I have a problem with you being gay? No, but I have a problem with you being a jerk to girls."

"*What?*" How dare she!

She sat next to me. "You think I don't know you so well by now? You only look like that when you know you're in trouble but don't want to own up to it."

Fuck her! Not even when she lightly smacked my shoulder and told me to shape up and tell her what happened did I flinch. With someone like Yumi it's difficult to not admit what you've done. She would make a great mother in that respect. How could you lie to her?

"We were doing it…"

"Uh huh."

"And I wasn't into it."

"Oh no."

She was thinking of the situation from "a woman's" point of view. Imagining what it would be like to have sex with someone and they weren't into it. You think I didn't know she saw me as a man in these situations? Yumi was accepting of my life, but she in no way understood it. Just like I didn't understand hers.

"Well, she took it personally."

"Of course! How is she not supposed to think it's her you're dissatisfied with? I hope you at least lied to her."

"It *wasn't* her fault!" How could I tell Yumi that the reason I didn't want to do it was because… "I have my own issues."

"The gay issues?"

If only she had known! "You wouldn't understand."

She wrapped her arms around me and leaned her head on my shoulder. "I can try."

That was the thing. She couldn't even begin to understand how much I wanted her above every other woman in the world. When I thought about that, I really did cry. Having my best friend squeeze me tighter both helped and hurt in more ways than I can explain.

Lest anyone think I had no other friends during this time, I will say that my life did not revolve around only Yumi and whomever I was seeing on the side. While I've never been the friendliest person on the planet – nor have I ever found making friends easy – I did have one other acquaintance I was becoming closer with: Koto.

Love, Yumi

We didn't see each other often due to our schedules, but when we could every few months, we met up to have drinks and talk about our lives. She was more open to talking about the group since she recently signed on with a local indie label. "When I told them who I was, they were excited to sign me on," she explained to me in Athens. I kind of liked the place when it was just me and one other person. "I get to have solo releases!"

That surprised me, since Koto could not sing. This isn't a knock against her. Really. She couldn't sing. She was a dancer first and foremost. A respectable actress second – I had seen her local commercials. So I asked her what she meant by solo releases, and she said her label was going to have her put out dance videos. I thought that was strange, but went along with it. Maybe she was becoming an instructor like Mayu.

After we went out I invited her back to the dorms. Even though I snuck her in, Beppu still caught us, but he didn't get angry or try to kick Koto out. Instead he stopped and talked to us in the lounge, and Nezu and Reika showed up to chat as well. When Yumi returned home from her work, she spared Koto a few minutes that made her face light up in happiness. She stuck around long enough to join us in watching the debut of *The Secretary of Shibuya*, and we all laughed at my appearance. Everyone told me that I was a natural. Of course. I was playing myself!

Three weeks later Yumi and I were back in Tokyo to continue filming the drama, which had good ratings. On one of our first days off we went to Shinjuku to hang out, eating foods we weren't supposed to touch, shopping for new designer threads for Yumi and gaudy jewelry for me, and even stopping at a photo booth to make faces and bunny ears. Yumi joked that I acted more in those pictures than I did in the drama.

On our way through Shinjuku she got the bright idea to duck into an adult shop. Groaning, I followed her, careful to keep my hat and sunglasses on so the paps wouldn't recognize me. Gag.

I've never cared for adult shops. If I want to shop for those kinds of things (ahem) I will do it online. The last thing I want is an audience, especially men, while I look at the kinds of things those places sell. Yumi, on the other hand, is absolutely shameless when it comes to toys and games like that. When we were kids, she was the same way in children's stores, going up and touching everything, and in this place she was no different. I followed her around before finally hanging back and trying to not be seen. If they did see me, they would see the pinkest cheeks on the planet, I was so embarrassed.

"Yo, Chi-*chan*."

Yumi was standing in front of a rack of DVDs. The kind with pixilated genitals and nipples, but otherwise are super graphic. I avoided looking at any of the jacket covers because I didn't want to see naked men or the women they were grabbing.

My best friend made me look at one though. She plucked a DVD off the rack and held it in front of me, as if I should have cared. "Look who it is," she said.

I took off my sunglasses so I could see the model's face. Sure enough, it was Koto.

"You're kidding."

We looked at the title *Dancer's Hard Night*. In it Koto played a down on her luck dancer who fucks her way to the stage in one night. Yes, it was hardcore. I wanted to throw up.

Our fun day off ended after that.

***

It's hot here. This place has no air conditioner, so I'm left to melt in my own sweat until it's cool enough to open my windows. It really is the humidity that kills you, and where I'm at is sweltering right now. I'm used to hot summers. I grew up in Seki. But oh my God, this room is a hotbox and I'm its latest victim.

Pardon me for sounding dramatic. Part of the problem is that there's little I can do to stay cool. There's a river flowing nearby that looks delightful, but I can't go out until it's dark enough to not be seen, and then I steal into the nearest convenience store to get some snacks. I can eat meals here. I also have my own private bathroom, but I don't want to be a burden and use up a lot of water, even if it's cold.

I'm whining because the heat is getting to me and I just want to take a nap. I'm lonely and I'm hot. I need to find out if I can at least get a fan in here. You never realize how much you miss air conditioning until you need it. At least if it were cold I could pile on some blankets and sweaters… this is torture!

Chapter 23

The label began preparing our eighth single entitled "Out of It / Dawn," the latter of which was my original composition. Some of the lyrics were reworked by the label to fit a theme they wanted for our album, which was to follow this single.

We recorded "Dawn" first. When the rest of the group found out that I was the one who wrote it, they either feigned indifference or congratulated me for finding a better use in the group. (If you were Dolly, you did both.) Yumi was the only one who was excited to record it. I was glad the label gave her the choruses, because it was her voice I had in mind when I wrote it.

"Congratulations, Chiharu," Beppu said after recording was complete. "Not only do you have a lead song on your hands, but you can expect some nice royalties for a while. That's where the real money is in this business."

I smiled. "I thought it was endorsements and concerts?"

"Sure, but those are harder to get. You have to be charismatic, pretty, and able to perform on command. Not saying that you can't do those things. Just that composers have the steadier job over the long term."

"Out of It" was the main promotional track and had a strange flair to it. The dance was difficult to the point I often lacked the motivation to go to practice, but I was in the back of the formation, as usual, and it didn't rely on footwork as much as the previous dances, so I had a better time of it. For once, the instructors didn't constantly yell at me.

On top of that, I was given the second largest amount of lines in the song after Nezu. Even Dolly and Yumi didn't have as many lines as me. We all thought this was surely a mistake and went to the producer, who told us that no, they really wanted my voice for both extended bridges. Nezu had an opening rap and a refrain in the chorus, giving her the most lines, but that was not unexpected by now. But me? I couldn't understand it. I had the deepest voice in the group, but it was hardly ever utilized outside of harmonies.

"Because you have a powerful voice when you concentrate hard enough," the producer said. I was not used to such praise. "I want to hear it lead up to the chorus both times. Entice the listener. Seduce the person on the other end of the line. Invite them to come into the spiral that is the chorus. Hold that note for five seconds before the drop, and we'll have them hooked."

Yumi was the happiest for me. "You're such a great singer, Chi-*chan*," she said at dinner that night. "It's a shame that they haven't been using your voice more. And to get so many lines on a lead track! I wonder if it's because of the drama? Maybe you're getting more popular!"

I was not getting more popular. I had the same amount of fan mail from before. Yumi knew this, since we usually received our fan mail all at once, and she and I would stay up late some nights reading our letters to each other. Like that night, when we sat on the floor in front of our beds, going through neatly handwritten notes and typed letters that lasted pages upon pages. Usually we read letters from female fans, which were most of my letters. Women and older girls who wanted to emulate my style or gush about how cool they thought I was. Yumi got a lot of letters like that too, although she also get love letters from guys. She did not read these out loud. Instead we focused on the silly or really sweet ones, like a letter from a girl who said she, "really looks up to Yumi-*oneesan's* talents and wants to sing and dance too one day."

We put our letters away before getting ready for bed. I was ready for sleep by the time Yumi returned from the bathroom and hovered behind me, crouching on the floor like she was about to pounce.

"I'm not sleepy," she said.

"Drink some tea."

She poked me in the back.

"What?" I rolled over enough to look her in the face.

It was dark in our room, yet she managed to find my nose with the tip of her finger. "Scoot over."

Don't get me wrong. Even at that point in my life I still yearned to hold and touch her – I still waited for her to kiss me again. That didn't mean I always wanted her bothering me. Just like you can be madly in love with someone for most of your life, you can also be so annoyed with them that you don't want to be around them at all for a while. That night I wanted to sleep. Normally I wouldn't think twice about Yumi pushing me against the wall and hogging half my bed, but she was in a slumber party mood, not a cuddling mood.

I obeyed anyway, giving her enough room to crawl in beside me and pull my comforter up around her chin. Even though I couldn't see her movements, her leg rubbed against mine and her hand wrapped around my side. Her nose was only two centimeters away from mine, her breath blowing against my upper lip. I wanted to close my eyes and sleep to these sensations, the intimacy we could share from just being near each other more soothing than a lullaby.

She spoke, her words hot against my skin. "Do you ever wanna do it with a guy?"

My eyes snapped open. Good grief. "No," I said without hesitation. "They have never interested me."

"Why not?"

Really? "Because they don't. There's nothing complicated about it. I've never wondered about men, and I don't have any inclination to find out about them. I would hate it."

I half-expected her to say, "How would you know if you don't try?" I wanted her to say it... if only so I could throw back, "Well, why don't you try it with a woman?" It would be the most forward I had ever been with her. Not that I was delusional enough to think that she would try it with me... even though I wanted her to. *Badly*.

"I envy you," she said after a short period of thought.

"Why?"

Her hand squeezed me tighter. Before it could become too distracting, I plucked it off me, holding her hand within mine between us. "Men and boys are so difficult," Yumi said. "They only want one thing from me."

The thought made me shiver. "Sex?" I whispered.

She nodded. "Sometimes I don't feel like a person around them." Her hand went to her throat, pulling out her necklace where the character for "person" danced between her fingers. "One time a guy saw this and wondered what I was trying to say. I never thought of it until then. He was so aware of what he was doing to me that..."

"It's okay." No, really, I didn't need her to elaborate. "I'm sorry." What else could I say?

"Is it the same with women?"

"There probably are some out there like that. I've never felt that way." I never felt like I was being taken advantage of. Only once in my life have I ever in that context, and it was not a woman who did it.

"Jealous."

"Are you seeing anyone right now?" The last I heard, Yumi was still seeing Yohei off and on. He was convenient, since they were under the same label and thus at many events together. The leader of Boytasm was becoming quite popular himself. Pretty soon both he and Yumi would be appearing on shows together, and the media speculated that they were dating.

"Yeah. A couple of guys here and there. Nothing serious."

"Yohei?"

"Yeah."

My hand nearly ripped hers off her arm. "He doesn't make you feel that way, right?"

"Forget I said anything."

When it comes to Yumi, I am often overwhelmed with conflicting feelings. There's the Chiharu who is in love with her, full of petty jealousy because terrible men take advantage of her and she seems to like it off and on. Then there's the Chiharu who is her best friend who wants to punch a fucker in defense of her honor. When these two sides of me collide, it's a wonder that I'm able to function.

"Have you ever been in love, Chi-*chan*?"

Her question came so out of nowhere that I didn't know what to say at first. Yes, yes I had been in love. I'd been in love with her for so long now that I didn't know how to fall in love with anyone else. Back then I often worried about being able to have a healthy relationship with someone. What if I met someone really great and we got serious? How would my feelings for Yumi affect that? Would I eventually fall in love with someone and forget about my love for Yumi? Did I want that to happen?

"I've been in love before." I still was.

"Oh, with whom?"

"I should ask you that," I deflected.

She grew quiet, her eyelashes batting at me above the comforter. "I think I've been in love. Sometimes it's hard to tell what is real love and what is something else."

"Tell me about it."

I put my hand on her cheek, caressing her skin and feeling her hair crinkle between my fingers. She did not flinch, nor did she roll her head into my palm. It was as if she couldn't care one way or another about my touch. I thought about what I had done with other women in bed, the sometimes rough and eager ways I had bruised their skin with my lips or thrust against them until they were sore. I couldn't do that with Yumi. If I did it with her, it would be tender, slow, and passionate. Real lovemaking. It frightened me to think that this was the only woman who made me feel that way.

Just like that, Yumi kissed me. Tender. Sweet. Needy.

One year and nearly four months. That's how long we went between kisses. That last one on my nineteenth birthday was so tentative compared to this one – not to mention I had quite a bit of experience now – that I almost fell deep into the abyss of my famished desires. Neither of us were virgins anymore. I could do it with her without any guess work. She could be mine.

Of course I held back. As nice as the fantasy was, I knew I couldn't just roll on top of her and use her like those boys did. Nor could I do anything that wouldn't let me savor the taste of her lips and the way her leg moved between mine. There, in that tiny bed where we had done this three times now, I could only think of her warm body, her soft lips, and the gentle way she always initiated love with me. I could feel her yearning beneath her skin. I was ready to show her what real, unyielding lovemaking was like.

"Chi…" Yumi gasped between breaths as I eased myself onto her. She lay precariously at the edge of my bed, my hand holding her up and traveling even more precariously down toward her rear. She wasn't going to lead this time. I was.

Until someone shook the lock on our door and helped himself inside, shining a flashlight on us while yelling, "Room check!"

The last of that word was barely out of Beppu's throat before he stopped, staring wide-eyed at the scene before him. Me. On top of Yumi. In my bed. My lips close to her throat and my hand squeezing her shoulder.

"Holy shit," he said. Yumi yelped, shoving me off her and squirming to get away from me as if I were dirty. "Holy fucking shit. Now I really have seen it all."

Even with everything else I could have felt, the first thing to enter my head was that I wished just once someone wouldn't be summoned every time I tried to have sex in my own bed.

***

As if she knows what I'm writing about, Yumi texts me, wondering what I'm doing. So I tell her. That night in our dorm room, when Beppu walked in on us doing something no two good girls were supposed to do.

It takes her a while to respond. *"I hope you make sure the world knows you were the really filthy one that night. You grabbed my ass."*

"I did not," I write back. *"You're misremembering."*

"I don't forget that night." That's the last message I receive from her for a while. I wonder if she's distracted with something or suddenly no longer interested in talking to me.

Chapter 24

For once Beppu was left speechless. He also frightened Yumi so much that she avoided him – and avoided me.

This meant the only one available to talk about what happened was me, Chiharu the sometimes-responsible tomboy. Or, as Beppu now saw me, Chiharu the horny lesbian.

Two nights later he cornered me in my room after Yumi left to go somewhere. Probably out on a date with Yohei, who was in town for business. As Beppu sat me on my bed and then sat across from me on Yumi's bed, I imagined her in Athens with that guy, having sex in a dark and empty hallway. *"He's just using you,"* I wanted to say. *"You said so yourself."*

"So," Beppu began, rubbing his legs and tapping his fingers against his knees. "About the other night…"

I was not in the mood for this. It's like your father sitting you down to talk about birds, bees, and vaginas. Neither of you want to do this, but for some reason he has this idea that if he doesn't talk about pussy with you the world will stop spinning and call him the world's worst dad. I can't help but wonder if he's ever had a conversation like this with his own daughters, who are only a few years younger than me.

When I didn't answer, he got antsy – clearly not in the mood to be the one who started this awkward conversation. "I'm not gonna pretend I understand what two best gal pals do in their private time. *Maybe* girls who grow up together really do those sorts of things with each other. The fuck do I know? Ask my wife. I'm never home."

I wasn't about to ask his wife anything.

"I've got this hunch though that you two aren't exactly normal best friends. I've known that from the beginning. That's why you two get away with so damn much. And look, I don't give a shit if you two are cuddling or practicing kissing or what the fuck ever you all do at your slumber parties, but for fuck's sake Chiharu, that wasn't *practicing* anything. If I walked in five minutes later, what the hell would I have seen?"

Probably what Yumi had seen a few months before.

"She know you're gay?"

"Yeah." That was the first time Beppu ever outright called me gay.

"Is she gay? Because if she is, she's doing a shit job at it with all the boyfriends I see her sneaking around with."

Now wasn't the time to give Beppu a lesson on sexuality and how it was possible for someone to like both guys and girls. Although until that point I never considered if Yumi was bisexual. I know it's strange. We had made out three times, each her own instigation, but I never wondered if she was anything but straight. I couldn't imagine Yumi doing those things with any other girl but me. In a way, Beppu was right. Our relationship was weird.

"She's not gay," I said, head down.

"Fuck." He put his hands up. "Not that either answer would have made me happy. Gonna be hard enough as it is keeping you clean with the media. Hearing she's not like that isn't good news for you."

I knew what he meant, and yet I still said, "What do you mean?"

"You keep that mess up and she will do nothing but break your heart."

Love, Yumi

How could I tell him that she had been slowly breaking my heart for years? I think he saw it in my eyes when I looked up at him. Felt the frustration and anger that had been bubbling in me since I was a kid, an inexperienced virgin who didn't know how to physically express herself, and an ignorant country girl who didn't even know lesbian love could exist.

"Look, I have to say this both as your manager and as someone who gives a shit about you. As your manager, I need to warn you that any animosity that brews between you because of this will only be bad for the group. As someone who cares about you, well... I don't want to see you heartbroken. These other girls, they don't even know what love really is yet. They're young. They haven't grown up with a person they love. When someone burns them, they hurt for a while, and then they're back at it. Might be a rocky while, but I almost always know they'll get through it. You? You're in deep if you fall in love with your childhood best friend. You've got about five forms of love competing for your heart. Give in to the wrong one, and I don't know if you'll ever get out of that darkness."

I didn't say anything. I could have told him he was wrong, what did he know? But I didn't, because I knew he was right. Falling in love with Yumi was the worst thing I could possibly do. Yet how does one stop the heart? How could I tell my soul and my brain to stop feeling happy around her, stop feeling fulfilled? How could I tell my loins to stop wondering what it was like to worship her body and give her the pleasure she deserved? That was darkness. That reeling sensation of falling into those fantasies, where I wondered what it would be like – *really like* – to make love to Yumi. To hear her say she loved me. To have what so many people in this world have. I wanted to cry in front of my manager.

So I did.

He didn't say or do anything while I sat there, leaning against my knees and covering my shame with my hands. I wish I could tell you that I'm a tough girl who doesn't cry often. Except I do cry. I cry a lot. I'm that asshole who, if she's particularly hormonal, will sob over commercials and God help me if some sappy drama or movie is on. Yumi says it makes me more human and personable, but I hate crying.

"Shit." Beppu lowered his voice, as if that were supposed to soothe me. I continued to cry into my hands, my tears running down my arms, staining them with my disgrace. "It's too late."

At that point in my life, I both knew exactly what he meant... and had no idea how late it was for me.

The release of our eighth single meant we had to take a quick break from filming the drama finale so we could properly do promotions. For this round we were on all of the top music shows: *Music Tonight, The Music Factor, Hey to You,* etc. Some of those aren't around anymore, so it's nice to say that I was a part of something like that.

We debuted at #2 again. While proud, we were also frustrated because we wanted this to be the time we finally hit #1. An actual #1. Not from one of those reader polls in magazines that asked people who their favorite girl group was, which we won a couple of times. This was before AKB48 took over the country and we would have never stood a chance. Also, Korean groups.

I didn't pay attention to the Korean groups at first. Some groups like Tohoshinki had been popular for a while, but since I wasn't interested in guys they flew under my radar. Then suddenly that year it became more popular to talk about K-pop, as it was called. The Hallyu wave. For a long time some Korean artists popped up here and there to have a career in Japan, but now it was becoming a trend. Like I said, I ignored it at first. Then some rumblings echoed at headquarters as the executives talked about whether or not to sign a Korean group before somebody else picked them up. Nobody knew how big Korean groups would be for three or so years.

Except for Dolly, who liked to constantly remind us now that she was Korean, after two years of trying to hide it.

"I have lots of fans there, you know," she said to no one in particular while we were backstage at *The Music Factor.* "Maybe when this gravy train comes to an end, I should go to South Korea and start up a solo career.

Travel back and forth." She flipped her red hair and touched up her makeup in the mirror next to mine. "I could be the next Hyori Lee."

I had no idea who that was. "You think this thing is gonna end sooner rather than later?" None of us were in denial about it. No girl group lasted more than a few years without some big upheaval, not counting the cutting of Koto and Mayu.

Dolly snorted as she put on her fake eyelashes. "Yes, and not all of us can be sitting back making royalties on songs. Unfortunately, I don't have a songwriting bone in my body. Rather have other people do it for me." She batted the one fake eyelash at me before putting on the other. "Like you."

It was true. "Dawn" was doing well digitally as well as on the physical copy of the CD. I got a cut of every sale for having composed it. "What are you gonna do?"

"Model. Act. Sing, if anyone will let me. Save as much money as possible because I'm only going to get older. *Mou,* now I wish I could write songs like you. Don't have to be good looking or young for that." She sounded eerily like Beppu.

Promoting the single was a good break from the drama, especially after I got the script for the final episode and saw that my worst fears had come true: my character was ending up with one of the male ones. There was no God.

"Oh, Chiharu," Yumi said in our hotel room in Tokyo. She peered at me over her copy of the script, neither smiling nor frowning. "There's a kiss. With you."

I had already seen it in the script and was contemplating the ends of the universe.

"You never kissed a guy, right?"

"No." I wasn't looking to start.

"What are you going to do?"

"I have no idea." Riot. Demand a rewrite. Cry.

I didn't think about it until the day of the shoot. Now, even if you thought I was good in that drama, I have to say that I am not a great actress. Not even that good. Like I said before, I was basically playing myself. So there was no way I could escape into my character and just kiss a guy because she would. When my costar approached me with his love confession, I could feel the room tense up. Would Chiharu do it? Would Chiharu kiss this average looking guy?

"Ha-*kun*," I said, addressing the character. He looked up at me, eager to hear me say those words. "I think I like you. I guess."

This was it. When he got up with a smile on his face, I was supposed to jump into his arms and kiss him. Half the staff was watching to see if I would actually do it, and the other half just assumed I would. Yumi sat in a chair behind the camera, hand to her mouth and eyes wide.

Confession: I tried to kiss him. I was going to be a professional and at least peck his lips. It would be haphazard and fake, but I was going to try. Yet when my lips got near his, I froze, my mind going "*What the fuck?*" and my body saying "*Ew. Gross.*"

My head remained stiff on the lean in. Either the director would call cut, or the actor would finish the kiss for himself. No matter what, I couldn't win.

"*Iya da,*" Resigned to my fate, I pulled away from the actor. I assumed that the cameras had stopped rolling and I could truly be myself again. "Can't do it. Kissing a man is too hard."

He struggled to maintain a straight face. "So no kiss then."

"Not today!"

I gave him a condescending look, wobbling in the heels that were too tall and thin for me. Finally, I heard "Cut!" and assumed my professional death was imminent.

Groans went around the room as people prepared for a second take. Yet the director stopped them, his lips dry as he licked both of them and stood from his seat. "Brilliant!" he cried, clapping his hands once. "Great job, Chiharu! You're really in the character!"

The stupid episode aired with that in it. Soon enough I got more letters from people, each of them praising me for my cool acting abilities. Some of them heard that it was "ad-libbed" and congratulated me. I had no idea what was going on. I just didn't want to kiss a guy!

Love, Yumi

***

Even now I can confidently say that I never kissed a man out of desire. I have never had desires for a man. I've met many lesbians over the years who had been with men before, and those who even loved them for a time before realizing women made them happier, but as for me? I could live the rest of my life without knowing the tender touch of a man.

I find it curious that I live in a world where most women can't relate to me. Not on the romantic front. They can empathize with my plight to find lasting love, but they can't understand how much I love the scent and the caress of a woman. It's funny that growing up I never wondered about my disinterest in guys. I just assumed that I would meet a guy one day who did it for me. Or not. I didn't care.

Then Yumi kissed me on her birthday, and suddenly the whole world made sense.

I'm fortunate that I know this about myself. There are many people in this world who feel like they are missing something. They don't realize that what they need is a different perspective on love. Beauty. Romance.

Of course this doesn't only extend to sex and love. Many people are dissatisfied with their jobs as well. Where they live. Their families. Again, I am fortunate to be able to do what I love and to pursue the relationships that I want. Could life be better? Naturally. Compared to some other people I knew in the industry, however, I got off very easy. Some didn't even make it out alive.

Chapter 25

The label didn't waste time preparing our second album. Why would they, when we had two #2 singles and a growing fan base that loved us? *The Secretary of Shibuya* was getting good ratings, and Yumi was up for a New Face award. We were on fire, or as much a relatively new girl group from Nagoya could be. Even me, in my unmarketable variety, had a solid core of fans who continued to send me roses and fawn over my compositions. "You're so talented," both men and women would say. "I really admire your musicality, the way you play piano, and your flair for working in A minor." What did that mean? Sometimes I think those fans just felt smart for knowing what A minor meant.

It was important for these things to be capitalized on. Of course, everything in this world is capitalized now, but in the entertainment industry, it's king. Timing is all. If we waited too long to put out an album, people would forget us and move on. If we went too quickly, not only would the quality suffer too much, but sales for the latest single would drop.

This meant the label needed all hands on deck. They had a variety of compositions and lyrics to choose from, but it was me they called in to ask my opinion and perhaps use more of my songs. "We will be honest, Chiharu," Mr. Kawaguchi said in a meeting with him, Beppu, and the producer of the album. "We are seriously considering not only including 'Tonight,' but making it the lead promotional track."

I couldn't believe my ears. First I had a title in a double A-side single, and now the group may be using my track to promote a whole album? That they were banking on making it to #1? Not just any track! "Tonight" was a very special song to me, given to the label before I started keeping my most personal tracks for myself. It was a song about Yumi. The lyrics told a sordid tale of being so in love that the singer is working up the courage to make "tonight the night the magic happens." Yes, I used that actual English phrase. I could see why the label wanted to use it. They could make it sexy and danceable. And I could be mortified that we were all up there singing about fucking my best friend.

Even knowing these perfectly sound reasons, I couldn't help but feel that something was off. Why were they taking such good care of me? After the meeting, Beppu was optimistic, saying that my time had finally come to grow as an artist in an industry that stifles growth. I had no idea back then, but he was grooming me to become a professional songwriter and producer. You know, where the real long-term money was. That's why I spent half my days in practice studios and half my days in meetings and the control room at the studio. When Dolly walked in to lay down her vocals on a track and saw me behind the controls, she cackled like a witch. I still have no idea what that was about.

Finally we entered the period of time between finished single promotions and anticipating album ones. Everyone was contributing in some way. I was helping to write and compose tracks. Nezu also helped write lyrics. Reika became our visual spokeswoman, touring the country and making appearances in CD shops and on radio shows. Dolly took a turn starring in a movie that would come out when the album dropped, meaning she was pulling double-promotional duties. And Yumi? She was everywhere again. Magazines, TV shows, one-man lives, you name it, she was doing it. The only time I saw her was when she came back to Nagoya to record or do something else local.

One particularly lonely night in the dorm I sat on the couch watching TV and drinking a beer. Yumi was on a variety show with Yohei, whose group was promoting a single that managed to crack the top five. The hosts loved teasing them. While they weren't officially a couple to the public, the media loved them. There was something "romantic" about the two leaders of a label's most popular groups going out. The label was careful in controlling that image. We were still idols, and openly dating even at our age could damage our image. People wanted Yumi to be accessible and virginal (ha!) and people wanted Yohei to be single. They weren't even publicly dating and there was slime all over the internet about Yumi. Just because she was possibly dating Yohei! Some fans are nuts.

"What do you look for in a girl?" the host, a middle-aged balding man with buck teeth asked. He slapped a fan against Yohei's shoulder. "Come on! Your fans are dying to know so they can run out and become that type of woman!" The audience laughed.

Yohei sat up straight in his seat, Yumi still slouching beside him. Even though the camera gave him a close-up shortly thereafter, I could still see them sitting close together. It made me jealous. After waking up on the wrong side of the bed that morning, the beer was supposed to help me relax, but it was just making me antsier.

"I like a girl who is a lot of fun." When the hosts laughed at him and implied something dirty, he merely waggled his eyebrows, making Yumi sink down in her seat next to him. "A girl who is pretty and not afraid to be herself around me. Isn't a girl like that great?"

Everyone gave him a hard time, and the audience ooh'd and aah'd at how reasonable he was. Of course a guy like him wanted someone pretty and fun. And he wasn't too specific, so they could all project themselves into such a position. *"Maybe he means someone like me!"* I didn't doubt he meant it, but it was such a coached answer.

"Eh, and what about you Yumi-*chan?*" The hosts were quick to point out that she was halfway down in her chair, covering the blush on her cheeks. "What kind of guy do you like?"

"Oh, I can't wait to hear this."

Beppu stood behind me, holding a raided beer from the fridge in his hand. He rounded the couch, sat on the opposite end from me, and took a drink. I kept my eyes on the TV.

"I like a cool guy." Yumi immediately laughed, holding her hand in front of the gap in her teeth. "You know, someone who makes you feel like you're pretty and wants to have a good time. Ah, maybe that's not good boyfriend material, but it's fun in the moment!" Once she realized what she said, she laughed harder, and the audience lost themselves as they related to her dating plight. The hosts were so rude about it that someone got censored.

"Maybe you should date!" The middle-aged host said, motioning to both Yumi and Yohei. "You seem like a good match."

He was only saying what everyone else was thinking. What everyone else knew. The way Yohei looked at Yumi... he wanted her. And the way she looked back at him, with those adoring big eyes smeared in eyeliner? No. No, no, no. My heart tried to burst from my chest as I recognized that stupid fucking emotion called *love*.

"Here." Beppu handed his half-drank beer to me. "You need this more than me."

I didn't take it. I stood up, tossed my bottle in the recycling, and went to my room. The room I shared with Yumi. That smelled of her.

Thankfully I was too tired to care.

Somehow I managed to get over myself within two days. It helped that I was probably a hormonal train wreck and had also accepted the fact that Yumi dated and had sex with guys. I had no real opinion of Yohei yet, since I only knew him through what Yumi said and the few occasions I hung around him. Naturally this didn't mean I had to *like* it. But I accepted it. Like Yumi went out and did her thing, I did as well. Although during that time I didn't do much of my own thing besides work. It was difficult finding girls to date in Nagoya, especially when there was one gay place I knew of and it was co-ed. Not too safe for a celebrity, either. Without someone like Ichiko hanging around the studios, I was alone with my own devices.

One night I sat in the living area, watching an American drama while eating a granola and yogurt snack. A relaxing evening after a long day in the recording studio and then the gym. Beppu was there, since it was early enough in the evening for him to have not gone home yet. He ate a microwavable meal at the table while reading something on his phone. It was not an unusual night around there. Quiet, but not unusual.

I got a call from Koto. A call I will never forget.

"Chiharu?" She sounded weak, weepy. "Are you there?"

Something churned in my gut. You know that feeling you get when something's wrong, like something horribly bad is about to happen? Sometimes you can't really explain it. Call it a sixth sense. People tell me I'm really empathetic, so maybe that's it. The moment I heard Koto's voice, I knew something bad was about to happen.

"I'm here. *Doushita?*"

"I don't want to be alone."

I told Beppu I was going out. He didn't fight me, since I was back to being responsible Chiharu. Plus the ban had largely been lifted as long as we weren't stupid about it. And aside from that one time in Roppongi, I was never stupid about it.

Koto lived a ways into the suburbs, in a high-rise low-rent apartment. I hadn't seen a place like that since I lived in Seki, but didn't think much of it as I entered her unlocked door. I expected to find her curled up in bed, depressed or something, but instead…

Instead she was lying on the living room floor, blood spilling from her arms.

This was the first of two times in my life I thought I was looking at a dead body. The revulsion, the *fear* welling inside me was terrible enough that I can never forget it… the sight of Koto's long, lanky dancer's body sprawled out on her floor, marinating in a pool of her own blood as a razor dangled from her hand. I almost threw up and ran. Instead I went to her, calling her name.

She was conscious, but barely.

The cuts on her arm were shallow, but she had been bleeding for a while. I did the first thing to pop into my head and grabbed some towels from the kitchen, staunching the trickle until it stopped. As I did this, I saw the scars on other parts of her arms. How had I never seen them before? Were they recent? Did she just do a good enough job at covering them up?

"Koto!" Once she was bandaged, I propped up her head and willed her to wake up. "I'm gonna call you an ambulance." I had my phone out, but she found the strength to lift her arm and knock it to the floor.

"I've been to the hospital," she said. "They can't help."

"What's wrong?" She was coming to, but still weak. What if I had been late getting to her? Would she have died? This would not be the last time in my life I wondered this.

While I sat there with her, her head in my lap as I remained shocked at what she had been doing to herself, she told me. Everything.

After she was let go from the group, Koto had no job prospects and considered returning to her hometown. Then a man approached her on the street and said he recognized her from the Butterfly Tops. He offered her a job under his agency. A dancer. Koto signed up without looking into it because she was so desperate to dance again.

She started in bars, dancing in skimpy outfits for businessmen. Then she graduated to illegal stripping in underground clubs. Eventually she was hired to dance in erotic videos, until she said one day she found herself on a porn set, drugged up and taking on three men at once. She had only been with one guy before that.

I didn't tell her that I knew about the adult videos. While I always suspected that it was not her choice, I still didn't know the whole story. Like even though she got paid a lot on paper to star in porn, the agency found sneaky ways to keep most of it, charging her for "lessons," props, costumes, etc. Idol groups could work much in the same way, but I can't say I remember being asked to fuck three guys at once for an hour.

Eventually she didn't want to talk about it anymore, so she asked me about the group. "I still follow you guys," she said, one of her bandaged hands on me. "It looks like a lot of fun."

While she had told her tale, I texted Beppu, asking him to come here. I didn't know what else to do. I told him it was an emergency... that I was all right, but someone else wasn't. I felt like I was calling my father to come pick up my drunken ass from the club. Something Dolly had done multiple times to him over the past year.

"The group is fine..." I held her close, remembering how she said she didn't want to be alone. "Our album is coming out soon... I wrote some songs for it..."

"Good. That's good."

The door, which was still unlocked, burst open thanks to Beppu's frightened strength. "Chiharu!" he called, and soon found us sitting on the floor in Koto's dried blood. She started crying when she saw Beppu there, and I knew she thought that I had betrayed her.

What else could I have done? I couldn't just leave here there like this. I needed someone who could help me, who would know what to do. Koto wouldn't go to the hospital with just my help. I need someone who could take charge. Someone to absorb her anger and shame. Beppu was good at that. He had absorbed about 100 girls' anger over the years.

"Okay, Koto," he said gently, pushing his jacket beneath her head. "You hang tight, sweetie. I'm going to call someone to come help you."

"No, no hospitals..."

"No hospitals. He's a medical professional. You really need someone to make sure these cuts don't get infected. That sound reasonable?"

Her bottom lip trembled as her matted hair crinkled against my arm.

Beppu made his call, and I helped Koto sit up and get in a chair. While Beppu ran around the small apartment looking for disinfectants, I found some cleaning fluids and started mopping up the blood. Koto sat in the chair and watched me, tears silently falling down her cheeks as she watched me wipe away the pain she spilled not once, but probably many times.

"I'm hot," she said. "Can you open the window?"

I opened the sliding door to her balcony. The late night breeze took away the smell of cleaner. It couldn't wipe the hollow look of pain on Koto's face.

She was once a very pretty girl. Young. Vibrant. Full of her dreams of being a dancer on stage in front of thousands of people, entertaining them and bringing them joy. It was a dream many girls shared. I was starting to understand what Beppu was always talking about. These girls too young to know any better, to see the threats coming for them in the form of people in suits with the tickets to their dreams... what chance did they stand? What chance did *we* still stand? Dolly slept with executives to get as far as she did. Yumi did God knew what. Koto had been so taken advantage of by one man who saw her dream and pounced on it, that now here she was, cut up and staring with a horrible visage of pain. Not even her tears shone, as if they too had given up trying to connect to what was left of her soul.

Beppu called me to the front of the apartment. "This is bad," he muttered. "We shouldn't even be here..."

I thought he was saying we should leave her to whatever demons haunted this place. Before I could protest, Beppu's medical friend showed up and wished to talk to him in private out in the hallway.

Just as I turned in Koto's *genkan,* fully intending on going back to her side, I heard the most terrifying sound of my life: a car alarm down on the street. The apartment was empty.

I don't have to tell you what I saw when I ran onto the balcony and looked over the edge.

***

I need to take a break. I thought I was ready to tackle that moment, but after writing it, I find myself too detached. I'm sorry. The image of what I saw is too real in my mind right now. After burying it for so long, it's like I ripped off a terrible scab and now I see Koto like that again.

I'm sorry. I'm so sorry.

I don't know who I'm saying that to.

Part 8

EVERY PEAK HAS ITS VALLEY

Love, Yumi

美しいバラにはとげがある

I feel better today. It's not as hot and muggy, and sleeping helped rid my brain of those horrible images I had been carrying around for much too long.

The first thing I did after logging in was read your comments. I've learned how to avoid the terrible ones. Thank you to my diligent readers who make sure good comments stay on top. They really help give me the motivation to keep going, especially after reading everyone's thoughts and feelings on Koto's tragedy. I didn't realize some of you had been fans of her when she was in the group. I'm sorry to those I made cry. Please don't remember her as someone who lost a war within herself. Remember her as someone who fought for so long. Sometimes we fight so much that we just run out of energy and the will to keep going.

Remember her as someone who was in love with dance. Someone who loved to move her body in grace and energy. I don't want to point fingers on who is to blame for what happened. There were too many factors. By the time I saw what was happening, it was too late. I have to tell myself this so I don't blame myself every day.

Hildred Billings

Today I want to move on. It began happily, with a call from my mother and the little one. We arranged to have a video chat later when they get back to their room. My mother is taking her granddaughter out for the day. Like I said, she is going to spoil her silly. Thank goodness.

I haven't checked what the media is saying. Don't know if I will. I just want to get back to writing this pain in the ass story. Don't know if you noticed, but it's all I have going for me right now.

Chapter 26

All of us went to Koto's funeral a few days later. Even those who were in other parts of the country dropped their schedules to come and pay their respects to someone they barely knew.

I was glad to have Yumi there. Beppu did a bang-up job keeping my name out of the media kerfuffle that happened. "Ex-Member of #1 Girl Group Butterfly Tops Leaps To Death!" was one disgusting headline. None of them mentioned that I was there. That I had stayed, shell-shocked in the very chair Koto had been sitting in, while the police and such came. They took my statement, but it was never released publicly. I have the label to thank for that.

The only people who knew about Koto's interim between the group and her death were me, Yumi, and Beppu, whom I told the details to later. We were sitting in the dorms, and he didn't say anything. All he did was pick up a piece of garbage left on the table and smack it against the wall.

The funeral was the first time I saw Koto's parents. They came from Fukui Prefecture, two nondescript parents mourning the loss of their only child. Seeing a haggard woman who hadn't slept or eaten in four days standing up there with her daughter's picture was one of the most heartbreaking things I ever saw in my life.

Although Koto was no longer a part of the group, the label put up a media barricade, probably because the whole group was there. This meant nobody took pictures of Yumi holding my hand or me hiding my face against her shoulder. I didn't cry. I was still too shocked. The first night Yumi came back after hearing what happened, I climbed into her bed for a change and wept against her chest. I told her what I had witnessed. What Koto told me. She didn't say anything, but she coddled me, and it was enough for one night.

Everyone else went back to their duties, some of them saying, "How tragic." But me, who had nothing outside of Nagoya to distract herself with, sat in the dorms, refusing to get out of bed. I got a few days off for my emotional troubles, but they were going to expect me to come back to work quickly. So Beppu got me in touch with a therapist who I saw once a week for a while. You see, going with Yumi to her therapist wasn't my first time doing such a thing.

Finally, the time came for finishing up the album and going into promotional mode. The title was chosen. "Top of the World." Play on words and making a big, if not generic statement. I didn't have a hand in choosing it, but I did have a lot of co-writing credits on the album. Not to mention, our lead track would prominently feature my vocals as well. I don't know how that happened. First I was given bridges, and now I was singing main vocals with Yumi. I wasn't that popular. I guessed they wanted to use my voice more, particularly on a song I composed.

Thank God for the album, because I was still trying to deal with Koto's death, and the distraction helped me get through it. We shot the jacket covers the same day we shot the video for my song. Before that, they touched up the looks for Yumi, Dolly, and me. Dolly became the official blond of the group, taking on a platinum look for this round of promotions. Yumi went back to her natural hair color of black. As for me, they dyed my hair for the first time. I barely recognized myself! Not only was my hair brown, but it was a light brown. When they put me in a designer outfit for the jacket shoot and music video, I nearly had a heart attack. My mother later said I looked so grown up she nearly cried.

The lead promotional video was mostly glamour shots of us looking good in our loaned designer wear, complete with some artistic camera shots to add interest. Since they sexed up my song there was a lot of lounging on beds and pillows, looking forlorn in cars, and a few dance shots that were more titillating than impressive. I was just glad there were no men.

As for the other promotional track, which was not my track, we were put in a wedding setting. At first I groaned at being dressed in a tacky bridesmaid dress and sitting at a table with a bunch of extras, but for the dance shots we were all put in suits at various stages of undress.

You may think it strange, but until that point I had never worn "men's" clothing specifically. It wasn't something that appealed to me, either on myself or other women. Yet the first time I saw Yumi walk out of the dressing room, wearing everything sans the jacket, I nearly fainted. Her slick black hair was tousled just enough to give her a bit of an edge, and compared to the other girls, who were still extremely feminine with their hair and makeup, Yumi looked like she was about to go marry a woman herself.

I screwed up the dance moves a lot that day. That's what happens when you put me behind Yumi dressed like that. I think the director was about to throw me off set based on how many takes we had to do. Assuming Dolly didn't jump over and strangle me first.

We waited with bated breath to find out the results of the first week sales. Daily, we jumped between #1 and #2, and so did another artist. When the results did come in, I thought Dolly was going to throw up from the anxiety.

We were #1. We had the #1 album in the whole damned country.

I cried to hear it. Not just because I was proud of my group, but because I was personally proud as well. Those were my compositions resonating with people. The videos had lots of comments saying, "This song has a great melody," and "I can really feel myself in this song." People who said it was stuck in their head all the time made me really happy. How could it not?

To celebrate, the label gave us a nationwide tour to promote the album. We had done small tours before, but this was our first time performing in stadiums. No, we didn't get that Asian tour, but we were given the next best thing. The first time I walked out on stage in a stadium, performing a song I had composed, I felt like I was the closest I would ever get to truly being on top. The only way it could have been better was if Yumi had kissed me more, like when she kissed me on the cheek during one of my piano solos. The crowd went nuts in appreciation.

The tour was over within two months. Much too soon. Eventually we would go on to create a ninth single, hopefully with one of my compositions again. Yumi would go around promoting something and starring in another drama while the other girls did their own activities as well. It seemed that we fell into a groove.

You know that feeling when everything is going great and all it takes is for one thing to make it all come undone? In the back of my mind, I knew a shoe was about to drop. I held on to what I had for as long as I could.

Then one early Tuesday morning back in Nagoya we were all summoned into the meeting room. I knew it wasn't good when I saw Reika standing at the front of the room, looking somber, flanked by two executives. Her first bow was deep, and I knew it. She was leaving the group.

It wasn't hard to acclimate as a group without Reika, who said she wanted to go to university. That's what she said, but I wasn't surprised when two months later she announced her engagement and impending nuptials to her boyfriend. Good for her, though. She still seems happy with him and their kids.

Of course an idol can't be married, unless they're, what, forty? If Reika wanted to marry her boyfriend without already being knocked up, she had to drop out of the group. It sounded like something she thought long and hard about, so it was clearly what she wanted. She had a good run being in a popular girl group and wanted to do something else with her life. Sometimes I wonder if what happened to Koto influenced that decision at all. She wanted to get out before she got stuck in a situation she couldn't escape.

Anyway, as I was saying, we acclimated quickly as a business. Since Reika didn't have many lines, it was easy to redistribute them. I soaked up most of them in our older songs. The hardest part was changing our dance formations to compensate. Dolly finally got what she wanted, and that was dual front-and-center with Yumi, with Nezu and me bringing up the rear.

The label had to scrap their plans for the ninth single and start over again, taking into account our new image. With a five-member group, you have some anonymity when you're not a shining star. The focus is more on the whole group and how you work best together. When you pare it down to four, suddenly people are looking more closely at you. We were four sides of a square. Well, maybe a rectangle is better. Dolly and Yumi were the long sides. More visible and more important to the structure of the group.

We all had strict roles. Yumi was the main dancer and vocalist, the undisputed star even if Dolly argued. Dolly was another important singer, but she also brought her own unique flair and became the central visual without Reika. Nezu was our rapper and the silliest member, always cracking jokes in interviews and charming the audience. As for me, I was suddenly a lead songwriter and given more lines than ever before. People liked my voice, apparently.

This meant our next single had to reflect a new stage for the group. We were no longer five girls having fun. We were four young women in charge of our lives and our sexualities, even if the label was really the one in power. We matured more in our image. Dolly became our first official not-a-virgin when she starred in a movie about a call-girl and started a column in a magazine about sex and relationships. Yumi hinted at her dating life in many interviews, although she never mentioned names. Probably because only half of those names would be Yohei. The other boys I hardly knew. She got around so much, I blocked them all out.

Nezu got more involved in hip-hop culture and started, amazingly enough, her own clothing line. I was invited to co-host a radio show in Nagoya that focused on the musicality behind pop songs. It was a fun show to do while I was involved. Finally, I got to talk about what I knew best. Shit that my group mates would roll their eyes to hear. I also started writing songs for other artists on the label. I groaned to write a love ballad for Boytasm, but I told myself the royalties would be worth it.

I also recorded a few more piano MP3s, some of them officially released through the label and others I uploaded on my own. Playing the piano so much was a good release for me.

Eventually the label settled on a new direction for our four-piece group. Our ninth single would be another double A-side, "Making Love / Being With You." Damn you if you couldn't see what image we officially now had.

I couldn't help but be content with such a direction. As long as I did not have to grind on guys or pretend to like them, I didn't care. I liked dressing up in fancy clothes and singing in front of a camera. I liked the sensual beats of our new songs, even if I didn't write either one. It was preferable to being back in that school uniform and dancing for old men.

The video was really similar to "Tonight," only this time the sexuality was overplayed more than usual. They actually let Yumi climb on top of me for "Making Love," the implication being obvious. Let me tell you, having the girl you're in love with climb on you wearing nothing but a bra, stockings, and a sheer jacket just about drove me insane – and in front of all those people! It only lasted a few seconds, but all of those seconds are available for viewing in that video. Please go watch it and look at my face. It doesn't get more genuine than that.

That night we had a party with the production staff. All four of us went with the director, the cameramen, and our producer to an exclusive club where we got our own VIP room in the back. I hated those kinds of parties. I had to watch Dolly and Yumi flirt with everyone, pouring drinks and stroking fragile egos. Nobody expected me to do that, but I still had to be courteous to men I didn't care for. And when we were all still dressed in our fashionable young woman clothes and fancy hair and makeup? Men started to think we owed them something.

They flattered us with petty compliments. Yumi was cool, Dolly was beautiful, Nezu was amusing, and I was surprising. Some of them still couldn't believe I wrote songs. So young! An idol! Who knew it was possible?

Sometime during the evening Yumi disappeared. I didn't think much of it. She came back from the bathroom long enough to have another drink, downing a whole beer in one gulp, her face tired and her body languid. "I'm heading out," she told me. I wasn't going to stay much longer either, but before I could offer to go with her, the producer said he would escort her out.

I stayed twenty more minutes. Long enough to pour one drink and finish the one I had. The director of the video complimented my hair, and that was my cue to get out before he started breathing on my neck or trying to touch my thigh. (This had happened before.) I left Nezu and Dolly to it, the former telling bawdy jokes and the latter rubbing up against the director in my stead. Dolly wanted more camera time in the video for "Being With You," I'm sure.

We were so far back in the club that there were many empty VIP rooms between there and where I would sneak out, hail a cab, and go back to the dorms. Now, before you get riled up, I will tell you right now – I had recently started smoking. I know, I know. Ever since the incident with Koto I found myself sneaking cigarettes to deal with the stress. That night I stopped in the middle of the hallway to pull a pack from my pocket and a lighter to start it with.

I accidentally dropped my lighter, cursed, and bent down to pick it up. This allowed me to see through a crack in one of the VIP room doors, where a very familiar form was bent over a couch, some half-drunk man fucking her from behind.

Oh joy. I was right in time for the finale. The producer of our music made a pathetic sound as he finished, Yumi's face contorting in both disgust and boredom, as if this were just another day, another lay with the staff. I had not forgotten what Dolly said to me that one night. Far from it. I thought about it every so often whenever Yumi came back from work late. To see it for myself? Someone our age like Yohei was one thing. A fully grown, married man who was in control of so many fates? Seeing that for yourself is something else entirely.

I wanted to look away. I almost managed to, that image burned in the back of my brain forever, but the producer walked away, zipping himself up, and Yumi pushed herself off the couch. "We have a deal, right?" she said, straightening out her dress and fixing her hair. "You use one of her songs for the next single. She also gets at least a quarter of the lines."

"Yeah, yeah, how many times we gotta go over this? Geez, you're some good friend. Now get out of here. I need to call my wife and tell her I'm coming home. Won't do me much good to hear you bumbling around in the background."

I was frozen, my lit but unsmoked cigarette dangling from my hand. Even when Yumi opened the door and gawked at me, I couldn't walk away. The first thing out of my mouth was, "I hope you used a condom."

That, my dear readers and friends, was the night the last of my naiveté was destroyed. The old, cynical bitch you know now was born. It was the only way to survive.

***

I do not enjoy revealing this about Yumi. At the same time, I don't feel too ashamed on either of our behalves because, as much as you may not want to believe it, such a thing was unavoidable for numerous girls. Many people abuse their sexual power in that industry. Not just men either. While I never met one, I heard tales of some women being gross with young idols. It's a rough life whether you're taken advantage of or not, but if you are, it's a special kind of hell that you become numb to.

Love, Yumi

Sometimes I can't shake the look on her face out of my head. The one she had on while that man used her in exchange for my career advancement. She looked so *bored*. How many men had she put up with like this? How many times with the producer? When did she stop feeling frightened, ashamed, or disgusted with herself and these men? How many encounters does it take? How many months? Years?

Dolly had been right. Yumi was screwing executives, staff members, and other guys in charge pretty much since our first album. To hear her tell it, it happened as often as twice, sometimes three times a week. "There were times I fucked a different guy every day of the week," she confessed to me one night. "My boyfriend of the moment, the producer, some executive, another boyfriend, the producer again... ah, but I got what I wanted from them." Even now, so many years removed from those times, Yumi looks bored with the whole thing. I know it bothers her, deep inside. She doesn't want to show it. She's tried to put it behind her.

And me... she did so much of it *for me*. Not just herself. Not just for the group. When they started taking my work more seriously? When I got more prominent lines? Yumi started screwing the producer around the time "Out of It" went into recording. I had no idea. If I had known she traded her body for my lines... I would have quit before letting her do that again. I can't dwell on it though. That my career got its boost so I can be where I am today thanks to Yumi doing those things. If I dwell on it, I feel disgusted. Like my songs, like my talents were all lies. I have to remind myself that she helped me get started, but I'm the one who has maintained my profession because of my skills. Nobody would have paid attention to me if she hadn't done that. It's a terrible thought to get stuck in.

I don't know if Yumi is reading these posts right now. If you are reading this Yumi, I'm sorry. You knew this part would be coming. We promised that I would leave nothing out. I take full responsibility for what comes out in the papers tomorrow. Wherever you are, whatever you are doing to hide right now, know that I have never stopped loving you any less than I ever did.

Chapter 27

I don't know what happened. Maybe it was Reika leaving and taking so many fans with her. Perhaps we pushed a sexy and mature image too hard, too fast. It could have even been lackluster songs. Whatever the cause, our ninth single barely made it to the #8 spot on the chart.

Granted, there were some issues with the promotion. The general music shows deemed the song too sexy for their audiences, so we were relegated to late night shows where we could wear our costumes and do our dance moves without worry. Although I got a concerned call from my mother saying she had stayed up one night and couldn't believe I spent half the song touching myself and grabbing Yumi from behind as if we were going to start grinding. I reminded her that we were both over twenty now, although I agreed it was strange for the label to feed into the idea that Yumi and I were some forbidden couple. (If only.) Should it turn out that we actually were, it could mean the end of our careers. The public *liked* the idea of us, but that was only because we portrayed some level of friendship others hoped to achieve. We weren't actually supposed to be lovers. Young women who practiced on one another, maybe, but as Beppu pointed out, what we sometimes did could hardly be called practicing.

Plans for a tenth single were scrapped. I was brought into a meeting and asked for a couple more compositions, which left a bad taste in my throat. Did they really want them, or did Yumi arrange this? Either way, I delivered them, and soon I caught wind that the label wanted to hurry out a mini-album.

I couldn't help but worry. We assumed that the label wanted to switch image again, perhaps going back to what we had before. We were clearly alienating our fan base with the sexy concept. "They just want to put out a quick end to this era, make some cash, and move on to the next thing," Beppu reassured us. I wasn't sure if he believed it himself.

Tension echoed in the dorms. Even Nezu, who was usually the most cheerful one, was sour when things weren't going our way. It was like we knew if our next release wasn't a hit, we were through, a quartet of has-beens only two years into the game. Dolly was lining up acting gigs, and Nezu called her connections in the underground hip-hop community. I spent half my days in my own piano room, churning out pop songs in an effort to build up royalties, which were finally starting to come in – those checks weren't shabby, either.

Yumi was the most restless. She paced in the dorms, her magazine shoots dried up and her latest drama finished. Sometimes she went out with guys, other times she stayed in the practice rooms dancing and obsessing over her appearance. More often than not she asked me to go with her to the company gym. Since I was still keeping my muscular body, I almost always agreed to go and spot her.

One afternoon I commented on how thin she was while she struggled to pick up a weight. For the past few weeks she had become leaner, her skin hanging oddly on her hips and her arms so bony that I could practically break them in half. She told me it was stress killing her appetite. In my infinite wisdom I said, "Who's encouraging you to do this to yourself? Those men?"

Neither of us had brought up that night after the video shoot in the weeks that had passed. It was verboten. I knew what I had witnessed, and Yumi knew I had seen it. What was there to say or explain? It was best to never bring it up. Unless I was trying to insult her, of course.

"Nobody encourages me to do shit." Yumi dropped the weight, twisting her mouth in contempt. If I were smart, I would let it go and get back to working out.

Me? Smart? Haven't you figured out by now that I'm an idiot?

"You can't live like this. It's not healthy." What was I talking about, exactly? The sex with many men who carried God knew what? The thinness? The smoking and drinking? Yeah, I was a hypocrite. I have long since quit smoking, but back then I was up to three a day. Not a lot by some standards, but now that I think about it, I want to throw up.

"You're not my doctor." Yumi fussed with the weight rack. "Or my mother. You're not even my sister."

"No, but I'm your best friend."

She snorted. "Then you know that there are some things your friends can't control." Yumi looked at me, her makeup-less face more foreign to me than all the eyeliner and blush. "Like you can't control your perversion."

"My what?" No way did she mean what I thought she meant.

I had never seen Yumi turn the corner of her mouth up at me like that before. "You're a fucking queer. You really think you've got room to tell me about unhealthy habits?"

Now I can look back on that moment and realize she was deflecting her own issues onto me. What a difference several years make. Back then, I was a defensive snot who didn't want to hear something like that from someone who made half her living fucking married guys for both her and my career advancements. "You take that back." What was I, eight?

"Fuck you, Chiharu." Yumi ambled out of the gym. I should have let it go. Let her go back to our room and snooze it off.

I should have done a lot of things in my life.

Love, Yumi

"What the hell is your problem?" I followed her, my bravado about to undo me.

Yumi turned, her brows furrowing but otherwise still hinged. "My problem? My problem is that stupid cunts like you think you're so fucking above the rest of us because you never had to demean yourselves. Ever think that maybe I *like* doing that? Maybe I like sex with guys!"

One could feast on her defensive outburst. I felt the pain welling up inside her, saw it twisting on her face like a pustule come to burst. My best friend was hurting. She was being used. She needed someone to give her reassurances. Not call her a slut.

"You know who likes sex? Sluts."

It was enough to piss her off and slap me across the cheek. Her grunt of denial smacked against the walls, the doors to empty dorm rooms, and my own heart.

"Bitch! The shit I fucking do for you!"

I had never heard her scream like that before. Crazed, delusional, *angry at the world*. I was the target for every emotion she felt. Because in the sting of her slap, I felt her desire for me to understand her, to tell her that everything would be okay. She needed me to be the cool, rational one who could keep her grounded in a place where at least someone in this world wouldn't hurt her.

"I never asked you to do that." I held my hand to my cheek, biting my lower lip. "I never asked you to spread your legs on my behalf!"

We were loud, and I had no idea if anyone else in the dorms heard us. I didn't care. I was the last one to know everything. Dolly, Nezu... they must have known exactly what Yumi was doing for me.

She stood back, her anger fading and replaced with exhaustion. Yumi was defeated, but not destroyed – a warrior who needed to go lick her wounds and sleep for a week before getting back on the battlefield. "Better me than you. You wouldn't even know what to do, dyke."

Never before had Yumi called me that. It stung, more than the slap. And then I realized what she really meant.

"Yumi," I said, lowering my hand and reaching for her. She pulled away, eyes locked on mine. "I care about you."

Her lip trembled, but she did not cry. "Let me live my life, Chiharu. I make my own decisions, just like you make your own." Limp, she went into our room, shutting the door behind her. I did not go after her. Instead I sat in front of the TV, watching images but not absorbing them. Not until a couple of hours had passed did I go into our room and sit with her on her bed, rubbing her shoulder and kissing the spot beneath her ear. She did not push me away. Nor did she invite me into bed with her. In truth, I didn't want her to. Not like that.

***

I took a quick break to eat, and against my better judgment I turned on the TV. Sure enough, there was a panel of people discussing my blog.

"What pushes a person to do this sort of thing?" the hostess asked one of her guests, a therapist who claimed to have a doctorate in something or other. "What makes someone throw away everything they have to tell such a private story?"

"Well, you see…" I didn't want to hear it. So I changed the channel, and there was a celebrity gossip show talking about how…

Our CDs, although they had been removed at some stores, were selling like crazy online.

I had to look again. Even the newscaster on TV wasn't sure what was going on. "CD albums and singles by YUMI and Chiharu Morita have been removed from some stores, both online and off, but counters are recording a spike in sales. Specifically, downloads for YUMI's biggest songs have gone up so quickly that they are taking four of the Top 10 spots. On the other hand, Chiharu Morita's most recent album, *Surface of the Sun*, is currently at #15 nine months after release. Explanations for how this phenomenon occurred have not been given."

Honestly, I couldn't believe it. I heard that we had been temporarily (or permanently) blacklisted at a few of the big chain stores, but I never expected for people to take interest in our music because of this. It certainly wasn't a promotional thing. Yet if the sheer number of comments I get on each post are any indication, I suppose things are really happening out there. It's hard to tell when you seclude yourself in the middle of nowhere. Now I'm going to wonder if the school kids passing by are listening to YUMI's music on their phones. Are people really supporting us in that way?

Why is it? Are people curious about us and want to know what kind of music we make? Are they buying it as a way to show the record label that we are supported? To not give up on us, no matter what we say? I have no idea what's going on. All I know is that hearing that news report has given me some renewed fervor.

Since the day is still young and I have nothing else to do until my video chat later, I guess it's time to get to more recent events.

Chapter 28

Working on our mini-album was bittersweet. On one hand we were ready to see what direction our image would go in next, but on the other we had an axe swinging above our necks as we slept. We had lost three members in one year. We were over twenty. We pushed a sexy image instead of remaining "pure" and young. We evolved too much, too fast. If this mini-album tanked…

I especially felt the pressure ten-fold. As one of the lead songwriters, it could be my neck that bled first. Not to mention I was still reeling from discovering that the only reason people were choosing my songs was because of what Yumi did for me. People liked my songs, right? They wouldn't keep picking my songs if they weren't doing well. Yumi didn't sleep with someone to get my songs chosen for other artists, right? Just our group, right? I refused to bring these questions up with Yumi. I didn't even tell Beppu – hell no! Although I often wondered if he knew. Probably didn't want to think about it.

In the end, two of my songs were chosen for the mini-album. Because I was so stressed out over them, I don't think they are my best tracks. They sound forced to me. One is the piano ballad closing out the mini-album, and the other was used as the promotional track, "Heaven." You might think that this sort of song is about Yumi from the title alone. It's not. It's one of the most generic songs I've ever written. It was the first time I came up with the bare bones for that chart about song lyrics and chord progressions. Maybe this is why the whole mini-album sounded flat to me.

"Slow & Easy," regardless of how hard we promoted it, only managed to make #7 on the album charts. We breathed a sigh of relief that we stayed in the Top 10, but Top 5 would have been much better for our lifespan.

Things were quiet after the album's release, and we didn't hear a word about the next stage. We barely had a tour. Fanclub only in smaller venues. No more arenas. The fanclub angle meant that the label was guaranteed to make back the money while conveying a sense of intimacy – not panic.

I saw the signs all around me. And yet I was still not prepared for the bomb that dropped on us the week before my birthday.

The thing that surprised me the most wasn't the disbandment of Butterfly Tops, the group I had been a part of for over two years, but the restructuring that happened afterward.

Yumi had heard rumors from the executives that we were going to be split into two. Naturally, we assumed that we would be together. People loved us. They loved our friendship and how we worked together with music. Me writing songs and playing instruments, and her singing and dancing while oozing charisma. We assumed we would become a duo of some kind. Not that we had any idea how Nezu and Dolly would work on their own, mind you.

So when Dolly, Nezu, and I were summoned into a meeting one day after being told the Butterfly Tops were over, I had no idea what was going on.

Mr. Kawaguchi broke the news to us, just as he had told us our group was done the day before. "Don't be sad, girls," he said to us, three young women who barely got along and had nothing in common besides being members of the same group. "Your career isn't over. The three of you will become your own group. A trio. See? It's not bad."

We looked at each other, disgust washing over Dolly. "Me. With just *these two?*" I could see it on her face. The perma-kid and the dyke. Not like I was glad with this development either. I had no idea how a group with us would work. What was our dynamic? And furthermore…

"Wait, what about Yumi?"

Mr. Kawaguchi smiled as if he had been expecting that question. "Yumi will be joining the hallowed halls of the solo artist."

"Oh, *fuck* her!" Dolly slapped her hands down. "Who the fuck is she blowing now?"

That kind of outburst could have gotten her kicked off the label. Except Dolly was apparently blowing the right people too – Mr. Kawaguchi, perhaps? – because she never got in trouble for that as far as I know.

When I asked Yumi if it was true that she was getting a solo career, she sat next to me on my bed and said, "In truth, we've been preparing my debut single for a while now."

"You said you thought we would become a duo."

"I was always going to have a solo single. I didn't tell you because I wasn't allowed to."

"You couldn't tell *me?* I thought we said no more secrets."

"This wasn't a secret. It was supposed to be a surprise." She put a hand on my knee. "I'm debuting at the end of next month."

"With what song?"

"Not one you composed. Believe me, I asked, but they had another song in mind already. It's quite sexy."

"I bet."

"Don't be that way, Chiharu."

Love, Yumi

I didn't want to fight again, so I stopped. Instead I leaned my head against her shoulder, afraid for the future. Happy for her, but afraid nonetheless.

The label got this brilliant idea to release our new "debut" singles on the same day. A built-in rivalry, if you will. Of course the last thing I wanted was to have a rivalry with my best friend. We tried to take it in stride, but now that we were no longer working on the same projects I rarely saw her anyway.

Except for on my birthday a week later, which happened to fall on a Saturday. Yumi took me out to Athens, plying me with alcohol and asking me what girls in there I thought were cute. I was half passed out on the floor when I pointed out a young woman on the other side of the club. I don't even remember what she looked like now. But within five minutes Yumi went and talked to her, and next thing I knew me and that girl were making out in the same spot I caught my friend fucking Yohei so long ago.

Embarrassingly enough, I was so drunk that I couldn't tell you if I had sex with that girl. If I did, nobody said anything. Including Yumi.

I woke up the day after my birthday with a raging headache. Not only was it the first time I had been properly *drunk,* but this was also my first hangover. Dolly laughed her ass off and said I reeked of pussy. I'm pretty sure she was being facetious. Or so she assured me.

I still had a headache Monday morning when my new group met for a meeting. We were given the name Celestial, a name I now laugh at. I laugh even harder when the words, "We want to take an edgy hip-hop route with you three," echo in my head. How great for Nezu! What were Dolly and I supposed to do?

A song was already prepared. We finished recording by the end of the week, and soon enough we were in the stylist's chairs having our looks redone for the new concept. Nezu finally got the street look she wanted, although her trademark pigtails never went away. Dolly was given darker makeup and her hair teased and colored a soft red. Me? They didn't have to change much. I still got to be a tomboy, only now with a new contract.

Yeah, we got new contracts at the start of the new year. A lot of it was the same standard numbers, only now we had income from other sources. The biggest change was that a lot of our old bans were lifted. We were allowed to openly date. We could be seen coming in and out of bars and clubs since we were all over twenty. We were discouraged from smoking since it didn't look good as performers. All four of us smoked, including Yumi. She and Dolly smoked the most, but that didn't mean much.

With our new styles and new terms, we tried to give the new group our all. But Nezu was the only one with any heart in it, as evident when she had half the lines of the first single. I was expected to suddenly be an expert hip-hop dancer, which frustrated both me and the instructors who were on a strict deadline. The music video was in a week, and there I was, floundering like a fish to the point one instructor told Beppu, "I can't do anything with her! It's like she has plastic bags on her feet!"

Shit, Beppu. He was still our manager. When he heard what they had done, he expressed his condolences to me, patting me on the shoulder and saying we all saw it coming. I could only roll my eyes at the time. Silly me, I thought he was also Yumi's manager, but that was ridiculous. How could he manage two acts at once? If he was Celestial's manager, then that meant Yumi had a new one.

We called him Koji, because the first time we saw him, waltzing in with his clean suit and fresh young face, he reminded us of an eager tiger cub ready to pounce and leave the ambush behind – whether he was really ready or not. At first we couldn't believe that he was assigned to be Yumi's new manager. He was too young! Okay, early thirties. We were so used to seeing old and grizzled managers like Beppu running around that this much younger guy in a suit was both a breath of fresh air and hardly any fun at all. He tried to be serious with Yumi, but it was clear from the beginning that his job was to not control her like Beppu controlled a pack of teen girls at any given moment. No, his job was to be her personal assistant who made sure she got to her appointments on time.

Even though Yumi and I were both in Nagoya preparing for our separate debuts, I hardly got to see her. We had different meetings, different times in recording, different dance practices… I was no longer a part of her world until it came time for bed. And even then Yumi would be up at all hours going over songs and texting people on her phone. When I saw she was working with our old producer, I wanted to shake her and say, "You don't have to do that! You're a solo star now!" When she was in recording with him, I would wait impatiently for her to return to the dorms, assessing her personality. Was she down? Was she cranky? And were these moods different from when she left?

One night I asked her if she was comfortable around that man. She looked at me on the couch – we were alone, for once – and laughed. "Comfortable?" she spat, while a commercial for fabric detergent played on TV. "That man is *mochi*. He'll do anything I say at this point. Well, unless the orders come from the higher ups. Not much I can do about that. Yet."

I didn't like the implication of that.

The farther apart we worked, the less I was able to protect her. Not that I believed I could protect her from anything anymore. If I didn't try, then it felt like I was condoning what happened. Like I didn't care that men took advantage of her. She could tell me that she liked sex all she wanted. There was no way she liked sex with *those* men.

I didn't need her to be gay or bi or whatever. I just needed her to be safe and healthy. Practically impossible in that fucked up world.

When I wasn't fretting over Yumi, I was becoming detached from my personal work. My compositions came to a crawling halt. I didn't like the song we were debuting with as Celestial. And I hated – *hated* – the choreography. There was nothing stimulating about swaying my body back and forth while I twisted my feet in opposite directions and moved my arms like noodles. It had nothing to do with Nezu and Dolly both being way better than me at it either. I swear.

I wasn't needed for recording and nobody cared about my opinions for the music video, so I was told to practice the choreography every afternoon. Sometimes someone helped me, but for the most part I was trapped in a practice room by myself for hours, playing the same shitty song over and over as I tried in vain to not look like a moron. We were supposed to perform on *Music Tonight*. It was the same ol' fears again.

That winter the weather was especially cold and rainy, but on one Wednesday the sun broke through the clouds and illuminated my practice room when I managed to open the blinds. That awful song continued to play on the stereo, but I ignored it, leaning my elbows against the windowsill and staring at the dreary Nagoya skyline.

"Having fun?"

Yumi's voice hit my ears as I watched a plane descend toward the faraway airport. I waited until it was behind a building before turning to see her standing in front of the closed door. She wore yoga pants, like me, implying that she just came from another practice room. The fact that she wore a long-sleeved shirt for dancing didn't mean anything those days. She never got hot anymore. If anything, she was always freezing, complaining in our room that she wanted more blankets and using it as a convenient excuse to crawl into bed with me. Over the months it became easier to share a small bed with her, and it had nothing to do with my body.

"*Tanoshikunai,*" I said with a sigh. There was nothing fun about torturing myself with this stupid dance to a stupid song I never wanted any part of. "You?"

We remained on separate sides of the room. "Just got done with my practice. Was gonna go hit the shower, but thought I'd bother you first."

Finally I turned, leaning against the wall as I folded my arms across my chest. The song started over again, and Yumi attempted to hide a smile behind her knuckles. I quickly bent down and turned off the stereo. "Think it's funny, huh?"

She shook her head. "That's an awful song."

"That's my life now. I do faux hip-hop. Even Nezu is pissed about it, and I think they did it to appeal to her."

"Are you rapping, though?"

"God, no!"

Yumi stepped forward. At first I thought she was going to come to me, but then she bent down and took out the CD from the stereo. "Bump It," she said, reading my handwriting on the burnt CD. "I'm so sorry they did this to you." I couldn't see her face, but I could hear her muffled laughter. "Let me guess… the dance makes you want to quit."

"How did you know? I'm so bad at dancing."

She stood up, placing the CD on the windowsill. "You're not a bad dancer, Chi-*chan*. You're just not as good as everyone else. That's not a bad thing in the realm of the world. Except in this business it has to cause a lot of pressure."

"You don't say." Yumi was a triple-threat. Dancing wasn't her strongest suit, but she could still dance better than any other girl at the label now. Koto had been better than her. I moved away from the window so I wouldn't look seven stories down.

"*Mou*, you're too hard on yourself." Yumi pulled out her MP3 player and hooked it up to the stereo. Lots of girls did that. They would go in the practice rooms on their own time, plug in their music, and freestyle for hours. I never did this. Dancing was a job I had to practice at, not something that came naturally or even brought me joy. I wanted to express myself through music, not my body. "You know how to dance. What you lack is confidence."

She fiddled with her player while I scoffed in her direction. "I have confidence…"

A song started rumbling through the floor. "Do you?" Yumi placed her player on the windowsill next to the CD. "Show me."

I thought she wanted me to do the dance while she critiqued. Just as I went to get into position, however, she gently took my arm and pulled me against her.

Until that point I had never danced with another woman before, let alone her. I don't count the music videos, which are highly choreographed. This was real dancing, the kind where the movements come naturally… and although Yumi and I were nearly the same height, she shrank before me, taking on the submissive role while silently encouraging me to lead. Not because that's the dynamic she wanted in our relationship, or because

I was more masculine, but because she thought it would improve my confidence if I led us in a dance.

An *intimate* dance.

The song playing was slow, sultry, and in English. I couldn't understand the lyrics, but I could understand the intent of the song. Probably about sex. Falling in love. Yearning for someone you can't have. Most of those songs are the same, but the reason we write them over and over is because those emotions burst from our veins and spill on our skin when we think no one is looking. I felt it now, both in the music and in the way my body responded to having the love of my life put my hands on her waist and urge me to do whatever I wanted to her – within reason, of course.

Yumi is a professional. It's the one bit of praise everyone heaps whenever they work with her. She's mature on set, listens in the studio, and doesn't get weird when her dance partners do what they're told to do, even if it means grabbing her ass or rubbing her breasts. Even if it's on camera. *Especially* if it's on camera. I didn't do either of those things, but I did notice the way she looked at me when I put my muscles to good use and dipped her toward the floor, my body tightening even though I needed to relax. How could I relax when I was so close to her face, the glow in her eyes sharp while her lids remained languid like the rest of her? Even during the darker times of her health she was still strong. She wasn't going to pick me up or anything, but she could lift herself into someone's arms. She didn't try that with me, but she did relax in my sideways embrace, my knuckles digging into the cotton of her shirt.

"Chi-*chan*," she said gently. "You need to loosen up. You can't do those moves if you're so tense."

This was supposed to make me *confident*. She was demonstrating how to be graceful. Or something. I don't know anything about grace. I know it when I see it, but trying to be graceful myself? It's a joke.

I relaxed my muscles, which made her dip lower toward the ground, the short length of her hair scraping the floor. My knees buckled, but the rest of me held firm. "That's better," she said, the song still playing and still fucking with my head. "Now pull me up without looking like you want to slam me against the wall."

That notorious smile on her face made me smile as well. I felt like we were back in high school, creating a new inside joke that we would reference for years. *"Now text me and don't say you want to slam me against the wall." "Now take out the trash without looking like you're going to slam it against the wall." "Now go pick up the kid without making the teachers think you're gonna slam the stroller against the wall."* My face betrayed me once again, but at least I could laugh about it.

I snapped her up into my other arm. Like a ballerina she turned mid-movement, her back landing gently against my limb. Beaming with pride, I made her laugh, if only because I had managed to do the motion without moving my whole body like I usually would.

Yumi stood up, placed her hands on my shoulders, and instructed me to put mine on her waist. She stepped back, waiting for me to step with her, and the rest was a blur of beats and music as I gave in to one part of my desires. The one that begged me to touch and hold her as long as she smiled at me.

What is confidence? Is it when I can do something without fear or hesitation? Truly? I thought that's what confidence was before that day. I thought it meant I could go on stage and play my part without betraying my fright to the audience. I also thought it meant hitting on a woman without the fear of rejection. And then Yumi drew me into her world of movement, where she showed me that the confidence I needed didn't come from how someone responded to me, but from how I responded to someone else. Namely, her.

Even then we still rode a wave of solidarity and childhood friendship. There was little we didn't know about the other up to a certain point. Things most people never find out about anyone else in their lives. I knew, without having seen it since she was sixteen, that she had a mole on her thigh. Except that was when we were kids. We were adults now. We had kissed and come close to sharing something more. I knew some of the darkest things she had been through – for herself and for me. The closer we grew together, the farther we also grew apart. There were things we couldn't talk about even though we both knew them. I suppose what happened is that we reached a plane of our relationship that cut off words altogether. We didn't need words to say, "Someone hurt me today," or "I had to do something with someone that I didn't really want to," without knowing they were true. Words only slowed things down. Why say in words what you can express with your body? I was beginning to finally understand it.

"See? You're a beautiful dancer." Yumi took my hand and wrapped it in hers, our fingers intertwining as sweat slid across our palms. "Don't let the instructors get to you. Show the audience what you show me, and they'll love you."

I understood, but she didn't. I couldn't show the audience what I had just shown her, because she wasn't a part of it. It was because of her I could find grace in the moment. The shimmy of her body was unlike anything – or anyone – else I danced with. It inspired me. It woke me up. I wanted to fall to my knees and worship her frame and the soul within. Why didn't she understand? I was better at expressing what I saw in the world because of her. She was beyond a muse. She was *Yumi.*

And now, as the song faded into another, she put her hand on my cheek before asking me to dance with her some more.

The confidence I drew from her led us around the room, twirling, stepping, and stretching against the barres lining the walls. As we descended into madness, our bodies becoming sweatier with each passing moment, I felt something akin to lovemaking come over my body. Whenever I touched Yumi, a spark burst within me, bringing me closer to her until I could smell the scent of her skin and hair. When her breath covered my mouth, one of her legs hooped around my waist as I pushed my fingers beneath her thigh, I felt a greater nirvana than any other woman had given me. It wasn't orgasmic, but it was ethereal nonetheless.

We stayed like that, her hand creeping up the back of my neck and pressing into my head. She brought me closer to her, and I squeezed her flesh, every one of my fingers fighting to break through her clothing.

Love, Yumi

For the first time I was not surprised when she kissed me. In truth, I kissed her just as much as she kissed me. For the first time, I took the initiative, and was gladly rewarded.

This wasn't my bed. We weren't in pajamas. We weren't clean from showers or feeling nervous about one another. I was sweaty and grimy; she was beautiful and glistening. Yumi's muscles tensed while mine became more languid, her leg wrapped hard around my waist as I pressed against her and kissed her with every shred of confidence she gave me.

I thought I was going to die when her tongue entered my mouth.

We were still dancing, weren't we? It was okay to put my hands on her body, right? I slipped one from her thigh to her rear, grabbing what she had there while I fought to feel her chest against mine. Her leg eased down from around me, and soon we sank to the floor, Yumi pushing me onto my back as she straddled my hips and ripped off her shirt. I barely had time to stare at her breasts, encased in a sports bra, before she was kissing me again, the urgency behind her love as great as my own.

You may laugh at me, I was ready to have her, even there in the practice room covered in sweat. I didn't care. I had been waiting to make love to her for years, whether I knew it or not. It didn't matter if it was in the privacy of bed or in some practice room somewhere. I told her this not with my words, but with my body as I toppled her to the ground and took my place on top of her, my lips on her stomach and boldly going elsewhere.

Imagine me, then, when she stopped, sitting up and pulling me so we could lean against each other's shoulders. I put my hand on her chest, feeling her bare skin there for the first time since I could remember. I wanted to kiss her, but she turned her head away.

"Why?"

"I'm sorry." Although the music kept playing, it lost its sensuality.

"I don't understand."

Yumi cupped my face in her hand and brought me down for a tender kiss. "Me neither."

If I could, I would tell the Chiharu of back then to not beat herself up over it. That's easy for me to say now. I'm not a twenty-one year old hopelessly in love with her best friend anymore. Back then, I would have punched myself in the face to suggest such a thing would be something I eventually got over and moved on from.

***

The foreign woman is back. She's sitting outside of my window, dipping her toes in the cool river water before pacing back and forth. I won't pretend to know what foreigners fret about when they're in Japan. I suppose they fret about the same things everyone else does. Money, loved ones, the future. But because I doubt she knows who I am, I feel compelled to talk to her. Not that we probably speak the same language. For all I know she's German.

Still, I yearn to go out at some time that isn't twilight. I pay the proprietress to bring me food so I don't have to deal with cashiers. My face is all over the news right now. So is Yumi's, but she has always been recognizable.

How much longer will I have to hide here? Eventually I hope I can meet up with Yumi somewhere so we can at least keep each other company. At some point I'll have to arrange for my mother and the little one to be with me. Not until things die down a bit. They're not going to die down until a while after I've finished writing this.

So I need to keep writing, but I'm tapped out at the moment. I stare at the computer screen but I'm still hung up on that day in the practice studio. I know that Yumi didn't mean to play with me. Not on purpose. She has a habit of falling into something and then scrambling to get out of it again. I was too much for her that day, I guess.

Maybe I'll take this time to finally answer some questions in the comments.

When you look back on your childhood, do you see signs that you were gay?

Love, Yumi

I don't know how to answer this, really. I never thought about sex or romance until I was well into my teen years. So I guess it depends on your definition of "childhood." In my case, I suppose I remember some times when I was so captivated by a girl or woman in ways that no normal child would be. Did that mean I was gay? When does one become gay, or are they born that way? I don't have the answer to that question, sorry.

Have you ever had a real girlfriend?

Yes.

Who do you think is surprised by your coming out confession? Your mother?

My mother knew I was gay before I started writing this. (I'll go over the day I came out to her later. It was a painful day, and not one I will overlook.) Everyone who is close to me knew that I was gay. Beppu, my students… it's not something that I hide from them. I don't run around talking about it until situations like this, but I also don't hide my girlfriend in my own home. I'm sure some people who knew me were surprised. I don't know who, though.

I'm confused. Is the child yours?

She is mine in the sense that I am her parent helping to raise her. I did not give birth to her. I don't feel comfortable disclosing her name right now.

Have you thought about moving somewhere that is more accepting of gay people?

I have thought about this a lot, but the truth is Japan is my home and I am not familiar with other cultures that well. Yumi is the well-traveled one. She tells me about these foreign countries she goes to for work and pleasure, and I'm always amazed that she feels so comfortable there. I've been to some foreign countries as well, but none of them felt like anything more than a short vacation. I don't think I would be happy moving somewhere outside of Japan. Besides, I would rather stay here and try to make my home a better place for others.

That foreign woman is looking up at my window. What does she see? A frumpy, sweaty Japanese woman who can barely keep her glasses on her nose? I wonder if she has any idea what I am hiding from. Then again, she may be thinking the same thing about me.

Chapter 29

Although Celestial and Yumi were set to debut on the same day, the label took very different turns in promoting us. As soon as our video was ready it was released on the internet. Within 24-hours it had over 500,000 views, but interest waned after that. Nezu pounded the pavement doing radio shows while Dolly appeared on multiple magazine covers. In comparison, Yumi's music video was kept under wraps until a few days before her single dropped. She never even told me about it, other than what day it would be uploaded.

She was in commercials to promote her single, and I didn't see her for a few days while she filmed episodes of variety shows, sometimes with Yohei. Boytasm was now the most successful group under the label, and Yumi was set to feature on their next single.

Yumi returned just in time for her video to be uploaded. We stayed up in bed that night, waiting for midnight, Yumi pressing the refresh button over and over on her laptop. Finally, it came on, and I scratched at the imaginary pearl necklace around my throat.

Everyone knows her debut song "Delicious." And everyone definitely knows the waves the music video caused, due to Yumi wearing skimpy clothing and enough makeup to change her identity. But mostly the clothes! Or lack thereof! I gasped, scandalized even at that age, to see my best friend strut down a sidewalk wearing denim cutoff shorts, strappy sandals, and a thin, cropped tank top that hugged her breasts. In the video she approached various men doing their jobs, receiving flowers and fruits from them as she sang about how "tasty" love and sex is. The final shot was of her slowly peeling a banana and biting off the tip while some guy turned on a hose behind her.

"Well?" Yumi asked when it was over. "*Dou?*"

I could barely speak. "It was... shocking."

"I figured you would say as much. That's why I didn't tell you about it. Didn't want to make you pass out." She patted my stomach. "This is the kind of image they're launching me with, I guess. I don't mind it."

In the years following people would discuss Yumi's provocative image at length. While she is a talented woman, the public often wondered if most of her fame came from her skimpy clothing or sexual songs and dance moves. Of course she didn't only sing sexy songs. She also sang popular love ballads and cheerful, positive songs, but this was the first image people knew. Yumi claimed to not mind it, but I often wondered if that was true... or was she just so desensitized to being Japan's sex kitten that she hardly noticed the gross comments that always came her way?

As her best friend, I wanted to encourage her. As a jealous woman, I wanted to tell her it was terrible to pander that way. I didn't want to whole world seeing her as nothing but an outlet for sex, as a dehumanized robot that performed on command. She was already so taken advantage of by people who saw her that way.

I took her hand and said, "No matter what, don't forget you can do anything you want." She had the talent. I hoped the label would actually let her use her talents, and not just her body.

"I could say the same thing to you, of course." Yumi squeezed my hand.

Love, Yumi

That night I got pretty brazen and outright invited her into my bed. I did so before we even got to our room, whispering into her ear that it was a cold night and my blankets were thicker than hers.

I was flirting with her. A part of me was stupid enough to hope that we could resume the fervor we felt in the practice room a few days before. Sadly that did not happen. But I did come back from brushing my teeth to find her already in my bed, as if that was a natural place for her to rest. In my mind, it was.

Is it any surprise that my group's single did terrible on the charts? Okay, not *terrible*. Yet we only made it to #9 on the weekly charts, and that was enough to make us groan, the trio accustomed to hitting the top five.

No one let us have time to deal with it, however, for someone we knew managed to hit number fucking one.

Yumi crumpled to her knees and began sobbing when the report came in early one morning. "Delicious" hit an all-kill, meaning it was #1 every single day that week. So it was no surprise that she got #1... yet she still did not expect to hear that report.

What is it like to have the #1 single all to yourself? I don't know. The highest I've ever charted as a soloist was in the Top 20. I can't say I ever pined for the top spot. I'm the type of person who wants to be successful but not necessarily famous. I don't feed on people's adoration like Yumi does. She needs the energy of the crowd to fuel her performances, whether she's in a stadium or a small venue for her fanclub. She can be selfless with her energy. If someone is having a down day, she will spend the last of her reserves to cheer them up and take pleasure from their smile. I've rarely seen her so happy as when she's interacting with her fans.

Written correspondence is enough for me. I get flustered when fans of my work talk to me in real life, even if it's at a meet and greet set up by the label. (Sometimes I wonder if this is a remnant of that attack. The place I was stabbed does get sore when I'm meeting fans.) This is a reason I love digital releases so much. I can just upload a track and move on to the next one. With CDs there is the constant pressure to promote. I don't even like doing solo music videos. If you've ever wondered why I rarely do videos or concerts at all, let alone appear in the few videos I have, that's why. I'm too nervous for that sort of thing.

So I was okay with Yumi moving on to develop her next single while Celestial pulled back to regroup. There was a tremendous expectation that our next single do much better. We didn't want to think about what would happen if we failed the label like that again.

They asked me to write an RnB song. I had never written one before, and I'm ashamed to say that my contribution was not that inspiring. I mostly wrote it to suit Dolly's voice, which she complained about, saying, "Chiharu doesn't know my register at all!" I just think she was upset about being stuck in this nowhere group.

Quickly, Celestial became a job. There was nothing fun about this life anymore – not if I couldn't work with Yumi or sing songs that appealed to me. The dances were complicated and our lives lackluster. The only thing I liked was the occasional photo shoot that had a cool concept, like the time we wore blacklight makeup and I got to experience life with bright orange eye shadow and hot pink lipstick. Then they would do something to make me hate my appearance again, like when they bleached my hair. It was so awful! I had never been blond before, let alone that crazy bright shade. It did not suit my face at all. Even Yumi twisted her lips at it and said, "Well, it certainly doesn't look much like you." Thankfully it only lasted for a couple of months, and then it was dyed brown again to transition to my natural black. From then on, the only time I let them dye my hair was if it was brown.

In my spare time I devoted myself to my songwriting. I was offered more gigs to write for other artists, so I threw my all into it. Even writing ballads for Boytasm was preferable to working on Celestial dances. I acquired quite a few writing credits in a short amount of time. When I received my first big figure check a few months later, I had no idea what to do. What twenty-one year old thinks they're ever going to have that much money? My mother told me to put it into a secure account, so that's what I did. I think I splurged on some nice clothes and that was it. Everything else went into the bank.

Yumi made her money off endorsements, and I made mine off royalties. Her money was immediate and bigger, but mine was steady if in smaller amounts. Either way, we were both becoming rich. When we set out from Seki nearly three years ago, we never imagined that we would come this far in such a short amount of time. When we both happened to have time off together, we went to Okinawa for three days, staying in a guest house by ourselves. I remember thinking the price tag was ridiculous for such a short stay, but at that age the money meant nothing to me. Especially when I got to enjoy the fresh weather and food with my best friend, who had issues keeping to her bed at night. A part of me pined for this to become a romantic getaway, but the most intimate we got was when she accidentally thwacked me in the breast during a vivid dream. I had a bruise for days.

For every single Celestial put out, Yumi put out two. By the time we had to put out albums, Yumi had a tracklist twice as long as ours. It also didn't help that she was excited to promote her debut album with a tour, whereas Celestial was lucky if it would get one concert at all. The only way they were able to get me on board with a live in Tokyo was by promising me a small set list of piano performances. Hardly went with our hip-hop theme, but I didn't care.

Our album didn't even break the Top 20. Yumi's hovered at #3 for two days before zipping to #1 the rest of the week. That weekend we all went to Athens to celebrate, but she was the only one having any fun at all.

When your career is in a downturn, you learn to cope. For some people, that means using substances. For others, it means picking up a new hobby.

For me, it meant flirting with girls through text message, vainly trying to get them to go out with me.

"Times sure have changed," Beppu said as we both ate dinner in the kitchen one evening. He sat across from me, flipping through a folder detailing our next round of promotions. I hunched over my phone, talking to a girl I met at that one gay bar in Tokyo Erina had told me about a long time ago. The girl was in Nagoya, and I thought it would be worth it to go on a date. For sex, of course. "Back in my day girls never flirted with other girls... er... I don't think, anyway."

I looked up long enough to give him a blank stare.

"Okay, fine. What do girls do on dates together anyway? I'm intrigued now."

Beppu liked teasing me about my sexuality. He meant it good-naturedly, but it annoyed me then just as much as it would annoy me now. I realize that it was a new thing for him to know a lesbian, but I wasn't a sounding board. "What the hell do you think we do?"

"I dunno. Paint each other's nails. Listen to records. Practice kissing." That was a low shot. Granted how busy Yumi was away from Nagoya now, he knew none of that was going on in our lonely room. "I'm jealous. I always wanted to paint a girl's nails."

I went back to ignoring him in favor of my fruitless flirting. It was a Friday night, though, and I wanted to have some fun that weekend. If fun meant getting half-drunk and knocking it with a girl I barely knew, hey, I wasn't complaining.

The quiet of the kitchen was rudely interrupted by a shrieking alarm blasting from Beppu's phone. I leaped out of my skin, knocking my phone onto the floor as I gasped in fright and nearly tumbled over the back of my chair. When I realized it was just Beppu's ringtone, I calmed myself, although that chilling sound still zipped up my spine.

I expected Beppu to look the same as always as he checked his messages or answered his phone. Except his face paled, and I realized this alarm was not a good thing at all.

Beppu is the kind of manager who has a different ringtone for every person on his phone. He told me this was important for his job, because he has to know how quickly he must answer at any given moment. After all, he could be in a meeting, backstage at a show, in the recording studio, or driving a van between Tokyo and Nagoya. If he recognizes a buddy, he ignores it. If it's his wife or an executive, he answers it. I found out once that the ringtone he's always had for me is Beethoven's Symphony No. 5, because, as he put it, "If Chiharu is calling me, then it must be pretty urgent. That and it matches her face." I didn't want to imagine his phone going off when I called him from Koto's apartment.

For someone to warrant a screaming alarm, it meant they only called in an emergency.

"Yes?" He answered, gritting his teeth. "What have you gotten yourself into?"

I watched as his face went from grim to possessed by a ghost. The few times I saw Beppu that shocked, well… it usually had to do with me. "What is it?" I hoped it wasn't a family member, for his sake.

"I'll be right there." Beppu stood up, grabbing his jacket off the chair behind him. "Stay there and don't say a word to the police. Don't fucking move either! You might be hurt!"

"Huh?" I stood up too.

Beppu hung up and hurried to put on his jacket and grab his wallet off the table. "Dolly," he mumbled. Oh, no.

I knew he didn't want me following, but what else could I do? Dolly was in trouble, somehow. No way the label wanted me tied up in whatever was going on… yet I couldn't just let my group mate stew in whatever trouble she was in.

It wasn't unusual for Dolly to be in some kind of trouble. The only thing was that she was good at getting herself out of it. The only times she called Beppu was when she was too drunk to function and needed someone to pick her up from Athens or a house party. However, from the way Beppu was acting, this wasn't a pickup call. Something bad had happened, and he wasn't telling me what even after I got into the van and we pulled out of the company garage.

We didn't have to go far. It was a not-so-busy road in one of Nagoya's suburbs. I recognized it only as the area Dolly's boyfriend lived in. I also recognized his car. His car that was completely totaled, the front end smashed against an equally smashed railing. Both doors were opened, with

Dolly and her bright hair sitting on the asphalt and her boyfriend shouting at somebody on his cell phone. Blood poured down his forehead. Likewise, blood poured down Dolly's, dribbling into eyes and making her look like a tragic ghost from one of her dramas.

"Fuck you," she said the moment she saw me. I was out of the van before Beppu, dashing to her side to make sure she wasn't bleeding elsewhere. She tried to push me away, but she was so weak that all she could do was scowl at me and shed some tears.

"What happened?" I looked over my shoulder at Beppu, who ambled up to the scene whilst shaking his large head. "Were you drinking?" I already knew the answer.

Ultimately, it was a miracle that this had never happened before. It was also a miracle that nobody was killed, maimed, or otherwise injured more than a concussion and a cut on the head. That's not why we were there, though. Dolly didn't call Beppu first because she was scared and didn't know what to do. She called us before the police because of her status as a celebrity. If Dolly got caught up not only in a traffic scandal, but one related to alcohol…

Her boyfriend screamed murder at us as we gingerly loaded Dolly into the back of the van. Did we take him with us? Of course not. He had been driving, and it was his car that was totaled. Sorry, guy, it's your ass that was about to be toasted and served to the police. Now, don't think I took any glee in this. Dolly's idiocy should've been punished as well, but the world I lived in dictated that I help Beppu strap her into the back of the van and make sure she got to the hospital in one piece. *Before* the police or the media showed up.

We told the emergency room personnel that she fell down some stairs. They did not question us. It wasn't until years later, when Dolly was caught in another traffic accident and went to rehab after her tearful confession that anybody besides us found out what really happened. Maybe you don't remember that. By the time that scandal happened in her life, she wasn't so famous anymore. She really did turn into Anna Matsuda. A bitter, once-young talent who thought she should have had it all. When she didn't, the world became a hateful place, where only drugs and alcohol could make things better. I don't mean to be harsh. This happens to a lot of girls in the business. Dolly really was (is) talented. She's a triple threat like Yumi – acting, dancing, singing… I couldn't tell you why she never got as far as my friend. Maybe it was because of her race. Maybe she was too brash and honest. Too sexual, and not in a marketable way on her own. Whatever the reason, that was the hand she was dealt. The way she played her cards, however, was her own fault.

It was almost my birthday again when Celestial was called into a meeting. Almost a year since we got the news our old group was dismantled. Three and a half years since I graduated high school and left Seki. Two months since I quit smoking. Five weeks since I last got laid. Two minutes since I last heard Dolly bemoan her terrible fortune.

"I'm so fucking over this," she groaned, tossing her fried hair – partially shaved so doctors could stitch her up – behind her shoulders. Celestial's lackluster sales meant her popularity had fallen. She didn't get as many endorsements or magazine spots as before, and her drama pickings were slim. The last drama season she didn't even get a starring role, whereas Yumi was headlining not only a one-man concert but one of the most anticipated dramas of the upcoming winter season. "Just put us out of our misery."

She got her wish. Celestial was disbanded, and our fates up in the air.

I had no idea what would happen next. My career as I knew it was over. For three and a half years I breathed the label's training, its schedule. I had always been part of a group. Now my group was going away. Nezu declined a new contract and had the old one dissolved in the wake of the group's dismantlement. Within a week, her dorm was cleaned out and she went on to join an independent hip-hop label, where she still is today.

Dolly tried to negotiate a solo career like Yumi's on the label, but her demands were too high and thus rejected. Instead of taking a hint, she stormed out of the office with her things. Next I heard she signed with a competing label and spread herself between the occasional solo single, lots of dramas, and quite a few magazine columns. She has done well for herself since.

That left me. I wanted to stay on the label simply so I could be near Yumi. That and I had no idea what else to do. I had no training in any other vocation, and at that point I didn't think I would be up for going to school. So I was offered a new contract. A low-key solo career with an emphasis on composing for the label. Like Mayu, I was offered to become a full-time staff member, focusing on songwriting above all else. No more dance practices. No more *Music Tonight*. I could release some tracks and even albums on a steady basis, since they knew I was talented. But I wasn't a cash cow. They didn't really care what I did as long as it didn't affect the company's image.

It was the end of an era for me. I grew up and transitioned into a fully realized adult. I was turning twenty-two and finally making my own decisions instead of having the label breathe down my neck to create the perfect product out of me. It was both liberating and downright terrifying. What does a girl thrown into that kind of situation do?

***

I don't think many people are capable of saying, "This is the moment I became an adult." For someone like me, it's easy to look back and see. Of course, when I was that age I already thought I was an adult. I managed my own money, followed through on my promises, drank alcohol and was mostly responsible about it, and had sex like most adults do. As you can see, however, I was still naïve in some aspects. Not naïve to what people wanted from me and what dangers I may have been in, but naïve to simple everyday things like managing my own schedule. When you go straight from the regulations of high school to the regulations of a corporation, what chance do you have to find out about yourself?

Sometimes I wonder what life would have been like if I went on to college and had a "normal" life. After Celestial I lost a considerable amount of celebrity, so it's not hard to imagine walking around at that age, nobody recognizing me or caring about what I did. Yet I will never know what it's like to go to a college class, hang out with friends afterward, go on a date with a classmate, and go job hunting with the best of them. In many ways I am fortunate that I came into my dream career easily, but sometimes I can't help but wonder.

Beppu says I was a good person to have under his care. You see, after Celestial, Beppu was no longer my manager. We still talked regularly, especially when we were both at the label building, but he was no longer watching over me all day… nor was I reporting to him about what was going on and making sure that his other girls had someone to take care of them. He once said that after I left the idol life he realized how invaluable I was. "I panicked a little," he said. "Only for myself. Not for you. I knew you would be okay out there in the world. But you felt like one of my daughters, so I had to worry, at least a bit."

"Why would you worry about me then?" I asked.

"Because you're smart, well-rounded, and grounded in reality… until it comes to that girl. Then you throw all reason out the window and make the dumbest decisions I've ever seen someone make. The one time you ever needed me to protect *you* was when Yumi was involved."

I knew what he was referring to, and yet I couldn't think about it. That story is still a ways off.

Chapter 30

The hardest part about being let go from Celestial was hearing the words, "Please leave the dorms within thirty days."

They told Yumi the same thing. Well, they weren't necessarily kicking her out, but she saw my departure as her big chance to claim some independence as well and buy her own home. Since she was spending a lot of time in Tokyo for work, she rented a small but beautiful place in Shibuya, the trendiest ward. "Whenever you are in Tokyo, you can stay there for free," she told me over lunch at a fashionable café in Shibuya after I came to see it for myself. "I want to get a place in Nagoya too. What do you think?"

My chance to tell her what I had been thinking came up. "Why don't we get a place in Nagoya together? You're not going to be there all the time, so it wouldn't make sense to have your own empty place there."

She tilted her head and gave me a disbelieving smile. "Come on, that's silly. Besides, don't you want your own place? Like, truly your own? Now's the time for the real Chiharu to come out!"

Except the real Chiharu was already out. She was the Chiharu who had lived in a small room with Yumi for three years and didn't want to know any different. I didn't want to admit it, but I was scared to lose her. Out of everything else going on, the thought of being cut off from Yumi hurt me the most. I doubted she thought the same way. She was probably happy to get rid of me for a while. Yumi had her own career and busy schedule to adhere to. Soon enough, meeting like this in a café would become a luxury.

I can't say I didn't try to get her to live with me, however. I was serious. Getting a place in Nagoya with her could appease us both. I would have my own privacy most of the time since she would either be in Tokyo or traveling elsewhere. She spent about one week a month in Nagoya. When she was gone she would have someone to take care of her living space and to keep it warm for when she did come through. It wasn't that I wanted her to help pay the rent. I could pay for my own place easily. I just… wanted to be around her essence. I didn't need her there every day. I'm pathetic.

Depressed and defeated, I called my mother and had her come to Nagoya to help me find an apartment. I had never lived on my own before, never paid rent or negotiated a lease, so I needed my mother's experience anyway. The concept excited her, and before I knew it, we had an agent hauling us around areas of Sakae and Kamimaezu. It overwhelmed me, because I didn't really care about where I lived. They would ask, "What about the ambiance? Do you see yourself living here? How about this dishwasher? It's nice, eh? Not everyone gets a dishwasher!"

The only things I cared about were a Western feeling and enough space for a grand piano. This limited the places even with a generous budget, which was good for me so I could not be so overwhelmed. My mother found this boring.

You may wonder why I wanted a Western apartment. Did I have something against the way I grew up? No, but I am such a lazy housekeeper. It's easier for me to take care of hardwood floors as opposed to tatami, and a big, Western kitchen is more freeing than cramped Japanese ones. I needed a work space that had an open feeling and good acoustics. I can't think of any Japanese-style apartment that can do that for me. You should have seen me when shopping for a home. By that point I knew what I wanted, and the real estate agent had the damnedest time trying to please me. I can't help it. I'm high maintenance!

In the end I chose an apartment in Chikusa Ward. The view of the zoo and the big park were stellar, and it was an easy commute to Sakae in case I needed to visit the executives. Yet I was also far enough away that I didn't feel like they were looking over my shoulder.

The apartment was high, on the twelfth floor of a residential building that catered to finicky people like me. There was a world class gym so I could continue my rigid regimen from my idol days. The security was good enough that Yumi could visit me without the paps getting past the gate. The apartment was open and brightly lit thanks to a south-facing window, and had enough space to put the piano of my dreams as soon as I could afford it.

I became very serious about this piano. I knew how much it cost, and even knew where to get one in Japan. However, it was very expensive. I won't tell you how much I paid for it eventually, but I will say... it's a Steinway. If you know about pianos, you are probably laughing at the thought of affording one. If you don't know anything, let's just say that I could have bought into a small franchise with the money instead. (I wouldn't say that's a better investment though. Steinways are excellent investments as long as you take proper care of them. Which I do. Religiously.)

Yumi happened to be in town when I moved into my apartment. She insisted on helping me move in, although I didn't need the help. I hadn't accumulated many things in my three years in the dorm. Mostly clothes, jewelry, makeup and a few small items from my travels. No furniture, and certainly no housewares. So after we quickly wheeled in my suitcases and took a look at the emptiness, Yumi insisted on taking me shopping for furniture and things like dishes.

My original plan was to gradually buy things as I could afford them. Don't get me wrong. I was making great money thanks to my royalty checks, but I wanted that piano like a dog wants a bone. This meant keeping careful track of my spending and only getting what I really wanted. I bought a lovely bedroom set to start off with, and it was moved in the first day. I didn't care about living room furniture yet, since I could easily relax in my bedroom. As for dishes, that's why we have 100 *yen* shops. I'm not above shopping at those places. I could spend 2000 *yen* and have a full dining set that would last me for years.

This wasn't good enough for Yumi. When I told her this plan, she scrunched her nose and said, "We're going to the department store." I protested, saying that I was saving money. What do you think she replied with? My best friend insisted on buying some things for me. She said it would be an early birthday present. Knowing how much some things cost, I was horrified. Especially when we arrived at the department store and she went straight to the designer stuff.

I wouldn't let her buy me frivolous things I would never use or really appreciate. So we settled on a five-piece dining set that was to my tastes, some sturdy and easy to clean cookware so I could feed myself, and basic living room and guest room furniture.

Any attempts to be polite and go cheaper were met with consternation. "Don't insult me by having me buy crap you won't even like or use," she said when I refused to pick a better couch. "I *want* to spend this money on you. We're fashionable young women and should live like it!"

She was the fashionable one. I had seen her Nagoya and Tokyo apartments and wanted to salivate over the pristine interior designs. The Nagoya one was dark, with black walls but bright, sophisticated decorations that brought a bit of fun. The Tokyo one was brightly lit like mine, showcasing minimalist designs. In the end, my apartment became a fusion of the two. Bright walls and floors, but dark furniture. I've picked up an affinity for leather over the years, whether it's fake or not.

We couldn't get same-day delivery, so we sat in my empty apartment watching the sun go down through my big, wide windows. I was already getting used to the view of the sun setting over the southern Nagoya suburbs. No high-rises in my distance, but not too far away was the ocean and an expansive world that called to me whenever I felt constrained in my own home. Airplanes often flew by, but instead of finding them a blight on my view, I often came up with stories about where they were going and what kind of people were on them. Do you know my song "Traveler?" That song was written while I imagined such things.

I thought Yumi would leave in the evening, but she remained long past dinner and eventually wandered into my bedroom, the only place to sit on something soft – my bed.

"Come here," she called, motioning to me as I remained standing on the other side of my door. "I've got something to give you."

What the hell was I supposed to make of that?

I went to her, of course, closing the bedroom door behind me. The room was dark since I only had one lamp that first night, and neither of us turned it on since the moonlight was bright enough to light the way. I sat next to Yumi on my bed, wary of my feelings but also willing to give myself over for a while.

She pulled something out of her pocket. A string. A red string.

"Remember when we first came to Nagoya?" She tied the string to my finger, letting the rest of it fall across her lap as she stroked it between her fingertips. "I said that this string would always keep us together."

"Yeah, and I told you that it was weird to use a red string."

As if to defy me, Yumi tied the other end around her finger. There it was again. The red string of fate binding us together. "Even though things have changed, I still feel that way. You're my best friend in the whole world, Chi-*chan*. We'll be apart more often now, but that won't change. If you get lonely, just think of me, and I'll probably be thinking of you too."

But I was always thinking of her. I loved her, the girl of my dreams, the love of my life, my destined soul mate. Having anyone but her in my thoughts seemed ludicrous. Wasn't I always in her thoughts too? "Okay."

Yumi pulled her bare feet up onto my brand new bed, the string still holding us together. "I love you," she said, head resting on my shoulder.

You would think that hearing such a phrase would elate me. I knew she meant it in the platonic sense. We were close enough over the years that it was natural to say that we loved each other when emotions were high. Sometimes I translated it as romantic love so I could feel stronger for a night. In the morning, however, I was always back to my senses. Without Yumi's real love.

"I love you too." I meant it in the romantic sense

We slept together that night. The first night in my new bed, in my new apartment, and I was with Yumi, her forehead touching mine as she kissed me gently, my body willing me to embrace her and make love in a way I had yet to experience. So please congratulate me on my extreme reserve... especially when Yumi began kissing the rest of me, from my cheek to my throat, her hand pressing against my side and breast.

I let her kiss me until she brought it to an end, head resting against my chest and our hands intertwined. The red string of fate remained tight around our fingers. My beautiful Yumi, what would have happened if I kissed you back that night? Would we have pulled the string apart in lust, or real love?

***

I think I'm done, even though the day is still relatively young.

My phone is buzzing with a text message from my mother. I answer it, expecting bad news or a question I'll have to answer soon. "*Is the little one allergic to shellfish? I forget!*" "*Is she afraid of clowns? Oh no, she's crying now!*" "*Doesn't she watch Doraemon? How come she doesn't know this character?*" My mother loves to pester me with these questions. She'll then follow up with how much the little one is like me. "*Not only does she make the same unsatisfied face as Chiharu, but when she doesn't get her way she starts pouting silently until I can't stand it anymore. This is my granddaughter, all right. She knows how to sway me like you did.*"

This message isn't a question. It's just a picture of the child standing in front of a viewpoint eating cotton candy. Wherever they went today it's sunny and a cool enough temperature to not upset the girl, who is sensitive to the heat.

I stare at the picture before forwarding it to someone else. When I hit send, my laptop lights up with a video call from my mother.

Greeting me is the little one, the shoddy internet at this place making her jerk and blur from moving too fast. My mother appears, holding back the child. Their movements may be slow on the camera, but their voices are loud and clear.

"There's Chi-Chi!" My mother points to me. I haven't seen her smile this much since the last time she came to visit in Nagoya and took the little one out for a day to spoil her. "Have you missed her, Sattchan?"

My daughter – some days it still feels weird to say that – waves at me again while nodding. Her hair shakes in front of the camera until the image completely freezes on her baby teeth. "Chi-Chi!" she calls, holding something blurry in front of the camera. "We went to the beach."

"I see." I try to put a smile on my face for her sake.

"Where's Mama?"

"She's not here right now."

There isn't much to note from this conversation. I barely retain any of it. I'm too focused on watching my mother and daughter try to vainly get their internet to work while telling me about their day so far. It's not until the little one puts her hand on the camera and says, "Why can't I touch you?" that I finally have to hold back the tears.

Not long after they hang up I find myself in bed, curled up and wishing I was back home with my family. I regret doing all of this, just for a second, because right now I want nothing more than to hear my mother's voice in the kitchen, to feel my daughter climb all over me for a nap, and to hear Yumi come through the front door of my house unannounced, complaining to anyone who will listen about some shitfuck at the label making her life difficult.

I pick up my phone again and text her. *"You should call my mother."*

"Why?" I receive. *"Something wrong?"*

It takes me a few seconds to punch in the next few words. *"Because your daughter misses you."* Wherever Yumi is right now, I'm sure she's about to reach through the phone and strangle me for the reminder.

Part 9

I AM NOT A VICTIM

Hildred Billings

僕は犠牲者ではない

Why did I turn on the TV this morning? Why did I log on to the internet? You would think I know by now. Nothing good comes of doing such things when your name is being smeared across the media.

Thankfully, there are some other things going on in the world today to take the spotlight off Yumi and me. Then every news anchor and morning show host finds a way to shoehorn us in, especially after last night's updates. My blog posts have become a phenomenon. So many people visited my blog last night that it crashed the server and people thought I had been hacked or deleted by the host. No, just really popular. I did get a nasty email from the host, however, asking me to join a paid program to give me more server space or something. Fine. If that's what it takes to keep the word out!

A part of my seclusion has been blocking people from the label from contacting me. Probably not a good move for my career (what has been?) but I don't want to deal with their anger right now. I'm sure when I turn it back on I'll have five million messages saying my contract has been dissolved and that I'm welcome to go fuck myself off a cliff for what I've done. Ha, now you see why I'm not dealing with it!

Right now on TV there's a woman interviewing Dolly. I wonder if she was already slated to appear on this show or if she was a last minute addition after what I wrote last night.

"How do you feel about Morita-*san* writing these things about you? Are they true?"

Dolly – who has a new nose and new tits – squares her shoulders, her toasty, crunchy hair falling in coarse ringlets over her ears and past her shoulders. "How do I feel? I'm pretty pissed, naturally. Here I was, enjoying what I've got going on in my life, and suddenly Miss Chiharu comes out of nowhere airing dirty laundry from years ago! Would've been nice if she would at least have warned me I would wake up one day with a camera in my face and some pesky reporter asking if I'm really such a bitch."

I laugh. This is classic Dolly.

"Are they true stories?"

"I know you want me to say they're not, but honestly, she's not too far off. I mean, I already talked about my accidents and some shady shit that goes on in the business, though not quite in those details. That was a long time ago. I've been sober for over three years now. I can't comment on the other things she's said."

"Did you know she was a homosexual?"

Dolly looks like she can't believe she's being asked this question. "Duh? Everyone knew. Knows. There are a few queers in the industry. It's not a big deal. Really, it's people like you making it a big deal. Why don't we focus on the fact she's airing my dirty laundry, and not the fact she gets boners for her best friend? Who cares?"

I'm really laughing now. You may not understand, but that's Dolly's way of saying she more or less accepts what's going on. This is one of those times I'm okay with her making everything about herself. Less attention on me, or Yumi. Probably half her intention, half that's just how she is. Who needs real allies when you've got someone like Dolly to amuse the press? I think she's got a drama coming out soon too. What great timing for some personal promotion. You're welcome, Dolly!

EDIT: Shit, I just tried to post this and I'm getting a bunch of errors. Is everything all right on your end? I wonder if the extra server bandwidth or whatever it is has come through yet. My blog has been in and out all day. I just changed my password too (I've been changing it every day to be on the safe side) so I wonder if that has something to do with it.

I hope this clears up soon. I looked at the blog host's main page and I am apparently the most popular blog in Japan. Gee, I guess there's no denying there's an audience now. Where should I pick up the story next?

Chapter 31

Bear with me, I'm skipping ahead about two years.

A lot happened during those two years now that I think about it, but nothing special enough to describe in great detail. Instead, let me break down the small events in several points.

Within a few months of moving into my own apartment, I was nominated for a song of the year award for "In the Wind," a song I wrote for Boytasm. What a bittersweet feeling. Of course I was excited to be recognized like that, but of all the songs! While I did not win, I was offered so many contracts both within the label and from other enterprises that I was able to easily afford the Steinway. Not only did this make me extremely happy, but it now meant I could work at home instead of commuting to Sakae to find a piano to play.

I got my driver's license. So did Yumi. We actually took the class together when she scheduled some time off to do so. In the end, we both bought our first cars. Yumi bought a sporty one she rarely drove, and I bought a good but practical one I still drive today. I prefer public transportation, but I can't exactly take it anymore. And I'm not famous enough to have a company car and chauffer like Yumi does.

Not long after getting my piano, I released my first solo CD featuring two songs I wrote and sang myself. "Everything" was a song I had been holding on to for a while. Even though I buried the meaning in lyrics that seem to say something else, it's a song about my feelings for Yumi, plain and simple. It debuted in the Top 30 and quickly fell off the charts a couple of weeks later. The label didn't care. They made their money with me through my compositions for others. The solo releases were more to entertain my few remaining fans and to amuse myself with. It hardly cost them anything since I did most of the production myself.

When I had enough solo releases, I went on a tour through Japan. Small, intimate venues where I got to meet a lot of my fans for the first time ever. In the beginning I was nervous, because I had never headlined my own concerts like that, but once I started playing and singing I pretended that people weren't even there. My mother came to a few and said she cried seeing me on a stage performing for people who came just to see me. On the last night in Tokyo, Yumi made a surprise appearance to sing a song we were working on together.

Yumi's first solo album was not only #1, but one of the bestselling albums for a solo female artist that year. Not long after that Yumi became the label's #1 source of revenue, and everything she did received a large budget and lots of promotions. By the time her second album came out, she was so popular that other labels planned their releases around hers, giving their headlining acts a large berth under the assumption that Yumi would dominate for a week or four. That second album was the bestselling album by a solo artist, male or female, that year. She went on tour and changed the style of her name to YUMI. I went to two of her shows, which were quite theatric and spectacular. In exchange for what she did for me, I appeared in the final show of the tour to perform a song with her.

Yumi entered this strange space where she was both heavily controlled and where she had enough clout to make her own decisions. Before, I wrote some songs for her, but the label rejected most and sent them to other artists. With the second album, however, Yumi started taking more control over which songs she worked with. This meant choosing mostly my songs. Every so often a lead single would be carefully selected for her by the label, but all other songs became hers to command. She once put out a four-song single that was 75% my compositions.

I always enjoyed working with Yumi, and not just because she was my best friend. As an artist, she was easy to get along with. All the composers said as much. We would lock ourselves up in the studio, just us and a piano, coming up with melodies and lyrics to go with them. This was how we wrote songs like "Something With You" and "Hot Panic." Yumi was becoming a talented lyricist, so I was rarely offended when she wanted to take one of my songs and change the lyrics that I wrote. Usually hers were better.

These songwriting sessions were sometimes the only moments we had together, depending on how busy she was. There were times I didn't see her for two or three months aside from short video calls or on TV. These were usually during her tours or overseas activities. Otherwise she would get Wednesday and Thursday off every week in Nagoya, and on Wednesdays we would hang out at my apartment, watching dramas, cooking dinner together, and gossiping about people at the label and in the industry. Every week she would ask me, "Do you have a girlfriend yet?"

Our love lives were not discussed much, which may sound strange for a pair of best friends who shared everything else. We were vaguely aware of each other's lovers, but they weren't serious, and we didn't understand each other's predilections in the bedroom. Every week Yumi was paired up with a new guy in the tabloids, and she would comment on whether or not it was true or just a poorly timed photo. She slept around some, but she was also so busy that once she mentioned she hadn't had sex in over a month. That was a long time for her.

I suppose I should mention that I saw some women here and there, but for the most part I was single. This bothered Yumi, who wanted me paired up with someone. I don't know why it bothered her. Well, not back then I didn't.

Thanks to my earnings, my mother was able to retire from her job in Seki. She still lived there, but I sent her money every month to pay her bills. Eventually I was able to pay the mortgage on her house, which took a lot of weight off her shoulders.

My songwriting took me to the point that I had other labels asking for my work. This created a bit of a riff at the office. I had worded my contract carefully enough that I was able to write certain songs for others. For example, a game company approached me about doing a soundtrack, something I had never done before. The label had to let me because my contract with them said nothing about soundtracks.

I think that's about it. Two years is a long time, but I quickly fell into a routine that gave me a rather mundane life, all things considered. It wasn't until after those two years that things began to undulate in the earth again.

I'm pretty sure it was February. I had just turned twenty-four and was in Tokyo for work. Specifically, I was meeting with executives at the Tokyo office and then having some radio interviews to promote my latest concept album. (The one I wrote when I was really drunk.) It was the end of my trip and I was in Yumi's Tokyo apartment, alone. She was in Osaka, I believe, although I can't remember for what. It doesn't matter. All that matters is that I had been spending a few nights in her apartment, cleaning it up in return for my stay there. Not hard to do when she barely lived there herself.

It was the last night of my stay. Since it was cold and I didn't want to crank the heat, I piled some blankets from a closet on top of me and buried my face in Yumi's pillow. That's right, I was sleeping in her bed and not in the guest room. She knew I did it, we didn't think it was weird, and what else is there to say? Are you really surprised?

So I was sleeping in her bed. Or at least nodding off to sleep with about four blankets on top of me. Just before dreams could take me elsewhere, however, a hand touched my shoulder.

I couldn't tell you what I thought in that moment. In my groggy state I probably thought it was Yumi. Then I realized that the hand was large, strong, and quickly going for my breasts while a big, hairy nose dug into my neck. Once I realized what was happening, I jerked up, my elbow going into a hard stomach and my voice echoing in the room. I was being attacked!

"Holy shit!" A man fell to the floor, and I panted like a scared dog, covers wrapped around me as I scrambled to turn on the nearest light. Once the light hit his face, I recognized Yohei, and he recognized me. "The fuck! It's you!"

"What the *hell*." I wasn't sure if it was better or worse that Yohei was the perp. "The fuck you think you're doing?"

"Excuse *me*." He planted his hands on the bed and stood up, brushing himself off. What a scruffy looking asshole. Boytasm was still together, but Yohei was enjoying a successful solo career as well. I had nothing to do with the duet he and Yumi did that sold so well. As if. What the hell has she ever seen in him? "Thought you were someone else. Don't know why I would ever think that!"

"You just come into Yumi's place and feel her up whenever you feel like it?"

"I have a key, bitch."

Ah, yes, as you can see, Yohei and I had a wonderful, mutually respecting relationship. He called me a bitch to my face and I told him his dick was made of dog sausage. (An insult to dogs, I know.) We hated each other for what we had with Yumi. I was jealous this scuzzy piece of shit was sleeping with her off and on, and he was jealous that sometimes she would ditch him to come hang out with me. We were both possessive freaks like that. At least I kept my activities, I dunno, legal?

"I've got a key too. Don't you know she's in Osaka anyway?"

"Sure thought so, but then I come in here to crash and here's some woman sleeping in her bed. The fuck am I supposed to think?"

"I'm staying here. Go find somewhere else to sleep."

"Why the hell are you in her bed, anyway?"

I turned off the light and pulled the covers over my head. "I was here first, asshole."

Grumbling, Yohei trudged out, used the bathroom (and left his piss everywhere, thanks) and then slammed the door to the guest bedroom. I did not sleep well that night, even after getting up and locking the master bedroom door. I was afraid that he would still be around in the morning, but thankfully I woke up late and he was long gone.

Halfway home to Nagoya on the bullet train I got a call from Yumi. "There's a meeting I need you to be at Monday," she said, clicking a pen in the background. "It's all good news, but I want you to be surprised!"

Sighing, I leaned against the train window and watched the countryside breeze by. It was an overcast day, and I could see patches of sunlight here and there... but not enough to cheer me up any. "Sounds good. I'll be there." If I was really supposed to go, I would get a text or call from my manager soon enough.

"What's wrong?"

I sat back up in my seat. "Last night I was sleeping in your room and Yohei came in and tried to have sex with me. He thought I was you."

At first I wasn't sure she heard me. Maybe she didn't believe me. Just as I held my phone away from ear to see if I still had a signal, Yumi said, "*Ehh?* Did he really? I'm so sorry!"

"You didn't tell me that other people had keys to your apartment."

"He almost never comes over there. Oh God, Chiharu, I'm sorry!"

"He peed all over your toilet. I cleaned it up for you. You're welcome."

I'm sure she could hear the condescension in my voice. "I'll talk to him." About what? About sneaking into rooms? About feeling me up? I shuddered. I could still feel that man's hands on my breast, squeezing it until he realized it was too big to be Yumi's.

Sure enough my manager called me later that day, telling me to go to the office Monday morning for an important meeting. My manager at the time was a woman we called Uma because she had a long face like a horse. I didn't see her that much. Only when I was touring or doing heavier promotions than usual. I was low enough in the artist ranking that I was just one of a few artists Uma managed. Not like Beppu who managed full groups at a time.

Yumi was already in the meeting room Monday morning when I arrived. She nursed a coffee and gave me a small smile as if it were an apology for what happened with Yohei. "Got any for me?" I asked, pointing to her coffee as I sat down next to her. I didn't have to ask again. Uma waltzed into the room with coffee for both me and her. Koji followed.

A few executives walked in as well, all of whom I recognized. Mr. Kawaguchi was one of them. As the only two original members of Butterfly Tops still performing under the label, we were somewhat of a curiosity to him. As a pair, that is. Individually we were as different as night and day in terms of interest. For him to show up... it was either interesting or important.

The only person there I didn't recognize was a man sitting at the other end of the table. He came in later, slumping in a chair he twirled around in while everyone else sat up straight in preparation for the meeting. At one point this man, who looked to be about forty with dark stubble and a stained cotton shirt, dozed off and fell farther into his seat. Appalled, I looked to Yumi, who shrugged her shoulders as if to say, "What can we do?"

It didn't take long to get down to business, even if one person was checked out. Mr. Kawaguchi stood at the front of the table and said, "We are here to discuss the cover album project of YUMI."

Yumi had mentioned once or twice that she might be doing a cover album. Not surprising, since she was at the peak of her career and covers were really trendy at the time. Combining the two was a guaranteed smash hit. Yumi glanced at me with a knowing smile, her hand grazing my elbow between our chairs. No, it was too early for feelings of longing.

"Yes," said another executive, his voice joining Mr. Kawaguchi's as they went into detail about the forecasts of cover albums, especially when sang by young female artists. The idea was narrowed to love ballads both past and present. Yumi was slated to record heartfelt covers of such classics like "I Love You" and "First Love." They also wanted her to do an original song that would be released as a single ahead of time. I figured that's where I came in. My ballads were my most successful compositions. Why did I need a meeting for this? Usually they would just send me a letter or Uma would tell me herself.

"Turning them into emotional piano ballads is how YUMI will stand out from the others," a man said, gesturing to me. "That's why we want you to collaborate on this project."

"For the single?" I asked.

"For the whole album."

Well, there it was. Yours truly would be playing piano on every song of Yumi's cover album. They were going for broke. Peak of her career, a cover album of love ballads, a piano with her best friend... the public would gobble it up like New Year's dinner. I would also get a nice boost in sales and I didn't doubt that a small tour would be on the docket. The way Yumi looked at me again, I figured she already knew all of this. Perhaps it was her who came up with the concept.

"That's not all," Mr. Kawaguchi continued. "Mr. Asada is here to help us with this project. His expertise will surely wow the audiences."

The grungy man at the other end of the table perked up at the name. Asada? *The* Asada? The reclusive producer who once created many famous tracks for idols and songwriters alike? I took a long, hard look at the man scratching his stubble and running his hands through greasy hair. Nobody knew much about Asada because he didn't make public appearances, preferring to work his so-called magic in studios.

"As the first time I will be working with Mr. Asada, may I say that I am humbled." Yumi bowed in her seat. "I look forward to the three of us working together." She gestured toward me, who hurried to bow as well.

Asada scratched his arm before interlocking his fingers behind his head. "Couple of kids from the sticks, eh?" he said, referring to our much publicized background. "Yeah, this'll be interesting." He looked at Yumi as if she were a project – he looked at me as if he didn't know *what* to make of me. The feeling was mutual. Now I wish I had gotten up and clocked him in the head as I should have done those few years ago.

***

I'm about to get the most bizarre phone call of my day. It's from Yumi, and I can tell just from the sound of her voice that she was up half the night over thinking everything.

"Did I make you gay?" she asks, before I've even had my lunch.

I look out the window, as if I could find the proper answer floating by in the river or shaking in the trees. "It doesn't work that way," I tell her.

"Yeah, yeah, I know. But think about it. You realized you were gay because I kissed you that first time, right?"

"It helped me realize it, but I was already gay. I would've figured it out eventually, with or without you."

"So me kissing you didn't make you gay?"

I clear my throat. "No. Why are you asking me this?" Yumi is usually more intelligent than this about these matters. For her to have such cloudy thinking... something must be bothering her. "Were you up half the night thinking about kissing me?" I tease her.

"I don't understand. I don't understand what makes people gay. Especially women. How can it happen?"

It's a conversation we've had multiple times over the years. We're to the point I have my speech memorized, and I give it to her now, also reminding her that a woman can like both men and other women if they are inclined that way. I'm not, which I think confuses her sometimes.

"Sure, I get that. Except what made someone gay to begin with? Were they made that way in their mother's womb?"

"Yeah." That's what I believe, anyway.

I know what she's thinking. At this point, I just know. She's wondering if the little one could have been made a certain way without either one of us realizing it. Yumi must be fretting that she's attached to this child that could possibly be gay as well. Something she doesn't understand. "So your mother made you a lesbian."

What a fantastic line out of context! "I sincerely doubt she went out of her way to do so. It's not something done on purpose." Already I'm weary of this conversation. I know she doesn't mean any harm, but it gets frustrating trying to explain this to anyone, let alone her.

"You know I don't care about you being gay, right?"

"Of course."

"I'm just trying to understand how that came about. That's all."

Even though she is being serious, I can't help myself. She's opened herself up to this comment. "If it's possible to make someone gay, then I really suck at it, because I tried on you for years."

She laughs, embarrassed.

Chapter 32

The creation of this cover album went beyond anything Yumi and I have ever done before. Not only was my schedule cleared to make it – good thing I had just handed in a soundtrack – but hers as well. Mostly because Asada had another project in a couple of months and needed to get this cover album from hell *done immediately*.

Even though I self-produce some of my own solo works, I am used to working with producers. It helps that the one Yumi was sleeping with left the company a while ago, so I never have to feel uncomfortable around him. Most of the producers that are left from when I first started are Beppu-approved, and he, like me, is an excellent judge of character. There are even some female producers now, although they mostly work with lower-tier artists.

So I was used to producers, but my relationship with them was pretty casual. We would go into the studio, I would talk about what I wanted to do and create, and together we would find a balance between my artistic vision and the mechanics of it. Sometimes they would have great suggestions I never thought of, and sometimes I thought they were full of shit and ignored them. They respected me as a songwriter and a self-producer, but they also were easy to get along with for Yumi and most of the other artists I knew at the label. So in my mind, working with Asada should have been simple. He was there to add his signature sound to make it more marketable to the public, but for the most part it would be Yumi and me doing our usual thing.

I was so wrong.

"These songs? These songs are shit!" When Asada looked over our list of proposed songs for the cover album, he laughed and crumpled it up. "Do you want to be a laughing stock? We can't do obscure B-sides from 1985. You wanna do a Miho Nakayama song? We do 'You're My Only Shining Star' because that's the only ballad she has worth a shit to the public. But that one has been done three times this year by other artists. Even the glorious and oh-so talented YUMI cannot get the public to care about that song yet again. Here. Look at these songs. Pick at least three of those so I have *something* to work with."

He handed us a clear-file full of music notes and scrawled sheets of music. "I like 'Swallowtail Butterfly,'" Yumi says tentatively. "Not sure how good I am at singing it though."

"Doesn't matter. You fuck it up, and I fix it."

I ignored his assumptions, looking through the sheets for a song that fit both Yumi's and my styles. The idea of a cover album full of ballads is that it must appeal to today's youth and the aunties and uncles stuck in the past. This meant looking for smash hit songs from the previous millennium and well-known songs from the past few years. Not much room in between.

The next challenge was finding songs within Yumi's range. And songs that I could embellish on the piano. Of course "I'm Proud" was on the short list, but Asada said that song was no longer remembered and much too simple to make cool again. Yumi was crestfallen, but I jumped in with, "Then we find a way to make it interesting. If we have to, we put it on as the B-side to the forthcoming single. Look, it's her favorite song. People know she sang it at our audition years ago. The fans will eat it up."

Asada rolled his eyes but finally relented. I couldn't get comfortable. It was the first of many arguments we would have during the creation of this album.

I don't like bossy and pushy men. Men who throw their weight around, even if they are talented and smart. Do you really have to puff yourself up in front of a woman like that? I never see them do this in front of other guys. Only me and other women in the business. It's pathetic.

So of course Asada was one of the bossiest, pushiest producers I ever had the "pleasure" of working with. When we came up with a new shortlist of songs, he vetoed half of them again. Slowly I realized that the songs he was kicking off the list weren't necessarily forgotten by the public, or too hard for Yumi to sing. They were just songs he didn't like! Look, I never got the hype around Mika Nakashima's "Snow Flower," but if Yumi says we're doing it, I go along with it and try to make it as interesting as possible for me. Why couldn't he do the same? You should have seen our argument over Akina Nakamori's "Shipwreck." He said it was too depressing, too close to the original singer's suicide attempt which still left a bad taste in people's mouths, and then went on to whine that getting the rights would be too difficult. Too difficult? Did he miss the part where we were in talks to get the rights to perform songs by singers who hated having their songs covered? I just don't think he liked the song!

If I still sound burned up over something that happened a few years ago, it's because I am. Thinking about Asada and the bullshit he pulled in and out of the studio infuriates me to this day. The guy was a grade-A ass. When we finally, *finally* started recording some songs, can you imagine what happened?

"What is this shit you're playing?" He interrupted me while I tried to record the instrumental to a song. Through the window to the control room I saw him, still greasy, flailing his arms around as if I had offended his ears. "Could you maybe, I don't know, take this seriously for a minute?"

Grumbling, I tried to play the intro again. Sure enough, his cracking voice came in over the speaker.

"You fucking piano players think you're such hot shit. Who the fuck are you? Beethoven? Do it over!"

I tried venting to Yumi, but she kept saying, "Some people in this business are like that. You just have to learn to work with them, even if it means sacrificing a few things." The only person I could go to was Beppu, who was recently busy managing the label's new up and coming girl group in pleated skirts. They looked like babies to me. I could only imagine how babyish they looked to him.

He had me meet him in a bar down the street from the label. Nothing like Athens. This place wasn't for celebrities, and it showed in its dive bar chic – except it wasn't chic, it really was a dive – and cheap beer. It was a haunt for the staff members at the label. Managers, producers, even personal assistants and secretaries. I guess I did kind of fit in there, even if I was still a talent on the label. I was a songwriter and sometimes producer, after all.

"Yeah, I can hear you two yelling down the hall while the new girls are recording their tracks," Beppu said over the rim of his beer bottle. "First time it happened one of the girls asked me what was going on. Told them it was the recording equivalent of a marital spat." He almost choked while he laughed. "Did you win the argument?"

"Which one?" I asked, exasperated. "The man isn't a perfectionist. He's a sadist."

"He's one of the best in the business. He produced five #1 singles last year. Even more in the top five. That's gonna create some egos."

"Fuck his ego."

Beppu could tell that I wasn't enjoying the banter. As he watched me down another beer, he rubbed his mouth and leaned against the bar. Around us were numerous colleagues. Hell, any manager who didn't have to work that night was there, including Uma, who sat with some friends in the far corner. Here, we ignored each other, and it was fine with me. I never considered her a friend, although I never disliked her and she does her job well.

"Eh, Chiharu..." His voice was low, serious. I sat up to attention. "I've heard lots of things about that guy. He's the type of man who makes the rounds in the management circles."

"Oh?" I wasn't sure I wanted to hear this.

"Let's put it this way. I would be wary having him work with one of my current girls. Wary about him being with *you* girls back then. The guy's got a reputation as a playboy. And he likes them, shall we say, young."

Playboy? Who the fuck was sleeping with Asada? He was brash, aggressive, and ugly to boot. I don't think he bathed. Unless he counted bathing in a vat of chicken gizzards.

"Don't make that look. You don't get it. He's a powerful man in the industry. Girls, especially impressionable ones, look at him and see someone who can change their lives. Not just professionally, but romantically. He knows this and takes advantage of that. Feel lucky that you and Yumi are in your mid-20s now. Too old for his general tastes."

I couldn't take it anymore. So he was just another sick fuck who coerced girls into sleeping with him in return for favors. My mind flashed to that night I saw Yumi and our old producer, the look of sheer boredom on her face as she went through the motions and expected no pleasure, no affection in return. Was Asada worse than that guy? The old producer seemed like the type to creep, but behind the scenes. Asada was reckless.

"Stick it out for this album project or whatever, and you'll probably hardly see him again. Just don't make a huge scene with him. I hate to say it, but he does carry a lot of clout in the industry right now. There's a reason they hired him for this project. Don't shoot yourself in the foot over your own ego."

If only I had known that it wasn't my ego in the greatest danger.

***

Love, Yumi

The worst thing about being trapped out here for now is that I have no creative outlet. Not for music, anyway. No piano to vent my frustrations on, let alone write some songs about what I'm feeling. I'm the type of person who can hear it in my head if I must, but it's nowhere near as satisfying as hearing the notes explode from the piano and echo in my home.

I've got this program on my computer that sort of simulates it, but it's not the same. I just spent ten minutes trying to make it work for me. There's a melody bounding around in my head that I can't let go of. With my state of mind as it is right now, this probably means I'm burning to write a song about this whole ordeal. I don't know. I usually write the lyrics last, if I write them at all. Hence my frustrations.

Don't feel like writing again yet, so I'm watching TV. People are reporting on my blog going down and being the most popular in all of Japan. Yumi's albums are taking up the top three spots digitally, and some of mine are creeping into the Top 10. Last night while we talked for an hour, Yumi implied that her album had been put indefinitely on hold. "Not shelved entirely," she said. "They're making too much money on this to not start it up again once the frenzy dies down. Right now they're punishing us for hurting their image."

That's easy for her to say. She's still a superstar. Everyone remembers when Noriko Sakai made a fool of herself in the industry. Nobody wanted to work with her anymore. Yet she still managed to have somewhat of a career, and she broke the law! Or how about Ami Suzuki? Blacklisted at the top of her career. She never fully recovered, but she seems to be enjoying some career today. Yumi can do the same when this is over. What is her biggest crime in the industry? Being my friend? I know guilty by association is a huge thing, but I'm the one taking the brunt of this. It's what we agreed.

As it is, I've lost my current outside-label contracts and jobs. I haven't really talked about it, but I've been dropped or had my contract voided from all of them. I'm still a part of the label, as far as I know. I doubt I'll be releasing music through them anytime soon.

It's kind of depressing, isn't it? What am I living for right now? To tell this story? I'm not home. I don't have my family. I don't have any outlets except this computer. The whole world is watching me, but I can't do anything.

Yumi, if you're reading this, hear my plea. I wanna get out of here, but I need somewhere to go and someone to be with. Let's hide together. If I'm dying of loneliness, then you must be about to explode. I don't care if they find us. After this next part of my tale, I'm going to need somebody. I need you.

Chapter 33

All told, it took about five weeks to produce the cover album. It took another week to compose the new original track to release as a single ahead of time. Usually Yumi and I would come up with something together, but Asada insisted on "helping" by sitting in on our sessions and telling us everything we did sucked. He refused to associate his name with anything not up to his standards.

The twelve track album covered an assortment of ballads from the 1960s to just two years before. The lead track (aside from the pre-released single) was Mieko Hirota's "Dollhouse," which surprised a lot of people. It's such an old song, but still very powerful today, especially coming from a strong and single woman like Yumi. I sang backing vocals in the chorus, which was something Asada didn't like at first. He was outvoted by everyone else who heard the track with my vocals in it. I'm proud to say the public agreed with him, as it was the bestselling track off the album.

The other leading track that we filmed a video for was a proper duet. Seiko Matsuda's "Hold Me" happened by accident in the studio. It was one of the contending songs suggested by Asada, and while we made a demo of it Yumi said she had issues with deciding what key to sing it in. I laid down some vocals as guidance, and the label decided it was now a duet. Isn't it funny? A song like that being sang by two women? Of course it was marketed as two women pining for their separate lovers, but even back then Yumi and I joked that it sounded like we were in love. (I was.)

The biggest surprise for me was the label giving us double-billing. Of course Yumi was the star of the album, and she sang the only vocals on many tracks, but the album was credited to Yumi Nishikawa and Chiharu Morita. Not even YUMI appeared. I think they were trying to give it a different image than usual. But because of how famous she was at the time, the album sold well anyway. So well that we hit #1, and that is the first and only time I've had a #1 album credited to me in any way.

Because of Asada's involvement and the scope of the project, we took a different approach to the promotions. Yes, we did appear on *Music Tonight* (my first time in three years) and did the usual photoshoots, but there was something different… that something was Asada.

We were his foray into being a public persona. Everyone knew his name, but now they would know his face. I admit, he could clean up well once a stylist got a hold of him. When he appeared in some magazine photos with us and took to TV talk shows, he was articulate and well-groomed. Where was this guy when we were recording?

And why couldn't we shake him?

I mean, it made sense that he would be at radio shows and TV sets we were all scheduled to attend. Except then he was also at the after parties. He showed up to radio shows that were just for Yumi and me, looking through the window as if he were still producing our album. You would have thought he was our manager from the way he hung in hallways and never took his eyes off us. Since Yumi and I had almost identical schedules for a few weeks, we were not only always together, but I was temporarily assigned to Koji to manage as well. While I find Koji to be harmless if not full of himself, it was nothing like Asada. Even when Koji asked him to back off for a couple of days, there he was, chewing on sunflower seeds and sipping black coffee as he watched us answer questions and sing ditties for show hosts.

The last straw for me was when Yumi didn't even notice.

"What is that guy doing?" I asked one night, when we were finally in the privacy of her Tokyo apartment. "Feels like we can't breathe without him saying we're doing it wrong."

"What are you talking about?" Yumi was getting ready for a shower, half her clothes off as she wandered around her bedroom deciding on a robe.

I leaned in her doorway. "You haven't noticed? He wasn't scheduled to be at that interview today, and yet he showed up anyway."

"He didn't barge into it."

"No, he just hung around like a total creep." Why? Why was he so interested in us? This went beyond promoting his own image.

"*Mou*, Chi-*chan*, you're too distrusting." She didn't finish her statement. *Of men.*

I didn't think this was a natural mistrust of men. Something about Asada creeped me out and I couldn't say what exactly. There were many excuses for his actions. Even when I brought up my concerns with Beppu over the phone, he told me I was probably moody. "Show him more of that constipation. That'll send him running."

They laughed, they joked, and they made excuses, but I knew something was off. I was proven right when I returned to Yumi's apartment one night after a day in Tokyo with my mother and found Asada sitting on the couch, his star singer cooking him dinner in the kitchen. I did not hide my disdain that he would be staying for supper.

"Didn't know you two lived together," he said, getting grease all over the leather couch. "How... quaint."

I didn't like what he was implying. "We don't live together," I said. "I just stay here when in town."

"Still quaint."

That night I got further proof of something I long suspected. Asada avoided talking to me whenever he could, instead focusing his conversation on Yumi. She served him dinner with a laugh. The same laugh she gave everyone she entertained, but I didn't like how it encouraged him to start flirting with her. He complimented her cooking, her hair, and her pretty, pretty smile. He never complimented me. Not that I wanted him to, but the disparity was so obvious I felt like a mother watching her kid dig the biggest hole ever and claim, "Oh, I had nothing to do with it!"

He finally left late, one hand clasped on Yumi's as they went to her door and shared a joke I couldn't hear. I thought I did hear, however, a reference to them working together again in the future. You should have seen the red on my face as I sat at the table and flung daggers from my eyes at that asshole.

"Yumi," I said that night, sitting on the couch. "Are you sleeping with Asada?"

She was both offended and yet not surprised at all. "No." She smacked my knee. "It's not like that. It's purely business."

"You have said that before." She knew what I referred to.

Her eyes narrowed at me. "Those days are behind me. I don't have to do those things anymore." *Because I'm famous and they're scared to touch me unless I say they can.* "I'm not screwing him. Last dude I did it with was Yohei like two weeks ago."

Too much information. "Just be careful, okay. I've heard some things about that guy."

"You need to stop being so distrustful of people. I know you and he had some rows, but he'll be out of your hair soon. I need to think about my career. If he continues to make hit songs, then I may need to work with him again soon. The more he likes me, the better."

Poor Yumi! Didn't she get that's what I was afraid of? I clasped my hand on her thigh, looking into her eyes as I said, "He creeps me out. Please, be careful."

"Yes, big sis."

She joked, but I was dead serious. I didn't like the way he looked at her. Smacking his lips at her beauty, her fame, her fortune, and what they could do for one another. She may not have been a teenager anymore, but

Yumi was still young, lithe, and very sexual both on stage and off. She couldn't help it. It was natural for her, even if her concept was supposed to be more mature and innocent at the same time. Even when we were in full suits for the pictures of the cover album, people commented that Yumi was sexy and beautiful, and it wasn't like the poses were more provocative than leaning wistfully against a piano. So she wasn't a young and helpless girl, but it was no wonder why someone like Asada would set his sights on her. This wasn't just about their careers and how they could prop each other up. I didn't care about that, even if I didn't like how he worked. This was about sex and control. If he was like that in the studio, then what was he like in... *ugh*, the bedroom!

"Come on," she said, getting up and pulling on my arm. "You need to go to bed. Your head is all *muri* with bad thoughts. Get some sleep."

I thought I was being sent to my chambers in the guest bedroom, where I usually slept when she was also home. Yet she led me to her room, where I slept when she wasn't there. (And when I wanted Yohei to feel my breasts.) I didn't question it. It frustrated me how easily she fell asleep against my side, while I was left to stare into the darkness and wonder what threat I would have to brush away next.

Try as I might to believe what everyone said about Asada being a temporary annoyance, I eventually discovered I was right all along. One month after promotions for the cover album ended, we were at one of those executive and staff people parties. Something about building good feelings. This wasn't like the creepy, predatory parties we went to after music video and album wraps. These were the usual business parties everyone has to go to, from the talents to the managers to the execs. They're usually a bit noisy for me. Not to mention the smoke.

I sat between Yumi and Beppu, my two favorite people at these things. At least Yumi was my friend (who liked to keep my drink filled for me) and Beppu was hilarious when he was half-intoxicated. His latest gripe was about one of the young teen girls he managed. Apparently she hadn't started her period yet – a real late bloomer, I guess – and she woke up recently covered in the crimes of the masked murderer. The story would've ended there, except Beppu was the one who had to take care of her and explain to her what was going on. Oh, and go fetch the usual girly things for her, only this time instead of just buying them and saying, "Here you go. Don't complain that I got the wrong ones if you were too shy to specify," he had to tell her how to use them because nobody else had before.

"It's wrong, I tell you!" He flung his empty bottle into the air as our half of the table listened with rapt and amused attention. "Why is it I have to tell other people's daughter's about puberty when I couldn't damn well tell you when mine went through it? I need a proper vacation. I think my youngest daughter is in high school now. I have no idea!"

Although I'm not big on these types of parties, I put up with them now because they're only once in a while and I get free food and booze. However, that night I didn't get to relax and idly wait for time to go by until it was appropriate to go home. Because halfway through the evening? You-know-who showed up and stuffed himself between Yumi and another woman.

When I grumbled about this to Beppu, he said, "Haven't you heard? They're in talks to do a series of singles and even a whole album together. He's taken a real… shining to her."

I looked over Yumi's head and flinched at the sight of sweat on Asada's forehead. He was leaning in toward Yumi, his voice low as he lit a cigarette for her and whispered something into her ear. She choked on laughter and patted him on the arm. Buddy buddy. How charming.

"They ain't… are they?"

I glared at Beppu. "She says they're not, so I believe her. But…"

"Yeah. *But.*"

For the rest of the party I had to watch as those two canoodled like bosom buddies. I knew that Yumi was just being her usual sweet and flirtatious self, but Asada didn't know that. He probably thought, based on how he kept finding excuses to touch her arm and leg, that she was genuinely interested in him. Or he didn't care if she was or not. Those kind of men don't take a woman's wants too seriously.

I kept my eye on them but also kept my distance. Yet my trust in Yumi could only go so far when she told me she was leaving and, wouldn't you know it, Asada was escorting her out of the party, his hand on her lower back. Flashbacks to that party from before swarmed my brain, and I couldn't let that happen again.

Please don't get me wrong. Indeed, I was jealous of any guy Yumi was with, but I also respected her sex life in that she could go have it with whomever she wanted. It was best for the both of us that way.

That's the thing. I didn't care (in theory) who she had sex with willingly. I hated Yohei, but I never told Yumi to stop fucking him, or any of the other guys I knew about. Those men were her choice. Someone like Asada? Even if Yumi entertained the notion – and she had made it clear she didn't think of him that way – I highly doubted she would go through with it. Flirt with to beguile him into better business deals, sure... but actually have casual sex with him? No way. I knew that. She knew that. Did *he* know that?

Did he care?

I waited a minute before excusing myself as well. Beppu gave me a look but didn't say anything. I bowed to everyone else at the table and made my way out, my feet hurrying to catch up to the two supposed lovebirds.

They were walking toward Yumi's apartment there in Sakae. I stayed back. My only intent was to make sure he didn't go in there with her – alone. I would barge in. I swore it. Then the moment I got him to leave I would tell her my fears. If Asada was supposedly forcing teen girls into such situations, what would stop him with a grown woman? Clearly he did not have morals one way or the other when it came to such things.

Yumi is a strong girl. She's an even stronger woman now. She's to a point where she can tell men no and mean it. But it took her a long time to reach that point. Back then, she was still saying meek yeses even when I could tell she didn't want to. With men in power over her – producers included – gray areas emerged. So when they reached her building and she hung outside to keep him from going in, I stayed behind a bush to make sure he didn't try anything.

Sure enough, the bastard tried to kiss her. Yumi yanked her arms out of his hands and turned away, flustered enough to say, "Asada-*san,* I don't think it's right."

He put a hand on her shoulder. She shrugged it off. His voice rose in an effort to woo her over, as if it worked that way in his world. (Maybe it did.) I was ready to intervene when he finally put his hands up and backed away. Yumi bowed slightly, said goodnight, and hurried into her apartment building. I hoped for her sake that there were no paps around that night.

After making sure she was inside okay, I then followed Asada down the street, just to see where he was going. I didn't mean to follow him all the way to his hotel, partly because I didn't know it was so close. When he reached it, I thought about going to Yumi's to make sure she was okay. Then that man started a loud phone conversation with some unknown person.

"She's such a fucking bitch," he grumbled on a cigarette. "Yeah, man, women like her are total sluts, up for anything until you make your move. Then suddenly they've got a clamp on their cunts. Why do you think I like them young? Easier to get them open that way."

I almost vomited.

"It's not a big thing. I'll get her eventually. There ain't a woman in this business I haven't worked with and fucked at least from behind. God, except that mean looking friend of hers. You saw her on those promo tours. Everyone knows she's a dyke but doesn't say anything... nah, but that would be pretty hot if they did do that for me!"

Bile in my throat.

"Listen, I'm gonna do some tracks with her in the coming weeks. *Without* the chaperone. I'll pluck her pretty pussy then. I'll make her beg for more. That's my favorite part."

I choked behind my lamppost.

"I've gotta go. Call up one of my girls, I guess. Been raging downstairs all night thanks to that whore almost grabbing my cock under the table all night. I'll write a sexy song just for her. By the time she's done recording it, she'll be begging for it in the mouth. I have it on good authority she gives great head."

Vomit. *Vomit.*

"So what if she says no? Never stopped me before."

Something snapped inside me. Did I hear him right? Did he imply everything I feared was true? That he would hurt Yumi, and not just debase her if she had a lapse in judgment? Oh God, I couldn't let that happen.

Since becoming a parent I fully understand the need to protect someone you love at whatever the cost. Back then, I felt it with Yumi, but I did not understand it. All I knew was that my best friend was in danger. The more she was around this guy, the more likely he would try to take her against her will. Perhaps he was all bluster with his friend. Could I take that chance?

I don't know why. I don't know how I found the strength... but I stepped out from behind that lamppost and approached Asada the moment he put his phone away.

"Well, well," he said with a yellow-toothed grin. "Look who it is. The chaperone. How much did you hear, stalker?"

I was equal parts frightened and emboldened. He was a man who could hurt me, but really, he should've been afraid of *me* hurting *him*. "Stay away from her." I tried to keep my voice steady, menacing, like I was the tough shit I believed myself to be. Yet it warbled, and I knew instantly that he could smell my fear. He probably smelled it on countless girls.

"Now why would I do that? She and I have something special going on." He puffed on his cigarette before blowing smoke into my face.

I turned away, eyes burning. "I'll do anything."

"Ah." That smile almost admired me. "You're one of those. Altruistic and selfless to a fault. What is with you and this girl? You love her or something?" He didn't let me answer. "Ha! How about that. Well, you have very good tastes. She's quite the pinch of woman."

"I mean it. Stay away from her."

"Or what? I'm not afraid of you."

"What do you want? Money?" I doubt I had enough to appease him. Didn't have to guess that he made much more than I did in royalties. "I'm serious. Tell me what it will take to keep you away from her. Forever."

I expected him to laugh me away. What could I give him that he didn't already have? That was worth more than Yumi? He smoked his cigarette thoughtfully, looking me up and down in the dark night. I wasn't wearing anything special that day. Jeans, a plain blouse, and a cardigan to keep out the chill. I was hardly dressed like the fashionable idol I used to be. This was my style now, and it worked for me, but I was hardly conventionally attractive. I quickly learned that such things did not matter to men like Asada.

"You know what you could give me."

I stepped back, the blood draining from my face and into my gut. My brain knew what he meant. The rest of me? It denied it. In fact, my body was so disgusted that it wanted to run away, to leave my poor friend and the woman I loved to the wolf that was Asada. *"Take her! She's yours! Just stay away from me!"*

"Why?" The word was a mere whisper on my lips. Suddenly the air was cold, and I clapped my arms over my chest.

"Why, she asks." Asada extinguished his cigarette. "Come on. You're a smart gal. A gal who understands what people see in other women. I don't think I've ever had a dyke before."

Typing those words makes me want to retch now.

"You think I'm not serious? Oh, this is fun." He brushed his hand against my shoulder, and I shook him off like a pile of ants. "The ones who want it least are the most fun for me."

I could have cried just from the suggestion. This man... what he was suggesting... with *me!* But I am Chiharu Morita. If there is anything in this world I will do, it is something to protect Yumi. A woman who had been through worse hell than me – for my sake – already. "If I do this thing," I said, my throat dry and my cheeks frozen in shock, "then you won't go near her ever again. You won't talk to her. You won't ever work with her

- 340 -

again. If she or the label approaches you to work together, you will make up an excuse. Say you hate her for all I care. Just stay away from her. If I do this and you don't do that, then I will... I will..."

"You'll what, sweetie?"

"I'll fucking kill you."

By the look on his face, I could tell he was serious. Perhaps that threat alone would be enough to deter him from showing his face again. Yet he saw my bluff in that moment. He had already made up his mind about what he wanted... and it wasn't the thrill of the beautiful and super famous Yumi. It was the thrill of breaking Chiharu instead.

To this day I remind myself that I am strong. I am not a victim. Did I want to do it? God, no. Did I want him to yank me by my wrist and take me up to his hotel room? No! Did I want to take off my clothes and do whatever disgusting and degrading things he told me to do to myself and to him? No. No I didn't. I never wanted any of that in my life. When it happened... while I saw the satisfaction in his eyes while he was on top of me that first time – while he broke and demeaned poor little Chiharu – I remained resolute that it was not something I would ever regret. I am not a victim. *I am not a victim.*

I went into it willingly. I never cried once that night. Even though it hurt, both in my heart and my body, no tears came. I thought of Yumi and how much I loved her. If I had managed to spare her this pain or worse, it was worth it. I hold fast to that truth today.

***

I'm going out for a walk, people recognizing me be damned. I need to clear my head before the bad memories paralyze me. When I get back, I hope I can continue.

Chapter 34

This may sound strange to many other females out there, but I never thought much about my *seiri*. It was an inconvenience in my life, sure, but besides some dull aches and related hygiene attention, I never paid much attention to it. It was there. It was a part of me. I was one of the youngest girls in our class to get hers, so even though I'm not so old it feels like another lifetime ago when I never had this sort of thing at all.

So to be a few days late was rarely a cause for concern. It would come when it came, and hopefully I wouldn't be trying to do something fun. Then I finally did have cause for concern when it was four days past due, and all I could do was stare at my calendar, trying to make sure the math added up. Being late was not unusual. When the label had us on toxic diets, I skipped two in a row.

I know that I am not the only woman to have this fear wrack her body. If you do not want to be pregnant, then every day late is like another day closer to giving birth. Especially if you might be pregnant with the child of some man you only gave it to because you had to.

Yumi was coming over that night, and I tried to distract myself until then by doing work or cleaning up my apartment. We were going to watch the latest episode of her drama, and she was bringing the ingredients to cook dinner. I should have been excited... until I woke up that morning still concerned for the state of my body.

"Get through today," I kept telling myself. "Tomorrow I'll go to the doctor and get a test. Then I will decide what to do." I didn't want to think about the options. I knew which one I would choose, but not only was that scary, the interim was too frightening as well.

I had left the door unlocked, so when Yumi burst in early, I nearly had a fright. She held up two plastic grocery bags and dashed into my kitchen, her voice pealing in the air. "I got stuff for curry!"

My pants were frozen to my piano bench. "Why are you so cheerful?"

Yumi dumped a pile of carrots and green onions onto my countertop. "Why shouldn't I be happy to be with my Chi-*chan*?"

She shed her fuzzy black coat and draped it over a barstool. My jaw dropped. I had never seen Yumi so thin, and this was the girl who did so well on that crazy diet and dropped two sizes when she was already skinny. When I had asked for a distraction earlier that day, this was not it!

"Yumi, you're..."

After perking her head up from one of the grocery bags, she glanced down at her body and said, "I was on a juice cleanse for a few days so I would look good for today's photo shoot," she explained, referencing her cover shoot for a high profile magazine. "This is gonna be the first meal, so we better get cooking! I want a food baby!"

Did she really have to say that?

At least it gave me something to focus on. Going into the kitchen and cooking dinner with Yumi was one of the few real pleasures I had in life. So what if it was tainted that night... so what if I couldn't match Yumi's enthusiasm as she hurried to start the rice cooker and start chopping vegetables as if she hadn't eaten in days. (Never mind that she hadn't, apparently.)

She talked up a storm, and I let her, choosing to focus my energies on cooking dinner. Yumi chatted about her parents, her manager, her latest single (which was not produced by Asada, thank God) and even Yohei. I nodded along. Even when dinner was ready and we took our plates to the table, she continued to chat, stuffing her face with curry while I tried not to think about my uterus.

Fretting wouldn't change my fate. If I was pregnant, than I was pregnant and would have to go from there. If I wasn't, fretting would only make my period later. Of course what petrified me wasn't taking care of a pregnancy, per se, but having a piece of that man inside of me still. The event was still fresh enough in my mind that I could clearly remember the sensations of him inside of me, and… well, I don't want to talk about it.

We sat down to watch her drama after the dishes were done. Yumi pulled her legs onto my couch and pointed to her stomach, rounder after eating most of the food. "*Yokatta*," she said, patting her stomach like a drum. "This is the fullest I've felt in *days*." As if she knows how to really fuck with me, she talks to her stomach. "How are you, my food baby? Long time to see!"

The drama came on. I don't remember which one it was, but I do remember Yumi talking through the first half, chatting about what the set was like, what she thought when kissing the lead male on camera, and how good the food was even though she didn't get to eat it most of the time. I was only half listening. A commercial came on advertising life insurance, showing a new father concerned that something could happen and his son would have nothing.

If I were pregnant, was it a boy or a girl? Did those things have sexes yet that early? I bit my lower lip and tried to think of anything else. Soccer. Game shows. Cars.

"What's wrong?" Yumi asked. "You okay? You've been quiet all night."

I kept my eyes on the TV so I wouldn't think back to that terrible night. "I'm fine."

My voice betrayed me. Thick, rough, and shaking. The last time I sounded like this was when I was on the verge of coming down with the flu. Instantly I know that I have failed in subverting my friend's inquiries.

"You sure?" Yumi leaned near me, and I slumped more into my seat. "You really don't sound fine. Or look it. You look upset. Did I do something?"

"No," I quickly said.

She kept her words in her throat for a while. "Is it your mother?"

Of all the words to use. My legs shook; my fingers dug into my arms. "It's nothing."

"Chiharu."

I could feel the tears burning behind my eyes. My elbow propped up on the arm of the sofa, my hand covering my face. I debated telling her. It felt like if I said it out loud, it suddenly came true. That I was pregnant and the cosmos wanted me to have that man's baby. And at any rate, how could I explain such a thing to Yumi? I never told her about what happened with Asada, and for good reason!

She was my friend, and the one person in the world I trusted the most. Back in high school, who would I tell? Yumi. Even now, though she was styled from head to toe and was skinnier than a lanky kid, I could still feel the concern coming from her eyes and the way her fingers brushed against my arm. "I'm late," I finally uttered. Tears broke free.

"Late? Late for what?" Yumi sat up. "Am I keeping you from something? If you need to leave, go ahead. Don't let me keep you!"

"No, no... I mean... I'm *late*."

It took a while for my meaning to sink in. Not because she didn't know what it meant, but because it's such an impossibility with someone like me. The Chiharu she knew did not sleep with men for any reason. Why would she be pregnant? "You mean your..."

"Yeah."

Yumi snatched the remote and turned off the TV just as her character appeared on screen again. "You're pregnant?"

I didn't want to answer, but I had to. "I don't know. I hope not."

"How could it happen?"

The look I gave her said she shouldn't play so dumb. "You know how it happened."

"I know *that,* but it's just so…" Yumi shook out her head, tossing whatever words in there around. When she spoke again, it was with a gentle hand on my shoulder and a kindness I never heard before in her throat. "How many times?"

"What?"

"I mean how many times did you do it? I'm sorry, I'm trying to figure the odds."

I didn't look at her. "Just one night." In all honesty, I had no idea if a man could become infertile the more he went consecutively. I don't want to say why I wondered that. "You know, once is enough."

"Did you use protection?"

My muscles flinched. "No." I struggled to keep my voice from trembling. Growing up, I made such a big deal about safe sex. It wasn't taught in school, so I had to learn about it through my mother, who made me promise that if I had sex with a boy that we would use a condom, no matter what he wanted. She didn't want me turning out like her. Who knew that when I was finally with a man, it would be so… "He didn't want to." It was the truth. I had to get myself tested just to make sure I wasn't infected with something. I didn't think to get a pregnancy test.

At least she did not berate me for that. "Who was it?"

No way was I going that far. "You don't know him," I lied.

My whole body shook, as if I was overcome with cold. Yumi curled up beside me, and for the briefest moment I felt serene next to her warmth and the scent of her expensive perfume. "What can I do?"

She didn't pry any further than that. For the next hour we sat on the couch in silence, Yumi leaning against my shoulder until gradually curling up in my lap. It was a sensation that should have pleased me, but all I could feel was apprehension. "I don't want to be pregnant," I muttered beneath my breath. "I can't."

"It's not a death sentence," she whispered back. "I know a doctor."

What did that mean? That she knew a gyno who could help me have a healthy pregnancy? A doctor who could give me an abortion? A doctor she had experience with in these matters? I wanted to believe that if Yumi had ever been pregnant, she would tell me. I can't imagine her keeping something like that to herself. Even if she went to a clinic alone, she would have told me, right? "I don't want to think about it."

I asked her to stay the night with me. She mentioned an appointment in the morning, but eventually relented and agreed to sleep with me. I went into my bathroom to get ready for bed, my door open just enough to see her dress down to her T-shirt and underwear. Even after I told her she could borrow some of my clothes, she still crawled into my bed dressed like that. For a second I was able to forget my worries.

Five minutes later, I erupted from the bathroom, my body falling against my bed as Yumi jerked up and looked at me as if I had lost my mind.

"*Yokatta!*" I said, grabbing her arms. "I'm not pregnant!" Finally, the most obnoxious part about being a woman came!

Her eyes remained wide until she gradually came back to reality. Tired, soft and relieved, Yumi's look told me that everything would be okay again. "*Omedetou*," she congratulated me. "It's a uterine lining."

I slept soundly that night, Yumi nestled against my chest, her hand on my stomach. I was too happy to sleep. Asada tried to break me, but he couldn't. Not only was Yumi safe, but she was with me. For the first time in my life, I kissed her without prompting, a mixture of celebration and love pouring from my lips. She entertained me for a few seconds before pulling away and patting my cheek. That's that. I wasn't pregnant. Now I could focus my energies and worries on more important things. Like how thin Yumi was in my arms.

***

"I'm so sorry you went through that, Chiharu-san. It's difficult being a woman, isn't it?"

"*Please don't get too sad to continue. Don't listen to the haters. Even if your company gives you grief, please find a way to continue the story. I want to know if it has a happy ending!*"

"*I don't know why people are so surprised about Asada. Don't you know where he is now? Ever since he was charged with molesting a teen girl in the USA he's been hiding out in some country that won't extradite him. This is just another nail in the coffin trying to bury him. I'm not surprised at all. In fact, you're a brave woman Ms. Morita. I hope more people can come forward so the international police will do something about him.*"

"*People in the media call you obsessive, but I think you're a good friend. You did what so many people would do to protect their loved ones.*"

"*Our bodies are the only real weapons we have as women. Is it our fault they work so well on men? We've been using them for thousands of years to survive.*"

"*I was raped by a coworker a few years ago. I know you say you're not a victim, but please be strong. Thank you for sharing your story.*"

"*This is my first time commenting, but I've read your story up until now. It's fascinating. I mean that in a nice way. It feels like I'm reading a fictional tale, but I can see all of these things really happening thanks to what I know from the news over the years. I admit I don't really listen to your and YUMI's music much, but I appreciate you both a lot more as people.*"

"*I've been a fan of YUMI's ever since her first album. To think that these sorts of things were happening… what is wrong with the industry?*"

"*A few years ago I went to YUMI's Budokan concert. I hope she can perform there again one day so I can support her. You too, Chiharu-san.*"

"*When I think about my best friend growing up, I realize that I would do a lot of these same things if I had to. Isn't it hard to watch someone you care about and know so deeply go that way? This makes me want to call my friend for the first time in a long time. We grew apart over the years, and that bothers me. We don't even live too far away from each other. I wonder if she's reading this too.*"

"*Please pardon my Japanese. I am not so good. I am from Canada and want to say I have been reading and support you.*"

"*As a man this is uncomfortable to read. But it's good to feel uncomfortable. I knew a guy like that Asada brute. Although I like many of the songs and artists he produced, I feel sick listening to them now. I knew about his past transgressions, but this... I guess reading a personal account, even if it may be biased, makes it hit home a lot harder. I hope those other artists weren't touched..."*

"If he is finally sent to trial, I hope you will testify against his character."

"Maybe now people will understand why this blog is so important. You're not just talking about your homosexual love. You're talking about other issues that affect so many people, especially women. I hope that people who don't understand the former can at least understand the latter."

"Thanks for your story. I just wanted to say that."

"Ms. Morita, I am a lesbian too, and in the beginning I read your story because I rarely hear a woman coming out in this world. Then I had to keep reading because it's a tale I can't look away from, especially now that everyone is talking about it. Please know that in many lesbian communities you have everyone's full support. What you're doing is something only most of us can dream of being able to do."

"You don't know me, as we have never met, but please know that you and your story matter. If you ever feel like giving up, know that you are helping so many people."

Thank you for everyone's encouraging words. They mean the world to me.

Hildred Billings

Part 10

ONE NIGHT: A TALE OF JEALOUSY AND DESIRE

一宵: 情熱とジェラシーの物語

I'm sorry for my absence these past few days. Things have changed once again.

The night I last posted an entry, I got a call from Yumi. She was with Koji, driving out to find me and take me away from my hiding spot. "We're leaving the country," she said, without letting me decide for myself!

So now I'm not even in Japan. Obviously I won't say where I am so local media can't find us, but it's warm and our room is on a calm and peaceful beach. It was two days of traveling and then one day of settling in. I'm still a bit jet lagged, and the warm weather and gentle rolling sea waves are not helping me stay awake.

Yumi told me to take a break from writing anyway. When she first saw me back in Japan, I nearly started crying on her shoulder, out of both relief and the terrible memories I dredged up. All she said was, "I had no idea." It was true. I had never told Yumi about what happened with Asada. Reading my blog was the first time she heard of it. I think she might be angry at me for hiding it from her.

We are sharing a room together. Just her and me… and all the people on her phone. Even though she spends half her day "working," I am still happy to have her by my side. I don't feel so lonely anymore. If I have Yumi, I can get through anything.

Your comments have meant everything. I don't let the bad ones get to me anymore. Yes, it's true that Asada is currently hiding somewhere so he won't have to answer for his crimes elsewhere. You have no idea how much relief I felt when he left Japan a year ago, though. In our industry, you never know when you'll run into those people again. I didn't trust myself to not punch him if we were ever in the same room again.

People rise and fall so quickly in this business. I hope Yumi won't be one of them. She was past her peak already when this started, but now I constantly fear that I've doomed her chances at a steady if not superstar career for the rest of her days. Then we got online this morning to see that our cover album was #1 on the digital charts. On one hand we were happy, and on the other it made us think of Asada, and I couldn't bring myself to write. We still haven't talked about it. I'm sleeping or she's working.

"What are you going to write about today?" she asked earlier, while I brought my laptop out onto the sunny balcony.

I settled into a lounge chair and balanced my laptop on my legs. "That one night."

She didn't have to ask which one I meant. At this point in my tale, there can only be one night I mean. Although first I must start a while before that to give you the proper context.

Chapter 35

It was late summer, a few weeks after I celebrated my *seiri* for the first time in my life. Because of what happened, I became needier for proper companionship. A woman's touch. I never found it too difficult to pick up a lover here or there, but for the first time in my life I was dating someone somewhat seriously.

I'll call her Naomi. She worked for the label, but through the Tokyo branch so we only saw each other when we were in either city for business. It started off pretty casual, but when my need for companionship burst I found myself calling her more often. We were friends as well as lovers. Don't ask me which happened first. Not only was she easy to get along with and talk to about everyday things, but she was also a tender but adventurous lover. When this story picks up, we had known each other for most of the year, but heading toward exclusive for about two months. Granted, we never discussed it. It was just sort of happening. I never anticipated finding someone I could see myself calling my girlfriend.

She often stayed with me when she was in Nagoya for work. Sometimes just to see me. That's when I knew things were starting to get more serious – when she was taking the bullet train down on the weekends to spend time with me before going back to Tokyo for work. I made the effort in turn, and soon enough Yumi started saying she missed me staying with her when I was in town.

Reaching that level of comfort with someone means it's not unusual to become physically closer to them. When Naomi came to stay with me while she was in Nagoya for meetings, we often sat on my couch watching TV. And not watching TV, even though it was on in the background. Ahem.

We weren't doing anything more scandalous than cuddling on my couch, Naomi's long brown hair draped across my shoulder and lap as we watched one of her favorite dramas on TV. It was a relaxing night, the kind I needed after the stress earlier that year. Naturally, I had a lot of hopes that we would soon take the night to the bedroom.

Just like I had a key to Yumi's apartments, she had a key to mine. Before I could start singing along to a jingle in a commercial, my door flew open, Yumi waltzing in with cake.

"*Ara!*" She sounded like a scandalized auntie when she stopped and stared at the scene before her. Like I said, it was just cuddling, but by the look on her face she caught us mid-coitus like that one time in the dorms. Naomi sat up, startled, her face like that of a deer's as it's about to meet an unfortunate end at the other end of a moving vehicle. Yumi ripped off her sunglasses and cleared her throat. I could only roll my eyes. "I'm sorry," she said steadily. "Hi."

"Hello." Naomi kept her head low and looked to me for help.

"What are you doing here?" I got up, wrapping my sweater around my body as if it were the middle of winter. "Were we supposed to be doing something?" Wouldn't be the first time I forgot we had plans.

Her smile was forced, the kind of fake smile she puts on for the camera when she's in a bad mood. "No, I was going to surprise you. I see I accomplished that."

"Indeed." I tried not to show any annoyance.

"Sorry for interrupting." Yumi waved at Naomi again and left a bag on my counter. "There are some strawberries… I'm sorry. I'll knock or call next time if we don't have plans."

She scuttled out of my apartment. The moment the door closed, Naomi let out a sigh of relief. Was I missing something?

A few days later, I met up with Yumi in one of our favorite cafés. Located at the top of a high-end department store, it was one of the only places we could hang out in public during the day and not be inundated with paps and nosy fans. Sure, some other celebrities hung out there too, but that day Yumi was by far the most famous one. We sat in a corner by the window overlooking the central Nagoya park by the TV tower.

"All right," she said, flipping open a notebook and pulling out a piece of copy paper. "I wanna know about this girl you're seeing." No hellos. No how are yous. The moment I sat down I had a piece of paper in front of me asking some of the most invasive questions Yumi has ever had the balls to ask.

"What's this?" I flipped the paper over when a server came by with my coffee. Once she left, I looked at the paper again. The very first question was "WHAT IS HER NAME???" I almost laughed in disbelief. "Why?"

Yumi wasn't laughing. Her arms were crossed and back planted firmly against her seat. She just returned from the salon and had perfectly plucked eyebrows and hair gelled until it couldn't move anymore. Meanwhile, I sat there with shaggy hair and a pair of jeans I was pretty sure had tea stains on them. The longer we lived, the further apart we drifted when it came to such matters.

"You've never had a girlfriend before. Not like that. So I wanna know about her."

She wasn't teasing. Nor was she joking. Yumi wasn't going to let me leave that café until I started answering her questions.

"Naomi," I said. "You probably see her around the offices." I mentioned which staff department she worked in, but Yumi merely shook her head. Unless it was someone directly involved in her career, she never remembered anyone.

"How long have you two been going out?"

I shrugged. "About two, three months."

"And you never mentioned her until now?"

"It's not serious."

Scoffing, Yumi plopped her purse in her lap so she could rummage through it. She pulled out a pad and paper, as if she were a reporter getting ready to interview me for the local fashion magazine. "She's cozy with you in your living room and it's not serious at all? I've never seen you do that with one of your, uh, buddies."

I sipped my coffee. "Sure I have. You just never barged in like that before." I didn't tell her that it was a rare occurrence. What? I can be a really private person. If you're relaxing on my couch, it's because I trust you.

"How old is she?"

Another shrug. More coffee. "Twenty-six."

"Older than you!"

"By like two years. It makes no difference at this point." I would be twenty-five soon enough. Hell, Yumi's birthday was about a week away. "What is with all of these questions? I never pester you about your dates."

"This is different." Yumi put her purse back into the basket by our table. "Is she gay? I mean, is she out and not stringing you along?"

"I have no idea." We didn't talk about those things. Most lesbians I knew didn't. Whether we wanted the world to know or not, we couldn't really say anything out of fear of reproach. "She's not married as far as I know. We're moving toward exclusive, I guess."

"You guess? Exclusive?" Why the hell was she writing this down? "You're either girlfriends or not."

"We're not. Not yet. Look, Yohei and those other guys aren't your boyfriend, right? This isn't much different. We're getting used to each other before making any further decisions."

"This is totally different!"

Love, Yumi

I was starting to get annoyed. The fact I had drunk half my coffee by now didn't help with the frustrated jitters. "Why?"

"Because I've never seen you with someone like this before."

She said it loudly enough that I looked around the café. Nobody outright looked at us, but I saw well-dressed businessmen and café employees glance at us through the corners of their eyes. Great. Now they had a story to sell to the tabloids. "Yumi Goes Nuts On Friend!"

I tilted my head as Yumi realized how loud she had been and hunkered down in her seat. "Yumi... I see women a fair amount of time. Not every day or even every week, but often enough that you should know this."

"I know, I know..."

"She's not the first woman I've dated. It's not serious."

Yumi stared at me through new eyes. New in the sense that I had never seen her look at me like that before. It was almost as if she didn't know or recognize me. Like I was a stranger she was on a first date with... like a child who had gone through puberty and now confused its parents. "*Who are you?*"

"If you want to meet her, I can arrange something, I'm sure. Though she may be a bit put off because of how famous you are. She doesn't know you like I do."

"But she works for the label..."

"How many office workers for the label actually meet and hang out with the talents though?" I was a fluke. The only reason I met Naomi was because she was assigned to help me negotiate a contract.

I thought she would ask me anything else than what she actually did ask me. "Do you have sex with her?"

Here's the crazy thing – the way she asked it? It was like she had never considered me a truly sexual being before. Yumi. The girl who sometimes made out with me, who had walked in on me fingering another girl, and who had asked me about lesbian sex before. In great, hilarious detail. I didn't get it. She knew I actually had sex with people, right? What was different now?

"Yes," I said, leaning across the table to make sure she heard my lowered voice. "Naomi and I have sex. A lot." Not really a lot, but I wanted to mess with this new Yumi.

For some reason Yumi didn't want to continue the conversation from there. She took the paper she handed me, stuffed it into her purse, and hailed the server so she could order a mimosa in the early afternoon. I watched her gulp it shortly before I left to run some errands.

What was it? September? It must have been September when Naomi and I were walking through some backstreets in Tokyo, heading to her apartment for an evening after dinner and a movie. Since she was not famous and I wasn't so famous – especially with a hat on at night –we braved holding hands. The talk was minimal, but when we did speak it was about the movie and what parts of it we liked or didn't care for so much. Idle chit-chat, really. Filling the air before we got back to her place and turned in for the night, if you know what I mean.

My phone rang. One of Yumi's songs buzzed in the air. Not just any song, either. A ballad I wrote for her a year ago about being lonely in the wintertime. I pulled my phone out of my pocket and glanced at her name on the caller ID, as if I didn't know it was her.

"*Moshi moshi?*" I greeted, hand still in Naomi's. "What's up?"

I could hear a party going on in the background and the grumblings of Yohei's voice as he implored Yumi to put the phone away and pay attention to him. "Chi-*chan!*" she called, giggling into her phone. "Where are you? You should come party with us!"

"I'm in Tokyo for work," I said, squeezing Naomi, who continued to look forward as we strolled down the street. I didn't say I wasn't in the mood to party, let alone around Yohei who was probably pawing my best friend as we spoke. "And I'm on a date."

"A date? With that girl?"

Girl? Naomi was older than the both of us! "Yeah. Why? Something you need?"

"I got my nails done today," she said. Oh God, she was drunk. Or at least really tipsy. "My stylist couldn't believe it! I had the fake ones taken off and the real ones filed down. You should see them. Doubt I'll be getting any Nail Queen awards soon…"

I held my phone away from my ear and stared at it as if it were infected. "You okay?"

Couldn't tell you what happened, but she hung up on me. Whatever.

"Everything okay?" Naomi asked. My phone went back in my pocket just as we reached her building. "Friend trouble?"

She smiled, wanly, but it didn't feel reassuring. "I have no idea. I think she was drunk."

We went upstairs to her place, where Naomi turned on a single light before I followed her into her bedroom. I took off my jacket, intending on taking off much more within the next half hour… depending on whether or not my sort-of-girlfriend wanted a bath or not. I had been building up the nerve to ask her to do such an intimate thing with me. Until then, I had never bathed with another woman. Not romantically, anyway.

"You and Yumi-*san*…" Naomi stood in front of her mirror, removing her jewelry. "You guys go way back, right?"

"Yeah." I sat on the edge of the bed.

It took a while for Naomi to continue her thoughts. "I never know what to believe when it comes to the label's PR machine. Everyone 'knows' that you two are childhood best friends, but that could mean anything. Like, maybe you happened to go to the same schools and were in the same classes, but not really best friends, right? Or maybe you just went to the same high school and met there because you both did theater or something. Apparently you guys really were best friends since forever, right?"

"Yeah. Since kindergarten."

"*Uso!*"

"Not lying. We've been best friends since then."

"That's crazy. I couldn't even tell you who my best friend in kindergarten was."

"We lived in a small town."

"So did I."

The bed creaked. "She implied that she wanted to properly meet you."

"I see." Naomi opened her closet and hung up her sweater. She was a petite woman with prominent shoulder blades, and without her heels on she easily only came up to my chest. Now wearing nothing but her bra up top she looked a lot younger than she actually was. "Maybe."

"Why not?" Being nervous was one thing, but to flat out refuse? That was silly. Yumi could be intimidating because of her fame, but she was still a kitten when it came to me.

Naomi stood in front of me but did not join me on her bed. I won't say I knew her so well that I could read her body language easily, but I was aware that something was off. Off enough to make me shift again. "You and her got a thing going on?"

It was such a random question to ask. "A thing?" I had no idea what else to do or say. "The hell are you talking about?"

"You know what." Naomi turned around, went back to her closet, and pulled out a sweatshirt to wear. "A *thing*." The sweatshirt went on, covering her half naked frame. "You fucking her?"

Unbelievable! She garnered something like that just from a couple of interactions? And the fact it wasn't even true… "We don't have a 'thing' like that. We're very close, but not like that." Sadly. I won't pretend that I wouldn't dump a girl to be with Yumi. "We've never had sex. She's straight." I shook my head. "Why would you even seriously ask that?"

And why wasn't she coming to join me in bed? Naomi was more standoffish than usual. She was never forward to begin with – she preferred to make me work for everything – but this was her putting up a barricade, not playing a game. "I've heard the rumors."

"What rumors?"

She laughed at my face. "You don't know about them? People say that you two sleep together. In the same bed."

"Who is saying that?" My brain searched its archives and could only come up with Beppu having any idea. No way he would gab about it. That left someone in the group who may have seen or put something together. Damnit. Dolly would totally gab if she had seen.

"Does it matter? It's what people think they know about you two. Of course few think that means you're fucking. I had to wonder. That's why I was surprised when we started dating. I never thought you would actually date someone if you had a girl like Yumi."

"Like I said. It's not like that. We're just friends."

No matter how many times I reiterated this, she didn't seem to believe me. It took another half hour before I finally coaxed Naomi into bed, and only then did we lightly cuddle as we went to sleep. No romantic bath, and definitely no sex. I wondered if this was something stewing inside my would-be-girlfriend or instigated by Yumi's call earlier. Maybe I didn't want to know.

***

"How's it going?"

I look up from my laptop and see the ocean undulating with peaceful waves. It's a private beach, but not too far away is someone walking his dog, picking up driftwood and tossing it into the surf for the dog to happily fetch. It's not until the dog does this twice more that I finally look over my shoulder and see Yumi standing in the sliding glass doorway of our room, her eyes fixated on me. "Fine," I say.

She steps onto the balcony, drinking in the warm sunshine. There's an empty chair next to me, and sure enough she pulls it over and sits down on the edge. Thankfully she does not try to look at my laptop screen. "You wanna talk about it?"

At first I have no idea what she's referring to. "Talk about…" It dawns on me. Not hard when she's got that pitiful look on her fair face. "No. I don't want to talk about it."

We still haven't talked about *it*. What happened between Asada and me a few years ago. All this time I let Yumi go on thinking it was some random guy I slept with for one reason or another. I didn't want her to worry like I always worried. Besides, I wanted to put it behind me. No sense dragging up something I did when it could no longer hurt me.

"I wish you had told me."

God. We have to do this. I sink deeper into my chair, my sunglasses firmly on my face. "Why would I have told you something like that? You never told me that you were doing things with producers until I saw it for myself."

She flinches. Good. Now she knows how it feels. "That was different." I hate that phrase. "It didn't really bother me once I got used to it. Sometimes it was fun, in its own perverted way. Yes, I know they were taking advantage of me, especially when I was younger... but that in no way compares to what you went through."

What I went through. My cross to bear. My burden. My blight in my sexual history. "It's in the past. Let's not drag it up."

Although she's now wearing her sunglasses as well, I can still tell that she's bothered by my deflection. "You kept it from me. You went through something horrible to protect me... it wasn't me willingly walking into a situation to help the both of us. You put yourself in harm's way. For *me.*"

"I had to." That was all I was going to say on the subject. Until...

"Don't pretend it doesn't bother you. You thought you were pregnant with his child! You think I don't notice how it's affected you, even if I am only now realizing it. Sometimes when we..." She stops, something in her throat. "I can tell. Your thoughts aren't with me. I used to think I was boring you, but now I know it's because you're flashing back to that night. Well, don't hold back from me. You know the pains I've been through. Why can't I know yours?"

I chew on the inside of my cheek, staring through my sunglasses at the calming sea and sky. Everything is so bright, so blue in this place. It should be refreshing. Gentle. And yet all I can think of is that dirty night not too long ago.

A shudder rips through me. Yumi puts her hand on my shoulder. No, no, not here... I don't want these memories here. Not in this beautiful place. I don't want the woman I protected to look into my mind and see what I went through. She was never supposed to know. I don't delude myself into thinking that Yumi is some naïve virgin. But she doesn't need to know this. She doesn't need the images that I have in my head. I don't want her to look at me and see...

"Don't be ashamed," she says, stroking my cheek and then my hair. Damn her! Doesn't she know that by preemptively soothing me she's just making it worse? "And don't be scared to tell me whatever you want. I'm here. If you can't tell me, who can you tell?"

She leans forward, pressing her forehead to my shoulder. A shudder goes through me again, and I realize it has nothing to do with my own body. It's her. Yumi is holding back some pain, some trauma she's felt and is dragging up even though it's going to hurt her. God, was she feeling it earlier and that's why she came out here? Am I supposed to comfort her?

I can't. I'm frozen to my chair, shivering even though the warm sun is beating upon me.

Yumi presses her hand against my midriff, forehead still on my shoulder. "We're so fucked up. Can you imagine what we would have thought about all of this when we were kids?"

Kids can mean so many things. Does she mean when we were children? Teenagers? Young idols? "No."

We sit like this for a few more minutes, my chest tightening and my throat going dry. I need a drink. Water, alcohol... it doesn't matter. My throat is parched and I want to die. With her touching me like this, however, I almost feel invincible. Pained, yes, but able to withstand the torrent going on in my brain. Damn her for dragging this up.

I have no choice. I have to tell her now.

Gradually I tell her what happened. I tell her about the way that man dragged me around like his prize, his piece of meat to round out his day. I was nothing to him. I wasn't human, and I definitely wasn't someone worth respecting. The way he used my body was bad enough. I could have handled it. Thought of something else as he used me over and over again, this way, that way, here, there. Who cared if I was sore or if it hurt. That didn't matter.

No, what made it even worse was the fucking shit he said, and I couldn't block that out. He called me a whore. He called Yumi a whore. He said we were nothing more than dogs meant to be whipped and tied until we knew how to properly obey. Which is funny. I obeyed him plenty, like a good bitch. I just wanted it to be over. You read these stories about women who grin and bear so much from men, especially on the other end of their sexual anger. Our bodies are mere vessels. What we must protect are our hearts and spirits. He wanted to break both of mine. He wanted me to think of him every moment of every day. If I were to deny him Yumi, then he would deny me freedom from him.

Yumi's hands clutch my shirt as I tell her what kept me sane through the whole ordeal. "I thought of you," My voice is soft. "That's it. I reminded myself why I was doing it. Why I consented to be with a bastard like him, even though I knew it would hurt and make me feel like filth for far too long. Don't think you owe me. Don't think for a moment you need to run out there and protect me like that. I don't want you knowing what this is like..." My voice trails off, my best friend's face against my chest as she embraces me, her tears melting through the cotton of my shirt.

"Chi-*chan*," she says, and I know she wants me to stroke her hair. I do so, and it's like we're in another world where it's just the two of us, protected by this paradise. "I had no idea. Really, I had no idea!"

"You weren't supposed to have one. I could have gone my whole life without you knowing, but... I couldn't leave it out. We promised I would share everything."

She sits up, wipes the tears from her cheeks and takes my hand. "There's nothing I'll ever be able to do to make it up to you."

I squeeze it back. I briefly think of that night I squeezed Naomi's hand, and it doesn't compare at all to this moment. "I wasn't raped," I say. "If you pay me any honor... don't ever think of me as a victim. As a survivor. Or something like that. I knew I would live. I hated him, and I hated what he made me go through, but never once did I think I was being raped." My lip is trembling. There are tears in my eyes now. I mustn't. I mustn't look weak right now. I mustn't let her see me for what I really am.

"Me too," she says, our fingers turning white as they cling to each other as if we're going to fly away. "I'm not a victim either. Nobody did anything to me against my will."

I force a smile, for her sake. We'll get through this. We'll get through all of the pain, all of the grief, and all of the lies we tell each other. Together.

We have to.

Chapter 36

Unsurprisingly, Naomi broke it off with me a few weeks later. By that point we rarely saw each other anyway. There was always some excuse, and I admit, I saw someone else a couple of times while waiting for her to get back to me. Please don't think I cheated. Our understanding was that we could see other people, but what I was waiting to hear back on was whether or not we wanted to be more serious and exclusive. I guess not.

I took it surprisingly well. After all, it wasn't love. But she was the closest I ever got to a real girlfriend. It hurt a bit at first, but I powered through the disappointment by distracting myself with work. Plentiful, that late autumn. I had a game, a short animated movie, and the usual deadlines for the label. The breakup fueled a few winter love ballads that were sent straight to Boytasm, Yumi, and others. Three out of five of such compositions were chosen right away to be included on upcoming releases.

The days were quick. Whenever there was no work I was exercising, visiting my mother, and taking some time off with Yumi. She was busy too, however. She had just announced her first Budokan concert, which was set to happen right after the new year. While she prepared a new single (using one of my ballads) she practiced for and arranged this glorious concert. Few solo artists, let alone women, get to headline a Budokan event so early in their careers. It was big news all over the media, with tickets selling out in record time.

"It's a lot of pressure," she said over the phone. "I want to give the best performance of my life, but what if I can't?"

"You can't think that way," I said. "Just go out there and be yourself. People love you."

"You'll be there, right?"

"Of course." She had already given me my special box ticket. Like I would miss it!

"I'm sorry I couldn't get you a second ticket. I figured you would want to bring your mother… or your girlfriend."

This was the first time Yumi had referenced Naomi in a long while. In fact it had been so long that she apparently didn't know that we had moved on. "I'm not with her anymore. She broke it off."

Silence, followed by, "I see." Yumi quickly changed topics after that.

We still spent our Wednesdays together whenever we could, although Yumi rarely had a full "weekend" of any kind. The first time she had one was in late November, and we immediately made plans to hang out at my place. I figured on the usual. Make dinner. Watch dramas. After that we usually played it by ear, which meant Yumi either went back to her own place or stayed the night with me. I always hoped for the latter.

She was late that Wednesday night. Just as well, since it let me finish up some work in preparation of a deadline. By the time she finally did show up at seven, my stomach was empty and I was ready to cook some damn food.

"Sorry I'm late," she said, idling in my kitchen. I took the grocery bags out of her hand and started putting together our dinners of salads. Fresh salmon, spiced croutons, juicy tomatoes, crisp cucumbers, and my mother's homemade dressing that she always sent home with me. Yumi was kind enough to bring some cheese, a delicacy even at our income levels.

She was oddly overdressed that night, and I figured that's why she didn't want to get dirty in the kitchen. Today she wore a tailored jacket and trouser combo over a bold blue blouse. Usually she came over for these hangouts wearing jeans and a sweater. "You're not that late." I slid her bowl of dinner across the counter. "Eat here or on the couch?"

After dinner we settled down to watch TV. When I asked her what she wanted to watch, I got, "I don't care," followed by a blank stare. So I turned on a Hollywood movie with subtitles and grabbed my glasses. I drew my legs up on my couch, my fingers absentmindedly picking at a bump on my bare ankle while Yumi sat up straight on the other side of the couch, her eyes trained to the screen.

She was acting so weird. Late. Dressed well. *Smelled* good too. Not to mention she was unusually quiet for someone who liked to gossip and whine about work. I mean, this was my own home so of course I was relaxed, but why the hell was Yumi acting this way? She was never so uptight in my home. If anything, she would drape herself over my couch, over me, burping and yawning and sometimes even snoring if she was worn out. We weren't afraid to be our natural selves in front of one another. (You think I was a saint in her apartments?) For Yumi to not even take off her jacket was strange in and of itself. Acting like she was in her *senpai's* home was even stranger.

"You okay?" I asked, leaning against the arm of my couch.

"Yeah."

"You don't seem very relaxed."

She forced her shoulders to slump. "How's this?" Her voice cracked.

I patted my lap. "You need a massage?" I was referring to her scalp. Sometimes she would put her head in my lap and I would knead her scalp with my fingertips. When she was particularly stressed out, she would spend a whole hour there in my lap while watching TV.

"I'm good."

So be it. I went back to watching TV, and she sat like a student on picture day.

Shortly before my usual bed time, I did the dishes and contemplated a bath. Before I could go take one, however, I needed to ask if Yumi would be staying the night. It was only right to offer her a bath as well. Or she could go on to bed while I took one. It didn't matter to me...

"You staying over?" I asked, looking at my friend as she gazed out of window.

She turned around, face pale and eyes wide. The hell was wrong with her? Was someone out there? This high? "I dunno..."

"It's pretty late. If you want to go home you should head out now."

"Oh..."

I turned around.

"Chi-*chan*..."

Her voice was pitiful. Almost frightening. I couldn't move at first because I was afraid I would turn back around and find her crying or fluttering her eyelashes to butter me up for something. When I did look, I saw the woman who graced newsstands and CD jackets. Not Yumi, but YUMI.

I froze. Why was she looking at me like that? Why was I only now noticing *just* how done up she was in makeup and carefully combed hair? Wasn't it her day off? Why would she be at a photo shoot or other major work function before coming here?

Why did I care? She was beautiful.

Yumi must have sensed my reaction to her, for she narrowed her eyes and pursed her lips. What in the world? What was going on? Why was she slowly approaching me, as if she were about to slam me against the wall?

God help me. She was about to do just that.

You may not believe me. You may think that I'm making shit up. But I swear upon my life that Yumi, my best friend, the woman I loved, my unbelievable soul mate, clasped her hands around my head and brought me in for a kiss that made me trip on my own feet.

I had kissed her numerous times. Been kissed *by* her. None of those kisses – so simple, so demure, so fucking passive – compared to the one which hit me like a punch to the mouth. No way had I been expecting *this*.

Nor was I expecting her tongue hurling against mine, her gasp in my throat, and her body bumping against mine where it stood. I had no choice but to wrap my arms around her to keep my balance.

Her teeth pulled on my bottom lip before she let me go, those dangerously darkened eyes studying me. Yumi's hand lowered to my neck. My breath left my body. "I'm staying the night," she said, voice low. It washed over me like warm water, caressing my intimate spots and making my lower joints tremble under the onus of holding me up.

Yumi released and watched me stumble. Before I could say anything, even touch her, she was sauntering across my apartment, her jacket sliding off her arms and landing on my floor. She closed the bedroom door behind her. I fell against my couch, breathless, but alive.

I hadn't been kissed quite like that since Erina. I thought I knew what it was like for Yumi to really kiss me. I had a sweet taste of it in the practice room at the office, but this was... *wow*. That was a premeditated kiss. Nothing spur of the moment. Everything laid out carefully in her mind in order to...

No. No she wasn't.

I waited two minutes before collecting what sanity I had left and going to my room. Lights off, I stood in front of my door, hand poised above the handle. What was on the other side? I was scared to find out. Whether it was my sweet Yumi dressed in lingerie or curled up in my bed asleep, I knew I would not be able to bear it.

Oh, I was right. When I opened my bedroom door, I nearly choked on my own foolishness.

She lay propped up on my bed, hands folded on top of her stomach. This was not the tentative Yumi I was used to in bed, on the few occasions she shared such intimacy with me, as fleeting as it was. This was a fully realized and sexual Yumi who stared me down in the darkness of my own room.

Not a word passed between us. Only that biting look and the even more biting hook of her finger as it motioned for me to come to her.

I went, slowly, my legs trudging through sludge as my brain told me this was a trap, and my heart yearned for it to be true. When I reached the bed I sat on the edge, my eyes never leaving the breathtaking outline of her body beneath that blouse.

Her hand grazed my arm, each of her fingers pressing against my sweater as if to yank it away. She took my hand, now clammy, and brought it to the buttons of her blouse. My nail shook against the seemingly frail plastic.

"Come to bed." Her back arched just enough to entice me some more. "I want you to."

Have you ever had someone you love so much suddenly want you back? I never had until that moment. When I imagined us making love, I thought of it in abstract ways – the emotions flooding my body, the neediness, the drive making me want to pleasure her. Now I had to be practical. If I wanted to finally know what it was like to press my lips against Yumi's skin, I needed to ground myself in reality and... who the fuck was I kidding? I wanted her so much my body only knew that it was blinded by this sudden mutual desire.

I lowered my lips to her chest, fingers fiddling with buttons and heart slamming against my ribs. "We won't be able to undo it," I said with confounded clarity. Yet I found a patch of skin between her buttons, my lips feverishly tasting her salty skin for the first time there. I was riled, my body aching to wrap around hers and take her to a place she had never been before.

"Lots of things can't be undone now." Her hand was so gentle against my cheek that I almost didn't feel it there. "*Daite.*"

The jubilation elating my heart in that moment could have killed me. Her scent, her touch was already enough to send me over the edge. Now she wanted me to embrace her. Not just embrace her. A more intimate, passionate embrace that only we could give each other.

Except I was also afraid. When faced with something you want so much, it's only natural to be afraid – that it will disappear on you. Yumi had been so generous with her affections at times, only to pull away when it became too much for her to bear. I thought of that night Beppu found us. I thought of that day in the practice room. We were losing ourselves to lust, and yet Yumi always found a way to regain her self-control with me.

"I want to." Meek. Feeble. What was I ashamed of? No, I wasn't ashamed. Only that I was showing Yumi a side of myself that she rarely saw. "If you'll let me, I will."

Her hands were soft on my head. When Yumi wants to be soothing with her touch, she will make you feel like you're in a world where no one can hurt you. It's electrifying.

"I won't leave. I won't stop it." She tilted my head up and eased the devouring look on her face. "I want this."

Could it be true? Did Yumi really want me like that? We had known each other for so long that it didn't seem impossible. If she really did want me, wouldn't I have known it before? It's difficult to determine, since we were two women who didn't grow up knowing such love was not only possible, but viable. Nobody told us that lesbians existed outside of the West. Nobody said that we could give our hearts to girls instead of boys. And nobody ever, ever told us that making love to another woman could be good and healthy. I had accepted myself years ago. I had no idea what was going on in Yumi's head. Aside from the kisses and tender affection she gave me since first coming to Nagoya, I had no inclination to believe she was attracted to women. In my mind, she was straight. The practical, logical, *lesbian* Chiharu knew this was probably nothing more than my best friend going through a… I dunno. A phase? A thing? Something deep and meaningful… perhaps nothing in particular?

She wanted it, she said. She *wanted* it. She wanted *it*. Desire. Sex. Passion? What?

"You want this," I said, pushing myself up, looming over her. "But do you want me?"

It wasn't enough for her to want sex. Or sex with a woman. If I was going to bare my heart to her, I needed to know it wasn't just because I was the most convenient one. I know, I was over thinking it. Every time we almost went all the way before, it was completely organic. She also taught me during those times to not assume she would go farther than a kiss and some heavy petting. Those were the boundaries she established.

Yumi's hands cupped around my face, and I fought the urge to bury my nose in the scent of her throat. "There's no woman in this world I would want more than my Chi-*chan*."

How do I respond to that? Tell her I love her? Tell her I feel the same way about her? Tell her I want to make love until the sun comes up and we're too tired to keep going? I had no idea what to say. My heart was beating so fast that I almost gagged. I wanted to believe her. I wanted this to be the night where everything changed.

I wanted so much to be happy. With her.

So I kissed her, falling deeper and deeper into the desires I harbored for so long. One moment I abandoned my fears and kissed her so hard that she whimpered against my breath; another moment I protected my heart so rigidly that she asked if I was okay. Where was the in-between? How could I love her without hurting myself?

"Touch me," she said into my ear, her tongue wild as it hit one of my most dangerous places. Self-control meant nothing when my body was told it was time to go for it. "Please."

I did touch her. I touched her with my lips, which covered her throat, he shoulders, and the top of her breasts. My legs straddled her waist, gently undulating against her as she grabbed my arms and threw her head back against my pillow. The craziest part was touching her with my hands. What they discovered both unnerved and thrilled me. Beneath those tiny buttons holding her silky blouse across her chest were both her breasts, unrestrained, and completely unlike her – the girl who would haul me into lingerie shops so she could squeal over and buy loads of cute and colorful bras. If she came to my home without wearing one of them... then... then was this her plan all along? Did she come to me with the idea of seducing me? Was that why she was so nervous and standoffish all night? Nervous? About seducing *me*?

Lest you think I spent most of my time pondering these mysteries as opposed to worshiping the beautiful body in my grasp... ha! I barely had time to register what she looked like beneath her blouse before I went for it, my mouth suddenly disinterested in the contours of her face and throat. She wanted me to touch her? She had no idea what she asked for when she said that to Chiharu Morita, the woman who had been stuffing her face in boobs for a good five years now.

That night was the kind I often fantasized about. And as I explored the body I wished to adore for so long, I couldn't just think of my own needs. I never asked for her to touch me back, to undress me with her dexterous fingers, or to kiss me all over. But she did. Yumi was not a woman content to let everything be done to her and give nothing in return. She had the confidence I often lacked, but it pleasured me anyway, because it was her. She could tap my cheek and I would find a way to make it take me to heaven.

The first time she undressed me, taking off my sweater and pulling up my shirt, I thought I would lose all consciousness. I almost did when her lips met my flesh, her tongue easily doing what we both wanted it to.

I will spare us the embarrassment of sharing too many details. Just know this: that night I not only discovered how deep my desires could go, but I explored them with the only woman I could ever see myself spend my life with. I had never had sex with someone I *loved* before. The idea that it was possible to feel this level of intimacy with anyone was beyond the scope of my reasoning. Our naked bodies together weren't just for the sake of getting off. I wanted to feel all of her become one with all of me. I cursed my female body because I couldn't connect with her in ways men could. Even though I lacked in some departments, I showed her how good a woman could feel in others. Hearing her husky voice – because God help me, I had never heard this tone from her before – tell me how good I felt inside of her while we rocked together, my bed covers falling to the floor as moonlight covered our skin… I came undone. I wrapped my body with hers, kissing her tenderly, hungrily, and urging her to do the same to me. Yumi confessed that she was afraid of disappointing me, but I assured her that nothing could be terrible. She was easy to teach in the world of female pleasure. Because, as I discovered when she told me how beautiful I was when her fingers brushed against me, she wanted to make me feel good just as much as I wanted to hear my name with her words of yearning.

No way could I tell you how long it lasted. The greatest moment was not taking my own ultimate pleasure toward the end, but hearing – and feeling – Yumi orgasm beneath me, her eyes closed, shoulders shoving into the pillow while her body rolled and writhed from the feelings inside her. The heat of her skin, the scent of her body, and the sound of her panting throat taught me, in turn, that I had loved her well.

Perhaps this was the natural evolution of our old friendship. Perhaps this was something more growing between us. Perhaps I was still a foolish girl who believed everything would change because the person I loved the most was finally in my arms and kissing me like I had changed her fate.

"I love you," I confessed into the crook of her neck, my body limp against hers as she stroked my head and touched the tip of my ear. "I don't care if you don't love me. This is the happiest I've ever been."

She eased me off her and then rolled onto me. Without a word she kissed me, and I knew that we didn't need those words. Everything we needed to say flowed through our hearts and bodies in ways no one else could understand.

So when she pulled me on top of her one last time and said, "Chi-*chan*, do that one thing to me again. No one's ever done it in a way that feels like that," I didn't need her to elaborate… but I couldn't help myself.

"What do you mean?"

"Anything."

There are many ways to tell someone that you love them. That night I told Yumi with my lips – but not in the way you think.

***

"Feeling better?" Yumi is back again after going inside to take a call from someone at the label. She's about to get another call regarding what I just posted.

"Yeah." I push my laptop to the side and relax in my chair. Finally, the sun starts to feel nice. "Feels good ruining our careers."

She puts a hand on my shoulder. "I'm hungry. I'm gonna call up some dinner."

"Sounds good."

Before she goes back inside, she looks at me and says, "Let's catch the sunset from the Jacuzzi later tonight. The one on the deck."

"Gotta wear my swimsuit for that, and I didn't bring one."

"You can wear mine."

"You brought two?"

Yumi stays in the doorway before flashing me a knowing smile. "I didn't say that."

I think this is a good place to leave off for the day.

Part 11

THE THREE FACES
OF HAPPINESS

Hildred Billings

Love, Yumi

幸せと仮面の何方が現実ですか

It's amazing how public perception of a person can change overnight. I knew what I was doing when I posted that story, and yet here I am, still shocked at some of the questions Yumi and I received when we returned to Japan yesterday. I hadn't wanted to, but I wasn't going to let her return by herself, either. Still, we were promised a quiet return late in the evening… someone at the airport must have leaked the information to the media, for the moment we stepped into the terminal cameras were flashing and voices rose into the air.

"Yumi!" they called, chasing us as we hurried down a clear path set up by the airport personnel. Bodyguards sent by the label and security both held them back, and a man I did not know shielded Yumi and me with his large body as we progressed to the parking terminal. "Yumi, are you gay? Are you a lesbian?"

"Are you still working on a new album?"

"What does your label think of this?"

Amazingly, nobody asked me anything, even though I was the source of the commotion. They were taking pictures of Yumi, who wore a hat and sunglasses as if they could protect her from this fracas. I took off my jacket and draped it over her head, my hand in hers as we hurried even faster through the airport.

"Are you two in a relationship?"

"Yumi! What does Yohei think about this?"

The only clear picture someone got of me that night was when I turned my angry face to the reporter who asked that super dumb question.

We didn't get any peace until we were in the private parking terminal, where a car waited for us. We got in the backseat, Yumi taking my jacket off her head as the car pulled out of the garage. I had never been so grateful for tinted windows.

"Please tell me this will be over soon," Yumi said halfway to her Tokyo apartment. "You must be nearing the end."

The driver glanced at us in the rearview mirror, but pretended he wasn't listening. "I am. This will be over soon. The truth will be out."

She laughed, pathetically. "It already is. Whether or not I'm actually gay, the public now believes it."

"I'm sorry."

Yumi looked out the window with a sigh. "Even with all this truth and whatnot... a part of me had hoped that such a night could've remained private between us."

The driver glanced at us again. Pervert. "You know I couldn't gloss that over."

"Did you see the papers? They called your blog entry porn. You talked about my breasts and what I sound like having an orgasm."

"Did you read it?"

"No. I haven't read anything since that awful entry about that man. I'm scared now!"

I couldn't tell if she was angry or frustrated. Either way, the driver tried not to smile. I'd be glad when we got home.

We got to the apartment, which was guarded by even more security than usual. Not just the building's security. The label's, too. I wouldn't be surprised to find out if some of them were on Yumi's payroll. No reporter would penetrate that building. No pictures would make it through the window, even from the neighboring rooftops.

One hour later, when we barely had time to settle in and argue about where I'm sleeping, my mother and the little one arrived, escorted by security. I nearly forgot they were going to stay with us for a while. Yet I was so happy to see them both that I crushed them, letting tears of happiness flow down my cheeks as I got a kiss from both my mother and my daughter.

Yumi didn't speak to either one of them. I think she was embarrassed.

After their arrival there were few arguments to be had. Only one guest room existed, and of course my mother must sleep in it. Yumi wasn't going to sleep with the baby, so that left the little one with my mother, and me to contemplate shoving myself in there as well. Yet Yumi left her bedroom door ajar and said nothing when I entered.

"I'm sorry," I said, putting a hand on her shoulder. "I shouldn't have said those details."

"Whatever." She got up and went into the master bath, latching the door behind her. I climbed into bed and waited for her to return. When she eventually did, she took over the other side of the bed, hugging the edge and refusing to face me.

Now I am here in the daylight with my little one napping in my lap and my mother cleaning things up around the place. Yumi went to deal with the label on both of our behalves. While my hand strokes my child's hair, happy to feel her breathing with me again, I open this blog and glance through the comments on my last post. As expected, most of them are perverted.

It's imperative I quickly move on. The last thing I want people remembering is me talking about what I can do with my mouth.

Chapter 37

Go on. Tell me what an idiot I was. Not like I'm well aware right now.

When I woke up the morning after Yumi so easily seduced me, I thought I had dreamed the whole thing. One reason I thought this was because of how soundly I slept. If in fact we had made love, then it stood to figure that it knocked me out. My memory said that Yumi and I were up a while. Plus, I tend to sleep like a boulder after sex.

The other reason I wondered if I had dreamed our tryst had to do with Yumi's disappearance from my bed. After falling asleep with her locked tight in my arms, I now found my bed empty save for me. The sunlight said that it was morning, but my bed said that I needed to keep sleeping. Maybe I would find Yumi in my dreams again.

Except that I was naked. And I never slept naked unless something good happened the night before.

The bathroom door opened and Yumi stepped out, dressed in her clothes from the night before and made up to look soft instead of overtly sexual like yesterday. Our eyes met across my bedroom. I thought she would turn away and leave, but she came to my bed, leaning across it to smile at me.

"I thought you had left already," I said, my throat sore from how vocal it was earlier. "Are you leaving now?"

She nodded. "Work."

Thursday should have been a day off for her, but I didn't ask for further information. Instead I leaned forward, letting my forehead tap against hers while my fingers searched for hers to hold.

Yumi let me touch her, but I did not feel the passion in her reciprocation. She kissed my cheek and said, "last night was just…"

I waited for her heartbreaking words, but they never came. Probably because I grabbed the back of her head and kissed her as if a night's sleep changed no feelings between us.

She indulged me, but not for long. When she pulled away, she tugged on my bed sheets so they properly covered my breasts. "I have to go." Yumi left my bed. "See you later."

What was I supposed to think? If we only knew each other from work… if we weren't such close friends… if we had no history like we *did*… then maybe I would easily suck it up and say, "Well, it was a good night anyway." This wasn't a woman I met through work. This wasn't Ichiko, Honoka, or Naomi. This was Yumi. Didn't she know what she was doing to me?

I wish I could tell you that Yumi came back later and we made love again. Or at least fell into each other's arms as a wave of happiness overcame us. Hell, I wish I could say I saw her again that week. With a new single coming out and the Budokan preparations happening, she was busier than usual. Or so I told myself when she wasn't answering my texts or calls.

November passed. December came and went, with only my birthday to note. That was the next time I saw Yumi in the flesh. She couldn't hang out with me very long, but there was no mention of what happened the last time we saw each other. I wanted her to kiss me. I wanted to kiss her. No birthday could have been better than that. I settled for meeting her in a private room at a Tokyo restaurant, where she brought me a cake... and a few other people. I had hoped it would just be her and me. Even if nothing happened, I wanted to spend some private time with my friend on my birthday. But she brought some mutual friends from the label and we got half drunk and made jokes about me being Christmas Cake at twenty-five. I reminded Yumi she was the same age, but she could only say, "That's different. I can get any guy I want even at forty." Gee, thanks.

When everyone else left and we finally had two moments to ourselves, I thanked her for the party and asked if she wanted to go back to her apartment together. I had been staying in a hotel since I could never get a hold of her to find out if it was okay to stay at her place.

"Eh? You should get your money's worth from that nice hotel." She put her hand on my shoulder while she packed up her purse and hoisted it over her shoulder. "Besides... Yohei is at my apartment right now."

"I see." So she was still seeing him. Somehow I was not surprised.

Don't misinterpret me. Even though I wanted to fall head first into my fantasies of more sex, dates, and getting married to Yumi, I never actually thought that would happen. So while it hurt to find out she was keeping Yohei cooped up in her apartment, it didn't faze me. I also knew what that meant. If I stayed there, I would be sleeping in the guest room while she shacked with that guy. To the hotel it was.

"Happy birthday." Yumi kissed her fingers and then placed them on my lips. "I don't know when I can see you again. Things are so busy, right? Even you're busy right now."

True, I had an album coming out in January, right before Yumi's Budokan concert, but I wasn't busy like she always was. I had to approve some things before they were sent to print, and then do a few radio shows and maybe a late night performance on a niche music program. There would be no magazines, except some interviews I already completed. "Yeah, I'm busy."

Before she could lower her fingers, I snatched her hand, holding her to my cheek as we looked into each other's eyes. *"You know I love you, right?"* I had to convey that to her, and from how intensely I stared, I knew I couldn't try any harder. Yumi's visage went from relaxed to uptight, her mouth opening and her breath turning ragged in her throat. I'd never seen her eyes turn from up to down so quickly.

She pulled her hand away from me. "Chi…"

I'm a fool. An idiot. Don't let anyone ever tell you otherwise… after all, I'm sitting here confessing these private things to you and the rest of the world. You shouldn't be surprised when I say, like the fucking idiot I am, I yanked Yumi into my arms and kissed her.

It lasted longer than I anticipated, her lips holding fast against mine as I held her so closely that I could feel her heart thumping in her chest. My blood coursed through me backward, tearing down my own heart, deep into my stomach. I was going to die, and I wanted her to be the last person I shared a breath with.

Eventually Yumi turned her head away, her hands still clinging to me but in that disbelieving way. I embraced her, my hands on her back and my nose in her sweater as I held on to her distinct scent that could take me to places in my head I could never find with anyone else. Just a little longer. I just wanted to have that moment for…

"*Dekinai.*" Yumi eased herself away from me, looking down. "I can't. I… I have to go."

She went home to Yohei. And I went back to my hotel room to a frustrating night full of bad dreams and me screaming into my pillow.

***

Way back in high school, Yumi and I were in a play called "The Three Faces of Happiness." Well, she was in it. I played piano and helped with the set design, since by that point I'd given up being on stage myself.

In it, Yumi played a peasant girl named Jinga who was not happy with her lot in life. Her parents were poor, they lived in the woods, and bandits had a habit of ripping through their property to steal their livestock and the few valuables they had.

One day, Jinga went for a walk in the woods to mope about her fate. Yumi was always good at playing whiny, silly girls who made good morality tales. (Who knew?) I can still remember her sitting on a fake stump, elbows on knees as she sang a short song about how much she hated looking at the soot on her face whenever she saw her reflection, like the pond she sat by while she sang.

"Why is this my life?" she asked her reflection. "Why are my parents poor and the bandits so many? I want to move to the city and meet a guy who will treat me like a princess!"

As these traditional morality tales tend to go, a talking animal showed up. Now, you, me, and the audience all know that this animal – in this case a frog – is going to be a god or other spirit of some kind. But Jinga didn't know that. Because in these plays the stupid girl never knows when something bad or good is staring her right in the face.

"Why are you crying?" the frog asked. "A pretty girl like you has nothing to cry about."

"My family is so poor and the bandits are always taking what we manage to amass."

The frog – which was a puppet on a stick and some disembodied voice off stage – tsked and said, "There are three faces of happiness, and this is not one of them."

Since the gods can't help but meddle with pretty girls and their sorry fates, the frog soon turned Jinga's life upside down. First, he made the local administration build a road through the forest, and soon travelers from all over the region were stopping by Jinga's house for shelter and sustenance until they built and opened a proper inn. Jinga found happiness serving the travelers and hearing their stories.

Next, the frog sent Jinga a man caught in the rain. He was a young, handsome man who quickly fell in love with the pretty forest girl. Since she was low class and the man was a young scholar with good prospects, Jinga's parents had nothing against them getting engaged. Finally, Jinga was blessed with a baby, who would go on to become one of the emperor's top courtesans, making Jinga's later life quite comfortable even after her husband died.

One day Jinga, in her elderly form, returned to the pond where she met the frog. He was there again, and this time he asked, "Why don't you look happy? I sent you everything you needed to be happy. The energy of people, the energy of love, and the energy of a child. You should be grateful!"

Jinga shed a tear, which Yumi did quite dramatically by turning her head and applying an eye drop. "This is my face," she said. "What makes you think I'm not happy?"

"You do not wear one of the three faces of happiness."

"But I have worn them all. Don't you see? I have no faces left to wear but my own."

"Stupid girl!" This was when the frog showed his true form, a mighty god in flowing silk robes and gills on the side of his face. "You never cast away the faces of happiness." His face turned, revealing that his head was a cube, and each face was different in its expression of happiness. Aside from his natural face, which was grim and plain, he had a face of shy elation, a face of blushing romantic love, and a face of full-hearted adoration. When he returned to his original face, he said, "If you throw away your faces, you will never have them again. How could you be so stupid? Come here!"

The frog god pricked Jinga with a spear and let her bleed out in the pond. A full life lived, and what was there to show for it? Jinga did not understand that happiness was something to hold onto, to treasure, to be reminded of constantly. She was always looking for some other happiness. When her spirit, now young and pretty again, rose from her tattered flesh, the frog god took her by the hand and said they were off to find her missing faces of happiness.

They found the faces of the travelers she used to admire so much. They found the face of her departed husband, now young again himself. Finally they found the face of her daughter, who had also just passed away from a plague that swept through the emperor's court. These people surrounded Jinga, and eventually she shed a slew of tears that said she finally understood what it meant to wear the different faces of happiness.

At the time I didn't think much of the play. It was just one of those seasonal plays we did in high school, in between lessons and riding bikes along the river's edge. Now looking back on it, I realize how true that story was. If I had frog here with me now, I would say, "You were right, frog king. We must hang on to the faces of happiness to keep us going 'til the end of our lives." If Yumi were here, I would tell her to remember it, even when she's angry at me.

Even though I felt the biting pain of her rejection after my twenty-fifth birthday, I still tried to hang on to the happiness she gave me for one night. What I didn't know was that I would see her wear all three faces soon enough – and struggle to keep them in her possession.

Chapter 38

I didn't get to see Yumi again until the night of her Budokan concert. We barely talked in the interim, but I chose to attribute that to her super busy schedule and not because she was avoiding me. The few times we did talk it was strictly about work, entertainment, or our families. We never brought up each other's love lives. It was utterly taboo now, and not just because we couldn't relate to each other. Not that I had a love life during that time. I was too down to go pick up a woman from a bar or flirt with someone from work. Sounded awful.

As we got closer to the night of her biggest concert ever, however, I received more and more messages from her while she was at rehearsals. *"I can't wait for you to see the set!! You're going to be amazed!" "Like half the songs are ones you wrote, Chi*-chan. *I didn't realize how many of my biggest hits were ones you wrote. Thanks so much! You're a genius!" "There's gonna be a special new song that night so you better make sure your ass is in that VIP box. I don't care if your arm is cut off and you're bleeding all over your seat. BE THERE."*

On the day of the concert, I woke up late. For some reason I found it difficult to drag myself out of bed – the bed I made love to Yumi in – and shower. I should have done some work in the morning, but I just sat and stared at my piano as if it were a foreign entity. The day was cold and drizzly, so I couldn't go for a walk to clear my head. No, at noon I had to board a bullet train and head to Tokyo. Then from Tokyo Station I would go straight to the Budokan hall. I didn't dare assume I would stay at Yumi's place that night, so a hotel would have to do. The things I did for her.

For those who have never been there before, let me tell you about Budokan. Performing there is one of the highlights of any artist or band's career. Every young and budding singer wants to perform in Budokan one day. So few people get to say they did it… let alone to a sold out crowd… let alone under their own name! This was a huge night for Yumi, and I was sure she was both nervous and excited. I was driven there by someone from our label and then given special treatment going in. I walked by the humongous crowds lining up to go inside and buying her merchandise, both authentic and knock-off. I asked if I could see her backstage before the concert started, but the man from the label said it was too close to show time.

The VIP box was right in front of the stage, in the midst of the fanclub. There were only a half dozen seats, and I shared mine with two of the executives from the label and Yumi's mother, who sat by me and chatted about Seki and how proud of her daughter she was for half an hour before the start of the show. "Your mother sends her love," she said with a languid sigh. "Too bad she couldn't come. She would love to see this!"

Most of you have probably seen that concert. It's her bestselling DVD, and some of her most iconic performances have been cemented in time thanks to social media and things like YouTube. Did you see it from my point of view? Sure, the camera can give you close-ups and perfect sound, but from where I sat right in front of the stage, I could see anything I wanted at any moment. There was no camera to dictate my view of the performance.

Love, Yumi

Yumi was right when she said over half the songs on her set-list were written by me. While I enjoyed her spunky personality and the way she flirted with the thousands of people in the audience, what really struck me was her performance of the winter love ballad I wrote for her a few months ago and had just come out in single format. For this performance she wore an ethereal icy blue dress that took up the whole stage. I mean the *whole* stage. The skirt poofed out around her, covered in reflecting crystals that twinkled beneath the cool lights. It pooled at her feet, circled the stage, and was held up behind her by hooks hanging from the ceiling. As the song went on, her vocals becoming more powerful as she threw her whole body into it, her skirt revealed a strange design that took me a while to interpret. Eventually I realized they were the lyrics I wrote.

"When it's cold at night, who do I turn to? It's you, in your arms, where I find the fire of winter. It burns and cuts like glass, but I keep returning, afraid to feel any pain but the exquisite one you give me. Hurt me, hurt me until spring comes and this fire melts away like snow."

That song was always meant to reflect an aching love that never goes away. Sound familiar? Even though they were my thoughts put into Yumi's mouth, I never really thought about what that meant when I heard the recording on the radio or even watched her other performances. I was usually too enthralled with the music they picked or looking at the woman I loved. But now I was fixated on her voice and the words that came out.

When I wrote that song, I had her range in mind, but I wanted her to sing it because of how heartfelt it was. It was about the nights we spent together wrapped in each other's arms, and I wondered if she realized that. We rarely talked about the contents of the lyrics I wrote. She would say, "Oh, it's beautiful and hits me right here!" but that's about it. We never talked about what inspired me to write them. I used to assume she thought they were stock lyrics based on basic life experience, but now I wonder... I truly wonder if she knew those songs were about our relationship.

"When I come to you, do you know how cold I am? Can you sense my frigid life? Do you hate me for taking your warmth? Yours is the only warmth that can stave off this winter."

That was the night I realized "Winter Serenade" would be one of the greatest songs I ever wrote. When she sang it, I felt my own pain, my own inhibitions toward love come flooding out in that hallowed hall of music and culture. The whole audience was spellbound... not even the usual waving of lights occurred, since they thought it was too inappropriate during such a powerful ballad.

"The more I come to you, the more your spark fades. You shield me from the cold, but at what price? What will I do... when your fire is gone, and the guilt I feel is too much?"

She looked in my direction. I looked away.

"I will fade with you, letting the cold claim me a final time. A final time, to be with you in the warmth of eternity where we will both glow."

I could feel the sadness in the audience. Thousands of people, all of them reacting to my words, to the soul Yumi put into them. I glanced around, at the monitors showing tears on cheeks and hands holding among all of these people.

My ego has never been big when it comes to my music. I appreciate the kind words people send me, but I don't think much about them. I don't write for praise or even the money (although the latter helps me keep writing). I'm more interested in expressing these bottled up feelings, whether it's just through my music or also the lyrics.

Yet seeing a whole auditorium tear up and feel my work that strongly – let alone coming from the woman I adored – filled me with more than pride. It also reminded me of my pain, especially when Yumi looked at me and smiled, ripping her veil of heartache she wore for the show.

I loved her. I needed her. I forgave her in that moment for screwing with my feelings. How could I stay upset with someone who smiled at me like that on the biggest night of her life?

"That was gorgeous," Yumi's mother said once the stage went dark and the final notes of our song dissipated. "Did you write that one?"

"Yes."

"Ah, you know my daughter's strengths so well. She owes a lot to you."

The rest of the concert was a blur. I remained stewing in my feelings from "Winter Serenade," even when Yumi burst out for a happy set full of songs I didn't write. Her smile was big and genuine, and when the audience joined in on a chant that echoed for eternity, her whole face lit up in jubilation. The audience gave her their energy, screaming her name, holding up their signs, and belting along with the lyrics to every song. Before the encore, they continued to scream, afraid that the night was already over.

We all know that the encore is full of personal thoughts, old fan favorites that didn't quite fit the rest of the show, and lots of sweat and tears on behalf of the performers. Yumi came out in jeans and a cutoff shirt, showing off her model's figure that was both captivating and worrisome if you knew her like I did. But she was happy, encouraging the audience to sing along with more songs until she toned it down for an announcement.

"There are lots of people I would like to thank who helped make this night possible." She wiped her brow, drenched in sweat. The names she listed were the usual families, executives, other creative minds that people probably didn't know. She thanked each member of her live band and the dancers that had been with her through the years. "Finally," she continued, cheeks pink. "There is one person I really want to thank."

I bristled, and I'm not sure why.

"This person has been with me since I knew I wanted to be a singer. They never judged me or told me I couldn't follow my dreams. In fact, they came with me so both of our dreams could come true. I wouldn't have half my favorite songs if it weren't for them."

The crowd whistled. A good chunk of them probably knew she was talking about me.

When Yumi looked right at me, her microphone to her mouth and her eyes watering, I had no idea what was going on. "Thank you, Chiharu," she said, and the audience clapped in my... what? Honor? "For always being there for me."

The camera briefly showed me on the screen, my cheeks pale and Yumi's mother beside me, clapping as well.

"I want to sing you all a new song." Yumi finally looked away from me. "It's going to be on my upcoming album this spring. Oh, did I mention I'm working on an album?" She laughed, and the audience applauded. "Please enjoy my new song, 'Nothing Without You.'"

I didn't know this song, as I hadn't written it. When the instrumental started up, full of piano, I knew it had been inspired by my compositions.

The lyrics were common, talking about someone the singer deeply trusted and understood. Even though I knew this song was about me, I couldn't help but pretend it was about someone else.

Does that sound terrible? After what happened on my birthday, I had a hard time believing that she cared about or needed me that much. Of course, we were still best friends. Except it had been complicated by, I dunno, sex? That seems wrong to say. The whole thing confused me. Did she or did she not love me as more than a friend? Was I so caught up in my emotions that I couldn't think clearly? I would always be thankful for her friendship and the love that came from that. We were beyond pesky fights threatening our friendship. We were *long* past that. No matter how much we disagreed or argued over stupid details, we knew that the next day we would be back to normal. This wasn't normal now! Your best friend isn't supposed to make your heart twist in your body, dragging it out of your chest and making you watch it bleed in front of you. Because you know what? That was the night I realized I loved her. Truly, unequivocally loved her. This wasn't a childhood crush. This wasn't me clinging to someone who showed me affection. I loved Yumi more than I could possibly love anyone else. Who was I fooling dating other women? None of them would fill my heart the way Yumi did. If I couldn't have her, then I couldn't bear to be with anyone. She was my soul mate. I never believed in such things before. Now I did, when I looked into her gleaming face and saw the only person who would ever give me true, unrelenting joy.

That sort of realization fucks you up!

Love, Yumi

I don't even remember the end of the concert. Yumi's mother escorted me to catch a taxi, and I received a text from Yumi thanking me for coming and saying that she had to go to an after party with her staff. Since Yumi's mother was staying at her daughter's place, I knew I couldn't go there. (Where would I sleep? In her bed? Ha!) So after the cab dropped her off there, I told the driver to take me to Shinjuku. I wanted a drink.

Even for the weekend, the one lesbian bar catering to closeted celebrities was empty. And I mean *empty*. I was the only woman in there for a good hour, meaning I got my liquor fast. The proprietress had chores to keep her busy as she periodically checked in on me, my elbows on the counter as my fingers pulled on my hair.

"What's wrong?" she asked. "Or can you talk about it?"

Most bartenders act as a cheap therapist whether you're gay or straight. In that place, things were slightly different. Many of the patrons couldn't say who they were dating or give away too much information about their work. The bar had a good reputation for keeping secrets out of the press, which was how it stayed in business for so long, but even I wasn't privy to say how much I loved Yumi, specifically. "Just a girl."

"It's never just a girl. Especially if you're looking glum like that."

"What do you want me to say? That I love some girl who will never love me back like that? Fuck it. So I do. And now we finally do it, and next thing I know she's going back on everything we've built over the years to... I dunno. I don't know what she was doing. Experimenting? Jerking me around? Building up enough sexual frustration that she finally got it out of her system with me?"

The proprietress considered my words before drumming her fingers on the bar. "Did you happen to write that song 'Winter Serenade' for her? Because I can tell."

"Yeah."

The following silence was quite unfair. She grinned at me, and I felt like the biggest idiot in the universe for falling into her trap. Great. Now she knew I meant Japan's biggest star.

"Don't worry, I won't tell anyone. Though I feel pretty bad for you now. Isn't she dating that one guy from the boy group?"

"Yeah. She's straight."

"Ouch."

Someone came in around that point, so I closed my mouth. A girl, not that much younger than me, sat down at the end of the bar, exchanged greetings with the proprietress, and ordered a tame drink. She was texting on her phone the whole time, but all I could do was stare at her cool clothes, slick blond hair that was dark at the roots, and poised way she sat even after she had a drink to nurse.

She reminded me of Yumi, even though their faces and voices were completely different. Yumi was new-money, and this girl had the air of someone who had been sophisticated her whole life. When she caught me staring at her, she flashed a smile and went back to her phone.

"How's the girlfriend?" the proprietress asked. This girl must either not be that famous or her girlfriend was a nobody. Or maybe she was the rare minor celebrity who had no closet.

"She's fine. At a function tonight so I decided to come here to relax. Been a while, eh?"

"Sure has. Missed your photogenic face."

When the proprietress went into the back, the girl looked at me from the other end of the bar and said, "Haven't seen you around here before. Then again I haven't been here in a while."

I forced a smile. "I'm not from around here, so I don't come often."

She shut up, thankfully. One of the unspoken rules at that bar was that you didn't pry into other people's lives unless they offered the information freely. I wasn't about to. "You look kinda familiar," she said. Well, there went that rule. You weren't supposed to speculate on who people were either. "I mean recently familiar. Ah…" That light bulb of knowledge went off behind her big, blue-contact eyes. "You're Chiharu Morita, aren't you? I just came back from YUMI's concert. Saw you on the big screen."

"Uh huh."

"Wow. My girlfriend's a big fan of yours. She plays piano professionally." The girl laughed. "She'll flip when I tell her about this."

About what? Meeting me? At a gay bar? "Tell her I appreciate it." It would've been rude to let the conversation drop when we were the only ones there, so I continued, "Sorry, I don't know who you are."

"I'm a model." That explained it. "You ever see those alternative wear magazines? Luxe Du Jour and Zing Zing are the main ones I model for."

"I've heard of them." Didn't read them, as I wasn't into those styles.

"I also sing professionally now. Trying to get my girlfriend to play piano with me on a track, but she's too embarrassed. Maybe I should tell her that you said she should do it."

How lovely. Putting words into my mouth. "I don't know if I recommend it. That way leads to heartache."

She was quiet for a while, studying my sorry, constipated face as I finished my drink and made sure my things were in my bag. "I see," she said again. "That bad, huh?"

"The worst."

Who ever means to be such a downer? That was me that night, making the smile fall off that pretty girl's face as she contemplated my words. Did she know I was talking about Yumi? She had been to that concert. She saw the way Yumi looked at me from the stage. She knew I wrote songs and often played piano for Yumi.

"I'm sorry."

"Consider yourself lucky." I slipped off my stool and picked up my bag. "Love sucks."

And that, my friends, was me being my usual cynical self. The look on that girl's face was one I would never forget. The way she twisted her brows was just like Yumi; the way she sighed was just like Yumi. This girl was dangerous. If I hung around much longer, I would be enticed to make this girl cheat on her lover. All for the wrong reasons.

Yet what could I say was the right reason? Was there one?

***

I'm lying here in bed with my little one when my mother appears in the bedroom doorway. She doesn't enter because it's Yumi's room, and my mother is an appropriate woman.

"Lunch?" she asks. I tell her it's okay to come in, and she does, standing at the end of the bed. "I'm going to make egg sandwiches and *miso*."

The little one perks up at that. "I'm fine," I say, but urge the child to get up and go to her grandmother. "This one clearly needs food, though."

"Ah, Sattchan." My mother takes her hand and helps her off the tall bed. "How's it going?" she then asks me. "I mean the... you know."

"It's fine. Have you... been reading it?"

She shakes her head so quickly I think it's gonna pop off. "No, no. Some things I don't need to know. If you wanted me to know specifically, you would have told me." The baby hits her legs to get her moving. "*Hai, hai*. What do you think? After lunch, let's watch your favorite show on TV." My mother glares at me. "By the time I'm done with her, she will have seen every episode of *Doraemon*. Really, how could she not know it?"

"I have no idea." I wait for them to leave the room before I go back to my computer. I've only talked about one face of happiness so far, and the next two are too hard to write about in front of others.

Chapter 39

Yumi and I found some sense of normalcy once again. Well, normal for us. We did not bring up our night of passion, much to my frustration, but I wasn't about to open that line of dialogue. We did, however, start hanging out on a regular basis again, which was welcomed in my lonely life. After all this time, Yumi was still my only real friend.

Having sex, however, changed a few things that I could never reclaim. For one, we were not as touchy as we used to be. She kept to her side of the couch and I kept to mine. We didn't hold hands anywhere – not that we had for a long time, anyway – and we definitely didn't kiss or cuddle. When I used her Tokyo apartment one weekend, I slept in the guest room even though she wasn't there. It felt wrong to curl up in her bed when she had rejected me.

We also certainly did not sleep together, even platonically. That point of no return had long been passed. Yumi no longer asked to stay the night at my place when she was over, and when I was in her Tokyo apartment with her neither of us brought it up. I went straight to the guest room after brushing my teeth.

Not until late March, when Yumi was preparing for her album coming out later that spring, did things begin to slip back into a dangerous direction.

I was in Tokyo with her, going over some details about a track of mine she was using for the album. We didn't have to do it in Tokyo, but since we were there at the same time it made more sense than waiting until we both returned to Nagoya. After a long day at the Tokyo branch offices, we had dinner at a neighboring restaurant and then returned to Yumi's apartment in Shibuya. Since it was late, I showered and got ready for bed quickly. As I opened the guest room door, dressed in my pajamas, Yumi said, "What are you doing? Come be with me tonight."

She stood in her bedroom doorway, smiling, dressed in sweats and a T-shirt just like me. I knew she had to be up early in the morning, so I doubted she was flirting. Yet she left her door open as she climbed into bed and turned off her light.

Like the dumbshit I am I went into her room, closing the door behind me and watching her turn over in bed. Yumi drifted off to sleep, the covers pulled down on the other side of the bed. Was she serious? This used to be commonplace for us, but since *that* night neither of us were comfortable sharing a bed. Until now.

I climbed in on the other side and stared at the back of her head. Within minutes I had an arm around her. When she did not protest, I pulled her close to me and whispered good night into her ear. Yumi stirred, but did not ask me to stop holding her.

Any elation I felt was marred by my need for sleep. I dozed off quickly, the scent of Yumi's skin filling my nose and placating my heart.

I don't know how long I slept. I couldn't tell you if I ever truly slept before it happened. All I know is that one moment I was lying content with Yumi in my arms, and the next a half-intoxicated voice demanded, "What the fucking hell is going on here?"

My eyes snapped open. Yumi sat up, breaking free of my grasp. The light switched on and there was Yohei, standing in disbelief in the doorway.

"Yohei!" Yumi pushed out of bed. Thank God she was wearing conservative PJs. "What are you doing here? You said you were in Osaka."

"I got back early." That man's eyes did not leave mine as I sat up in Yumi's bed. "Too early, apparently. What is she doing here?"

"You know she stays here when she's in town."

"In bed with *you*?"

They took it out of the bedroom, shutting the door but not shutting out their voices. I drew my legs up to my chest and strained to listen.

"Don't be like that," Yumi hissed. "What would you know? Chiharu and I are best friends since we were kids. We've been sleeping like that for years. Long before I met you!"

"That's weird. That's fucking weird. Nobody does that shit. She was spooning you like she fucked you. For fuck's sake, you're not having sex with her, are you? You a queer?"

"No!" Yumi answered it much too quickly. "Don't sexualize it!"

"I know she's a damn queer, so why shouldn't I think you are as well?"

"Would a queer swallow your junk for you?"

Gross. Definitely too much information. "I don't know, would she?"

"What do you care anyway? We're not serious. I know you're fucking other girls."

"That's different!" God, is that where Yumi picked up that phrase? "I'm not queer."

"You're disgusting. You should leave."

"Whatever. This time next week you'll be begging for some real cock again. Get this friend of yours out of your system before she totally turns you."

"Watch your mouth!"

"I'm just saying. You're too perfect to be a queer, baby."

I don't know what either of them said after that. Long had I since slammed my ear against the pillow and plugged the other one with my hand. If I heard that shitty word one more time, I was probably going to cry.

Eventually the front door slammed shut, and Yumi came back, grumbling and clearing her throat. The bed sank beneath her slight weight. "I'm so sorry you had to hear that," she whispered. My hand entwined with hers.

"Yumi…" I couldn't contain the thought I'd been carrying for years. "I don't like that guy. He's not any good for you. There are lots of guys who would be better for you…" See? I wasn't delusional. "I don't know what you see in that guy." Prayers erupted inside of me. Prayers that she wouldn't mention his dick.

"Don't worry about it right now." Yumi buried he nose in my chest before wrapping her arms around me. "You'll always come before him."

I had no idea what that meant. That she loved me more than him? That she valued me more than him? I wanted to tell her those were dangerous thoughts to travel with. But then she was asleep, and I slowly followed.

The closer Yumi got to her new album release, the busier and more distant she became. This was normal, and I understood entirely. Albums took a lot of my own time, let alone someone who was a superstar and doing a hundred times the amount of promotion. I won't pretend it didn't make me sad that I only saw a glimpse of her once every other week, but I knew that it would eventually pass. The album would release, she would heavily promote it for two to three weeks, and then things would slow down until it came time to prepare her nationwide tour. A cycle I was familiar with.

When Yumi did manage to come over, we watched movies, cooked dinner, got half-drunk and silly, and sometimes fell into bed together… but not like that. Basically, it was the old times again. If we had never made love at all a few months ago, it would be as if nothing changed. Of course things changed – in my heart, and between us.

We were fast approaching the release date of the album. A royalty check had just come in, and since "Winter Serenade" was one of the biggest singles of the winter season, I was planning a glorious Golden Week in May for my mother and me. The plan was to take her to Ireland, a place she always wanted to go. Then she called and said she had "met a guy" and was going to Okinawa with him. Well, fine.

Yumi was tearing her hair out because the label wanted her to keep her #1 streak and was worried that a huge boy group releasing an album the same day would be bad news. So they pushed her album back not two weeks, but a month. When she called me and asked, "What are you doing for Golden Week? I suddenly have it off," I nearly passed out. We hadn't vacationed together in years.

Yet no plans formulated. Yumi disappeared for a week without a word. Again, not unusual, especially with work consuming her. I saw some reports on TV that said the paps caught her and Yohei drunk at a bar. It was a blip in the entertainment section, and I tried not to think about it.

One night, a week before Golden Week, I was in Yumi's Tokyo bathroom getting ready to go out to Ni-chome. I hadn't been there since that night after Budokan, and well, I had needs. Let's just say I don't sit in front of the bathroom mirror grooming and putting on makeup to go out to get groceries and see people at the label. Pretty much the only time I do this now is to go on TV or go out to meet a new friend, if you catch my drift.

While I was judiciously applying eyeliner, trying to look a bit mysterious, a bit sexy, my phone blew up with one of Yumi's songs. I waited until I finished with the eyeliner before picking it up.

"Chiharu!" Sure enough, it was Yumi. She sounded drunk. "You won't believe it!"

Was she crying? It was hard to tell between Yumi crying and her just being drunk, especially on the phone. "What?" I checked my face for pimples.

She sobbed. Oh, so she was crying. You may think I sounded heartless in the moment, but this wasn't the first time Yumi called me drunk-crying. Wasn't the first time she called me drunk. Remember when she told me about her nails? "Yohei and I had a fight…"

Fantastic! Who would have ever guessed? "I'm sorry to hear that."

"It's over! I'm serious." Yumi sniffed, and I could see her sitting on her couch in Nagoya, wiping tears as she struggled to put on her best acting face. "I'm never seeing him again. Do you know what he did?"

"No." My imagination could fill in so many blanks, though.

"We were out on a date and I caught him making out with another girl. On a date with me! You know I see a few guys, but I would *never* do that while on a date!"

"Uh huh." This wasn't the first time Yumi said she was dumping Yohei. For good, or whatever. This happened about once or twice a year, and a few months later they were back together again. So pardon me if I wasn't riveted by the story.

Another pathetic sniff. "I'm serious. I'm so sick of his disrespectful shit. Now I wish he hadn't done that feature with me on the album. It was going to be one of the promoted tracks."

"I'm sorry."

"Where are you? I tried reaching you at home, but you weren't there. *Mou,* I need you…"

I can't lie. Hearing her say it that way pulled on my heartstrings like only she could accomplish. "I'm in Tokyo, remember? I'm in your bathroom right now."

"Eh? You taking a bath?"

"No. I'm getting ready to go out."

"Go out? Where?"

I sighed, looking at my lipstick and debating between colors. "Ni-chome."

"*Ehhhh.* I wanna go."

"What? Why?"

"It's bars full of women, right? I don't want to see another man right now. Being surrounded by women sounds great."

"They'll all want to have sex with you."

"Is that so bad?"

Love, Yumi

But you're not gay, I thought. In reality, I said, "I've got one goal tonight. Dunno what I would do with you once I found a girl."

Yumi was silent for a while, aside from some quiet sniffs that echoed over the line. "Well, hurry back here, okay? And... be safe?"

"What do you think I'm doing? Fucking random guys?" I realized what I said right after the words came out of my mouth. "I mean... without protection..." That hole I was digging sure looked deep. "I'll be back in Nagoya in a couple of days."

"Okay..."

I didn't want to leave her like that, but what could I do? I couldn't go to her, and I couldn't stay on the phone with her forever, especially when I knew it would degenerate into nothing really fast. After I hung up and went to Ni-chome, I kept thinking about my best friend, alone and upset in Nagoya. If I were there, I would be at her side in a heartbeat. But I wasn't there. I couldn't go there. Worrying about Yumi ruined my evening and the furthest I got was two drinks and one girl telling me my makeup looked nice. I can't say that I was disappointed.

When I returned to Nagoya, I was afraid that I would find Yumi either a wreck or back in Yohei's arms. But she had work to distract herself with, and I learned to forget about her frantic phone call that one night.

The day before Golden Week began, I was at the label office the same time she was. Since most of the staff would have Golden Week off, we both had loose ends to hurry and tie up. She was going over her schedule for her return after the holidays, and I was handing in some last minute compositions I was up half the night finishing. She stopped by my meeting room to look them over, telling the department head that she wanted first dibs on them for future singles.

Yumi waited until my meeting was over to walk me out of the building. She was driven to work by a company car – her preferred mode of travel – and I drove my own car. I offered to give her a ride home and she accepted, but as we got into my car in the parking garage she asked, "What are you doing tonight? Or this week in general?"

I turned on the ignition and wiped some debris off my rearview mirror. "No plans. I thought you and I were making some but I never heard back."

"Well, shit. I have no plans either because I've been so distracted. How pathetic are we? It's too late to go traveling now. Everything will be booked." Funny how money wasn't a concern now. "Let's go to your place. I don't feel like going home."

"And what are we going to do?" The car idled in its parking space. "Watch movies? Pop some popcorn?"

"Fuck yes. Let's go."

I really didn't have any plans that night beyond relaxing in the tub and maybe ordering in. I could still do the latter with Yumi around, but with her tastes we had to order some fancy cuisine I still couldn't tell you the name of. Not that it wasn't good... it was delicious, I remember that much. She paid for it too, so what did I care?

From the moment we sat down on my couch, I knew she was feeling clingy. She didn't sidle up to me, or climb on me, or even use her pathetic child's voice on me, but she whimpered in her corner, legs drawn up and hand on head as if she had a headache. As the movie started, I asked her what was wrong, and she said, "Nothing."

"I don't believe that. Did you fight with Yohei again?"

She sighed, covering her stomach with her hands. "I haven't talked to him since that night. I told you. It's over."

That surprised me. She usually caved much sooner than that. "Good for you." I meant it.

"*Nee...*" Yumi leaned over and put her head on my shoulder. Soon enough she was wrapped around my arm, frowning at the credits on the screen. "Why is love so messed up?"

She was asking me, of all people? "Because it fucks with your heart. Anything that messes with your heart isn't going to be good." Didn't I know it.

"You're so smart." Yumi rubbed my arm. I had a cup of tea in my hand and she played with the bag in it, the string twirling around her finger as she sighed. "You have the right approach to love. You don't jump into things. I've never seen you in a real relationship… but that also means I've never seen you during a breakup. Feh! You're doing it right."

I didn't mention that the reason I couldn't get a real relationship was because of my hang-ups for her. "I'm also lonelier than you," I said.

It took a few moments for her to respond. "I'm lonely too. Even when I have people… even when I'm with these guys… I'm lonely. I hate it."

"Well…" I doubted she wanted my advice, but I was going to give it anyway. "Maybe it will be good for you to be single. I'll write a song for you about being an independent woman."

"God, you would know better than me about that. I feel like I rarely make my own decisions. Someone is always making a decision for me. Mostly men. The executives tell me when I'm releasing a song and what kind of direction it will have. Boyfriends tell me where we're going and if we'll have sex or not. I'm tired of it. I can deal with one or the other, but not both. I should dump the boyfriends… you're right."

"If you feel like you have to choose, that would be the one."

The movie played. I drank tea and felt Yumi's breath against my arm.

"I don't have anything to wear," she said as we wound down for the evening.

"You can borrow something from me." I took a large T-shirt out of my bottom drawer and handed it to her. It was big on me, so it would be a sack on her. After she thanked me, I went to take a bath.

Yumi was in bed in the guest room by the time I got out. I was surprised, since I expected her to be in my bed, but whatever. It was for the best. Yumi crawling into my bed would only mean more confusion for me.

I had no idea what was going on the next day. Yumi seemed interested in doing something fun for Golden Week, but she was right when she said it was too late to make travel plans. Oh well. I figured it was something we could sort out in the morning, so I went to bed thinking of drives to the mountains and maybe taking her back to Seki to see her folks.

"Chi-*chan?*"

I opened one eye to the darkness of my bedroom. I lifted my head off my pillow and looked toward my bedroom door, where Yumi stood in nothing but my shirt.

"What?"

She scratched her arm. "You awake?"

"Yeah…"

"Can I be with you?"

I rubbed my eyes and slapped my hand against the other, empty pillow. "Uh huh."

Even as I listened to her step lightly across my room and pull back my covers, I wondered what was making her act this way. She never asked if she could get in bed with me. She just did it. At this point we assumed it was fair game unless the other said something about avoiding it. Like I said before, I was surprised she went straight to my guest room.

"You okay?"

She buried her head in the pillow and pulled the covers up to her neck.

I closed my eyes again without reaching out to touch her. When she was weird like this, I tended to let her lead our interactions. My Yumi could be finicky about how people touched her.

Just as I was falling asleep again, I felt her hand on my shoulder.

And her lips on the nape of my neck.

"*Nani?*" I couldn't move. It was like I was back in that mystical dream world where Yumi and I made love without shame or consequence. Especially when her hand wrapped around and touched my breast, her weight coming on top of me from behind. "Yumi!"

Her hunger was palpable. Yet this wasn't the same woman who seduced me months ago. Not the one who came to my apartment dressed in her finery and laying herself on my bed until I came to her. This woman pined for affection, hands pushing beneath my shirt as her moans echoed in my ear.

"Please." That wayward hand cupped around my chin and turned my head toward her.

"Please what?" Maybe I wanted to hear her say it. If she couldn't acknowledge what we were doing, then I knew I would feel nothing but pain right in my soul and heart.

Although the kiss did not surprise me, the intensity behind it did. This was indeed like that night she seduced me: passionate, determined, and unrelenting. It took me about two seconds to fold beneath her whims, sinking into my bed with this woman overcoming me in ways I could have never expected. What she whispered into my ear before biting it surprised me even more.

"Hitotsu ni narimashou…"

Do you think that I believed her? Or do you think that I pushed her away, determined to find out once and for what she really meant to me?

We've established that I'm a stupid idiot who would do anything to believe that Yumi wanted me. How could I not believe it when we were in bed like this, her asking to make love?

Think that I'm a fool all you want. I wouldn't blame you. I damn well thought I was a fool – a giddy, glorious fool – when I brought her down into my arms and gave her what she wanted. A kiss here, a kiss there, a forbidden kiss to her other lips that made her lose her mind. I had never felt her light up so quickly in my arms. There was no hesitation. No worry that what we were doing was scary or wrong. I knew that the only experience she had with women was with me, but she was just as eager as she had been the first time we did it. Gentle, malleable… she wanted to please me as much as I was pleasing her. Not tough to do when my heart was leaping over the moon at her tender – and not so tender – affections.

Actually, I wasn't a fool. I knew what I was getting into. I knew what heartbreak I was setting myself up for. But when the person you love asks you to share one of life's greatest joys with them? Are you going to walk away? Are you going to say, "No, we can't do this even though I want you so much?" Maybe some people have that much self-control. Not me. If Yumi climbs into bed with me and says, "Let's make love," I am going to make love to her even if I know she'll run away in the morning and pretend that what we shared never happened.

Because I knew she would. I knew, even as I consumed her body and brought us both to the heights of pleasure, that I would hurt in the morning. Someone like Yumi... she knows how to hurt me better than anyone else. The funny thing? Neither of us could have predicted what would come between us this time.

***

"You wear the second mask of happiness," the frog god says to me, "and yet it doesn't look happy at all."

"I'm happy, I swear. The love of my life is with me. We'll be together. Just her and me."

"You say this, and yet your face betrays your worry."

"I'm happy, can't you see?"

"All I see is a girl who wears a fake mask. Where did you get it? Who gave it to you?"

"I got it myself. I woke up one day with this face. It must have been the day after she came to me and said she wanted me."

"What's this now? What is this other face?"

"Huh?"

The frog god is not a patient sort. He scrunches his amphibious face at me and says, "You have another face. Don't you see it?"

"No, I don't."

"Ah. *Ah*. She doesn't yet know the meaning of this happiness. Yet it waits for her in the wings. The happiness that only the future world can bring."

I don't know what he's talking about. Why must these gods always be so cryptic? Maybe a face is just a face, and happiness is just happiness. "I feel no other happiness. Only for her."

"And for your fans, right? Don't you enjoy performing for them?"

"Not as much as she does. I suppose it's all right."

"Even a bit counts. The happiness we curate from those around us will feed into our souls for all eternity. Don't be fooled by temporary happiness."

"Don't patronize me. You think I don't know what happiness is? You think I can't feel it consume my soul and tear me apart… alive?"

"You think happiness is supposed to do that?"

"Maybe not happiness, but love."

"Who said anything about love?" The frog god scoffs at me. "Love is something else entirely. Not my realm."

"I get happiness from love."

"Be careful saying that."

"Happiness can be born from love."

"Indeed that's so. Happiness can be born from hate and violence as well."

"What are you saying?"

"Wear your third face and find out."

I try to put on the third face but struggle to fit it on my head. It's like a mask all right. This one doesn't quite match my cheekbones or the way my eyebrows arch. It's quite uncomfortable, as if someone is trying to slowly suffocate me.

"Chi-Chi!"

I wake up with my laptop warm against my legs, the screen dark. The little one is beside the bed, slapping my hand as it dangles near her.

"*Ara*, Sattchan!" My mother swoops in and picks up the child. "Can't you see she's trying to rest?"

"No, no, it's okay," I say.

"Chi-Chi…" She reaches to me, cheeks puffing. "Watch TV?"

"Hm? I'm sorry, I can't. I have to finish this."

Her pout is almost enough to gnaw on my heart. My mother shields her from me, chuckling. "Maybe later, eh? When Mama gets home, we'll watch something good. Maybe some Disney, eh? Chi-Chi always liked Disney movies. *Ne?* You would sing along to the songs and try to play them on piano."

I barely remember. "Sure. We can watch Disney later."

This appeases the little one enough that she clings to her grandmother with a silly smile on her face. What kind of happiness is that? Is there a mask for it? "Piano?"

I realize that I haven't played piano around her in a long time. Well, a long time for a three-year-old. "I can play you some piano later. Go with *Baa-chan* for now." I try to give her a soft grin to let her know that everything is all right, but she looks at me as if I wear a mask of pain instead of happiness.

"Do you feel it now?" the frog god asks me as my mother and daughter leave the room. "Do you feel the third mask you wear?"

"Every day," I whisper. "I've felt every form of happiness since the night we made her."

This makes the frog god happy, and he leaves me alone.

Chapter 40

What if I told you that my fears were for naught? What if I said that I woke up the next morning with Yumi still nestled in my arms, her breath warm against my chest as she dozed and I briefly woke to a sunny day?

I didn't want to move. Say I woke her up and she suddenly remembered what happened the night before? I would never forgive myself if I ruined something so exquisite like her bare skin pressed against mine with the morning light warming our bodies.

My eyes closed, and I let myself drift into a slumber that was neither dreamful nor barren. The only thing that woke me up a few minutes later was the feeling of Yumi's lips lightly touching my skin. A part of me wanted to cry. After what happened last time, I wanted to believe that this time would be different. She was here, wasn't she?

"Chi," she said, too sleepy to finish my name. "I don't want to get up."

"Who said we have to? It's a holiday."

Her hand was strong against my abdomen. "Then let's not get up. Just kiss me."

Hildred Billings

I rolled on top of her and gave her what she wanted. I had never made love to someone in the morning before. Usually my one night stands saw themselves out, or women like Naomi were not morning people and thus wanted nothing to do with sex until after the sun went down. Granted, Yumi had never been much of a morning person either. Who knows why she wanted to do it then? You think I was complaining?

Afterward I lay on my stomach, cheek resting against pillow as my eyelids became heavy again. Yumi's finger traced the scar on my back. "I thought maybe this had faded."

Sometimes I forget I still have that scar. Since it's hard for me to see, the only times I'm reminded of it is when people comment on it, like then. "It won't ever fade," I said. "Some things just don't fade." I slipped back into sleep, her fingers stroking my skin.

When I awoke again two hours later, it was to a wild scent coming from the kitchen and the sounds of Yumi's feet thumping on my carpet. "Chi-*chan!*" She called, hopping up onto my bed and shaking me. "Wake up! I made breakfast."

Was that what I smelled? I forced myself up, looking through groggy eyes into Yumi's cheerful face. Her hair was still mussed, but her eyes were wide and her smile too happy to bear. I thought I was dreaming. Did we really make love again? Was she really still here with me, taking my hand and trying to pull me out of bed so we could have breakfast?

Yumi dragged me halfway out of bed before dropping my limb and going back out into the kitchen. I rose, and within a few minutes I had thrown on a baggy sweater to wear out into the rest of my home. The moment I stepped out of my room, I saw her in front of the stove.

There are some images that stick with you forever. For some reason the image of Yumi standing there, wearing nothing but my black T-shirt as she added too much salt to eggs and swayed between feet, has stuck with me like a vivid photograph since it happened. I always thought she was beautiful... but in that moment she was utterly radiant, her skin glowing and this positive energy that I hadn't sensed from her in *years* surrounding her like an aura. I fell in love with her again that day. I loved her every day, but that morning it was like having a rock pelted at me. "Hey!" it said, leaving a dent in my skull. "That woman is really gorgeous! Go get her!"

Yumi turned off my stove and put the eggs and ham on two separate plates. She opened the fridge, took out some orange juice, and then rummaged through my cabinets in search of clean glasses. I had no incentive to tell her where they were since I was enjoying watching her stand on her tiptoes.

"Breakfast's ready," she said after catching a glimpse of me. Yumi found the glasses and left them on the counter. I approached, my arms instinctively wrapping around her from behind, and my nose grazing the back of her messy hair. Yumi seemingly ignored me, moving the dirty pan to the back of the stove and wiping her small mess with a cloth. "Are you gonna eat it, or should we just stand here like a couple of sillies?"

I relented, but only because my stomach was starting to growl. While I would never say that Yumi is a great cook, that morning even her over salted fare had me on cloud nine as we sat at the counter and fed each other food like we damn well were a couple of sillies.

"Let's go out," Yumi said after we cleaned up the dishes. We were still dressed for bed, but trust me, my hand was trying to coax that shirt off her again. The thought of putting on *more* clothes and going out in public where we couldn't do whatever we pleased with each other was not what I had in mind. "I wanna enjoy this fresh air."

"And the crowds? As ourselves?" Cameras would be everywhere. If people caught wind that someone like YUMI was in their midst, we would not be safe.

She took my arm. "If I have my Chi-*chan* to protect me, everything will be all right."

Eventually Yumi convinced me to put on some clothes and go out with her. But she listened to my reasoning that we shouldn't mingle with the holiday crowds and took me to some of her favorite department stores, where she was on a first name basis with the staff.

I'm not someone who wears designer clothing. Not on purpose, anyway. If a designer puts out something I like and it fits into my budget, I will get it, but I don't make a point of buying only designer clothes. Yumi, on the other hand, only wears designers. She's not particular, although I know for a fact that she loves Hermès scarves to the point she doesn't even wear them anymore. Instead she uses them to decorate her apartments. You ever walk into someone's home and see beautiful, colorful scarves draped over shelves, tacked in delirious patterns on the wall, and even hanging off random hooks here and there? Then you've clearly been somewhere Yumi lives.

"This one would look good on you." A pastel springtime pink scarf was wrapped around my neck when I wasn't paying attention. The auntie clerk applauded Yumi's good taste and told me that the pink really brought out my complexion. "You need more color in your wardrobe. Too much black and gray."

"I have color. Just not bright."

"Look at it this way, Morita-*sama*," the clerk said, smiling sweetly as she slowly approached and touched my white sweater. "Wearing such basic colors like black and white open you to a whole world of colorful accessories. A scarf like this…" She arranged it so it draped around my neck and down one side of my chest. "Gives just a hint of fanciful color while still retaining your original style."

Oh, she was good. Not good enough to convince me to buy it, but good nonetheless.

Yumi did her shopping in a carefree manner, flitting from one department to another with the biggest smile on her face. I knew she loved shopping, but usually she didn't have quite this much energy for it. She also didn't really buy anything, aside from a hairpin and one scarf to add to her collection. It took me a while, but I gradually realized that much of her happiness came from… being with me? She was always touching me. Not sexually, but her hand on my arm here, her fingers with mine there, and her nose rubbing against my cheek as she became excited about something a clerk said. If we hadn't just spent half the night making love, I would think she was on drugs!

Love, Yumi

Here's something I had never considered: that Yumi, the woman I pined for and loved beyond measure for so many years, would love me like a silly girl in return. In my fantasies, if my love was ever reciprocated, it was always quite serious, or a non-issue. "Yes, I love you, Chiharu," she would say with a straight face before kissing me. "Now let's get dinner and then take a bath." See how practical I am?

Even now I don't really understand the kind of girlish love that takes some people over. I had seen Yumi moon over boys before, but the idea that she could be acting like a lovesick, clingy girl around me was unfathomable. Nobody had acted like that around me before. Girls (and women) saw me as a sex partner, someone to talk to over dinner, or maybe both. Dates were personified with touchless nights out until we got home and could unleash our closeted tendencies. I knew Yumi was open with her love, but to have it directed toward me?

Was she falling in love with me? *Already* in love with me? What was going on? And why did it make me embarrassed?

No, not embarrassed. I wasn't angry that she dare show me any affection in front of other people. The public knew we were feely friends who sometimes held hands, and it meant nothing. To them, it meant nothing. To me, it now meant everything.

She took me to lunch at her usual spot, and we laughed about our childhoods, about the early years at the label, and even found something hilarious about the day we were detoxing from the drugs. "You looked like such utter shit," Yumi said over her cider and salad. "I'd never seen you look so sick before."

"You didn't look so great yourself. It wasn't my head trapped in the toilet bowl."

"Hmm." A piece of lettuce rolled over Yumi's fork. "Why was I the only one throwing up so much like that? Sometimes I wonder if I was on something else from the rest of you. I can't imagine my constitution being that weak."

It was something I often wondered as well. But I didn't dare ask Beppu or anyone else what they thought. Some things were best left unknown.

"Why are you wondering that now?" I asked.

For the first time all day, she frowned. "I haven't been feeling my best this past week. I feel fine today, but yesterday morning, for example, I felt pretty nauseated for a while. I wasn't sure I would even be able to go into the office."

"You seemed fine in the evening." More than fine.

"That's the strangest part. It goes away pretty quickly."

Are you laughing at me? At my ignorance? I feel ignorant just typing up this exchange and going *if I only fucking knew!*

I was afraid that the fun would be over after lunch. Yumi yawned in the early afternoon and mumbled something about going home and taking a nap. Yet when we got into the elevator by ourselves, she surprised me by saying, "Let's go to your place. I've got something to give you."

"At my place? What are you talking…"

She pushed me against the wall and kissed me, right in front of the camera!

We got in my car and went back to my apartment. I sat on my couch, staring at my piano, out the window, and wondering what the hell Yumi was up to in my bathroom for the past ten minutes. Then I realized she wasn't in my bathroom when the drawers began opening and closing in my bedroom. What in the world?

"Chiharu!" Yumi called, a drawer closing. "Get in here and explain this to me!"

Those words seem angry and sinister, while her tone was anything but. Still, I took my time peeling myself off the couch and going to my bedroom door. I cracked it open a bit, seeing her stand beside my bed in the same clothes she had worn the night before. Minus the blouse. And the pants. And everything but her underwear.

"Yeah?" Dare I ask why she was almost naked? She was getting my hopes up.

What she held up in her hand should have given me a heart attack. In truth, it nearly did. The words tossed in my mouth like a hot candy, and God knows I felt like a scandalized auntie about to rip an insolent girl a new perspective on morality. "Chi-*chan*..." Yumi said, grinning as she slapped the other end of a woman's most private possession against her hand. I jerked at the sound, at its implication. "This is a really naughty thing to have just lying around. I had no idea you were that kind of girl."

"You just going through my drawers?"

She shifted on her dainty feet, that grin almost ominous as she kissed the tip she held in her hand. "I wanted to see your secrets." Yumi held out what she had and nearly scoffed at it. "You're a woman after my own heart. Big."

"Oh my God."

"*Nee*," Yumi approached me, her hips swaying back and forth in her lacy lavender underwear, "how do two women use something like this?"

I blushed so hard that she had to stifle a laugh. "Well, you see..."

"Oh, this here goes in one person, and this one in the other? Like this?" She held it up. Like a pro. Damn her.

"You've been through my drawers already!"

"Now, now." She was close enough to smack me in the chest with my own device – which she did. "I don't follow directions very well. You're going to have to show me how these things work."

"I..."

She turned around, signaling for me to unhook her bra. "Let's get going. We only have all day."

Thank God, because it practically took the whole day for me to wrap my head around what was happening.

It was the greatest week of my life. Every day Yumi and I were together, and every single day was a new adventure in our... romance? Love? Blossoming affection in newfound ways for each other? I didn't care. I was a girl in love and expressing it for the first time in my life, and nothing you could have said or done to me could have changed a *damn* thing.

On our third day together, Yumi and I spent most of the day in my apartment, coming up with bullshit songs on my piano and watching our old drama *The Secretary of Shibuya* on TV. I hadn't seen it since it aired, so seeing a much younger me try and fail at acting while Yumi made her impressive debut was a laugh and a half. I laughed so hard that by the end of the fifth episode I had to go excuse myself to recollect my sanity in the bathroom.

"Look at you, refusing to kiss that guy." Yumi was halfway in my lap, pinching my cheek while younger me did everything in my power to not kiss my male costar. "Remember how much the director praised you? I'm surprised you never got more acting offers."

"I'm a one-trick pony," I said. "That's the only character I can play. Myself."

Yumi rubbed my chest with those nibbling lips at my throat. "I like you, though. Might as well play the best character."

I wavered between accepting her affections and being wary of them. She hadn't said this was a permanent thing between us, and I was afraid to ask. For all I knew this would be a Golden Week fling and we would be back to just friends after she returned to work. In that moment, however, I felt pretty smug wrapping an arm around her as if that was what one did.

We went out later, to Athens. For the first time ever I felt comfortable there, probably because I had Yumi's undivided attention and it was like a date. We knocked back a few drinks and tried our hands at pool, but since we got tipsy too quickly the cues were slipping through our fingers and we kept losing track of the balls. A guy offered to help us "find the balls" and Yumi merely shrugged him off while laughing at one of my really bad jokes.

I don't remember how much we drank that night. All I know is that I woke up the next day with a mild hangover and Yumi was sick enough to spend half the morning in my bathroom. Having partied too hard, we decided to switch locations and go to her apartment, where she had better medicine and a darker environment for battling headaches. By the late afternoon, we both felt much better.

Yumi was naughty and showed me some confidential things from the label. We sat at her dining table, looking at the photos and concepts for her upcoming album. "I don't know what to do with my hair," she said, running her fingers through it as she spoke. The blond hadn't been touched up in a while, so it was half platinum and half black. "I like blond, but I've been this color for so long."

"It's pretty much your trademark," I said. "That and black. Maybe it's time to go back?"

"Black is so boring!" Her face immediately colored. "I mean on me. Sorry."

"No offense taken." I hadn't dyed my hair in years, although sometimes I thought about going back to that soft brown. As happy as I was at the moment, it didn't seem like a bad idea.

"Maybe red?" Yumi picked up one of her pictures and studied her own face. "Not shocking red, mind you. Something dark. *Maa*, I dunno. That pink hair I had for two weeks was a bit much."

I picked up the photo showing the track list. "Eh, you really are putting that song on there," I said, referring to the song she sang for me at Budokan.

"Of course I am!" Yumi snatched the photo from my hand. "I told those people it was going to be on the album."

"Who wrote it?" Not me. Not even the music.

"One of the other staff composers. I wrote the lyrics."

"You really love me, eh?" I smiled, letting her know it was a joke. Although I would be lying if I said I didn't want to know the answer.

"Of course I love you."

For her to say it so matter-of-factly and with her eyes on her pictures meant that she meant it in a friendly way. "*Of course I love you. We've been together since we were six. How could I not care about you?*" I loved her the same way. Only in the past few years I also loved her like a girlfriend. No, a wife. I didn't need her to perform "wifely duties" like cooking and ironing my shirts. I wanted to grow old with her in my arms every night, my name on her lips every time she wanted to make love.

My name was on her lips that night. After dinner, Yumi took me by the hand and guided me to her room, where she latched the door shut and started unbuttoning my clothes. "You're really into it this week," I said, trying to maintain my cool as she pressed her lips against my skin. "Not that I can't keep up."

"What can I say?" Yumi stepped back toward her bed, my shirt in her hands as she pulled me with her. "Another day goes by, and I want you again."

My shirt came off and we fell onto her bed. "You ever have a naked woman in your bed before?"

"Only me." Before I could have an image of her sleeping with a guy, she said, "It gets hot in the summer."

"It's about to get hot in mid-spring."

"Well I better take off my clothes then!"

I could get used to this. My bed, her bed, any bed in the country. All we needed was each other and enough time to explore what made us fit together so well.

On a lark we packed two overnight bags, got into my car, and drove up to Seki to revisit the old haunting grounds. Since my mom was still in Okinawa, we went to Yumi's parents' house to surprise them with our smiling faces.

It was my first time seeing them like this in many years. Eight years, when I thought about it. The last time Chiharu came to the Nishikawa house she was still wearing a high school uniform. Now she wore fashionable clothes and jewelry, her body filled out and her face done up in light makeup.

They asked me how my music was going while they doted on their star-studded daughter. Yumi had gone from being their spoiled only child to their darling baby who would take care of them forever. Both parents only worked because they wanted to now. Yumi's money was more than enough to set them up for the rest of their lives. Like me for my mother, Yumi paid off their house, their car, and her mother's remaining medical bills from her illness years ago. They were both debt free and enjoying life. To a daughter, that's tremendous.

Love, Yumi

Together we ate lunch at the old kitchen table, the same one Yumi and I did homework at growing up. We looked at a stain on the far end from when we tried to make a volcano for a science project. Who knew that those two bumbling, arguing twelve-year-olds would one day be music stars? Yumi and I went to her room to take a trip down memory lane — awards, photos, ribbons, and plenty of dolls that she forgot she had.

In the afternoon we grabbed Yumi's old bike and figured out how to ride in tandem like we used to. Back then, we would choose who drove and who clung based on who the bike belonged to. We quickly found out that I had grown too big in my adult years to ride on the back of the seat. After switching, Yumi wrapped her arms around me and said, "Let's pretend we're sixteen again."

We biked through Seki, retracing the roads we once used to get to school and waving at the same people who sat outside of cafés and produce stands. Some of them mindlessly waved back while others gawked as they recognized us. The aunties and uncles had seen us as teenagers every day. They would brag to one another and to the press, "Remember when Yumi and Chiharu would ride past here to school? Thick as thieves, those two. It's so sweet that they're still friends." Now they looked twice to make sure it was us they saw. "Remember when Yumi and Chiharu sped by here during Golden Week? Wearing those nice clothes, too! I can't believe they're still friends like that. Bosom buddies are alive and well."

Soon the roads took us out of Seki. Pavement gave way to dirt, but neither of us complained when our clothes got dusty and our lips became chapped from the wind. I pedaled until we reached the old magnolia tree we once climbed when we were children. It had grown bigger since and was in full bloom… it's those kinds of places, where time has stopped and nostalgia has a chance of thriving, that a grown woman truly feels home again.

We didn't go tree climbing, but we did inspect the tree, looking for the initials we thought we had carved a long time ago only to discover we made that up.

"Those were good days," Yumi said wistfully. "Even though it felt kinda boring back then, now I often find myself wanting to return to those days so I can feel that freedom with you again."

Out there in the middle of nowhere I felt comfortable putting my hand on the small of her back. She deferred to my embrace and held me close to her. "I'm glad I met you." My voice was softer than the warm breeze blowing against my cheek. "I'm glad you talked to me that day when we were kids."

I did it. I managed to make her blush. "You're my favorite person," Yumi said. "I knew you would be."

We walked through the fields of our hometown, holding hands, splitting up to pick flowers and make chains out of them, and then coming back together to drape strands of dandelions on each other's heads and arms. I felt silly, but Yumi was radiant, like a springtime princess in her bold hair and bright smile. When she trotted away in her flower crown and hid behind a tree, her big round eyes peering at me in the descending glow of the sunlight, I thought that she was for sure the most gorgeous girl in the world.

"You're glowing," I said, standing on the other side of the tree. Our hands locked around it, and I fought the urge to take her in my arms and kiss her until we fell to the grass and made love. "Positively."

"I'm so happy this week." Her voice almost disappeared into the tree bark. "Promise me we can keep this week forever, Chi-*chan*."

I stole a kiss from around the trunk. "If I could stop time today, I would."

My heart was so heavy with love that time did stand still for me. I gazed at every line of her body as it twirled in the setting sunlight, her smile as she looked up to the sky both wondrous and saved just for me. To touch her, to kiss her were my only goals, but I could also settle for watching her enjoy her youth like a girl again. I remembered teenaged Yumi and her knack for getting us into mischief, such as bothering farmers and teasing boys. Harmless stuff in the long run. Back then, when the whole world was Seki, it was all I wanted to be familiar with.

Love, Yumi

If I could go back in time and tell my much younger self that Yumi and I would be like this today, I would be shocked. Confused. First, what was it to be in love with a woman? With Yumi? I didn't think of her explicitly in that way back then. She was my best friend. We painted each other's toenails, shared homework, gossiped about our classmates on rainy days, and went to bed together as if it were natural to do so. The idea of not only making love but also creating a life together was beyond me. Sometimes I caught glimpses of the same understanding from Yumi as we strolled through the sunset and reminisced about those days. Her hand was tight in mine, and when we stopped on a hill to watch the final descent of the sun, Yumi put her head on my shoulder and her hand on my thigh.

Overall, the perfect day. The original plan was to go back to the Nishikawa house, but Yumi said she couldn't bear the thought of her parents butting into our new love life. "Take me somewhere we can properly be together," she said, helping me find her bike again.

So we went to my childhood home, which I still had a key for and was empty that week. We snuck upstairs into my old bedroom and made love in my old bed, giggling at the scandal of our younger selves walking through the door and seeing what adult us were capable of doing when adult love heated up and we couldn't keep our hands off each other anymore. The only problem was that my bed was not built to take two grown women undulating together in the dark. The sound of the squeaks and the thumps of the bed against the wall made it worth the slight fear that we would go tumbling to the floor at any moment. "Thank God we didn't do that in high school," Yumi said when we basked in our exhilaration. "Your mother would've definitely heard."

She lost me at the implication we could have done this back in high school. To this day, I wonder what would have changed, what would have been different if I had told Yumi early on how much I loved her. Would she have reciprocated? Was this even reciprocation right now? I would have to ask soon. Golden Week only had a single day left.

On the last day of our vacation, we drove back to my apartment in Nagoya and decided to be as lazy as possible. Yumi said she felt weary so it worked for her, and I needed to do some light cleaning so it worked for me. While she dozed on my couch with the TV on, I wiped down the kitchen and went through a load of laundry. There was a domestic comfort to it that I never considered before. A part of me wished that Yumi wasn't so famous, if only so we could be together like this more often. Once the album came out, and once the tour started, I would see Yumi maybe once or twice a month.

I made a small dinner, which we ate with wine. If there's one thing dangerous around me, it's wine. I don't just get giddy – I get sentimental, and very, very touchy. Wine is a great drink for me to have on nights like that one because all I want to do is wrap my arms around someone and tell them how fantastic they are. Good thing for Yumi I loved her so much. No one benefited as much as she would from these feelings welling up inside me.

The dirty dishes were left in my clean kitchen as we kept our flirting to the couch, this time with the TV off. Even after a full week of indulging ourselves, I didn't feel as peaceful as I did then, pressed against the back of the couch with her nestled in my arms. I tried not to think about us parting the next day. Well, not *parting*. Why did it have to be now? I wish it could have happened during a lull in both of our lives. I am aware that every relationship has a honeymoon phase, but we hardly had time to enjoy ours.

Yumi got up to use the bathroom and I put the wine away before I became too intoxicated to function. As I waited for the effects to wear off, Yumi returned, putting some music on my stereo. At first I thought it was our cover album, but then I realized that no, it was a mix of the original songs we sang.

"*Nee*, Chi-*chan*," Yumi said, turning from the stereo and looking at me in my kitchen. "Do you remember when we danced in the practice studio?"

I didn't have to ask her to get more specific. "Of course." Given recent events, I wondered if I should bring up what we did in that studio.

Including her admission that she didn't understand why she always had to stop our affections.

Apparently I wasn't supposed to say anything, for she extended her hand to me and said, "Dance with me."

I hid my reaction behind a plate. "I haven't danced in years." Thank God. Best part about ending life as an idol.

Her fingers motioned to me some more. "Even better reason for you to dance with me. You obviously need the practice."

Deep down I knew I couldn't embarrass myself in front of her, but on the surface it was all I could think about. Even so, I put the last of the dishes away and went to her, if only so I could feel her hand against mine again.

She pulled herself into my embrace just as a slow song started. Arms wrapped around my neck, she rested her head on my shoulder, and we began to sway back and forth. Now this kind of dancing I could do.

"I feel so safe with you," she mumbled into my sweater. "I can barely understand what I feel right now, but I know that I feel safe."

I wrapped my hand around the back of her head and pulled her closer to me. "I understand what I feel." For years now.

"Because you're Chiharu. You don't overthink things. You just follow your heart and don't care what anyone thinks." Yumi pressed her forehead against mine. "I want to be more like you. I wish I didn't care so much about what other people think."

"You're in a different place from me," I reminded her. "You were always the face of the group, and now you're one of the biggest stars in the country. What am I? Nobody cares about me in the tabloids, unless it has to do with you."

"That's not true." Her lips brushed against mine, gently, not an invitation to initiate more. "I care about you."

I couldn't tell you what song was playing on the stereo. Maybe it was "Dollhouse" or maybe it was "Hold Me." It didn't matter. The only music in my head was the fluttering of my heart as I kissed Yumi and asked, "You'll stay with me tonight, right?"

"Of course."

We made love in my bed, for one hour, for another, sweet and gentle so we didn't wear each other out too quickly. For our last night together, I wanted to memorize every part of her body, beginning with her blushing cheeks and ending at her delicate ankles. I know I say this all the time, and I am biased, but Yumi Nishikawa is the most beautiful woman in the world. If you don't agree with me, it's because you don't know her like I do. You haven't seen the way she's grown over the years, from a spunky girl rallying kids to play make believe in the schoolyard to a fit young woman inspiring half the world through the power of her voice and dance. She's always been that way. Enticing. Entrancing. Think about it. Even if I were not a lesbian, I would have never stood a chance growing up with Yumi. I would have loved her in other ways. The fiercely protective older sister (even though I am four months younger) or the clingy best friend who could never be separated from her. Romantic love adds a layer to those feelings that can't be tainted.

Late into the night I found my lips against her stomach, searching for the firm muscles beneath as her breaths made her body ease up and down against my mouth. Mesmerizing. I could tell Yumi wanted me to venture farther south, and I did tease the top of her mound whenever I found it fitting, but my attentions were captured by the slight movements of her abdomen as it reflected how quickly her heart was beating.

It was like I knew back then. There was something more to share my love with than just the woman I worshiped with my meager body.

Long after we settled in for the night, something weighed heavy in my chest. No, not just my lovesick heart. Something more toxic. Doubt. Worry. Insincerity.

"What is this?" I finally asked, clutching Yumi's body close to mine. Her hand and head were on my chest, my arm wrapped tight around her back, the perfect position for us to ponder when near one another. "What does this mean?"

Yumi lifted her head enough that her chin pressed into my rib. "You tell me."

Love, Yumi

How dare she! I was the last person who should be making that decision. Yumi was the one holding all the cards. If I had it my way, she would be my girlfriend. Not my girl who was a friend, but my lover, my partner, the woman I built a life with. I wanted to live with her. If not here, then somewhere. I would move into her apartment if she asked.

"All I know is that this has been the happiest week of my life," I said carefully, trying to not betray the desperation lurking beneath my voice. My arm squeezed her tighter, and Yumi pulled herself up to my level, her nose digging into the nape of my neck. "Do you know how long I've loved you?"

There it was. The desperation. I couldn't believe that Yumi didn't know I loved her – like that – but who knew how she rationalized things? She never even said that she was gay or at least considering some other sexual identity. I wouldn't ask her to stop being attracted to men. That wasn't my business. But if she wanted to be with me, I wanted her to at least acknowledge that side of herself. I've been with women in denial. They never last more than one night.

"I know," she finally murmured against my throat.

"Then don't fuck with me." I eased her off me, my body pinning her to my bed so she couldn't run away from the dilemma I was about to present. She looked at me with those wide, startled eyes that said she wasn't ready for this side of me. "Don't be like last time and get my hopes up just to pretend this never happened. This happened, right?"

Her face softened, and my heart melted with it. "Of course it happened." Her hands were on my cheeks, and I kissed one of them, that same heart wishing I would shut up and give myself over to this woman who owned it. "I don't want to forget it either."

Just say it, I thought. Just say you love me. She had to, right? These moments wouldn't exist if it weren't for any love she held for me, right? "I love you," I confessed again, my lips hitting hers with more force than I intended. "No matter what, I'll stick with you as your best friend, but I want to love you like this too. Forever."

She raised her head and kissed me, bringing me back down with her. "You can," she whispered between my lips. "Forever."

I don't have to tell you how happy that made me. Finally, for the first time in my life, I had someone to love wholeheartedly. That night I showed her exactly what she had to look forward to with me.

"I can't tell you when we can be together again," she said the next morning, getting ready to return to her apartment before going on to the office. "I'll call you later. We'll figure it out."

That goodbye kiss before she went out my door was just what I needed to fuel me for the rest of the day. And the rest of the week. The month. I held onto those memories, even after I realized I should have never let her leave me at all.

I'm sorry, Yumi. I wish I had known.

***

It's evening when Yumi returns, her face flustered and her designer handbag slamming against her couch. Her anger is palpable enough that my mother jumps in her chair and the little one's lip quivers. Seeing the storm about to explode, I tell my mother to take the child into the guest room. She does it just in time.

"Fuck those bastards," Yumi mumbles, channeling her energy through the nearest dining chair. "Fuck them!"

I stand on the other side of the table, trying to muster a calming mood for her to feed off. "Didn't go well at the label, I take it."

"Gee, what makes you think that?"

She looks like a petulant child. Like the girl who would throw a tantrum in front of her mother to get what she wanted. Those days are mostly over, but now adult Yumi keeps it behind closed doors. I'm probably one of the few people who sees this side of her now.

"They've suspended me," she says. "And I mean *suspended*. If I am then you're probably getting booted from the label altogether."

I have yet to hear anything. I'm probably next, though. "What do you mean suspended? They've already put your album on hold."

"Oh, it's been shelved indefinitely. They're also cancelling all of my upcoming interviews, spots, and…"

"And?"

She bites her lip and clenches her fists. "I've been dropped by Kosmetics."

"Oh God." Yumi's Kosmetics endorsement is the biggest one she's had since Butterfly Tops hit #1. She's represented them for *years*. Her face is in every magazine, every commercial, every poster in the trendy districts. For them to drop her and cancel her contract means they're really pissed. "Well, we figured that might happen."

"And you? What have *you* been dropped from?" She doesn't want an answer. She wants to stomp back and forth like a tiger cooped up in a cage. "Nothing."

"Yumi…"

She holes herself up in the bathroom. I have to shrug off her words and go back to fixing dinner. Even if she's pissed and I'm not that hungry, my mother and the little one both need to eat. I fix something simple and let them eat before going to fetch Yumi.

"I'm not hungry!" she calls through the door.

"Come on. You have to eat."

"No I don't."

Even so, she comes out and joins me at the dining table within ten minutes. She eats silently, but forcefully, like the small steak is going to sprout cow legs and run out the door if she doesn't stab it, chew it, and devour it quickly enough. She barely touches the salad. Someone wants blood.

"Wanna talk about it?"

Yumi glares at me. "You're the last person I want to talk about it to."

"I'm sorry."

She shakes her head. "You should have heard what they said." Her voice is softer, but I can hear the tears about to start. "They told me to 'professionally and personally sever ties' with you. They gave me this whole list of conditions to follow if I wanted to be treated like a second-class artist on their label. One of them was denouncing you and your blog. Another was going on TV and officially apologizing while saying most of what you wrote was lies. They're coming for you next."

"*Sou ka...*"

"They're reading everything you post. They've got people trying to take your blog down. You better hope it stays so popular simply so the blog host has more incentive to keep it up than to let it come down."

"I've got backups."

"God!" Yumi drops her silverware as a sob almost overcomes her. "Is this really worth it? Fuck it. It has to stop."

"It can't stop. We're fucked with the amount that's come out. It will mean nothing without the whole story."

I don't expect it. How can I? When Yumi's hand lashes out and slaps me across the cheek, I feel like I've been hit by a meteorite.

"The whole story will destroy me." She leaves the table.

My cheek still stinging, I do the dishes and check in on my family. My mother is reading a story to the little one in the guest bedroom, and when she sees the red mark on my face she invites me to join. For ten minutes I curl up next to them and listen to the tale of a frog prince and his three faces of happiness.

"Chi-Chi was in this play when she was in high school," my mother says. "Wait, were you in the play?"

"No. I did some sets and played the piano."

"Good enough for me."

I tell the little one that Yumi played Jinga. "She was a beautiful peasant girl," I say wryly. "Even more beautiful old lady on the brink of death." This makes both my mother and daughter laugh, albeit uneasily.

Eventually I leave them to go find Yumi and clear the air for the day. I hear her splashing in the bathtub and knock lightly, surprised to find the door unlocked. To some great amusement, she's buried beneath an ocean of bubbles, head resting on a towel as she stares at the ceiling of her luxurious bathroom. I latch the door behind me and sit on the covered toilet next to the tub.

We're silent for a while, and I'm pretty sure Yumi is ignoring my existence. She has a glass of wine she knocks back when she thinks I'm not looking. She also has a bowl of chocolate covered raisins. If she hadn't just come back from an awful meeting with label executives, I would think she was pampering herself because she can.

I'm surprised when she hands the bowl of raisins to me. Wordlessly I decline, and they return to the other side of the tub. Guess it's okay to talk.

"Feeling any better?"

She looks at me as if I just asked if she grew a third leg.

"Look, I'm sorry. I don't know what else you want me to say."

"Don't say anything. You don't have to always be apologizing to me." The wineglass is against her mouth.

"This is clearly bothering you…"

"Whatever. You were right. We knew going in to this that the repercussions would be real. It's just…"

"Hm?"

The bubbles float up higher as she moves her legs beneath the water. "I wish I had more control over it. It's not fun wondering what you're going to write next and then finding out the next day. In your words. Not that you don't have a way with words, but it's my story too, and none of it is my words."

"We could fix that."

Yumi considers this for a few seconds before snorting hard enough to create a bunch of bubbles by her face. "No thanks. I'm anxious enough. Just for the love of God, finish this soon."

"I'm trying. I can only write so much at a time."

"What did you write today? I turned my phone off so people will leave me alone."

I tell her. She neither flinches nor smiles.

"Do you remember that play we did in high school? The Three Faces of Happiness?"

"Vaguely."

"I've been thinking about it a lot. About what the three faces are."

"All I remember is people, romance, and babies."

"That was the basic gist of it."

The only reaction I get is a judgmental glare as her eyes travel up and down my body.

"You've gotten pudgy."

"Excuse me?"

Her wet hand grabs my upper arm and squeezes it. When she lets go, I'm not surprised that there are water droplets all over my sweater. "You used to be a lot more muscular."

"Ever hear of getting older? Plus I haven't had time to work out lately." All the traveling, the stress, and the sitting at my computer has not been good for my figure. "If you're so offended by my body, I may be able to squeeze in a workout tomorrow."

"You better. If I'm going down in the history books as your lesbian lover, then you better look damn good."

"Yes ma'am."

"Now get the hell out of here. I'm stewing in the remnants of my career."

I leave, shutting the bathroom door firmly behind me. Suddenly I'm overcome with fatigue, and I don't know if it's because I'm just tired or mentally drained.

Part 12

ONE-THOUSAND SPRINGTIME PETALS

Hildred Billings

Love, Yumi

春の落ちている花びら

I woke up to find a packed suitcase next to the bedroom door. I didn't think much of it at first until I stepped out into the living room and saw Yumi cleaning out her purse – something she only does when she's about to go on a trip and doesn't want "junk" in her bag.

"Where are you going?"

She looked up, startled. Yeah, I was up early enough to catch her trying to sneak out. "I'm going back to Nagoya," she said as if it had been planned for weeks. "I'm no use to anyone here. My mom's gonna meet me and we'll go somewhere. Maybe home, if it's safe enough."

"Okay." I was still groggy, but as the situation came over me I woke up little by little. "Give us an hour and we'll be ready to go."

"No." Jacket already on, Yumi hoisted her purse strap on her shoulder. "I'm going alone. You and the others stay here for now. There's security. Especially if you get called into the principal's office."

I couldn't tell if she was being purposely cheeky. Neither one made me happy. "You just don't want to be around me right now." At that point it was merely a fact.

She didn't dispute it. Sunglasses and head covering on, Yumi said goodbye and headed for the door.

"Mama?" The little one hopped off the couch and ran toward her. "Mama, *doko iku ka?*"

Yumi stood in front of the door, one shoe on and the other languishing on her left foot. "I'm going to Nagoya. Sorry."

Yumi's always been brusque with my daughter. Usually the little one takes it in stride, but that morning, overwhelmed with her child feelings, she started crying, crumpling to her knees as she grabbed Yumi's ankle.

"Mama *ikanaide!*"

While the little one threw this tantrum, Yumi gave me an exasperated look. "*Do something about this, would you?*" her eyes said. I bent down and plucked my child off the ground, holding her to my chest as she got tears and slobber all over my nightshirt. I tried to soothe her with a pat on the head, but that only made her cry louder, summoning my mother from the guest room. When she saw what was happening, she frowned.

"Nobody wants you to go," I said to Yumi. "At least take her with you."

She seemed to consider it for a moment, but whether a small child would cramp her glamorous style or she just didn't want to deal with the little one's unique whims, Yumi shook her head and gave the child a half-assed kiss on the forehead. "You're better at this," she told me. "She's better off with you."

"Whatever you need to tell yourself."

I'm not proud that those were our parting words. With no idea when I'll see Yumi again – or if she'll even call tonight when she gets wherever she's going – I will sit here on her couch in Tokyo and watch the clouds roll by. My mother took the little one out to cheer her up, bodyguard in tow for good measure. He looks close enough in appearance to my mother that the average person would think they're mother and son. Let's hope the reporters think so too. The last thing I want is them showing up in the tabloids tomorrow, or to have my mother harassed with questions she can't even answer.

Love, Yumi

Today I'm gonna need a drink before I start writing. Time to find out where Yumi kept that bottle of wine. Advanced apologies if things get a bit incoherent toward the end. My mother's gonna come home to find her daughter at least halfway intoxicated.

Chapter 41

I took my separation from my girlfriend (because that's how I thought of her) in stride. Even after the first two weeks passed, during which I had received at least some texts or a phone call every day. Then when suddenly Yumi disappeared from the face of the earth, I was content. Her last message to me was that she was going into full-album-release mode and may be scarce. I looked forward to seeing her on TV promoting the album.

The album went straight to #1. Not surprising, since YUMI was still hot and the label took extra care in choosing a release date when she didn't have as much competition. They didn't have to worry. She sold over 100,000 copies that first week, one of the best album drops of the year and already solidifying her a top 10 spot on the end of the year charts.

It was June, about a month after Golden Week. Yumi was in the first week of promotions, going on variety and music shows to perform. The lead track wasn't a song I composed, but it was mature and lively, the exact image she was going for at the time. However, her performances were a bit lackluster. Even me, with my love blinders on, could see it, and the general populace said the same thing. Yumi would get on stage and stand in one spot instead of dancing. Her voice wavered on high notes as if she were about to start crying. I sent her a million texts and voice messages asking her to call me in case something was wrong. I was concerned when she never did.

"I've been a bit ill these past couple of weeks," she told one interviewer on a late night show. "Nothing serious, before people worry about me. Just some seasonal stuff. I'm sorry about my performances as of late. By the time of my tour I should be up to snuff again."

The interviewer, an older man known for his candid way of asking questions, said, "Your image has changed a bit since you began your solo career. As you come upon your twenty-sixth year of life, are you making strides to change how the public perceives you?"

Yumi smiled sadly, although I was probably the only person in the world who saw that pull on her lips before she recovered. "I am going through many changes this year. Sometimes it's easy to forget that I'm a grown woman who can make her own decisions in her personal life. I'm so used to other people telling me what to do that it's difficult for me to be honest at times. But yes, many changes have happened this year alone. For example, I'm in love."

I perked up in my seat, and the audience gasped before minor applause erupted. "Love? You know I have to ask with whom."

"That I can't share right now. It's a person who will take good care of me, and I'm sure that you'll be seeing us together a lot in the near future." Yumi looked right into the camera and smiled. *"You know it's you, right?"*

Although this had been recorded a few hours ago, I still smiled back at her and nodded my head. As soon as the show went to commercial, I texted Yumi that I had seen it and that I definitely still loved her. Oh, and for her to call me when she had the chance.

Mid-June she did her final TV performance for her album promotions. She surprised everyone by performing "Nothing Without You," the song she wrote for me. I should have been elated, but she was so pale, so fragile looking on stage that my stomach was in my throat the whole performance. Every close-up on her face included a desperate look from behind her eyes, as if her soul were crying out to me, begging me to find and rescue her from whatever bothered her so much. All I could do was touch my TV screen and send her even more frantic messages. Why wasn't she answering me?

And why was she falling on the stage, her body crumpling on the ground as staff people shouted, the crowd gasped, and the studio quickly cut to commercial? I called and called. I even called Koji, but all he would tell me was, "She has the flu. I'm sorry you had to see that. Yumi sends her regards and wants me to tell you that she'll call you soon." She never did.

I should have known that something was terribly wrong when a tour was never announced. Usually the news would have hit by July at the latest, but July came and went without a peep about Yumi's condition or any tour.

The only reason I knew she wasn't dead or in the hospital was because she still did radio. I would tune in to shows just to hear her voice, but nothing beyond generic questions were asked. "What was the hardest part about working on the album? Which song means the most to you? What kind of style would you want to try next? What's your favorite TV show at the moment? If you could perform in any country in the world, where would it be?"

Her answers, while heartfelt, were scripted to the point I could anticipate the next word coming out of her mouth. It felt good to hear her voice, but I prayed that she would call me herself. This wasn't just about Golden Week. Something was going on… either she was being kept from me, or there was something she didn't want me to know.

Did the label find out that we were an item? Maybe she told someone she thought she trusted and the word got out to the executives. Except I would have heard something. My work flow was the same as always, and nobody said anything to me beyond work related issues.

My worries buried themselves in my gut as the summer wore on. By August I was still concerned – beyond concerned – but I stopped blowing up Yumi's phone and waited for her to contact me. When she did, about one week before *obon,* it was a simple text message.

"Turn on the seven o'clock news tonight."

Why the news? I went online and saw that Yumi would be holding a press conference that night. Fans speculated everything. Most assumed that it had to do with a world tour, and that's why the original tour was put on hold. Yet if that were the case, wouldn't she have told me long before? No way would she be able to hold that in!

My fears returned. Maybe she was sick. No, no, no. I didn't want to believe it. Cancer. It had to be cancer. Both of my hands shook when I turned on the news that night. I expected to see Yumi looking skeletal and with a bald head.

Instead she sat at a table, full in the cheeks and wearing a baggy black blouse. She had a full head of hair that was almost to her shoulders… and black. Apparently she decided to cut out the blond and let her natural hair color reign. She also wore minimal makeup, and kept her hands in her lap.

Members of the staff got into their places. Koji sat to her left, dressed in his usual suit and tie with his head bent low. The seat on her right was empty until a late arrival showed up.

Yohei.

Fucking Yohei.

I knew. I knew what had happened. Bile shot up my throat, but my brain tried to tell the rest of my body that it wasn't anything to panic about. There were many reasons for Yohei to show up at a last minute press conference with Yumi. Maybe they were going on tour together. Maybe they were doing a duet album. I wanted to believe anything. *Anything.*

"As of this morning," Yumi said into a microphone as she forced a pretty smile, "Yohei and I have filed marriage papers. We're married now. Please support us."

The reporters went wild, flashing pictures and shouting questions at the new, happy couple. I sat on my couch, horrified, frozen in place while I focused on my breathing and tried to convince myself that this was a terrible nightmare.

"Furthermore," Yumi continued, waiting for the rabble to die down, "there is another piece of important news." She and Yohei smiled at each either. He motioned for her to continue while Koji sat up straight, preparing for an oncoming onslaught. Still smiling, Yumi turned back to her microphone. "I'm about twelve weeks pregnant. I'm going to be a mother."

That was bigger news than the marriage announcement. The TV turned into a giant camera flash as people asked to see the wedding ring and when the baby was due. Yumi held up her left hand, but I couldn't make out the diamond ring on her finger. I was too busy slipping off my couch and landing with a thud on the floor. Someone had walked by and clocked me in the back of the head.

How could she smile like that? How could she wrap her arm around Yohei's as they smiled for the cameras and promised to be good, dutiful parents?

"Suffice to say any plans for a tour have been canceled," Yumi said a few minutes later. "I apologize to my fans who were patiently waiting, but right now I want to focus on my new marriage and having a healthy baby. I hope that you will understand."

Koji and a bodyguard escorted her out of the room. The press conference ended with a network reporter commenting on the surprising news.

Have you ever been so shocked that you can't move or think for long periods of time? That was how I felt that hot August night as I tried to process what happened. Yumi? Pregnant? *Married?* After everything we had been through… after the promise we made to each other before she left at the end of Golden Week… this was how it turned out? She couldn't even tell me herself? Me, the woman who loved her. Me, her best friend in the whole world. *This was how I found out?*

When the shock wore off, my body collapsed onto itself. My heart ached to the point I had to lie on the floor, covering my face with my hand as I held back my tears of weakness. I couldn't hold them back forever.

Love, Yumi

When they burst through, I was lost to my heartbreak and the blinding rage settling into my soul. "Why?" I sobbed into the sleeve of my shirt. "*Why?*"

At some point I grabbed my phone and called someone. Anyone. Not Yumi, obviously, but someone else I could talk to.

My mother answered after only one ring. "Chiharu!" she greeted, an obnoxious happiness layered in her voice. "I just saw the press conference! Isn't it wonderful? How long have you known? Must've been hard keeping that a secret!"

The first sound out of my mouth was a garbled screech of defiance against what the cosmos had just thrown at me. My mother tried to get me to calm down, but I couldn't. Hearing her like that took me back to my childhood, when someone or something hurt me and I cried into my pillow, my mother reassuring me that I would be all right.

"I love her," I sobbed, on the brink of hyperventilating. "It hurts so much…"

I told my mother as much as I dared, confessing that I was gay and that Yumi and I were an item more than once. She listened quietly, and I wondered what she looked like. Was she at the kitchen table? In the living room? Was she more concerned about how upset I was or what I was saying?

"Chiharu," she said softly. "I'm so sorry."

I was sorry too. So sorry that I let myself be swindled by that no-good thing called love.

***

One time when we were promoting the cover album, Yumi and I went on a talk show aimed at adults. Since we were singing songs from twenty, thirty years ago, this made sense to do from a marketing perspective. However, I was not prepared for the types of questions they asked.

"What kind of person do you most want to date, Chiharu-*san*?" the hostess asked me. "A cool girl like you must have a particular type."

I glanced at the camera, at the audience waiting for my answer. "The person I date has to be someone I can be myself around. It's not usual for me to show someone my true self."

"That's right, she's very guarded," Yumi interrupted. "We've known each other since kindergarten, and sometimes I still feel like I don't know her so well."

The audience chuckled. Thankfully the hostess moved on to Yumi, who would surely give out a better answer. "What kind of person are you attracted to, Yumi-*san?*"

"Oh, that's easy." She patted my arm. "I want someone like Chiharu."

Laughter bounced around the set, but not because they thought it sounded gay. To them, they thought Yumi meant someone with my personality or knowledge of her. Me in male form. "Sometimes it's best to be with someone you know, right?" the interviewer asked.

"Of course! I often think, 'Gee, if Chiharu were a man, I would totally date her!' Wouldn't that be great?"

The audience laughed until the hostess had to ask them to quiet down. I sat in my seat, slightly horrified that this felt like it was at my expense.

"Let's get married." Yumi squeezed my arm as part of the joke. "I'll never do better than Chiharu! We can get married and have lots of babies. Just be a man, please!"

Man, woman, I never felt good enough for her.

Chapter 42

"Please come over tomorrow," a text from Yumi said. *"I'll be back in Nagoya late tonight. I want to talk. I have lots of time off now."*

"I bet you do," I muttered, tossing my phone onto my bed as I rolled over and tried to pretend the day wasn't happening. It was three days later, and my anger still hadn't abated. Well, I shouldn't say *anger*. A mixture of despair and a sense of being betrayed simmered inside me. I had cried out most of my overt feelings so now continually basked in my own foul mood.

Nevertheless I replied with, *"I'll do my best."*

I thought a lot about what I would say to her. In my head I saw a million scenarios. I even acted out a few of them in the shower. None of them reflected well on me, to be sure. Just know that at the end of every scenario I said, "That's no good." Ultimately I knew that it would depend on my mood, Yumi's mood, and how we approached the topic.

Work didn't get done. (It hadn't been done since the press conference.) I skulked around my apartment, skulked around the supermarket, and then skulked my way to the watering hole the label staff loved to frequent. Some people said hello to me, and others were unknowing assholes who asked me if I was happy for Yumi. I told them I didn't want to talk about it as I sat at the far end of the bar and ordered something strong.

I didn't want to get drunk. I wanted to numb the pain overcoming me. The TV above the bar was set to some local baseball game, and for a while that placated me... until I saw Junpei's face coming up to the plate. I tapped my forehead against the bar before asking the proprietor to change the channel. He set it on some animal show.

"Not surprised to find you here."

Beppu sat beside me. I hadn't seen him in over a month, and yet I couldn't bring myself to get excited about it. Especially when he knew about my feelings for Yumi. "Not in the mood."

"Taking it pretty hard, huh?"

I glared at him before putting my head down again.

"I'll have the usual," he told the bartender. "And get her a double of whatever she had earlier. My tab."

Thanking him should have been my priority, but how could I when he was making light of my misery? This wasn't a bombed single or my favorite outfit ruined. This was something that would change my life in ways I could never be prepared for. Yumi, pregnant! Married! I couldn't decide which one was worse. Was it her marrying a man she said was out of her life forever? Was it her becoming a mother? Some people may think I was heartless... well, I was trying to turn off my heart so it would stop hurting.

"Surprising that she's the only one so far to get a *dekichatta*. I'm sure someone owes someone money. My money was on Dolly being the first."

"Reika had a baby."

"I said a *dekichatta*. She was married to that boyfriend for a full year before any pregnancy rumors."

I sat up, my back aching. "You mean I wasn't a high contender?"

"Not from anyone who knew you. Some people would bet on you though just because you seemed the least likely. Good money to be made in a betting pool."

Love, Yumi

"Gee, thanks." The idea that staff members took bets on things like this regarding the talents didn't surprise me, but it wasn't flattering on their behalf either.

The bartender dropped off our drinks. I looked at mine, wondering if I could down it in one gulp. "Don't," Beppu said. "I'm not dealing with drunk Chiharu. Depressed Chiharu is already enough."

I scoffed. "Depressed? Try emotionally mutilated."

"Is that the song you're writing right now?"

"How could you guess?"

He tapped his fingers to his lips. "You really didn't know before the press conference? That surprises me. I heard from Koji that she told her staff three weeks ago. She must have known she was pregnant longer than that. Twelve weeks... that would be..."

"Early April. Trust me, I've done the math." That meant she was at least one month pregnant when we were together during Golden Week. I should have known. The morning sickness. Eating more than usual. The radiant skin. The need to feel protected. Hell, her bubbling sex drive, which I attributed to me at the time. Now I knew she just had carnal pregnancy cravings. That was probably why she came to me to begin with. No men on hand to satisfy those physical needs.

"And you didn't know?"

"No. She hasn't talked to me at all since May."

"Ah."

We drank in silence, the crowd behind us getting rowdier as people got more intoxicated. Most were there talking to friends or having small parties. Me? I was there to forget Yumi just for a bit. "She wants to talk to me tomorrow, though. I don't know what I'm going to say or do."

"You're taking this a lot harder than I expected, to be honest."

My snort burned with alcohol. When the unpleasant feeling passed, I said, "The woman I love has married some useless jackass because she's pregnant with his kid. How am I supposed to feel? Blessed because now I know I will never have her?"

"Chiharu."

His tone insinuated that I was still that stupid teenager he once watched over years ago. Well, I wasn't. I was a grown woman with a career and other responsibilities. One of them was to myself: find happiness. That happiness was going to be with Yumi. Until now. "You don't get it," I said, tears welling behind my eyes again. "We were... were..."

"Hm?"

I glanced at him and became embarrassed. There wasn't enough liquid courage in the world to get me to confess my relationship with Yumi. Not until I cleared my throat and looked around to make sure nobody was listening. "We were girlfriends. *Girlfriends.*"

"I see."

"I'm serious. We started a romantic relationship over Golden Week. She couldn't have known she was pregnant yet. I told her I loved her... and she said she wanted to be like that with me. *Forever.*"

The only sounds came from the happy crowds behind us and the show about big cats on TV. Every so often someone cheered at one of the tables. Their merriment made me feel worse, so I took sip after sip of my drink. Finally I just knocked the whole thing back.

"I'm sorry." It was all Beppu could say.

"One week. Is one week all I get?" Not just the lovemaking, but the flirty words, the looks of adoration, and the slow dancing. I wanted my best friend and my lover. Yumi and I were going to cook together, watch TV with booze and sugar, and have late night talks about our dreams until we were too sleepy to keep chatting. We were also going to make-out half the night before taking it to the bedroom. There were still so many things for me to show and teach her. She had loved everything so far. "And now she wants me to go to her place tomorrow and 'talk' about this. What am I going to say to her?"

Beppu placed a reassuring hand on my shoulder. "You're going to say that you still love her and will support her through this. Chiharu, do you think she married that guy for love?"

"I don't want to believe it. She finally dumped him for good last April. What is this cosmic joke?"

"It's the cards you've been dealt. Play the best hand you can. That's all you can do."

What could I say?

"She probably never told you because she was afraid to. I can't tell you how she really feels or what's going to happen, but I can tell you that you need to step up as the best friend right now. That girl doesn't have a lot of good people in her life. You're one of the best for anybody, let alone her."

"But I..."

"She's having a baby. She's going to become a mother. Being married to some guy right now isn't nowhere near as big as those other things. You're one of the only people she can trust as this huge moment happens. You need to put aside your romantic feelings for her and be the *friend* she needs."

He was right. It hurt, but he was right. Yumi didn't need her lesbian lover. Yumi needed her best friend in the whole world. She needed me more than anyone else.

I arrived at her apartment an hour early the next day. My reasoning was that it didn't matter if I dropped in early, late, whenever. Of course I wanted to be polite and not late. Being late was akin to saying, "I don't care about you anymore." The truth couldn't be farther away.

But I was nervous. I hadn't seen Yumi in the flesh since we last kissed at the end of Golden Week, when she left my girlfriend but now returned as some other person's wife. As I rode up in the elevator and fished for my copy of the key to her apartment, I wondered how I could possibly look her in the eyes and not combust.

I helped myself inside, and at first I wondered if nobody was home. The apartment was quiet, sterile, and devoid of the markings of someone living there. Except for some cards on the kitchen table, one would have thought that this was a stage home to sell other apartments.

"Yumi?" I called, slipping off my shoes by the door and putting on the slippers I always used in my friend's home. Wouldn't it just be my luck if she had disappeared off the earth again?

Heavy footsteps thumped behind the bedroom door before it flew open. Yumi stood on the other side, her face pale and feet shooting out from beneath her in an attempt to come to me.

We met in the middle of the room, my arms wrapping around her and pulling her into my strong embrace. I held back my tears of relief that she was alive, okay, and *here* again. Over three months since I last saw her. The thought of being apart that long again made me shudder.

"I missed you so much," I said, pushing my fingers into her growing black hair. It was the longest I had seen it in years, reaching to the base of her neck and curling around her ears. I knew pregnant women weren't supposed to dye their hair, but it surprised me to see it this long. "Do you know how much I've worried about you?"

She didn't answer. Not with words. Haven't I told you before? We don't need words in moments like those.

Instead she kissed me, luring me back into a world of beating hearts and rushing blood. I didn't care if her stupid husband came waltzing through that door to find his pregnant wife *in flagrante* with the local lesbian. Reporters could have stormed the door and I would still kiss her, bringing her closer to me until I felt something bump against my abdomen.

"*I'm sorry,*" she told me in that kiss. "*I missed you too.*"

I didn't get a good look at her until after. Aside from her hair, her appearance had not changed much. She was still thin everywhere… except for her stomach, which had the smallest bulge against her sweatpants. If you didn't know her body as well as I did then you probably wouldn't have thought anything of it. Even celebrity women can pack a small pooch when they're taking time off. Except I knew that was the baby growing inside of her.

"Just tell me," I said, cutting her off before she had the chance to speak. "Did you know when we…?"

She shook her head. "I didn't know until the album came out."

Two months. Like me during my idol days, Yumi missed the occasional monthly visitor due to stress and poor diet. She probably didn't think much of it when she missed the first one. By the second, however, she may have begun to suspect. "Why didn't you tell me?"

I sounded pathetic, and I felt pathetic. My only hope was that I didn't *look* pathetic standing in front of her for the first time in three months. "What could I have said? No, let me finish." Yumi held up her hand to my face. "I just found out I was pregnant. The first person I told was my mother. She told me to do the right thing."

"Which was…"

"Once I realized Yohei had to be the father, I told him. I thought he would be angry and tell me to get an abortion, but he was surprisingly… serene about it? He told me that he always wanted to have kids and that he was excited for the future. I had never seen him like that before. He treated me delicately and… he proposed to me!" Yumi laughed at the preposterous memory. "I didn't say yes right away. I thought about it, but it was difficult with the album promotions going on. When I fainted on stage I realized I had to do *something*."

"Tell me. You could have told me."

She turned away, and from the back all I could see was a worried woman who had too much sitting on her chest. "I wanted to tell you. If we hadn't… if Golden Week never happened, I would have told you first. But I couldn't. Don't you see? I didn't want to break your heart."

"Bullshit!" Even though I told myself on the way over there that I wouldn't get angry, here I was, yelling in her apartment and flailing my arms around like a kid not getting her way. "So you made me find out with the rest of the world? Do you know what that did to me?" My lip trembled, but I refused to cry. Beppu's words kept echoing in my head. "*You need to put aside your romantic feelings for her and be the friend she needs.*" I couldn't show that level of weakness. "I was so worried about you." Getting my voice to level out was no easy task. "I didn't hear from you for weeks. I saw you getting worse on TV. I thought you had something like cancer, for God's sake!"

"Cancer?" What the hell? Why was she smiling? Let alone that devilish grin she gets when she's about to make fun of me? It was the same one she gave me in the bathroom last night, telling me that my muscles were getting soft and she deserved to be linked to someone better. She had been joking, but because she was my best friend for so long she knew how to dig under my skin. "Goodness, I'm sorry! But cancer?"

"Like I said," I stood there, humbled, "I was worried and my brain was thinking up these crazy scenarios. Which is why I wish you told me before I found out that way."

The smile faded. "I wanted to. Every day I thought about picking up that phone. I didn't just want to tell you. I also wanted to be with you. I've been so petrified these past few weeks." Yumi leaned against her sofa, one hand on her abdomen. I couldn't look away from it. "Whenever I felt like I was about to stop breathing, I thought of you. When I was in the doctor's office hearing my test results, I wanted you to break down the door, punch him in the face, and scream at him that he was wrong and to do it again. When Yohei proposed to me, I wanted that same thing to happen. Basically, every time my life seemingly slipped further and further from my grasp I wanted you to come save me." When I approached her she shrugged me off. Didn't she just say she wanted me to come to her? "Then I saw your face when I told you the news. How devastated you would be. I was weak. I couldn't do it."

She cried into her hands. No sobs, just a few tears that dripped down her skin until she managed to compose herself again.

"I'm sorry."

You don't know how much I wanted to grab her and run away together. I didn't care if on paper she "belonged" to some man. I just wanted to be with her, somewhere safe, somewhere nobody would care about who we were or that we were in love.

Instead I had to sit next to her against the couch, my hand on her shoulder. A best friend's touch. "You're right," I said. "It would've crushed me. It did crush me. But I still wish you would have told me yourself long ago. At least when you made the decision to keep the baby and marry that man. Even if you decided against it, I still wish you would have told me." I would go with her to the clinic for either a checkup or a procedure. All that mattered was that she trusted me enough to go with her either way.

Becoming mothers was one of the few things we never talked about growing up. I'm not sure many girls really do talk about it. What's the point, when most of us assume it's inevitable? What power do we really have in stopping something like that? Look at Yumi. Look at me. We both suspected we were pregnant for very different reasons. Hers from her lifestyle, and mine from abuse. Not only is it pointless to talk about as foolish girls, but either outcome is scary when you barely know how your body works. When I thought I was pregnant, all I could think about was getting an abortion. Not just because it was that man's thing inside of me, but because I'm not the type of woman who can do that sort of thing – the pregnancy and childbirth thing. If it had been conceived out of love, perhaps I would have thought differently.

With Yumi, who could say? I never heard her talk about having children. Getting married, yes, but maybe that was included with children. After all, so many of us assume that's how it happens. Marriage, children. Sometimes the other way around, especially in this day and age. "From now on," I said, my hand pressing against her back, "promise me that you'll tell me when something big like that happens again, okay?"

She promised, patting my knee and getting up from where she leaned. Yumi went to the table and sat in a pulled out chair. I stepped away from the sofa and glanced at the cards.

"What are these?"

One by one she picked them up, reading each line before setting them off to the side. "Wedding invitations. We're having a ceremony in a few weeks."

Something clogged my throat, but I hurried to swallow before it choked me. "I thought you were legally married already."

"We are. The ceremony is for the press and our families." Sighing, Yumi flipped over a card and made a correction on it. "You'll come, right?" She handed me another card, this one marked with *For Chiharu Morita.*

The card shook in my hand. On it I was invited to the grand and joyous occasion of Yumi Nishikawa marrying longtime boyfriend Yohei Yoshizaki. Friends! Family! A pregnant woman in a wedding dress! I thought of all the press, the well-wishers, the aunties cooing over Yumi's belly and giving her advice on how to make sure it turned out to be a boy. I wanted to scream. Yet I remained docile, my head slowly nodding as I quipped, "Of course, Mrs. Yumi Yoshizaki."

I got an admonishing laugh, a request to never call her that again, and half the cards on the table thrown at my head.

"Be the best friend she needs. Be the best friend she needs."
If only Beppu knew that his words would become my mantra over the next few weeks. With nothing else to do, Yumi lost herself in planning this wedding while I worked and tried not to think about it. Yet I could only use work as an excuse so many times. On weekends I went to Yumi's — and Yohei's, since he moved in permanently just to piss me off – to help her pick out flowers, dishes to serve, and to listen to her complain about her growing stomach.

This served the biggest problem, and was why we waited until the last minute to rent her a wedding dress. Yumi's mother, who already spent half her time in Nagoya to fuss over her married and pregnant daughter, said that getting married at five months pregnant was one of the stupidest things Yumi could do. "Even if we rent you a dress a week before the wedding, you won't fit into it in another week!"

Yet Yumi had to try, so the weekend before the wedding we went to an upscale wedding rental boutique in Sakae for the sheer fun of it all.

Everyone else had fun anyway. Yumi, her mother, Yohei's sister, and some other girl I didn't know. They gathered around the clerk to tell her what was needed, kindly specifying that Yumi may be slightly bigger even a week from now. "No issue," the clerk said. "We have dresses just for such a thing." I had no idea the shotgun-marriage business was *that* strong.

Yumi's mother helped her change into the sample dresses while I and these two girls I had never met before sat in the gallery. They chattered, going over their own dream weddings and talking about the men they wanted to bag. I sat on the other side of the guest sofa, trying to not let my jaw clench too much. My dentist was already in the habit of yelling at me for it.

I swear every dress looked the same. Of course Yumi was radiant in each of them, but aside from some different beading the styles were the *same*. Yumi always looked best in dresses that highlighted her lines. These dresses were full, poofy, and more often than not started the skirt right beneath her breasts in order to hide her stomach. She looked like a princess, but Yumi was never the fairy-tale princess type. More like the older, more charming princess who could schmooze with diplomats.

The clerk knew how to butter up women high on pregnancy and wedding hormones. "This is most gorgeous," she said, pulling back Yumi's hair to give her an idea of what to expect at her wedding. "See how the beadwork creates an illusion of romance?" The fuck did that mean? "Anyone seeing you in this dress would be stunned into silence."

I was looking at her right now and had plenty to say.

"Chi-*chan?*" Yumi turned to me. "What do you think?"

"I think you're beautiful."

"But is this dress the one?"

"I can't tell you that."

She furrowed her eyes at me but said nothing more. When she told the clerk she would like to try on one more dress, her mother said she was getting tired and needed someone to help her in the dressing room. Yours truly volunteered like the good, doting best friend I now was.

Between Yumi's mother and I, we were able to get her dressed in the next outfit within only a few minutes. The moment she saw herself in the mirror, however, she declared she hated it, and had us take it off her immediately. Rolling my eyes, I helped her get the bodice over her head, followed by the waves of beaded tulle and satin suffocating the both of us.

"Why do these dresses have to be so ridiculous?" I muttered a bit too loudly. "Really. You could probably feed a small village in Africa for life based on the cost of these dresses."

Out of line? Probably. The truth? Maybe. Yumi, now devoid of any dress at all, touched me on the shoulder and said, "Maybe you should wait outside. You need some air."

I waited just outside of the changing room. Couldn't say I felt like joining those other girls with their prattle about imaginary men and weddings they probably wouldn't ever have. Yet if I had joined them, I would have managed to avoid the prattle *behind* me.

"What is wrong with Chiharu?" Yumi's mother hissed to her daughter. "She should be happy for you."

"She is, Mama. You know how she is. She's not very expressive."

"She's jealous, if you ask me."

My breath caught in my throat just as Yumi gasped as well. "What do you mean by that?"

"I'm just saying, she was never much of a pretty girl. Homely... though that isn't bad. She's just not the kind of girl who is going to get a lot of men her way."

"I don't think she cares about that."

"Doesn't matter if it's what she *really* wants. Jealousy can rear its ugly head in these situations. Don't let her bring down your happiness."

Yumi didn't say anything. I wondered if she would ever defend me to that woman. I guess not.

The wedding was the first Sunday of September, in an upscale hotel banquet hall. Members of the press were allowed into one small conference room, but only one professional photographer was hired to take pictures to be later released as PR material.

I didn't recognize most of the people. Members of Yumi and Yohei's families made up a chunk of the people, but also industry professionals and staff members they both worked with over the years. The reception hall was packed with men in suits and women in formal gowns. I showed up in the nicest thing I had – a red silk blouse to go with some plain trousers. My hair was styled and I put on some makeup, but for the most part I felt woefully underdressed compared to the other people there.

Love, Yumi

Since I wasn't officially a part of Yumi's family, I was not given the highest honors. This also meant I didn't have to serve drinks or make sure things were running smoothly. No, I was allowed to sit at one of the front tables with some other people from the industry, stewing in my own misery while I tried to put on a happy smile.

"Chiharu!" It was Yumi's mother, kneeling beside my chair and shaking my arm. "It's Yumi. She needs to talk to you."

Neither Yumi nor Yohei were out to greet the guests yet. I didn't know exactly where she was, but I knew she must be getting ready in that rented wedding dress, something the female members of her family should have been helping with. So why was her mother here?

"What is it?"

"I don't know. She won't come out of the dressing room until she talks to you."

To the sounds of pleasant laughter, tinkling champagne glasses, and the man on my right talking about his trials with indigestion, I got up and followed Yumi's mother down a quiet hallway to where the bride's dressing room was.

I knocked on the door. "Yumi?"

She opened it a smidge, caught sight of her mother and said, "I need to talk to her privately. Please go."

Not until Yumi's mother slowly retreated down the hallway did the bride open the door far enough for me to slip in. She closed the door – and locked it.

Yumi was already dressed, from the flowing ball gown to the long veil covering her otherwise bare shoulders. Her hair and makeup had been done by her personal stylist just before her mother came to get me... but it looked as if the eyeliner was about to start running down her cheeks.

"You're really beautiful."

She sniffed. "Thank you."

I gently took her hand, trying to be the rock she needed on this emotional day. "You wanted me for something? Everyone is waiting for you out in the hall."

Before I could see her coming, Yumi flung her arms around me and kissed my lips as if the world were going to end in ten minutes. Startled, I stepped back and fell onto a stool, but Yumi was still there, kissing me with both of her soft hands clutching my cheeks.

I had never kissed a bride before. I somehow doubted Yumi had kissed other people – let alone a woman – on her wedding day. Yet here we were, going at each other like a couple of kids unable to contain themselves until the wedding night. It was our first kiss since reuniting a month ago. From the way Yumi slammed herself against me, I had a feeling that bad news was coming.

"No, no…" I tried to keep her with me, but she pushed herself away and huddled in the corner of the dressing room. Right away I got up and went to her, my hands on her side and then searching through that monster of a skirt to find the bump on her stomach.

"Chiharu." Her hands were on either side of the corner, head bowed and shoulders slumped. A bride was not supposed to look so defeated. "I'm sorry." She hiccupped. "This has to stop now. I… I can't do it anymore."

She did cry now. Bitter, salty tears that marred her makeup until her cheeks were covered in black and deep purple. I rubbed her shoulders, cooed at her, did everything I could think of to calm her down and get her to explain herself. Pretty soon her mother would be back to find out what was taking so long.

"I'm doing the right thing, right?" Turning, Yumi showed me the damage on her face. Even then, I thought she was lovely. I was concerned, but also hopelessly in love. For a second I pretended that we were dressed up to get married. Yumi, my bride. "Getting married is the right thing to do, right?"

"You're already married. This is just a formality," I reminded her.

"I know. But this makes it feel so much more official. I'm telling the world that I love Yohei and am going to be his wife. And you…" She took me by the wrists and squeezed as hard as she dared. "I'm breaking your heart."

Love, Yumi

This was it. This was the moment Beppu warned me about. I had to cast aside those feelings of sex and romantic love. Yumi needed me. To be her rock, her foundation. She needed me to once again be the voice of reason, to reassure her that she was on the right path. I couldn't think of my own feelings. I had to drag out of me the selfless Chiharu I rarely got to see.

"As long as I can be near you, I'll be happy."

She almost believed me. My poor Yumi, with her tear and makeup stained face, smiled and pressed her forehead to my chest. And then a transformation. When she looked up again, her tears were gone and her visage determined, as if she were about to charge out onto a music stage and give the performance of her life. This wasn't Budokan, though. This was personal.

"I have to do what's right for this baby," she said, squeezing my arms. "I can't have it be born a bastard. I can't, even with my money and connections, bring it into this world already that disadvantaged. So I'm going to do it. I'm going to marry Yohei in front of the whole world. I'm going to smile and kiss him. I'm going to fuck his brains out tonight like everyone expects. I'm going to be a good wife and better mother. I'm doing this for my baby. You understand, right?"

No. No I didn't understand. I didn't yet know what it was like to be given a child and told, "You have to protect it. You have to make sure it gets the best in life." Yumi has never struck me as a maternal soul. Yet I couldn't look into her heart and see what she was feeling with that baby growing inside of her. How scared was she? How conflicted was she? I wished I were a man. As a man I could have had sex with her the right way. Maybe the baby would have been mine. Maybe Yumi would have lied and said it was mine and not Yohei's. Then we would be getting married. *We* would be feeling happiness today.

Except I wasn't a man. I couldn't have gotten her pregnant. She couldn't even lie about that.

"I understand."

She stood up straight, our heights similar enough for her to look forward into my eyes. "What happened during Golden Week... I'll never forget it."

My resolve started to weaken. I pushed my hands into her coiffed hair, disrupting the veil set gently on her head. "It was the happiest week of my life."

"And it has to stay in the past. I know what I told you then... but that was before..."

"The baby." I kissed her cheek, inoffensively. "You're doing the right thing." I put on a smile to get her to believe me. "A baby needs all the help it can get. If you're having it, it's only right that you marry the father and give it a good record when it's born."

"I'm doing the right thing," she repeated, holding herself to me as I stroked what hair I could find and kissed her neck. I had to. It was probably my last chance to do so. "And you..." Yumi stood back, fingers digging into my shoulders. "Promise me, Chiharu. I want you to find someone who can make you happy. Fall in love with someone else. Let me meet her and tell you how darling she is. You will have my blessing. All I ask for in return is that you give me your blessing as well."

We shared a last kiss before I left her, off to fetch her mother and the stylist so she could fix her "marks of happiness," as I called them. Throughout the wedding, Yumi was all smiles and big charm for the hundreds of people come out to celebrate her marriage to a man who could barely put himself together for the day. I watched them kiss. I watched them dance. I watched them cut cake and talk about the child they were going to have together. When I was asked to give a speech, I only wished her happiness.

After the reception they got into a limousine, waving at the crowd and making bawdy jokes about what they were going to do that night. You would have never guessed that just a few hours ago Yumi and I were kissing in her dressing room, making promises that we might be able to keep, but only if we kept lying to ourselves.

Love, Yumi

I walked home. It was late afternoon on a warm September day in Nagoya. The air was fresh and the world still spinning. I had lost Yumi. Yet it was better to have her for that one week than to have never known her kiss and touch at all.

I'm not a religious person. I wouldn't even call myself spiritual. When I was a kid, my mother took me to shrines to pray for good test scores, and when I was an idol we would sometimes stop by a shrine to pray for a strong release. Since those days, however, I never stepped foot on holy grounds outside of playing tourist. So I surprised myself when I stopped in front of a neighborhood shrine and stared at the red *torii* gate, chipping in paint but not losing its luster.

The water of the purification well was cool to my fingertips. I walked around the grounds, nodding at priestesses and aunties out for a stroll alike. Really, I just wanted somewhere peaceful to sit and contemplate my future without Yumi as my lover. I was drawn to the *ema* for sale and bought three of the wooden plaques. The priestess gave me a thick marker to use, and I sat down at the end of the stall to write my wishes.

On the first one, with a picture of a Momotaro bursting from his peach on the front, I wrote for Yumi, *"May you have a safe childbirth and a healthy baby. May your child bring you endless joy."*

The second one had a picture of a horse since, assuming Yumi didn't have a late pregnancy, her baby would be born in the Year of the Horse. *"I hope you grow up strong and brave in the face of adversity. May you be clever, quick, and good looking enough to get ahead. Know that your mother has done everything in her power to give you the best starting step in life, even if it meant her own happiness. She loves you. I love you too."*

For a long time I stared at the third plaque. On the front were painted cherry blossoms. On the back was my delicate handwriting.

"I hope that I can find happiness. I hope that I can be near her always."

The priestess took my three plaques and helped me hang them up by the statue of the local goddess. I thanked her, went home, and prayed in private for everything to work out in the end.

You know what they say about The Horse? They say that The Horse is friendly and charismatic. That they always have friends flocking to their side. Horses are easygoing to a fault. They endure independently. Society loves a good Horse because a Horse embodies the spirit of a group of people coming together for the greater good.

I'm a Dragon. You wouldn't guess it from looking at me. Yumi is much more a Dragon than I am. Either way, we both prey on horses.

That little one never stood a chance with two Dragons circling overhead. No wonder she is too shy to use her Horse side!

Chapter 43

October is usually one of my favorite months, because the weather finally cools down and the Chubu humidity isn't as suffocating. It doesn't rain much, but it's the perfect time to admire the fall foliage, like a mini-hanami with friends down by the cherry trees.

That year, however, I found it difficult to enjoy that month. Yumi was in her sixth month of pregnancy and second month of marriage. Even though I was welcomed at her place anytime I wanted, it felt wrong to be there most of the time. Especially with Yohei there, soiling the kitchen and commanding the television. He now slept full time in Yumi's bed, so I didn't dare go in there out of fear of smelling his presence where I once made love to her.

Her mother wasn't much better. Since Yumi's doctor expressed fear that she wasn't gaining enough weight for his liking, she was told not to do strenuous things like housework or traveling. This meant a return to her natal home in Seki to be pampered by her family was out of the question. Instead her mother came to stay with her in Nagoya.

A woman like that can't butt out of anybody's business. She was constantly asking Yumi how she was doing, if she was eating enough, exercising enough, and using her creams to make sure her stretch marks weren't permanent. On one hand it was good for Yumi to have someone with pregnancy experience around her, but on the other it created a somewhat hostile environment every time I came over, even if it was just to watch TV for two hours.

"Don't sit that way," Yumi's mother would say, her daughter leaning against my shoulder on the couch. "Do you want my grandchild falling out sideways? Its brains will be all pushed to one side."

Whenever Yumi called me and asked me to bring her things she craved, her mother would confiscate them the moment I walked through the door.

"This is too much sugar!" or "This is too much salt!" Whether it was cake or crackers, Yumi wasn't allowed to eat anything other than on an approved list. She often complained about being sick of everything. Sometimes literally. It wasn't unusual to walk into her apartment to find her curled up in bed or hovering around the toilet. "The things a mother must sacrifice for her child," Yumi's mother said more than once, "include her body, her sanity, and her peace of mind. Now you know how I felt."

The more insufferable Yumi's place became, the more I retreated into my own apartment. I had work to do anyway. I had just told the label I was *not* writing a love ballad for Boytasm in the vein of Yohei pledging his love to Yumi, and now was tasked with another slew of winter ballads to make the Christmas rounds.

I didn't always stay in my apartment to work those days. My fame had died down enough that I could go out in public without glasses or a hat, so I often took to a café at the end of my street. I went there once, twice a week to read or work on lyrics. That one early afternoon in October, I toiled away on a song that I was having trouble with. The label wanted one about feeling melancholy in spring, but it was autumn. Sometimes my brain didn't want to reconcile what was right now and what was impending.

"*Ano, sumimasen…*"

Love, Yumi

To this day I remember the melodic softness of that voice. I normally don't like being interrupted when I'm songwriting, but I couldn't help but glance up and see a lovely young lady in front of me. Twenty. Maybe twenty-two. She had glossy brown hair that shimmered in the sunlight beaming through the café windows. Her fashion was expected for the times, lots of subdued browns with only splashes of pastel colors.

"Can I help you?" I asked, removing my reading glasses.

The young lady stepped back. Was she shaking? In all my years, I never had a girl approach me like this before. What did she want? It almost reminded me of those dramas where a girl goes to give her crush a love letter, but that was ridiculous.

"Are you Chiharu Morita?"

My shoulders slumped. "Yeah," I said, already wondering if that was a mistake to admit.

Her face lit up with a bright smile. "I can't believe it. You're one of my favorite composers in the whole world!"

I never had anyone say that to me, not counting Yumi. "That so?"

She bowed as an afterthought, her need to be polite even as she approached a minor celebrity almost delightful. "My name is Asuka. I study piano at the music school."

That was how I met my first student. When I told Yumi a few days later that I decided to take on Asuka, the first words out of her mouth were, "Are you fucking her?"

No, I wasn't. I never have. Asuka was (and is) a student and a kind assistant, nothing more. I've had the pleasure of meeting her equally polite boyfriend several times. The only mutual love we share is one for music.

Trying to tell that to Yumi while she festered with pregnancy hormones, however, was something else entirely.

"Oh, so now you get to have a cute girl in your life? How old is she? Eighteen?" Asuka was twenty-one at the time. "Don't bother answering. I'm not in the mood."

Luckily my first lesson with Asuka went without a hitch. From that day on, we entered an arrangement where I would teach her what I knew about the piano and composing, and she would act as my occasional assistant in return. I had no idea how much I would come to rely on the shy but eager girl.

***

I never considered myself a good enough musician to have students lining up to take lessons from me. Asuka was my first student, but she wasn't my last. Since then I've had a few more come and go, some of them sent to me by the label once they caught wind I was interested in doing that.

Growing up, I knew that piano teachers came in two breeds. The first was the in-home tutor who taught children on a casual level. Sure, they could be serious about the craft, but they were chosen because they were the cheapest or the only ones available in a rural area. My piano teacher in Seki was a nice woman who taught me a lot, but I can confidently say today that I would be much more advanced than her. No, I'm not a master pianist, but I do know my skills on the piano, and I'm not afraid to show them off a little.

The other breed are the true professionals. Those who have gone so far that they're either performing around the world or teaching at a collegiate level. Those were the people I wanted to study under had I not been accepted into the idol group.

I always saw myself somewhere in between. A professional pianist in many ways, but not cheap enough for the average family or advanced enough to be taken seriously at a music school. Knowing this, I never considered being a teacher. Ask anyone who knows me... do I seem the teaching type to them? Probably not. At the end of the day I'm a serious woman who prefers to hole herself up in her apartment to work all day. Who has time for students?

All I know is that learning the patience to tutor prepared me for so many things. One of them was becoming an instructor on a more visceral level. The other was becoming a parent.

Chapter 44

"Thanks for bringing me here."

Yumi's hand grazed my arm as she lay on the exam table. Me, with my dry winter skin, sat next to her in a chair and judiciously applied moisturizer to my elbows and forearms. That November was particularly cold and dry.

"Don't mention it. Least I could do." When Yumi called that morning asking me to take her to her checkup because her mother was busy, I had to make arrangements, but agreed nonetheless. I was supposed to meet Asuka for lessons and for organizing my address book, but that wasn't happening today. "Besides, I always wondered how these things went."

"Lucky you don't actually have to do it."

I put my moisturizer back in my bag just as the doctor walked in. She was an older woman with a few gray hairs but a friendly demeanor that quickly smiled at Yumi and glanced at me. "Doing well?" she asked. "Who's this? Certainly not your mother."

Yumi introduced me as her best friend. Even then – hell, even now – I consider that title a point of pride. No, it doesn't feel as good as being called her girlfriend or lover, but how many people can say they've been her best friend? Only me.

The examination was two parts interesting and five parts stomach churning. I normally don't have a weak constitution for blood and guts, but for some reason seeing that gel slathered on Yumi's stomach and the blob of the baby appearing on a monitor made me woozy. Maybe it was the sound that came with it, reminding me of an old and worn out video game at an arcade near our high school.

"Everything seems okay," the doctor said, staring at the monitor. I didn't notice until then that Yumi was clutching my hand between the table and my chair. "Looks like a healthy twenty-six-week old kid."

Yumi was relieved to hear it, and so was I.

"Should we show your friend the baby's sex?"

Before I could perk up, Yumi said, "No, I'm keeping it a surprise." Really? Was that why she hadn't told me yet? Come to think of it, Yumi's mother had been badgering her about it as well. I squinted and tried to make out anything that looked remotely like a penis but couldn't tell heads from tails.

After the exam, the doctor wanted to have a consultation. "Your baby seems healthy, all things considered," she said. "It's you I'm more worried about."

I looked at Yumi and then the doctor. Should I be hearing this?

The doctor told us that due to Yumi's weight, frame, and the size of her growing baby, bed rest was advisable. This didn't mean she was confined to bed, apparently. She just wasn't supposed to walk more than a few minutes at a time, and lying down or sitting on the couch was preferable to taking out the trash or lifting weights. "However, I will reassess as we near your due date. Don't be surprised if confinement to bed during the last few weeks is necessary."

Yumi took this news a lot better than I did. When we got back in my car and I pulled out of the hospital parking garage, I said, "Bed rest? What's going on?"

"Nothing." She looked at her ultrasound photos, her expression unchanging. "Just something we've been talking about since my second trimester started. Guess I suck at safely carrying a kid by myself."

Traffic was heavy, meaning I got to sit at every light and creep along the avenues until we reached Sakae only two kilometers away. "You don't suck at anything." I then had another thought. "Why won't you let me know the baby's sex?"

"I'm not letting anyone know. I know. That's all that matters."

"Not even me?"

She glanced at me. "No matter how I answer, you'll treat me and this baby differently."

"Eh?"

Sighing, Yumi flipped the folder shut and stared out the window. "If it's a girl, you'll treat me more delicately. If it's a boy... well..."

The terrible thing was that she didn't have to finish her sentence.

"It's the same for everyone. People will make enough assumptions about this baby after it's born. Why do I want to be inundated with gendered bullshit before I even get to hold it in my arms? No thank you."

I eased my foot onto the gas pedal as another light changed. "You gonna be one of those parents who tries to raise their kid gender free?" Fat chance of that happening.

"No. I just want as much peace as I can get before delivery."

Peace did not come easily to someone like Yumi. Upon hearing about the doctor's recommendations for bed rest, Yumi's mother flipped a few lids and insisted on moving into Yumi's apartment to take care of things. Yumi flipped the lids right back, telling her mother that she would rather starve to death than put up with her twenty-four hours a day for God knew how long. Insulted, Yumi's mother stayed in Seki, visiting on the weekends while bringing more baby crap over.

I was the one chosen to help Yumi when she needed it. In the beginning, it was easy enough. She could still get up and walk around, so all I had to do was some grocery shopping and get the mail. I would do this after lunch, leaving any paperwork to Asuka as I took off for Yumi's for the rest of the day. We would watch TV, cook, go through the boxes of crap her mother brought over, and fuss about in the guest room that was now being turned into a nursery. Yumi long ago had the walls painted cheerful yellow and dark wood furniture brought in. But as she entered her nesting phase, she would have me move a chair here, this table over there, and oh my God we had to completely change the linens only to change them back again later. Clothes needed to be put away. Toys had to be checked and rechecked to make sure they were safe. I never thought in a million years I would spend the bulk of my afternoons in a damned nursery.

This wasn't so bad. When my birthday arrived in late December, Yumi had a cake waiting for me. She also gave me a present: a new chain for my necklace, which I had worn whenever I could since the day she gave it to me almost eight years ago.

"We're both twenty-six now," she said, watching snow fall outside. "I hope we have a good year." Her hand went to her bulging stomach. There was no hiding she was pregnant now.

Yes, it wasn't so bad. Then the new year came and went, and Yumi entered the final few weeks of her pregnancy. The doctor confined her to bed as we both feared.

Now I was not only Yumi's assistant, but also her maid, cook, and nurse. You may be wondering where Yohei was in all of this. Would you laugh if I told you he was touring with Boytasm? An Asian tour! A stop in Canada! When Yumi told me he was going, the first thing I said was that he was going to miss the baby's birth. She didn't seem to mind.

I still didn't like going into the bedroom, but that was where Yumi lived now. Luckily Yohei hadn't been there in so long that it hardly smelled like him, and the only reason you could tell he lived there sometimes was because of shaving cream and razors.

Yet I was not alone in this. People came and went all through the day. While I did laundry, a trainer came in to help Yumi exercise her unused muscles. When I put the clean dishes away, Koji or some other label person entered to discuss business, like the single that came out while Yumi was pregnant or the remix CD the label was putting out to keep the public's interest up. Best of all, sometimes Beppu would drop by just to tease me for being a homemaker while he gave Yumi a hard time for ballooning and looking like bored death on her bed all day.

I didn't always do chores. When they were finished I would sit with her, and we would watch TV in her room or work on songs together. Oftentimes she would close her eyes and listen to me play her upright piano in the living room. I still had work to do, after all. Some of this work included a piano version album of her songs I was putting out. Not my idea. All the label's.

"It's my gift to you!" I called to her from the living room. "Not me practically wiping your ass. Just a shitty CD of your songs on the piano."

I waited for her to say something testy back, but all I got was, "I like your piano playing."

Every day I gave her a massage, helped her change clothes, and sometimes helped her bathe. The doctor was right about her frame. As her stomach grew bigger and bigger, the rest of her couldn't keep up with hauling it around. She would stumble from the weight on her way to the bathroom. Sometimes she told me that she had dreams of rolling down a hill like an inflated ball. Her feet were so sore that I had to rub creams on them while we watched travel shows on TV. She complained that her breasts hurt too, but I let her do that herself.

There were worse ways for me to spend my time. I got my wish in that I wanted to be close to my best friend. We were with each other for hours almost every day. Sometimes she took care of me too. Like when I was tired from the weather or work, she would let me curl up next to her in bed and stroke my head. More often than not she would start singing a pretty tune, stop when she felt a kick, and then put my hand on her stomach so I could feel it. Bizarre. Frightening. Utterly amazing that such a strong life could be acting up inside her body.

She slept more as we entered February. I began to wonder if the baby would come before or after the Chinese New Year. My tribute CD had come out, and sometimes I would walk into the bedroom to find it playing in a Discman while the headphones were wrapped around Yumi's stomach, her eyes closed and chest slowly heaving up and down.

"I want it to like music," she said when she woke up. "Your music."

Our hands interlocked on the bed. After a gentle kiss to her cheek, she asked me to go play piano, and I did, wondering what my new role in her life would be after the baby came.

February. Normally I didn't think much about that month, but after that year, it suddenly became very important.

Not just because Valentine's Day came and went either. On that day I bought Yumi some gourmet chocolate because she had been such a good sport. Six weeks of confinement to bed and she was about to go mad. Yumi's not the kind of gal who wants to stay inside all day unless she has a date. Actually, even if she has a date. Growing up I was content to hang out in our rooms, watching tapes and listening to music. Sometimes we would read magazines, talking about how we wished we could be pretty like the women in them. (Or in my case, sleep with them.) Then she would get cabin fever and insist we go outside, rain or shine.

She scarfed down the chocolate and then complained about a stomachache. I made her some of the drink the doctor prescribed to "settle her nerves" or whatever they talked about. By then it was snowing again, and I huddled up in bed with her, where the heater was on and a thick afghan covered us both.

"For the love of God," Yumi grumbled at her stomach. "Come *out*."

"It's not even your due date yet."

"I don't care. I'm sick and tired of being pregnant. All I know is that I'm never doing this again. This is the only kid I'm having."

"I'll get you a pack of condoms then."

"Ha ha, very funny!"

"Well you got pregnant somehow."

"I don't even remember. We were probably drunk and forgot the condom."

"I thought you were on birth control."

"That's how drunk I was."

"Lovely. Baby will love to hear that blessed story of conception." I had my share of intoxicated sex, and every time I was thankful I didn't have to worry about pesky things like contraception. Some of those women could really do it, too...

"Wake up." Yumi smacked my stomach, although the afghan softened the blow. "I need you to tell this kid to get out. Chinese New Year is in five days and I'm not raising a Sheep."

"What's wrong with Sheep? At least then it will be docile and obey you." Listen to us! Talking about astrology as if it were true. "A Horse may be more trouble."

"I think it will be a Horse. It's been kicking a lot."

"You know it's okay then."

A silence fell over us, and I considered turning on the TV to see if some hilariously bad *taiga* drama was on. "*Nee*, Chi-*chan*."

"What?"

Yumi rolled onto her side, kicking off the afghan because she claimed to be hot. "I'm scared. Like, a lot."

This was the first time she expressed the fears I knew were bubbling inside her. That's how she was though. Yumi would take things like stage fright, shyness, and those other socially crippling emotions and push them down inside until she couldn't feel them anymore. Then she would jump out on stage, go talk to that boy, or finally open up to me. I looked at her, saw her fearful eyes, and couldn't help myself from touching her cheek and wrapping my fingers around the back of her neck. "What are you scared of?"

"I'm having a baby! If not the actual birth... there's someone I have to take care of for the rest of my life. What if I'm terrible at it?"

"You have one of the best doctors in the whole country. Everything looks fine."

"Yeah, yeah, that's just one event. What about its life?"

I know that it's not uncommon for a new mother to fret about how good she'll be at raising a child. But Yumi sounded more scared than I had heard her in a long, long time. "You've got lots of money. It will have the best opportunities. The best care. You'll love it and it will love you, even when it's fourteen and claiming that it hates you."

"Thanks."

"I'm serious." I pushed myself up, my nose just centimeters away from hers.

"That's not what I'm worried about."

"Oh?"

She bit her lip. "I'm worried that I'll have to do it alone."

Even then she knew that Yohei would not be a good father. The man wouldn't even come home for the due date. For all that bullshit he fed her months ago about wanting kids and being excited, he sure was scarce now. When I confronted him about it before he went on tour, he brushed me off saying, "Eh? And should my career stop while I'm at my peak? I'm not carrying the kid. What can I do? You know that next to royalties the best way to make money in this business is to perform. Well, I'm not a composer like you. I don't get royalties. So I've gotta go gyrate my ass on stage for a million teenage girls so I can make sure the kid goes to a good school." He seemed proud that he thought to say such a thing. How altruistic.

I was with her most of these months, but Yumi was lonely. It was probably part cabin fever, part fear. Her mother cared more about the unborn baby than the daughter carrying it. Her husband was already largely absent, doing God knew what. The label was mad that she got pregnant at the top of her career. There was no delusion that her job would be the same when she returned to it. The public saw her as a mother now. She was no longer the "pure" and bubbly entertainer of old. A good chunk of her male fans would no longer find her sexy, and lots of her female ones would lose interest due to her absence. It would be a miracle if her comeback album had half the sales of her last one, especially with the industry as it was.

"You're not alone." I held her head to my chest. Her stomach kept us apart down below, and if possible, I would have wrapped my legs with hers and kissed her forever. "Don't you see that I'm here? I'll always be here."

"No, don't say things like that." Yumi's fingers clutched my shirt as if she were about to rip it off. "Don't stop your life for me."

"I'm not stopping my life. It's just going to change."

I didn't expect her to do it, but Yumi pulled me in for a kiss, her lips melting against mine as I gradually rolled against her, hands on her, my body wanting to desperately make love to her. It was impractical. I also knew she would push me away before it got too heavy. Yet right now, in that moment, she was mine again.

No, no, she was always mine. Even if she married someone else, even if she went on tour around the world for a year and I never saw her, even if she threw me out of her apartment so we wouldn't be led into temptation. She would be mine. And more importantly, I would be hers.

"Hey, you," I said, pressing my ear against Yumi's stomach. The gurgling, the heartbeat, the inner workings of a new life being formed echoed in my ear. "Don't give your mama grief. She's done a lot to make sure you get the best in life. I'm sorry that man is gonna be your father, but know that he doesn't have to matter. Your mother is gonna love you. I'm gonna love you too. Two people who love you. Isn't that what most kids want?"

Yumi's hand was on my head, the pressure of her fingers burying into my scalp.

"I didn't have a dad growing up. It's not so bad only having your mother. Your mother will die for you. But it probably is better to have two people you can count on. I'll take care of your mother. You know why? Because I love her. Any child of hers I'll love too."

"It's a girl," Yumi said weakly. She clutched my hair, and although it was uncomfortable, I was too busy mulling that information over.

"I know," I finally said. As I kissed her stomach, the girl kicked against my mouth. Yup. She was a Horse all right. That meant Yumi would go into labor anytime now.

"Leave them on my dining table," I told Asuka over the phone as I perused the vegetables in the nearby supermarket. "I already told the label I'm taking this next week off from work to help Yumi. They'll get over it. My old commitments have been honored."

My student assistant confirmed that she would leave some documents from the label on my kitchen table. The girl had a key to my home, that's how much I trusted her by now. Since I was spending so much time at Yumi's place, I had Asuka keep my place tidy and take care of any mail. Apparently she just signed for some legal documents.

I hung up and stared at a display of radishes. What the hell was I making for dinner? Yumi couldn't have anything that would upset her stomach, and that was everything now. She would be lucky to get a salad.

My phone rang. It was Yumi.

Last I left her she was napping in bed after her stylist came over to cut off the hair she had been growing for a year. Something about starting the new Chinese year not looking like a sweaty ghost. Now I listened to that ringtone and knew she was doing anything but napping.

"Chiharu!" she shouted into my ear. "Get here, now!"

Screw dinner. We were having a baby!

I rushed back to her apartment, bursting through the door expecting to see some gory scene straight out of a horror drama. Blood, broken water, some guts for good measure. Instead I heard Yumi's warbling voice calling to me from the bedroom, where she sat on the edge, doubled-over and clutching her stomach.

"*Daijyoubu?*" Really? Did I think she looked okay? "How far apart?"

She gritted her teeth and grabbed my arm. "Not far enough!"

We had a packed bag by the front door. I grabbed it, went back to her, and tried to help her stand up. "It will be faster to drive," I said. "We need to get you into the car first."

Love, Yumi

That was a special trial in itself. Yumi could barely move since she was so bottom-heavy and not used to moving more than a few meters in that condition. She hanged off my arm as I helped her put on shoes. A groan of intense pain echoed in the *genkan* as she almost sat down on the floor. I persevered, getting her into her hall and calling for a security guard to help me get her downstairs.

The first real blessing was the lack of traffic that early Wednesday afternoon. I sped, fully expecting to get into trouble, but we were at the hospital in fewer than five minutes.

"Yumi Yoshizaki," I announced to the woman at the counter. "She's going into labor. Her doctor is…" I couldn't remember her name in that moment.

Luckily Yumi was high profile enough for everyone to know what she needed. Not only that, but she got special care and treatment from the moment they brought out a wheelchair. When they tried to wheel her away, she grabbed my arm, begging me to come with her.

"Don't make me do it by myself!" Panic swiped her face away. "I swear to God!"

"*Hai, hai.*" The nurse pulled us apart and patted Yumi on the shoulder. "We're going to get you ready for delivery. Then your sister can come in." Neither of us corrected her.

The nurse told me to meet them there in half an hour. While I paced in the waiting room, I called everyone I could think of, including the people we agreed upon, such as Koji, her mother (who was getting in her car right now), *my* mother and, yes, Yohei.

"Your wife is having your baby!" Spit flew from my mouth. "Get your ass here!"

"I'm in Tokyo at the moment." He sounded way too calm for my tastes. "I'll get there as soon as I can. Watch over her for me, will you?"

What did he think I had been doing for the past twenty years?

I called Asuka to tell her I probably wouldn't be home for a long time. After that, I phoned Beppu because I needed someone with experience in this mess to calm me down.

"What are you doing calling me?" he asked. "Your woman's in labor and you're making pleasure calls? Even I was there for the birth of my kids, and I was managing some shitty girl group on tour for the last one. *Go.*"

I reassured myself that both Yumi's mother and Yohei were on their way. I was the only one Yumi had, so it was me who went to the room and told the nurse that I was expected.

"Is that Chiharu?" Yumi sounded like she was being dragged bloody and mauled through a muddy street by a pack of wild horses. "Let her in!"

The nurse jumped. So did I.

Within five minutes I was washed and prepped. Normally they require the mother's companion to attend some class, but as I have learned over the years when it came to Yumi and hospitals, being stupidly famous lets you get away with a lot of shit with doctors.

There was some dithering about whether or not to go ahead with a natural birth. The doctors thought I couldn't hear this – and I barely could, because Yumi was crying into my arm, her face contorted in ineffable pain as she did her best to keep her screams in.

Eventually the doctors agreed to go ahead with a natural birth. Good timing, because I'm pretty sure Yumi was at the stage of horror where she was going to rip off my arm if something hadn't been done soon.

In the months leading up to this moment, Yumi's mother did a number on making sure her daughter went through as much torture as possible. In order to have an epidural, Yumi had to find a hospital not only willing to do it, but schedule it in advance. So no epidural for her today! Instead she was left to hold in every scream trying to take her prisoner. Something else she wasn't allowed to do. "Whatever you do, don't scream in the delivery room," her mother told her more than once. "Do you want that baby coming out scared of its own mother? You want it to come out thinking the whole world is nothing but pain and anger? I never once screamed while I was delivering you. Of course it hurt like shit but I made sure you were born a happy girl."

What would happen if she screamed? Nobody told us. To be honest, I didn't want to hear her scream. And she didn't, for the first half hour while they waited for her to be dilated and the contractions to lead to a baby popping out. Her only hope was that the baby came out quickly.

"Chi…" she whimpered between contractions. Her brow was already sweaty, and I was glad for her sake that she got her hair cut earlier that day. "You're not gonna leave me, right?"

"No. I'm not going anywhere."

"Mother?"

"She's coming from Seki right now."

"Yohei?"

"He said he's coming from Tokyo."

Her head hit the pillow. Her hand squeezed mine until it turned red.

I've never seen a baby being born, and I'm pretty sure I never want to again. Not with Yumi, anyway. Once the procedure began, it was like a dam broke in her vocal chords. After the first scream I could see the panic on her face. The doctors glanced at each other, and the attending nurse held her hand to her lips. None of them said anything. They weren't going to stop her from screaming. Just judge her for it.

Scream, scream, scream. Once the first came out, the others followed, and soon I felt like I lived in a world where Yumi's screams would echo for eternity. Her sweaty hand was all over mine, and sometimes her other hand smacked against me as she whimpered and tried not to die.

"Fuck it hurts!" In case nobody knew.

There were times I felt like I was giving birth as well. Now if Yumi reads this, she will probably come back to Tokyo just to smack me across the head. *"The fuck do you know about it?"* she would say. It was true! The nurse not so politely asked me to control Yumi's outbursts, "For the safety and comfort of the baby." I squeezed her hand back, tried to get her to breathe with me, and kept a towel on hand to wipe her brow.

"You're gonna be fine," I told her during a much needed lull. "I love you."

The room grew quiet. One doctor and the nurse exchanged glances before staring at me. What? I glared right back at them. If they wanted us out of there, they would hurry their asses up and get that fucking baby out. How long had it been? Six hours? Where was Yumi's mother?

Another hour passed. Yumi was too tired to scream anymore, and instead she wept, tired tears streaming down her face. "I don't wanna do this anymore." Yumi released my hand and almost passed out. I shook her gently. *Where was her damned mother?*

Finally, after what felt like twelve grueling hours (in reality, eight,) the doctors let out a relieved cry – and so did someone else. The pathetic wails of a new life never sounded so sweet.

"Thank God." At first I thought she was dying. Yumi's head rolled over and she fell unconscious. The nurse told me that she would be fine. My heart was torn between my half-dead friend and the baby crying in another room.

One doctor remained behind to take care of the final moments of birth. The other tended to the baby, and when the nurse brought the little one out, swaddled in the white of the gods, I thought for sure we were going to wake Yumi up to see her daughter.

Yet it was me the nurse came to. She placed the child into my arms, told me how to hold her, and I sat there, utterly stunned.

You know what they say about holding your child for the first time? That you're filled with these crazy hormonal endorphins that instantly bond you to a new life? When I held that child, looked into her red, wrinkled face, and heard the most pitiful sounds in the world, I knew. Those endorphins filled me, released by my heart instead of my brain, and all I could do was look into the midst of this blanket and think *"My life has been changed forever."*

I didn't think it was possible to love somebody so quickly. I knew what lust was. I knew what slow-burning love was. This was new. And to this day I wonder if I did something wrong. By being the first person to hold the baby, did I absorb those endorphins from Yumi? She should have been the one to hold her daughter and feel that wave of love wash over her. Instead it was me. Big, incompetent Chiharu. From that moment I became a parent.

When the nurse tried to take her away, she said, "She's lucky to have an aunt like you."

I didn't correct her. I was too stunned.

The nurse showed me where to clean up and kindly asked me to give Yumi some peace to recuperate. I left the delivery room, still in a daze, my feet tripping down the hall until I reached the waiting room, where two men waited. Neither of them were who I expected to see.

"Congratulations," Beppu said, clapping Koji on the shoulder. "You've got a baby to manage now. Enjoy that."

I fell into Beppu's embrace, my pent up emotions bubbling out as I sobbed. I don't think they were tears of happiness or sadness. Just *tired* tears. I was there for every grunt, every push, every loud and shrill scream that came from the woman I love. If I weren't the father, I was damn near close.

"Good job, kid." Beppu held me tight as I cried. "How's the other kid?"

"Fine... I think."

"And Yumi?" Koji was ready for the worst news imaginable.

"Worn out, but I think she'll be okay." I stood back, bedraggled in my clothes and sweaty hair. "Any news on her mother?"

"No, sorry. We've been the only ones here."

"So no Yohei then."

Beppu frowned. "No."

"I called him and told him to get his ass here. I know he was coming from Tokyo, but..." I didn't finish my sentence. We all knew what I meant. "*What if he's not making the effort?*"

"He's on tour, right? We're lucky he was even in the country." Koji put on that salesman smile he used in executive meetings and to schmooze producers backstage at a show. "I'm sure he'll be here by tomorrow."

Beppu set his jaw and gave Koji one of the most fatherly faces I ever saw in my life. "I was working both times my wife went into labor. You know what I did each time? Found someone to take my place and rushed to see her. The second time I was clear on the other side of the country with some girls on tour. I didn't make it back in time to see the birth, but God fucking damnit I was one of the first people to hold my daughter." Before Koji could say something, Beppu continued, "A man who can't care about his wife and newborn child ain't a man at all." He looked at me. "You know what that means, right?"

I nodded, woozy but not delirious. "I know."

"Good." He put his hand on my shoulder, steadying me, looking at me man-to-man. "That kid's gonna need somebody as sensible as you."

Koji appeared as if Beppu told me to marry Yumi and make off with her into the sunset. If only I could! "Like I said, I'm sure the father will be here as soon as he can." We ignored him.

Yumi's mother finally arrived twenty minutes later, hollering about a road accident that she, if you were to believe the way she put it, single-handedly solved with the brute strength of her mother's resolve. After demanding I tell her everything, she rushed to Yumi's room, and I didn't see her again that night.

Everyone told me to go home. I couldn't see mother or child until the next day.

The first time I saw Yumi holding her newborn daughter was on Chinese New Year. The little one avoided being a Sheep by five hours, which meant nothing to anyone except us.

"Look," Yumi said, tilting the baby so I could see her pink face.

I gently touched the fuzz on the baby's head before kissing Yumi's. "I saw her yesterday. You passed out."

"For twelve hours. I woke up this morning in this room feeling like I had been run over by a delivery truck." She realized what she said and strained to laugh. "This is my first time holding her."

I wondered if she felt the same way I did. Just looking at the baby again made me happy, since I could see Yumi in her already. The way she wrinkled her nose, the wide eyes that could shrink in disgust at a moment's notice… when Yumi passed her to me, I knew she was bestowing me with a great honor.

"What's her name?" I asked.

Yumi stayed mum on that for a while longer. "I've had one picked out ever since I knew it was a girl," she said. "I'll tell you later. I'm too tired to explain it right now."

"Baby Yoshizaki" was the child's name until further notice. Mr. Yoshizaki finally graced us with his presence late in the afternoon, sauntering in like he should be congratulated because he drunkenly popped a nut ten months ago.

"There're my girls!" he cried, startling both myself and Yumi with that booming singer's voice. He practically pushed Yumi's mother out of the way to stand over his supposed family, giving his wife a long kiss that made me gag and staring at the child as if that would make her any more attractive. "Came as soon as I could, babe."

I bet he said that before many times.

As weak as it may make me sound, I couldn't stand and watch that mockery. I went into the waiting room and called my mother, telling her everything that had happened and that I wished I could see her soon.

"Her name is Chisa," Yumi told me two days later. She was sitting up, her strength slowly returning but not enough to release her from the hospital. "I made Yohei tell the doctors so they could add it to the family registry."

Nothing seemed out of the ordinary about that. "It's a pretty name," I said.

Who knew I missed that sarcastic way she could look at me? "Are you dense?"

"Eh?"

Yumi pulled a piece of paper off the nightstand and handed it to me. It contained the *kanji* for the little one's name, and must have been the slip given to the officials to make sure it was recorded correctly.

It took me a while to figure out what Yumi had done. The first *kanji* for "Chi" was the same as mine: one-thousand. The "haru" in my name means springtime, and my mother said that she wanted me to bring a thousand springtimes wherever I went in the world, because someone was always living in a perpetual winter. But this nod to me didn't stop with the first *kanji*. The second for "sa" was the *kanji* for petals.

The little one was "One-Thousand Petals" and I was "One-Thousand Springs." I didn't need Yumi to tell me what it meant. It was more than an acknowledgement of my existence. It was her saying that this child came from me.

She didn't say anything when I wept and placed my head on her breast. The next time I saw the baby, I wept again.

***

I'm weepy right now. Remembering those beautiful moments with Yumi and the baby, I am transported back to a time when I believed everything could be better, easier. I had it in my mind that someone like Yumi could be with me, even if she was married and a mother. We would find a way to make it work.

I think about these pleasant things while my phone rings. I don't know who it is.

"Chiharu." It takes me a bit, but I finally recognize Yumi's mother's voice. "What have you done?"

Suffice to say, I have no idea what she means. After all, she could be referring to any *number* of things. My blog? My involvement in Yumi's life? My falling in love with and making more love to her?

She tells me that I'm a terrible person who should be ashamed. Okay, she doesn't say it that bluntly. Yumi's mother is a master wordsmith. She finds words, metaphors, and allusions I never thought would apply so aptly to me. Not just "dog shit" either. Something about a rainbow reaching into the cosmos and dying from a lack of oxygen. Maybe not that. I've completely detached from her verbal abuse and am thinking about lunch.

"There always was something wrong with you. I should have never let you play with my daughter to begin with. Do you know what she's been doing since she got here? Crying! What have you done to her, Chiharu?"

Love, Yumi

By this point I'm only vaguely listening to her rant. I should hang up, but I don't want her talking too much crap about me to her daughter, whom I still love. And, well, I hope she still loves me. Who knows anymore.

"Please understand," I eventually say, almost not believing my own voice, "Yumi and I made this decision together."

"Together! Don't drag her into this. My daughter isn't well, and you know that. She's not responsible for any stupid idea you two had. You should know better than to drag her into your debauchery. Damnit, Chiharu, you've ruined her life!"

Those words sting. In many ways I do feel like I've ruined her life. Not just with this blog, but also with everything else I've done. Like falling in love with her. I don't regret it. I wouldn't know my own life without my love for her. Thinking about a life without having ever known her… it sounds so empty. Unbearable.

"Put her on the phone. Let me talk to her."

"I don't think so. She exhausted herself crying. And anyway, that's just a bad idea. If I had my way, she would never talk to you again."

I've never considered Yumi's mother, per se. She took care of me sometimes growing up, but in that "friend of my daughter's" sort of way, not as a second mother. When things changed later in life, I noticed that my mother was the one including the both of us in her thoughts and plans. Yumi's mother has always been focused on her daughter. I am an afterthought. That never really bothered me before, but there it is.

She has a few more choice words for me, but eventually I just hang up. I can't take that shit anymore. I lie down on Yumi's couch, hoping that my mother and daughter come home soon. Seems like a good day to do something with them.

Somebody pounds on the door. Once, twice, thrice, in quick succession like bullets firing from a gun. I sit up, wondering who the hell that could be. The knocks come again, followed by an intimidating, "Open up!"

Oh God, no, not now.

Still, what can I do? I must be a good citizen and open the door to the police, who rush in, serve me a search warrant, and go about Yumi's apartment searching for… well, according to the warrant, drugs.

This is my own fault. All I can do is stand to the side while drawers are ransacked and closets emptied. Do they find any drugs? Of course not. There aren't any. When they ask me where Yumi is, I tell them the truth. She went back to Nagoya. I'm sure there's a raid going on there as well.

Without apology the police decide that there's nothing to be found and start heading out. My mother and daughter choose then to return, and Chisa is crying, her little body shaking against her grandmother's leg as the police badger them about who they are.

"Whose child is this?" they ask, pointing to Chisa.

"Mine." I cross my arms, daring them to scare her some more.

After brief consideration, the last of the police march out, and my family goes into the apartment to see the mess.

"Drugs?" my mother asks.

"They didn't find any."

"Call her."

I do. After seven rings Yumi finally answers, weary and in no mood to talk to me. The fact she does, however, gives me hope.

"The cops just raided your place here. If there are any drugs at home, get rid of them."

It's not until I hang up that I realize something even more disconcerting: my laptop is missing from the couch. The cops have fucking taken it.

Part 13

THE REBIRTH OF YUMI NISHIKAWA

Love, Yumi

西川裕美の新生

I can't believe what's happened. After panicking for a good two hours, my mother finally found my laptop pressed between two sofa cushions. You would almost think I hid it there on purpose when the police arrived. Shaken, I called Yumi again, but all she would say to me was, "I don't have any fucking drugs. Thanks."

Did the police raid this place because it was simply time to? Or was it because of all the things I've been saying in my blog? I don't want to think about it. I tried to sleep last night, but I tossed and turned in Yumi's bed, wishing she would come back here and tell me, for once, that everything was going to be okay. I slept with Chisa, because I needed someone near me, and the scent of her mother on the pillow calms her down too.

I looked to your comments for support when I logged on. I refuse to turn on the TV or to go to any other website. We're nearing the end of our tale. Finally, you will learn the truth Yumi tried to hide for all this time. I need to get it out before someone manages to stop me.

Chapter 45

Chisa went home after two weeks in the hospital with her mother. I visited almost every day, partly to visit Yumi, partly to see the baby. As she aged, she lost some of the pinkness to her skin and looked more, well, human. Yohei's family arrived, talking about how much she looked like the members of their line. That's where their interest in her ended, however. Yohei was the baby of his family and his older siblings had plenty of children already. There was nothing special about a Yoshizaki girl, even if she was the "famous" one.

The label released a statement saying that Yumi and her baby were healthy. They didn't share her name, just that it was a girl. Fan letters poured in, and Koji brought them by once every other day. These letters told Yumi that she would be a wonderful mother and that she was lucky to have such a beautiful and healthy baby.

There were little things, however. Little things that made me worry.

The baby was fine. Underweight, but not enough to concern the doctors. No, what was wrong had entirely to do with Yumi. First, she couldn't get her daughter to latch to her breast. Then they found out that her milk had no nutrients anyway, and Chisa would have to be bottle fed until she weaned. Everyone reassured Yumi that it wasn't something she could have prevented, but behind her back they whispered that this was terrible for the child.

Second, when he thought they were in private, Yohei mumbled that she should try harder next time to make a boy. "My family isn't going to care about a daughter," he chastised her. "She'll be good to soften my image for a while, but soon the public won't care. So we should be careful to have only boys from now on."

Third, Yumi didn't show the amount of interest typical for a new mother. It wasn't because she was tired. She just handed off the child whenever someone else was in the room, which the nurses mentioned was unusual. Their stay in the hospital was meant to promote bonding time. Yumi was supposed to hold Chisa as much as possible. She gave her bottles and occasionally changed her diaper, but for the most part she seemed completely distant from the situation. I hoped she was overwhelmed and would return to normal when she went home.

Yohei did not stay. He had a tour to get back to, after all. So it was up to Yumi's mother and me to help them transition to home life. My vacation was over, meaning I left this to Yumi's mother. Fine by me. I loved that child, but I knew nothing about caring for one.

I still visited at least every other day, taking time off in the late afternoon to stop by. Yumi always lit up to see me, and when her mother wasn't around would say, "It's good to have someone who doesn't drive me crazy around." On the rare night Yumi's mother went out, I stayed in and held Yumi on the sofa, enjoying her presence until the baby started crying and one of us had to do something about it.

Personally, I liked taking care of the baby. Then again, I didn't have to live with her. I didn't doubt that being kept up half the night with feeding and diaper changes was hell. I think Yumi appreciated having me over because she liked me interacting with the baby. Sometimes she would sit and watch us talk, almost in awe that I was such a "natural," as she put it.

It all seemed easy enough. Then Yohei's tour ended and he came home. And then Yumi's mother went back to Seki, only to visit every other weekend.

My life returned to normal. Yumi's went somewhere else entirely.

It was April. Chisa was almost two months old and I fell back into routine. Work picked up big time so I spent most of my days either at the office or at home with Asuka helping me keep my life in order. I visited Yumi when I had the chance. Already she was in the process of getting back to work. "Write me a song about anything," she said. So that's what I did.

When I couldn't visit, I called, usually late in the evening. If I were over at her place, Yohei was more or less behaved. On the phone, however, I could hear him yelling in the background, sometimes at the TV, other times at Yumi. "Shut the kid up!" I heard him say once. "It's your turn!" Yumi shouted back. This continued until Yumi finally went into the nursery with a huff. Honestly, I could have saved them both the grief and done it myself if I were there.

Things didn't happen in front of me until one night in late April when I went over to spend time with Yumi and the baby. She was more tired than usual, attributing it to the vigorous workouts she did to get back in perfect shape. We sat at the dining table while Yohei and three of his buddies – including Junya, if anyone remembers him – played video games on TV. Loud, violent video games that made them shout and curse every time something happened. Their ruckus was so disruptive that the baby cried more than once. The first time Yumi got up to take care of it, while the second time I went into the nursery to do something. The third time, Yumi insinuated that Yohei do it because he was the one scaring the child.

"Who's the mother?" He then gestured to the TV. "I'm busy! You're just gabbing."

Junya sent us a sympathetic look. Teeth gritted, Yumi got up and went to check on her child. While she was gone, Junya lost the game first, and he got up to get some drinks out of the kitchen, passing me along the way.

"Hey," he said. I looked up from my phone and smiled. "How's it going?"

It was a simple question that he didn't have to ask. I appreciated it, though. Really, in another life if I were attracted to men at all, I could see myself dating Junya. In the few interactions we had over the years he came off cool, polite, and attentive to what was going on.

Which is probably why he then said, "Sorry about that." He gestured to Yohei.

Before I could say anything, Yohei snapped, "What are you doing with that queer? You ain't getting anywhere with that pussy. You'd have better luck with Yumi. She's easy."

"*Sou ka...*" Junya nodded to me and went to get the beers.

At first, I didn't think Yumi had heard anything. Then after the guests went home she confronted Yohei in their bedroom. I was holding Chisa, who had been crying again.

"How can you say those things in front of people? I don't care if they're your friends. Don't disrespect me."

"You're too sensitive. It was all in good fun."

"And don't disrespect Chiharu like that."

"What the fuck do you see in her? Besides free babysitting?"

"What do you mean by that?"

"I have no idea anymore. She's fucking weird. I don't like her being around the baby."

"Why not? Sometimes she's the only one the baby responds to."

"You know why. She's gonna make my kid queer, and that's the last thing I'll allow."

"Listen to you. All high and mighty about shit he doesn't know."

As they continued to argue, I looked down at the baby, now snoozing against my breast. "Don't worry, Auntie Chiharu doesn't care what you turn out to be. I don't think your mother does either."

Voices rose to shouts, and I took the baby to the nursery where she wouldn't be scared.

Yumi didn't come over to my place very often anymore. She didn't like going out with the baby, so either stayed home or found someone else to watch over Chisa. The few times she did venture out with the kid, she mostly came over to my place. Like one Sunday morning when she arrived unexpectedly while I had a raging hangover.

I was making something to relieve said hangover when Yumi walked through my door, packing her baby in a large carrier. It was half the size of my friend, making her wobble until she was able to put Chisa up on my kitchen counter. I would have helped, but my headache was too strong to move that quickly.

We said the usual pleasantries, I played with the baby until I felt dizzy, and then my bedroom door opened to admit one pretty and confused lady who was missing half her clothes.

She looked at me, then Yumi, then me again. "Which one of you did I fuck?"

Clearly, it was the other hungover one in her pajamas. I raised my hand, trying not to smile – or flinch in front of Yumi.

"Wait… aren't you a woman?"

"Guilty."

"Holy shit! I'm not gay!"

I held my hands out, sickness be damned. "You were in a gay bar!"

The girl's face paled. Granted, I didn't remember her well. I was half shitfaced when I bumped into somebody and took her home. Good one, Chiharu.

"That was a gay bar?"

I could have laughed, if this weren't happening in front of Yumi. "Well, shit."

The girl scurried to find her things and leave. As she helped herself out she mumbled, "I thought you gave really good head for a *guy*."

My door slammed shut, and my apartment fell into awkward silence. Yumi, who had been quiet until now, refused to look at me as she said, "I didn't know you had a guest over."

I could hear the pain in her voice. Pain and a hint of jealousy. The night before, when I went out to get drunk and possibly laid for the first time in a year, I didn't feel any remorse about it. Yumi had given me her blessing to find some form of love somewhere else. Right now I wasn't interested in searching for romantic love, but sex? Hell yes.

"First time in a while," I said. "Sorry you had to see that."

"Still..." her face contorted in what I thought was disgust. "How stupid did she have to be to not realize she was in a gay bar *or* with a woman?" Nope. It was amusement. Even now she was teasing me.

While I dressed and tried to shake off my hangover, Yumi pulled the little one out of her carrier and held her up in the light.

"Look at silly Auntie Chiharu. Don't be like her. She picks up sillier girls in bars and gets drunk with them. Then does God knows what with them."

I dried my hands off after washing them and came up behind her, wrapping my arms around her midsection and rocking the three of us back and forth. "You know what I was doing."

I expected any other reaction than the one I got. "Don't say that sort of stuff in front of the baby."

"What stuff?"

"Stuff about you and me."

I didn't release her, although I sure wanted to at that point. "What's wrong with that?"

Yumi held Chisa close, shielding her tiny baby ears as she hissed at me. "It's best that she doesn't know about that."

"Why? You saying there's something wrong with it?"

My tone was rough, but my embrace remained firm around her. "No... just... it will confuse her if she sees me being affectionate with both her papa and auntie like that."

I won't pretend that it didn't hurt. Of course it hurt. I loved Yumi, and deep down I knew she loved me back, even if she had never said it in earnest. Why shouldn't the baby see at least one loving relationship? I doubted she ever saw one at home.

"Please, Chiharu."

There was no sense in arguing. I kissed her quickly on the neck and walked away, off to nurse more than my hangover wounds.

For Yumi's great return to the industry, she was having a double release. The first was a brand new single to celebrate the approaching warm weather. I hadn't written either song, but I was glad she was getting back in the game. Hopefully work would be able to shake her out of the funk she found herself in lately.

The other release was a photo book. Not just any photo book, either. A *sexy* photo book. Even in jeans and a cutoff T-shirt Yumi looked devastatingly beautiful in a studio, her body as lithe and flawless as it had been before getting pregnant. I'm sure most of you remember how controversial "WITH YUMI" was when it came out. She told me she trained for weeks to get her body limber and fit again in time for her return to the public eye. She dyed her hair a light brown and did her own makeup for the shoot, which resulted in sultry eyes to match a come-hither look that had conservative fans up in arms. Wasn't she married? Wasn't she a mother? How could she appear like this in a giant photo book meant to clearly titillate and give half the men in Japan erections? (Don't get me started on what it did to lesbians. Especially the semi-nude shots.)

She gave me a copy. Signed. When I opened it at home, I saw a note in the front that said, "For when you're lonely." Really, it only made me lonelier.

Her official comeback single hit a modest #2 on the charts. Modest for her, anyway. Yumi appeared on TV for the first time in nearly a year. Her performances were energetic, but I got the same bad feeling I had a year ago. Maybe I was just paranoid she was going to faint again. She wasn't pregnant, was she?

"Fuck no I'm not pregnant." Yumi laughed at that insinuation over lunch at my place one mid-June day. "I was serious when I said I wasn't doing that ever again. I'm on a pretty good regimen right now. Besides…"

she waved any other concern away with a flippant hand, "that requires fucking."

"So you and Yohei aren't…"

"Ha! He barely looks at me anymore. We only have sex when he's bored. Trust me, he's got a lot to keep himself amused. Boytasm is still #1 throughout the country and he's got lots of friends in every major city. I'm glad when he's gone. More quiet for me."

Things weren't always quiet even when Yohei was gone. One night I stopped by Yumi's place to the sound of a crying baby. And I mean *bawling*. Chisa's lungs were pretty powerful at almost five months old. Her mother's willpower, however, was fading fast.

"Why does she keep *crying?*" Yumi sat on the couch, legs drawn up and head in hands. "Make it stop!"

I entered the nursery just in time to have my ear drums almost burst from the shrill cry coming from such a tiny person. I picked the baby up and cradled her just how I knew she liked. Within a few seconds she was silent, choking on some tears, but appeased for now.

Yumi stood in the doorway. "How the hell do you do that?" She backed away when I approached with the baby. "Why does she always respond to you? She never stops crying for me…" Tears welled in her eyes. Another way Yumi and Chisa looked so related.

"Yumi…"

She retreated into the other room, and eventually I heard the master bedroom door shut. I made sure the baby was clean and otherwise taken care of before going after the mother, who had holed herself up in her bedroom.

"Go away," she said, face in her pillow. I opened the door the rest of the way, prepared to face her wrath. But she had no wrath to give me. Her eyes were red and heavy, her skin pale, and her hair limp against her head. I went to her, kneeling beside the bed and taking her hand.

"What's wrong?" I asked as softly as I could. "Tell me."

It took more coaxing, but eventually, as I sat on the bed and held her to me, Yumi said, "I feel like the worst mother in the world."

"Why?"

"My baby is always crying and I can't *do* anything. I hold her, I rock her, I sing to her, I take care of her… but she never stops crying. She will for anyone but me. She hates me."

"She's a baby. She can't hate anybody."

"And what about the rest of me? I can't give her my milk. It's like even my body is rejecting her. Ever since she was born I feel like there's this hole inside of me. Like she ripped out a part of my soul when she emerged from my body. Does that sound stupid? I'm pathetic."

"You're not pathetic." I tilted her head up. "You're doing the best you can."

"Then I go and put out a photo book showing off my skin and my post-baby body? The media was right. I'm disgusting."

"You're not disgusting."

"You have to say those things because you're my friend."

"I'm serious. You're a beautiful person, both inside and out. Chisa-*chan* is incredibly lucky to have you for her mother. You do your best. That's all anyone can ask. Have you talked to a doctor about this?"

"Why? So they can tell me how I fucked up? You heard me in the delivery room. I screamed so much I disrupted my baby. My mother was right. I shouldn't have screamed."

"I was there. And you did everything fine."

"Chi-*chan*…"

"Hm?" I didn't want to let her go, but she sat up, pulling away from me as she grabbed her pillow and held it in her lap.

"I lost the umbilical cord a few weeks ago."

Now, I'm not superstitious. I talk about the zodiac more than I should, but it's all in good fun. I don't even buy into blood type boohoos. (I'm an AB, so I can't.) Western zodiac says that I'm a Capricorn, but I don't know what that really means. At the end of the day I believe we make our own fates with some help from cosmic chance.

Except what Yumi admitted was very serious, even to someone like me. The umbilical cord is the mother's connection to her baby. Even my own mother still has my umbilical cord in a wooden box on her dresser. I'm sure Yumi's mother has her daughter's in safekeeping as well. It's said that losing the umbilical cord means mother and child are destined to drift apart because there is no string tying them together. If Yumi had it in her head that losing the cord meant her daughter hated her, well, there was little I could do to make her believe otherwise.

"You love your daughter. You want the best for her. Don't beat yourself up over things you can't control."

"Chiharu…"

I was afraid now.

"I don't feel anything for my baby."

The tears were strong now, coursing down her cheeks as she clung to my arm and tried to hide her shame in my shirt. Stunned, I could only hold her tighter, telling her that what she said couldn't be true. She loved that child. I saw it for myself. She tended to her and took care of her. She kissed her. Held her. Sang her lullabies and read her stories over her bed. But…

She was right. There was no feeling in any of it.

To this day I don't believe that Yumi is a bad mother. In fact, I blame myself for this. On the day the little one was born, I absorbed all the feelings of love and protection that were supposed to go to Yumi. How could I have been so selfish? How could I have saved it all for myself and not let the real mother learn to love her child in those pivotal moments? I will never forgive myself. I don't regret loving Chisa, but I do regret not letting Yumi love her too.

"Rest," I said, lowering Yumi to the bed and pulling the afghan up around her. It may be almost July, but it was cold in there.

Yumi dozed off, and I went about the apartment trying to clear my head and find something to do. I started with folding the laundry – yes, including Yohei's clothes – and prepping the baby's next meal. I wiped down the counters in the kitchen, rearranged the chairs around the table, and then went on a hunt for the wooden box Chisa's umbilical cord was in.

I was determined – I was going to show Yumi that the universe wasn't trying to tell her anything. She loved that child. Finding the box would go a long way toward proving it.

I didn't find it that night. What I did find was much worse.

Beneath Yohei's socks was a bag. A bag full of white powder. Beneath his tie collection I found another one. Deep within the closet was a hat with another bag. Then in the nightstand. An unused kitchen cabinet. *In the baby's fucking dresser.* I didn't know what any of these things were. I may have been twenty-six and an ex-idol, but I had never seen cocaine before.

Once I realized they were drugs, I freaked out, rushing them into the bathroom to flush every bit and then wash my hands until no evidence remained. It wasn't until afterward that I realized Yohei would be angry.

***

What is it about motherhood that affects women so differently? Some just seem like naturals at it, whether they showed a maternal bone before having kids or not. They're the mothers enjoying their roles and making the most of every moment with their child. Sometimes they even make it look effortless. When I take the little one to the neighborhood playground to see her friends on the weekend, I see these other mothers swoop in and take control of everything. Maybe they're natural born leaders, but why is it that some women are born to be parents and others aren't?

I feel for women who try their best but are criticized from the moment they do something for themselves. Being a parent is beyond difficult. Not only do you have to make sure the child is healthy and happy, but you have to constantly watch out for dangers around every corner. When I realized how much work was necessary in my house to make it safe for the little one, I almost called my own mother to throw a toddler sized fit. How was I supposed to make sure every sharp corner and wall socket was covered? It was an impossible task, because once I thought it was done she would make a beeline for the one thing I forgot to cover!

Love, Yumi

We still live in an era in which women are expected to give up everything the moment they become parents. In a way, you want to. Suddenly everything is about this child in your life, and you're the only one it can depend on. Does that mean the rest of your life ends? I don't doubt that some women want to do nothing but caretaking. For every woman who slips right into the role of mother, there's another who constantly worries that she's a failure. They work too much. They have outside interests. Even if the father stays home, it's somehow a failure on the woman's part. It wasn't so long ago that one of the national slogans was "Good Wife, Wise Mother." Those sentiments still run deep in the undercurrents of society. Not even the undercurrents.

I'm probably never going to give birth myself. I don't know what it's like to try to hold in your screams while your body tears itself apart. I don't know what it's like to breastfeed. I do know what it's like to love a child as your own.

I keep thinking back to when Yumi left yesterday. The way she treated Chisa was cold, but I know she loves her. I was the foolish one. How could I suggest that Yumi take on custody at a time like this? That wouldn't be good for either of them. Even now, when my world crumbles around me and I type up stuff like this, I am still the better parent for this situation. It also helps that both Yumi and I trust my mother.

That doesn't change the fact that she was cold and hurt Chisa. Can't you see it, Yumi? Your daughter is reaching out to you. She wants to be with her mama. It doesn't matter if you cuddle her or keep her at a near distance. She feeds off your presence. We both do.

Shit, maybe she really is my daughter after all.

Chapter 46

"Do you want to meet up sometime soon?"

"I think I have some time off this weekend. Would Saturday be okay with you?"

"Saturday is fine for me. It's gonna be warm, so wear cool clothes. ;)"

"What are you saying?"

"I'm saying that you don't have to cover too much up."

"I could say the same to you."

"Saturday, then?"

"Saturday."

Not often did I forego sex on the first date, but I did for this girl I had been seeing for about two weeks. I met her through another acquaintance, and we hit it off enough that we had lunch in a café. That lunch turned into dinner. And then dinner was drinks at a bar. I didn't get lucky because she likes to wait a bit.

God knew I needed a girlfriend to keep me away from other drama. Ever since I threw away Yohei's drugs, Yumi was on a tear every time I went over. One night I visited to find him going through every drawer and shoebox in search for his precious treasure. All while his daughter cried and his wife blocked out the noise with headphones. He shook Yumi until she paid attention to him and asked, "What did you do with it?" When she genuinely had no idea what he was talking about, he slammed the closet door shut and stormed out of the apartment.

He didn't suspect me, which was good. Perhaps he suspected one of his own frequent guests. As long as he didn't hurt Yumi or Chisa, I didn't give a single shit. All I knew was that I wasn't letting those drugs anywhere near a child.

But now I had a date to look forward to. Yumi had been prodding me lately, saying that for her birthday she wanted me to go out all proper with another woman. "You can't waste your life with me like this," she said, gesturing to her apartment. "For the love of God, go on a date. And make sure she's actually gay this time. And knows she's in a gay bar."

First, however, I was due at Yumi's to help her pick out new clothes for the baby. Chisa was still small for her age, but she was starting to grow a little. A few days before I picked up some fuzzy onesies for her that made her look like a stuffed animal come to life when she flailed on the changing table. She was in a giggling phase, and looking at her in those outfits, so was I.

It was still early evening. Yumi told me her husband was out late doing work, so we had plenty of time to get tipsy and watch our latest favorite drama while perusing catalogs for baby clothes. If the little one was in the mood, she could join us in her swing. Wearing one of the fuzzy onesies I got her, of course.

That image made me smile as I stepped out of the elevator. I was excited to see the baby, and Yumi, my two favorite girls in the whole world.

One of whom was currently throwing a box of tissues across the room when I opened the front door to her apartment.

"Spineless fuck!" Yumi, cheeks blotched red and eyeliner dripping from her eyes, picked up a paper ball next and let Yohei have it on the head. "You go around sticking your prick in anything that moves, huh? How old was she? Sixteen?"

He dodged the paper, putting up his hands to get his wife to calm down. Yumi wasn't having it. To my horror, she picked up a glass and hurled it at the wall just beside Yohei's head. It shattered into a thousand pieces and made him jump out of his rubbery skin.

"Holy shit, you crazy bitch!" He hid behind a chair as Yumi looked for something else to throw. "Get over it!"

"Get over it? *Get over it?* You think it's cute to fuck some groupie who bats her eyelashes?" Yumi slammed her hand on the back of another chair. "You're a married man!"

"Oh yeah? Well you're out there shaking your ass on TV and selling those pictures of you rolling around on the floor and showing off your tits! You ain't got no room to talk!"

"I'm not cheating on you!"

"Why would you cheat on me? Nobody would find you hot enough to stick it in. You're soiled goods. What guy hasn't had his cock in you?"

"Take that back."

Yohei laughed like that kid in high school who is trying to hide the fact he's reading a comic book in the back row. "When word got out that we were married, half the guys at the label laughed at me and asked if I knew for sure the kid was mine. Got to find out that day that they all fucked you at one point or another. You know how good that feels?"

"Like I said, I never cheated on you. Since we got married it's only been you, and I expect the same courtesy."

He scoffed. "You can't cheat on me because nobody wants you. Don't flatter yourself. Photoshop can't change what happened to your cunt. Looks like a crime scene, feels like hell."

Yumi's lip quivered as her knuckles turned white against the chair. "Please stop seeing other girls…"

He rolled his eyes at her pathetic attempt to make him stop being a cheating bastard. "And what are you going to do about it? You haven't been interesting since you had that kid."

"*That* kid? That's your daughter!"

"What good is she to me? The public is already bored with the idea of me being a girl's father. If I want my career to continue, I need to get back out there and make them remember why they love me. Can't do that stuck at home with the old lady and a..." Finally, he saw me. "Old lady and her queer."

Yumi didn't defend me. She looked too tired, too defeated to say anything back to him. I didn't defend myself either. What was the point when reacting to that word just made him want to use it more?

The baby started crying. None of us moved. I would have gone to the nursery, but Yohei was glaring at me, as if daring me to go near his child that he was so afraid of becoming contaminated. I tried to give the man the benefit of a doubt when he married Yumi. I thought that maybe I would see what she saw in him, about how much he wanted to be a father and take care of her. I never saw that. Deep down I knew I never would. But for Yumi's sake I *tried*. Now I saw a man who didn't care about his kid except for how she reflected on his image. That was all little Chisa-*chan* would ever mean to him.

"Somebody shut that kid up." Yohei grabbed his jacket off the back of a chair and walked out, stopping only to put on his boots in the *genkan*. He didn't spare me a look as he left.

Yumi sank into the nearest chair, and I went to get the baby. When I brought her out to her mother, Yumi said, "What have I done?" Her elbows leaned against the table, her face in her hands. The little one reached a hand toward her, but neither Yumi nor I moved. "That man doesn't love me. He never did." She lowered her hands, looked at me with clear eyes, and took her baby into her arms. Chisa gurgled against her mother's shoulder, those manicured fingers stroking soft black hair. "He doesn't love our baby. What am I going to do?"

I pulled out a chair next to her and sat down. Although Yumi firmly held her child, I still feared that the growing baby would fall out of her mother's arms, and so I put one hand on the small of Chisa's back as I told Yumi what she needed to hear.

"Divorce him."

She shook her head.

"It's been a year. The baby is almost half a year old. You did what had to be done to give Chisa-*chan* the right start in life. Now you need to make sure she grows up in a happy and healthy household. That can't happen with that man around."

"I know, but..."

"What are you afraid of? Losing the baby?" That seemed absurd. Children almost always went to the mother unless Yohei managed to prove without a doubt that she was unfit. We could throw that right back at him!

"No..."

"Then what?"

Yumi didn't answer me. I don't think she could. Whatever her fears, she did not have the words for them yet. That left me to embrace her – and the child – trying my damnedest to feel her emotions course through me so I could better understand.

"I'm scared. I don't want to be alone. I don't want to be a divorced single mom in an industry that vilifies them. What if my career is over? My life? I don't want to be alone."

"You're not alone," I said, one hand on her shoulder and the other on the baby's head. "You've got us. I'll stand by you."

The baby whimpered when Yumi squeezed her too tightly. How could I reassure her? How could I make her see that a better life could happen soon enough? I don't like seeing people hit rock bottom. One of the hardest things in my life has been accepting that sometimes people have to hit rock bottom before things can get better at all.

Things improved only because both Yumi and Yohei were working and thus away from one another. Yumi was in the midst of a brief comeback tour, and Yohei and the rest of Boytasm were gearing up for a high-profile album release. Yumi featured on one of their songs. A love ballad, of course. I wrote it.

Love, Yumi

Yumi's mother mostly took care of the baby, but sometimes I brought Chisa to my apartment and watched over her for a weekend or however long was necessary. I didn't mind it. Aside from having to do other things like playing piano, I liked having her around and having my chance to watch her grow. Yumi and I joked that as soon as she learned to walk she would be kicking stuff over like a true Horse. For now, it was amusing to watch her sit on my floor and then try to stand up. She was nine months old and a happy baby as long as no one was shouting.

One night Yumi got off work early and came over to my place to pick the baby up. She walked in to find us sitting on the couch together, Chisa propped up in my lap and giggling at the cartoons on TV. Yumi stood off to the side, staring at us as if we were strange creatures she had never seen before.

The next time she came to pick up the kid, I was in the bathroom, having just left Chisa crawling around her playpen. I was washing up when I heard an excited, "Chiharu! Hurry!"

I rushed out, expecting to find the baby unconscious or bleeding. Instead she was standing, chubby fingers wrapped around the web of the playpen as she took one tentative step forward. Yumi and I had a collective heart attack, the mother searching for her camera while I dashed forward to keep the baby from falling over. We tried to get Chisa to recreate the act once Yumi found her camera, but the baby merely sat there laughing at our antics.

Yumi's tour came to an end by my birthday. The news reports said it was successful, with most shows sold out and reviews good. I didn't get to see any of the shows since I was busy with work or taking care of the kid, but I knew it must have been enjoyable since Yumi was starting to cheer up again.

She made me dinner for my birthday. This surprised me, since Yumi has never been big on cooking on her own. She prefers to make it a social thing or to not cook at all. So when I walked into her apartment the night of my birthday and smelled spaghetti, one of my favorite dishes, I couldn't help but smile.

While we ate she gave me my present, a pair of sparkly earrings that added a touch of femininity to my look without overpowering my natural personality. Yumi put them on for me, taking out my gold studs and admiring her own good taste.

"You're in a happy mood tonight," I said as she brought out cake. Chocolate with white frosting and fresh strawberries on top… another favorite. "Did you really enjoy your tour?"

"I had fun, yeah." Yumi served me a piece and then sat back down with hers. "I need the crowd's energy to get me going. Also helps that the doctor gave me some new sleeping pills to help me actually, you know, sleep."

"Sleeping pills?"

"The baby cried so much those first few months that I never got any sleep. And when she finally started sleeping more, my body just didn't want to sleep too. So I went to the doctor and he gave me some sleeping pills. It's no big deal."

I dropped the subject. If they were helping her sleep and be happier, then I wouldn't speak out against it. When it came to taking such things from a doctor, though… forgive me for being a bit jaded.

After dinner she announced she had something to give me in the other room. I checked in on the baby and then followed Yumi into the bedroom, where she left the door only slightly ajar. I expected to see another present, but what I got was hands on my face and lips on my mouth.

Like a fool I succumbed to her immediately, pushing her to the bed and crawling on top of her as she whispered, "Quick. We have to be quick." Quick, slow, some bastardization of in between… I didn't care. It had been a year and a half since Golden Week. If I had known then how long the wait would be, I don't think I would have ever let her go back to work.

Things like morality didn't enter my head. By that point in my life, Yumi could have been happily married to someone else and I wouldn't think twice about doing this with her. Let alone someone she was miserable with. Who cheated on her. So what if she was cheating on him with me? That's probably why she decided to give in to her desires for me again.

"I'm not exactly the same from before," she told me as my hands fumbled with her jeans. "You heard what he said…"

Yeah, I had heard. And I knew he was full of shit. "There's nothing that could have happened that I won't find beautiful. Relax."

I didn't think about what she said on her wedding day. About how we had to keep our romance in the past. I didn't think about her telling me to keep this away from the baby so it wouldn't confuse her. All I could think about was sharing pleasure with the woman I loved. My lips traveled to her throat, where they kissed the necklace she put on almost ten years ago.

"Well, hell! I fucking knew it!"

That awful voice hit me like a brick, knocking me off Yumi as we turned to see her darling husband standing in the bedroom doorway. He dropped his backpack and jacket on the floor, arms wide as he gave us a disturbing smile. I froze. Yumi shuddered beneath my grasp. Neither of us could move.

"You tell me that you don't fuck her. And yet here we are, her hand down your pants and you panting like a fucking whore. When did this start, huh? When'd you turn queer?"

Neither of us answered him. I wanted him to be angry. I could handle angry. But he was laughing. Smiling. As if he just won a big bet. I held Yumi closer to me, and while I was glad we were both still fully clothed, I felt like we were naked anyway.

Yohei stumbled away from the door. He didn't appear drunk, but a terrible combination of tired from work and irate to find his wife in bed with another woman. The refrigerator door slammed in the other room. I got off Yumi and stood up.

She didn't release my hand. "I'm sorry, Chi-*chan*," she said, kissing my hand before holding it to her face. "I can't confess it."

At the time I didn't know what she meant. I assumed she meant confessing her would-be affair to her husband, who had seen it for himself.

These days I know what she really meant. If I had known then, perhaps I would have done things differently.

I had to leave. Nobody told me that, but I knew I would only cause more problems by being there. I asked Yumi if she would be all right alone with him, and she promised. Why did I believe her? After a brief kiss goodbye, I sneaked into the main room, where Yohei drank milk from the carton and waited for something to heat up in the microwave.

"*Oi.*" He slowly approached me as I hurried to put my boots on. Boots! Why did I wear fucking boots that day? If I had slip-on shoes I could have been out of there in ten seconds. But nooo, Chiharu Morita, your resident idiot, had to wear fancy boots for a fancy birthday. I was trapped in the *genkan* with that man as he glared at me. Until then I never noticed that I was actually a little taller. "I'm gonna look this shit over for now." How kind. I tried to keep a straight and even face so he wouldn't sense the flecks of fear poisoning my heart. If I was scared of him, then how terrified was Yumi? I hoped she would take my advice to divorce him soon.

"Good night." I shouldn't have said anything.

As my hand reached for door knob, his hand snatched my wrist.

"I don't want you near her ever again."

All I could do was stare at that hand on me. The last time a man touched me like this... suddenly I saw Asada in Yohei's place, his promise to "do me good" echoing between my ears.

"Don't go near my wife. Don't go near that kid. Go spread your shit somewhere else, but not to my family."

It was the only time I ever heard him refer to Yumi and Chisa as his family. "Or what?"

He shoved me against the door, my shoulders squeezed to the point of bruising. I thought he was going to hit me, but all I felt was his breath on my face as he said, "I'll fucking kill you."

Should I believe a man like that? Regardless, I would never abandon Yumi to such a piece of lint. I tried to give Yohei my best look of determination. The one that said I was not easily frightened… and that I could be a threat myself.

"I know it was you who flushed my goods," Yohei continued, his teeth dangerously close to my nose. "You really need to learn how to stay out of a man's business. Nosy bitch like you can't help herself, can she?"

At least I managed to keep my mouth shut. Don't get me wrong – I wanted to scream about five foul things in his face, but I knew it would only make matters worse. Yohei wasn't easily intimidated. He thought women were so beneath him that no matter what I did he would only laugh. What had Yumi ever seen in this guy?

When he let me go, I hurriedly opened the door and escaped into the hallway. I wasn't running away. I was running toward an answer to save both Yumi and the baby.

The next three days were some of the most anxious of my life. I didn't dare go over to Yumi's, and she didn't dare come over to my place. I texted her, but I never heard back. A call got me lots of yelling from a man who told Yumi to block me. He was isolating her from me. She still had end-of-the-year plans on TV, and the only way I would see my Yumi again was if I tuned in to see her fake a smile through a lackluster performance.

On Christmas I released a digital single that had been in the works for a few weeks. Normally I would get online and spend some time with my fans, but I was too preoccupied with my worries that it took Asuka prodding me to realize I had forgotten.

"Not this year, apparently," I said with a sigh. "What are you doing here anyway? It's Christmas. Go on a date with your boyfriend."

After arguing a bit with her, she finally relented, and her boyfriend stopped by my place to pick her up. The way he nodded, smiled, and held her hand like a gentle lover's made me angry. Why couldn't Yohei be like that with Yumi? If I were losing the only woman I truly loved to someone else – let alone a man – then that person better be one of the kindest, most loving around. I could have lived with that.

Christmas never meant anything to me. Since I didn't date much, I never had a Christmas date. Growing up, my birthday was so close that my mother didn't bother to hold some festivities until that time. Living in Nagoya, however, means I'm obligated to eat the local fried chicken and mashed potatoes... which I did that evening, sitting in front of my TV and watching badly dubbed American Christmas movies.

Sometime around seven, I got a call from Yumi.

"Chiharu," I could barely hear her, "please..."

A shriek from the baby interrupted her. Yumi tried to get her to calm down, whispering that they needed to be quiet. Then I heard it. Far in the background, but still too close to comfort, was Yohei drunkenly screaming that he was going to kill Yumi if she didn't get the kid to shut up. Something hit the wall, and a sob filled my ear. I was off the couch in less than a second.

"What's going on?" I grabbed my jacket and looked for my keys. "Did he hurt you?"

"Please do something... I don't know what to do..."

"Call the police!"

"I can't! What if they..."

"Who are you on the phone with?"

"Oh, God!" A door slammed shut. Yohei pounded on the door, which pounded into my phone, and soon the baby was crying even louder. "Please hurry! I think he's going to kill me!"

The phone cut off. Somehow, while the adrenaline burned inside me, I reasoned that I needed to call for backup. Strong backup.

"What the fuck are you two in this time?" The sounds of a party played behind Beppu's voice. "I know you're not calling to wish me a Merry Christmas."

I told him what was going on. I was so frantic that I tripped over my own shoes and almost cut open my hand on the umbrella stand.

"Jesus. I'll meet you there. *Don't* do anything brash, Chiharu!"

I knew what that meant. Don't go inside. Don't get myself involved in that mess. Don't call the police because they probably wouldn't do anything, only cause a PR nightmare that made things worse for Yumi. (If she wasn't dead!) I flung myself into my car and tore through the avenue toward Sakae. My heart was about to explode in my chest as I continued to try to get through Yumi's phone. She never answered.

Who knows what I thought I was going to do. Knock down the door and pacify Yohei with my superpowers? Subdue him with my brute strength? Knock him out with a pan and run away with Yumi and Chisa? All I knew was that I had to protect them both. I would risk my life if it meant I could save either one of theirs.

I could hear the commotion outside of their apartment door. Both Yohei and Yumi's voices were raised, although I couldn't make out their hateful words. My key faltered in my hands enough times that I cursed my incompetence and ended up entering the scene calling myself a stupid bitch.

Truly, I was not prepared for what I saw. Yumi's usually impeccable and stylish apartment was trashed, every drawer in the kitchen pulled out, silverware scattered on the floor and food spilled on the counter. The couch cushions were torn to shreds, their innards left to create a trail to the bedroom, where the mattress was overturned and both lamps broken. The dresser drawers were also ransacked like the ones in the kitchen. In the bathroom I found exactly what I feared: a bag of drugs, including a nice, even line ready for consumption. Something had interrupted Yohei before he could use it, and I was afraid to find out what it was.

This search of the apartment took about fifteen seconds. When I popped back out into the living area, I saw Yumi hit the floor in the nursery. My legs had never carried me so quickly.

I had never seen a man high on coke and alcohol before, and I never want to see it again. Although I've been frightened many times, the sheer violence in this moment will never leave me. Yohei, who was usually much more bark than bite, looked crazed enough to beat his own head. Indeed, Yumi had taken at least one blow, her cheek red and arm limp at her side. She groaned into the carpet when she saw me, and used the last of her voice to tell me to run the moment Yohei saw me too.

"The fuck are you doing here?" He stayed on his side of the room, sweating and sticky, his knuckles pricked with blood. Even the baby was too scared to cry, her body huddling in the corner of her bed as if doing so would hide her from the man who was supposed to protect her. I willed her to not move or make a sound. Yumi whimpered against the carpet, lifting her swollen head and then falling down again. "Didn't I tell you to get out of my house?" He stepped forward, kicked Yumi in the abdomen, and cursed, "Did you fucking call your girlfriend?"

"Hey!" He backed off before he could kick her again, Yumi clutching her stomach and shedding fresh tears. She wasn't just in pain. She was embarrassed. Ashamed. I knelt beside her and looked for signs that she was dying. Although wounded, it did not seem fatal. "The fuck is your problem? Beating women and scaring kids the only way you know how to be manly?"

Those dark eyes of his were full of an insanity I had yet to encounter. This was my first time seeing both alcohol and drugs behind a man's eyes, and... dear God it scared me to my core.

I never meant to be so transparent in my need to protect and shield Yumi from the dangers of the world. Yet it seems like every man I know can sense it from across the street. Beppu knew from the moment we moved into the dorms. Asada called me her "chaperone." And now Yohei looked at me, then her, and it was like the light went off that told him exactly how to destroy me.

Athletic I may be, but even I couldn't stop him in time from slamming his foot into his wife again. The most pathetic sound in the world came from her lips as she clutched my leg. At first I thought she was asking for help, but then I realized, as I leaped up and pushed on him, that she was trying to keep me from going after him.

She knew firsthand how strong he was. I found out when he shoved me against the wall and I was too stunned to move again.

Until that moment the baby had not made a sound. When I slid down the wall and hit the floor, she cried. Loud. Louder. Her fingers wrapped around the bars of her bed, and all I could think was what Yumi said about screaming during childbirth: she had brought Chisa into a world of pain and suffering.

I wanted to move so badly, especially when Yohei turned on the little one and shouted at her to shut up. That only made her cry more, and he raised his fist to his own child.

I wanted to get up.

I wanted to stop him.

I wanted to kill him.

A different scream, a scream powered by the last bit of steam in an engine erupted in the nursery as Yumi leaped off the floor and jumped onto Yohei's back. She clawed his face from behind, legs wrapped firmly around his waist as they moved backward. "Don't touch my daughter!" Yumi was as I had never seen her before. The protective mother inside her finally came out, and it was her own husband who was about to face her unholy wrath. Yohei slammed her against the wall, repeatedly, shouting back at her until she fell to the floor, unmoving.

No, no, no she could not be dead. I refused to believe it as I finally found the wits to stand up. I tried to go to her, but that man grabbed me by my sweater and spat into my face. "You want to be with garbage like that? What did you do with the stuff?"

"What stuff?" Did he really think I had something to do with his latest crop of drugs? How high was he?

"Don't play dumb! You flushed it before!"

"I didn't do anything! I swear!" His hands held me so fast that I could barely move. Then, so slowly that I didn't notice until it was too late, both hands were around my neck.

"Stupid bitch. Stupid fucking bitch." Those hands didn't wring my neck, but they threatened to, and I saw my end in his scowling, strung-out face. "What is your problem, anyway? Why do you care about that girl so much? She's trash! She doesn't really love you. She fucks anything that moves, even girls."

"I don't care," I said, hands on his forearms. "I love her. That's all I care about."

When I die, I will need someone to create a sign for my funeral that says, "Today we honor Chiharu Morita, the woman with too much defiance." I would not be afraid. Or at least I would not show him the fear thumping in my chest. Like a good martyr I would willingly set myself on fire and feel the flames eat away my skin and sinew if it meant a better end for someone else. That's what I was doing when I looked Yohei in the eyes and told him I loved Yumi. Not a frivolous girl's love. Not a best friend's love. *Love.* The strongest love in the universe that anyone could have for someone they met on the path of their life. It was friendship, yes, but it was also an intense sisterly bond from our childhood, peppered with respect of someone also in the same industry. Yet the real power came from how much I wanted to sacrifice myself as her lover, as someone who wanted to show her nothing but tenderness and undying passion. Two things Yohei was not capable of.

He saw that in my eyes. My defiance has always been fueled by my love for Yumi, and he saw it now. I was as good as dead.

A jealous, enraged man, let alone powered by drugs, is a terrible thing to behold. It's even more terrible to have him tear you apart, to split your lip, to blacken your eye, and to throw you across a room until half your body can't move anymore. He tossed me out of the nursery, throwing me to the carpet in front of the windows overlooking the Nagoya cityscape, a serene city full of violence and horror.

He called me worse names than Asada had. When he claimed he would "fix me," I cried, fighting to keep his hands away from my buttons and zipper. Why is it men like that have to resort to that kind of violence? Is it because they know it works so well on us? That we're powerless to stop it most of the time? That nobody will believe us or care how it's made us want to die? For all I knew, Yumi was dead. Who was I sacrificing my body for now?

I begged him to stop. I knew it was futile. The only saving grace was that he was so high he could barely do more than punch and kick, let alone rip apart my pants or sweater. It gave me time to crawl away, my lip dribbling blood on the carpet as I tried to reach for my phone. I didn't care if the police were useless. I had to try calling them anyway, if only to take the baby far away from here.

He struck me in the back of my head, grabbed my phone, and threw it across the room into the kitchen. Renewed with purpose, he groped me until I began to succumb, my body too worn out to fight him any longer. My only hope was to let him abuse me and hope that he didn't kill me in the process. Maybe if he thought he had broken me he would leave us all alone.

Yohei never got that far. As soon as he grabbed my breast, Yumi clobbered him over the head with the wooden umbilical cord box that had been missing for so long. It didn't knock him out, but it sent him rolling across the floor and dashing for the door. He left it ajar on his way out.

I sobbed, relief pouring from my battered body as Yumi fell on top of me, her whimpers all I needed to know that she was alive, and we would make it through a night like this together.

***

Anyone who has been in this business wonders what life would have been like if they never got into it. Consider that, on the talent side especially, most of us got in at an early age. For many it's the only job we've ever known. Even many of the staff people got their start right out of high school or college working for their company. They probably don't wonder as much as we talents do, but that's because they either don't see the dark side of the industry... or they're contributing to it.

What happened that night remains one of the worst experiences of my life. It hurt me, physically and mentally. When I went with Asada, I knew what to expect. Yohei? That man wanted to kill me. Rape me. Find some way to decimate me so he would never have to look at me again. What about me made him so angry? That I loved his wife? That she loved me more than him? The man treated her like shit, cheated on her countless times, and he was jealous about that?

Dredging up those more recent memories makes me think of everyone else I knew who felt the cold sting of this world. I think of Koto, who wanted nothing more than to bring people joy through her dancing, and ended up taking her own life in one of the most brutal ways possible. Dolly drove herself to alcoholism until she almost lost everything in a car accident. Every year we hear about some idol – usually a young girl – who either takes her life, tries to take her life, or is so beaten down that she goes out of her way to get kicked off her label. Most of them can leave any time they want, but are too ashamed to instigate it.

Why does this happen? Well, I know why it happens. The truth is that the industry is full of kids who want to do whatever it takes to become a star like YUMI. The adults in charge know this, and some of them are attracted to the roles because they know they can take advantage of and do sick things to them.

Obviously I am not saying that every girl goes through these things, or that every staff person is terrible. But it's much too easy to destroy someone before they've even had the chance to see their dreams come true.

Yumi and I left our relatively safe hometown to pursue a dream to make music. We were young, naïve, and all we knew was what talents we had and that we wanted to make people smile. Yumi wanted it the most. She was also prettier and a better dancer than me. So when some people in charge caught wind of that, they decided to offer her a deal that set her on a path to self-destruction. All of those terrible things Yohei always said about her? I've never once heard her refute them.

We smile on stage. We shake our fans' hands. We dream of winning awards and going down in history as one of the country's most beloved stars. Yet even those who achieve those dreams probably went through something terrible that you don't even know about. Then there are the others whom you've never even heard of. The ones who were driven out too early and either found a normal life before it was too late… or found nothing but darkness.

Love, Yumi

My love for Yumi kept me powering through the bullshit for so many years. If it weren't for her, I probably would have been cut from the group anyway and done something like college. I would now be working some other job. Hopefully happy, but probably struggling to pay my bills and agonizing over my sexuality. Every time I think about how "normal" I am for an ex-idol, I am reminded of all the horrific things I saw and felt in fewer than ten years.

The thing that scares me the most? I wouldn't trade any of it for the world.

Chapter 47

Beppu found us crumpled on the floor. I had never heard him as panicked as I did that night. The only time he expresses large emotions is when he's angry or happily drunk. Scared? Beppu? It's like finding your father crying.

I don't remember how the four of us got into his car. All I remember is that one minute I was lying with Yumi in her apartment. Then the next we were in his car, me propped up in the passenger seat while Yumi moaned in the back. After that, things were a total blur until we reached a private clinic where I saw the man who tried to help Koto that one ill-fated night.

It's humbling, being the one he looks at.

Both Yumi and I had concussions. My lip was cleaned, a gash on my forehead stitched up, and my swollen eye tended to before having a patch placed on it. Two of my ribs were bruised, but I hadn't broken anything. Later on, I would find cuts and bruises all over me, but they healed fairly quickly.

Yumi, on the other hand, had other issues. There were some things I heard that night that I never want to hear again. For her sake I won't share what they found. Just know that if I had the strength I would have gone out with a knife and found the bastard who did it to her.

The only saving grace was that the baby was fine, physically. Emotionally she cried for the both of us, sitting in Beppu's lap as he patted her back and even changed her diaper once. Sometimes I forget he's actually a father. Then nights like that happen, and I see a whole new side of him.

We should have gone to the hospital for a few days, but that was too risky. The reason we came to that clinic was because we could be treated off the records and nobody at the label or in the industry would know. We didn't even call Koji. We did, however, have our injuries photographed as evidence. I entertained the fantasy of the police going to pick him up for assault, but I knew it would never happen. He was too famous. Too rich. Nobody cared about that kind of assault. We were doomed.

The only person outside of us who found out was my mother. Beppu called her for me, and the next morning my mother was there, crying over what had happened and demanding to know who did it. When she heard, she said, "I knew there was something cruel about that man. He always looks so shifty on TV."

We made her promise not to tell Yumi's parents before we agreed to let her and Beppu take us to my apartment. She put us to bed and said she would take care of the baby while we slept and tried to recover. First I made her lock and barricade my door in case Yohei showed up. I instructed her to call the police if he did. At the very least I could get his ass for trespassing.

Yumi fell asleep first. I followed, wrapping my hand with hers just so I could assure myself that she was there.

The most surprising thing was that Yumi filed for divorce almost immediately. I say almost because the city hall was closed for the holidays.

The moment they opened their doors again, however, Yumi put in a petition citing irreconcilable differences. I'd say.

She told the label that she was getting a divorce. I was at that meeting, wearing my eye-patch and holding the baby. Although I should have been paying attention to Chisa, I couldn't take my one eye off Yumi, who calmly told the executives that she was divorcing their star male artist and she would not be working with him anymore. They tried to raise some protests, but she firmly said, over and over, that she would no longer be a Yoshizaki by the end of the month, hopefully.

Then she got a lawyer. The best in Nagoya. He advised her to keep the child with her at all times to prove her dedication to custody. This put some holes in plans since we intended to hand the little one off to Yumi's parents for safekeeping. Instead both Yumi and Chisa temporarily moved in with me, since it was too dangerous to stay in her own apartment, even in Tokyo. Yes, Yohei could easily find us, but he didn't have a key. I informed building security to keep him out, but he never showed up, thank God.

Yohei was scarce. We thought he would come after us, but after that night I hardly saw him again until the divorce proceedings. That we couldn't hide from the media. A carefully worded press release was concocted by the label's PR team. They had to be quite careful since Yohei and Yumi were their star couple, and the members of the public who supported their marriage might turn. Overnight Yumi was labeled "single mother," which dropped her popularity a bit, but also then increased it later as she pulled in some other mothers into her realm of fans.

Commoners get to divorce fairly quickly, but it's a bit different for celebrities. We have the same problems of dealing with property and children, but we also have to do it in a way that does not conflate with our images. I say we because I was with Yumi every step of the proceedings. The property was easy to deal with. She had the foresight to get a prenup, which, while not common, made sure she kept all of her shit. We expected there to be a problem with custody, but when Yohei was asked if he wanted to contest Yumi receiving full custody of Chisa, he said no. No!

Not that I wanted him to be anywhere near the child, but I had to admit his lack of concern for her appalled me.

The grave injustice that happened next appalled me even more.

Both Yumi and I filed for restraining orders against Yohei. We provided the photos of our injuries and gave our testimonies of what happened that night. (I left out the part about the drugs, but kept in the alcohol.) However, since we did not have a doctor's or police officer's report, the judge held up his hands and said there was no way to determine that our wounds came from Yohei.

All told the divorce took about three weeks. I expected longer, but the power of their lawyers and Yohei's willingness to get it over with sped things along. By the little one's first birthday, both she and Yumi were Nishikawas.

"Look at me, a divorced hag," Yumi said the night her divorce was finalized. We were back in her apartment, cleaned up since that terrible night. I opened a bottle of champagne to celebrate her severing ties with that man once and for all. "What the fuck do I do now?"

For someone who remained so strong and resolute during the divorce, she now finally cracked, showing me the tired side of her for the first time since the previous year. "You move on," I said, pouring us both a drink. "Get back to work, if that's what you want."

"Ha. Work." Yumi took the glass I handed her but didn't drink anything. She was slumped in a chair in front of the blank TV, her demeanor that of a woman who had just lost everything in a divorce as opposed to almost entirely getting her way. "I asked them when I could put out a new release. It's been almost two years since my last original album. That's almost has-been time."

"You had a baby and then had to come back."

"Yes, yes. Well, I was originally gonna prepare for an album this spring, but then the divorce happened. Now they want me to lay low for a few months. Something about a *digital single*. You know what that means. No risk, no faith in my name." She glanced at me. "Sorry."

"No offense taken."

"Anyway," Yumi sipped her champagne, but we were hardly in a celebratory mood. "I don't know what's going on. By the time I get back into the game, I'll be nothing. My career as I knew it is over."

I couldn't argue with her. Her career as she knew it was over when she married Yohei and gave birth to their daughter. Very few women can bounce back from that much time off and out of the public eye. Plus those fans who turn their backs on the celebrity they claim to love because she's no longer their attainable girlfriend dream.

"Your last tour did really well," I pointed out. "There's no shame becoming an artist who mostly tours."

"No shame, but I'm not looking forward to barely scraping the top ten with my next album. It's going to suck no matter what."

Again, I couldn't argue.

"Tell you what." I sat down at the upright piano and opened the lid. "I'll write you a great comeback song. Independent woman or nothing about that sort of thing at all?" Spring was coming. Time for a song about cherry blossoms and shit.

She sat with me on the bench, holding the drink in her hand. "I don't care. Just play me something pretty."

So I did. I played the prettiest tune I could think of off the top of my head. One of these days I'll get her to finally sing "Magnolia."

Stupid me thought that things could go back to normal. I should have known that as long as certain people were around, drama would follow.

Yumi and I were both at the office the same day, although for different reasons. As I was coming out of my meeting, however, I got a front row seat to an altercation between her and the label's top male star right there in the hallway.

"Leave me alone!" Yumi tried to walk away from Yohei, but he grabbed her wrist.

"You think I'm done?" he hissed at her, as I approached from behind. I'd like to see him try to smack me around again at the office. "This ain't over. Your career is done."

Love, Yumi

"*Oi.*"

He turned, grimaced at the sight of me, and said, "The fuck you want?"

"For you to get the hell out of here. Go on. Scram."

Yohei snarled at the both of us, as if that was supposed to make us scared in a public place like this. Just then a number of executives approached, and the next thing I knew Yohei left to go bow in respect to them and chat one up. Yumi and I had to nod to all of them before sneaking out of there.

"How many times has he done this now?" I asked her in the elevator.

She had to wait to answer, since on the next floor two trainees boarded, gave us both deep and respectful bows, and quietly rode with us five floors down. Yumi cheerily said goodbye to them and waited for the doors to close.

"Don't worry about him." I'd heard that before.

"Don't worry? He's still harassing you."

"I changed the locks on my apartment."

"He's harassing you *at work*."

I don't know if Yumi really didn't see the problem or if she was too weary to deal with it. Either way, she got off on a different floor and left me to stew in my worries.

Yohei needed to be taken care of. I wracked my brain trying to come up with ways to get him out of Yumi's life forever. This wasn't like Asada, though. Yohei was more ingrained as Yumi's abusive ex-husband. Asada could be swayed by sex, but not money. I doubted Yohei would take my body in exchange for leaving Yumi alone. This wasn't a game to him. This was personal.

It wasn't until I was at home, washing my dishes, when I realized what had to be done. I wish I could tell you that I went to where he was living now and intimidated him, but I knew that wouldn't work. No, what I had planned was better. More permanent. Well, not quite *assassin* permanent, but something that would make him go away for a long time.

Once I dried off my hands I picked up my cell phone and called the police. "Hello? I'd like to report a drug dealer."

"Oh my God!" Yumi frantically called me two nights later, the baby crying in the background as many male voices barked orders at one another. "The police are in my fucking house looking for drugs!"

I had warned Yumi to make sure Yohei's stashes were cleared out. While I hadn't told her what I did, the idea was that she needed to keep that stuff away from Chisa. This was true, of course, but I hoped she would understand when the police inevitably showed up to check on Yohei's known acquaintances and previous addresses.

"Just do what they say," I said. "Do you need me to come over?"

One authoritative voice called out that everything was clear. Someone apologized to Yumi for the intrusion and asked to have some questions answered. She had no choice but to hang up the phone.

The next day, Yohei's face was all over the news. The public was shocked to find out that one of their male idol darlings not only ingested harmful substances, but was also a known dealer in the industry. Footage of the drug bust at his current apartment complete with coked out friends and a new girlfriend who shrieked her way through the raid was shown, and the news anchors direly reported that Yohei faced serious charges. Yumi was of course brought up. They said that police had questioned her and had no reason to believe she was involved. Still, I knew it would not mean the best for her image anyway. Members of the public would say she should have known better than to get involved with a guy like that.

When I finally met up with Yumi again, she had a headache the size of her shame. The cops had left her place in complete disarray when they searched for drugs – that she would have been charged for possessing, even if they were Yohei's – and she had yet to clean most of it up. I offered to help, but she declined, saying she would get around to it eventually.

"I can't believe this is going on right now." She helped herself to a hug, her head resting on my breasts as I leaped at the chance to embrace her. "This is too much too fast. I didn't even know about the drugs until a couple of months ago."

Love, Yumi

We rocked back and forth for a bit, my heart reaching for hers as my body demanded I kiss her. Not since my birthday had we shown affection like that. Too tired. Too worried. Too hurt to make love. Yumi was officially single again, but she never insinuated that we were going to rekindle our relationship. I was waiting. I would wait forever, if that's how long it took.

"He's going to jail," I reassured her. "He can't bother you or the baby anymore."

"*Yokatta.*" Yumi lifted her head. "Thank you for always being there."

I buried my nose into her shirt, willing her to understand how much I loved her and needed her to be one with me. Like a lovesick dog I obediently waited for her to tell me to follow her to her room, to kiss me until we couldn't help ourselves, or to whisper words of love into my ear. None of those things happened. But I got to hold her, and that was an improvement over the past few weeks.

I thought things could only keep improving. In my head, I saw us gradually moving toward a happy ending. I could be optimistic like that.

***

The "post" button has barely been pushed when I get a phone call from Yumi. Considering everything going on right now, I have a bad feeling.

"Chi…" Just as her mother said earlier, she's been crying. "Please. Stop."

I imagine her sitting in front of her computer or looking at the screen on her cell phone. She's reading my blog, and the moment the page refreshes to show the latest entry, she knows what's coming.

Sympathize I do, but we've come too far to stop now. We're almost to the end of our tale, but this is going to be the hardest part for Yumi. "How can I stop now?" I keep my voice as gentle as possible, and I wish until the end of time that she was there with me, so I can show her my sincerity. If necessary, I'll hold her until she's brave enough to continue. I know that's too idealistic, though. There's nothing I can do to assuage Yumi's fears right now.

"Just… please. People don't need to know about that."

"You said so yourself when this started that it was the most important aspect. Can you go back on that now?"

She sniffs, and I feel bad. There must be some way to make her feel better. If I can't do it, maybe the little one can. But she's not here. "I dunno…"

"Yumi," I say, packing that name with as much compassion as I can, "you know I have no desire to hurt you, right?"

"Of course."

"Remember when we talked about this? I asked you a hundred times if you were sure this was what you wanted to do. Remember?"

"Yeah."

"I wish you were here."

She doesn't answer. All I can hear is her sniffing and her mother yelling at her from the other room to hang up on me. "I can't talk much longer. Just… please, Chiharu… don't make me sound weak."

"I would never."

Yumi hangs up. I need to fill my glass with some harder alcohol before I can continue. My heart is breaking as I write this…

Now I will tell you the truth about Yumi Nishikawa. The truth she never wanted anyone to know, least of all the people reading this right now. I will do my best to not make her sound weak.

Chapter 48

For the little one's first birthday we threw a party more for adults than for the child. Sure, her grandmother piled her with presents, but it was cake we liked and enough alcohol to make the child sober for life. Chisa tried strawberries for the first time, her face making a puckered expression as she spat out the rest and started crying. Her grandmother picked her up and said she got her lack of taste from her father.

"What do you say, Sattchan?" Yumi's mother asked. We started calling her Sattchan to differentiate her from me. Otherwise Yumi, the child, and I would all be confused to hear Chi-*chan* too often, and it seemed cute to call her Little Petal. "What do you say when someone gives you a present?"

She waited patiently for a thank you, even a spittle of one. Yumi and I glanced knowingly at one another. The baby hadn't spoken yet, aside from the usual mindless prattle an infant tosses over their tongue while they're practicing speech. She could stand and toddle around for short distances. As far as we were concerned, that was good enough development.

"Eh? What's wrong with her?" Yumi's mother put Chisa back in her highchair and looked to anyone with an answer. "You were saying whole words by this age."

Yumi shrugged. "She's only a year old. Doctor said we have at least a few months before we start worrying about something being wrong with that. She's starting to walk. That's enough to deal with."

The look we were given suggested that Yumi's mother thought we were full of shit. You know, growing up I had no real opinion of the woman. She could be kind and tough, attentive and distant. Since she wasn't my mother, we accorded each other a certain respect. She fed me, gave me shelter many nights, and even bought me presents for my own birthdays as a kid. Nothing fancy, but I always appreciated being thought of. Now? I noticed more and more that she would look at me strangely, as if I were to blame for all the ill in her daughter's life. Was it because I was twenty-seven and still single? Did she suspect something? Surely she was thankful that I took such care of her daughter and granddaughter. Actually, that was probably why she never gave me shit outright.

"She should be saying at least simple words by now. Hasn't she called you Mama yet?"

Yumi, who had been lazily drawing pictures in her leftover cake icing, stopped doodling and looked into her lap. "Not yet. Like I said, we're not worrying about it right now."

"We?"

"You know Chi-*chan* helps a lot. She's like a second mother."

Before Yumi's mother could glare at me again, I joked, "She'll probably be calling me Auntie Chiharu. Actually, it wouldn't be so bad."

"Look, her dad's going to prison and is a lowlife I never want around her. She should have two people she can look up to. I can't do it all myself. I have my limits as a human being."

Now her mother returned her attentions. She patted her daughter's idle hand and said, "Don't worry. You'll get yourself a decent man next time. Someone who will love raising such a precious child with you."

Love, Yumi

Yumi sighed heavily enough that her whole frame moved. I merely shifted in my seat.

At this point I still didn't know what our relationship was. We were like a sexless married couple who lived apart but came together almost every day to either bullshit or take care of the child. (Or both, really.) I'm not complaining. Back then I was more than happy to do these things if it meant helping both Yumi and Chisa out. Yet I wouldn't be honest if I said I didn't care about physical affection. The girl I was trying to see a few months ago disappeared into the void, and I hadn't been seeing anyone since. In my heart I had this idea that Yumi would eventually invite me back into her bed – intimately – and we would pick up where we left off after Golden Week two years ago. After all, hadn't she initiated such things on my birthday? I guess after what happened with Yohei she wasn't ready for any physical affection yet. I could wait.

Yumi's mother left shortly after dark. Considering I thought she would be staying the night with her daughter, I was relieved. The moment that woman left, Yumi turned to me and said, "She has some opinions, huh?"

"It's natural for her to want to give you parenting advice."

I got *the* look. At least she was smiling, even if at my expense. "And it's natural for me to want to tell her to shut the hell up."

"That could be you and the kid one day. When you're a grandmother."

"Don't go there." Yumi picked her daughter up out of the highchair and put her in the playpen by the couch. Chisa immediately sat down to play with a stuffed sheep that squeaked whenever she smacked it against the floor. Those squeaks peppered our conversation. "She's never having kids. It'll be my mission in life to make sure that doesn't happen."

I didn't respond simply because I had no idea how to.

The TV stayed off as we sat at the table and did some work. Yumi was working on a digital single – much to her chagrin – and only agreed to it if we composed it. We had half an idea sketched out, but the label wanted the whole thing by the end of the next week. A theme continued to elude us.

"*Nee*," Yumi said later that evening, when half the table was covered in music sheets, "I do worry about her development."

- 535 -

I looked up from my notes about cherry blossoms and new school years. "The baby's?"

She nodded, sadly. "I know the doctor said wait a few months before worrying about her speech, but what if something really is wrong?"

Laughter bubbled within me, simply because this was a fantastic example of how Yumi truly did care about her child. Wasn't it normal for a young mother to worry that her baby wasn't meeting the benchmarks? "Why would there be something wrong?"

The way she studied our papers was as if she expected the answer to be written on them. "I read that drugs could make a baby's development slow."

I scoffed. "You said you never did those drugs. Let alone when you were pregnant."

"I didn't, but Yohei probably did. Wouldn't that contribute?"

"She's fine."

"And I did drink those first couple of months. You remember."

Golden Week. Of course I remembered. "Uh huh."

"So what if I fucked up my baby?"

"You're not the first woman to ingest substances before she knew she was pregnant. Everything is fine. She wasn't premature."

"She was underweight."

By like two grams, but I wasn't mentioning that. "You can't think like this. She's born. If something did happen, it was done. You have to concentrate on the child as she is."

"I know."

Did she? Yumi still often confided that she was worried the baby would grow up feeling unloved by her. Even today I wonder how she could ever think this. Could Yumi have been – and be – warmer toward her daughter? Yes. Oftentimes I don't think she instinctively knows what most mothers naturally gravitate toward. Yumi has a distant, albeit vested interest in the little one. She researches the best schools, buys the cutest clothes, and changes and feeds Chisa as needed. Back then, I assumed that as the girl grew older, developed more of a personality, and became someone Yumi could actually talk to that their relationship would improve. She never was a baby or small child person.

Sitting there thinking of underdeveloped children wasn't going to get us anywhere, so I stood up and went into Yumi's kitchen to start some tea. When I came back, I stood between the playpen and the table, stretching while Yumi looked at me with passing interest.

"Chi-Chi."

I lowered my arms. Yumi's ears perked up. Behind me, standing against the edge of the playpen, the little one extended her hands and made a grabbing motion. "What was that?" That grabbing meant she wanted to be picked up. Yet I swore I heard...

"Chi-Chi!" Her feet stomped in her pen and she almost fell down from the effort. Chisa looked right up at me, her hands furiously trying to grab my sweater as it dangled toward her. A brief look of frustration overcame her, and I thought she was going to cry. "Chi-Chi!"

I scooped her up into my arms, and she instantly smiled. No other words came out of her mouth now that she had me, and I turned to Yumi in utter disbelief.

"Did she just say..."

Nodding, I held Chisa close to me, stroking her hair as I tried to contain my excitement. I mean, she just called me... she called me...

Father? No. Doubtlessly she was asked to call Yohei that when he was around, but a baby was more likely to say papa as opposed to something more difficult like *chi chi*. Combined, however, with hearing Chi-*chan* every time her mother was around me, and I could only guess that she associated the sound with me.

A part of me wanted her to call me father. Not that I thought of her as her *father*, per se. I still don't think that way. Nor am I her mother. I'm her second parent, but not in a way that I take a male role. I wouldn't even know where to begin with that, as I'm not a man!

"Oh my God." I gently bounced her in my arms, my own smile finally bursting through as I looked at Yumi. "She spoke!"

I expected her to jump up in glee, to phone her mother, anything. But she only sat there, one leg resting over the other, fingers drumming on the table as she studied my face and then her daughter. "*Omedetou.*"

Why was she congratulating me? Her daughter had spoken her first words! "Who's that?" I asked, pointing to Yumi. "Is that Mama?"

Chisa smiled at her mother, but it was me she looked at again while she said, "Chi-Chi."

No matter how many times she said it, Yumi would not react. I went to her and tried to give her the baby, but Yumi got up, her jaw and fists clenched. She went into her room and didn't come out for a few minutes. How could something that should be so joyous make her so upset? I couldn't understand.

"Happy birthday, little one." The baby laughed in my arms as I kissed her cheek and patted her back. "One year ago today your mama suffered to bring you into this world. She'll work very hard to make sure you grow up big, strong, and really smart. She loves you. Don't forget that, okay?"

I thought of that Valentine's Day one year ago when I put my head to Yumi's stomach and listened to the baby swim and gurgle inside. Yumi had been through so much, not just with the pregnancy, but even going so far as to throw herself on the man who was about to hurt her child. Every time Yumi claimed she was unloving and no good as a mother, I thought of a time when she showed this child the meaning of a mother's undying love.

Time passed quickly. Soon enough it was spring, and I was making the rounds at radio shows and some late night local talk shows to promote my latest full-length album. Even though I was busy, and even though I was tired of looking at Uma's long face sitting outside radio booths, I still found time to call Yumi and check in on her. She was also back at work, having released that digital single we finally wrote and now allowed to work on a proper album for the summer. I thought she would be excited, but every time I brought it up or otherwise asked how it was going, she would sigh and say, "What's the point? My fanclub numbers are half of what they used to be. My last one-night live didn't even sell out. I'm tired."

We don't talk about depression enough. Maybe that's why it was hard for me to realize what was going on with her. Little by little, however, I understood that there was something wrong with Yumi. Not just the stress of trying to fix her career or raise a child. Something deeper, darker, and more sinister. A demon lurked in her shadow, and I wasn't powerful enough to exorcise it. I don't think anyone was.

All I could do was be there for her. Even then, two years after that conversation with Beppu in the bar, I heard his voice telling me to be her best friend first. Everything else? Second.

After a while she stopped answering. When she did, the conversations became shorter, more curt on her end. I would spend more time talking to the baby than talking to Yumi. Whenever she went to hang up, I told her that I loved her. Not once did she say it back to me. Sometimes she said thank you, and sometimes she said nothing at all.

At one of my radio shows the DJ asked if I missed the idol life. Uma gave me a sour look when I almost snorted my answer. "It was fine for when I was that age," I said diplomatically. "Though I'm happier now. I can go at my own pace and express myself artistically."

"You have always been a piano player, right?"

"Yes. Since I was a child. My special talent at my audition was playing the piano."

"You auditioned with YUMI, right? She's your good friend?"

I nodded, glad that there were no cameras to catch the expression on my face. People always ask me about this, but now it hurt as I thought about what she was going through. "We grew up together. It was her idea to audition for our label. We performed an original composition and were invited to be in our group."

"And you're still friends today?"

What a stupid question. Anyone knew the answer to that. Every time Yumi was caught by the paparazzi now, I was with her half the time.

Hildred Billings

"We're still good friends. That sort of friendship is hard to end. Even if we fight, we usually make up quickly and move on. There are a couple of people at our office who call us that old married couple because we just do what the other says, and when we disagree one of us always relents right away, because what's the point of fighting? Recently we had a stupid argument over a key change in a song and I got really mad, because I like to believe I know more about music than she does. We really ended that on a sour note. But we were having lunch together in an hour and her manager couldn't believe that we had made up already."

"Did you have the key change?"

I laughed. "We worked something out."

The DJ commented that he couldn't wait to hear the song that made us fight. Then, "I don't think I'm still friends with anyone I grew up with. It's amazing to think that such a friendship could last so long. Let's take a call."

Normally people didn't call in to these shows to talk to me, so I was surprised to have one on the line. Who wants to talk to Chiharu? Even my fan mail is terse. "I love your music," they will say, signed by someone from across the country. "Thank you for your music." "The last single really spoke to me." "We play your songs in my café all the time and people ask who it is." These people are like me. Short and to the point. The few times in my life I wrote my own fan mail to celebrities, I was just as terse.

"Hello?" A young lady's voice arrived in my headphones. "Yes, I just wanted to say that your friendship with Yumi-*san* is really inspiring to me. I'm thirty-four and still best friends with a woman I've known since third grade. Sometimes it's really hard since two people change a lot during those years, but at the end of the day she's like my greatest sister. No matter how we change, we still find ways to relate to each other's lives. So, thank you for showing the world that it's possible."

"My pleasure."

"Eh?" The DJ chuckled. "Suddenly this is a feel-good therapy show. I thought we were here to talk about music!"

After the show Uma and I walked back to our hotel, said goodnight, and went to our separate rooms. I wasn't halfway done filling the bathtub when I got a call from Yumi.

"I listened to the show," she said. That was new. Yumi didn't usually listen to the radio. "Is it really unusual that we've known each other for so long?"

"Is that a bad thing?"

"No. Is it usual for people to be like that?"

The first thought to enter my head was that she wanted to take a break. She felt stifled and wanted to know what life without Chiharu was like. She was spring cleaning and I was the first thing out the door. These were irrational fears, I know, but Yumi was becoming more unpredictable over the years. "I'm glad we're still friends."

She hung up without replying.

You should know by now how paranoid I can get that something is horribly wrong. Although Yumi had been like this for so long now that I kept telling myself it was another mood of hers that would pass. She would see. Her next album would do more than fine and people would start loving her again. This funk would pass. Sure, the baby would become more of a handful, but Yumi had lots of money to find people to help her take care of Chisa.

I sat in the bath that night wondering what I could do to help. Yet it seemed like no matter what I did, what I said, or what I suggested, Yumi became someone I didn't know.

"Look over here!" I trained the camera on my phone at Chisa, who waved at me before slapping the carpet and drooling on her hand. "Can you say hi?"

She giggled, grabbing her foot and shuffling in place, which was utterly adorable, but not what I was looking for. Since she first spoke on her birthday, I was determined to get her talking more. So far I wasn't having much luck.

"What are you talking about? The deal was three music videos for twelve tracks." Yumi walked out of the bedroom, phone attached to her head. "Not two videos for ten tracks. The only people who put out ten track albums are has-beens and newbies. You saying I'm a has-been?"

I knew she was talking to Koji because he was the only one at the label she spoke to like that. Usually. She had gotten mouthier with a few of the staff members and was building a reputation as a hassle to work with. No longer the professional princess of old. "Come on, Sattchan," I coaxed. "Tell everyone hi!"

She was distracted with one of her toys now. I left the camera on, got up, and went to Yumi who was in the kitchen.

"Trouble at work?"

The fires of a crematorium burned behind her eyes. I shuddered, imagining her decimating half the people at the office and turning their bones to ash as she avenged herself. "They're neutering me. I was supposed to have a twelve track album with three videos. The lead track video, plus a ballad video, and then one of my choice. Now they're taking away two tracks and the video of my choice. They don't want to spend the money on me. I bet they're halving my marketing budget too."

"I'm sure they know what they're doing."

"Do they? Oh, I bet they do. Fuck it. They're having a summer festival this year. I'm invited, but they're not going to give me a top spot." She laughed. "At least I know Boytasm won't get it either! It's gonna be that new girl group making waves."

Since Yohei was arrested and put in jail for his drugs, Boytasm was disbanded to the tears of young girls everywhere. No matter what we did we couldn't quash the news of his abuse getting out, and rumors appeared on the internet that he beat the both of us. Luckily the pictures never leaked. Some people also speculated he hurt the baby. *Those* rumors really made me mad.

"You'll still headline," I pointed out. "That has to mean something."

"Would you knock it off?"

"Eh?"

Love, Yumi

Yumi threw her hands in the air. "You always do this. You refuse to see what's happening. Everything is always explained away and you fucking coddle me until I feel like I'm suffocating. What are you? My mother? No." Few times in my life had I seen such a look of pure spite hurled my way. Let alone from Yumi's narrowed eyes. "You're *her* mother, aren't you?" She pointed to the child, now toddling underfoot.

Tears welled in Yumi's eyes, but she didn't let them fall down her cheeks. I wanted to comfort her, but what could I do? She just said that I was suffocating her. So I packed up my purse and headed out the door, not saying a word or waiting for an apology.

"Don't you want your kid?"

I glared at her as I put my shoes on in the *genkan*. "Watch her for me, would you?"

That was the last time I spoke to her for nearly two weeks.

Yumi's new album was announced during that time. Ten tracks. Two promotional videos. A picture of her looking sultry at the camera in a black dress was released with the news. The title, "My Future," was meant to invoke the image of a woman starting life over again stronger than ever. I knew she wasn't stronger. If anything, Yumi was becoming weaker as time went by.

Before the album promotions could rev up, she called me. No apologies. She invited me over for dinner. Said her mother was taking care of the kid for the weekend. "We need to talk," she said. "About us."

I was scared. Nervous. Excited. We hadn't talked about our relationship for far too long. I had been waiting, and now we were going to address it. My hope was that she would want to rekindle the romance. So obviously I was scared that she would tell me that, after much reflection, she not only didn't want a woman, but she definitely didn't want me. I prepared myself before I went over. Yes, I dressed up, and told myself in the mirror that whatever happened, I would take it like a fucking adult and promise to be there for her anyway. If that meant watching her date men and possibly marry one again, so be it.

Would it hurt? Without a doubt. A part of me would always want her more than anyone else. That was my own issue to deal with. Preferably before I started seeing other girls.

It was like my birthday again. The apartment was cleaned and dinner set on the dining table. Food she cooked. Candles lit. Yumi dressed up as much as I was. Okay, so maybe things were going in my favor after all.

We didn't talk about "us" for a while. The topic jumped from the meal she cooked, to my new blouse and how we should go shopping sometime, to the high points of her new album. It was refreshing to hear her softly talk about it for once. A smile even crept on her face at times. "Some of those songs I put a lot of soul into. I convinced them to release the other two tracks as bonus material online. Why not? Those tracks are finished. I really wanted one of them to be on the album. It's about you."

"Another song about me?" I hid my embarrassment behind a snorting laugh. Well, so much for not embarrassing myself. "You're going to make me blush."

"Good," she said, taking my hand. "You're cute when I manage to make you shy."

I had no idea what to say. My mouth was dry, my heart fluttering at the return of the old Yumi I knew. This time I wanted to be the one who cried, if only to show her how happy and relieved I was. But I was a good girl and kept those emotions to myself.

To make it even more like my birthday, Yumi reached into her pocket and pulled out a piece of paper. "I have something to show you."

I had no idea what to expect from a piece of paper. That night I was wearing the earrings she had given me for my birthday, and I put a finger on one as I picked up the paper and read it.

A page from Yumi's will and testament stared back at me. You may think it's morbid for someone as young as her to have a will, but since she's rich and famous it's a practical thing to do. Even I had a will. The unusual thing was that she was showing me hers. It wasn't something we talked about, aside from recommending this lawyer or that.

Love, Yumi

The legal jargon was too hard for me to decipher, so I asked Yumi to tell me what it meant. She pointed to a small clause about her daughter should something happen.

I was named Yumi's primary choice for guardianship, even above her own mother.

This didn't mean I would automatically get Chisa should something happen to Yumi. Doubtlessly there would be legal issues out the ass if I decided to pursue it. (Which I probably would.) This country favors blood relatives above all others to a fault. Yohei's parents would probably get the child before I did. Hell, some distant second cousin was more likely! However, that wasn't the point. The point was that Yumi named me her personal choice. I didn't think this was a stab at me. It was an honor, and one that made me put the paper down and gape at Yumi.

"You're the only person I trust." Her hand gripped my arm, her other arm propping up her chin as she looked at the paper I dropped. "I don't even trust my own mother anymore. I sure as hell don't trust anyone at the label. How can I after everything I've been through?" Her eyes clouded with bad memories.

"I don't know what to say." Is this what she wanted to talk about? Yumi acknowledged that I was a parent to Chisa. Or at least as good as one. Maybe that was our relationship now. Two parents raising this child the best that we could. "Thank you." That seemed like the wrong thing to say.

"I just want the best for her. Honestly, you're a better parent than I am right now."

"Don't say that."

"It's true, though. If you're not in her life, then I worry about her." See? She was a worrying mother after all.

Her hand slipped down my arm and to my wrist. Our dishes remained dirty before us, and one of the candles burned low. "Yumi?"

She snapped out of her thoughts and flashed me a fake smile. "You're always so concerned for me. Sometimes I worry that I've run out of concern for everyone else. I should have been more like you from the beginning."

"We are different people." I braved shaking her hand off me and taking it with my own. She did not protest. "We're two sides of a Dragon."

"I guess so."

"You know I looked into our Western signs once. Yours says that you're really vibrant and enigmatic. You like to be with people and express yourself." I left out the part where it also said she liked being sexual. A lot. "Mine says that I'm practical and like to think things through, to a fault. I don't take as many risks as you. I guess we balance each other out."

"I guess so. Yin and yang?"

"Now we're just getting too metaphysical."

"I like yin and yang." She leaned in close, her perfume overwhelming me, inciting my endorphins to fuel my brain until I was under her spell. My eyes fluttered closed, then open, my lips dangerously close to hers. I didn't dare go for it though.

She did it for me.

It was our first real kiss since my birthday all those months ago. The thing about her kisses is that they get better every time. The more she realizes her feelings, the more she becomes comfortable with herself... well, the better the kiss is. That night was thus far the best, her passion rushing into me as my hand nearly ripped hers off her body.

We left the dirty dishes on the table. We didn't even blow out the candles. The urge to go to bed overpowered us as we wordlessly got up and went to her bedroom, now devoid of any sign of her ex-husband. Knowing that he couldn't interrupt us this time made me bold as I wrapped my arms around Yumi from behind and kissed her neck, her gasp striking me right in the heart.

There was nobody else there. We had no obligations that night – or that weekend. Time was ours. Yumi knew this. As we eased ourselves onto the bed, me on top of her, she said, "Go slow."

I wanted to go slow anyway. As much as I missed and wanted her like this, I also wanted to savor everything. Who knew when the next time would be? Every time I thought we were reaching the next stage of love, something came between us. If not tomorrow, then perhaps six months from now. Maybe a year. God, had it been two fucking years since that Golden Week?

"I said go slow, not treat me like a porcelain doll." Yumi yanked my hair, forcing me to look at those same sultry eyes I saw on her recent album cover. That was it. I was done. There was no shutting off my desire after that.

All my fears that she didn't want me or was too scared to love me were assuaged that night. I felt the same need and want from her that I did two years ago, our bodies coming together in that ethereal way that tears a heart apart if you let yourself go too easily. Losing myself in lovemaking is too easy with her. My heart is full of joy and, as much as you would think it's the opposite, I never have to worry about impressing her. I know that anything I do will make her happy. Sometimes she says, "Do this, please," or, "I like it when you…" as a gentle hint, and I am so happy to oblige that things carry on as before.

Pleasure is different with everyone. With some women I enjoyed the different sounds they made, what got them going most, or the surprising ways they spoke to me or acted during sex. With Yumi the thing that makes me happiest is feeling her warm body against mine, her whimpers on my lips and her groans in her throat. The way her sweat tastes on her skin is exquisite, not to mention other heady things that no proper woman discusses in public. The best part? When she's so involved with what we're doing that she clings to me, every kiss a step closer to ecstasy, those thrilling moments where physical pleasure meets love, and the next thing I know I'm losing my mind and all control of my body, and she is too. I don't care how loud we are. I care that she feels good first and foremost. My pleasure is secondary. But when I feel it, I'm never happier to be alive and sharing this most private side of myself with her.

Sex. Fucking. Lovemaking. Whatever you call it, I wanted to do it. With her.

When my strength faded with my climax, I stilled on her, listening to her hard breaths and the quick beating of her heart. Eventually some strength returned and I rolled off, drawing her into my arms as we embraced and tried to remember who we were besides "one."

"I love you." I swore it to her until my throat was hoarse. Didn't she know that she could always depend on me? That I would protect her? She was the love of my life, and I would never forget it. Even if I woke up with amnesia one day, I would always instinctively search for her.

Her finger pressed against the healing gash by my mouth. The one Yohei gave me a few months ago. Then her fingers touched my shoulder, near the scar from that one man's blade so many years ago. "I'm sorry," she said, rubbing her head against my shoulder. "You're always getting hurt because of me."

"Because of you? You're not creating these situations." I rolled against her. Had I the strength, I would have made love to her again. I settled for kissing anywhere I could reach.

I didn't ask her what she was thinking. What she feared. If she loved me. I was so in the moment that those kind of things didn't matter. In my heart I knew this was finally the beginning I waited for.

Sleep overcame me as she stroked my cheek and caressed my hairline. Those simple pleasures born from love could seduce anyone into a drowsy interlude. It wasn't until she got up that I awoke again, my head full of dreams but my eyes focusing on the outline of her naked body as it sat on the edge of the bed, contemplating the air before it.

Yumi reached into her nightstand and pulled out a pill bottle. She popped one, waited a few minutes, and then climbed back into bed where she finally fell asleep in my arms.

The next day we had lunch in one of the most beautiful rooftop cafes in Nagoya. We were given preferential seating next to a big bay window that towered over the skyline, the natural light illuminating Yumi's bright hair and the white sweater gracing her gorgeous body. Throughout the

Love, Yumi

meal we held hands across the tiny table, not caring what the wait staff thought or gabbed to the press.

Yumi was in a nostalgic mood, chattering about old memories from school. She wondered what some of our classmates were doing now. Were they happy? Did they have good careers? Families? What was this old boyfriend doing? Did I know anything about Junpei? I entertained her because I was happy to see her laughing and thinking of times before life became painful.

Eventually we progressed to our idol years. Most of that conversation focused on me.

"I remember that one time after *Music Tonight* when you snuck out to go get laid, although I didn't know that's what you were doing at the time." She had to cover her mouth with her hand because she laughed so hard. "Beppu was *so* mad at you."

"Can't say I regretted it."

Yumi studied my face, and I knew she was about to ask me something personal. "How many women have you been with, anyway?"

It was a cheeky question. She didn't want to impart judgment, so I answered honestly. "At least ten."

"What do you mean at least?"

"Well, some of them I'm not sure what really happened…"

"Drunken slut."

Low blow! I laughed with her, concurring that I was, in fact, too drunk during those times to know how far I went with any of those girls. If I went anywhere at all.

"You never had a real girlfriend?"

That might've been judgmental. It was hard to tell given the mood she was in. "Not really, no."

"Why not?"

Should I tell her the truth? No, I think she knew why, but I couldn't bring myself to say it. *"Because I love you too much. I could never give a woman the proper attention she deserves if there's even a chance with you."*

"Never met the right woman, I guess."

Pensive though she was, Yumi shook it off and insisted we order something for dessert. We split a piece of chocolate cake and headed out.

I walked her back to her apartment, where my car was parked from the night before. A part of me hoped she would invite me to stay, but she told me she had to head into the office for some reason on a Sunday night. I didn't think anything of it. After all, weirder things happened when an album was coming out. Maybe they were doing an emergency do-over on a track.

A kiss on my cheek turned into a real kiss. We stood there in her entryway, my arms around her as I kissed her as hard as I dared. Any harder and I would be tempted to drag her off to bed again.

"See you later," I said, pushing my lips against her. "I love you."

Yumi lingered in the doorway. The door slowly closed, her big eyes peering through the last of the crack. "Sayonara," she said. I didn't think anything of such a heavy goodbye.

It was late evening when I sat on my bed, perusing the photos and videos on my phone. A call came in from Koji. Strange that he would be contacting me. Not like I worked with him.

"Have you seen Yumi today?" he asked. "I can't get a hold of her. It's not important, but I'd rather she hear something tonight than at the office tomorrow."

"I had lunch with her today. She said something about going into the office tonight."

"What? There's nothing on the schedule for something like that."

"Don't know what to tell you." After I hung up I texted Yumi, playfully chastising her for giving Koji the runaround. I didn't get a reply, but this was Yumi's usual bath time.

I went back to looking at the videos. The most recent one of Chisa popped up. I watched it for a few seconds before cameraman me put the phone down and went to go talk to Yumi. The baby continued to play with her toy, and I focused on that instead of paying attention to her parents arguing in the background.

Chisa looked up. Smiling, she pushed herself into a standing position and hobbled over to Yumi, who had come over to tell me that I was more Chisa's mother than herself. The baby put her arms up and said, "Mama."

We had both ignored her. "Mama," the baby said again, growing distressed. She pawed at Yumi's pant leg, that grabbing motion eager for her mother's affection. "Mama!"

Yumi and I were really arguing by then. I grabbed my phone and stormed out the door. The video ended.

Now, I could only stare at the black screen, my brain trying to catch up with what my heart already knew.

Mama! The little one spoke that pivotal word, and even knew that Yumi was her mother. If I was elated when I heard her call me Chi-Chi, then I was doubly so hearing Yumi receive such honors. Yumi! She had to know!

I didn't bother calling. If Yumi were having a night alone, she could bear me butting in to show her this video. So I threw myself together, hurried to my car, and drove all the way back to Sakae to her apartment.

Three times I knocked on her door. I rang the bell twice. Finally I texted her to tell her I had something important to share. When I didn't receive an answer to any of these, I pulled out my copy of the key and helped myself in.

The lights were on, but it didn't look like anyone was home. Everything was spotless. No trace of our night together remained, not that it was odd.

Something wasn't right. An eerie fog replaced the air, and I felt like I was breathing in the poisonous fumes of a ghost wafting through a reality it refused to depart. I stood in the living area, trying to figure out what was wrong.

Chiharu.

My hair stood up on the back of my neck. The ghost was whispering in my ear. My face paled. Bile crept up my throat as I finally accepted what I saw before me.

An empty wineglass. An empty pill bottle. My beautiful, beloved Yumi sprawled on the floor as if she were sleeping. Except there was no color in her face, and my head knew better.

"Yumi!" My scream echoed in her cold apartment as I knelt beside, trying to shake her awake. No. A nightmare. This had to be a nightmare. I slapped her. I listened for her breath and couldn't feel any. I pressed my hands against her chest and tried to resuscitate her.

"What the hell happened?"

Koji was in the open doorway, his irritated visage turning into panic.

I stopped CPR long enough to yell, "Do something!"

He called an ambulance. Within ten minutes they were there, shoving me out of the way as they checked Yumi's vitals, pronounced her "alive but critical" and took her away. I was ready to fight Koji to the death over riding with her, but they wouldn't let either of us in. Instead they told us which hospital to go to, and we climbed into my car to head to the nearest one. The same one she gave birth to Chisa in.

Everything was a toxic, heartbreaking blur. I became hysterical in the emergency room when I saw a team of doctors working on her, Koji yelling at them to do their fucking jobs and then being escorted away by a frantic nurse. She tried to take me too but I fought her off. I wouldn't let my eyes leave Yumi's face as tubes, masks, and a million hands covered her and struggled to save her life. They pumped her full of something, or maybe they were pumping something out of her. I don't know. I'm not even sure if I was there anymore. Maybe I was told all this later. Like I said, it was a disgusting blur that I never want to relive.

They took Yumi somewhere. Maybe to surgery. Maybe to a room. She was still alive last I heard, but who knew what had happened? Brain damage. Heart or other organ damage. I was so ignorant about that sort of thing that I could only think of the worst case scenarios. I paced around the waiting room.

"I heard what happened."

Even though I recognized that comforting voice, I couldn't bring myself to lift my head out of my sweating hands. Beppu's shoes appeared before my eyes as I stared at the floor. "How?" My nose ran and my voice cracked.

"Koji called me. Poor guy had no idea what to do." He sat down next to me. "They don't exactly go over this sort of thing in our training. Even though at some point we all see it."

I had been thinking of Koto all night. Flashes of what happened to her appeared on the back of my eyelids every time I tried to see anything but Yumi passed out on her floor. "I thought she was dead," I whispered, hands pressing against my face. "The moment I saw her, I knew she was dying."

Beppu put a reassuring hand on me, but it didn't help. "She would have if you didn't show up in time. Because of you she has a chance."

That was the thing. Yumi didn't want a chance. Ever since I arrived at the hospital, everyone was ignoring the ivory white elephant storming back and forth in the waiting room. "She wanted to die." Saying that brought on clarity I didn't expect. "I should have seen it."

"How could you have known? People who are determined will hide it from their loved ones."

"I should have known. Nobody knows her like I do."

"Tell me how it went."

I gathered the courage to recount the past few days. How we had fought and then made up, gloriously so. Then our lunch today before I dropped her off at home and went on my way. How I found something good to show her and that's why I went over to her place... only to find her passed out from drugs and alcohol.

"I'm sorry." What else could he have said?

We stayed there until a doctor came out to tell Koji that Yumi was alive, but would remain under intensive care for at least a day. "It was almost the point of no return," he said. "If she pulls through these next twenty-four hours things will look optimistic. Until then..."

The decision was made to keep it a secret. There was no hiding that Yumi was in the hospital. We had called an ambulance, after all. Her reason for being there, however, could be manipulated. If the public found out that she tried to kill herself…

"It'll ruin her career once and for all," I said. "Everything she's worked toward rebuilding would mean nothing. We can't let it get out that she tried to commit suicide."

Beppu grunted. "You're more cynical and jaded than even I took you for. You're right, though. The last thing she needs is this getting out. The label knows how to spin this sort of thing to the media so it sounds like she's passed out from something not of her own fault."

I wanted to stay at the hospital in case there were any developments, but nobody would tell me anything after that. Other than "Go home," and "What can we know before morning?" Koji had to stay, but Beppu convinced me to leave, escorting me to my car.

The night sky was clear. I sat there in the driver's seat staring at it, trying to imagine a world without Yumi to look at it with. How? How was such a world possible? Since we were children we looked at the sky together. Since becoming a songwriter, I've noticed how many pieces in our collective memory focus so much on this concept: that no matter where we are in the world, or how far apart, that special someone is still under the same sky as you. What happens when that person's soul transcends this world? If Heaven is beyond the sky, then how can we be beneath the same one? Those songs are supposed to be comforting because we're reminded that we can see each other again. If that person's dead…

I started my car and drove away. I didn't go home.

Yumi's apartment was just as we had left it. We were in such a hurry that Koji and I forgot to lock the door. Be rational, I thought. Be logical. I had to be the responsible one right now. My heart was aching, my soul weary, and my brain fried from the night, but I had to muscle up and get rid of the evidence. I washed the wineglass and threw away the bottle. Those weren't that incriminating, however. Not like the pill bottle, which required putting the few white pills back into and hiding in the rear of her medicine drawer.

Love, Yumi

Everything felt heavy inside of me, like I was carrying around a sack of sand in my chest and gut. I could feel a torrential cry coming on, but tried to stay strong. I told myself that Yumi would be okay. *She's alive. She's alive.* A sutra to keep me moving, cleaning, and focusing on what was most important: preserving her image so she had something to return to.

No matter how many times I recited it, however, I was not prepared for what I found in her bedroom.

There, on her pillow and upon the bed we made love in the night before, was a folded letter – addressed to me.

Yumi has beautiful, meticulous handwriting. As a child I was often jealous that she had such penmanship, when I had to practice twice as hard to be legible. Homeroom teachers praised her and she was always elected the class record keeper up through graduation. During our idol years, she impressed fans with her stylized signature that incorporated both *kana* and Roman letters. The only time her handwriting got sloppy was when she was so tired she could barely hold a pen in her hand. The writing in this letter was careful and attentive. She took a long time to write it. For me.

I still have this letter. I've been carrying it in my bag just for this moment.

Chiharu,

All of my life you were a constant by my side. Now I ask the impossible of you – to continue to live without me by your side.

Do you remember when we were little and said that we wanted to die together? We didn't understand what that meant back then. We were dramatic children with no idea what it meant to die or to even grow up into adults. To be honest, did we really think we would keep being such close friends after high school? Most people drift apart. I wonder if that would have been us had we done different things after graduating.

But it wasn't. We became idols together. We did things for each other that were dangerous and thrilling. Had we never become idols and lived together so closely, I never would have kissed you on my birthday. When I did it, I meant it as a joke. Then we both felt it. That intoxicating spark of love.

Hildred Billings

You embraced it. I ran from it. From a distance I watched you pursue your sexuality while I tried to force mine. Boys my age, much older men... if I told you how many there were or who exactly some were, you would hate me. Sometimes it really did feel good and there was so much relief that I could be normal. Men were a promise. A toxic promise.

You see, I couldn't have a good man. He had to be strong, bullheaded, a bit of a bad boy. The Yohei type. I needed men to control me so the power was out of my hands. If I did something disgusting and liked it, it wasn't my fault. Even if I pursued that man, it was up to him to finish the job. Sometimes more than one man at a time. Whether I gained something professionally from it or not didn't even matter after a while. I wanted men to own me so I would be liberated from the real feelings in my heart.

Every time we kissed I felt myself come more and more apart. What was originally a joke became something I wanted to explore. I often fantasized about you controlling me like those men did, but it was wrong. Not in a moral way, but from the idea that you would never do such a thing. You were safe. You were pure, even when you were being naughty. As time went on and kissing you became more desirous, I ran farther and farther from what life intended of me.

And every time I fucked up, you were there to save me. You took a knife to the back for me. You held my hair back when I threw up because I was too drunk. You took a beating from my husband to take his attention off me. You took care of my kid when I couldn't. And every time you saved me, I was reminded of how much of a danger I am to you.

Do you know the moment I fell for you? Earnestly, and honestly? It was when we recorded that cover album together. That one afternoon we spent in the studio, laughing at how ridiculous some old songs sounded, especially set to piano. You made so many funny faces to the point that you started screwing up the melodies, and we laughed so hard and for so long that my sides hurt. You were still laughing even after I calmed down. I saw such a joy in your expression that I had never seen in anyone else before. You were so beautiful. I always thought you were pretty, but in that moment my heart began to accept that it could be you and me.

Seducing you was the best thing I ever did. You showed me that sex could truly be tender and still hot. You were my first woman. The only woman I've been with. And I love you. Not just as my friend, but as someone I would have married in an instant if you were a man.

Forgive me. Although I love you, I'm scared. I don't know how to live the life you do. People expect me to be with men, so I am with men. I don't understand the word lesbian. What other woman have I desired? None. Only you.

And you! I've known how much you love me for so long. The moment I saw you through those eyes I only took advantage of you more. You were someone I depended on too much. I consumed your life. You could have died countless times because of me! It wasn't until this past Christmas that I realized how much of a danger I am to you. Hearing you talk about your bleak dating life told me that you would never have a proper love life unless I was out of the picture. The only person who really "needed" me was my daughter, but what good am I to her? She doesn't know me. When I hold her, I feel broken. I feel wrong. Every mother told me that I would feel this wave of euphoria when I first held her. I FELT NOTHING. My soul was empty as I looked into that ugly face. I selfishly thought of my own pain and exhaustion. I didn't know how I was supposed to look at her until you walked into the room and smiled at her. Then I smiled because you were there.

I am useless to everyone. A danger. A nuisance. My daughter is surrounded by people who love her more than I do. Not knowing me won't be too hard on her. When I kissed her goodbye yesterday, knowing it would be the last time we saw each other, I felt relieved. She was going to have it better and easier from then on. I didn't feel sad or guilty at all. She was free.

When I kissed you goodbye earlier, I also felt relieved. Sad that this would hurt you, but it's for the best. Without me, Chiharu, you'll be free too. Free to pursue a life that isn't dictated by where I am or who is hurting me. You can date and fall in love with someone who is better for you. Just promise me she won't look just like me, okay? I can be vain, but that's not healthy.

I do love you. I meant it two years ago when I said I wanted it to be forever. Back then, maybe it was possible. Not now. This darkness hovering over me is too consuming to subject to another person. Even you. I won't bring you down with me. You've protected me from everyone else. Now I must protect you from me.

I'm sorry for hurting you. I'm sorry for the grief I have brought upon you. But I'll watch over you, okay? If you miss me, just say, "Where are you, Yumi?" and I'll find some way from the spirit world to let you know I'm there. I'll do it if it brings you comfort. But you have to promise that you'll live a great life without me. Take my daughter and build a beautiful family with her. I don't mind her having two moms. The more love, the better.

*Good bye, Chi-*chan. *You were the greatest person I ever knew. My last few heartbeats will be for you, and I will go into my eternal sleep thinking of all the wonderful memories we had together.*

Love, Yumi

I couldn't stop the tears. They dripped onto the paper, still there today. Or at least you can see the weak spots in the letter, some smeared ink, and a crease or two from where the letter crumpled in my hands. I collapsed onto her bed, my hands grabbing her pillow so I could smell her, pretend that she was with me and not in some limbo where she may or may not die. *"Where are you, Yumi?"* I prayed. Even though I don't really believe in prayer, I prayed so hard that every god in the universe must have heard my pleas for mercy, for I soon slipped into a heavy, dreamless sleep. The last thing I recalled was the familiar scent of her body on her pillow. I craved the comfort until unconsciousness relieved me.

***

I need to take a break.

Chapter 49

There was both good news and bad news the next day. The good news, which I received while sitting in the waiting room at the hospital, was that Yumi was finally in stable condition. Uncertainty remained considering potential brain damage, but the doctors were no longer afraid that she might slip into a coma or even die. They moved her out of the intensive care unit and put her up in a private room as necessary for someone of her celebrity.

The bad news was that she still hadn't regained consciousness. The doctor said it might be another day or so before she woke up, and after that they would have to run a number of tests to gauge her mental health. The hospital, of course, knew what had happened. Even the executives found out early that morning. The damage was done there. Mr. Kawaguchi stopped by to talk to the doctor and to Koji before going back to the office to handle the media. By the end of the day it was announced that Yumi had "fallen ill" and needed temporary medical attention. To read the press release, you would have thought she had a bad flu. Nevertheless, I was grateful the secret was safe.

Yumi's parents arrived in the early afternoon. I called them. It only seemed right that they know their daughter was in the hospital, although I didn't tell them what for. Nobody did, not even the doctors. I don't know if you can get away with that in normal people situations. If the label requests that the doctors not tell her own mother and father the truth, though, they don't. So I'm sorry you had to find out this way, Mrs. Nishikawa.

They brought Chisa with them, and I held her while they visited their daughter, still unconscious. Embracing the baby – although she was quickly growing out of the baby stage – brought me a much needed sense of relief. She clung to my jacket as she slept against my shoulder, which is how Beppu found me when he stole some time on his lunch break to see how things were going.

"I didn't even consider that updating her will could mean something," I told him, after mentioning Yumi had made me the little one's guardian. "All the reminiscing that day… sending the baby away… how long had she been planning it?"

He shrugged. "You know her better than anyone."

Did I? I declared it the night before, but I hardly knew now.

Asuka came to visit me in the hospital. Funny, someone visiting a visitor. She brought me some of my mail to look at, but I was so distracted by the baby and what was going on around me that I snapped at her and made her wince. I apologized and told her that I was worried about Yumi. "Please only call me if there is something important," I said. "Now's not a good time."

She bowed and showed herself out, but not before saying, "I hope Yumi-*san* recovers soon. I know how much she means to you."

"How do you know that?"

Asuka looked askance at me. "From your music, of course."

Love, Yumi

When she left, Beppu crossed his arms and turned his lips inward. "Yeah, your music. Anyone who spends five minutes with you knows that your world revolves around her."

It reminded me of what Yumi said in her final letter to me. "*I'm setting you free... I have to protect you from myself.*" I hadn't told Beppu about the letter, and I wasn't going to. It was in my bag, buried deep at the bottom with my wallet and appointment book. That letter was only meant for me to see.

I offered to take care of Chisa that night so the Nishikawas wouldn't have to worry about two people. All I asked was that they call me if there were new developments. I went back to my place to pack some fresh clothes and toiletries before going to Yumi's and putting the girl down for bed. That night I slept in Yumi's bed again for the third night in a row. For some reason I couldn't bring myself to pull away from her scent.

Yumi was still unconscious when I returned to the hospital the next day. However, they were now letting non-family visit with her for about an hour at a time. While Yumi's parents went to go eat lunch, I sat with her, my hand taking hers.

I didn't know what to say. What should I say? Could she even hear me? The doctors said she was in a deep sleep that she would wake up from eventually. If she wasn't awake by the end of the day they were going to try to induce it, but for now they didn't seem to be worried. Her vitals were normal and a feeding tube kept her nourished. She was breathing on her own. I wondered if she was dreaming.

"Yumi." I put my head down on the bed, my forehead brushing against her arm. "Please wake up. I want to hear your voice again."

The machines beeped. Her chest rose up and down.

"Where are you, Yumi?"

It felt like a long shot, but I wanted a sign. If I sensed nothing, I would assume she was fine. But if static zipped up my spine, or if something foreign beeped or clanked, I would know that she was in a coma or otherwise spiritless. Either way, I had to know.

I didn't expect to feel pressure against my hand. Her thumb was tight around it, causing me to lift my head up and look at the miracle holding itself to me. When I sat all the way up, I met Yumi's faded, drowsy eyes looking at me through heavy lids.

"Thank God." I brushed my fingers against her cheek. "You're awake."

Her head rolled away from me, and I thought she was going to fall asleep again. Yet her eyes remained open, and she looked at the machines, at her clothes, and then back at me. A new sadness overcame her demeanor, and I knew that *she* knew. Where she was. What had happened. Her plan that had gone wrong. "Chi-*chan*..."

I didn't want to stress her out so I merely sat there, smiling at her while keeping her hand warm. "Welcome back."

She was too weak to converse. After we remained there holding each other's hand, my other one tenderly touching her, I summoned a nurse so the next round of bullshit could begin.

I was asked to leave the room. Yumi's parents were summoned so they could receive the happy news. The label was informed that Yumi was conscious again, and they shared the news with the world in their own words. Even the Nishikawas were evicted from their daughter's room, however, and the doctor informed us that they needed to run their tests and let her get as much mental rest as possible. We were basically told to go home yet again.

So I went home. To Chisa, whom I left with a sitter, and Yumi's bed, which I hadn't made in over two days.

"The baby is doing fine, see?" I showed Yumi a picture I took that morning of her daughter sitting in her highchair eating breakfast. "Maybe I'll bring her in tomorrow to visit."

I was gauging whether or not Yumi wanted to see her. Based on the way she only glanced at the picture before looking out the window again, I guessed not.

Still, I persisted. There was no way I was going to sit there in the depressing silence Yumi offered. Since I arrived, she had barely said

Love, Yumi

anything to me. According to the Nishikawas, she wasn't talking to them either. The doctors hardly got anything out of her. They said her scans and other tests checked out, so they didn't think it was brain damage, but I already knew what was wrong. Yumi didn't want to be alive.

Well, she could be depressed about surviving all she wanted. I for one was grateful she was alive. Determined, as always, I got it in my head that I would do everything I could for her going forward. Then I realized that I was part of the problem. Too nosy. Too involved. I didn't have a magic wand to make her depression disappear. I never would.

"How's the food?" I asked. Yumi glared at me through the corners of her narrowing eyes, as if to say, *"The fuck do you think?"* The only saving grace during that lunch hour while her parents were away was that she didn't yank her hand out of my mine. I don't know if she was too weak, if she didn't care, or if it brought her comfort. Maybe she didn't even feel it.

The silence sucked so much that I rambled on and on about nothing. Updates to our favorite TV show. "You won't believe what Yuko said to Gun in last night's episode." Gossip from the office that I overheard from Koji and Beppu in the waiting room. "That secretary in accounting flirts too much with the male talents." A scandal involving a local politician. "Something about him going to Bermuda on taxpayer money…" Yumi sometimes gazed at me, but for the most part she looked blankly at the ceiling or out the window.

"It's bright in here," she mumbled. "Too bright."

I got up and closed the curtain enough that the sun no longer shined on her face. When I sat back down again, Yumi had both hands in her lap.

"You shouldn't be here," she finally said, picking beneath each of her nails.

I took a deep breath. "Why not? Don't you want me here?"

"No."

"Tough." I wasn't falling for her manipulative bullshit. "You're stuck with me for another forty-five minutes. Then you'll have your blessed parents *all* to yourself."

"Fuck them."

"Don't make me send in Beppu."

"Why the hell is he here?"

"Because he cares about you."

The sheer amount of hatred she shot at me through those watery eyes should have shaken me in my seat. Yet it didn't. I let it wash over me, like a stubborn crane standing in a rainstorm. What was she thinking? That she was embarrassed? Upset? I've never been in that much darkness. While that makes me fortunate, it doesn't help me understand her on that level. All I could do was be there, whether she liked it or not.

The longer I stared back at Yumi, daring her to rebel against me, to express her anger in the unhealthiest way possible, the more her lips twisted. I thought she was snarling at me. Then a grimace. Neither. She was trying to hold back her tears, which exploded from her eyes as she wrinkled her face and slapped her hand against it.

My heart cried out for her, but I kept my distance. Yet every whimper hit me in my gut, and I couldn't hold myself back from grabbing her other hand, both of mine now in her lap.

"I'm so sorry," Yumi sobbed, her tears and the hiccups in her throat making her sound hysterical. "I did it wrong. I did it all wrong!"

What was she talking about? The suicide attempt? I stroked her hand, which clenched around my fingers. "Don't be sorry."

Her breathing slowed as she gulped some big breaths and tried to calm down. "I don't want you to see me like this," she said, avoiding eye contact. "You weren't supposed to see me like this. You were supposed to see me as I was, not as I am."

"I found you, Yumi."

"Oh God…"

"When I saw you, I thought I was dying with you. I thought you were dead."

"Why wasn't I?"

I couldn't answer that. As I've said before, I'm not a spiritual person. I don't necessarily believe in predestination or fate or someone looking out for us. In the West I guess they call them guardian angels. Doesn't mean I believe *everything* is coincidence, but I wasn't going to give her some utter crap about how she wasn't meant to die or it wasn't her time yet.

"I planned it all so carefully." Yumi was back to looking out the window, toward the Heaven she thought she should be a part of. Or maybe the Heaven she would have been denied. I don't know how that works. "The baby was taken care of. I tied up my loose ends... the album could come out on schedule and people would get paid. I told you I couldn't hang out so you would go home. I didn't know how long it would take for people to know, but it wasn't going to be you..."

"Then who? Who else has a key to your apartment besides me?"

"I don't know..."

"You know I would have found you alive or dead. You had to have known."

"I didn't want you to!"

"That's what would have happened. I wouldn't be able to contact you. Koji was already calling me talking about how he couldn't reach you. I would have started worrying pretty quickly. I would have gone over within a day. If not because of that reason, but another." I didn't let her yank her hand out of mine. Instead I leaned forward, lowering my voice in an effort to be comforting. "After what happened the night before? I would want to be with you."

We were silent for a few seconds, Yumi sniffing and looking down at her chest.

"I found your letter."

The tears started again. This time she didn't try to hole herself away in whatever oppressive force built inside her. She rolled onto her side, searching for my shoulder so she could cry into the warmth of my body.

"I love you." I wrapped my arms around her shoulders. "You're worth loving. Don't ever feel like you're a burden to me or anyone." When she shuddered, her hot tears dampening my T-shirt, I continued, "I *want* to love you. I *want* to be with you. You're my best friend in the whole world and I can't leave you behind."

The curtain may have been closed, but sunshine continued to pour through the hospital window, warming the far end of the bed where Yumi's feet twitched beneath her blanket. Her fingers clamped against my head and grabbed chunks of my hair, her forehead pressing against mine as I tried not to cry as well. "I love you too."

Finally, *finally*. How many times had she thought it? How many times did those words bubble in her throat before she finally found the courage to say she loved me? Unequivocal love, filling her heart and making her day, her life just a bit brighter. I could have kissed her, but in the hospital that was risky, and besides, it was better for her to initiate it right now.

Yumi didn't kiss me, but she held onto me for another minute, her apologies wafting through my ear. "*Gomen ne.* I'm so sorry. *Gomen, gomen.*"

I don't know what she was apologizing for. Many things, I suppose. It didn't matter. Yumi finally said she loved me, and she was going to get better. I had to believe it.

"That night I found you, I was coming over to show you something." Yumi sat back, and I pulled my phone out of my pocket to show her the video I took of the baby. We watched it together. When the past us began to argue, Yumi grimaced, and I told her to keep watching. Soon enough she saw her daughter get up on her feet and gesture to be held. "Mama," Chisa said. "Mama!"

The change in Yumi's demeanor was instantaneous. She smiled, her hand reaching out to my phone, taking it from me and playing the video again. "She called me Mama..."

"You see? She knows you. She knows you're the person who loves her the most, the most unconditionally in this entire world."

"And I just ignored her."

"Don't do that to yourself."

Yumi handed my phone back. "I want to see her."

"I'll go get her when your parents return."

Before my hour was up, Yumi took my hand again and said, "Thank you, Chiharu. For everything."

Love, Yumi

We kissed, lightly, because who knew when that door would open or what cameras might see. In that small kiss I felt a new spark. Not the spark of love and desire that ignited almost ten years ago in our tiny dorm room, but the spark of life returning to Yumi's body. I knew it would be a long journey out of the darkness. Yet I thought of nothing but holding her hand and making sure she didn't lose her way.

Yumi was released from the hospital a week later. However, a social worker arrived the day before, and we took Yumi to a room in a grungy office on the other side of Sakae.

It was about her child. There were concerns that, due to her recent "episode," Yumi was not fit to parent until she could be reevaluated by both the child welfare department and her doctors. Since Yohei was awaiting trial still, Yumi asked her parents to take Chisa back to Seki. "She'll get fresh air, at least." That's what she told herself, but I knew the idea that she was an unfit parent only reaffirmed some of her worst fears.

You may wonder why she didn't ask me to take care of the little one. That's because Yumi was temporarily moving into my apartment so I could look after her while she went through various therapies and took a break from work. Her album was released without any promotion on her part. Even then, she still managed to hit #4 on the charts. Her #1 streak was over, but she smiled to hear from Koji that she still managed to sell that much on name alone.

Yumi's official reevaluation date was four months from the day she moved in with me, taking up residence in my guest room. She said she wanted to take things slowly. "I don't think it's a good idea to jump into a romantic relationship right now," she said, perching in a nook by one of my windows. That became her favorite spot. Sometimes she would spend hours sitting there staring at the city and the sky above it, stewing in her own thoughts, whatever they were. I didn't ask, and she rarely shared. "So for right now, you do what you want."

I wanted to wait for her. So I did, patiently, watching over her as much as I could without being in her business every minute of every day. In the beginning she stayed in my apartment, as recommended by her new therapists. I was given explicit instructions on what to do or not to do regarding safety. Yumi was still considered a potential suicide risk, so I had to keep my balcony doors locked, only taking out my key to hang up laundry to dry – which I did when she was napping in the guest room. That last part was probably paranoia, but after what happened with Koto, I wouldn't in a million years risk it.

She was given medicine that wouldn't hurt her in large doses aside from possibly upsetting her stomach. I got rid of all alcohol. I kept my kitchen knives locked in a drawer. Other sharp objects like scissors also went in there as I found them lying around. If Yumi really wanted to die, she would find a way, of course… there were plenty of things to hang herself with, and she could starve herself, but I did what I could.

It was morbid to think this way. To look around my apartment and find different ways the love of my life could kill herself. But I did it. Even if she found a way, I would know that I did everything in my power to keep her alive.

That first month was precarious at best. Yumi would be fine one moment, watching TV and eating chips, and then the next minute she was locked up in the guest room, crying loudly. I eventually learned to give her the space she needed to cry out whatever was bothering her. I would say, "I'll be in my room," or "I'm going to do some work in the kitchen," just so she would know where to find me.

Her doctors came to us that first month. Once or twice a week a therapist made a house call just for YUMI, and they would talk in the guest room or in the living room while I hid out in my own bedroom. In those instances I pressed my ear against the door to try to hear what they were talking about. I know I shouldn't have, but the curiosity was too great.

"Have you ideated suicide recently?"

"Not really. If anything, I just feel guilty that I didn't succeed that time. I have these feelings of 'I want to die,' but not in a way that I want to kill myself. Does it go away?"

Love, Yumi

Sound bites like those made me want to weep. How could someone who was once so vibrant and determined in life suddenly feel that way? Even though I knew what kind of history she had, it was still hard for me to reconcile the Yumi I knew growing up with the one that existed now. I didn't love her any less. Love couldn't stop my confusion.

Asuka did my errands for me since I wasn't supposed to leave Yumi alone. If I really needed to go out, such as to sign documents at the office, I had Koji or Beppu come over if they could spare the time. Otherwise it was just Yumi and me in my apartment, her contemplating whatever she needed to think about while I tried to work.

I didn't hesitate to play piano all day like I usually did. If I were finishing up songs and thus playing them through to completion, Yumi would hang around, sitting in her nook, dozing on the couch, or sitting on my bench with her head on my shoulder. Although if I was in the beginning stages of a piece, thus playing the same notes over and over as I made changes, she would grab headphones and go into the guest bedroom. She never complained or praised me.

She also didn't talk about much. We would comment on TV shows, on what we felt like eating, or that sort of thing, but we never got much deeper than that. If I complained about work she would listen and give minimal responses. Three weeks in she finally said, "You talk a lot."

Hilarious, considering she used to be the absolute chatterbox!

After a month the doctors said she should start going out. The reason it wasn't earlier was because of her celebrity status. They were afraid the public attention would make her anxious and panic. So that first time we left the house was when I took her to the office and we said hello to some people. I went into the recording booth while she stayed in the control room, fiddling on her phone and reading a book. For someone living such a shadowed life, she never once grumbled about it. If I asked her to wait somewhere, she did. Aside from one moment where I came back to find her gone to the bathroom (a lovely panic that was) she always obeyed, even if she sighed to do it.

It took me a while to realize that she was basking in relying on people. For years she was told what to do but resented it. She didn't trust those people with her health, safety, *well-being.* To figure out that she trusted me so much that she didn't begrudge my guardianship was a breakthrough for me. Until that point I always worried that I was butting in too much. Now I knew it was probably the right amount.

We graduated from safe places like the office and her therapist's place to more public areas like supermarkets and cafés. I don't know if the timing was a coincidence or if getting out and about helped improve her that much, but she started smiling on a regular basis, her posture became more confident, and soon we were in my corner café talking like we did before… well, I don't know what to call that time.

One day I went to the office alone. Yumi didn't feel like going so I called Koji to look after her. When I returned I found her on the couch, reading letters out of a box labeled "Fan mail for YUMI."

"Look!" she called, a piece of lined paper in her hand. "This is all the mail I got since I was in the hospital."

She told me to help myself to the contents. I sat in my chair, grabbed a letter, and opened it to find stationery dotted with hand-drawn thistles, one of Yumi's favorite plants.

"Dear Yumi," I read aloud. "I hope you are feeling better since falling ill. I was really worried when I heard on the news that you were sick in the hospital. Right before your comeback album, too. Please know that I bought your album and really enjoyed it. I listen to it every day on the way to and from school. I hope I can see your smiling face on stage again soon. You're really cool and one day I want to be a musician too. Take care, Hinata F, age 17."

"Read this one." She handed me the letter she had been reading when I walked in.

"To Yumi. You don't know me, but I am a fan of yours. Half of my iPod is your songs, and I listen to you when I do my work. Your songs really give me the energy I need to finish my projects. I don't know what it is… maybe it's the tone of your voice or the energy behind it. I'm just a humble civil servant so I don't expect you to find it impressive that I listen to your music, but it would be a shame if your voice was no longer heard in new and exciting ways. I look forward to your return and to find out what kind of songs you put out next. I like the more mature sound of your new album. Please take care, and I hope your family is doing well too. Ryosuke M."

"They're all like that." Grinning, Yumi dug into the box and showed me the rainbow color of papers, the gel pen ink, the animal stamps, the origami cranes and stars... so many people had written to Yumi in the span of a month just to tell her how much they cared. There were even letters written in other languages.

"*Sugoi*," I said. It really was amazing. For every person who actually took the time to write a letter, buy a stamp, and put it in the post, there were probably a hundred more who felt the same thing in their hearts. How many people had heard the news of Yumi's condition and felt scared, sad, or worried?

"Koji said there are also some gifts waiting for me!"

Gifts weren't unusual, but from the way Yumi talked about it you would think she was getting a diamond ring in the bundle. Perhaps to her those kind sentiments were diamonds. "What a fantastic surprise." I smiled, letting her know that I approved.

Something like that was all it took to give her another boost in her recovery. Knowing that most of her fans were patiently waiting for her return to the stage, Yumi became invigorated, asking me to play a melody she had in her head on the piano. I laughed, thinking of all the times I tried to teach her how to play. And now I was her dancing musician. Whatever it took!

We spent a week writing some songs together. The next time she went to the office, she asked to return to work behind the scenes. Meanwhile, her therapist suggested she start recording, even if the demos were crap. He thought that letting Yumi express herself even in a booth would be enough to help her recover some more.

Things were gradually returning to normal. We were fast approaching Yumi's main reevaluation, after which it would be determined whether or not she was fit to parent again. We had seen Chisa occasionally, mostly through video chat but also when we went to Seki one weekend and they came to visit us another. Yumi was reserved around her daughter – more so than she had been before. I don't know if she was scared to feel nothing or scared to feel anything.

The only thing I was not happy about was Yumi's renewed smoking habit. After quitting when she learned she was pregnant, she had started up again. In the beginning, I didn't say anything because I figured she needed some vice to take the stress off. Smoking was terrible for her voice and long-term health, but she couldn't drink and we agreed on no sex until she was sure she was emotionally ready. So I sat by and watched her smoke half a pack a day for weeks until we came close to the evaluation period.

"You need to quit." It was the first time since the incident I criticized her at all. She stood on my balcony – a privilege granted after two months living with me – doing her usual contemplation while smoking two in a row. "It's not good for you or your career." If she wanted to get back to recording and performing, she needed to lay off the smokes.

Ah, there was that glare I never knew I missed. "You sound like my producer."

Saying that I worried about her or that I personally found it disgusting was not going to win her over. I had to try another tactic. "I won't have that shit around my kid."

For the first time I asserted my guardianship in front of Yumi. Her eyes widened, the smoke curling away on the breeze as the cigarette burned away in her hand. "Yes, ma'am." She extinguished her cigarette and went back inside. To my pleasant surprise, she managed to quit within two weeks.

On the day of her evaluation I escorted her to the hospital, where she was welcomed into an office full of her medical professionals and the child service representative. We were told this was mostly a formality, but it didn't stop us from being nervous. Going there, Yumi said while we were stuck at a red light, "What if they say I'm hopeless? Maybe I shouldn't be that child's mother after all."

"The fact that you're so concerned is a good sign." I smacked my hand against the steering wheel to reiterate how confident I was. "Look how far you've come in just four months." I was sweating, thanks to the hot summer sun pouring through the windows. The air conditioner was on, but it didn't feel like it. "Besides, she needs you. Shouldn't she have the both of us?" I didn't tell her how much I missed Chisa. According to the Nishikawas, she was learning more words. Slowly, but she could now ask for her hugs, toys, and food. She had called her grandmother "baa-cha," which got us an excited phone call at seven on a Sunday morning. Poor little one was still working on her Ns, apparently.

Yumi retreated to the inside of her mind, eyes glazed over and fingers twiddling in her lap. "I suppose."

I was only invited to the first part of the evaluation, to give my testimony as to how Yumi had done over the past few months in my home. I told them that she had made gradual but astounding improvements, and went out of my way to recite the different milestones she achieved. They knew this, of course. They established those milestones on paper.

"Do you feel that Yumi Nishikawa-*san* is of sound mind and no longer a threat to herself or to others?"

"Yes, I do."

"Do you feel that she is prepared to resume her parenting responsibilities to the child in question?"

"Yes."

After that, I was kicked out of the room, but I could still hear bits and pieces of what went on inside. Mostly the part where they sat Yumi down and gave her an hour long evaluation, complete with invasive questions.

"Is your cycle regular?"

"Yes."

"When was the date of your last menstrual cycle?"

"August 2nd."

"Are you, or do you plan to become pregnant in the foreseeable future?"

"No."

"Are you currently dating someone?"

She paused. What would she say? I wouldn't feel bad if she said no. Technically we weren't dating or resuming our romance anytime soon. "Possibly. We're on a break right now."

They asked her about suicidal ideation, her general mood these days, her plans for work and how well she was doing keeping up with chores. (That last one made me glad I started asking her to do some chores around my apartment that past month. She volunteered to do dishes and the like, but I gave her some vacuuming and laundry to do on top of that.) At that point people were starting to come in and out of the room so I had to sit off to the side for a while. When I went back to eavesdropping, I heard them asking about her parental desires.

"Are you prepared to take care of this child as its mother?"

"Yes."

"How old is the child?"

"Eighteen months."

"What is her name, including the *kanji*?"

"Chisa Nishikawa. Her name means one-thousand petals in the western river."

"When is her birthday?"

"February 18th."

I knew why they were asking such simple questions. They wanted to make sure that Yumi not only knew basic facts about the child, but that she showed any interest at all. They continued to ask about schooling, diet, developmental milestones, and all sorts of other things that she answered promptly. My only worry was that her answers sounded dry and rehearsed.

In the end we waited another thirty minutes for them to come to their conclusion. We were called back into the office where we heard the following words:

Love, Yumi

"After much consideration on behalf of Nishikawa-*san's* medical overseers and the child welfare representative, we find her fit to parent with the aid of another trusted adult until further notice."

Yumi cracked her first smile all day and bowed deeply to each of them, thanking the doctors and representative for believing in her. She then thanked the doctors for helping her recover, even though she would continue to see at least half of them for a long time.

There were other results. The doctors kindly told Yumi that she was probably okay to ease herself back into public work. Nothing strenuous on the body or the mind, which is almost impossible to do in our industry. Yet she had been hoping to do at least one fanclub concert and release a proper single, so this was good news.

We returned to my place that night and opened a bottle of champagne. Yumi only had a glass – her first since the empty bottle of wine – but it was enough to make her giddier than I had seen her in so long. Before she went to bed, she kissed me goodnight and thanked me for being there for her. I didn't have the chance to tell her to stop thanking me. Just seeing that smile on her face was enough.

It was the day before we were due to pick up Chisa in Seki when Yumi hit a new turning point. Nothing particularly special was planned that day. We had just moved in some of Chisa's important things, since Yumi said she wanted to keep staying at my place. "That apartment," she said, referring to hers, "has too many bad memories. I want to move." I didn't know if she meant permanently in with me or somewhere else entirely – with or without me – and I didn't ask.

She was resting in her nook by the window, dreamily gazing at Nagoya as if some humorous secret lurked in a nearby building. I was in my room, door open, sitting on my bed as I went over my most recent transcriptions with a pen. Asuka had come by earlier for her lessons and to give me some requests from the office. They now recognized her as my "official" assistant, which amused me greatly.

Yumi could sit in that nook for hours, so I didn't think much about her. Not when I was so brain-deep in work. The air conditioner worked to keep the main living area and my bedroom cool, but I still sweat in my cotton shorts and loose shirt. No idea how Yumi could sit in the sunlight wearing a baggy sweater. I swear she does not retain heat at all.

I didn't even see her get up. Her silent footsteps brought her to my room, where she stood in the doorway and gazed at me for a time. I tried to not let her distract me as I read over staff notes regarding a soundtrack I was working on.

Yumi didn't say anything. I waited for her to ask a question, to tell me she was going out (she had been allowed out by herself for about a month now), or to coyly insinuate that she was hungry and we should have an early supper. None of those things happened. Instead she sauntered up to my bed, ripped the paper out of my hand, pushed me back, and climbed on top of me with a kiss that rivaled the passion of the old Yumi.

Oh, but this wasn't the old Yumi. That girl was gone. Sometimes I still struggle to accept that the happy-go-lucky girl I grew up with has turned into a different kind of mature woman. The one who slipped on top of me and between my legs now, her lips caressing my throat as she smoothed down my shirt as an excuse to touch my chest.

"Excuse me," I said, her tongue somewhere near my navel. "I am working."

As if my work meant nothing more than scraps of paper, Yumi shoved everything onto the floor and tackled my shorts. "Write a song about this." Honestly, I don't think I could possibly write a song about what she did next without tripping the media censors.

I thought our first time making love again would be like the last time: slow, gentle, and attentive. Sure, I guess it was attentive this time too. So attentive that I quickly forgot where the hell I was and that I had almost lost this precious person four and a half months ago. The world no longer existed outside of my bed. Why should it, when all I ever wanted was right here, undressing me, caressing me, and making love to me as if it were so natural?

Love, Yumi

The thing that brought me the greatest pleasure, however, was feeling the life ripple through Yumi's body, her ardor matched by the purrs in her throat and the beat of her heart. Impossible to resist, even for someone usually levelheaded like me. I should have told her we needed to take it slow. That maybe I shouldn't be having an orgasm in fewer than five minutes. Or maybe it was okay to say we loved each other first.

But what was the fun in that?

In all my worries and concerns, I had forgotten that sex was supposed to be *fun*. I got a wild taste of that with Yumi during that one Golden Week, and now here it was again, over two years later. Being reminded of what it was like to let go of my cares and just go for it led to me quickly taking control and giving her the sensations she deserved.

She wasn't, but I was left breathless afterward, as if she sucked the life straight from my lips and took it into her own body. I was fine with that. She could take all the life she wanted from me. I was relieved to finally lie back and feel her resting in my embrace again, her naked body entwined with mine.

"*Suki yo*," she said. Those words had never sounded so sweet.

"I love you too."

When she finished giggling, Yumi sat up, her visage glowing with a sense of beatitude I could *definitely* write a song about. "Chi-*chan*," her voice soothed the last of the butterflies swarming my stomach, "I want to make it work. I'm ready." Her lips tightened. "Are you?"

"I've been ready for ten fucking years."

"Don't remind me!" She playfully slapped my stomach before flinging herself back onto my bed. "From the first time I kissed you, right?"

"How did you know?"

Her nose touched my skin. "Because you're sentimental like that."

We lay there for a while, my eyes growing heavy for a nap. There was a lot for us to discuss, but we could do it over dinner. The next day we were going to Seki to pick up Chisa, and knowing that we would do so as a unified pair gave me strength. I knew it gave Yumi strength as well.

"You know," she began, "I was really confused for a while. I mean a *while*. The letter I wrote you contained some of that, but I didn't have the energy to tell you the extent of it."

"Confused, huh?"

"Can you blame me? I never in my life considered I might like a girl. Not even you. Why? Did you just accept it as fact the moment you felt it?"

"Kind of."

"I'm envious. Maybe if I had accepted it that quickly as well things would've been drastically different. I could have avoided so many mistakes. We would've been together a while now, and maybe happier."

The words of her therapist entered my brain. "You can't linger on the past and what-ifs," I reminded her. "Know who you are now and move forward with it."

"It's true, though. I was so confused partly because I accepted loving you, but I wanted it to be non-romantic. You were my best friend. How could I want to have sex with you? When I made the decision three or so years ago to finally do it with you, I…" She faltered, either stifling a laugh or bile. "I did some research because I didn't want to embarrass myself in bed with you."

"Eh? Research?" I thought she said I was the only woman she had ever been with.

"I watched a lot of porn, Chiharu."

My mouth turned downward. "I'm so sorry."

"It's awful, isn't it? I couldn't believe what those women were doing to each other. They weren't having fun. They barely touched each other. I know porn is stupid anyway, but this was so bad it actually made me wonder if that was how lesbian sex really was. You made it sound good, so then I second guessed my own desires. If I didn't find that porn appealing, did that mean I didn't really want to do it at all? Also, I was scared. Were you going to want to do some of the more frightening things with me? You don't know how nervous I was going into that situation that night. I wanted to make love to you, but I had no idea what to actually expect."

"None of it was bad, if I do say so myself."

"*Deshou?* Once we got going, it became so natural. There were things I didn't instinctively know, but I didn't with guys either. I was just relieved that I could do simple things with you and have it feel really good."

"I'm glad."

A kiss pecked against my skin. "I'm still confused sometimes." Her voice was neither wistful nor depressed. "For example, what am I? Am I a lesbian? It doesn't feel right to me."

"Then don't use that word. Don't use any labels if you don't want to."

"Maybe I'm bisexual. It wasn't that I detested men's bodies. I just threw myself at the wrong men." She stopped, probably thinking of her past. "Except that doesn't feel right either. I'm attracted to you. When I see you, I want to touch and kiss you. If you wear the right outfit or look at me a certain way, I feel myself come undone inside. I'm confused because no other woman does that for me. I've been around some of the most gorgeous women in the business. Why didn't any of them excite me like that?"

"I don't know." I really didn't.

"*Mou,* my therapist doesn't know either. I told him about my relationship with you, which surprised him. He said you might just be an exception for me, because we are so close. I fell in love with you as a child and developed a sexual attraction to you from that."

"Is that why you kissed me?"

"Who knows? I'm glad I did, though. You're the best kisser I've ever known."

That sounded like a request for proof. So I kissed her, once, twice, a thousand times in one day. By the time I was done with her, she had little red marks all over her neck and shoulders. Good thing she had so many scarves.

Chapter 50

The instant we pulled up to the Nishikawa house in Seki, the door burst open, and Yumi's mother unleashed the terror of a year and a half old child bounding onto the path leading from the door.

"Mama!" she called, her smile half the size of her face. "Mama *kita!*"

Yumi ran up to her and plucked her off the ground. Not only was I surprised that Chisa called her mother, but that she said a whole phrase. A short one, but a phrase nonetheless!

"*Hai, hai.*" Yumi kissed her daughter before squeezing her tight. "Mama finally came." There were tears in her eyes. It was the first time she heard Chisa call her mother in real time.

From that moment on, I had a family. Of course I always had *family,* but now I wholeheartedly thought of Yumi as my more than my girlfriend – perhaps my life partner – and Chisa was without a doubt my daughter. I fell into both roles naturally. Our relationship was a secret to everyone but Beppu, Asuka, Koji (who never made a comment on it,) and my mother. I'm sure many at the label suspected, but they said nothing, thankfully.

Love, Yumi

We split our time between our apartments, assuming we were both in Nagoya. The reason Yumi didn't just sell her Nagoya apartment and move into mine had to do with our short-term goals. With Chisa now walking and our family expanding, we decided it was best to find a new home for the three of us. In between recording sessions, concerts, and lazy days at home, Yumi and I went out to find a house in the close-in neighborhoods that would give us space and privacy, but also a quick jaunt to Sakae.

The house we picked was perfect, although we both made concessions. Yumi didn't like how suburban it felt, but I told her it was good for giving the little one some room to grow and privacy from the hustle and bustle of downtown life. (In truth, I loved the quiet.) I didn't like how upscale it was, since most of the neighbors had high security fences and wore sour faces when I encountered them in the street. Yumi reminded me that we needed the security due to our fame. Indeed, quite a few of the residents were board members of local companies and even other celebrities. The nearby nursery school was renowned for its good early education and for being mindful of celebrities' children. Chisa could even get an early start learning English there, something that was important to both Yumi and me.

Honestly, all I *really* cared about was that the house had enough room for my Steinway. Nothing stressed me out more on moving day than that.

I got my work space, Chisa got a downstairs bedroom that we could later turn into a playroom or study, and Yumi got a large master with adjoining Western bath. We both got the large Western kitchen we had become accustomed to since leaving Seki. The yard wasn't as big as I liked for the child to play in, but there was a nice, large park nearby complete with play set. It was a good excuse to go out for some fresh air while the little one socialized with other neighborhood children.

Our roles were set from the beginning. I stayed home with the kid most of the day, unless I needed to go to the office or studio, in which case Asuka babysat or I found someone else. Yumi was determined to work like she did before, which meant she was at the office every day or even touring around the country. After we settled in at our new home, we focused on putting together a new album for her. It debuted at #3, and she went on a nationwide tour to support it. That was our first time being apart like that since deciding to make our relationship official. At least this time she didn't disappear off the planet.

As for us, there have been many difficulties. No relationship is easy to maintain, but Yumi and I come from a unique background that I don't find much support for online or in the advice books. We deal with the intersection of romantic needs and being the best friend sounding board. You would think they are seamless, but they're not. We wear multiple hats at any time, and if I forget to take off my composer's hat when we leave the studio, I risk hurting her feelings because I'm not wearing my girlfriend hat. Yumi is not fully recovered from her issues, and I doubt she ever will be. She's making improvements, but I have to constantly remind myself that deep inside there is someone afraid of losing everything and retreating to that darkness.

As a lark we went to an astrologist, mostly because we kept arguing about whether Chisa was a Horse or a Sheep. (Does this matter? For some reason, it mattered to us.) The astrologer told us that Chisa was a Horse but may also have attributes of the Sheep, which can lead to confusion in the early years of her life. She also told us that we should consider ourselves lucky that the Horse and Sheep are used to getting along in the world.

Then she asked us what our signs were, and when we told her we were both Dragons, she grew listless and said, "Two Dragons can be a good match. You both understand each other's need for action while challenging each other's intellect. But you have powerful egos and that can cause plenty of tension."

She didn't say!

Yumi took the astrologist's words personally and said we needed to "mind our egos." Who was talking? Yumi has always had the biggest ego between the two of us. I took it to mean that she needed to mind hers the most.

For the most part I have been too happy for words. Every day (well, until recently) I wake up with Yumi by my side if not in my arms. When we have the chance we get away for a while, sometimes just the two of us. There are times I worry that she is unhappy or will suddenly realize that she doesn't romantically love me anymore. I've told her as much, and she's said, "The kind of love I feel for you can't be compromised. Is there anyone else on this God forsaken planet that will love me like you do? I'd be a fool to shit on that." Yumi has done many foolish things, but I am the designated fool of the relationship.

Everything seemed blissful – or as much as life can ever be – until one day about two months ago.

It was a lazy Sunday, the air warm but the weather too drizzly to go out and do anything. I was home with the little one, who was now three years old and big enough to climb onto chairs by herself. Such as her habit of climbing onto my piano bench beside me and interrupting my work by banging on the keys when I was in the middle of composing a bridge. I would look at her, those parental eyes of *"Don't do that"* peering into her, and she would smile sheepishly before doing it again.

I was about to put Chisa in her room when Yumi came home from the therapist. It's impossible to miss her pulling into the driveway because her latest car is a Porsche with an engine loud enough to piss off the neighbors – if they weren't driving around in fancy foreign sports cars too. Chisa hopped off my bench and ran to the *genkan* in preparation for her mother's return. Whenever Yumi announced her arrival like that, she could bet her daughter would be precariously close to the dirty part of the *genkan,* waiting for either her Mama or Chi-Chi to tell her to stop being filthy.

Yumi was so focused on finding me that she nearly missed the little one leaping off the edge of the *genkan* and grabbing her mother's ankle. A shriek echoed in the house as Yumi backed up against the door and dropped her purse. It took me plucking the child off her to get her to calm down again.

"She did that to me earlier," I said, hauling the kid to the couch. I dropped her on it, Chisa squealing from the thrill as she rolled from one end to the other, giggling. Our kid skipped the terrible twos and went straight for the terrible threes. She still didn't talk much, though. "Looks like we know what her new favorite thing to do is." At least she wasn't pulling the shoelaces from our sneakers anymore.

Yumi collected her bag and sank into one of the kitchen tables. "I can't wait for more of that. Especially after days like today."

I readied some tea on the stove and sat next to her. "What happened?"

The sigh consuming my girlfriend's body told me it would be a doozy. "I'm tired. Not with work or the kid or anything. That's normal. I'm just tired of hiding it all."

I didn't have to ask what she meant. For a few months now she mentioned it bothered her to always be matched with male celebrities. As far as the public was concerned, YUMI was single. It was easy to play it off for the first year we were together. She could tell the press she was focusing on rebuilding her career and raising her baby. After that first year the tabloids took every piece of news about her working with or being seen with a man as proof she was in a relationship with him. There was a new up and coming male soloist on the label that Yumi did a duet with. Right away the headlines said, "YUMI about to make the same mistake twice? Ex-husband still in jail."

"Maybe it's time to come out," I said, knowing she would gripe.

Oh, she did. I was reminded that being labeled a lesbian – whether if only in relationship and not identity – could mean the end of her career. While being in the closet was easy enough for me, it bothered her a lot. Yumi is the type of woman who wants to be open with everyone around her. Even her parents didn't know we were "like that." They had never seen us hold hands, embrace, or kiss. Of course they knew we lived together, but they treated me as the nanny and maid in Yumi's life, not her partner.

"That's not what really makes me tired, though." The kettle whistled, and soon enough we had hot tea and some crackers I scrounged from the cupboard. "I can't stand putting on a front all the time. It's more exhausting than I thought it would be." When I gave her a concerned look, she said, "I'm happy, don't get me wrong. Just sometimes I feel like I'm trying so hard to come off as everything always being okay. My fans still think I had the flu two years ago. I don't want to scare them or ruin my career that way either but…"

"What did your therapist say?"

"He just gives me the bullshit about keeping journals. If I write one more diary entry, I will break my pen in half and smear the ink on the wall. *Fuck* journaling."

The little one stood beside her mother. "Don't say that word," I told Chisa. Last thing I needed was her nursery school teacher telling me what a foul mouth my child had. Chisa would say it, too.

"Fuck journals."

"Oh my God."

"See what you did?"

I got up and put Chisa in her room, telling her to not say bad words she heard from her mother. One week later I would be getting an earful from the teacher.

"A part of me just wants to tell the world everything." Yumi had been waiting for me to return. "*Everything.* All the shit. The things I did as an idol. What Yohei did. What I did. You."

"What I did?"

"No, I mean being with you."

I recognized that look on her made up demeanor. She was focusing on the negative thoughts and feelings swelling up inside of her, and if she stayed on that path, well… I had no idea what she would do. I put my hand on her shoulder and said, "Then do it."

"Hello? Did you miss the part where I said it would destroy my career?"

"If you're becoming depressed again because of the secrets you're keeping, then it might be time to just do it."

"How?"

"You could do an interview… or release a statement… or…" I stopped when I saw that exasperated glare. "Never mind."

I thought that would be the last I heard of it anyway. A week later, though, I found Yumi sprawled out on our bed, staring at the ceiling and mumbling about the pressure to put on a smile for an upcoming magazine interview. I found her journal on her desk, opened to the last entry. *"Seriously FUCK this!!! What good is this doing me??? Writing in this piece of shit doesn't get rid of my problems."*

Would it really be so bad if she came out? About everything? Would her adoring fans really say, "Whoa, don't know if I can support a possible lesbian who once tried to kill herself?" It gave me a headache to think about. People could be cruel, I know, but I also wasn't in her position. I was never a superstar. Even when I was an idol I was only as famous as the rest of my group. The fans I still had were fans of my music itself more than me. YUMI was a whole product. Those people were fans of her and the music to a lesser extent. She was a personality who appeared on variety shows and sold out concerts. I was nobody.

"I'm going to come out," I announced, standing over her. "I'll announce on my blog that I'm a lesbian."

However I thought she would react, I did not expect her to laugh so hard that she had to roll over and grab her stomach. "What the hell will *that* accomplish?" she asked, shortly after I told her to knock it off. "You have nothing to gain from that."

"There aren't many out lesbians in this industry," I reminded her. "Visibility is important. Maybe I can help someone out there feel more comfortable in their skin."

"People know we live together."

"I know. That's part of the point."

"So instead of me owning my life, you want to start up nasty speculation instead? The moment you come out people are gonna wonder if I'm gay too."

"Maybe it's better that way."

"No." Yumi sat up, swung her legs over the side of the bed, and grabbed her phone off the pillow. "There has to be a better way."

"So you want to do something?"

She sat there for a few seconds, taking one deep breath after the other as she glanced between me and her phone. "Yes," she finally said. "I just don't know what."

We discussed it off and on for two weeks. What we should do. Who we should tell first. In the end it was decided that I would be the one to do it. I would tell our story here on my blog, one piece at a time until the whole truth came out. "People knowing that I love you doesn't scare me as much as them knowing what I did to myself," Yumi confessed in bed one night. "Is it weird that I fear that judgment more than the gay thing?"

I held her close to me. "How you feel about me or any other woman is something millions can relate to. What you personally went through in that moment... not even I can say I know what it feels like exactly."

Once we made the decision to do it this way, Yumi became more distant. I don't know if it was fear or her trying to preemptively stave off a media shit storm, but I made the decision to not tell her when I started. Otherwise she might try to talk me out of it.

I started one evening when I was home with the little one already in bed. Yumi was working late in the recording studio and I couldn't concentrate on my own work. I kept thinking that tonight was the night I started our mad descent.

My laptop sat on the kitchen table, plugged in and charging. I paced back and forth, staring it down, wondering what kind of crazed power it took to sit and type out one's life story. I had decided to tell it entirely from own thoughts and feelings. Take the responsibility off Yumi's shoulders. If I distracted the media then maybe she wouldn't get in trouble. I know it sounds like stupid thinking now, but I had to psych myself up if I were going to do this.

I texted Yumi. *"Tonight."* I then shut off my phone to escape the barrage of texts I was sure to receive in return.

After making enough coffee to kill myself, I sat down, opened my blog page, and started typing. By the time I finished for the night, Yumi barged through the front door, her face pale and growing paler as she saw where I sat and how empty my coffee cup was.

You know the rest.

***

What have I hoped to achieve from all this? As Yumi and I discussed, it wasn't only about sharing our relationship or the horrible truth of what really happened the night she went to the hospital. For me, anyway, I wanted the world to know what really happened to those two innocent girls from Seki, full of dreams and the promise of an exciting future.

There are people more fortunate than us, and people less fortunate. I don't know what's going to happen now, but I know that if I have Yumi and the rest of my family, I can brave anything. I hope she can be as strong. I know she can.

Please, whether you were a fan of her or not before, know that she's a good person who has always tried her best to be happy and to bring more happiness to others. Awful people took advantage of her. Many hurt her. She doesn't deserve hate or other such feelings of ill-will. If you supported her before, please continue to support her. Yumi's biggest fear was people turning on her because of who she is and what she has been through. Please prove her wrong.

It feels strange to be done with the past. Lying here, in Yumi's Tokyo apartment, feels both comforting and alienating. I close my eyes and try to sleep, but sleep doesn't come easy after you've done what I have. Now the whole world knows that my partner of nearly two years and best friend of so many more once tried to kill herself to save me from the life she lived. Every day I strive to help her see the beauty in life. Some days it's pretty thankless, but ultimately I am happy, and I believe we're building a great home for our child.

I doze to these thoughts. In the morning I'm sure I'll be called into the local office. It's not enough that I've called out the abusers in the industry, outed myself and Yumi, and now told the world that Yumi almost committed one of the most unspeakable sins. I've done so unapologetically. Selfishly. These types of businesses don't like it when you do that.

Not five minutes later I'm awaken by somebody's breath on my cheek. I open my eyes to see Yumi hovering over me, her half of our necklace dangling from her throat.

"What are you doing here?" I push myself up as she backs away, still dressed in her stylish travel clothes. Her perfume wafts before my nose, and I am convinced that I'm dreaming. "You're in Nagoya."

"I came back." She unties the front of her coat and lets it slip off her shoulders and onto the floor. "I wanted to be with you."

"Your mother…"

"God, don't remind me about her." Yumi looks so thin in these tiny, baggy clothes she wears. As we've grown older I've become thicker in muscle and, well, other things, and she's only gotten skinnier. I often worry that there's something else going on, but I see her eat. The doctor told me that it's not her diet as much as it's her mind tearing herself apart from the inside. Sounds like horse shit to me. "When I left, she was saying such awful shit about you. I couldn't take it anymore. I told her that I loved you. Can you believe it? After all this time she finally drove me to it."

"And?"

"What do you think?" Yumi snorts. "She told me I was foolish and didn't know what I was about. You had poisoned me, etc. etc. I don't know, I don't think she means to be that cruel." She climbs onto her side of the bed, pulling back the covers but not getting in them. "I think she's scared. The media circus going on right now is not going to be kind to us. She's scared for me and Chisa."

"But fuck that Chiharu bitch."

A hoot of laughter shoots out of her mouth, and she slaps her hand over it, looking toward the closed bedroom door as if she can see our daughter waking up in the other room. "She ain't a fan of you right now."

Yumi wraps her arm across my chest and settles in with her head on my shoulder. "Things will settle down," I tell her.

"How far did you get?"

"I finished."

She looks up with disbelief in her eyes. "All of it?"

"Yup."

Her head goes back down. We lie in silence until she says, "What happens now?"

"We're free now."

I know I'm being optimistic. There will always be people fighting against us, refusing to work with us, and maybe even telling our daughter that she can't play with their children. Yumi will always be a celebrity of some kind, but whether or not her fame is soiled will remain to be seen. Yet I choose to believe that getting everything out in the open means we can now grow better as people and as a couple. I tell her as much, and to my sweet surprise, she smiles, the first genuine smile I've seen in weeks.

"Remember when we rode the train from Seki to Nagoya?"

"Of course."

Yumi pulls on the necklace around her neck and then looks for mine. All these years later, I still wear it almost every day. Tonight was no different. She holds my charm against hers, the two of them spelling out Best Friend.

"I got these because I wanted the whole world to know that we were best friends."

"Well they definitely know now."

"Back then I didn't think it was possible for us to become even closer. Then we did. Do you think it's possible that one day we'll be even closer than we are now?"

I roll on top of her, kissing those chatty lips until she gets the idea to kiss me back. Now we're talking. "I don't know. Let's try to find out."

Although I know sex doesn't solve anything, at the very least I want to prove to Yumi that, no matter what happens out there in the world and who tries to hurt us, there is at least one place we can wholly be ourselves and find both love and pleasure. Yesterday, today, and certainly tomorrow.

I have no idea what to expect when I wake up. But I know Yumi will be with me, and that's enough.

Epilogue I

A BIRTHDAY ENGAGEMENT

エピローグ 第一：誕生日の縁談

Surprise! Bet you didn't expect to see me again. It's been a couple of months since you last heard from me. I'm sure you've seen some of the fallout of my confession on the news. I decided to come back and talk about what happened in my own words. I might update this a bit to tell you about any good news we receive.

First, I want to mention that the three of us are back in our home in Nagoya. Most of the frenzy is over now. What's done is done, and all that. Yumi and I are trying to bring a sense of normalcy back to the little one. It's summer break right now, so she's home almost all day while I try to get things done. But it's good for her to be at home after so many weeks of moving around the country.

You'll be shocked to know that I was summoned into the office to be told that I was in very, very deep trouble. (I was shocked, truly.) In order to stay at the label I was expected to do three things: issue a formal apology to the executives, be suspended from all work for at least six months, and adopt a secret penname for all compositions I continued to submit to the label. Suffice it to say, I told them to go fuck themselves and had my contracts terminated.

It was strange severing myself from the company I had been with since I was eighteen. Eleven years. Maybe twelve. The last time I walked out of the building, I felt pretty damn free.

Also, unemployed. I could still release music under my own name, and I would always have my royalties, but I like to be busy. Yumi told me that it was my chance to truly do things the way I wanted to. So as of last month I have started my own company. My first employee was Asuka, who graduated from university this year and was looking for employment anyway.

Under my company I am my own boss. It's a small company, mind you. Its purpose is to not only market my releases but to also net me independent contracts with other companies. Beppu told me not to expect any job offers right away given the reasons I left my old company, but to both of our pleasant surprises, I received an offer from a small gaming company. They couldn't offer me as much money as I was accustomed to, but it was a start, and I took what I could get.

Who cares about my career? I was prepared to become a stay-at-home parent if it came down to it. It's YUMI's career that people are interested in. Well, I already said that she was at the label today. Yes, she's still with them. They were going to punish her similarly to me, but here's the thing: thanks to my "little stunt" as they put it, both of our album sales jumped so high that we singlehandedly boosted the company's stock to record levels. People from all over the world were purchasing YUMI"s CDs and downloading the tracks. I didn't sell as much as Yumi, of course, but we laughed at the payday we were going to receive while the label frothed at the mouth and tried to come up with ways to punish us. In the end, they decided to take capitalism by the balls and milk Yumi for all she was worth. They put out a remix album, best and compilation albums, and an album full of uncompleted demos that was sold exclusively in MP3 format. They opened her fanclub worldwide since they expected international interest to take over the loss of Japanese fans, and that's exactly what happened. Yumi was invited to perform shows in San Francisco and Hong Kong. She hasn't gone to those yet, but it was very exciting to hear.

Love, Yumi

In the end, Yumi renegotiated a new contract with the label. They argued for two whole days, her lawyer and their lawyers going at it until they finally came to an impasse and the label relented. Yumi took a tiny hit in royalty share (as her "punishment") and in exchange earned more control over her image and release schedule. One stipulation was that they allow her to use my compositions. So now she's the only person at that label I write songs for.

That's about it really.

***

Actually, I have a quick confession to make. I'm planning a party for Yumi. It's her thirtieth birthday today and she's spending it at the office. I know her staff is throwing her a small party there, but I want her to come home to a nice one here. Not many people are coming over, but I think after a long day at work she'll be okay with that.

Most of the preparations are done. Before I logged on today, I went to the bakery and picked up her cake. I went with chocolate because she's mentioned a million times recently that she wants some chocolate. I also picked up a present that I've already wrapped, but it's a surprise. I'm not really doing decorations because Yumi will complain about the mess later. (Even though I will be the one to pick it up anyway.) All that's left to do is get ready and text Koji that he's not to let her walk through that door before seven. Yumi will be impressed that I got her manager in on it.

For some reason I can't decide what to wear. I search through my third of the closet (because Yumi clearly needs two-thirds of it) and my dresser to find something presentable for my own girlfriend's birthday party. That I'm throwing. If I don't know what level of formality it is, then who does? I could just go wearing what I am now, but I want to look a bit nicer than cotton pants and a plain T-shirt. It was fine for running errands in the sweltering August heat, but now I want to look nicer.

Eventually I settle on my one pair of really nice jeans and a jacket that Yumi often says looks good on me. Before we were a couple, I rarely listened to her fashion advice. Now that I get a thrill out of being attractive to her, I take note of what she comments on and am more likely to listen to her suggestions when out shopping. Is it normal for couples to be like this? It doesn't go the other way around because she has such a firm grasp on her own style. What can I contribute?

"Chi-Chi!"

Oh no. I've left the closet door open and now the little one is in there going through our stuff. She's in that grabby-everything-is-mine phase and really likes to go after her mother's heels if given two seconds of a chance. Like a dog she'll sit on the floor in the closet and chew on the shoes. Assuming she doesn't stab herself with a stiletto first.

"Come on." I pick her up, and she's already getting drool on my clean jacket as I haul her out of the master bedroom. That'll show me to leave a bunch of doors open. I also need to do something about her scrambling up and down stairs. She's not even supposed to be upstairs but Yumi refuses to get a child gate because they annoy her.

People start to arrive around five-thirty. My mother brings a present and takes over watching Chisa so I can focus on dinner. Beppu insists on sticking thirty candles in Yumi's cake just so we can burn the house down. Asuka shadows me, asking if there's anything she can do. By the time I get a text from Koji saying they're on their way home, dinner is ready and I'm convinced this is all going to backfire.

We turn off the lights and huddle in the dark living room. It's still twilight outside, but I can't see anybody's faces in here. Chisa starts giggling and requires more than one person to get her to quiet down. I hear the company car pull into the driveway and two doors open and close.

"Why are you coming in?" Yumi asks her manager. Her voice grows louder as she approaches the door. "And why the hell is it dark inside? Isn't anybody home?"

The door opens and we all give her the fright of her life.

Once she realizes what is happening, she smiles, taking in the sights of all the people who came to celebrate her birthday with her. She bows at some, kisses others, and responds to happy birthday greetings with gleeful surprise. I'm the only one she kisses on the lips, which gets us much teasing from the guests.

Dinner is fabulous, if I do say so myself. Lighting the cake requires a blowtorch and the fire department on speed dial. A dozen cell phones whip out to take pictures of Yumi blowing out the fire and smiling through a fog of smoke. She hands her cell phone to my mother to take a picture of me and her posing with the cake. Yumi mentions uploading the picture to her blog later.

The party lasts well until last train, when guests start filing out and we're left with a mess to tackle tomorrow. My mother is staying in our upstairs guest room, but she says she wants to spend more time with Chisa while Yumi and I decide to go to bed.

"Thank you for the lovely surprise," Yumi says in our room. She's tired, but happy, her clothes shedding off her body as she roots for a robe to put on. I'm in the bathroom brushing my teeth. "I didn't expect it."

I finish up and join her in our room. "How's it feel being thirty?"

"Eh? You're not supposed to bring that up." She's radiant in her lavender silk robe she likes to wear on warm summer nights. Part of the reason she liked this house so much was because of the small nook in the window that, like the one in my old apartment, she perches in when the mood strikes her. Like now. "My website is going to say I'm eternally twenty-nine."

"What happens when I surpass you and I'm thirty-five and you're still twenty-nine?"

"Magic."

I go over to her and kiss her, because I can. Okay, and because she's gorgeous enough that I can feel that red string tugging at my heart. I'm sure the other end is in her hand. "Happy birthday."

"Happy anniversary."

I step back. "Anniversary?" Funnily enough, Yumi and I don't have a designated anniversary. Our relationship is so spread out across different dates that there's no way to tell when we became a couple. When she was officially ready two years ago? When we loved without abandon over that Golden Week? When we first made love?

"Eleven years ago today I kissed you. It took me much too long to accept it, but I loved you even back then." My hand lingers in hers as she looks up at me adoringly. Sometimes I still can't believe that a beautiful woman like her has chosen me as her partner. "If I can't share my birthday with something like that, then life is pretty boring."

Another kiss. Another touch to the hand. The sweetness of love is overcoming me, and I need to get the bed ready for sleep even though I have yet to change my clothes.

As I go to pull back the comforter on the bed, I find a red string tied in a circle on my pillow. "What's this?" I ask, picking it up and looking it over. "The baby's?"

From the way Yumi smiles at me, I know it's from her. "Chi-*chan*," she says, her visage a terrible union of mischief and love, "let's get married."

Just like that, I'm engaged.

Epilogue II

THE HAPPIEST DAY OF HER LIFE

Hildred Billings

エピローグ 第二：彼女の一番好きな日

I don't know the first thing about planning a wedding. Let alone a wedding that isn't legally binding. Let alone a lesbian wedding! When I long ago considered the idea that I might marry a woman someday, I thought of it as a small ceremony with our closest friends making merry with us. Something relatively inexpensive. Easy. Delightful.

Do you think Yumi does anything *small*? No!

It's a good thing she's a natural planner. From the moment I agreed to marry her – which, I must confess, used a good portion of my body as opposed to my words – we were thrown into wedding planning mode. I thought it was a bit soon, as I would have liked to enjoy calling Yumi my fiancée, but she insisted that the venue she wanted for the party needed to be booked. By God she booked it. One month away.

One month! Did I mention I only had one month before I was *married*? Yumi gave me a laundry list of things I needed to prepare while I tried to run a freakin' business. I had studios to reserve and employees to manage. Those employees were now booking the studios while I accompanied Yumi to our local Shinto shrine. Can you believe it? She wanted to have vows there! She didn't have religious vows for her first marriage. "Because

I didn't care about that," she told me on our walk. "I couldn't bring myself to care. With you? I wanna do it right."

Neither of us knew how it would go at the shrine. As anyone can tell you, it's important to use the local shrine as that's where our family is registered and those are the gods supposedly watching over us. Shinto doesn't say anything against gay people, and I've heard of many gay and lesbian couples having vows at various shrines around the country. But you never know about the prejudices of the people working there. They won't bother the neighborhood deviants like us, but they might refuse services that aren't related to purification. Pretty sure two women winging a wedding isn't pure.

We walked into the shrine holding hands, my throat dry and my skin sweaty. Yumi, however, charged ahead and found the local head priest right away. He recognized us, but I couldn't tell what his expression was.

"Tell her we can get married here," Yumi said, pointing at me. "She's nervous and thinks you'll say no. It's okay, right?"

What was this? Had she already talked to the priest about this matter? She had! The way they talked said that this was something they discussed before, and now the priest told me that there was no issue with us having marriage vows at the shrine, assuming we were serious about it. When we both insisted that we were a real couple, the priest asked us for the date to make sure there were no double-bookings.

It was in my best interest to defer to Yumi on the wedding planning front. Her vigor for it was so great that I couldn't help but wonder how long she had been fantasizing about this. Even though we had been together for two years, I never once considered that she was thinking about these sorts of things – with me! The way she scooped up venues, made reservations, tapped into services, and charmed her way into having a custom gown fitted in fewer than three weeks told me that she had the things ready to go long before she suggested we get married. The only thing I was required to do was figure out what I wanted to wear.

A dress was out of the question. Yumi would steal that show, and I wanted her to have the honors of being the visual at our wedding. Besides,

Love, Yumi

I haven't worn a dress in years. Not since my idol days. I don't have anything against dresses, but at this point I do feel uncomfortable in them because it's been so long and they're not my style anymore. Nevertheless, I felt like a stereotype when I told Yumi I would wear a suit. Nothing extravagant. Just a simple three piece suit, no tie, but I decided to feminize the look with accessories and a ruffled collar. Yumi kept her dress a secret. I don't know where she was keeping it. Perhaps in the guest room, which I only entered to dust and change the linens.

The most stressful part was curating a guest list. We quickly exhausted the people we knew wouldn't have a problem coming to our wedding. Of course we also sent invitations to people we work with (it's not like we're exactly closeted anymore) and family members. My mother was one of the first to know the day after we became engaged, and she nearly cried as she hugged us both and said we were a beautiful couple.

Yumi's parents, on the other hand, reacted just about how you would expect.

They would come. For their daughter. Yumi's mother made it clear that she didn't approve of this "spectacle" and wished her daughter would move on. "You've already had one embarrassing marriage," she said, and this was after she knew about the abuse! "Why do you need another one? Is it even really a marriage?" Even Yumi's fans were more accepting of the news than her parents. The ones who had stuck by her after my confession either supported our relationship or were indifferent.

As the day grew closer, I became more nervous. I couldn't work, even though Yumi took over much of the planning so I could focus on my business. How could I when she was at the kitchen table talking to florists on the phone and shushing my piano playing? Chisa was back at nursery school and I still couldn't work. When Yumi hung up, talking about roses and carnations, I thought I had my chance to lose myself in music again. Then her damn phone rang and I slapped my fingers against the keys to create a cacophony of noise.

"*Hai, Yumi desu.*" So she didn't know who it was? Whoever had her number could have only gotten it through her or the label, so if she didn't know them it had to be business. "Eh?" She sat up straight in the chair. "*Hontou desu ka?*"

She wasn't panicked, at least. I sure was, as I leaped off my bench and hovered around her, preparing to hear some awful news. Yumi held her phone close to her mouth and lowered her voice, agreeing to a meeting somewhere before hanging up.

"Who was it?"

Yumi stared into nothingness before shaking her head. "That was the editor-in-chief of Hayari Magazine."

"What?" One of the most prestigious glamour magazines in the country? Why were they calling Yumi? Even during the peak of her career before she got pregnant she was never contacted by them. "What did she want?"

"They want to feature us in their upcoming issue!"

"*What?*"

Yumi launched herself from the dining room table and came to me, grabbing my arms and nearly shaking me where I stood. "They want to photograph our wedding and then later in our home. The want to take pictures of our family and write an article about us!"

I don't think I fainted, but I definitely felt woozy after that.

***

So now here I am on my wedding day, dressed in my suit and sophisticated jewelry, sitting across from a reporter from Hayari Magazine. Risa is better dressed than me, as befitting one of the country's top lifestyle reporters for a magazine that sells to the elite and wannabe elites around Asia and beyond. Their articles are even translated into English! Are we going to be in American magazines too? I'm too nervous to ask.

"Congratulations on your big day," she says with a professional grin. I'm assuming she doesn't mind being here, but she's so respectful that it could easily be a front. I shift in my seat, my suit closing in on my skin and making me sweat more than I should. "This is your first marriage, right?"

The fact she deigns to call it a marriage means something. Yet I can't miss the tone in her voice, implying that I am Yumi's second. "Yes, this is my first marriage." I quickly have another thought. "My only one."

Risa raises her manicured eyebrows, but says nothing. What can I say? Should something happen to Yumi (God forbid) or if for some reason our relationship ends, I already know that I don't want to have another. I'm a one-woman kind of gal... for life. If it's not Yumi, then who can it possibly be? I will always be pining after her and hoping that somehow I can be with her again. If we're separated, that's not fair to any new woman I date. If Yumi is dead, then my heartbreak will be so great that I don't think I could love again anyway. Not like that.

I don't say any of this to Risa. This is a happy day, and I want the article to be nothing but good things.

"Chiharu," my mother is beside me, putting a hand on my shoulder and nodding in apology to the reporter. "Yumi's in the dressing room and wants to talk to you."

Flashes of four years ago appear before my eyes. Yumi, pregnant and drowning in her wedding dress, crying because she was afraid for her future. Because she wanted to be with me instead. What could she possibly want this time?

I excuse myself from Risa's presence and follow my mother to the dressing room. After I knock, I hear a sweet tone that tells me Yumi is all right. Whatever this is about, it can't be bad.

The one thing I don't expect when I open the door is to see Yumi already dressed in her bridal gown. It's stunning, like her. And unlike her previous dress, which was large, ridiculous, and meant to hide a pregnant belly, this one hugs her figure from the collar to the hem. The bodice is sleeveless, high-collar, and beaded so thoroughly that she looks like she's wearing crystals on her chest and around her neck. The natural waistline is cinched with a thin belt before the pure white skirt sheaths her legs toward the floor. Yumi turns, showing me the open back that reveals the bottom of her shoulder blades. "Well?" she asks, giving a twirl. "What do you think? Am I a decent bride this time?"

Her stylist has been here. Yumi's eyes are dark and flirty, her hair combed behind the ear and roots touched up. I too have dyed my hair recently. After thinking about it for months, I finally decided to try the brown again for the wedding. I had black hair for so long that it felt right to start a new phase of my life with something different about my look. "You were beautiful last time too."

Yumi's earrings and bracelet sparkle with her movements. She's a princess. No, a queen. Maybe a goddess. Is there something greater than a goddess? I wouldn't mind finding out. "Last time was awful. I wasn't happy."

I approach her, making sure the door is locked behind me. Ah, this is really bringing back strange memories. It's hard for me to believe that *I'm* the one she's marrying. "You're gorgeous," I say, taking her hands. We decided against engagement rings since we were marrying so quickly, so her fingers are bare. That will change later. "Did your mother help you?"

God damnit, Chiharu! Don't I know what a stupid thing that was to ask? Yumi's smile fades as she swallows her sudden sadness. "I haven't seen her. They said they were coming, but I don't think they will."

I kiss her hand in an effort to apologize.

"Promise me something," she says, and I think of that promise I made on her last wedding day to find someone worth marrying. (I did.) "We won't be like them. We'll support our daughter, whether she brings home a boy or a girl one day."

Easy for her to say. You think I want my little girl dating boys quite yet? At least with another girl I don't have to worry about a major fuckup leading to something like Yumi's first marriage. "Of course we will." I smile. "Every time you call her our daughter, I'm happy."

I get a smile out of her in return. "Can I tell you a secret?"

"*Un.*"

Yumi takes my arms into her hands and draws herself closer to me. She's wearing a new perfume for the big day – I love it. "I like to pretend that she's really your daughter, as if we made her together." Her grip on my arms tightens. "That Golden Week was passionate enough to create someone like her. When I think of it like that, I'm able to forget Yohei and everything he did to us. And besides..." Yumi doesn't blush often, so when she does I feel like I've uncovered something fantastic. "I really do think of her as your daughter. She's lucky to have you."

I'm flattered, but now is not the time to fall over myself with platitudes. "She's lucky to have the both of us."

Our foreheads touch, and a soft giggle touches my lips. I lean in for a pre-marital kiss, but Yumi pulls away with a devilish grin. "That's why I have something important to tell you before we get married today," she says, her cheeks about to burst with the secret. "I'm pregnant."

Did a bomb just go off somewhere? Because I swear I've gone deaf and am either also dead or too shell-shocked to have heard my girlfriend correctly. "You're *what?*"

My face must be priceless. Yumi bites her lip and then explodes in laughter, one hand on her stomach, which I am staring at in an effort to see a baby bump. "I'm joking!" Her laughter makes her cheeks turn pinker beneath her light rouge. "Oh my God, your face!"

"That's not funny!" Images of who the father could possibly be had been swarming my head. It would have meant she cheated on me. Because even though I too can fantasize about being Chisa's biological father, I am well aware of certain limitations in the bedroom... whether I sometimes compensate or not. "*Mou*... how can you joke on a day like today?"

"*Gomen, gomen,*" she apologizes. "I just really wanted to see how you would react."

"Is that what you called me in here for?" I sigh, wondering what I have signed myself up for by marrying her. Yumi always had a bit of prankster in her, but I thought that was mostly gone by now.

She slips into my embrace, her hands on the small of my back while I stand there with my arms hanging out to my sides. I'm afraid to touch her. She's done up so well, if I put a hand on her it's going to displace some hair or smear some makeup. Maybe wrinkle her dress.

"Chi-*chan,*" Yumi says, lips grazing my cheek. "Today is the happiest day of my life."

I don't mean to laugh, but I do, and Yumi looks at me as if I've wounded her. "Mine too," I say. "I'm glad this is happening."

"I'm serious." I rarely see such resolve on her face, and as a bride it makes her look like a despondent princess deciding between war and clemency. "Before today, the happiest time of my life was that Golden Week. Before that, it was my concert at Budokan. Before that, it was when I released my first solo single. And before that? The day we were accepted into the industry. If I go back even farther, I'm sure they're all memories with you." Her hand is on my chest, digging beneath the ruffles of my blouse and touching my skin. "There isn't a truly happy memory that isn't thanks to you in some way. You've stayed by my side for so long that I don't know what the meaning of living without you is. From now on, let's make even more memories together."

I nod. "Do you know how lucky we are?"

My mother is rapping on the door, quietly asking if we're okay and if we're ready to start. We ignore her. "How lucky?"

"We've always had someone to rely on since we were small children. To fall in love on top of that? How many people can say they've been so fortunate?"

"I want you to be able to rely on me for the rest of our lives." Yumi finds my necklace and beams like the sun. "No matter what happens, we have to be there for each other."

In truth, I haven't relied on Yumi for much other than her love. I always thought that was enough. But when I think about it, I was always protecting her, listening to her, getting her out of trouble and supporting her career. She did things for me too, of course, but I love her so much that I do things without a need for reciprocation. "I love you."

"I love you too." Yumi kisses me, and we're ready to get married.

There are a lot more people here than I anticipated. They're gathered in a separate hall from where we're having our reception, because first we must exchange the vows we've written. Earlier we had a more official ceremony at the Shinto shrine, but it was quick, efficient, and only my

Love, Yumi

mother attended as witness and to take a few pictures that won't be sold to any magazines. For that ceremony, Yumi wore a simple white kimono. Now she walked into the ceremonial hall of this venue in her designer wedding gown tailored just for her in less than a month. Every time I think about it, I'm impressed. Her popularity has diminished over the past year, but she still commands attention wherever she goes.

We have no officiant. We simply stand in front of our friends and family and swear our love and loyalty to one another.

"On that day almost twenty-five years ago," Yumi says, her hands on top of mine, "I decided that I wanted you to be my friend. I don't know why. Maybe I liked how you looked or that you were more reliable than the other kids. I do know that you welcomed me without question, and not once in all those years since have you ever made me doubt your love for me. Where would I be without Chiharu? In a lonely world with no music to light up my life."

She says it so easily. I suppose it's her performer's nature. She's able to tune out the people focusing on us. My mother is crying. Our daughter is rocking on her feet in a pretty periwinkle dress Yumi picked out. Risa the reporter is writing down snippets of what Yumi said while two photographers vie for the best shot of us. I'm not used to this kind of attention. I'm Chiharu. I sit behind a piano offstage or stand in the back of the dance formation where hardly anyone can see me. I'm not supposed to be equal to Yumi. Yet here I am, standing before her and getting ready to spill my heart in front of the world.

"I've loved you for a long time," I say. "I don't know the exact moment I wanted to know you better, but my whole life has been spent loving you in some capacity. You were my best friend first and then my partner. You don't know how happy you've made me just by being yourself and sharing your love with me. I'll do everything in my power to make sure we're able to enjoy our new life together."

We exchange rings, but not the gaudy, expensive kind you're thinking of. Yes, we bought some rings. Just a simple band for me and a sparkly stone for Yumi to twirl on her finger, but for the ceremony we're more sentimental. I pull two red strings out of my pocket and hand one to Yumi, who ties it around my finger before I tie mine around hers. Then we kiss, and the guests clap for how clever we are.

I've been to my share of weddings over the years, and while some things rarely change whether you go Eastern or Western, I'm still surprised at how much this one mirrors Yumi's first wedding. For after the vows we go to the receiving hall to greet our guests. Yumi and I stand by a wall in a long hallway, staff people lining the guests up in single file and ushering them past us. We shake hands, bow, thank them for coming, and in our case, thank them for supporting us this long. Most of the guests are there out of professional propriety, but there are a few people who surprise us. Like two of the old and hardened executives, Mr. Kawaguchi in tow.

They're curt, but polite. We bow respectfully, we thank them for their continued support, and they thank us for… something. I like to think that Mr. Kawaguchi came to support us personally, but I'm not sure about the other executives. Of course we invited all of them, but we didn't think they would actually show up.

I didn't think half the people who came would show up.

"Eh, look at you two!" Nezu is dressed in a simple suit, her piercings removed and hair respectfully down. "Now I'm sad! I thought Chiharu would stay uncommitted like me forever."

"You two are the sorriest girls I ever had the extreme pleasure to work with." Beppu isn't a bower. He shakes my hand hard enough to rip off my arm before clapping me on the shoulder and winking at me. "When you weren't giving me heart attacks, of course. Now go be happy so I can have faith in some things working out okay in this world." He shakes Yumi's hand more gently than he does mine. She thanks him, smiling,

"Good Lord." Dolly lowers her sunglasses and glares at us through bloodshot eyes. "Put this on the list of things I never expected to see." No bows and no hand shaking. Somehow, I'm okay with that. "Never expected to see you married," she nods at me, "let alone married to *her.*"

"Thank you for your love." I can't tell if Yumi is being sarcastic.

I certainly don't expect the next guest in line.

Love, Yumi

"*Ohisashiburi*," Erina greets, her skin tanned but face no less cheery than I remember from ten years ago. "When I got the invitation in the mail, I knew I had to come."

Shocked, I look at Yumi, who hides behind her hand as if to say "*I would never.*"

"By the way…" Erina puts her hand on my shoulder, our first touch since she initiated me into the world of carnal delights. "Thanks for the kind words on your blog. My girlfriend got a real hoot out of the visuals." She winks at me before moving on.

As nice as it is to see both recent and old but familiar faces, I can't help but think of the people we don't see that day. I wish Koto were here to see the happiness that can come out of the lives we've lived. And Yumi's parents…

"Mama!" Yumi steps forward, her hands reaching for the woman and man approaching us in line. Even I'm surprised, since if they weren't here earlier, then clearly they weren't coming at all. A part of me dreads any comments that are bound to come from them, but at the same time I'm happy that Yumi has her parents on her big day. They give us soft smiles and apologize for being late, but I can tell from their taut lips and wrinkling brows that they're not too happy to be a part of our spectacle.

When the last of the guests have made their way through the receiving hall and into the main reception, Yumi and I join them, sitting at a high table with our families flanking us. Yumi's parents sit next to her, and our daughter and my mother sit next to me. I still don't recognize half the faces in the crowd, but I don't care anymore. I'm finally starting to relax, probably because I'm being loaded with champagne and food.

Then our parents get into a kerfuffle over tea and champagne.

"Aren't you going to help me?" my mother asks Yumi's, indicating the load of drinks that must be served to the guests. "It's our duty as their parents to make sure the guests are comfortable."

Yumi's mother balks at the idea that this wedding is real enough to command her attention like that. My mother perseveres, staring down the woman she helped raise two daughters with. Those same daughters who are now dressed in bridal attire and waiting for one of them to make the wrong move on our big day.

With so much attention on her, Yumi's mother has no choice but to politely bow and grab the nearest bottle of champagne. She and my mother make the rounds, filling up glasses and small talking with some of the guests. Without her grandmothers to mind her, Chisa tries to climb into my lap so she can better survey the festivities. She'll be bored soon enough, but for now I let her hog my lap while Yumi fixes our daughter's hair and tells her to mind her manners.

The speeches play out while we eat. People reminisce about us, how they had no idea we were "like that" or they totally knew we were "like that." I try not to roll my eyes too hard.

"Let's face it, I was one of the only people who knew," Beppu said when someone had the *bright idea* to hand him the mic. "Way back when I worked with them, this one here," he points at me, "had it so bad for that one there I knew it would be nothing but trouble. And it was! I'm not ever gonna lie and tell you lot that I just knew everything would be hunky-dory and we would have this moment today. Because life threw a lot of shit at these young women, and somehow they prevailed and made it this far. It's inspiring, isn't it? Look, you," he points to Yumi, "best appreciate what you have sitting next to you. Chiharu would take a damned bullet for you without thinking about it. And you!" He points at me. "Stop being an idiot and jumping in front of bullets. Or knives, for that matter."

The crowd is silent, aside from some shifting legs and clearing throats. It's me who starts laughing first, a snort shooting through my nose and then a gag as I try to quiet down my embarrassing giggles. Then Yumi starts up, her hand slapping across her mouth.

Uneasy laughter filters through the crowd. At any other wedding those kinds of comments would mean the end, but with us it's just another day dealing with our old manager.

The rest of the wedding is a whimsical blur of toasts, more speeches, and then some dancing as things begin to wind down. Heady with champagne and the good food, I lead Yumi to the dance floor where we sway back and forth in front of our loved ones. This is the first time we've danced together in public like this, and it's taking every bit of restraint I have to *not* kiss her like she deserves.

"So how was your first wedding?" Yumi asks, a flash to our left as someone takes a picture. "I have to say, this was better than my first one. For one thing, I'm not pregnant. For another, I'm finally marrying the right person."

I lean in toward her ear, my voice a whisper against her skin. "Remember when you told me to find someone that you would approve of? Well? Do you approve of who I'm with?"

"Eh, honestly, you could do better." Her fingers massage the back of my neck, and I'm lulled into a sense of security I rarely get to feel. "Although if I'm the one you want, well, I won't give you shit. I'll give you my blessing."

I'm about to reply when I feel something brush against my leg. We look down, our daughter now moved on to Yumi's skirt in an effort to get our attention. "Mama *dansu,*" she says, riled up on some sugar *someone* – I glare at my mother – gave her.

"Excuse me," Yumi says, pushing away from me so she can take our daughter's hand. "It appears that I am being called away by my other favorite girl."

I mingle, drink, and eat more cake than my personal trainer would like. It's my wedding day, damnit, and if I want to gain three kilos I damn will, thank you. I spend much time gazing at my beautiful bride, who looks much more glamorous than I ever could. I'm happy to let her hog most of the spotlight when we're apart. It gives me time to wind down and thank my mother for everything she's done for me.

"I should commend you for being such a sensible person," she says, trying not to cry.

"I'm not sensible. Do you see who I fell in love with?"

"Ah, to be honest, Chiharu, I'm not sure how you're not supposed to fall in love with someone like her. She was always a vivacious and pretty girl."

"She still is."

"Yes, yes."

Most people probably don't want their big day to end, but I am ready. Tired, and sore, I accompany Yumi to the limousine waiting for us. She stops to throw her bouquet of yellow lilies and tiny thistles, the few single women in the audience scrambling to catch it. In the end it goes to Asuka, who nearly drops it when she realizes her boyfriend saw it happen.

We go to a hotel downtown, where Yumi has reserved the honeymoon suite for the night. In the morning we'll fly down to Okinawa, where we'll stay a week before flying to New York to spend another week on our honeymoon. It will be my first time in New York, so I asked her to book somewhere a bit more familiar first.

But tonight we're staying in Nagoya, and the moment we step into our luxurious suite I'm overcome with fatigue… and some emotion.

"So this is it, huh?" I stand before the king sized bed, Yumi surveying the quality of the room before coming back to me. "We're married. Or as much as we can be. Does that make you my…" It feels weird to say. Somehow we haven't discussed this before. Wife? Wife sounds weird. I never thought of having a wife or a husband. She's more than my girlfriend now. Spouse is too formal, too distant. Partner doesn't hold the same power as saying we're married… but if I don't think of her as my wife, then what am I to her?

"Tonight I can be your bride." She loops her arms around my shoulders, a satisfied smirk on her glowing countenance. "You know what newlyweds are supposed to accomplish on their wedding night, right?"

"Once again, I can't knock you up."

"Yes but we can *try*. I'm not on birth control anymore. It could happen."

"I never did get you those condoms."

It takes her a bit to get my reference, but when she does, she taps my cheek in admonishment. She turns around, gesturing to the clasp on the high neck of her dress. "Unhook me, love. I want to get out of these stiff clothes."

Love, Yumi

Undressing her is a ritual tonight. I'm not just helping her change clothes efficiently. This is foreplay. When my fingers unclasp her collar I put my lips there, burying my nose in the scent of her perfume and the base of her sheared hair. She shivers in my arms, and I know I did well.

While I kiss the warmth of her neck the bodice slips down her torso and drapes around her waist. I'm not in the least surprised that my bride isn't wearing a bra. I make sure she's aware of this, my hands touching her for the first time since our vows. I didn't think it would, but it does feel different afterward. I've felt her like this a hundred times, and yet it seems so strange now… to think that this person, this woman is the one I'm going to spend the rest of my life with. We're not just friends. Or lovers. We're working together to bring about not only our collective happiness but that of a child's as well. It overwhelms me, and I squeeze her too hard.

"*Ita!*" I'm not supposed to be hurting my bride on our wedding night, and yet Yumi pulls away, surprised that I got so handsy. "What are you doing? Trying to maul me?" She covers her chest with her arms, grabs one of her bags, and heads toward the bathroom. "Hold on. I seriously need to take this off. And *no* you can't help any more until you learn to control yourself."

I wait on the bed, wondering what the protocol for wedding night sex is. You know me by now. I like it when things happen organically. All this build up and pressure to perform inhibits my ability to fully enjoy myself. It doesn't matter that I've been with Yumi enough times now to know exactly what we both like. If she's expecting something in particular for her mulligan of a wedding night, then I'm going to be waltzing in circles.

Yumi appears in the bathroom doorway dressed in sheer white lingerie. And I mean *sheer*. Not a single thing is left to my imagination. There's something to be said for what you imagine being more powerful than what you actually see and experience. Not tonight. Yumi is so beautiful that her lingerie is like a veil hinting at what I can discover beneath. The way it hugs her breasts and hips only accentuates both of these things. She's so deliriously feminine that I'm sure I'm staring at her like I can't believe she's mine.

"Well?" She puffs her chest out. It's cold in this bedroom, thank God. "You gonna say something or just look at me like I'm a centerfold?" At least she knows her worth.

Say something? This from the woman who showed me a thousand times that we didn't need words? Funny. "Yeah, I did good," I say, crossing my arms as if inspecting her. "Could have done worse picking a hottie. At least I can die saying I married someone good looking."

Yumi exaggerates her eye roll. "Should have figured."

I take off my jacket as she comes over, climbs onto the bed, and lays herself out in the most inviting way possible, one arm propping her head up while her toes curl in the air. Those seductive eyes are back. I used to stare at them in her photos, and sometimes I still can't believe that they're pointed at me – *me* – in a bid to get me to come over and make love to her.

She pats the space in front of her. Who? Me? She can't mean me. Sure, we just got married, and sure, we've been together two years, but she can't mean *me*.

"I don't tell you enough that you're beautiful," Yumi says, my body crawling up the length of the bed. "Even when we were kids, I should have said it more often."

"Why?"

She pushed some hair out of my eyes, her touch lingering on my forehead before returning to her side. "Just… you were always hard on yourself sometimes. People would talk frankly about your looks. I remember when Anna made you feel ugly. Stuff like that."

"Well, we're not all bombshells like you."

"Stop it." She lightly smacks my arm, but I am distracted by the way it makes her chest move. "I'm serious. You're really beautiful! Sure you were plain growing up, but so was I. As adults I think we've really come into our own. Ah, can you imagine the old us hearing that we would have a moment like this?"

"I wouldn't have believed it."

"Me neither! I imagined us growing up and marrying guys. We were going to live next door to each other and become old ladies like that."

"Were we?" I don't recall this.

Yumi sits up, and so do I. "I like this outcome a lot more. Not only do I love you, but I know you'll be good to me and love me back." Good ol' dependable and reliable Chiharu. That's me. "Not only that…" She puts her hand on my neck, her thumb playing with the bottom of my ear. "You ain't so bad in bed."

"Inspiration helps."

The first kiss we have in bed as a married couple is exactly what I need: tender, yet passionate, the sort of kiss that explores what we would like to do before we jump into it. I think that's exactly what we're going to do before Yumi slips her hand down the front of my shirt, one button after another coming undone. I suck in my breath, her fingers reaching beneath my bra and pinching my flesh. "Like that?"

"Yeah." I try to keep my cool, but the gasp in my throat betrays me.

"Uh huh." My blouse is open, Yumi's hand pulling one bra strap off my shoulder before she leans forward and kisses my skin. "Look at how beautiful you are. Now make love to your equally beautiful bride."

How can I say no to that? I can't. I'm absolutely weak and vulnerable around her. But if I can't feel that way with Yumi, then who can I feel that way with? Tonight, tomorrow night, and many more nights in the future I'll show her my most vulnerable side – the side that is hopelessly in love with her, sometimes to a fault.

Hildred Billings

Epilogue III

LOVE, CHIHARU

Hildred Billings

エピローグ 第三：愛、千春

Hello, everyone. It's been a while, hasn't it? Aside from the occasional work update, I haven't had much time to talk about what's going on in my personal life. Since I made such a big deal out of it earlier this year, it's not surprising that people always ask when I'm going to update the world on it again.

Well, today is my birthday. My thirtieth birthday. As always, I have caught up with Yumi. It's also about three months since I got married. While the weather isn't as warm as it was back then, it's pretty and sunny today. Winter may be here, but the sun doesn't show any signs of going away. Its shine is really lighting up the house this morning.

Let's see… a lot has happened, *ne?* After our honeymoon, Yumi and I returned to a flurry of things to do. She finally released that album that was pushed back from this spring. According to her, it was a good thing it got delayed, because she decided to change the theme in the end. Its title, "Decade," was both a nod to the length of her career and entering a new phase of her life. When she promoted the album she went on one of those late night talk shows. I watched it at home since I had work to do here.

"This has been a huge year for you," the hostess said, addressing Yumi who was gussied up in leggings, boots, and a leopard print coat. I informed her the tinted glasses were a bit much, but she insisted that she had a style to maintain. "Between the blog confession and your new marriage…"

"It was pretty exciting, huh?" Yumi looked relaxed in her seat. Even if she's dripping in sweat and telling me that she's nervous to be on TV, you would never guess just from the way she conducts herself once the cameras start rolling. "When this year began, I thought the only big change would be turning thirty. Then the blog thing happened, and the next thing I know I'm having this wedding that all of Asia wants in on. Did you see the Hayari photos?"

"I did! Congratulations."

"Thank you. I know my relationship is not conventional, and I know that I alienated a lot of people, but it was important for me to live openly and unconditionally. I hid so much in my life for so long that I just couldn't do it anymore. It was either come clean or retreat back into a dark place. With a family counting on me, I couldn't do that latter thing."

"How old is your daughter?"

"She'll be four soon enough."

"They grow up so quickly!"

"The older she gets, the more I realize I need to be a good example for her. I don't want her growing up and thinking that her mother is weak or stupid. If I can't be honest with the world, then how can she trust me to tell her the truth about things? Pretty soon she'll be going to school and learning all sorts of things beyond my control. I want her to know that she can be open with me about anything. I doubt she will be, because who is? But I don't want her to feel like I've shut her out. I guess even now I still worry about her not knowing how much I care about her."

The hostess nodded. "And the marriage?"

"What is there to say? It's a marriage. We're constantly changing how we approach things as we go through obstacles. This is my second relationship like this, but this time it feels a lot more serious. I married for love and practicality both, not because I had to protect my daughter from antiquated systems."

The hostess cleared her throat and the audience silently chattered. I could practically see Koji standing off to the side and tearing his hair out. Yumi was going to be a hell of a sound bite the next day. "Your marriage is not legal, though, correct?"

"Of course not. We're married in each other's eyes, and we don't allow anyone to tell us otherwise. We don't treat it any less seriously than anyone who has signed those papers and had them filed. I doubt we'll be allowed to legally marry anytime soon, but it's hopeful."

"You've been very quiet about your identity in all of this…"

"As public as my life has been this year, I still consider myself a somewhat private person. There are some things the world doesn't need to know, such as how I identify. What does it matter? I've been married to a man and I'm now married to a woman. I can't get hung up on these things. All I can do is what's best for my life and happiness."

"Is there anything that's fundamentally changed in you this past year?"

"I turned thirty this year. On my birthday, I thought about everything that had happened this past decade. All of it led up to that moment. Who I am, the scars I have, and the feelings that have flooded my heart. I spent so much of my 20s running and hiding from who I am that I wanted to embrace my 30s as a new woman. I want to be someone not only more mature but more sure of herself. The music I make is going to be a lot more heartfelt and the direction I want. I want to go at my own pace so I can enjoy work and my family. I'm not saying that the past decade was all bad, but I see this as a chance to start over and be a new me. When I'm forty, I want to look back and say that the past decade was pretty damn good."

Yumi doesn't think she has a way with words, but she does. She writes a lot of lyrics now. I doubt she'll ever be a big composer, but she doesn't need to be. She has me, doesn't she? The songs we create together are the best she has, I think.

The album sold decently. Not superbly. Not even great. I was afraid Yumi wouldn't take it well, but she acknowledged that her popularity took a big hit. There were some hateful comments and every once in a while we receive a letter telling us how terrible we are and how we should be ashamed to expose our child to our lifestyle. They bother me more than they bother Yumi. I daresay she's become more accepting of our life than I have. I never thought I would see the day. While her career has not been decimated, neither of us did it any favors... but she'll persevere. She told me that she feels like she has a lot more freedom now that she's no longer on top. The people who love her will continue to love her, and the people who didn't really weren't her fans to begin with.

"An idol is someone that people adore," she told me in the studio one day. "*Someone*. Not a thing. My job was to bring people joy and happiness. Why can't I still do that?"

We were afraid that she would lose some of her endorsements, and she did. In response, she picked up a couple more respectable ones, including cosmetics and fashion brands. Particularly Western ones that probably hoped to score brownie points around the world. She's now the spokes model for London Face throughout Asia. You can see her modeling their makeup in Tokyo, Seoul, and even Taipei, where they still love her just as much as ever.

She's also venturing into new realms of media. Recently she accepted an offer to be on stage in a musical for the first time ever. Yumi is nervous about it because she's never had to do something like that in her adult life. "What if I forget how to act on a stage?" she asked. "High school was so different!"

Yumi will also be filming a movie at the beginning of the year. It's not going to have a huge release, but she's excited about the project, as she still loves to act. She probably won't be in as many dramas as she used to be, but maybe once a year isn't so bad. Like she said on that talk show, she wants to slow down and live life with us as well.

I've been busy as well, and not just with my business, which is seeing more success than I anticipated so early on. Shortly after we returned from our honeymoon, I received a call from a publisher in Osaka who wanted to turn my blog confession into a book. I hesitated at first, but after discussing it with Yumi for a few days we decided to go ahead with it. It may cause another wave of negativity in our lives, but at this point we figure most of the damage has already been done. The publisher wants to translate it into many languages. The idea that people all over the world will be reading my confession in a way they can understand is positively terrifying. I'm just one woman in the grand scheme of things. How could my confession mean anything to anyone? Apparently, this publisher seems to think the world wants to know.

So I've been working on that. I just returned from a trip to Osaka to discuss this with the publisher, and they want to see the first draft by the end of February. I've written many lyrics in my day, but putting together blog posts in a coherent storytelling format is something else. At least most of the hard work is done?

I don't know if you've seen it, but our spread in Hayari Magazine came out a few days ago. I was surprised how long the article was, let alone how many pictures appeared. Even now I remember the photographer here in our home shortly after we returned from our honeymoon. He was the same fellow as from the wedding, and I can still remember that shoot like yesterday.

"Let's get a shot of you two on the couch," he said, motioning for us to sit in the living room. "No, no, more casually. Like you would normally sit. That's how you normally sit? Okay then. Not how you normally sit. Here, you try this..." he asked Yumi to cross one leg over the other and lean in toward me, "and you try this."

He took a million shots of us sitting on the couch, Yumi giving her best smile while she mumbled, "Come on, Chiharu, smile for the world."

"I am smiling." My cheeks were about to implode.

"Not the serial killer smile."

"You'd rather I look like I'm going to kill someone?"

"What did I just say?"

At least the picture they chose came out well. Yumi was beaming and I didn't look upset or predatory. There were also shots of us sitting at the kitchen table and "going about our business," in the most staged manner possible. The photographer shot me at my piano and Yumi going through papers with her glasses on. All this happened while our daughter was at school, since we weren't going to allow her face to appear in the spread.

The article talked about what I wrote in my confession, how it had impacted our lives, and what we wanted to do now. Given my initial reservations, I was pleased to find that the slant was either neutral or supportive depending on the context. Hayari focuses on an international readership where the kind of relationship Yumi and I have is more readily accepted. Overall, not terrible publicity.

As I'm winding down, I'm struck again by that story about the three faces of happiness. I got a great example of it earlier this month when Yumi had a one-night concert in the Saitama Super Arena. Even with everything that happened this year, she still managed to nearly sell it out. Five years ago she would have sold it out five times over. One year ago it would have simply sold out. This year, however, we are thrilled to hear that she has thousands of fans who still want to see her perform. Since it was a one-night only show, people from all over Japan and beyond came in to see her sing and dance. She may be thirty, a mother, and married (to a woman, no less) but she's still bringing joy to the masses.

I had told her that I couldn't go that night due to some other commitment. Well, I was committed that night. To being there anyway, as a special surprise at the end of her set.

"Hey, Yumi," her keyboardist, a man she often did MCs with during her shows, said while she was talking to the audience. "Did you know that there's someone here to see you?"

"Eh?" Sweaty, Yumi stood at the end of the catwalk jutting into the audience, her big eyes glistening in curiosity on the big screens. "What are you talking about? Who is here?"

I stood at the far end of the stage where nobody but staff people could see me. A stylist had just made me presentable to be on stage and probably recorded on camera. When Yumi started looking around, confused because this wasn't a part of the rehearsals, her keyboardist stepped away from his instrument. I took his place, and not only did the audience go nuts, but Yumi sank to her knees and covered her mic so it wouldn't pick up her laughter.

"What are you doing here?" she asked, her wedding ring sparkling in the arena lights. "Were you that bored at home you crashed my concert?"

The audience laughed. "Why do you get to have all the fun?" I asked, the mic attached to my lapel echoing until one of the engineers readjusted the levels. "Maybe I felt like bothering you today."

"Because you don't bother me enough at home?"

I shrugged.

"What do you think you're going to do? The next song on the list isn't even by you!"

"We'll make something up." I played the first note of "I'm Proud," which most people wouldn't recognize, but it made Yumi instantly laugh again, her rosy complexion making me smile in turn.

What was she thinking? Was she reminded of our audition to become idols? Or was she simply laughing because I was there? Whatever she thought, she readily stood up and nodded, ready to perform.

It was planned from the beginning that I would play this song. The label already cleared the rights for it, and it made sense to perform since it had been on that cover album we did. I wouldn't let memories of Asada into my head as I played the first notes and waited for Yumi to jump in with her clear vocals.

We only performed through the first chorus before I played the ending notes, signaling to my partner that we didn't have to do any more. Instead I jumped into "Hold Me," which made the crowd clap in approval since it was one of our signature songs together.

That song got played in its entirety, including my solo parts in the second verse and chorus. For the first time in my life I didn't have to hold back my feelings for her as I sang. I didn't have to close my eyes and simply imagine her in my mind. By some miracle – called being openly married, I suppose – I was able to sing directly to the love of my life, who continued to blush and crouch against the stage whenever she wasn't singing. The whole arena had their eyes on us, on our relationship, and I can't tell you how freeing it was to bare my heart in front of those people and sing to the woman I married.

I left the stage after that, and Yumi was supposed to return to her regularly scheduled set list, but she was so overwhelmed by what happened that she stumbled through the lines of her next song and had to stop while the crowd cheered her on.

After the final encore she came backstage, searching for me and instantly smacking me on the shoulder by her dressing room. "You didn't tell me you were doing that!"

"I didn't realize I was supposed to reveal a surprise."

"First my birthday and now that… I don't know if I can take more of your surprises."

"They always end well, don't they?"

She hugged me, the scent of her sweat overtaking me. Yumi then exclaimed again when she saw my mother and Chisa sitting in the dressing room. They both had watched the concert from backstage, Chisa's ears properly plugged but no less able to appreciate her mother's performance.

"Today was a great day," Yumi sighed against my arm. "Thank you for being here."

I saw them then. All three faces of her happiness. The face for the adoring fans who stuck by her through everything, the face for her giggling daughter, and the face for me – the person who loved her more than anyone else in the world.

I'll never be able to heal all of her wounds. There will always be lingering sadness within her, and I'm learning to accept that. It's in my nature to want to make her better. To turn her back into the girl I once knew growing up. When you've been through what we have, though, it's impossible to go back to those innocent ways. Of course everyone grows up in this world, but the way we matured would have killed most people. I suppose we should be proud that we made it this far and managed to carve out our happiness. We're together. We're strong. We'll make a warm and supportive home for our daughter. One day we'll wake up and we'll be old. I'll wonder where all the years went, and she'll wonder how she made it so far. Until then, we take it one day at a time. When she needs her space, I give it to her. When she needs comfort, I'm the first one there.

That sounds pretty one-sided, doesn't it? This whole time I've talked about our relationship in regard to how I support her. Don't get it wrong. She gives just as much to me. Without Yumi – her smile, wry jokes, signing voice, and the way she walks her fingers up my spine when we're alone – I am merely a shell. She's the one who makes me get up and think, "Today will be a good day," even if I don't see her because she's on tour or working hard at the office. Knowing she's out there, doing her best and sharing her love with others, makes me believe in a better world. If I'm having a bad day, all I do is look at her face and feel better.

We can't mend each other's wounds. We understand them. We're the only people in this world who understand each other so completely. Growing up together, surviving the idol industry together, and then becoming a romantic couple has made us completely incomprehensible to others. If something happened to me, I think that Yumi could move on and find love again, even if it takes a while. I've never loved anyone else. Since I was a girl I wanted to be with her, and now that I am, how can I imagine a life without her?

Now that my life has reached this point, I hope that I can get back to blogging about my work, with only the occasional life update. Do you guys really care about the details of my personal life now? I did my confession, and now I have told you how it all worked out in the end. From now on I would like to return my blog to its original purpose. I might post once in a while about my vacations and being a parent... or I could get really fancy and open one of those social media accounts that let you do that sort of thing.

Thank you to all of my readers who have gone on this journey with me. Without your continued support, I'm not sure I could have gone as far as I did, let alone complete the whole thing. It's because of you readers that

I've been able to be so open and myself in the world. I'm not exactly the most socially acceptable person around. I want to be happy just like anyone else. I've found my happiness. My goal from now on is to hold on to it and be the best partner and parent I can be.

The Chiharu I once was and the Chiharu I am now are two different people. I'm stronger, more assured, and happier than I could have ever imagined. If I could say anything to the past me, the one floundering in the idol life, wondering what the point of it all was, I would say, "There will be a lot of awful shit that happens, but it will be worth it. You'll see." I would say something about not worrying about Yumi, but worrying about her so much is what led me here.

Goodbye folks. May you find your happiness more easily than I did!

Love,
Chiharu

***

I close the lid on my laptop, grateful to be done with it. Relief floods me. Great! Now I can get back to my usual life.

It's cold for such a sunny day – then again, it is winter now – so I turn up the heater a little and wish I had put on a thicker sweater. Too late now. I look at the clock and realize it's time to go pick up the little one from nursery school.

"Yumi!" I ascend the stairs, since the guest room is the last place I saw her before I sat down to type my final blog entry. Sure enough, there she is, crouched with an open box and tricycle parts all over the floor. "I'm heading out to get Sattchan."

She looks up at me, exasperated, a wrench in one hand and a sheet of instructions in the other. The tricycle is Chisa's Christmas present. We were originally going to give it to her on her birthday in February, but decided there was no sense putting it off two more months when we already had the damned thing. The way the little one has been zipping up and down the stairs recently, it was inevitable she would find it eventually.

Although I can't stop laughing over the fact Yumi was the one who took it upon herself to put it together. Yumi. Perhaps the least mechanical and handy person in the world.

"Hang on a sec," Yumi says, standing up and brushing off her hands. "I'll go with you."

"Eh? You sure?"

Shrugging the bushy sleeves of her sweater, she says, "I should probably put in an appearance to the teachers."

She really doesn't have to. It's actually a nuisance sometimes to have her come with me to pick up the little one, or for her to do it herself. I'm recognizable enough now, but Yumi is a superstar, even if a tarnished one. Her going to the nursery school in the middle of the day usually results in small crowds as the other mothers gather around and try to get a look at her.

As if she's reading my mind, Yumi says, "I'll pop into the bathroom real quick to touch up my makeup and check my hair. If I'm going to show up in Twitter and Instagram photos, I best be looking good."

It's not just that. While Yumi is gussying up – not that she doesn't already look perfect to me – I go to the downstairs closet and pull out a hat and surgical mask for the little one to wear. Yumi and I try to keep Chisa out of photos, although this isn't always possible. We're not necessarily worried about her safety at this point, but we don't want her growing up with a camera always in her face. Luckily the law is on our side. Chisa might not mind posing for paps and the public when she's out and about right now, but as she grows older and starts dealing with self-image and esteem it will become more difficult for her to not be hard on herself. I'm not looking forward to those days. I know Yumi looks forward to her daughter growing up into more of her own person, but I would love for the little one to *stay* the little one for a lot longer.

Yumi comes down the stairs as if she's walking out onto a runway. She doesn't do it consciously, but this is what I'm talking about regarding self-image. Chisa is going to grow up with these edited images of her mother all over the place – all over our house! – and seeing the way Yumi carries herself and dresses. It could go either way, I guess. Chisa will either constantly compare herself to her mother or not care at all. I'm hoping for the latter but preparing for the former. It's completely different to be raised by someone like Yumi than to simply be in love with her. Too bad getting her to understand this is a losing battle.

"It's not cold, is it?" Yumi peruses the closet full of heavy coats and jackets, her fingers rejecting every one of them. I'm not going out in a jacket. By the time I come back home I'm usually pretty warm, unless it's cold enough to snow.

We leave the house dressed in nothing thicker than sweaters. Mine is gray and drab, but Yumi's is cream-colored with dark red stripes. Coupled with her bright hair and she is going to stand out amongst even the most fashionable mothers there. She'll also be the most famous by far – the other mothers aren't really celebrities themselves. They're the wives of boardroom men, media producers, and other celebrities like sports stars and local actors. Actually, I think one of them may be the new and younger wife of one of the label's executives. I'm sure she and her husband gossip about us extensively.

"*Waaa.*" Yumi steps into the yard, arms extended and head pointed toward the sunshine. I lock the door behind me and join her on the walk toward the front gate. "Nice day for your birthday, Chi-*chan.*"

"Glad you remembered." I open the gate for her and then step through myself. The street is empty at this time of day. That's why I usually choose now to step out to run my errands, even when I don't have a kid to pick up from school. It's crazy to think that in just two years she'll be walking herself to and from the local elementary school. Yumi is completely fine with this. Me? I'm already fretting about her getting lost or someone trying to kidnap her. That's it. I'm making nice with the other mothers just to form a going to school group.

"Of course I remembered." Yumi walks close but doesn't touch me as we go down the one-lane street. Just a few months ago it was full of reporters and policemen trying to keep them under control. I don't miss those days. "Your birthday is one of my favorite days of the year."

"That so?"

She leans in toward me, her booted feet curling over one another in a way that prevents her from tripping. "It always ends well, doesn't it?"

I know she means the kisses, the touching, and more recently the sex, but my brain goes back to that night she desperately wanted to make love and Yohei found us. That's my role in this relationship. Always think of the worst thing that can possibly happen – that *has* happened – and try to not let it occur. "I have confidence that tonight's will end well." I don't want Yumi to know I'm thinking bad things. It's best that I redirect my thoughts to her anyway.

"Not having the kid around will help." Her over exaggerated wink makes me laugh and rouse a sleeping cat nestled between two bottles of water in someone's yard. I often think that we should get a cat. Yumi would rather have a dog, but I don't want to take care of something that high maintenance. Yet it would be good for Chisa to be around a pet in her early years. Maybe an older cat would be good. They need homes, right?

"Thanks for the reminder of how much I have to do this afternoon. On my birthday."

"Why? I'll be home and don't have anything to do. I'll help her get ready for grandma."

I glance at her, that beautiful, reassuring smile doing its job on me. I don't deserve this woman. That's what I think every time I'm captivated by something she's doing just for me. How did someone like me not only get a girl like her for a best friend, but now as my lover and life partner? When I think about it too much, I become overwhelmed with the sense that it's not real. I'm going to wake up tomorrow and I'll be back in my old apartment, alone, or I'll be back in that dorm room, teenaged Yumi nestled beside me… platonically. I'm living one of my greatest fantasies. It can't be real.

"I still have to do her piano lesson." Chisa started taking lessons from me shortly after we moved into our house. However, she had a hard time concentrating or doing even the basics. After the blog thing started, I gave up for a while and only recently started her on it again. One of my fears is that she's as good as her mother when it comes to playing instruments. "Don't want to skip it since she needs to get back on track."

"Don't be so hard on her." We turn the corner at the end of the street. "I know you want her to be a virtuoso, but what if she's not? No matter, she starts ballet after the new year."

"And what if she can't do the movements?" Chisa is still not the most coordinated girl even for her age. She has made great improvements in the past year, but I still fear that she's not a late bloomer but... well... "For all we know our daughter's greatest talent will be beekeeping."

"Bees are important." Yumi points to a dormant flower bush hanging over someone's gate. "Otherwise we wouldn't have gardens like those. Or food. Did you know bees are dying?"

"You know what I mean."

"You worry too much."

"You don't worry enough." That was it. That was the summation of our relationship.

She unexpectedly takes my hand and rests her head on my shoulder as we slowly walk. The school is at the end of the road, but at our pace it'll be another few minutes before we get there. "I worry plenty. I worry about things every day. I even worry about you."

"What now?"

"Ah, I worry that you won't like your birthday present tonight."

My ears perk up. "Oh? What did you get me?"

"I didn't get you anything. But I am giving you something pretty good." Her eyebrows wiggle in my direction. I'm sure I'm not supposed to be flustered like this in public. "Skip the piano lesson and get your mother to show up earlier. I'll make your present last longer."

My mind is racing with so many possibilities. With Yumi, I honestly never know what to expect when she's so forward like this. She'll either want me to completely consume her or, well, she'll want to do crazy shit to me. I always knew she was kinky, but my God. We can make porn stars blush when we have a night to ourselves. "I would like to eat dinner tonight. Maybe take a relaxing bath. You can't tie me to the bedpost for hours on end."

"Why not?"

She says it loudly enough that a deliveryman looks up as he mounts his motorbike. He fastens his helmet and zooms away in a cloud of exhaust. "Besides, I've got some work to do this afternoon. Try not to distract me, and I'll finish it up earlier."

"You just made me want to bother you more."

"Then my mother will be my savior." She's coming to pick up Chisa and take her to Seki for the winter break. Yumi and I will go there a couple of days before New Year's to visit them and her parents as well. While Yumi's mother still hasn't completely come around to our romantic relationship, she does her best to not be rude, even when she asks inappropriate questions. I don't look forward to visiting her, but I can tolerate it.

"You don't get it. I need to mess you up good tonight because when I'm in Taiwan I'll be missing you like crazy." That's another thing. Yumi has been spending more time in Taiwan recently. Her management wants her to focus on international markets, where being in a lesbian relationship isn't as damning to her popularity. Since I can't really go with her every time, it will mean more time apart in the future. Not for long periods of time. A few days here and there. Nothing worse than when she's on tour or on location for something, but the extra distance makes it feel lonelier somehow. Luckily she calls me a lot and, well, sometimes we make do…

We separate when we get closer to the school. As anticipated, there are small clusters of women standing outside of the gate. The usual suspects. There's the group from two streets down. The group from across our street… that I would probably be a part of if I weren't a dirty lesbian. I think one of the other groups is actually a quartet of sisters who married a quartet of brothers and now all their children are awkwardly related to each other in ways God did not intend.

They look at us. Some of them have the decorum to only do so through the corners of their eyes, but others full-on stare, and I have no idea if it's because we're famous or because we're married. Honestly, it's both.

Some children are playing in the yard, but I don't see our daughter among them. She usually isn't there. It's not until the front doors open and a gaggle of three-year-olds emerge that the mothers begin descending. Some of them have kids in the yard and others are still inside, but for the most part we all had kids in the same freakin' year.

The head teacher sees Yumi and ducks quickly inside. This means they'll either usher Chisa out as soon as possible to make us leave or hold her back so the other mothers have to leave first. If the latter happens, it's because they want to talk to us. Probably to tell us that Yumi disrupts everything by breathing in the same space as common people.

Sure enough, every child but ours comes out of the nursery school. Don't get me wrong, they're pretty adorable – falling over each other, smiling, crying, flailing about in Mickey Mouse shoes and Hello Kitty dresses while their parents swoop in to catch them before they fall and scrape their knees. I tug on Yumi's sleeve and we go stand at the end of the fence, still in sight of the door but far from the fray. At this rate my piano lesson with the little one will be late, unless we eat lunch quickly...

Who am I kidding? You can't do anything quickly with a three-year-old!

Most of the parents leave with their children, but surprise, surprise, a few stay behind and continue to glance at us. Their voices are too low for us to hear outside, but I can see Yumi chewing on the inside of her cheek as she debates going up to one of them. I silently plead for her to do anything but. A celebrity! Gay cooties! Which is more important?

They not so discreetly whip out their cell phones and take pictures of us. Mostly Yumi. I think she's going to ignore them, but then at the last minute she turns around and flashes them a smile and peace sign. She has the desired effect. The mothers hurry to put their phones away and scurry off like ants.

Love, Yumi

"You're clearly too much for them," I say. "I mean, if you're too much for *me* sometimes…"

I don't get to finish my perverted thought before the school door opens again and there's Chisa, holding the head teacher's hand as they descend the small stoop and head toward the gate. Yumi and I go to meet them, where the head teacher bows graciously to one of her richest customers before handing Chisa off to me.

"Mama!" She slaps a piece of paper into Yumi's hand, her smile so proud.

"The children drew pictures of their families today," the teacher says sweetly. She doesn't mention that for Chisa "drawing" is a state of mind more than an actual function.

"I see." Yumi unfolds the paper and stifles a laugh. I glance at it. Yup. Two giant scribbles. One color. At least this time the little one attempted something that looks like a face. Last time Yumi and I were a giant black hole in the universe. While her classmates made passable attempts at stick figures, our darling daughter is still grasping the concept of, I dunno, drawing anything besides scribbles?

"Aw, looks just like your Chi-Chi." This time I stifle the laugh. On the surface it sounds like she's referring to me, but that tone and sour look says she's referring to Yohei, the messy tangle in our lives. "You did a great job, Sattchan." Yumi pats our daughter on the head before folding up the picture and keeping it secure in her hand. "Thank you for taking such good care of her." We both bow to the teacher, and Chisa smiles at her mother's praise.

I hold on to my child's hand as we turn and go back the way we came. The streets are full now. Full of the other children, their parents talking about play dates, husbands, shopping, and where they're going for New Year's. Everyone glances at us at least once, and at least half of them bow their heads to whisper one thing or another. We're famous. We're gay. We have a daughter who barely talks and can barely put one foot in front of the other some days. I worry about these things, but Yumi reminds me that the alternative is having a small child who never shuts up.

"Feels like it might rain later," Yumi says, glancing at the dark sky while ignoring the people staring at us.

"Mama!" Chisa almost yanks her hand out of mine. "*Te o tsunaide…*"

"Eh?" Yumi holds her hand palm up, and the little one slaps their skin together loud enough to make Mama grimace. "Are you just being lazy?"

We are each holding a hand, but our daughter is anything but lazy right now. She has to walk twice as fast to keep up with our slow steps, and without her other arm to help her balance she is wobbling more than usual. Yet her smile is unmistakable. Right now, on this whole street, Chisa is the happiest girl around.

I look at Yumi, who is minding the child before glancing up to meet my eyes. She flashes a soft grin and I shoot one back at her. Words, words, words. So overrated. I don't need words. Yumi doesn't need words. In that smile I saw her love, her desire, and her current happiness as our family heads home. Her wedding ring twinkles in the oncoming mist, and the necklace she's worn since that train ride twelve years ago hasn't lost its shine. I'm glad she always wears it still. Not because it's linked to mine, but because it's good for Yumi to be regularly reminded that she's a person who deserves to be loved and respected.

There's a lot to look forward to today, tomorrow, and a month from now. I have to remind myself of this every time I become overwhelmed with work or the stress of dealing with the media after what I did earlier this year. But I have it good. I have money. I have a good home. I have a happy child who will never want for anything, least of all love. And I'm married to my best friend.

Our lives will never be normal. We left normal behind in Seki when we boarded that train and first came to Nagoya to be idols. I don't know exactly what the future holds for our careers or health, but I do know that we'll get through it as long as we have each other.

We've been through so much worse already.

Hildred Billings is a Japanese and Religious Studies scholar who has spent her entire life knowing she would write for a living someday. She has lived in Japan a total of three times in three different locations, from the heights of the Japanese alps to the hectic Tokyo suburbs, with a life in Shikoku somewhere in there too. When she's not writing, however, she spends most of her time talking about Asian pop music, cats, and bad 80's fantasy movies with anyone who will listen...or not.

Her writing centers around themes of redemption, sexuality, and death, sometimes all at once. Although she enjoys writing in the genre of fantasy the most, she strives to show as much reality as possible through her characters and situations, since she's a furious realist herself.

Currently, Hildred lives in Oregon with her cat, with dreams of maybe having another human around someday.

Connect with Hildred on any of the following:

Website: http://www.hildred-billings.com
Twitter: http://twitter.com/hildred
Facebook: http://facebook.com/authorhildredbillings
Tumblr: http://tumblr.com/hildred